Seducing the Sheriff of Nottingham

A Kinda Fairytale

Cassandra Gannon

Text copyright © 2023 Cassandra Gannon

Cover Image copyright © 2023 Cassandra Gannon

All Rights Reserved

Published by Star Turtle Publishing

Visit Cassandra Gannon and Star Turtle Publishing at

www.starturtlepublishing.com

For news on upcoming books and promotions you can also check us out on Facebook!

Or email Star Turtle Publishing directly:

starturtlepublishing@gmail.com

We'd love to hear from you!

Also by Cassandra Gannon

<u>The Elemental Phases Series</u>
Warrior from the Shadowland
Guardian of the Earth House
Exile in the Water Kingdom
Treasure of the Fire Kingdom
Queen of the Magnetland
Magic of the Wood House
Coming Soon: *Destiny of the Time House*

<u>A Kinda Fairytale Series</u>
Wicked Ugly Bad
Beast in Shining Armor
The Kingpin of Camelot
Best Knight Ever
Seducing the Sheriff of Nottingham
Coming Soon: *Happily Ever Witch*

<u>Other Books</u>
Love in the Time of Zombies
Not Another Vampire Book
Vampire Charming
Cowboy from the Future
Once Upon a Caveman
Ghost Walk

If you enjoy Cassandra's books, you may also enjoy books by her sister, Elizabeth Gannon.

<u>The Consortium of Chaos series</u>
Yesterday's Heroes
The Son of Sun and Sand
The Guy Your Friends Warned You About
Electrical Hazard
The Only Fish in the Sea
Not Currently Evil

The Mad Scientist's Guide to Dating
Broke and Famous
Formerly the Next Big Thing

<u>Other books</u>
The Snow Queen
Travels with a Fairytale Monster
Nobody Likes Fairytale Pirates
Captive of a Fairytale Barbarian

*I have loved to the point of madness;
that which is called madness,
that which to me,
is the only sensible way to love.*

Françoise Sagan

Prologue

How It Happened the First Time...

Robin Hood hadn't come to save her.

Maybe that wouldn't matter to Maid Marion, though.

Maybe Hood had some passable explanation for why he'd left her in the church. Maybe Marion would forgive him for being such an unmitigated asshole. Maybe she'd vanish into Sherwood Forest, with her arrow-shooting True Love, and he'd never see her again.

The Sheriff of Nottingham muttered a resigned curse, resting his forehead against the window. He would die if he couldn't see Marion again.

Nicholas was obsessed with the woman. Literally *obsessed*, in the terrorizing-her-hairdresser-to-learn-what-kind-of shampoo-she-used sense of the word. It was a compulsion that he'd long since given up trying to control. Every moment of the day, Nicholas was *obsessing* over Marion Huntingdon. Where she was going. What she was thinking. Who she was smiling at. How she was feeling. When he might see her again. She consumed him.

And there wasn't a damn thing he could do about it.

In the distance, he could see the lights of Marion's home. It seemed impossibly far away. Unreachable and warm. He stared at the illuminated estate, always on the outside looking in.

Doubts and "what ifs?" swirled through Nicholas' mind. He should have closed the drawer to the nightstand better. If he had, she'd still be safely tucked into his bed. Or even if he'd been able to concoct an ingenious lie to somehow explain away the blatantly obvious. But Nicholas had never been good with words. Everything always came out wrong. And he hadn't *wanted* to lie. Not to Marion. She'd looked up at him, with huge brown eyes, and he'd told her the truth.

So, of course, she'd run away. Why in the world would she stay?

Nicholas wasn't even really *real*.

He was a gargoyle, carved from stone and enspelled to life. The vast majority of his body was flesh and human-shaped. If you shot a gargoyle, he would bleed and die. They could eat and think and have sex. But, it was impossible to miss that gargoyles' ancestors had been the granite statues that protected the roof of the castle. Thanks to Nottingham's ancient, proprietary magic, gargoyles now talked and breathed, like other beings.

But were they truly alive?

That was a question Nottingham was forever trying to answer. Had they created a race of vigilant warriors, steadfast and solid in their duty? Or were the gargoyles just empty stone carvings moving around like programed robots? Most people went with the latter. Gargoyles were nothing but burly vessels created to guard the palace.

Passionless, purposeless, and predictable. Those were the words usually used to describe them.

Although today, Nicholas had proved that bigoted stereotype wrong, once and for all. Things hadn't gone to plan, but he'd still ended up on top. He'd outmaneuvered all the humans in the land and he'd won. ...For all the good it did him.

Nicholas pinched the bridge of his nose. Marion was furious at him. She had a right to be. And she was heartbroken over Hood. God only knew why. The man was useless. Even worse, Nicholas had ruined Marion's pristine reputation. A Maid's reputation was *everything* in Nottingham. That had to be traumatizing for her. And then there was everything that came after...

He glanced over at the nightstand again, where his lamp had one stood. Now shards of it were all over the floor.

Broken.

Today had changed everything. Broken the uneasy

status quo between him and Marion and Hood. Nothing could ever change it back to the way it was. There was no rewinding the clock. No redoing it all.

Even if you could redo it... would you really want to?

Nicholas' jaw tightened. The mental voice of his worst-self sometimes flitted through his brain, guiding him on terrible, selfish paths. His reverse conscience. On his best days, he could ignore the dark drives that it urged him to follow. This was not one of his best days.

Nothing could redo what happened. But, if you were Nick Greystone, Sheriff of Nottingham, that indisputable fact was actually... good news.

Wasn't it?

Analyzing it dispassionately, he realized yes. It was *very* good news. His actions today were set in stone. Hood and Marion's relationship was broken. Irrevocably. Even if that son of a bitch wanted her back, it could never be what it was before.

Marion already sensed the permanency of their rift. Until now, she'd been endlessly loyal to her beloved outlaw, defending his every asinine move. But tonight she'd seemed willing to listen to the truth. She was angry at Hood. Enraged that he'd abandoned her. That was promising.

Nicholas' paranoid worry that Marion would flee into the forest faded. She claimed she'd hate Nicholas forever-after, but she'd also said that she hated Hood *more*. That was promising, too. To her mind, Hood was the greatest villain in this mess.

Which was obviously true.

The Sheriff of Nottingham was the least popular man in the kingdom, so it was a welcomed change to have someone else getting some blame. Especially, since Nicholas only became Sheriff of Nottingham because of three interconnected quirks of fate:

There was a war.

He was a gargoyle.

He never missed an opportunity.

Nottingham was a small kingdom, always on the look

out to grow in stature. King Richard had allied with King Uther of Camelot for the Looking Glass Campaigns, in far off Lyonesse. Richard didn't care much about Camelot, but he did care about power. So did the rest of Nottingham's elite. All the noble idiots happily went off to exert their will on the 'inferior races,' dragging the rest of the kingdom along with them.

It was a huge campaign. All the able-bodied, human men rushed to join, thanks to the chivalric propaganda being blared on every radio station and the promise of foreign riches. The gargoyles were soon drafted into the war effort. King Richard tried to use them as expendable troops. Gargoyles weren't really *real*, after all, so their deaths meant much less.

Sadly for Richard, the idea of gargoyle soldiers was doomed to fail. The gargoyles' stony features didn't conform to the heroic ideals crooned about by popular bards. Their hulking bodies didn't look so great in Nottingham's flashy blue and gold uniforms. And, worst of all, they were all terrible bowmen.

Gargoyles' fingers were often thick and large. That made archery difficult. They broke the bows. Nottingham's soldiers were all expert archers. King Richard took pride in that, so the gargoyles' inability to fire arrows was a huge disappointment for him. Then came the Battle of Kirklees, where the gargoyles were found at fault for Nottingham's staggering losses. After that, they were all shipped back to the kingdom in disgrace.

Nicholas wasn't surprised. Gargoyles were always convenient scapegoats at home, so why should war prove different? Still, he wasn't exactly heartbroken over the loss of a military career. He'd never seen the point in trekking to some distant desert and he didn't give a shit about expanding Richard's power.

Gargoyles didn't have a reason for existing, beyond serving Nottingham, though. Since that's all he had to devote himself to, Nicholas had thrown himself into the role of sheriff with relentless determination.

In every way that mattered, Nicholas was in charge of the kingdom these days. Not even Gepetta could've predicted he'd rise so far. Unfortunately, there wasn't much of a kingdom left to rule. Nicholas tried to hold things together, but it was another losing battle and even he knew it. Thanks to the Looking Glass Campaigns, Nottingham was broke.

And that asshole Robin Hood robbed what little gold the kingdom had left.

It made no sense to Nicholas. Hood could open an orphanage, if he wanted to help all those foundlings in the woods. Or work an actual fucking job and donate the money to the poor. Or do any one of a million other things to show off his compassion and selflessness. Instead, he was hunkered down in the forest, illegally shooting deer, and stealing from everyone who wandered by. What the hell went on inside the man's head?

Hood should have married Marion long ago! Nicholas certainly would have, if he'd had the option. Instead, that moron devoted himself to defeating the Sheriff of Nottingham and left his True Love vulnerable.

And Nicholas had seized the opportunity.

Marion was his now. He'd kidnapped the woman and he was keeping her. Was that still possible? Yes. Of course it was. The rock-hard determination at his core wouldn't allow for anything else.

Despite his smoldering obsession with a certain brunette, Nicholas was a logical man. Practical to the point of heartlessness. He relied on facts and strategy more than emotions. They were easier for him to understand. His straightforward mind began to analyze where he currently stood with Marion. It was mostly positive news, by any objective reading of the evidence.

Marion might not like what Nicholas had done, but the two of them were connected. They both knew it. He had years to persuade her to see things his way. Decades. He wasn't going anywhere. Surely, Marion could get over Hood in decades. The man wasn't *that* fucking special.

Nicholas had so much time to convince her. To fix things.

A knock sounded on his bedroom door.

Nicholas' head whipped around. As the least popular

man in Nottingham, visitors weren't usually an issue for him. No one came to his room. No one except servants used the stairs to his tower. No one even talked to him, most days. Maybe it was one of the palace guards. His men were the only people who'd ever seek him out.

Nicholas was painfully introverted. As a boy, his mother had insisted he was just shy and he'd outgrow it, but he never had. There was an awkward distance between Nicholas and the rest of the world. He could feel it like a force field, all around him. Nicholas only felt like he *fit* with Marion and she rarely talked to him, these days. His social skills were abysmal. He dealt with his discomfort by encouraging people to leave him alone in the most efficient way possible: He was hostile towards everyone. Mass hangings and silent stares tended to keep chitchat to a minimum.

"Go away." He snapped at the visitor, fully expecting his orders to be followed. His orders were always followed. The other gargoyles could deal with whatever the hell was happening.

Why was someone bothering him? He hated other people in his space, because the *noise* of them overwhelmed him. Sounds often felt oppressive, like he was drowning in them. His room was the one spot he knew he'd have silence. He wanted to be alone, brood about Marion and think of ways to...

Another knock, more insistent. A voice calling to him.
Startled, Nicholas opened the door.
...And his time ran out.

Chapter One

After two decades of reporting on Nottingham's most infamous intrigues, tragic tales, and sordid scandals, the murderous man-eater Maid Marion is the worst criminal I've ever encountered. Nottingham is sleeping safer tonight, knowing that she's locked up forever.

Alan A. Dale- "Nottingham's Naughtiest News"

Ten Years Later

"Do you ever wish you could redo your life?"

Maid Marion jerked awake. Once upon a time, she'd been able to snooze straight through blaring alarms, but those days were long gone. A decade in The Wicked, Ugly and Bad Mental Health Treatment Center and Maximum Security Prison had turned her into a light sleeper.

"Marion? *Psst!* Did you hear me?"

Her idiot cellmate always waited until midnight to start jabbering. Every time Tansy so much as whispered, Marion was wide awake for the rest of the night.

"Oh for God's sake..." She groaned, scrubbing a hand over her face. "Really, Tansy? *Really?*" In her old life, Marion had been sweet and refined. In her new life, here in the WUB Club, all of that had been burned away, allowing her to reach her full potential as a raging bitch. "I'm trying to sleep, you idiot."

"This is important." Tansy Hatta persisted, because the girl really had been sent to ruin Marion's already ruined life. "Do you ever wish you could do everything again and make different choices?"

Marion tried ignoring her, but it did no good. Tansy was like a perky, blonde pitbull. She'd been born a Hatter, a rare and mysterious race capable of altering time. Tansy claimed she could change it, in fact. That meant she spent vast portions of her day rethinking the events that had landed her in the penitentiary. Who could blame her? If Tansy ever got out, and had the magic inhibitor removed from her ankle, it was theoretically possible she could rewind all her mistakes and do things differently.

Marion wasn't sure the girl's magic would actually work, of course. No one knew much about Hatters. There weren't a lot of them and their ability to warp time frightened people, so they tended to keep to themselves. Some things that they obviously might have changed stayed terrible, though, so there must have been some limits to their ability to effect the past. Since Marion herself had no powers, she couldn't explain it all. She certainly wasn't bigoted against the Hatters, though. Marion wasn't bigoted against anyone.

Except every single asshole in Nottingham.

"Are you awake up there? Hey Marion? Are you awake? I said..."

"I *know* what you said." Marion snapped, trying to think of a downside to smothering Tansy with one of the uncomfortable pillows. Nothing came to mind. "You seriously don't want to know what I'm wishing for right now."

"No, I really mean it. Haven't you ever wished you had a second chance to fix all your mistakes?"

Marion muttered a curse. From experience, she knew that Tansy wouldn't stop talking until she got an answer. The two of them had been sharing the small space for over a year and the woman had been yammering nonstop for all four hundred and twelve days. She even talked when she brushed her teeth.

"What mistakes?" Marion asked sardonically. The prison never turned the overhead lights completely off, so she had a clear view of a roach skittering across the cracked ceiling and onto the wall. "I'm living the fucking dream."

Tansy tended to get philosophical at night and, no matter the time of day, she took everything literally. "Me? I would *definitely* make different choices, if I knew where I'd end up. I'd have listened to Momma and stayed in school... Said no to all those dark spells... Not helped my loser boyfriend to levitate a grocery store into that vortex..."

"Or at least hire a better lawyer, afterwards." A decade in the WUB Club had made Marion blasé about evildoing. She'd been born Good, but Badness had become a part of her through enculturation. It was part of the "being a bitch" thing.

"I'd never let Ricky into my pants, in the first place." Tansy continued seriously. "If I didn't go around with that bastard, I wouldn't be here. He wouldn't have hit me or bullied me, until I wasn't even me anymore. If I could redo my life, I'd be a whole different person." She paused. "And then I'd go to Neverland Beach."

"The beach?" Of all the crazy things Tansy had ever said, that one had to be right at the top. "You come from a trailer park in Wonderland. When did you ever see a beach?" Wonderland was second only to Nottingham in least desirable vacation spots

"I *haven't* seen a beach, but I always wanted to go to some fancy resort in Neverland. When I was a kid --after my daddy left us for that dial-a-witch tramp-- I used to dream about Momma and me movin' to the ocean. The endless blue sky, and sand in my toes, and shirtless boys, bringing us umbrella drinks." She sighed. "I miss my momma in here."

Marion could relate to that sentiment. Her mother had died giving birth to her, so Marion had spent her whole life missing the woman. She'd once treasured all her mother's belongings, because they made her feel closer to the beautiful, mysterious duchess. As the family's fortune failed, though, those belongings had been sold, one by one. First the priceless artwork. Then the antique furnishings. And finally even her mother's favorite necklace.

Marion had wept as she sold that ruby pendant. To this day, it was the hardest thing she'd ever done. But she'd needed the money to pay for her father's medicine and there was no other way to get it. It wasn't like any job would hire her. What skills did a Maid have, besides pouring tea? The duke had died anyway, of course, the year before Marion's arrest. But he'd died with a roof over his head, because of an unexpected tax exemption and Marion gutting the contents of the once grand estate to pay the other bills.

"Do you ever miss the beach, Marion?"

"Nope." She refused to miss anything about the outside world. Refused to talk about her old life or follow the current happenings in Nottingham. Her former lady-in-waiting, Clorinda, had once shown up on visiting day, but Marion had refused to see that duplicitous sow. Whatever gloating news Clorinda wanted to share, Marion was fine with never knowing it.

Once she was locked in a prison cell, the universe outside of the WUB Club had ceased to exist for her. It was too painful to dwell on what other people were doing or how the world was going on without her. The Maid Marion who'd visited the beach and slept through alarms and believed in happily-ever-afters was dead and gone. The woman who now lived in her body was harder and smarter and didn't waste her time on wishing for what could've been. Life behind bars was the only world she could focus on, if she wanted to survive.

Well, that and trying to figure out who murdered Nick Greystone.

All day, every day, the thought swirled around Marion's brain, no matter how many times she told herself that it was pointless to dwell on it. Every time she woke in a cold sweat, or she ate the gloopy porridge in the cafeteria, or she nearly got shanked at craft time, she wrestled with the same impossible question.

Who the hell had framed her for killing the Sheriff of Nottingham?

It was a pointless exercise, but everyone needed a hobby.

"Hell, you probably spend more time thinking about do-overs than anyone." Tansy continued, disregarding Marion's denial. "After all, you're --like-- the only one in here who's really innocent."

Tansy was a twenty-two year old, pain-in-the-ass, recovering mercury-powder addict, but she was also the one person in the world who believed that Marion was wrongly convicted.

Marion hadn't even told her the whole story of what happened. These days, she kept her mouth shut about anything that mattered. But, the two of them had been locked together in a twelve foot cell for over four hundred days. She'd figured out Marion's backstory and decided for herself that Marion hadn't killed Nicholas Greystone.

Tansy's unwavering loyalty was why Marion tolerated these late night chats. Why she defended Tansy's skinny ass against the other prisoners and made sure none of the crooked guards sold her drugs, so she stayed clean. Life had taught her that real friendship was something precious.

Marion ran a hand over her eyes. "I don't think it matters what any of us did to get here. All that matters is we're stuck in a cage and not getting out." She said wearily. "I've told you before that no good can come from thinking about this shit. Why don't you just go to sleep and forget…?"

Tansy cut her off. Apparently, she'd been waiting for an opening like that. "Because it's your birthday!" She squealed, as if she was springing some fantastic surprise. In fact, she actually yelled "surprise!" in a wincingly high-pitched voice. Up and down the row of Orange Level cells, other medium threat level prisoners shouted at her to shut up. Tansy ignored them and swung herself off the bottom bunk, clapping her hands together like a little kid. "Happy birthday, Marion!"

Marion was too tired to keep up with Tansy's lunacy. "It's *not* my birthday." She said automatically.

…At least she didn't think it was. Time lost all meaning behind concrete walls. Shit. She started counting off days on her fingers, trying to figure it out. Huh. Maybe Tansy was right. Maybe it *was* her birthday.

Like it fucking mattered.

She had forty-seven more years to spend behind bars, so she wasn't exactly marking her days on a calendar.

"I know it's still ten minutes to midnight, but I have to give you your gift, right now." Tansy's sunny smile shined at Marion over the edge of the mattress. Hatters loved birthdays.

And unbirthdays. "You're really going to like it!"

"Can you give it to me when it's daylight?" Marion tried, already knowing it was hopeless to quell Tansy's excitement.

At times like this she really missed some of her former roommates. Like Elsie, the tattooed ogre-derby champ, who'd tried to beat her to death one Merry Christmas. Or that damn elf who'd cried in the corner for two years straight.

"Here." Tansy shoved a package at Marion with the exuberance of a hyperactive Irish Setter. "Open it! Open it! Open it!"

Marion gave in. She reluctantly sat up and accepted the small bundle, festively wrapped in toilet paper. Tansy had drawn a square cake on the front with thirty-six spindly candles on top. Against her will, Marion's mouth twitched upward at one corner. Playing the role of bitchy badass came easy to her now, but not with Tansy.

Brown eyes flicked up to Tansy's beaming face. "Thank you." Marion said quietly. She didn't give two damns about the contents of the mummy-wrapped package, but she (grudgingly) appreciated the thought. No one had remembered the anniversary of her birth since Trevelyan died. Not even Marion herself.

Inside the wadded-up mess of a package was a necklace made of twisted string, dried pasta, and hazy glass beads. A cracked and semi-melted-looking pendant dangled from the bottom, with half its gold paint worn away. It looked like something tourists bought in some low-rent warlocks' spell shop. When they were drunk. *Really* drunk. Marion did her best not to wrinkle her nose in distaste.

"It's enchanted." Tansy announced proudly. "I know it's *super* ugly, but it has --like-- magic-powers."

"Of course it does..." Marion reached up to pinch the bridge of her nose. She was clearly going to need some of the fermented grog that Thumbelina bootlegged in her cell. It was the only way she was going to make it through this conversation without cracking. "Tansy, sweetie, you're a moron. Magic doesn't work in prison. It's part of *being in prison*. How much did you pay for this thing?"

"I traded that old lady with the glass eye over in Yellow Block two packs of cigarettes."

"Did you keep the receipt?"

"Would you just listen? That thing is *really* magical." Tansy insisted. "I can see you're all like," she adopted a sterner tone to imitate Marion, "'Here's Tansy being a gullible airhead, again. Like the time she thought Pecos Bill was coming here to put on a country music concert during visiting hours.' But I *promise* you this time is different."

"Uh-huh."

"I'm giving you a chance to redo your life!"

That caught Marion's attention. "What?"

"See, the magic inhibitor and all the alarms stop me from using any time spells. But it's still inside of me. I have level four powers." Tansy tapped her chest. "So, I had the glass-eye-lady make me this pendant at craft time."

Craft time was the highlight of Marion's week. She was amazing at it. This week they were supposed to be making picture frames, not shrunken-head-ish looking talismans.

"The pendant holds magic." Tansy went on. "So, I cast the spell, even though I can't enact it yet. It's inside the necklace. When my magic is restored..." She snapped her fingers, looking pleased with herself. "The spell gets carried out."

"And the glass-eyed-woman made you this pendant for *what* exactly? Two packs of menthols?" Maybe Tansy could get the cigarettes back. Marion would *way* prefer those as a gift. "Tansy, *think!* Why wouldn't she just keep a magical time travel necklace for herself?"

Tansy shrugged. "She and her sisters have their own magic. Besides, Hatters' powers scare a lot of people. This is a one way trip, Marion. You go back to *then* and don't come back to *now*. You override the person you were and she ceases to exist. A new timeline begins. It's just *this* you, in your old body. It can't be undone. Nothing will be the same."

"And that's a bad thing?"

"For some people, I guess. But not for you. I think

you're *great* now." Tansy smiled and folded Marion's fingers around the necklace. "Keep this." She urged. "Please? It would mean a lot to me. Ever since I got here, you've looked out for me and you didn't have to. Let me repay you by giving you a second chance."

"Life doesn't give you second chances."

Marion knew that better than anyone. This whole thing was a pipedream. But, she still found herself giving into the pleas, because this imbecile-on-a-perpetual-sugar-high was basically the only living person she loved. She slipped the Necklace From Hell over her head, epically unsurprised when she didn't disappear in a puff of smoke.

Tansy stared at her intently, like a kid desperate for the fireworks show to start. "I think the pendant is going to glow or something." She whispered in a properly reverential tone. "Don't you think it's going to start glowing?"

Marion waited a beat, just to humor her and then arched a brow. "It's not glowing." She reported unnecessarily. "Can I take it off now?" She lifted the heavy medallion off of her chest, repulsed by its undeniable grossness. "I don't want it laying eggs in my skin."

"You can't take it off until you get into the past. Then it can go, because the spell will already be cast. The magic will be used and gone."

"Seems like it's plenty gone, right now."

"Magic amulets have to link to you." Tansy argued. "Give it some time to boot up."

Marion began to seriously reconsider the smothering-Tansy-with-a-pillow plan. It wasn't like she had much to lose, given the length of her sentence. What was another couple decades, when you were pretty much guaranteed to die behind bars anyhow?

"I know!" Tansy brightened, some new thought flittering through her empty noggin. "You have to --like-- tell it where to send you. *When* do you want to start over? It has to be a birthday. That will lock in my spell. Do you want to go back to when you were a newborn baby, or the summer you got your first kiss or...?"

"The night I got engaged to the Sheriff of Nottingham." The words were out before Marion could stop them. "My twenty-sixth birthday."

Tansy goggled at her. "You were engaged to a *sheriff?*"

"Well, I wouldn't call it an 'engagement,' really. He kidnapped me to flush out my dumbass boyfriend. A week later he was dead and I was arrested for it."

And she'd been "unhealthily fixated" on the man ever since, according to her prison therapist. Marion didn't feel like she was fixated. She just thought about Nicholas eighty million times a day.

"Tell me about that first night with him, then. Be very specific about the moment you're traveling to. What were you wearing when he proposed?"

Marion frowned. "That night Nick --Nicholas Greystone was his name-- told me I was marrying him, I was wearing," she thought for a beat, "a yellow dress with dots, because I was a twit who bought yellow dresses with dots on them." She unconsciously jabbed a finger around her legs to indicate where the dots had been on her skirt. Marion talked with her hands.

"You wore a yellow dress with dots on it?" Tansy was delightfully scandalized by that idea. These days, Marion was the least yellow-dotted-dress-girl imaginable. She chain-smoked and wore a safety pin through her eyebrow. "*You?*"

"It was an extremely appropriate and demure dress, for an always appropriate and demure Maid." Marion said, with a sigh of self-disgust.

Nottingham was a small and old-fashioned kingdom. Unlike the blinking neon of St. Ives or the cultural modernity of the Four Kingdoms, Nottingham stuck to its ancestral roots. Men were blacksmiths and archers. Women were dutiful and chaste. Especially Maids. They were the highest-born class of highborn women, protected and untouched until they were safely passed to their future husbands. The daughters of nobility. Maids didn't wear pants. Maids didn't fight in wars. Maids didn't work or earn money. They were pristine prizes handed out to heroic men.

Men like Robin Hood.

"Back then I cared what people thought and what they'd say and what I wore and who I was seen with." Marion muttered. "I tried to do everything... *right.*"

"I can't really imagine you giving a damn about that stuff."

"It was before I became me." Marion disliked the old version of herself as much as she disliked everyone else. If going to prison had done anything remotely positive for her, it had at least forced her to grow up. "What did all that conforming get me? When the chips were down, I had no one to count on but myself. The whole kingdom turned against me."

Once a Maid was tarnished, everyone was through with her. She was ruined in the eyes of polite society. Not that Nottingham's opinion mattered to her, now. The whole dismal place could burn, for all she cared.

Fuck 'em all.

That was the family motto. Fuck. Them. All. Put it on the Huntingdons' ducal crest, in bold point font.

Marion's eyes narrowed. "If I got a do-over, I would make that horrible kingdom pay."

"Or you could just go back to the year you turned eighteen and move out of Nottingham, all together." Tansy pointed out with an uncharacteristic amount of logic.

"I could never leave my father all alone. He was sick for years."

"Well, go back to your twenty-sixth birthday, but let the sheriff deal with his own problems. Just get out of town."

"Whoever killed Nick, killed me, too." Marion snapped. "They buried him in a grave and me in this place, so I died in slow motion. They stole my future. We're both *dead* and they're going on with their lives? No! I'm *never* letting that go. If I got a chance to go back, I'd take my revenge."

"You *are* going back." Tansy promised. "But once you get there, I hope you can find peace and mercy and forgiveness."

"Doubtful."

"There are better things to accomplish with your second-chance than revenge, Marion. Maybe you can even find love."

For the first time, Marion began to feel like Tansy was serious about this whole thing. Hatters weren't known to be the sanest of people. Her eyebrows drew together, worried about her friend's mental health. "Tansy, you don't *really* believe that this amulet is going to…?"

"It's glowing, isn't it?" Tansy interrupted.

Marion looked down, her eyes widening. Holy shit! The damn thing *was* glowing. It was so bright, she was surprised it wasn't already setting off the magic alarms.

Tansy's grin was wide and tinged with secrets. "There's a breakout tonight. Did I tell you that? It's why I needed to make sure you had the necklace for your birthday. As soon as the magic inhibitors turn off, I'm going to the beach and you're going back to Nottingham. It should happen very quickly, so don't be afraid."

"A breakout?" Marion repeated, her mind whirling. No prisoner had ever escaped from the WUB Club.

"The Tuesday share circle is going to cut the power to the prison. In about…" Tansy pursed her lips and cocked her head, like she was listening to something only she could hear. "One minute."

Marion was in the Saturday share circle. Group therapy sessions were differentiated by color-levels and the Tuesday attendees were all Red. The worst of the worst villains. Today alone, they'd started a riot in the cafeteria and (according to rumor) torched the dwarf guards' security office.

Trevelyan had once been in the Tuesday share circle, for Christ's sake. Everyone remembered the havoc he'd caused. Red Level were all Bad news.

A feeling of foreboding hit Marion. "How do you know what Tuesday share circle is planning? You haven't been hanging out with Scarlett, have you?" Scarlett Riding was part of the Tuesday group and she was capable of talking smart people into doing very dumb things.

And Tansy wasn't that smart to begin with.

"Nope. I just know a lot more than everybody thinks." Tansy leaned forward to hug her. "I'll miss you, Marion. You're my sister forever! Maybe we'll meet up again, one day. In fact, I *know* we will! ...But not for a while, because I'm about to be fourteen, again."

Marion closed her eyes. "Tansy, honey, let's take a second and talk about..."

She stopped short.

Someone was playing *The Wedding March*. She could hear the violins and flutes, like she was standing right next to them. No one was allowed to blare music at this hour. In the WUB Club, no one was allowed to do much of anything except dried pasta crafts.

"What the hell is that?" She asked out loud.

"Is the music too much, duchess?" A dark voice mocked. "I want Robin Hood to imagine the full romantic scene, when he reads about our engagement in the morning papers."

Marion's eyes popped open and she found herself face-to-face with the Sheriff of Nottingham.

Chapter Two

**Kidnapping a Reluctant Bride: Traditional Meet-Cute or First-Degree Felony Abduction?
You decide in our insta-poll!**

Alan A. Dale- "Nottingham's Naughtiest News"

For several heartbeats, Marion was too shocked to move.

She was in Nottingham Castle. In the bedroom where the Sheriff of Nottingham had kept her, after his gargoyle henchmen had taken her from her own house. She would've recognized it anywhere.

The thick stone walls and heavy tapestries were exactly the same as they'd been a decade before. So were the Bandersnatch-skin rugs, and the moonlight filtering through the narrow windows, and the huge fire burning in the walk-in fireplace. Even with the flames, the room was cold. The whole castle was cold, although it had been May when she'd been stuck there. She could feel the draft, even now.

It couldn't be real. None of this could be real. It had to be some kind of trick.

"What the *fuck* is going on?" Marion demanded, leaping to her feet. The chair clattered to the ground behind her.

Her eyes darted, trying to identify the other people in the room. By the doorway, a scared assembly of palace musicians stopped playing *The Wedding March* at irregular intervals, so the music faded off with a disharmonious squawk. A tabloid reporter from *Nottingham's Naughtiest News* jotted down notes on a smartphone that was a decade out of date. Clorinda, Marion's genetically-blessed lady-in-waiting, had frozen in shock, a goblet of wine halfway to her lips. And directly in front of her...

"Did you really just say 'fuck'?" Nicholas Greystone's dark eyebrows climbed high on his forehead, looking more shocked than she'd ever seen him.

Holy *fuck!* She was actually seeing him.

Marion's eyes devoured this man in the Sheriff of Nottingham's blue and gold uniform, trying to spot some hint that he was an imposter and coming up blank. It was really Nick, alive and well! He stood by the massive fireplace, just as he had a decade before. She remembered it. He'd come in, while Marion and Clorinda were eating. He'd brought the musicians and a reporter to document everything for the morning papers, so Robin would be sure to see it.

It was all the same.

Nicholas even *looked* exactly the same. Only he looked different, too. His face was still all hard angles and shadows, with smoke-colored eyes that saw everything. His hair still fell to his collar, in granite colored waves. Thick and carelessly brushed back from his face, it was filled with every shade in the world. Layers of blacks and golds and everything in between. But, there was also something smoldering beneath the surface of Nicholas that she'd never really noticed, before. Something that had her gaping at him anew.

He met her wide eyes and Marion had the hysterical realization that he was actually... handsome.

The humans who carved the gargoyles seemed to take delight in making them look as hideous as possible. When one of the stone statues was enspelled to life, their faces were frozen mid-transition. Some parts of their bodies became warm, living flesh and some remained unyielding rock.

As a result of the humans' malicious stonework, most gargoyles looked like monsters, even after they were made living, breathing, mortal beings. Craggy hunks of stone often jutted out of their otherwise normal looking skin. Their features sometimes included fangs, or demonically pointed ears, or elaborate facial hair, which could never be removed, because it was chiseled right into their face. It seemed especially cruel to Marion, because gargoyles grew and aged, like humans did. So the carvers were disfiguring children.

Whoever had designed Nicholas must have agreed with her, because he'd been carved with care and artistry. There was a classic elegance to his features. The rough bits of rocky texture that remained just worked to give his otherwise too-pretty face an element of masculinity. The right side of his body was still dappled in places like living stone, but the texture of it was fascinating and exotic, not at all off-putting.

She might've been "unhealthily fixated" on Nicholas, but she hadn't remembered him looking like *this*. He was really... handsome.

"Were you this handsome the first time?" She blurted out.

His eyebrows climbed even higher, not answering that question. The man was always surly and taciturn, so the silence itself wasn't strange. For the first time, though, Nicholas seemed to be quiet simply because he had no idea what to say. No one called gargoyles handsome. Ever.

"Are you feeling alright, Marion?" Clorinda asked, apparently freaked out by Marion's freak out. She was stunning, from the glorious shine of her waist-length blond hair to the tiny soles of her perfectly-pedicured feet.

Marion ignored the prettiest girl in Nottingham, her mind buzzing.

Dr. Ramona, the prison shrink in charge of Saturday share circle's group therapy, had told Marion she was "teetering on the brink of madness" with her refusal to move on from the past. Maybe she was right. Maybe Marion had somehow toppled off the brink and fallen *into* madness, now. Maybe this was what madness looked like. A drafty castle, and a handsome kidnapper, and everyone wearing out-of-date clothes.

Except Marion was perfectly sane. Mostly, anyway.

She cast around for another semi-logical explanation for how this was possible. ...But there simply wasn't one. She could feel the heat of the fire and see the threads of the tapestries. No one could fake this kind of detail. Not WUB Club shrinks experimenting on unconscious prisoners. Not a TV studio filming some bizarre reality show. Not the most deceptive glamour cast by the most powerful witch. No one could do this, except a Hatter rewinding time and giving her a do-over.

Was it possible?

Was Tansy's magic that strong?

Marion looked down at herself and saw that she wore the stupid yellow dress. Also, she appeared to be at least twenty pounds heavier. She'd always despaired of her weight, before prison. But, now she couldn't help but notice that her breasts filled out the polka-dotted silk way better than they did in her prison-issued sweats.

"Wow." She automatically touched them, checking their size and happy with them for the first time in her life.

Nicholas' gaze dropped, watching her palms cup her breasts. His expression went taut.

Marion barely noticed. She switched her attention to her hands. Holding them out in front of her, she stared down at her pristine French manicure. Definitely *not* the hands of someone from the WUB Club's Orange Level cellblock. In fact, everything about her looked just as it had ten years before.

Except for the necklace.

The ugly pendant Tansy had given her lay against her (way nicer than usual) chest.

Marion gave a wild laugh, finally accepting what was happening. "It worked! The goddamn thing actually *worked!*" She looked skyward and spread her arms out, drinking in her freedom.

"Tansy!" She shouted in exaltation. "Welcome to Neverland Beach, you beautiful, crazy, genius!"

Nicholas' eyes flicked up to the ceiling, like he was trying to figure out what the hell she was screaming at. Everyone else was edging back from her in fear and trepidation.

"Her mind may have snapped from the stress of this kidnapping." The reporter in the doorway surmised, making a note of it in his ancient phone. It was astonishing he even had one at all, considering Nottingham was a technological black hole in any timeline. "Maids are notoriously feeble."

Marion recognized the guy as Alan A. Dale, the slimiest paparazzi in Nottingham. The man was an anthropomorphized weasel and wrote incendiary gossip stories for his rag of a paper. Half of them contradicted what he'd written before, but it didn't much matter. They were marketed to people who just wanted outrage and sex scandals. For once, she was pleased to see his rodent-y face, because she wanted all of this preserved for posterity.

"What worked?" Clorinda asked Marion, still looking baffled. Her skin was flawless, because she soaked it in sheep's milk each night to keep unfashionable freckles at bay. Clorinda was all about fashion... and random malice. "Who's Tansy? Are you...?"

"Oh, shut up." Marion interrupted, exhilaration sweeping through her. There wasn't a moment to waste in her second chance at life. She wanted to do everything, all at once. Everything she'd regretted was about to be fixed. Everything she'd missed would be experienced. Everything she'd wished for would come true.

And everyone who'd screwed her over was about to pay.

First up was the two-faced bitch in front of her. "You're *fired*, Clorinda." Just saying the words felt glorious. "Get the hell out of my sight before I throw you from the window by your ugly-ass extensions."

Nicholas glanced towards the window, as if gauging the dimensions, and gave a considering grunt. Apparently, he agreed that Clorinda's skinny ass would fit through the opening with room to spare. See? The two of them were already in synch.

Clorinda reached up to touch her long hair protectively, even as her mouth dropped open in shock. "I'm not wearing extensions!" She sputtered. "How can you talk to me like...?"

Marion cut her off. "You read my diary. You have copies of it." And she would gleefully recount the most salacious passages to Alan A. Dale. Reading her private letters had a tendency to set off Marion's temper, but selling them to the newspapers was even worse.

Clorinda's enviably full lips parted in outrage. "What in the world is wrong with you? Why would I read your diary? You're not interesting enough to hide any secrets!"

"You *betrayed* me. And *nobody* fucking betrays me. Not anymore."

"No, I did not! You're making all this up..."

Marion cut her off. "And I can't believe you won May Day Queen over me, last time through." It was the second biggest injustice of Marion's life. "I *know* you cheated. No way did you play the piano that well, without some magical fix."

"I have no idea what you're even talking about!" Clorinda shrieked.

That's because it wouldn't happen until Monday.

"Get *out*." Marion pointed towards the door. "And good luck getting another job, once I write your glowing reference, you vainglorious, clout-chasing skank. You'll be back working as a shepherdess in no time."

One of the musicians gave a half-suppressed laugh. Yeah... this exchange was definitely gonna get recounted across the whole kingdom. Good. For once, the gossip would be true.

Clorinda's mouth thinned. The woman might pretend to be a helpful companion, but under that feigned subservience there was haughty distain. Clorinda had been born very beautiful and very poor, which severely limited her job options as a lady's maid. Few noblewomen wanted to hire someone so lovely or lowborn. ...Or so calculating. She was a creature of perfect makeup and zero empathy.

"You're just jealous, because I'm a real woman and not some untouchable paragon." She hissed at Marion. "Your whole job is to be chaste and loved from afar. It's no wonder Robin let *him* kidnap you." She waved a hand at the sheriff. "Why wouldn't he? It's not like he's missing anything with you gone."

Nicholas glanced at Marion sharply. "You're still not sleeping with Hood?" He demanded in apparent surprise.

Marion shot him an aggravated glare. Of course he would focus on *that*. "Robin and I are not together anymore."

Their breakup was official in both timelines. In the last one, he'd told her they should "see other people." In this one, she'd just dumped that ass clown in absentia.

Nicholas shook his head, like he didn't believe her. Well, he was in for a surprise, wasn't he?

"Noblewomen never put out." Clorinda taunted. "Why do you think they call her *Maid* Marion?" She rolled her eyes. "But the Merry Men want someone they can *touch*."

Marion arched a brow. "Is that why Will Scarlett's wife caught you sucking him off, that time?"

Alan was writing notes so fast it was a wonder his stylus didn't go right through the phone screen. His wire rim glasses kept sliding down his furry, brown nose and he'd quickly shove them back into place, as he scrambled to get it all down.

"Will and I were both drunk! Sex doesn't count, if you're drunk." Clorinda blustered, but she flushed deep red. "Who the hell do you think you are, anyway?"

"I'm Marion. The one and fucking only. Get used to it."

Nicholas blinked.

Clorinda's head whipped around to look at him, like the sheriff might be able to intervene on her behalf. "This is *your* castle, until King Richard returns. Only you can kick people out of it. Marion's a spoiled brat and always has been. She drags down everyone who... *Shit!*" Her words ended in a panicked wail, because Marion hit her.

Hard.

And it felt frigging *great*.

The blow connected to Clorinda's cover-girl face with enough force to send the traitorous cow to her knees. It wasn't the slap of a well-bred lady. It was the four-knuckle punch of someone who'd done a decade of hard time. A goddamn barbarian had taught Marion how to hit her enemies like she meant it and she *really* fucking meant it.

"*Help me, Sheriff!*" Clorinda howled, as she theatrically collapsed to the ground.

Nicholas made no move to save her lying ass from Marion's wrath.

Good. She liked the man better and better. Just because she hated whiners, Marion grabbed Clorinda by the front of her favorite pink dress and hit her again. Years of dealing with lunatics and criminals had Marion putting her whole weight into the blows. Hit hard and fight dirty. Cartilage crunched as Clorinda's nose broke in two places.

Nicholas' gray eyes stayed on Marion, barely noticing as Clorinda rolled around on the carpet. He'd always done that. His burning gaze would focus solely on Marion, like she was the only thing he saw. It had confused the younger her. Now, she just felt a rush of energy and vindication.

The brink of madness never looked so sweet.

"You're insane!" Clorinda screeched at Marion, scrambling backwards on the rug like a crab. "I'm going to sue you!"

"Out!" Marion roared again. Alan continued joyfully writing down everything for posterity. Marion didn't even try to stop him. History would be *right* this time, so he might as well record the details.

Clorinda began to cry hysterically, fingering her bleeding nose. She was a drama queen, who loved playing to an audience. "You're going to pay for this, you fat bitch! You can't just..."

"Enough." Nicholas commanded.

Clorinda stopped her caterwauling mid-wail, blinking up at him in trepidation. Not even she was defiant enough to cross the Sheriff of Nottingham when he gave an order. Nicholas had a habit of hanging people who irritated him. ...And there were a lot of irritating people in Nottingham. He'd filled half the kingdom with gallows to deal with them all.

No surprise, Nicholas was incredibly feared and hated.

No surprise, Marion couldn't care less about his unpopularity.

She stared up at him, breathing hard and unable to believe he was really right there in front of her. Every bit of Marion was buzzed on adrenaline and excitement and impatience. All her senses felt like they were on fire, her mind going a thousand miles an hour. *Nothing* would stop her, now that she was free. When you got a second chance, you grabbed it and didn't let go. She needed to stop screwing around with Clorinda and focus on what really mattered.

"Get rid of the others, Nick. We need to talk."

Nicholas gave his head a slight shake, not liking the order. He'd put on this elaborate "engagement" production for the reporter's benefit, but now he was getting back to his usual surly self. "As the crying woman said, this is *my* castle, for the time being. I'll be the one giving the orders."

"Fine. We can do this with them here." Marion shrugged, not caring very much. Everyone else might be afraid of him, but she wasn't. Not at all. "Did you propose, yet?"

"I *told* you we were getting married. Does that count as a proposal?"

"Good enough for me." She righted her chair and flopped down at the small table, picking up her wine. "I accept."

Nicholas seemed confused. Excellent. Keeping him off-balance could only help her. "You accept?" He echoed blankly.

"Get me my ring, honeybunch." She smiled widely and drained her goblet.

God, she forgot how good *real* alcohol tasted, after drinking bootlegged swill for years. And chicken! Holy crap, there was roast chicken for dinner. Marion pulled the whole platter closer to her, eating with her hands. She felt like she'd been dying of starvation for a decade. All the WUB Club fed prisoners were bowls of lukewarm porridge. Everything here tasted incredible. Everything looked and smelled and felt *incredible*. Even the colors were brighter. This was the greatest day of her life!

Alan seemed similarly thrilled. He was so happy with this twist in the story, it was a wonder he didn't start crying in demented glee.

"You can't accept my proposal." Nicholas insisted, like she was wrecking the script he'd written. "Why would you accept?"

"I've fallen tragically in love with you, dipshit." Marion

told him with her mouth full. "Jesus Christ, this chicken is *fantastic*. Was chicken always this fantastic?"

Nicholas's eyebrows compressed, realizing he'd lost control of this situation. The man hated to lose control. He glanced over at the weasel-y reporter and the goggling musicians. "Leave." He ordered. "Now."

As usual, he didn't have to repeat himself. Even Alan didn't press for more details. He probably planned to just make up his own, but whatever. Marion had made her point. There was a scramble for the door and in less than a minute she was all alone with her secretive, handsome kidnapper.

Finally.

Chapter Three

Maid Marion Agrees to Wed Sheriff!
(Yep, you read that right, folks!)

Alan A. Dale- "Nottingham's Naughtiest News"

Nicholas' smoke-colored eyes stayed on Marion, until they were finally alone. "You're kidnapped. Deal with it." He pronounced, like he anticipated an argument and was trying to cut it off.

"I think I'm dealing great with *everything* that's happened. Super calm and rational."

"That bleeding shepherdess woman might disagree."

"Clorinda left here alive, didn't she? Considering she sold me out to the tabloids and cheated me out of my rhinestone tiara, I think she got off easy."

Nicholas crossed his arms over his chest, like he didn't even care about the May Day Queen debacle. Of course, he hadn't experienced it, yet. "What's your game, duchess?"

Only he ever called Marion that, although it was technically accurate. The title had passed to her, after her father died. Not that she was able to do anything with it. Thanks to Nottingham's chauvinistic, ass-backwards laws, the dukedom would go straight to her husband. The money and power were gone, so it didn't much matter. The Huntingdon name was just fancy wallpaper on a crumbling manor house.

"I'm not playing a game." Marion finished off a chicken leg. "You asked me to marry you..."

"I didn't *ask*. I commanded."

"...and I said yes." She went on, as if he hadn't spoken. "Most grooms would be happy."

Nicholas stared at her, like he'd never seen her before. He hadn't. She was new and improved, like a butterfly breaking free of her cocoon and soaring. "Are you drunk?" He asked after a long beat.

"Not yet." She told him happily, elated with the whole world. "I've just been upgraded."

"What does that mean?"

Marion saw no reason to lie to the man. This was their engagement party, after all. For better or worse, richer or poorer, time travel or no time travel... "What do you know about Hatters?"

Nicholas was trying to keep up as she sped through topics and punched people. "Hatters screw around with time, don't they? Change things. Those are the rumors, anyway. I've never met one."

"Well, it just so happens that I know a Hatter, named Tansy. Who just so happened to send me back here to redo my life. So, I can tell you from firsthand experience that the rumors are true."

He was shaking his head before she even finished that explanation. "There aren't any Hatters in Nottingham."

"I met her while I was doing time in The Wicked, Ugly and Bad Mental Health Treatment Center and Maximum Security Prison."

"Why in the hell would someone like you be in the WUB Club? Forgetting all the other reasons why that story is insane, you're *Good*."

His point was a fair one. There were Good folk and Bad folk in the world and the justice system treated them differently. The Bad were usually the ones who got locked in jails, because they were an oppressed underclass. ...And also they committed the most crimes

The Good folk tended to be insulated from punishment, even if they were total scumbags. They were the elites, who wrote the laws and stayed in power. There was a lot of inequity in the system. Marion hadn't much noticed it, when she'd been a cosseted Maid. But, ten years in the slammer had made her identify with the villains and had opened her eyes to a hell of a lot of problems. Bad folks didn't get a fair shake in this world.

They might still be better off than gargoyles, though. Nicholas' people weren't Good or Bad. They just... existed. It was one reason so many people insisted that gargoyles weren't really *real*.

"Turns out, when you assassinate a duly-appointed sheriff, they don't much care about Good and Bad designations." She told Nicholas. "They just toss you into the deepest hole they can find to set an example." Honestly, she was pretty sure King Richard had sent her there to die. Kong had insinuated as much. Instead, though, she'd found a way to thrive amid the Badness. It had become her natural state.

"You're threatening to assassinate me, now?" Nicholas didn't sound very worried.

"Not *me*." She splayed a hand on her chest, because most everything she said was accompanied by movement. It helped her to think. Her father had once told her that if he tied her arms down, she'd go mute. "But *someone* is going to do more than just threaten it, Nick. They're going to shoot you dead."

Nicholas' gaze narrowed.

Marion reached over to grab Clorinda's wine, so she could drink that, too. "Robin is my prime suspect. I can see him screwing us both over, because he feels so damn picked on." She waved her ex-boyfriend aside, because fuck that guy. "But, there are plenty of other suspects, too. You're not the most popular fella in town, sugarplum. I think it's all the gallows you use as lawn ornaments."

He didn't seem to care very much about his formidable reputation. Gray eyes watched her, cataloguing her responses and weighing them. The man used silence like a weapon.

Marion refused to buckle under the stony stare, needing him to understand. "Look, all that matters is this: You're going to be murdered on Thursday." There was probably a gentler way to break that to him, but damn if Marion knew what it was.

He was shaking his head again, denying it all.

"Believe it or don't. *I* know what's going to happen. And the only person I know for absolute *certain* didn't frame me for the crime... is you. How could you, when you're dead?" She moved on to decimating the bread basket. The butter was more beautiful than she could have ever imagined. And honey! She barely recalled what it even tasted like.

Nicholas watched her broodingly. "It's an ingenious tale. I'll give you that. But it won't work."

"Oh?" Marion sucked a bit of honey from her thumb.

Nicholas' eyes lingered on her mouth and he gave himself a small shake. "You're thinking this nonsense will confuse me into letting you go. But, your story is missing one key detail."

"Which is?"

"Gargoyles aren't really *real*. So nobody would go to prison for killing one."

"You seem pretty damn real to me." Marion tore a hunk of roll free and dipped it into the mashed potatoes' gravy. "One thing I learned in prison: Don't let other people define you."

"The kingdom's laws define me and every other gargoyle." His voice was flat. "And under that law, we're barely classified as alive. Gargoyles are passionless, purposeless and predictable, according to Nottingham." He ticked off the words on his fingers.

"Bullshit." Marion scoffed. "Everything about this kingdom is bullshit, but *especially* its laws. Thank Christ I don't follow them anymore." She might be free from prison, but she'd always be a felon. Embracing Badness was a part of her now.

"Laws are not bullshit," protested the man charged with protecting them.

"Nottingham's are. They're trying to erect barriers between us, when really Maids are treated the same as gargoyles. Everyone thinks we're just there to fulfill *their* needs. Never our own. They try to keep us oppressed, because they're afraid." She gestured towards him. "Passionless, purposeless, and predictable?" She pointed at her own chest "Meet passive, polite, and pushed-aside." She shook her head. "It's all a trap. Don't believe it."

"That's a ludicrous comparison. You're *incredibly* valuable. Anyone who's met you sees how special you are."

Marion paused in her snacking to stare at him.

"Meanwhile, I'm expendable to the world." Nicholas went on, not noticing her riveted gaze. "Gargoyles are *not* like Maids."

Marion cleared her throat. "You aren't expendable to me."

"Of course I am."

"Nope." She ate some more bread, carbs be damned. "Among other things, your life is linked to mine and I just got my life back. I'm in no hurry to lose it again, so you're staying breathing whether you like it or not, cuddlekins."

Nicholas still wasn't buying it. "Legally, a Maid would never be punished for killing a gargoyle." He insisted. Too bad he hadn't been her lawyer, because he was ready to relentlessly advocate for her cause. The man was relentless in *everything* he did. "Not in any court in the land."

"I was charged with murdering a *sheriff*." Marion clarified. "The prosecution insisted your title made you more important than an average gargoyle and that it was really the 'noble institution of sheriff' that had been murdered. We had a whole pretrial hearing on it."

"The judge would have to be the biggest idiot in the world to..." He trailed off, like he had no idea what they were even arguing about anymore. "No." He sliced a hand through the air, cutting of the discussion. "You always do this. You go off on tangents to confuse me."

"It only confuses you, because you're mentally undressing me, rather than focusing."

Nicholas blinked.

"It's okay. I don't mind. I'm doing the same thing to you."

The guy wasn't the best at communication. Maybe he was shy under all the menace. When his emotions were up, he always seemed to flounder for words. "What the hell...? What are you trying...? You can't just..." He stopped talking and blew out a flustered breath.

Marion waited.

Nicholas inhaled deeply and started again, in a more controlled tone. "No."

"No?"

"*No.* You're trying to muddy the waters, but it's pointless. All of this is *pointless*. We are getting married. Period."

Marion lifted a nonchalant palm in a one-handed shrug. "I said 'yes,' didn't I?" She reminded him innocently.

Nicholas kept going, refusing to accept her acceptance. "Our engagement will be announced tomorrow in every newspaper. It will piss off your precious Robin Hood. He will come to the wedding to rescue you. And I will kill him. *That's* how this will play out."

He ticked off each step on his thick, rocky fingers. When sculpting Nicholas, the carver had obviously tried to shape elegant hands. The magic didn't always work evenly over a gargoyle's whole body, though. Nicholas' left hand looked like everyone else's. His right was thick and stony, the fingers slightly malformed. It wasn't ugly to her. It just wasn't... human.

She kinda liked that in a man.

Marion chewed her bread. "You're like a big, blunt hammer, you know that?"

His forehead wrinkled at the non sequitur.

"As an instrument of destruction." She clarified. "You're direct and hard. You hit people, until they break. Then, you hang them. There's no subtlety."

His jaw ticked.

"Robin is an arrow. He comes at you when you don't suspect it and slams into some target you're not even looking at." She slapped her hands together to simulate the impact. "Calculating and distant. That's him. That's why this scheme of yours won't work. Robin won't come for me."

"Of course he'll come for you. *Any* man would come for you."

Marion glanced at him, again.

Nicholas looked away with a muttered oath, like he

was frustrated with his own words. Things always got interesting when he forgot to be silent and moody.

Marion studied the classic lines of his profile. A decade in jail would no doubt make any man look attractive, but Nicholas looked *really* attractive. How in the hell had she missed that before? Had she been so blinded by Robin's strawberry blond wholesomeness?

Her "unhealthy fixation" on Nicholas was getting bigger by the minute.

"I'm a match." Marion went on, thinking things over.

"A match?"

"I light shit on fire."

He grunted, like he completely agreed with that assessment.

"A match is small. Not much of a flame, when you first see it. But give it time and it can incinerate a whole city." She lifted a shoulder. "And I *have* time, now. I'll see Nottingham in ashes. I promise you. I will burn down every motherfucker in this dismal kingdom. Robin included."

His eyes flicked back to hers. "Or you could just break their noses, like you did with the vainglorious clout-chasing skank. It would be easier."

Her mouth curved.

Nicholas' lips parted in astonishment. He wasn't used to having people grin at him. Mostly they just hated and feared and mocked him for not being "real." (And, to be fair, the mass hangings of dissidents didn't help with his likability, either.) For a split-second, his handsome face reflected openness and longing, before he yanked it back.

Marion took it as a positive sign. The man's granite expression rarely changed, so anything that jolted him into a response was a step in the right direction.

"Someone around here is coming for us both, Nick. We need to work together to figure out who it is... and get them first."

"Together?" He repeated and there was something new in his voice.

"*Together* we can win."

"Win against who? Hood?" Once you got him talking, Nicholas was filled with snarky, suspicious questions about everything. So was Marion. It was good they shared interests. "He's your True Love. Why would you be fighting him?"

"I'm fighting *everyone*, right now." She shrugged. "Except you. We're on the same side. And you have resources I don't."

He was still looking for a trap. "And what do *you* have that *I* don't?"

"Well, I can tell you the future." She seesawed her hand in mock debate. "That's *kind* of a great skill for an ally to have."

"Unless you're lying about it."

"I'm not lying. Why would I lie?"

"I have no idea. I'm not as sharp as you are. No one in all of Nottingham is as sharp as you, Marion. I've always seen that."

Nobody had ever complimented her brain before. Maids weren't supposed to be too smart, because they might make their male companions feel bad. It felt amazing to be admired for something other than her ladylike decorum. Especially by Nicholas, who knew her inside and out.

Marion gave him another smile, feeling wildly optimistic. This conversation was going better than she ever could have predicted. "Right now, my sharpness is telling me that you're the only one I can turn to, because you're the only one I *know* isn't going to frame me for murder. That makes you my new partner-in-solving-crime."

"And your fiancé." Nicholas sneered.

"And my fiancé, cutie-patootie."

He scowled at her casual agreement, like it pissed him off. Or possibly it was the nickname. No "cutie-patootie," then. Not a problem. She'd just have to find an endearment that he did like.

"Why aren't you fighting me harder on this wedding idea?" He demanded. "I thought I'd have to lock you in this room all week."

"Oh, you did that already." She assured him. "But

42

everything *I* did before...? I'm doing the opposite now. Last time, I said 'no' to the proposal and you died. This time I'll say 'yes' and maybe you'll survive to get an annulment."

"It'll have to be a divorce."

Now, Marion was surprised. "Why's that?"

"Well, you didn't share my bed last time, did you? So this time, you'll have to do the opposite."

See, *now* they were getting someplace. It was a taunt, meant to terrify any virtuous Maid into submission. Nicholas must be getting worried, if he was trying to frighten her off. That meant she was already winning. Marion loved to win.

She grinned at him. "Oh, I was in your bed last time."

He scoffed at that and stalked over to sit in the seat Clorinda had vacated. Apparently, he'd decided to terrify her at closer range. It wouldn't work. A decade before, he'd been able to intimidate her, the way he did everyone else. Now, she knew better.

"You didn't sleep with your True Love, but you slept with the gargoyle who kidnapped you?" He slammed himself down in the chair. It occurred to her that gargoyles must weigh more than other races, because of their partially-stony exteriors. It seemed like the whole room shook. "Be serious."

"You didn't really kidnap me."

"That's not what you were shouting at my men, as they dragged you out of your home."

"That was the *old* me. The *new* me is happy to be here, having a dinner with her beloved groom." There was a small cake on the table. Marion hadn't noticed that the last time. It was white, decorated with red flowers and balloons. Nicholas knew May 1st was her birthday. Of course he did. Marion wasn't about to fully trust the guy, but something deep within her warmed. She cut a huge slice and plopped it on a plate for him.

He hesitated staring down at it and then at her.

"Is this strawberry?" She cut a slice of cake for herself. Silence.

"I love strawberries." She'd forgotten she loved them, because she hadn't seen one in a decade. "How strange and remarkable that you somehow knew they were my favorite."

More silence. Deeper and more complex.

Marion smirked and realized this was the best birthday she'd ever celebrated. "Thank you, Nick." She licked the frosting off her fork and sighed in pleasure. "This is... perfect."

Nicholas watched her savoring the cake for a long moment. "If you're really consenting to be engaged to me, doesn't that give me betrothal rights?" He asked out of the blue.

Marion frowned at that odd question. He'd never mentioned betrothal rights before. What was he up to, now? The man was so unpredictable. "Nobody really demands their betrothal rights." She told him, because it was true. "It's a ceremonial thing, so highborn noblemen can pretend they're *actually* noble, by resisting temptation."

He arched a brow and didn't respond to that.

"And I can't believe you're focusing on some stupid antiquated rules, when I've just told you that you're going to be murdered." She went on in exasperation. Being distracted by her awesomeness was all well and good, but he needed to concentrate. "Have you even been listening?"

"I listened. I just don't believe you."

"Think back over my decades of perfect decorum and scrupulous honesty." Marion suggested around a bite of cake. "How many times have I been interesting enough to make up a completely fabricated tale of...?"

"Once." He interrupted simply.

Marion blinked. He remembered that day in the woods? He must. He still called her "duchess," didn't he? Butterflies fluttered in her stomach.

Nicholas cleared his throat. "I may not be as sharp as you, Marion. But I'm not an idiot." She liked it when he dropped the "Maid" title and just called her by her name. "This little foray into creative fiction is a waste of time."

"I don't waste time. Not anymore." Marion wasn't going to argue about it, though. He'd realize the truth, soon enough. "Just keep your eyes opened for somebody who wants you dead, okay?"

"Besides you?"

"Why would I want you dead? We tried that last time through and it sucked. *This* time things will be different. That's why we're going to be joined at the hip for the foreseeable future, treasure squirrel. Where you go, I go."

"You think you're going to follow me around, spying on me?"

"Oh, I *know* I am." She'd shadow his cutie-patootie all over Nottingham. Her "unhealthy fixation" was positively swooning over the delightful stalking possibilities.

"No. You're staying in this room and out of trouble."

"I'm done staying in rooms and out of trouble. You try locking me in here and I'll get out. I promise you."

Smoke-colored eyes narrowed.

Marion smiled and ate another bite of cake.

"Have it your way." Nicholas got to his feet and pointed a stony finger at her, regaining his footing as a heartless abductor. It was just sweet as pie to watch. "But, if you disobey me, I'll assume you really *are* here willingly and I'll start *acting* like a fiancé." It was a warning.

"You will, huh?"

"*Yes*. And all your bullshit sagas about sharing my bed aside, you're not going to like it if I throw myself into the role." He shook his head. "Because no matter how confusing you try and make this very simple abduction, I know one thing for certain: You belong to Robin Hood."

"Except I don't." Marion assured him seriously. "Not since the wedding."

Chapter Four

How It Happened the First Time...

Robin Hood wasn't coming to save her.

Marion was standing by the altar, preparing to marry the Sheriff of Nottingham, when she suddenly realized the truth. The man she'd loved since she was sixteen wasn't going to rescue her from this insane, forced wedding scheme. She was all on her own.

Had Marion *always* been on her own?

Looking back on it all, she realized... yes. She always had. She'd been kidding herself about Robin. About his intentions and plans. About her place in his life.

To Robin, their story wasn't Robin Hood and Maid Marion having adventures. It was Robin Hood having adventures and Maid Marion *thinking* about Robin's adventures. And that was okay with him. *Not* being with Marion was okay with Robin, so long as she was focused on his daring deeds and pining for his boyish smile.

Because it was *always* about Robin.

Since they were teenagers, they'd been a couple in the minds of Nottingham. They'd seemed a natural fit. Robin was exciting and attractive, with undeniable charisma. Marion had always been pudgy and unathletic, but she was well-bred and people liked her. At least, she'd *thought* they did. She was popular with just about everyone, from household servants to earls.

Most importantly, no one could doubt her virtue.

In Nottingham society, virtue counted for *a lot*. Even girl-next-door Marion Huntingdon became a prize when you stuck "Maid" in front of her name. And Marion wasn't just any Maid. She was the *perfect* Maid. She was the cousin of a king. She came from the oldest family in Nottingham. She could dance a flawless waltz, knew every nobleman's favorite meal when he came for dinner, and was as virginal as a newborn unicorn. She'd been bred as a reward for Nottingham's greatest hero. And everybody agreed that hero was destined to be Robin.

He'd started courting her on her sixteenth birthday. One day *after* her sixteenth birthday, Marion declared herself totally in love with him and never even looked at another boy. How could she?

Robin was her True Love.

A True Love was the ultimate gift. The one person made just for you. When you were born a Good folk, like Marion and Robin, you didn't know your True Love just by looking at them. Evil witches, malevolent sorcerers, and other beings born Bad had it easier. They could identify their True Love on sight. For Good folk, it was harder, because they actually had to sleep with their True Love to feel the bond.

Of course, Maid Marion could *not* sleep with Robin Hood. Not before their wedding, anyway. If she did, she wouldn't be a Maid and if she wasn't a Maid, he wouldn't want to marry her in the first place. But she *knew* Robin was the one-and-only man for her.

Everyone accepted the truth, even if they couldn't yet confirm it officially. Robin and Marion were True Loves. They would one day be married. Marion had already bought a wedding dress. (Not the dress she wore today, of course. The gown Nicholas had provided for this farce was a scratchy, too small nightmare of ruffles. No, her *real* dress was safely stored in her closet, waiting for her *real* wedding.) Marion had told herself that Robin would become her betrothed, when the time was right, and that her dreams would eventually come true.

Up until this very moment, she'd been a stupid child.

Behind the lectern, Friar Tuck was droning on and on, trying to drag out the wedding service. Trying to give Robin Hood a chance to show up and save the day. Only he wasn't going to come.

There was no way Robin could reach the church and save her without risking capture himself. Marion always had unshakable confidence in Robin's abilities and even she knew that Nicholas had set the trap too well for anyone to escape.

The Sheriff of Nottingham had been ruthless in his preparations. Robin was clever, but Nicholas was proving to be smarter than anyone guessed. Gargoyles weren't so predictable, after all. Under Nicholas' guidance, Nottingham had become a literal fortress. There were too many gargoyle guards filling the streets. Too many traps laid. Too many cameras, pointed in too many directions. Robin would be caught if he came to rescue her.

For all of Nicholas' plotting, though, he'd misjudged the most important piece of his grand scheme: Robin didn't love Marion nearly as much as he loved himself. That miscalculation was going to piss the sheriff off. And a pissed off Nicholas Greystone was sure to be a very bad thing.

Even as a teenager, Nicholas had been hard. His hard face never smiling or revealing his thoughts. Hard words snapped out whenever anyone approached him. Marion had always tried to be nice to him, but, as time went on, that just seemed to piss him off more. Nicholas was the hardest, most isolated, unfriendliest man she'd ever met.

And he was in charge of the kingdom.

Nicholas and Robin had both gone off to war in the Looking Glass Campaigns, along with a generation of other young men. Robin had been placed at the head of the gargoyles troops, because it was assumed they needed a nobleman's leadership. While Camelot fought the formidable winged gryphons, Nottingham was tasked with subduing lesser opponents. "Inferior races" was what Camelot called them and most of Nottingham agreed. No one voiced much objection to the wanton slaughter.

Except for the "inferior races."

At the Battle of Kirklees, the centaurs had decimated Robin's battalion. Barely anyone survived. Nottingham was sure Robin's management had been impeccable, so the gargoyles had been blamed for the loss. King Richard declared the gargoyles unfit for such a glorious war and sent them all home, along with a wounded Robin. That somehow made Robin's behavior even worse.

The Sheriff of Nottingham was always a gargoyle, because they were the palace enforcers. The other gargoyles voted Nicholas to be their commander and, with many noblemen still at war, the job gave him real power. His influence at court pissed Robin off. Nicholas got more and more authority, as the war dragged on and on. There was simply no one around to stop him. Robin *hated* that Nicholas had control, but there wasn't much he could do about it.

Marion wasn't certain exactly what injuries Robin himself had sustained at Kirklees. He looked fine, from the outside, and if he was mentally tortured by what he'd seen, he did a good job of hiding it. Whatever had happened in battle, it must have been terrible, though, because it had been ages and Robin showed no desire to return to the front. All he thought about was "reclaiming Nottingham." He swore to her that they couldn't even discuss marriage, until he defeated Nicholas.

Robin had always been righteously idealistic, but now there was a zealotry to his beliefs. A certainty that he alone could identify and solve the problems of the world. He was convinced he should be ruler of everything, holding court from Sherwood. It was all he talked about. Robin's cause to rip down Nicholas' authority and replace it with some woodland utopia was just... *idiotic*.

A part of Marion had known how crazy it all sounded, but it had seemed harmless. A way for him to recover from war. A make-believe battle, where Robin and his men were fighting "evil," without really harming anyone. Nicholas wasn't in any danger from Robin, of course. Even at her most starry-eyed, she'd never believed that Robin could actually defeat an army of gargoyle guards. She told herself that he'd grow out of this idiotic phase, and stop living in the woods, and they could finally be together.

She'd told herself a lot of very pretty lies.

Somewhere inside of Marion, an emotion flicked off that could never be turned on again. A connection to Robin, that she thought would last forever, split in two. There was no going back for them now, because she could see him far too clearly.

It wasn't just that Robin hadn't come. It was *how* he hadn't come. No note telling her he loved her. No promise to return, when the coast was clear. No… anything. He didn't like this game, because there was no opportunity for him to easily win. So he wouldn't play, at all. Like none of it truly mattered, beyond his adventure out there in the woods.

All around her, in Nottingham's gothic cathedral, the wedding droned on. The two tiers of pews were filled with people who weren't going to help her. They were all too scared of the sheriff or maybe they were secretly glad to see her suffering.

She truly did have no one.

Marion stared at the front of Nicholas' blue and gold uniform, seeing nothing but her own stupidity. Her hands were shaking so badly the pedals were falling off the rose bouquet and onto the floor. She was allergic to roses, so the scent of them made her nose itch. In her misery, she barely noticed.

Her whole life, she'd been living in some idiotic dream world, where everyone got a happily-ever-after. Now, she was suddenly awake and standing alone, in the harsh light of day.

…Well, not *totally* alone.

Marion's eyes unconsciously traveled up to her "fiancé's" big, stony face.

Nicholas wasn't technically her fiancé, of course. Not according to Nottingham's very strict and codified betrothal laws for a Maid. Marion had turned down his proposal. (Which was really just him ordering her to marry him and her refusing.) That meant they *weren't* really betrothed and he had no rights over her. But, Nicholas didn't let facts stop him from holding the wedding. So, here they were, in a frothily decorated church filled with terrified guests, waiting for Robin to swoop in and rescue his True Love from her abductor.

What was her abductor going to do when Robin *didn't* swoop in?

Already Nicholas was getting concerned. His expression didn't change, but she somehow saw realization dawning for him. This plan was doomed to fail. Neither of her prospective grooms cared about her. To Nicholas, Marion was nothing but Robin's True Love, which made her a tool to use against him. Sure, his gaze followed her, whenever she was in the room, but he rarely spoke to her. Nicholas didn't like her, at all.

Now, his undeniably beautiful gray eyes suddenly met hers and he seemed to... blink. She couldn't really explain it, except *something* happened inside of his head. He'd finally realized that his scheme was over. That she was worthless as bait. Damaged goods. Rejected by her True Love. A damsel in distress that no hero would rescue.

"Robin's not coming." Marion whispered, just in case he still didn't get it. A tear rolled down her cheek. "You can stop all this now. There's no point."

Nicholas stared down at her. "Isn't there?" He asked softly.

Marion shook her head, desolation sending her into a state of semi-shock. She could feel herself disconnecting from the church and pulling inward. Trying to hide from all the pitying eyes and the smug whispers. Trying to figure out what in the hell she was going to do.

She had no backup plan for her life. She'd never even considered needing one. Maids didn't have amazing educations or big dreams of their own. She'd been fully invested in Robin's gallant words about chivalry and honor and True Love. She'd believed every lie she'd ever been told. If only she could do it all over again, she'd make so many different choices...

Marion heard Friar Tuck continue to talk and Nicholas snapping at him, but she wasn't sure what they were saying. She was too broken to concentrate.

Then, Nicholas was leaning closer to her. He had *such* beautiful eyes. She'd noticed that at the May Day Queen Pageant, much to her dismay. It had felt disloyal to notice anything about him as a man, but she couldn't help it.

His gaze was the color of smoke and now it seemed *bright.* His face wasn't hard for once, either. It was... impatient? Persuasive? Happy? Like some adventure was about to start and he wanted her to come with him.

His strange expression caught her attention. No one

else had ever looked at her that way. Did he want to include her in some plan? The novelty of that idea penetrated her fog of grief. Marion had always wanted to plan something, but Maids didn't get to participate in proactive strategizing. They were rewards for adventurous men after all the planning and adventuring was done.

Marion sniffed, gazing up at him. He wasn't even wearing the traditional bycocket hat that *all* grooms in Nottingham wore at their weddings. She had no idea why she noticed that, but she did. "Is it over, yet?"

"I've given up on Hood coming to your rescue."

"Me too." Her eyes filled with tears.

"When the chips are down, you can't count on True Love to save you, Marion." He said just to twist the knife. Even the Sheriff of Nottingham knew Robin was indifferent to his destined mate. *Everyone* knew.

Marion swiped a hand across her eyes. Nicholas was right. Mean, but right. There was no more counting on Robin to save her. She could only count on herself. Standing there waiting for her True Love was pointless. Humiliating. She needed to *do* something. Take some kind of action.

Only she had no clue how to start.

It was so hard to think. And everyone was staring at her. Marion wasn't sure how to handle that, either. Being the center of attention was abnormal for her. Maids were supposed to be modest and demure.

"You want to get out of here, duchess?" Nicholas' voice was low and filled with mysterious ideas.

Marion desperately seized on that vague question, trusting him even though he'd done nothing to deserve it. Her instincts took over. She nodded, not bothering to ask where they were going. She just wanted to leave. "Please, Nick."

Anyplace in the world had to be better than standing at the altar and realizing your True Love didn't love you.

Anyplace at all.

Chapter Five

Royal housekeeper tells all!
Which king made a sex tape with a troll? Which Maid isn't so pure?
Which royal pet had an affair with a centaur? We've got the scoop
on all the smut, right from a highly-placed source!

Alan A. Dale- "Nottingham's Naughtiest News"

Since childhood, the Sheriff of Nottingham had hated Robin Hood and that shithead had hated him back. Now, their feud was finally coming to a head and Nicholas intended to win.

The Looking Glass Campaigns had exacerbated the conflict, but the true source of the animosity was Marion. Both of them knew that. Hood was a moron, but even he was bright enough to notice Nicholas was obsessed with his True Love. Instead of being outraged, Nottingham's greatest hero always seemed smug that destiny had given him the woman that Nicholas longed for. For fifteen years, looking at the man's arrogant smirk had set Nicholas' teeth on edge.

Likewise, Nicholas' position of command seemed to piss Hood off. He'd vowed to defeat the sheriff, before he settled down and married Marion. So, of course Nicholas did everything in his power *not* to be defeated. He would've done anything in the world to prevent Hood from slipping his ring on her finger.

And killing the bastard was obviously his *first* choice.

The problem was, Hood always hid in Sherwood Forest, striking only when he could catch his prey unaware. He never fought in the open and had tunnels all over Nottingham to aid in his skulking. Nicholas needed to draw Robin Hood out and the fastest way to do that was to use Marion as bait.

If he took Marion away, Robin Hood would show up to get her back. Of course, he would! It was inconceivable to Nicholas that someone wouldn't fight for Marion. There were other pretty girls in the kingdom, if that's all you wanted. Other relatives of the king a man could court for power, if you were looking to climb the social ladder. Other Maids, if you were some upright, prig who had your heart set on a chaste bride.

There was only one Marion Huntingdon, though.

Hood understood that. He *had* to. Robin would certainly come for her and Nicholas would catch him. Action and reaction. This should have been a very simple and straightforward plan.

Only Marion seemed determined to screw it all up.

Nicholas wasn't sure what her new game was, but his lack of understanding didn't surprise him. Marion was mischievous and clever. Very clever. Sometimes Nicholas felt like he was the only one who noticed that fact. Maybe the rest of the kingdom overlooked it, because the true troublemaking brilliance of the woman had always been masked behind sweetness and ladylike manners.

Except, that seemed to be changing, now.

Looking into her eyes last night, Nicholas had seen the sharpness of her mind gleaming right out in the open. He'd seen someone who could outthink him *and* Hood, if she wanted to. He'd seen all the Bad ideas swirling in her Good little head and a teasing glint in her eyes. He'd seen the One-and-Fucking-Only Marion, washed clean of all the courtly bullshit.

And he'd wanted her.

He always wanted Marion, but showing his obsessive desire wasn't part of the plan. It also wasn't part of the plan for Marion to *agree* to marry him. Or for him to start thinking of his sudden betrothal rights, when she did. Or for her to smile at him and for his heart to start pounding in his chest. Or for him to spend half the night reading about goddamn Hatters, of all things.

His very simple and straightforward plan was being blown to hell by that too-clever woman. It wouldn't do. He needed to take control of the situation. He'd locked her in her room, but that wouldn't slow her down for long. Marion weaved trouble like a spinner turning straw into gold.

"Good morning, Commander." Rockwell, one of his

top lieutenants, came in.

The gargoyles who'd survived the war now lived in the castle. Most of them were palace soldiers, serving directly under Nicholas' five most trusted men. Those lieutenants – Gravol, Boulder, Oore, Rockwell, and Quarry-- then reported to him. (Well, Gravol wasn't technically in charge of anyone. He just floated between the other lieutenants and they took turns watching out for him.) In any case, the system reduced the number of people Nicholas had to speak to each day, which was always one of his main goals as leader.

Rockwell was an older man and the stone he was carved from tended to crumble, but he was still given to fits of optimistic nonsense. And he talked too much. Everyone talked too much, in Nicholas estimation.

"Your newspaper." He respectfully laid it in front of Nicholas on the table and didn't wait for a response. Everyone knew Nicholas hated conversation, especially in the morning. Rockwell hurried out of the banquet room, no doubt to read one of the romantic stories he favored, and left Nicholas to his routine.

Nicholas wasn't sure why he ate in the vast, echoing space, except it was on the official palace schedule drawn up for the sheriff. It made sense to continue with some of the traditions, if only to create the illusion of control. He spent every morning in the room, listening to reports from around the kingdom and reading the daily briefs.

Sitting at the head of the long table, Nicholas flipped the paper over and smoothed out the headline. "Maid Marion Agrees to Wed Sheriff!" was spelled out in block letters that took up half the page. His thick, rocky fingers ran over the words, feeling a surge of satisfaction that had nothing to do with his plan to lure Robin Hood into a trap.

"I've always hated that picture." Marion strolled in, glancing at the paper and rolling her eyes.

Nicholas looked up at her, through his lashes. She'd gotten free of her room. He wasn't even mildly surprised.

He wasn't going to answer her, though. The less he said, the less chance he'd make an idiot out of himself. Words didn't come easily to Nicholas. They got all mixed up somewhere between his head and his mouth. The results were a never-ending source of embarrassment and frustration for him, which added to his introverted tendencies.

Luckily, his quiet, stony stare usually cowed people into submission, so it all worked out fine. Except with Marion. With her, Nicholas had to press his lips together to stop himself from saying something back. Last night things had gone off the rails, because he'd been unable to just ignore her. He'd never been able to ignore Marion.

She was the only one he ever wanted to talk to.

"You couldn't have picked a better photo?" She went on blithely. "Or did you deliberately choose one where I look fat?"

He scoffed at that nonsense. The woman always looked beautiful.

"I look fat in a lot of pictures, though." Marion shrugged at his dismissive sound. "And I'm probably going to *keep* looking fat in them, because I don't care very much and I've developed a new addiction to non-prison-y food." She headed for the sideboard. "Hot damn... Waffles for breakfast. Who could've guessed those were my favorites?"

Nicholas' gaze slipped down her body, lingering on her lush posterior. She was wearing pants. Women in Nottingham tended towards dresses, in keeping with the outdated customs of the place. She must have stolen them from somewhere in the castle, because his men certainly hadn't brought them from her house. Nicholas had carefully checked all her belongings, making sure she had no ready means of escape.

He'd also taken the opportunity to examine her underwear. If he was going to be an obsessed bastard, he might as well do it full throttle. So he had a very clear picture of what silky bits of fabric separated her succulent curves from the pilfered clothes.

He wondered if it was the black panties with the lace.
Christ, he hoped so.

Marion turned and caught him staring. Looking over her shoulder, she studied her own behind and shrugged. "I was thinner in jail, but my ass was flat. It's an either/or kinda deal, for me. Starving and thin. Eating and ass." She moved her hands up and down, weighing the two options. "I'm choosing my ass."

Good choice.

Nicholas cleared his throat. He often talked to himself and the mental voice tended to encourage his worse impulses.

Being neither Good nor Bad, gargoyles existed in a perpetual gray area. It could be a struggle to balance for him. Ogling Marion seemed perfectly natural, but he knew it was wrong. Nicholas had his own vague code and he tried to follow it, regardless of what his reverse conscience urged. So, he pried his gaze away from Marion's lovely ass and hunted for something to say. Even conversation seemed safer than letting her continue to casually discuss her luscious body.

"Didn't I lock you in your room?"

"So?" She heaped waffles onto her plate and doused them with a quart of syrup.

"So, you are presently in protective custody, not a houseguest."

"Is 'protective custody' sheriff-talk for bolting my door closed?"

"You'd prefer I toss you in the dungeon? You're suspected of aiding an outlaw."

"Robin?" Marion snorted. "Please. I never aided him in anything. He didn't let girls into the sacred club of Merry Men." Her voice was dismissive, when she spoke of her True Love. "Nope. He did his thing and I did mine. Besides, if I was locked in my room, I couldn't be here with you. And according to my prison therapist, I'm 'unhealthily fixated' on your pretty self, love monkey."

Considering Nicholas was almost criminally obsessed with her, that joke was a little too close for comfort. "As opposed to a healthy fixation?" He heard himself mock.

"I guess." She didn't seem worried about her supposed diagnosis. "I feel great about it, myself. Totally healthy. But Dr. Ramona said I was 'teetering on the brink of madness' over you. I told her maybe so, but the view is awesome from up here."

She sat down at the table. ...In the seat directly next to Nicholas. As she did, her eyes scanned around the room, like she was cataloging each stick of furniture and measuring the length of every wall. She even angled her body so she could watch the door. Something about her intensity reminded him of soldiers just back from the war. He couldn't explain it, but it was all there in her gaze. A knowledge of darkness that was unusual in a gently bred Maid.

But then, Marion *had* had hardships in her life. Perhaps, they were weighing on her. Nicholas knew better than anyone how she'd struggled when her father was sick and the Huntingdon family fortunes dwindled. Not to mention her boyfriend was a narcissistic terrorist, covered in tree sap. That was sure to be a burden.

What the hell did she see in Robin Hood?

And why was that jackass not sleeping with her?

Because of some obsolete social customs that said Maid's had to stay a virgin? Were noblemen really *that* stupid? If Nicholas had been Robin, he would have been bedding the girl from the day she turned eighteen. Nicholas wasn't a man to miss an opportunity. Chivalric code be damned, he would have taken what was his, before someone stopped him.

The betrothal rights are yours.

Nicholas shook away that thought and tried to focus on something innocuous. "It's... unusual to see you sitting at my breakfast table." He told her, because it seemed a safe enough thing to say. God knew he wasn't good with small talk.

Why was she making him do this? Why was he *letting her* make him do this?

Those fathomless brown eyes flashed back to him, oddly fearless. "Well, I'm having an unusual couple days." She drawled out. "Yesterday, I was ten years older and rotting in a jail cell. Today, I'm engaged to a dead guy. I'd say I'm coping pretty well."

"I read some articles about Hatters, you know. No one has ever conclusively proven they can warp time."

"Pretty sure *I* just proved it. Hey, maybe I should hit

the talk show circuit. Make a fortune with my dramatic tale of love, spanning space and time." Marion cut herself a huge piece of waffle, smirking like his doubts amused her. "In the meantime, what's on the agenda for today, sweetie-nugget?"

"If I had to guess: You driving me crazy for about fifteen hours."

She laughed. "That's funny!" She popped the waffle into her mouth. "Have you always been funny? I don't remember you being funny before."

Her laughter was the most beautiful sound he'd ever heard. Voices and noise often felt suffocating to him, but never around Marion. She was a calm spot in the chaos and her laughter was magical.

Shit.

Nicholas' drummed his stony fingers on the tabletop and considered his options. His troublesome fiancée wasn't intimidated by him. He had no idea why. Since he was unwilling to force her compliance, he was in a quandary on how to proceed.

Marion had been right, the night before. Nicholas *was* a blunt instrument. If you built a wall, he'd stand there and hammer on it until it fell. That was how he'd risen in the palace guardsmen' ranks, at such a young age. Once he'd gotten his foot in the door at the castle, he'd trained harder and longer than any other gargoyle ever had. But there was no way for him to use his typical single-minded determination against Marion. She was clearly going to do whatever she wanted and how the hell could he stop her?

She was the only person in the kingdom he was powerless against.

Nicholas could corral her back to her room, but she'd figure out some new way to escape and God only knew what kind of mayhem she'd cause once she did. None of his men would be able to keep up with her and Nicholas couldn't stay at the castle all day to prevent chaos. It was probably better to let Marion stay near him, if she wanted. He could keep an eye on her and try to figure out what she was really up to.

Also, he liked seeing her beside him.

"I'm going to sit here until ten." He grudgingly said. "Then, I'm going into town to meet with Friar Tuck."

"Deliberately?" She made a face. "Ugh. Why? He was always such a jackass."

"He's officiating our wedding."

She snorted. "Oh yeah... I forgot about that. You know he's friends with Robin, right?"

"Why do you think I picked him to conduct the ceremony? I want Hood to hear all about our pending nuptials. The more pissed he is, the more likely he is to screw up and get caught."

"He's not going to rescue me." Marion insisted. "You're wasting your time on this shit, when you should be focusing on whoever wants you dead. We need to start narrowing down the suspects..."

She stopped talking, her whole expression changing as someone else entered the room. Her eyes tracked one of Nicholas' gargoyle soldiers as he marched in, saluted, and handed him a file folder without speaking.

Nicholas flipped it open, scanning it, as the man left, again. Boulder knew he preferred silence at breakfast, too. ...If only his stolen bride picked up on the social ques.

"There are too many people around you." Marion hissed, leaning closer in case anyone else was lurking nearby and eavesdropping. "This is what I'm talking about. You're not listening to me about how serious the situation is. Someone is plotting to *murder* you. Who was that guy? Do you even know?"

"That is Lieutenant Boulder." Nicholas told her distractedly. He knew the names of all his men and always worked to ensure their safety. Someone had to look out for the palace gargoyles, since the king sure as hell didn't. "I doubt he's going to murder me. If he was, I'm sure he'd mention it, because he's never shy about telling people that he hates them."

"It's always the ones you don't suspect who get you. I once got stabbed by a munchkin during group therapy." She shook her head in annoyance. "You don't stab people in share circle. You just *don't*."

Nicholas ignored that. "The latest treasury shipment was stolen, last night."

The only way to pay Nottingham's never-ending bills was melting down the castle's treasures. Most of the priceless objects had been accumulated over centuries, but paying for food was more important than a horde of shiny knickknacks. Even Richard thought the plan was sound, no doubt because the king squandered over half the profits on his endless war. Gold coins spent better than candlesticks and elaborate picture frames. So far, Nicholas had sold about a ton of heirlooms.

And Hood had tried to steal *all* of it.

Nicholas looked up at Marion. "Did you know about this theft?"

Marion frowned. "I don't think so." She lifted a nonchalant shoulder. "If I did, I don't remember."

"You don't *remember* your boyfriend pilfering a chest of antique jewelry, eighteen golden goblets, and a scepter shaped like a lion's head?"

"Well, I *have* had a lot on my mind, for the past decade or so." She sent him an aggravated look. "Like that time I *went to jail for fucking murdering you*."

Nicholas pinched the bridge of his nose and struggled for patience.

"But golly! A missing lion scepter?" Marion continued with exaggerated shock. "How could I *possibly* forget something so vital? It's a national tragedy. How will we ever go on, with such an important part of all our lives missing…?" She trailed off in mock confusion. "Hang on, what is a scepter even *for*? Isn't it just a stick?"

Nicholas wasn't getting sucked into her chaos. He *wasn't*. "Hood did this." He tapped his finger on the printout of stolen goods, inadvertently shaking the tabletop. He was so annoyed that he didn't even bother to worry about her reaction to the rocky surface of his right hand. "We both know it."

"Probably." She didn't seem to care about the theft or the living-stone texture of Nicholas' skin. "Robbery isn't the crime I'm here to solve, though. All I care about is keeping you breathing."

"If I die, Hood will be behind that, too.

"He's definitely a main person of interest, like I said. ...But, on the other hand, I can't imagine you letting Robin get so *close* to you." Her eyes narrowed in thought. "We'll find him and question him."

"Question him?" Nicholas saw her new angle. "Let me guess: I should let you go find your boyfriend and 'question' him. Then, you'll report back to me, right?"

"I was thinking more like we should trap him in a cage and let him sit there, suffering and alone, for ten years or so. It only seems fair, since someone did it to me." Her fork stabbed another piece of waffle with unnecessary force.

Nicholas stared at her. He'd watched Marion for so long, he could read her expressions and this one was clear. She was angry. For the first time, he processed that she was genuinely *angry* at Hood.

Marion arched a brow. "Robin and I have had a falling out." She reported. "Have I mentioned that? I feel like I've mentioned that."

Nicholas' heart started pounding with awful, pointless hope. "What kind of falling out?"

"The kind where I'm a vengeful bitch, out to wreck his life." She smiled prettily. "Wanna help?"

Yes.

"No." He snapped, overriding his own thoughts. This was an act. It had to be. Marion was plotting something. She had everyone else in Nottingham fooled, but he'd always seen deep into her mischievous little soul. "Whatever you're up to, I have my own plan and I'm sticking to it."

"Like a said: A big, blunt hammer. That's you." Marion made a little hammering motion, to illustrate her point. She liked to talk with sound-effects and hand gestures. Nicholas found it endearing, even when she was mocking him. "Fortunately, my 'screwing over Robin' agenda neatly dovetails into my 'saving you and exonerating me' agenda, so I think everything will come together. ...With or without your help, jellybean."

"I'm not letting you go." Just saying the words gave him a rush of shameful triumph. "You're kidnapped. Deal with it."

"I didn't ask you to let me go."

Nicholas wasn't appeased. Abducting her had been a personal low for him, brought on by years of frustration and bitterness. Marion had always been kind to him, even when he was a surly jackass to her. He'd targeted her *because* she was kind to him, for God's sake. Because she was the one he fit with. Because he was obsessed with every perfect hair on her perfect head. Because Robin Hood had what Nicholas longed for and it drove him crazy.

But now you have her.

Technically, that was true. His kidnapping plan had become more complex the second Marion said 'yes' to his proposal. Her agreement legitimized his crime. They were legally engaged. Really and truly *engaged*. That was a huge deal. Under Nottingham's backwards rules, Marion belonged to Nicholas.

With an engagement comes betrothal rights.

His head tilted. "Didn't I tell you I was going to start acting like your betrothed, if you left your room today?" He asked abruptly.

"You did." The pulse in her neck sped up, even as her eyes stayed level. "But, these days, I'm *very* Bad at obeying... Even when I know I'm going to be punished for it." She gave a teasing grin that invited all sorts of wonderfully dirty interpretations.

Every drop of blood in his body pooled southward.

Marion's smile grew wider, seeing that she'd just stunned him into a trance.

Nicholas shook his head, trying to clear it. What was she doing? He didn't understand her trap, but he *knew* it was all around him. There was no other explanation. "Are you wearing a wire?" He abruptly demanded.

"A *wire?*" She chortled. "Lord, you watch way too much TV."

"There are no TVs in Nottingham."

"Aw fuck. I forgot about that, too. Even the prison has television sets." She sighed in dismay. "I guess it doesn't matter. Everything will be a rerun for me, anyhow."

Nicholas refused to get distracted. "Are you recording me, as some kind of undercover shit?" He persisted. It didn't make any sense, but it was the only thing he could think of.

"That's the dumbest thing I ever heard and I did time with a leprechaun who only talked in limericks." She shuddered. "God, I was *so* happy when Trevelyan ate him."

Nicholas refused to back down. "Did Hood put you up to this plan?" Maybe she was lying about their "falling out," after all.

"When did Robin ever have a plan that didn't involve an arrow?" Marion rolled her eyes. "No, this is all me. You can tell because it's *working* and because no one is dressed in leaves."

Nicholas stood up. "Come here."

Marion's smug expression dimmed a bit, but she got to her feet. "You're being paranoid about all the wrong things. I haven't spoken to Robin since right after my trial. I think he put some gold in my commissary account at the prison, but he told me that we..."

Nicholas cut her off. "Face the table." He spun her around, nudging her legs apart with his boot.

Marion's hands went flat on the tabletop for support. "Hang on. You can't..."

"I *can*. I'm the sheriff of this kingdom. Who's going to stop me?"

"Shall I call my lawyer? Not that the bitch did me much good last time."

Nicholas disregarded that legal analysis. Despite his words, he was trying to keep his hands light and professional, as he searched her. He was actually a little proud of himself. Marion was bent over the table in front of him and he had the right to do all kinds of nefarious things to her pretty little body. But he was resisting temptation...

Until he got to her torso, anyway.

His thumbs brushed the undersides of her spectacular

breasts and he stopped. If he went any farther, he was going to be crossing a line he couldn't uncross. He knew it as surely as he'd ever known anything.

Marion looked up at him, her face flushed and her eyes bright. "I could have a microphone stuffed in my bra." She reported and it sounded like a dare. "I'm a D cup. There's plenty of room in there."

Nicholas felt his fingers moved upward, like they were drawn by a magnet.

No.

He yanked his hands away, before they made contact. Marion was tricking him somehow. He thought in straight lines, while her brain zigzagged all over the place. It was impossible for a purposeless, predictable, passionless man to keep up with her, but he was sure as hell smart enough to know she was scheming. Marion wasn't doing this because she wanted him so damn much, that much was certain.

Not like he wanted her.

Nicholas swallowed. God, he'd wanted her for so long. Her mind and feelings and body and smile. He wanted *all* of her. It really was an obsession. He thought about Marion every minute of the day. He'd memorized her schedule, so he could stand by the castle windows and see her go by. He knew which shops she visited and what she bought. Which books she checked out of the library, so he could read them, too. He even knew what color her goddamn toothbrush was.

Marion was everything to him.

Nicholas flattened his palms on the table next to Marion's, looming over her, her back to his front. He stood there for a beat, breathing hard, trying to stay in control. If she had some kind of recording device in her blouse, it would just have to stay there. No way was he looking for it. There was only so much a man could take without cracking.

Marion didn't try to push him away. Instead, she sighed, almost apologetically. "Sorry, I'm…" She swallowed. "I don't mean to pressure you, Nick."

His heart flipped at the shortened form of his name. She was the only one who'd ever called him that. He'd told her she could, back when they were children. It shocked him that she still remembered. Why would she?

"Is it Robin?" She guessed. "Is that why you're feeling hesitant about touching me? Because I *promise* I'm not pining after that douchebag." She shook her head. "You don't come back from the kind of falling out we had."

"He's your True Love." Nicholas forced the words out. "You'll forgive him for whatever he's done."

No gargoyle had ever found a True Love, as far as he knew. Few even bothered to look. Caring for a mate gave you a purpose and his kind were eternally purposeless. It was part of their enspelled DNA, according to Nottingham's scientists. Nicholas longed for a purpose, beyond serving the moronic king. Something bigger.

Something *his*.

His mother had assured him he'd find it, but Gepetta had been too optimistic about the world. She'd told him if he committed himself to something, with his whole heart and soul, he'd inevitably find his purpose. But Nicholas had set goals and reached them, again and again. He'd thrown himself into rising through the gargoyle ranks, pressing forward with sheer determination and plowing down everything that got in his way. No one could've been more committed than he was. Now, he was as high as anybody could go in Nottingham and it was still empty.

Meanwhile, Hood had just been handed everything Nicholas had ever wanted on a silver platter. God, he seriously hated that asshole.

"I'll never forgive Robin." Marion shrugged with total finality. "If you don't want me, I'll find someone else. But, *never* him. I'm going to experience everything that I missed, which includes sex, so..."

"No one else!" Nicholas interrupted loudly. "Are you out of your mind? You agreed to marry *me,* last night. No one else is allowed to touch you, Marion. Legally, you're already mine."

He wasn't sure why he said all that and he was even less sure why she didn't argue.

Instead, she tilted her head, in feminine challenge.

Nicholas stared back, his chest heaving. ...And for an endless moment, everything went still. Whatever feeble barriers he'd been able to construct inside of himself cracked open. That was all it took. Holding back from Marion was impossible, when she was pushing closer. He might as well try to stop the rising tide with a mop.

Guyla Gisborn, the castle's middle-aged housekeeper, came in with a fresh pot of coffee, only to stop dead in the doorway. Nicholas was still positioned behind Marion, his large body pressed up against her in ways no decent woman would allow with a gargoyle and a Maid wouldn't allow with *anyone*.

Unless he was her very demanding new fiancé.

"Leave." Nicholas told the housekeeper, barely looking her way. His voice was deeper than usual.

Guyla fled in terror and glee. The woman was a bigger gossip than *Nottingham's Naughtiest News*, so she was no doubt eager to spread this tale. Within ten minutes, the whole kingdom would hear that the sheriff had already begun exerting his betrothal rights on Maid Marion. The thought gave him a hot surge of possession.

"At least this time she won't have to lie about seeing us together, the miserable hag." Marion muttered.

Nicholas had no idea what that meant.

Instead of explaining, Marion arched a brow. "So, are you done searching me for secret wires?"

"What...? Oh. Yes." Nicholas stepped back from her and ran a hand through his hair. There were no microphones on her body. Just acres of flawless curves. "You're clean."

"For now." Another impish grin shined his way.

Nicholas blinked. The-One-And-Fucking-Only-Marion had somehow been released from her Maidenly shell and she was blindingly bright. He forced himself to look away and head back to his seat. What *the hell* was happening here?

Marion made a face at his brooding silence. "Why would I hide listening devices on my body, anyway? You barely say anything. What could I possibly record?"

"I've talked to you more than I've ever talked to

anyone else." With her, words just poured out of him. It had always been that way. It was why he should avoid her. It was *why* it was so damn hard to avoid her.

Marion stared at him. "Do you?"

He grunted.

"Why do you think that is?"

"I have no idea." But he unconsciously rubbed the spot where his mother's ring had once hung around his neck.

Marion looked pleased with that grumbled reply. "Okay." She sat down again, only now her chair seemed even closer to him. Was her chair closer to him?

Nicholas' frown deepened. "Hood won't like that you said 'yes' to this engagement, you know." Since intimidating her was useless, he gave up even trying and went with another plan. Maybe the reality of this situation would begin to sink in, if he mentioned her moronic boyfriend enough. Maybe Marion would start behaving like he'd expected her to behave and he could regain some functioning brain cells. "When he sees that you actually *agreed* to marry me, he's going to explode."

"I'll bet my virtue that he doesn't."

Nicholas' eyebrows rose. Maids didn't make wagers like that, even in jest. Their virtue was too valuable. "Deal." He heard himself say a little too swiftly. "I'll take that bet."

Marion looked at him in surprise. "I can predict the future, Nick. For real, Robin's not going to care."

"He'll care. ...Unless this is all some plot you two are perpetrating."

She forked up a bite of waffle. "Robin doesn't *care* enough about me or my opinions to 'plot' with me." She chewed her breakfast, like she relished the taste. "Maybe that's why I got engaged to you, snickerdoodle."

"You're trying to make him jealous? With *me?*" He scoffed at that idea. No one in the world would ever think that Marion would prefer Nicholas to Robin Hood. Especially not Nicholas and *especially* not Hood himself.

She considered him thoughtfully. "No, I'm not trying to make him jealous. I don't think I even could and I don't care enough to try. I don't want him to want me. That's not what this is about. I was over that asshat before I even got to jail."

Nicholas searched for a response to that and came up empty.

"Mostly Robin is in that 'ex-boyfriend space,' where you forget he exists for months at a time and then suddenly you remember and you're embarrassed all over again that you ever liked him, in the first place." Rather than pour herself a cup of coffee, she reached over to take Nicholas' mug. "But he fucked me over and *no one* fucks me over and gets away with it. Not anymore. Now, I'm just wrecking his life for the hell of it." She gave a nonchalant shrug.

He watched her drink from his cup saying nothing.

Marion's head tilted. "Are you going to be disappointed when you don't get under his skin with this silly plan?" She gestured towards the newspaper.

"I'm going to hang the man." Nicholas murmured, his gaze tracing all over her face. He could do nothing but stare at her for hours and never get bored. "It doesn't matter if it gets under his skin or not, because he'll be dead."

"You'll have to catch him, first." She sipped his coffee, pink lips on the rim that his own mouth had touched, her beautiful eyes shining with razor-sharp ideas. "You *sure* you don't want to team up with me, so we can do that together?"

Chapter Six

Maid Marion Moves On!
Robin Hood's former flame has cast him aside in favor of Nottingham's most infamous gargoyle and it seems like she couldn't be happier. The newly engaged couple was spotted out and about today, planning their nuptials. Maybe Sherwood's favorite bandit spent a little too much time polishing his own bow and left his lovely lady aching for the long arm of the law.

Alan A. Dale- "Nottingham's Naughtiest News"

Friar Tuck had always been a prick.

"Of course this is all highly unusual, sheriff." He anxiously watched Nicholas and the other gargoyle guardsmen inspect the church. Blue and gold uniforms circled the building like hungry sharks looking for prey. "I don't know what you hope to find. This is a place of worship, after all."

Nicholas shot him a dark look, not bothering to respond. It was like the man only had a certain number of words to say each day and so he didn't like to waste them on anyone other than Marion.

He'd been telling the truth earlier. He really *did* talk to her more than anyone else. Mostly, he complained at her and doubted her, but he was still *speaking*. That was a great sign for their partnership.

Inside the pocket of her stolen pants, she carried the hideous necklace Tansy had given her. Its magic was gone now, but she liked having it close. It felt like a good luck charm. She absently ran her fingers across the talisman. She would need all the luck she could get to seduce her surly groom.

"Nick wants to find all the ways Robin can sneak into the church." Marion told Tuck, willing to lend Nicholas a hand, even though he was still refusing to listen to her about Robin. He'd completely shot down her offer to team up over breakfast.

Sooner or later, he'd come around, though. And in the meantime, the quicker he searched the cathedral, the quicker they could leave. "Did you ever seal up that tunnel in the basement?"

Tuck's eyes went wide in horror.

Nicholas glanced down at her in surprise.

Marion shrugged and blew a bubble with the gum she was chewing. "There's a tunnel in the basement." She told him casually. Robin had tunnels and secret passages everywhere.

Several of the gargoyles exchanged confused glances, surprised by her willingness to switch teams. She was pretty sure none of them were behind Nicholas' murder. She'd been carefully watching them all morning and they seemed to idolize the man.

Nicholas glanced over at the closest one. "Oore, search the basement." He ordered.

"South wall." Marion called helpfully, as the guard rushed off to look. "Behind the wine racks."

That sent Tuck off on another jabbering rant about how he barely even knew Robin and how he never went into the basement, so he had no clue *what* kind of tunnels were down there, and how this was all *highly* unusual, and how blah, blah, blah...

Marion tuned out the nut-sack's rambling and looked around the interior of Nottingham's cathedral. It looked the same. The ornamental stone, and the stained glass, and the two tiers of ancient pews. It could have been a thousand other churches, in a thousand other lands.

Only this one was where she'd been publically humiliated.

Being back in the grand space wasn't traumatic, exactly. But the cathedral certainly wasn't on her Top Ten list of sentimental spots to revisit. All she wanted to do was figure out who was going to kill Nicholas and get the hell out of Nottingham for good.

And a cigarette. She wanted a cigarette.

That was all muscle memory, though, not an actual nicotine craving. Marion hadn't started smoking until six months after her conviction. At the time, lung cancer had seemed like a viable long-term escape plan. But now that she had a reason to live, it wasn't such a great choice. That knowledge did nothing to cut the cravings. After chain-smoking for a decade, it felt weird not to have a cigarette in her mouth.

Marion was making due with gum and watching Nicholas prowl around. He was even more handsome in the daylight. How in the hell had she missed that the first time through? Robin really had been a pestilence in her mind. Now that she was cured, everything looked different. Better. Her eyes drifted up Nicholas' large body.

Really, *really* better.

Her "unhealthy fixation" with the man told her to drag him off somewhere and ravish him. Then, set up cameras to watch him all day, so he could never escape or get hurt, again. And maybe steal his stuff and build a little shrine.

Huh.

Okay. That was going a little *too* far towards the brink of madness. Fine. Whatever. No shrine. That pontificating bitch, Doctor Ramona, would be very proud at her restraint.

Marion wasn't done with the "evidence gathering" phase of her courtship anyway, so there was time for her stalking-him-until-she-died instincts to calm down. A girl couldn't be too careful, after all. She wasn't ready to fully trust Nicholas, yet. So far, though, things were going more really, *really* better than she'd ever imagined. And ten years behind bars left lots of time for imagining. She kept telling herself to slow down, but it was hard not to throw caution to the wind and just tell Nicholas everything.

"We need to triple the security, all along the balconies." Rockwell, the gargoyle guardsman, told Nicholas, gesturing up at the top row of pews. He was an older man. His stony skin was cracked in places, like the rock he'd been carved from was flawed from the beginning and just grew worse with age. "Robin Hood could try and come in through the roof."

Nicholas nodded.

"Robin's not coming in through the roof." Marion assured them, for the millionth time. "He's not coming, at all."

Nicholas ignored that, for the millionth time.

"We should put men in the alleyway, as well." Rockwell went on, shooting Marion a wary glance. He didn't seem to know what to make of her shifting allegiances. "It runs behind the cathedral and Hood might be able to sneak in that way."

"He won't." Marion said easily, chewing her gum. "None of this matters."

"Do it." Nicholas told Rockwell, as if she hadn't spoken.

Rockwell saluted. Like all the guards, he either spoke to Nicholas in respectful awe or stood by in deferential silence... even while his moronic commander refused to listen to reason. Nicholas might be a moody grouch, but his men clearly worshiped him.

Robin couldn't say that. The Merry Men were mainly in it for the ale and wenches.

Marion sighed. She didn't blame Nick for not listening to her, honestly. They were both a little mistrustful, by nature. But, it was frustrating to waste all this time. They'd already gone through this whole using-the-wedding-to-capture Robin deal-y once, so she saw no reason for a repeat. Being left at the altar had sucked and none of the flower arrangements had been to her taste. Nicholas hadn't even worn a traditional bycocket wedding hat. If Marion was planning a wedding for really *real*, she'd...

She tilted her head, her thoughts trailing off. Huh. If Nicholas was determined to do this again, they really should do it *right*. "Hey, can we *not* have roses, this time?"

Nicholas looked down at her, with a slight frown.

"Flowers?" She prompted, because he seemed confused by the request. "For our ceremony? Because girls have ideas about what their wedding should look like, Nick."

He stared at her.

"We've already ordered pink roses, Commander." Rockwell chimed in, always eager to help his boss. A steady stream of dust fell from the cracks in his stone features, as if the ill-fitting rocky pieces of his face were constantly grating together. "I'm not sure how your betrothed knows the flowers, but changing the order now would be..."

Marion cut him off. "I don't want pink and I'm allergic to roses." Her eyebrows rose expectantly, her gaze staying on Nicholas. "Unless you have some other color scheme in mind, I'm thinking red and white tulips."

He shook his head, a strange look on his face. "I don't have a color scheme in mind. I've never thought about color schemes once in my whole life."

"You never thought about what it would be like, if I was walking down the aisle to you?"

Silence.

Marion inwardly smirked.

Nicholas blinked and glanced at Rockwell. "Order whatever makes her happy." He decided.

Rockwell gaped at him, but didn't question the command.

"Good. We'll do red and white tulips, then." Marion snapped another bubble with her gum, satisfied with the way that conversation had gone. "Very fucking tasteful."

Nicholas frowned a bit, but didn't comment. Huge surprise. His attention slipped back to Rockwell and he nodded. Rockwell quickly jotted down a note to change the flowers. Nicholas cleared his throat and went stalking off to examine the massive locks on the massive doors that Robin would never try to get through. The man was determined to focus on all the wrong things.

"*Such* a goddamn waste of time." Marion rolled her eyes.

Friar Tuck was shocked by her language and by her aiding the enemy. "Maid Marion, what in the blazes has gotten into you?" He demanded, lowering his voice so the gargoyles wouldn't overhear. He was a portly, bald man who had a tendency to sweat a lot. Since it was May, and Tuck was dressed in a brown wool tunic, that was a bad mix. "You don't even have your loyal lady-in-waiting with you, as you gallivant around with these ruffians! What will people think?"

Marion flashed him a dismissive look. Since he wanted

to chat, she might as well share some thoughts. "You're an asshole, Tuck."

His fishy-looking mouth dropped open in indignation. "What?!"

"An... ass...hole." She pronounced the syllables slowly, because he seemed to be struggling to understand. "You drink too much to hide the fact that you're a coward and incapable of fulfilling any of your vows to help people. When I was dragged from my house and locked in the castle, you did jack-shit to lend a hand. Instead, you got plastered and told me to wait for Robin to save me."

His face grew mottled, sputtering out excuses for himself and Robin. "I have no idea... This isn't you talking... The sheriff is filling your head with..."

Marion cut him off. "Leave Nick out of this. It's between me and Robin. Specifically, it's about me detesting Robin."

Tuck shook his head, like she was being an overexcited female and he needed to calm her. "Robin will come to rescue you from the sheriff, Maid Marion." He tried to give her arm a condescending pat, but she jerked out of range."

Nicholas' head snapped around, his eyebrows compressing. He must've been paying closer attention than she'd realized, because her evasive movement had his hackles up. He didn't like Tuck touching her. At all. He took a step forward, like he was ready to hang the friar right there in the church.

"I've got this handled, cookie-crumb." Marion assured him. She could handle anything that came her way, these days. "You just keep murder-plotting with your little friends."

Nicholas' attention stayed fixed on Tuck.

Tuck took a huge step back from Marion.

Nicholas grunted, still not thrilled, but at least placated with that outcome. He turned his attention to some map Rockwell was showing him.

Oooh, her groom was sexy when he got possessive.

Tuck was smart enough to keep a larger distance, but he wasn't through being a chauvinist dick. "You mustn't give into hysterics, Maid Marion. Just give Robin time to come up with a plan..."

"He's not coming to rescue me." Marion interrupted. "I don't even *want* him to."

Tuck frowned, not appreciating her dismissive tone. "You know, it hasn't escaped my notice that you *accepted* the sheriff's proposal." He said stiffly.

"What tipped you off? The giant newspaper headline or the fact that I'm helping him plan our dream wedding?"

Tuck ignored that. "You're using the sheriff to make Robin jealous. That's a dangerous game."

She rolled her eyes. Again with this shit? "I'm not trying to make Robin jealous. I'm done with Robin. I'm engaged to Nick. I'm perfectly happy being his hostage/bride."

Nicholas glanced at her sharply.

She made a face at him. "Are you eavesdropping, now?"

"No."

"Because it seems like you're eavesdropping. I told you I could handle this."

"I'm not eavesdropping. You're yelling. How can I help but overhear?"

"I'm not yelling." Were the sounds of the church all amplified for him? "My voice is echoing off all the frigging buttresses. A gentleman would ignore it."

"I'm a gargoyle, not a gentleman."

"You can be both, sugar-bean. I've seen you do it."

He blinked.

So did every gargoyle in the church. It seemed like maybe no one had ever claimed they were capable of honorable behavior before. Another huge surprise. Nottingham never missed a chance to be small, cruel, and flat-out wrong about everyone.

Tuck's scowled back and forth between them, not liking Marion's blatant flirting or Nicholas' uncharacteristic verbosity. "This situation brings up an interesting liturgical point." He declared. "It's not entirely clear to me that gargoyles *can* get married. They're not really *real* in the eyes of the church, you know. They can't even have children."

"So?" Marion couldn't care less about kids. She wasn't super maternal.

"*So*, that suggests that a higher power is seeking to keep them in check and our species separate, for the Good of the world. Who are we to question that divine wisdom?"

Marion waved aside that nonsense. "We'll get someone else to marry us, if you won't. I've never liked you anyway."

"First, I'll hang you by the neck and display your dead body from the portcullis." Nicholas corrected, his unyielding gaze on Tuck. "*Then*, I'll find someone else to marry us."

Tuck's lips thinned even thinner, but he didn't argue. At least not with Nicholas. No one argued with Nicholas, if they could help it. He had gallows erected all over the courtyard, making debate a bit one-sided.

The second her menacing groom turned away, again, Tuck's beady eyes were flashing back to Marion. "Robin is fighting to build a new utopia! A kingdom of nature and prosperity, where everyone knows their proper place. Meanwhile, you're playing this sad female game."

"It's not a game. And I couldn't give a troll's ass about Robin's utopian vision." His childlike idea of everyone living in the woods would stink in every possible way, if the Merry Men's camp was any indication. Marion had never been there, but she was pretty sure it was nothing but twig huts and smelly people. She couldn't imagine the stench of the full forest realm of Robin's imagination.

"You would stand in the way of Nottingham's future?!"

"I'm going to burn this whole kingdom down and *laugh*, you sanctimonious putz."

Now, he was angry. "I told Robin he shouldn't trust a woman." His voice was shrill with righteous fury. "I knew you were too weak. All you care about is your own selfish desires, just like your whore of a mother."

"Leave my mom out of this, too, jerkoff!"

The former duchess had been much younger than the duke, leading to constant speculation about her fidelity. In gossip, she'd been linked to affairs with every nobleman in the kingdom. In reality, the duke had been her True Love and she'd been ecstatically happy in the few years they'd had together. That was the story Marion's father always told and she saw no reason to doubt it.

Tuck kept ranting. "Why, I wouldn't put it past you to allow that ugly rock-monster liberties with your person." Rock-monster was a particularly vile and unimaginative slur against gargoyles. Just saying it proved he was a bigoted shit. "You'd allow him to touch you, out of nothing but feminine spite!"

"It won't be out of spite. I'm going to sleep with Nick, because I *want* to."

Marion hadn't bothered to lower her voice for that pronouncement. Every single being in the church turned to look at her. The jaws of the gargoyle guardsmen dropped. The various clerics cringed. Nicholas blinked.

Oh well.

They'd all get over their shock. When she was younger, being the center of attention had made all her modest, Maidenly insecurities go haywire. Now, she was over that crap. It took a lot to embarrass Marion, these days, and telling the truth wasn't enough to make her even flush. She stared back at them in defiance, not caring that she'd just blown her Good girl reputation straight to hell.

"Am I allowed to eavesdrop on this part?" Nicholas asked calmly.

She flipped him off.

Tuck's lips pinched together so hard they went white. "You don't care about the future of the kingdom or Robin's call to greatness. You aren't willing to pay the price for anything real."

"I'm the only one who's paid for *anything at all*." Marion shot back. "Don't pretend to be noble. Not with me."

"What's that supposed to mean?"

She leaned closer to him, so Nicholas couldn't eavesdrop this time. "If Robin is robbing from the rich to give to the poor... why is everyone in Nottingham still so fucking poor?"

Tuck's expression went thunderous. "You have no idea what you're talking about." He hissed. "Everything Robin does is for the Good people of Nottingham."

Marion wasn't backing down. "Everything Robin does is for *Robin*. When you see him and tell him about this conversation, which I'm sure you will, be sure to mention that I've dumped his selfish ass. Oh, and tell him I know about the letters."

"What letters?"

Done with this pointless outing, she headed for the door without answering. "I'm going to my house." Marion announced in a louder voice. It wasn't a request. Talking about Robin had reminded her how dumb she'd once been. How naive and trusting. She needed to make sure she didn't screw up, again.

Nicholas' expression went hard. Well, hard*er*. It was always hard, but now it was like granite. Literally. "No, you're not." It sounded like an order.

"I need to get something." Marion kept walking. "It'll only take a minute."

"You're not leaving my sight, Marion."

"Tackle me to the ground and stop me, then." She glanced at him over her shoulder. "Or you can come along. Take your pick, doodle-puppy."

Nicholas didn't tackle her.

The gargoyle who'd searched for basement tunnels came rushing back. Oore was apparently his name and he had carved ram's horns on the sides of his skull. He headed right to Nicholas, lowering his voice to speak urgently in his ear. Nicholas' gaze flicked to Marion, watching her with unreadable eyes, as he listened to Oore's report.

"Told ya." Marion gave a smug little curtsey. "I'm not lying to you about anything. Let's hope you can say the same."

He studied her with unreadable eyes.

"Coming?" She waltzed out the door, expecting him to follow. Why wouldn't he? She was *way* more interesting than some sweaty monk.

Nicholas muttered a curse. "Arrest the friar." He told

Rockwell. "Then seal the tunnel and finish securing the church." He stalked after Marion, ignoring Tuck's squawk of panic. "You have a very unique idea of what it means to be kidnaped, duchess."

Marion smirked as Nicholas caught up with her on the exterior steps. "My prison shrink says my brain doesn't work like everybody else's."

"I agree. It's one of your best qualities."

Butterflies fluttered in her stomach, again. "Thank you, Nick."

Gray eyes flashed to hers and then quickly away.

Marion was very encouraged. "So, you wanna walk or ride?" She gestured towards the unremarkable black coach.

Her big, stony groom wasn't the showiest despot in the land. He didn't use the king's blue and gold carriage, or bedeck himself in the royal coronet, or put his unsmiling face on all of Nottingham's currency. He did *everything* just a little differently than typical evildoers.

In jail, her theory had been that he was secretly shy, but now she thought it was more than that. His introversion was part of his core physiology. He'd once told her that he was very aware of sound. The echoes in the church had been making him wince, on and off, like he was uncomfortable with the loud noise. Social-situations seemed to make him physically uncomfortable, too. He felt crushed by all the talking and people.

Being Nicholas, he powered through his struggles just like he powered through everything else: Using the straightest lines possible and all by himself. He was determined and clever. Being scary meant he could keep people away and make things quiet, so that's what he did.

Also, he had an innate and *very* attractive wicked streak working for him.

He wasn't born Bad, but he'd clearly tapped into his latent potential for it. Nicholas' natural talent for wickedness probably helped him to survive in a world where he didn't quite fit. ...Just like Marion's had in the WUB Club.

They truly had *so* much in common.

Nicholas answered her question about their transportation by starting off towards her house with determined strides. The townsfolk couldn't get out of his way fast enough.

Behind them, Tuck was being carted out of the church, screaming about his rights. Hopefully, that weasel Alan A. Dale was somewhere in the crowd to get a picture of Tuck's ignominious exit. It would make another fabulous newspaper headline for her comeback tour.

"Why are you so upset, Tuck?" Marion called, because she was a spiteful bitch and proud of it. "Just have faith that Robin will come and save you. That's what you told me."

He lunged at her in wrathful anger.

Nicholas shifted so he was between Tuck and Marion, his hand going to his sword. From the expression on his face, an impromptu execution seemed likely. Sadly, Rockwell and a gargoyle with a pointed beard carved onto his chin hauled Friar Turd back, before Nicholas got to do any hardcore sheriff-ing. It wasn't like Tuck could run far on his stubby legs, so he was easy to catch.

Rockwell glanced over at Nicholas with a questioning expression.

Nicholas said nothing, which in gargoyle-ese must have meant "toss the bastard down the stairs," because that's exactly what Rockwell did.

It was wrong to grin, but Marion never claimed to be a super-great person. Tuck went tumbling to the bottom of the stone steps in a mass of unholy cursing and smelly robes. Before he even knew what was happening, the gargoyles were hauling him up again and roughly shoving him forward.

"I'm telling Robin about this, you traitorous harlot!" Tuck bellowed at Marion, blaming her for his humiliation and pain.

Rockwell sent Nicholas another look.

Nicholas said even more nothing than the first time.

The gargoyle with the beard on his chin was named Boulder. She remembered him testifying at her trial. He stepped forward and Tuck went down *again*. This time he didn't get back up. His unconscious body was haphazardly lugged off to the dungeon and Marion realized the gargoyles were her new best friends.

She waved a taunting good-bye to the little toad, not that he was awake to see it. "If I ever open a bar, do you think I should call it 'The Traitorous Harlot'?" She asked Nicholas happily. "Because I kind of like that name. I'm not gonna lie."

"I think if you want to live to open *anything*, you should stop pissing off people who outweigh you by a hundred pounds."

"Pfft. I could take that guy. Easy." Marion wasn't even worried about it.

Nicholas grunted.

"You know, it occurs to me that the new-and-improved me doesn't seem to faze you very much. You were a little confused last night, but now you're barely blinking at the change."

"What change? You've always been a troublemaker. Now, you're just showing it to everyone." He resumed walking.

Marion hurried after him, pleased by her groom's answer and with the general gloom permeating the town. Tuck's arrest seemed to be upsetting all the hypocrites who spent their days waiting for someone else to solve their problems.

At the edge of the crowd, Marion spotted her former lady-in-waiting. There was a bandage on Clorinda's broken nose, as she glared at Marion. When that shrew cheated her way to May Day Queen *this* time around, her coronation picture was going to feature two black-eyes.

Good.

Marion hated Clorinda, mostly because she had always *liked* Clorinda, despite her mean girl tendencies. She'd thought they were friends. That had clearly been a lie, so now Clorinda could burn along with the rest of Nottingham.

These upright citizens had found her guilty of a crime she didn't commit. It was nice to see them afraid, for once. God knew, she'd been scared to death during her trial. Everyone in this town deserved to suffer and Marion was happy to make their dreary lives a little bit worse.

Not that they could get *too* much worse.

Destroying Nottingham seemed almost redundant. Marion was going to do it anyway, of course, but the whole kingdom was already decaying. Its buildings weren't "historic architecture" that tourists took pictures of on expensive tour packages. They were just old and falling down. There was no money to fix them, so people still crowded into the listing structures and blamed everybody else for their dilapidated state. Royal banners, in Nottingham's official blue and gold color scheme, were plastered up here and there, but they did nothing to hide the endless gray of the town. And the surrounding landscape. And the people.

The abject misery was *exactly* what Marion wanted to see.

"Actually, I don't have to open a bar. Or do any job really." She told Nicholas cheerily. "I know who wins the next decade of Wolfball Championships. That should pay my bills, just fine." She leaned closer to him. "Bet on the Southlands, next year, by the way. There's a new kid named Marrok Wolf, just coming up, and he's going places."

Nicholas grunted again, not even blinking as Nottinghamers dispersed before him like a flock of frightened birds. Ducking into stores, hiding in alleys, covering their faces like that would somehow help them to avoid his notice. The dirty cobblestone streets cleared as he swept along. It was quite a spectacle.

Marion found herself smiling. "If you were in jail, you'd be running the joint within the first week, turtledove. It took me five years and a murder rap to inspire this kind of terror."

She looped her arm through his. It was half instinct and half just wanting to touch him. Maids always took the arms of gentlemen when they were out walking. She had to take two steps for every one of Nicholas', but that was fine. Marion was a girl with places to go.

Nicholas glanced down at her in surprise. Instead of freeing his arm, he slowed his stride so she could keep up.

"How could you possibly kill me? No one could believe that nonsense. You're a quarter my size."

"It was postulated in court that my stature allowed me to be stealthy. Maybe you were asleep and never saw it coming, the prosecution said. Which totally didn't match the forensics, but no one cared. It was a good story."

"I allowed you to kill me while I slept?" He snorted at that idea. "No."

"I *didn't* kill you and you *weren't* asleep." She stressed. "But, we'd had an argument on the night you died, so I was the most likely suspect."

He still wasn't buying it. "What did we argue about?"

"Secrets and stealing."

"What did you steal?"

"You were the one who stole, actually."

He shook his head. "I wouldn't steal from you." He sounded very certain.

"You literally stole *me*, Nick. Right out of my house."

"You just told Friar Tuck that you were happy being a hostage bride, remember?"

"Fine. You stole *old* me, right out of my house. And *old* me was pissed at you, for many justifiable reasons. There are things that you didn't tell me and you know it." She paused. "You want to tell me now?"

"Why would I tell you? You claim to already know everything. You're going to be the richest Wolfball gambler in Nottingham, because of Myron What's-His-Name."

"Marrok Wolf." Marion corrected. "We worked in the prison laundry together. Hell of a guy. Very handsome and prone to all kinds of charming Badness."

Another contemptuous snort.

"You still don't believe me about the Hatter thing, huh?" Marion debated revealing everything she knew, but he was already wary of her. He'd just come up with a thousand other ways she could've uncovered his secrets. If she pushed, it could backfire. She needed to go slowly with him.

And in the meantime, she had a lot of shit to do.

Her eyes went to the banner hanging across the town's

square and a new idea came to her. "Tomorrow is the May Day Festival?" Of course it was. The May Day celebrations went on all week in Nottingham. It was their biggest holiday.

Nicholas shrugged, clearly not a "festival" fan.

"I want you to take me." Marion persisted. It was perfect!

He frowned. "Why?"

"Because I love plopping an ugly hennin on my skull and listening to alternative music in a field." She mocked.

"What's a hennin?"

"A stupid, cone-shaped princess hat."

"Oh." He shrugged. "You *should* enjoy wearing those pointy hats. You look good in them." It was a grudging compliment, but she'd take it.

"If you think that, you're an idiot. A sweet-talking idiot, but an idiot non-the-less." Hennin were an unholy collusion between dark magic and the manufactures of migraine medicine. She was sure of it.

He flashed her an incredulous look. "Sweet-talking?" Clearly, no one had ever called him that before. The man wasn't known for his extravagant prose.

Marion rapidly snapped her fingers, trying to get him to concentrate on crime-prevention. "Focus on catching Robin and not Nottingham's disastrous fashion choices, okay? I'm trying to keep you and your silver tongue alive."

Nicholas hadn't wanted to hear her plan to capture her ex earlier, but now he seemed reluctantly interested in the idea. She was getting to him, despite his protestations to the contrary. "Do you 'remember' Hood being at the May Day Festival?"

"Nope. I didn't go to the May Day Festival, last time." She slanted him a meaningful look. "Some big, sheriff-y jerk had me locked in a tower."

"Your bedroom is not in a tower."

"Yours is, though. Pretty sure I recall a lot of steps, when I slept up there."

He shot her a glower. "You *never* slept in my room."

"Not yet." Marion smiled innocently, liking the feel of

Nicholas' strong arm looped through hers.

The citizens who weren't fleeing in panic were giving her scandalized looks. No Maid should be touching a gargoyle. It simply wasn't done. Of course, nothing interesting was "done" when you were doomed to be a Maid. Marion pitied the former her. Her life really had been a restrictive box, living in this kingdom. Even before she'd been sent to jail, she'd been locked in a cell of expectations and rules. Thank God she was free of everything now.

"The point is, this time we're doing things differently." She continued. "I'm going to help you reach your full potential for wickedness. You'll help me with blunt force. If we lure Robin to the May Day Festival, together we'll be able to flush him out. For once, he won't be hiding in the trees like a damn chipmunk."

Nicholas laughed.

Well, it wasn't really a laugh. He didn't make a sound and his expression didn't change and he didn't smile, but she *felt* his amusement at her snarking. That was enough, for now.

She grinned at him. "So, what if we held an archery tournament at the May Day Festival?" She went on, thinking out loud. Badness really did come naturally to her. "Robin's arrogance will make him attend. He'll be determined to win and then we can trap him."

"He's not going to just walk into the festival. He's an egotist, but he isn't a fool."

"No. He'll be in some stupid-ass disguise or something." She made a "God help me" face. "But he'll be there. I know it. Especially, if you offer him a prize that he can't resist."

Nicholas' brows drew together. "You?" He guessed in an irritated tone.

"No. Of course not. Robin has no problem resisting me." She flicked a dismissive palm. "This will be a whole lot easier if you understand that nobody except you sees me as important."

Silence.

"I was thinking a solid gold arrow." Marion went on.

She waved her free hand in front of her in a little arc, like she was revealing a new ad campaign. She could see the trophy sitting on a red velvet pillow. "Gleaming. Enticing. Useless. Robin will love that crap."

Nicholas didn't seem enthralled with her genius idea. "Where are we supposed to get a golden arrow?"

"Gold spray paint and a regular arrow." She shrugged. "Easy."

He arched a brow.

"What?" Marion challenged. "You think he's going to sue us for false advertising from his prison cell?" She rolled her eyes. "Relax. I'm amazing at arts and crafts. This is going to work. We'll arrest Robin, when he shows up to claim his glistening, gilded prize. He's never even going to get close to it."

"You really think he's dumb enough to fall for such an obvious ploy?"

"His pride won't let anyone else win. If you set up the contest, he'll show."

Nicholas grunted, obviously not trusting her. He didn't outright call her a liar, though. That was progress. Maybe ratting out that ass-wipe Tuck had bought her some gargoyle-y goodwill. "I'll take it under advisement." He muttered.

"Good."

A mural on the side of a crumbling wall caught her attention. It was a huge depiction of the former king, Jonathan, surrounded by flowers. Jonathan had been her mother's best friend and her father's cousin, so she'd known him well. When Marion was a child, Jonathan had come by the house sometimes to visit her and bring her gifts. He told her stories of her mother, his eyes filling with tears as he recalled their adventures. He'd been a wonderful godfather to her, until he tragically disappeared while hunting in Sherwood Forest, when she was fourteen. She still missed him.

Marion always thought Johnathan was dashing, with a loud laugh and modern plans for the kingdom. Everything would have been different with him alive. He'd be on the throne. Instead, his brother Richard had inherited the crown and things had gone downhill ever since.

Many people seemed to agree with that assessment. Jonathan's image increasingly appeared on t-shirts and buttons throughout Nottingham, in protest of Richard and the Looking Glass Campaigns. More and more poor, young men were resisting the call to arms and refusing to waste their lives in a pointless battle for noblemen's glory.

"You have his eyes." Nicholas said, studying the painting.

"Jonathan was my cousin. He and Dad were my only real family, growing up."

"Richard is your cousin, too."

"Yeah, but Richard let me rot in jail, so he can kiss my ass. So can the rest of this town. After I find out who kills you, my next priority is burning Nottingham to the ground."

"Figuratively, I hope. Considering we live here."

"For *now*, we live here." Marion murmured, thinking it all through. "Just for now."

That got Nicholas' attention. "You want to leave Nottingham?" His tone was more urgent than she'd ever heard it before.

"After I destroy it, I'm outta here." Why would she live amid the ashes and lamentations? She glanced up at him. "Want to come along?"

More silence. Brooding, worried, plotting silence.

Marion mentally patted herself on the back and moved on. "On a related subject, I jotted down a list for you." She reached into her pocket and came up with a folded piece of paper.

Pants were *awesome*. So much better than the dorky dresses she'd had to wear as a Maid. The black trousers she'd liberated from the palace laundry were about a decade out-of-style to her eyes, but at least they weren't prison-issued or a bulky skirt. Marion really had spent years working in a laundry room. She was comfortable stealing from one. She was fairly comfortable stealing from *anyplace*, actually. It was the joy of being a convicted felon.

"Happy day-after-our-engagement, pookie-pooh." She

held out the note to Nicholas.

He eyed it like it was a bomb. "What is that?"

"A list of some Merry Men. A couple of them I only have first names for. Sorry. We weren't that close. But, I'm sure you can track them down..."

Nicholas cut her off. "Why are you giving me this?" He still didn't move to take the paper, suspecting a trap.

"So you can arrest them?" Marion made it sound like a question, because it seemed pretty obvious. She waggled the page at him, tempting him to take it. "We can't have poor Tuck being all alone in the dungeon, can we?"

"Why in the hell would you want Hood's men arrested?"

"Because *someone is going to kill you*." How many times did she have to say it? "It's possible one of these nimrods is the murderer. Personally, I've got nothing against the majority of them, but if locking them up helps keep you alive..." She trailed off with a shrug. "It's not like they're going to die in prison."

"They will when I execute them."

Marion yanked the paper back from his reach, her mind flashing to all the ominous gallows he'd built on every free inch of grass. "You wouldn't dare."

He arched a challenging brow, refusing to show her anything but stone in his expression. "Of course I would. I'm the Sheriff of Nottingham. Who's going to stop me?"

Teaching him some more *creative* types of villainy might not be such a terrible idea.

"All you have to do is keep these guys in the dungeon until Friday. You get that, right? We can use them as bargaining chips, if they're alive. Dead, they're no good to anyone."

"They're no good to anyone *now*." He scoffed. "And once I capture Hood, I don't need them as bargaining chips. You might be soft-hearted about criminals, but I'm certainly not."

The man wasn't soft-hearted about anything.

"This is *logic*, not sentiment." Marion wasn't soft-hearted, either. Not anymore. ...Except she was heading back to her house to find that damn letter, wasn't she? She scowled at Nicholas, pissed that he had to complicate everything. "Do you want the list or not? Because I'm not going to give it to you if it sends you off on a mass-killing-spree. Some of these guys have families."

He weighed his options. "No executions of Merry Assholes." He promised. "But I reserve the right to conduct light torture on the more annoying ones. It is *my* wedding gift after all. I should be allowed some fun."

Marion was pretty sure that was a joke. She'd never known Nicholas to joke with anyone before. That charmed her enough that she handed him the paper. "The annoying ones are *all* of them. So, that'll add up to a lot of tortured Merry Men."

He neatly folded the list and slipped it into his own pocket. "I hope so."

Chapter Seven

Huntingdon family tragedy exposed!
The former duchess' torrid love affairs drove heartbroken duke to murder her!
Dangerous obsessions and loose morals doomed the once powerful couple.
Has Maid Marion inherited her family's diabolical madness?

Alan A. Dale- "Nottingham's Naughtiest News"

The Huntingdon estate was over two centuries old and its interior showed every single year. From the outside, the tasteful paint was chipping in places and some wear was evident around the windows, but none of that was noticeable at a distance. Any plebeians who walked by the iron gates and peered up at the big house on the hill would be impressed by its grandeur. The old duke had been a prideful man, so appearances had been important to him. The Huntingdons were the oldest family in Nottingham and he'd wanted outsiders to remember that.

Inside the manor house, where no one but family was admitted, it was a much different story.

Nicholas' stood in the formal living room, silently scanning the decaying interior. Wallpaper peeled down in curly sheets. The rugs were all frayed and discolored. The decorative shelves were empty, the pieces of art that had once occupied them surreptitiously sold off long before. The crumbling fireplace looked like it hadn't been lit in years. He'd known that Marion had been having financial problems, but this type of neglect was worse than he'd imagined.

He glanced at her and was surprised to see that she was looking over the room the same way he was. Like she'd never seen it before, even though she'd been taken from this very house last night.

"Was it always this bad?" She asked, almost to herself.

Nicholas said nothing, because he wasn't sure what to say.

Marion didn't take offense to his silence. She slowly moved towards the fireplace, her eyes on the portrait above the mantle. Her father, the old duke, glowered down at them in gloomy-toned oils. Marion hadn't inherited any of her father's heavy features, but she did have dark eyes. While hers were warm and glowing with ideas, his had been cold and filled with haughty judgement.

"He was so sad, all my life." Marion kept her eyes on the painting. "He never recovered from my mother's death, you know. When they were together, he was joyful. I wish I known that version of him. Everyone said he was always smiling and happy."

Nicholas wasn't going to upset her by disagreeing, but he imagined "everyone" was lying. He had a feeling the old duke had been born a miserable bastard.

Nicholas had only met the man once, when he was thirteen. Even as a young teenager, Nicholas had been a loner. He had a reputation for causing problems, because he didn't give a shit about... anything. Not after his mother died. She'd been an anchor for Nicholas. Without her, he began to spiral.

Unlike most gargoyles, Nicholas had been carved by a woman. She hadn't needed a guard or a stone servant. She'd wanted a son. Geppetta Greystone had been a gifted artist. She made stunning, intricate jewelry for the noble houses of Nottingham. And when it came to designing her only child, she'd spared no expense in making him attractive and ensuring that he'd have a quality education.

To Geppetta, that all meant her son was exactly the same as any other boy in Nottingham. It was why she gave him a really *real* name. The castle named most gargoyles, typically with a "rock" theme: "Slate." "Myneral." "Blok." Gepetta broke that tradition. "Nicholas" was a human first name and gargoyles typically didn't have last names, at all. No one knew quite what to make of it.

Or of Nicholas himself.

He'd obviously never fit in with the humans and he'd always been different from the other gargoyles. Plus, his natural impulses for silence and slight villainy were "wrong" according to the rest of Nottingham. Nicholas didn't care. The idea of talking to anyone overwhelmed him, loud noises made him cringe, and he saw no reason to pretend he was thinking Good thoughts when he wasn't.

Nicholas wasn't so great at following pointless rules, either. If you couldn't explain it to him logically, he refused to listen. Nottingham was built on unchallenged traditions, so his blunt questions were rarely met with satisfactory answers. Humans soon grew uncomfortable with his gray eyes pinning them, while they hemmed-and-hawed, trying to explain shit that they wholeheartedly *believed*, even though it made no sense.

Adding it all together, he'd never fit anywhere.

His mother had been his one safe place. Geppetta assured Nicholas that he had a wonderful life ahead of him and she worked hard to prepare him for it. She taught him everything she knew and, when Nottingham schools refused to enroll him, she hired the best tutors to teach him more. Nicholas adored his mother. For the first twelve years of his life, he'd been sheltered and loved. Every day, he was told he had a bright future. A *purpose*.

Then his mother died and Nicholas realized it was all bullshit.

Without Geppetta to shield him, the true bigotry of Camelot hit him full force. Gargoyles had no chance for advancement in the kingdom. No hope of bettering themselves. They were hollow and predictable, existing without passion or purpose. Some asshole pointed that out to him at least once a day, until Nicholas hadn't seen the point in even trying.

So, he'd kept to himself, brooding about his empty future and living alone. Refusing to give anyone the satisfaction of caring. The Good citizens of Nottingham took notice of his insubordination. His large size and surly attitude made him a target.

That day in Sherwood Forest, Robin Hood and the other kids were throwing rocks at him, because they thought it was the height of cleverness to throw rocks at gargoyles.

Until Marion Huntingdon had arrived to save him.

She'd come out of nowhere. He certainly hadn't asked for her help. He hadn't even wanted it. But at twelve years old, Marion had stepped in front of Nicholas and changed his life.

"Stop!" Marion rushed into the fray, her eyes fixed on the highborn boys in disappointment and anger. "What are you doing? Noblemen don't bully…"

Wham!

A rock hit her right in the forehead.

Marion fell to the ground, a bloody gash by her hairline.

Nicholas' mouth dropped open in horror. So did the other boys'. Maids were supposed to be protected. They were fragile beings, admired from afar and never touched.

Robin had thrown the stone that hit her. He'd been aiming at Nicholas, but that hardly mattered. Marion had been hurt and hurting a Maid resulted in severe punishment and eternal dishonor. Robin's face paled, knowing he was in deep shit. The rest of Nicholas' tormentors fled, disappearing into the woods.

Nicholas stood frozen for a moment, trying to decide what to do. He should run away, too. He was pretty sure that he'd somehow take the blame for all of this. But his gaze stayed on Marion's still form… and he couldn't look away.

"It was your fault." Robin insisted defiantly. "The stone was supposed to hit you, rock-monster!"

Nicholas had never hated anyone more. The force of the emotion was overwhelming and confusing, but there was no stopping it. The sight of Marion's blood triggered a fury that would never fully abate. "Get out of here before I kill you, Hood." He snarled.

"You're nothing but a gargoyle! You'll go to jail forever, if you kill me!"

"And you'll still be dead." In that second, he meant it. His rage was so deep that he almost wished Robin would try *something else, just so Nicholas could get rid of him, once and for all.*

Robin saw the intensity of his wrath and believed the threat. The other boy's eyes widened in fear. He took off running, but he'd despised Nicholas ever since.

Nicholas crouched down next to Marion's small body and hesitated, unsure whether or not he should touch her. Gargoyles weren't supposed to be alone with Maids and they certainly weren't allowed to put their brutish hands on them. But he also couldn't leave her there, unconscious on the ground.

He slowly reached out to smooth back Marion's dark hair and get a better look at her injury, when she made a soft sound. He yanked his ugly fingers back, just as her eyes blinked open.

For an instant, she looked confused and then she saw him next to her. Her attention centered on his face, everything rushing back. "Are you alright?" She asked. "Did they hurt you?"

Nicholas didn't understand the feelings that swamped him. Her warm gaze held his and it was suddenly hard to breathe. "I'm fine." He heard himself say harshly. He was always angry, but this was a new kind of anger born of shame. She wouldn't have asked that of a human boy. "I didn't need your help. I don't need anyone's help."

Marion studied him for a beat, like she could see straight through his wounded pride. She was young and ladylike, but her big, brown eyes missed nothing about the world around her.

"Well, I need help." She said. "Would you please give me a hand?"

Nicholas blinked and forgot about his embarrassment. "Me?" He blurted out.

"Who else?

"Right. I mean... Sure." Flustered, he carefully extended a palm to her. He used his left, because it looked less gargoyle-ish and he didn't want to frighten her.

Marion took hold of it and let him draw her to her feet. Her fingers were so tiny that Nicholas was afraid he'd crush them just by closing his hand. So, he left it open, with her hand on top, helping her keep her balance. To his surprise, she linked their fingers together, like they were... friends.

Nicholas swallowed. He'd never been so close to anything so breakable in his life. Gargoyles weren't allowed near breakable things, because everyone knew they'd break them. Her trusting, delicate touch did weird things to his chest.

"Would you take me home, please?" She asked politely and pointed the way. "My head hurts." Her hand stayed on his, just like he was a highborn boy giving her aid.

And because she treated him that way, he responded in kind. For the first time since his mother died, Nicholas' hardened exterior cracked. The manners that Gepetta had taught him instinctively came out. "Of course, Maid Marion." He softened his tone, liking the way it felt to care for her. He started walking, shortening his stride to match hers.

"You know my name? I'm so sorry, but I don't know yours."

"Nicholas Greystone."

"What a great name! Do people call you Nick?"

"My friends do." Or they would, if he had any. "You can call me 'Nick,' if you want." He wasn't sure why he offered that. His mother had never called him anything but "Nicholas" and no one else called him anything, at all. It just seemed natural for Marion to use the shortened name. Just like it seemed natural to talk to her, when he went through most days without speaking to anybody.

Marion seemed to fit *beside him.*

"Thank you so much, Nick." She sounded flattered. "You're lucky to have a nickname. I love nicknames, but Daddy says they're unseemly." She wrinkled her tiny, freckled nose in disappointment.

"You'll be a duchess, one day." He offered, because he didn't want her to be sad. "Then people will call you that."

That made her laugh and he swore he saw stars. It was the most beautiful sound he'd ever heard. "Do you think 'duchess' would be a good nickname?"

"I'll start calling you that and we'll see." Names were

important, so he was shocked at how quickly she accepted the one he proposed.

"Deal!" She enthused. "You're very nice. Why were those boys picking on someone so nice?"

"Because I'm a gargoyle. Obviously."

Marion blinked her huge eyes. "That's it? That's the whole reason?"

"Yep."

"Well, that's crazy." She made a twirly-motion next to her temple with a manicured index finger. He liked the way she moved her hands when she talked. "Goodness, I thought there was deeper motivation than that."

"People don't need deep motivations to be assholes. They're just born that way."

Her lips parted at the casual swearing. Maids didn't hear it a lot. They were too delicate.

Nicholas winced, hating that he was so socially-inept. "Sorry."

"No!" She smiled. "I like that you say what you mean. I wish I could do that. I think so many things that I'm not supposed to..."

"Marion!" A male voice boomed.

Nicholas' head whipped around to see Marion's father bearing down on them. Tall, white-haired and aristocratic, it was impossible to miss the blue blood flowing through his veins. The man looked like a duke. He also looked pissed about a gargoyle touching his pristine daughter. Fuck. Nicholas instinctively wanted to yank his hand back from Marion, but he was afraid she'd fall. So he stood there, his heart pounding, as the duke stalked up to them.

"Daddy, thank goodness you're here." Marion said before either male could speak. "I've been horribly injured."

She had?

Nicholas glanced at her in surprise, scanning for horrible, hidden injuries.

"I know. Some of the boys came running up to tell me you were hurt in the woods." The duke agreed, also looking her over for wounds. "And that some dirty gargoyle had..."

Marion talked right over him. *"I fell and hit my head."* She went on in a much fainter voice than she'd been using with Nicholas. *"I must have passed out and when I came to... I was so frightened."* Her eyes flooded with crystalline tears. *"I just want to go home, Daddy."*

"Of course, my princess." The duke soothed. He all but ripped her away from Nicholas, sending him a furious glower, and then turning back to his daughter. *"I'll take you home, right now. I've told you time and again that Sherwood Forest is no place for a Maid. You meet up with all kinds of undesirables."*

"I know, Daddy. That was why I was grateful to be saved by Mr. Nick Greystone here." She gestured towards Nicholas. *"I think I might've died of fright, had he not come along and rendered aid. Why, I was prostrate on the ground, sure I would bleed to death."* Her graceful hands swept out to indicate a pile of leaves, as if it might well have been her grave. *"He has been the very model of chivalric behavior. We owe him so much."*

The duke blinked.

So did Nicholas.

"Uh..." The duke seemed to wilt under his daughter's expectant smile. *"Well, of course we do."* He muttered uncomfortably. *"Come up to the manor house, boy, and I'll see you have some gold for your trouble."*

"I don't want any gold." Nicholas told him coldly.

Marion's father wouldn't have offered it to Robin or any of the human boys. It was only mentioned because Nicholas was a gargoyle.

"Of course you won't accept it." Marion agreed easily. *"No gentlemen would. But we must repay you?"* She turned back to her father. *"I know! Let's introduce Nick to Cousin Jonathan. The king always needs gargoyles to guard the castle."*

Nicholas' jaw dropped. Working in the castle was the greatest honor a gargoyle could hope to achieve. Even Gepetta would have been impressed with the idea of him working there. The boys chosen to train as guards were all highly accomplished and well behaved and not at all like Nicholas Greystone. He *could never hope to even enter the castle, let alone belong there.*

The duke frowned. "Those gargoyles are the very best their kind can offer..."

"So is Nick." Marion interjected. "I'm sure of it. And I know Cousin Jonathan will be so grateful that his favorite goddaughter didn't die in the forest, thanks to this brave young man. Family honor demands that we pay our debts." She paused, clutching her forehead. "I know that I'd feel inconsolable if I ever shamed the lauded Huntingdon name." She whispered weakly.

The duke picked her up, like he feared she was about to collapse. "Don't upset yourself, Marion. You could never bring shame upon the family name. Why you're the most virtuous girl in Nottingham."

That was true. Marion Huntingdon had always been the perfect Maid. It was why the duke doted on her, in Nicholas' estimation. The man was a showoff and she was his shiniest trophy. Everyone knew Marion's value, even as a young girl. She was destined to belong to the greatest hero in Nottingham.

"I'll speak to the king about training the boy tomorrow." The duke carried his little princess back towards town. "Let the men handle it and you don't worry about a thing."

"Thank you, Daddy." Marion simpered sweetly. Then, her brown eyes met Nicholas' over her father's shoulder and she sent him an impish wink. Like he was in on the joke.

Like he was her very best friend.

His lips parted in surprise. She wasn't close to fainting, at all. She'd been tricking her father! She'd gotten him to agree to exactly what she wanted, by acting exactly how he expected her to act and she wasn't even sorry about the lie.

Nicholas stared after the girl, a strange feeling in his chest. Marion Huntingdon wasn't just the perfect Maid, she might just be the sharpest person in Nottingham. The heroic bastard who won her would be crowing about it forever. He had a right to.

The man she chose would probably have to perform terrible trials to win her favor. Like slay fearsome monsters and write dopey poetry. But to feel her fitting happily beside him, he'd gladly overthrow kingdoms. His hand came up to touch the ring he wore around his neck on a chain.

Marion was a girl anyone would fight for.

Thinking of the memory, Nicholas found himself rubbing the same spot on his chest. The ring was now safely stored in his bedroom, but when he was around Marion he could still feel the weight of it against his heart.

"The last few years were especially hard on my father." Marion murmured, still gazing up at the old duke's portrait. "The estate was making *so much* less. He wasn't used to struggling with money and it destroyed him to think that other people would notice our diminishing circumstances. I kept up the outside of the house, as best I could. But, it was barely enough. We would have lost everything to taxes, if there hadn't been that new exemption."

Nicholas grunted.

"Robin was helping with the bookkeeping, trying to shift gold around to cover expenses." Marion went on. "I suppose he deserves *some* credit for that. But there was nothing to be done and my father was so depressed. I really think it killed him, in the end. The shame of losing generations of family wealth."

"Hood controls your money?" Nicholas asked, his eyes on her lovely profile.

It was easy for the Sheriff of Nottingham to know what Maid Marion did in public. She was suspected of aiding a terrorist. Surveillance was expected. Inside her gated estate, it was much more difficult to keep up on the day-to-day details.

For all her outward popularity, Marion was private. She didn't even employ any servants, except for her lady-in-waiting. In retrospect, he definitely should have listened to his reverse conscience and tried to bribe Clorinda for specifics on how this household was functioning. That horrible, vapid woman would surely have been receptive to an offer. Because he'd lacked adequate information, Marion had hidden how much help she'd really needed.

"Robin didn't *control* the money. There wasn't much *to* control, really. He just oversaw the distribution of funds. I wanted to do it myself, but Daddy and Robin were sure it was too much for me to handle." She made a face. "I was honestly kind of shocked Robin even wanted to help, since he was always so disinterested in my problems."

"An outlaw 'oversaw your funds'...and now you're broke." Nicholas summarized without inflection.

Marion rolled her eyes. "I know, right? He sucks at accounting. I was always interested in finances, so I'm *sure* I could've done better. I can't believe I didn't ignore all his sexist crap and learn how to..." She trailed off and Nicholas could see her brilliant mind suddenly shifting direction, thinking over his words.

He waited for her to become shocked and defensive on Hood's behalf.

"That thieving *son of a bitch!*" Marion hissed out in rage.

Nicholas' brows soared. He'd expected her to get angry at *him*, for his suspicions. He had no proof Robin Hood had embezzled anything, after all. But instead of defending her True Love's honor, Marion instantly found Hood guilty. That felt oddly gratifying.

Her beautiful brown eyes slashed up to Nicholas'. "He was stealing from me!"

"Maybe."

Probably.

Nicholas liked facts and figures in front of him, before he rendered a judgement. But with Hood, it always paid to expect the worst.

Marion didn't seem to need more evidence to reach a final judgement. "Definitely!" She turned on her heel and marched into the next room, slamming open the double door. "Do you know anything about bookkeeping?" She called over her shoulder. "I always thought I'd be great at it, but don't have time to learn, right now. I need answers!"

Nicholas cautiously followed her, wondering what she

was up to. The-One-And-Fucking-Only-Marion was fascinating. For a man who'd been called "predictable" over and over and over, her incredible *un*predictability felt like freedom. It always had.

"I audit the royal accounts, every month." Nottingham had so little money, that he had to be vigilant in how it was spent.

"Good." Marion started rummaging through a large wooden desk.

This had to be her father's private office, because there were stacks of books and heavy leather furniture everywhere. All of it was the best quality, though it had seen better days and there were pieces missing against the walls. It seemed obvious that Marion had sold all the other furnishings, before she touched her father's beloved sanctum. She'd shielded the old man as best she could from the Huntingdons' financial crisis.

The fireplace in this room matched the one in the living room and a portrait of a young woman hung over this mantle. Nicholas studied it for a moment. She looked like Marion, only her clothes were several decades out of date and her eyes were blue. He could only surmise this was her mother.

It was hard to imagine that pretty girl, with the familiar mischievous smile, married to the dour duke. She must've been miserable. According to all the rumors, she'd coped with her disappointing True Love match by sleeping with a score of handsome, young men. Having met Marion's father, Nicholas didn't blame her for it.

"I want you to look all this over and figure out what Robin did." Marion began piling ledgers on the desktop, incandescent with fury. "Tell me how much that bastard took. Right now."

Nicholas eyed the listing pile of accounting books. "Me?"

"*You*. You're the only one in Nottingham I like."

His heart flipped at her words. "Alright."

"I'd do it myself, but my misogynistic tutors insisted Maids didn't need to learn math. I learned a lot of useful shit in prison, but I have no idea how to audit anything." Marion was breathing too fast. "I can't believe this. I can't *believe* I can't believe this. Why am I even surprised that he was robbing me blind? Robin has only ever cared about himself."

Nicholas certainly couldn't argue with that assessment.

"But to steal from my dying father, when Daddy trusted him *so much*. When Robin knew how hard it was to even buy Dad the things he needed. When I think about what I had to sell..." Her voice broke and she swiped a hand over her eyes. "What a selfish *prick*." She turned slightly, like she didn't want him to see her crying.

Shit.

As much as he enjoyed listening to her badmouthing Hood, Nicholas couldn't stand Marion's tears. That was the last thing he'd want. He hunted for a proper response and only came up with one. ...And it was probably wrong.

Fully expecting to be shoved away, he hesitantly reached out and patted her shoulder. The rocky texture of his thumb rubbed against the smooth curve of her upper arm, soothing her as best he could. Hopefully, she wouldn't cringe away from his touch. Or flee the room, screaming for help. Or notice the stony texture of his skin.

Shit.

What had he been thinking? He should have used his other hand.

Instead of retreating from him in revulsion, Marion threw herself against his chest. Nicholas reaching out seemed to crack the last of her composure. Caught off guard, he froze, as she buried her face in his chest and cried.

Shit.

Nicholas had no idea what to do next. No one had ever needed or wanted his comfort before. Certainly not Marion. At a total loss, he automatically looked around, seeing if somebody more qualified for the job was hiding in the corner of the room. There wasn't anyone of course. He and Marion were alone in the house, which meant this was all up to him.

Going with instinct, he eased her closer to his body and encircled her smaller body with his arms. Okay. Now he was hugging her. Never in a billion years had he ever envisioned hugging Marion Huntingdon, outside of his own hopeless fantasies. He'd never hugged *any* woman, aside from his mother. Twenty-four hours before he'd kidnapped Marion and now she was sinking into his embrace like he was her lifeline. Trusting him to care for her. Marion's hands came up to grip the front of his uniform, clinging to him as she wept.

Nicholas' eyes closed briefly.

Considering she was in such distress, it was wrong to enjoy the soft feel of her in his arms. But how in the hell was he supposed to ignore all the curves of her body nestled against his hardness? Or how right it felt to be the one she turned to for support? Or that her hair smelled really, really good? It was impossible for Nicholas *not* to notice how perfectly she fit against him.

He sighed in self-disgust. "Um... Let's check the ledgers and see what Hood's really done, before you get *too* heartbroken." He tried, although he was pretty damn certain what his audit would uncover.

"I'm not heartbroken over *Robin*." Marion's voice was muffled by his shirtfront. "I'm upset because of my mother."

Her mother? Nicholas was more lost than ever. Talking to people was so complicated. Especially, talking to Marion. He always felt like he was struggling to keep up with her fascinating mind. "Oh." He said, awkwardly.

Marion sniffed, not discouraged by his inadequate help. "She was *wonderful*. Not like Friar Tuck and the others say. My father told me the truth, about how much they loved one another. They were True Loves. That's the kind of relationship I always wanted, too."

"And you found it." He said quietly.

The night she'd publically declared Robin Hood was her True Love, Nicholas had gotten so blackout drunk he'd lost four days of time. He hadn't cared if he ever sobered up.

"Daddy told me all about mother." Marion went on, as if she didn't even hear him. "She died when I was born, you see."

He nodded, feeling a bit more grounded. He knew that

Marion always missed and loved her mother. He knew everything about Marion, although she didn't know that he knew most of it. "My mother's gone, too." He offered, because it seemed like an appropriate thing to say.

"I know."

Nicholas blinked. She did?

Marion didn't notice his confusion. "All I had left of my mother was her ruby necklace." She blindly gestured to the woman's portrait on the wall. Sure enough she wore a large red pendant.

Nicholas frowned a bit, his eyes tracing over the delicate filigree work

"My father needed medicine and I sold it." Marion went on. "Robin *knew* how much it meant to me. He *knew* how hard it was to part with it. And he let me do it, even though *he* was the reason we needed money so badly."

Nicholas gave up on presuming Hood innocent. He wasn't sure why he'd even bothered, in the first place, except he didn't want to see Marion hurt. "Everyone knows the man is a thief. You shouldn't be surprised that he turned out to be untrustworthy."

That probably wasn't the most supportive thing he could've said, but it was honest. Nicholas preferred honesty to pretty words, which was one reason he sucked at conversations.

Marion didn't seem to take offense at his blunt phrasing. "You're right. Robin always says he robs from the rich and gives to the poor. But that fuck-head *made* me poor."

Hood's mission statement was idiotic. How the hell was Nottingham supposed to pay for any social programs, if outlaws kept stealing the tax revenue? Food kitchens and welfare checks stopped when criminals looted all their funding. Hood didn't care about the poor. He just wanted the citizens dependent on *him*.

"I was working so hard to keep my father alive. Thinking about my future with Robin was *the one thing* that gave me a little bit of hope. And it was all a lie."

Nicholas knew the strength it had taken her to care for

her ailing father for so long. She'd been struggling to survive and Robin had taken advantage of it, instead of helping her. Nicholas had a million reasons to hate Hood, but that bastard making Marion cry jumped to the very top of the list.

Marion moved one of her hands to swipe at her eyes. "Sorry. This is dumb. I think being in this house again is dragging up more memories than I anticipated. Mostly Bad ones. I don't ever want to live here, again. Do you want to live here?"

He squinted slightly at the strange question. "No."

"Good." She sniffed. "I haven't cried since the damn wedding, you know." She seemed embarrassed to show any weakness. "Not even at the trial. I wouldn't give them the satisfaction. Now, I'm crying over a necklace."

Nicholas said nothing. His hand moved of its own accord, brushing away a tear that was tracing down her cheek. The rough stone texture of his fingers caressed her satiny skin.

Marion stilled, her damp eyes finding his.

For an endless moment, they just stared at each other.

"You don't always have to be strong." Nicholas finally murmured. "I won't tell anyone you cried. I have no one *to* tell."

Marion gave him a slow half-smile of thanks. "I knew if anybody would understand about Mom's necklace, it would be you. I've seen how you treasure your mother's ring."

Nicholas froze, his gaze still locked on Marion. No one knew about his mother's ring. Absolutely no one.

He'd never spoken about it to a living soul.

Chapter Eight

**Countdown of the biggest scandals I've ever covered, as a seasoned and impartial reporter of truth:
Number 5: Nottingham's werewolf spy ring stalking our every move!**

Alan A. Dale- "Nottingham's Naughtiest News"

His shock seemed to improve Marion's mood. "*Now* you're starting to believe me, aren't you?" She guessed in a lighter tone.

"How do you know about that ring?" Nicholas demanded, his heart pounding.

"You told me."

Nicholas shook his head.

"You *didn't* tell me?" She translated. "That's what you're going with? Okay. Where did I hear about it, then? Gossip from your many close friends?"

He didn't have any close friends. She had a point. But he also couldn't imagine any circumstance where he'd tell Marion about his mother's gift.

She's the only *one you would tell.*

Marion didn't seem inclined to explain herself farther. "Whatever. You'll see I'm right, eventually. Ready to look over the account books?"

Nicholas debated his options. He couldn't explain Marion's knowledge of the ring, but *something* was certainly going on. He knew Marion and her recent behavior made no sense. She should be furious with him for abducting her, not playful and smiling.

Despite his earlier accusations, Nicholas seriously doubted the woman was running some complicated con on him. Why would she even bother? For Hood? She seemed genuinely enraged at that deer-poaching moron. Why would she turn on Tuck and the Merry Men, if she didn't want to help Nicholas defeat him? Why would she make up such an insane time-traveling story, unless she at least *believed* it was true?

Maybe she'd suffered a brain injury.

"Did any of my men bash your skull when they kidnapped you?" He asked, because it was a valid concern. She might've suffered a concussion. He would hang every one of those idiots if she'd been injured.

"No! My brain isn't bleeding, Nick." She sounded exasperated, now.

Well, there had to be some reason for Marion to be so confused. Somehow she'd forgotten a decade of devotion to her True Love and all her dreams of living happily ever after in his treehouse. Whatever was going on with her now, it was temporary. He knew that much. Sooner or later, reality would come rushing back to Marion and she'd remember that she was destined to marry Robin Hood, regardless of his thieving ways.

And remember that she hated Nicholas.

"Jesus, I told you what happened a dozen times." Marion persisted, refusing to see the truth. "A Hatter helped me travel back... Oh, never mind." She gave up on explaining it again. "You'll get there eventually. In the meantime, help me find Daddy's missing money." She wiped the last of the wetness from her face. Clearly, she wanted to move on from her show of unrestrained emotions. "And help me prove Robin took it."

Nicholas grudgingly made his way over to the old duke's massive desk. "What will you do if Hood *did* steal it?"

"Destroy his dreams."

He arched a brow.

"It's not a crime to destroy the dreams of someone who stole from you." Marion argued, like Nicholas had been hotly debating the issue.

"As sheriff, I can tell you that's true... so long as 'destroying his dreams' doesn't mean 'literally murdering him.'"

Marion crossed her arms over her chest, ready to be offended. "You'd arrest me for murdering that dildo?" She challenged.

"No." Nicholas wouldn't arrest her for doing anything. Marion could go on an arson spree and he'd just shrug his shoulders and watch her pull out marshmallows. The woman had a free pass for any crime she cared to commit. Especially, if she committed it against that asshole Hood. "But I can just hang him for you and save us both some trouble."

She grinned at him, like he'd brought her a valentine. "Thank you, squishy-boo."

As her teasing nicknames went, that one wasn't his favorite. Something in his face must've told her as much, because Marion's grin grew even wider. She always had been a mischievous little wiseass. How did no one else notice that?

"Sweet cheeks?" She suggested instead. "Fluffy-muffy? Feel free to tell me when we get to one you like. I'm open to feedback here."

"I prefer names that actually mean something."

"'Prince Handsome Pants,' maybe?"

Nicholas refused to even dignify that with a response. Instead, he began flipping through the old duke's ledgers, his thick fingers running down the columns of numbers. Marion paced around the room, a bundle of anxious energy. She went through three pieces of gum, waiting for him to audit her family's finances. He wasn't even sure what she was secretly hoping he'd discover. That Hood was innocent? That her father hadn't died in poverty for another man's greed? That her True Love wasn't betraying her trust?

If that was the case, he already knew she was in for a disappointment.

Nicholas wasn't a gifted accountant, but he knew enough about bookkeeping to get by. His mother had owned a jewelry shop and he'd helped her as a boy. It didn't take him long to start seeing problems with the Huntingdons' financial records. He frowned. That small flicker of expression was apparently all it took for Marion to know he was onto something.

"What is it?" Marion instantly hung over his shoulder, wanting to see the page. "Do you see how Robin stole the gold?"

Yes.

"Do you own a factory?" He asked instead of answering her.

"No." She leaned closer to his body to scowl down at the book. "Does Nottingham even *have* any factories? I thought its only exports were sheep and sadness."

Her breasts pressed against his shoulder and Nicholas tried not to notice. Well, he didn't actually try at all, but he at least knew he *should* try. That was the best he could do when it came to chivalry.

Marion's gaze scanned the ledger, her brows compressing. "What the hell is Doncaster Toys and Games?"

"Apparently, it's a toy factory in north Nottingham, co-owned by Marion Huntingdon and David Doncaster."

"Who the fuck is *that* fucker?"

The woman certainly had a way with words.

"I don't know. I've never heard of him." And Nicholas knew most of the kingdom's scumbags. "It's possible that the man doesn't exist, at all."

She glanced at him in surprise. "You think it's an alias?"

He paused, choosing his words carefully. "It's not unusual for someone to create a fake company to funnel money from legitimate enterprises into illegal ones. Or vise versa."

Her eyes narrowed, quickly understanding his meaning. "So, Robin is washing my money through this Doncaster Toys to hide his tracks."

Nicholas blinked at that blunt statement. She was instantly ready to believe her True Love was operating a sophisticated money laundering scheme, just on Nicholas' vague theory. She'd really believe a gargoyle over a nobleman? That was gratifying and shocking at the same time.

"I don't know for sure how Doncaster Toys is tied to Hood." He told her truthfully. "But I'll find out."

She nodded, her brown eyes staring off at nothing. "How much money did he take?"

"All of it."

She kept nodding, like she'd suspected as much.

"I'm sorry, Marion."

"Don't be. I'll get even with him." She gave her hair a toss. "This whole damn kingdom owes me and I'm going to collect. Fuck 'em all."

Those three words perfectly summed up Nicholas' worldview. "Fuck 'em all is my family motto." He deadpanned, just to make her smile.

Sure enough, her lips curved, the darkness fleeing from her eyes. "Mine, too. What do you think that means?"

"A psychiatrist might say we're both antisocial." Not that he gave a shit.

"My prison counselor said my brain doesn't work like everybody else's, actually." Marion reminded him. "Something about generalized paranoia, with a pathological pull towards Badness and a slight sexual dysfunction."

"Sexual dysfunction?"

"That part's probably true. Nottingham brainwashes Maids, so there's a lot of sexist baggage to sort through." Marion shrugged. "Dr. Ramona also said I was 'unhealthily fixated' and 'living in the past.' Literally, those were the bitch's exact words." She rolled her eyes. "If she could see me, now."

The woman had no idea what "fixated" really meant. Nicholas' obsession with Marion had started that day in the woods and had gotten progressively worse with each passing year. He could rattle off the name of every flower in her garden, every horse she'd ever owned, and every man she'd ever spoken to.

Marion straightened away from her chair, her tone lighter. "I like talking to you. I'm not sure I expected that."

Nicholas had no idea what to say in response. No one else had ever said such a remarkable thing to him, but he loved hearing it. He loved anything that hinted that she enjoyed his company even a fraction as much as he enjoyed hers. Spending this afternoon with her had been the best day of his life.

"I have to go up to my room and get my wedding dress." Marion continued, missing his silent adoration. "The hideous rag your minions get for me is too small and scratchy.

Since I've decided I might as well make this my dream wedding, this time around I'll be wearing my own gown."

That distracted him from all the warm feelings growing in his chest. "You own a wedding dress?"

"Of course! I was the Maidiest Maid who ever Maided. I started imagining my wedding when I was in utero. It was like the *one thing* I was allowed to plan, so I invested some real time into it. I have a binder full of ideas, just on linen choices." She waved a hand. "Don't worry about a thing, for Wednesday. I've got our whole reception covered and my wedding dress is already altered."

His brow furrowed and he rose to his feet. "But you altered it for your wedding to Hood." It wasn't a question.

"I bought it for *my* wedding." Marion corrected, sounding insulted. "It's *my* perfect gown. It has tulle and pockets and buttons on the back and a bow."

The wedding Nicholas had planned was a trap for Hood. Nothing more. So it didn't really matter what Marion wore to it. Logically, he knew that. "Has Hood ever seen you in this perfect gown, with a bow and pockets and whatever else?" He demanded anyway.

"Nope." Marion went up on tiptoes and brushed her lips across his, like she was charmed by his jealous question. "And neither will you, until the big day, nummy-muffin."

She was playing, but Nicholas felt her quick kiss like a hammer to the gut. His mind was wiped clean of all rational thought. Every muscle in his body tightened, sparks of energy arcing through him. The world slowed around him and everything --*everything*-- became Marion.

God, he'd been so stupid, trying to convince himself this wedding was about catching Hood. The truth was so much simpler.

The only truth was her.

Marion started to bounce away from him, pleased with her teasing. Nicholas' hand moved of its own accord. Instinct took over and he seized hold of her, dragging her back. His bulky fingers encircled her arm with room to spare. As always, he was morbidly aware of the difference in their sizes. He could damage her, if he wasn't gentle. So he was very, very careful... but he wasn't letting her go.

Rather than shove him away, Marion grinned. The perverse woman seemed to *like* it when he captured her. One day, she would go back to hating him for abducting her, but for now she acted like he was a friend. *More* than a friend. A man she wanted touching her. Someone she cared about. Having Marion smiling at him was even better than he'd always imagined.

Nicholas sat on the edge of the old duke's desk, tugging Marion towards him, so she was standing between his knees. She was so damn small, the new position made it easier for her to look into his eyes. He loved it when she looked into his eyes. She was the only one who ever had. The only one he'd ever wanted to.

"Yes, orange peel?" Marion asked, like she wasn't sure what he planned to do next, but she was eager to find out.

He had no idea why she was so bizarrely agreeable to being caught by the Sheriff of Nottingham, but he wasn't dumb enough to question his luck. He'd never gotten anywhere in his life by letting chances pass him by. He just pushed and pushed and pushed, until he reached his goal.

"Again." Nicholas wasn't sure whether it was a demand or a request, but it didn't seem to matter. Marion edged closer to him, instead of running away. That was all he cared about.

"Kiss you again?" She translated, breathlessly.

"Yes. Kiss me, again." *Now*, it was a demand.

Her arms wound around his neck and she obediently kissed him, again. It was that simple. Dear God... Nicholas groaned in surrender, as her lips parted against his. Marion tasted like bubblegum and magic. He deepened the kiss and she leaned against his body, giving him just what he'd always wanted. Her attention. Her touch. Her sweetness. *Her*.

This woman was the only really *real* thing in his life.

Marion made a humming sound of pleasure and the top nearly blew off his head. "You know, my father would *not* approve of us making out on his desk." She whispered against his mouth. "He was very proper."

The old duke wouldn't approve of Nicholas touching his immaculate daughter, anytime or anywhere. Gargoyles were an entirely different species than Maids, both literally and figuratively. No one in Nottingham ever forgot that.

Except Marion.

"Is it really Bad to *like* knowing he wouldn't approve?" She asked with a delighted wrinkle of her freckled nose.

"Christ, I hope so. I love it when you're Bad." From the time he was thirteen, her troublemaking side had entranced him.

She smiled impishly. "Wanna pretend we're kids and you snuck in here to ravish me?"

He wanted to push her to her knees and show her what happened to naughty little teases. He wanted to come all over her perfect body, just to mark her as his. He wanted to take her against the desk, while she sobbed his name. Then, he wanted her to curl up on his lap, so he could hold her while she slept and whisper promises into her strawberry-scented hair.

He wanted her to be his girl.

Nicholas' grasped the curves of her hips and drew her even closer. Flattening her against him. Any inch of space between them was too much. It always had been. She fit against him, just like he knew she would. Like she was meant to...

Marion jolted.

Too late, he recalled she was a virgin. She might be a mischievous little thing, but she was innocent. And gargoyles were big. They were carved that way. The rock-hard evidence of his desire caught her off guard. Marion gave a small gasp of surprise at the feel of him against her.

"Sorry." She blurted out.

He suddenly wanted to smile. "For what?"

"I don't know. I'm just not used to this. I should be way more experienced, at my age." She looked a little frazzled. "See? Slight sexual dysfunction. I told you. But, I didn't exactly date in prison. And Robin..." She shook her head. "I'm probably going to screw this up, because I'm not sure what..."

Nicholas cut her off. "Marion?"

"Yeah?"

"Kiss me, again."

That relaxed her instantly. She beamed at him and fell back into his arms. Literally *fell*, dropping her weight forward and expecting him to catch her against him. Which was exactly what happened. Nicholas wrapped her back up in his embrace, his lips unerringly finding hers. Starving for her. Marion laughed lightly and the sound was absolutely beautiful.

And suddenly Nicholas saw how his life was always supposed to be.

How it *could* be.

The stony determination that defined the very core of Nicholas switched on. It had driven him to heights no gargoyle had ever dreamed of. Now, it focused in on something even more crazy and improbable than running a kingdom. Something he'd never dared to consciously think about before. The glory of his idea swept over him like a tidal wave, washing away all the harsh realities that threatened to keep him from what he wanted most. There *had* to be a way and he would find it.

Nicholas was a man who never missed an opportunity.

Marion finally ended the kiss. Obviously, it would be her who pulled back first. He'd happily live and die in this room, if it meant keeping her lips pressed against his. The wonder of having her in his arms was almost a religious experience for him. Years and years of hopeless yearning and then --miraculously-- *this*.

But... *Now* what should he do?

Sexual activity in Nottingham had a transactional element. For gargoyles, that meant actual gold changing hands whenever a woman touched them. Payment was expected. It proved the physical intimacy was about *business* and that the woman herself wasn't tainted by unnatural desires for inhuman men. She just wanted their money.

Nicholas wasn't sure about the next step, when the woman touching him was *Marion*, though. She was special. Clean and kind and she'd seemed to like kissing him back. He wasn't imagining that, was he? This situation was outside of his experience.

Offering her any kind of payment felt wrong. But, Marion might be offended that he didn't give some sort of compensation. Any other woman would be. He needed to say something... maybe? That might work. Something very amazing, and possibly romantic, and that conveyed all the incredible emotions he felt for her.

Unfortunately, he sucked at talking.

"Thank you, Marion." He whispered, feeling like an idiot, even as the too simple words left him. He wished he knew poetry.

Brown eyes stayed locked on his, big and a little wary. "If you're toying with me, just because you want to take something from Robin, I will never forgive you." Her lips were moist, and her voice was breathless, and she was using the most serious voice he'd ever heard her use. "And if you think I'm a fixated bitch now... wait until I'm your ex."

"I don't think you're a fixated bitch." He said, because it was true and because everything else he wanted to say was beyond his capabilities.

"Then you haven't been paying attention."

"I always pay attention to you."

"*Why* do you pay attention to me? That's the question that I've been asking myself for years. If you're around, I know you're watching me. I can *feel* you watching me. It's always been that way, I think. *Why?*"

Nicholas stared into her eyes and reluctantly told the truth. He always wanted to tell Marion the truth. "I can't help it. All I see is you."

She studied him for a long moment, searching for something.

"When I kiss you, I am not thinking about Hood." He assured her, because that seemed to be what she was worried about, even though it was crazy on every possible level.

"You're positive?"

"*Yes*. Trust me." He'd always wanted her trust, too. Although he'd done literally nothing to earn it, he wanted it anyway. "Trust me. Just this once."

Marion blinked at the words, like maybe they weren't as inadequate as Nicholas had feared. As if maybe they actually... *meant* something to her. "You told me to trust you once before."

He hadn't, but he wasn't going to argue about it. "Did it work?"

She pursed her swollen lips in thought. "I'm still considering it." Her hair bounced enticingly, as she headed out of the room. "Wait here, honey-bunny. I'll be right back." She sashayed off to retrieve her precious wedding dress.

Breathing hard and aching with desire, Nick Greystone chose his future.

Right there in the Duke of Huntingdon's overwrought study, his life reached a fork in the road. One way led to continued achievement and peaceful solitude. He knew every inch of that path. The other was a hopeless morass of twists and turns, that would no doubt get him killed. Only a doomed idiot would venture even a step farther on that trail.

And he was taking it anyway, because Marion stood at the other end.

Maybe this crazy route was destined to collapse beneath his feet, but falling was better than never walking it, at all. He had *nothing* without that little troublemaker, so risking everything on Marion was a simple choice. When he inevitably self-destructed, he'd at least do it reaching for something spectacular. His new goal was worth the gamble. It was worth anything. Everything.

Fuck Robin Hood. Fuck the old duke and everyone else who stood in his way.

Fuck 'em all.

Nicholas was going to keep Marion for himself.

And he was damn sure claiming his betrothal rights.

Chapter Nine

Orphans of the forest: Lovable foundlings or cannibal outlaws?

Alan A. Dale- "Nottingham's Naughtiest News"

Marion hadn't been inside her bedroom in ten years, but it was like she'd never left. The smell of her favorite perfume clinging to the air, the familiar color of the pale yellow walls as the sunlight came through the windows, her fuzzy slippers haphazardly peeking out from beneath her four-poster bed... It was all exactly the same. The room had greeted her every morning for twenty-six years and she remembered every inch of it.

She especially remembered how to open the secret drawer in her vanity.

Marion marched over to the dainty piece of furniture, covered in pretty glass bottles and unpaid bills. She pressed the hidden button on one of the carved rosettes and then slid open the small compartment it revealed. Inside was her most prized possession, limp from constant re-readings and water-stained from her heartfelt tears. The only letter Robin had sent her from the Looking Glass Campaigns.

Before her life imploded, Marion had read the poetic words every night, dreaming about her perfect future with her True Love.

After her arrest, she'd lain awake in her dark prison cell, brooding about the note and growing increasingly suspicious.

Shoving the dog-eared paper into her pocket, Marion raised her eyes to look at her reflection in the vanity mirror. Rewinding ten years could mess with a girl's mind. It seemed strange to see herself looking so innocent. In her head, she still had a safety pin through her eyebrow, chopped off hair, and a "don't fuck with me" reputation around the prison. She could go back to a younger version of her body, but that didn't change the person she'd grown into after her murder conviction. Her hair might be longer and her face rounder, but inside she was still a thirty-six year old felon.

Good.

Marion liked who she was and she was fine with her "real" age. A decade behind bars had taught her some shit she never would have learned in Nottingham. Being a bitch was way funner than being a Maid. Besides, if you thought about it a certain way, she was actually older than Nicholas, now. That was kind of cool.

Marion tugged at her eyebrow, frowning slightly. She did miss the safety pin, though. It wouldn't be too hard to pierce...

The window behind her slowly swung open. In the mirror, Marion watched one gangly leg fumble over the sill, as someone tried to clamber into her bedroom.

Huh.

Rather than call for help, she grabbed the inexpensive floral lamp off her nightstand and stalked towards the intruder. She would never, ever wait for someone else to rescue her *ever* again. And she was great with lamps.

The second a shaggy head poked past the lace curtain, Marion brained it. Cheap glass shattered over the invader's skull and he gave a yelp of pain and surprise.

"Ow!" A long, skinny body tumbled into the room and splayed on the threadbare rug. "Damn it, Marion! That really hurt!"

Little John.

Crap.

Marion winced a bit, watching the teenager clutch his bruised scalp. If she'd known it was L.J., she wouldn't have used quite so much force. Unlike so many of Robin's Merry Men, she liked Little John. He was only fifteen, but he was tall, already towering over the others. That made his childhood nickname kind of silly, but there was simply no changing it. He was "L.J.," now and forever.

L.J. had been tagging along with the Merry Men ever since Robin got back from war. That was an obvious mark against his brainpower, but he was still a sweet kid. He just hero-worshiped her doofy ex, probably because Robin was an orphan, too. *Everyone* in Sherwood was an orphan. Robin had been raised by an earl, but the Merry Men seemed to see it as some kind of fated connection between them. L.J.'s devotion was a little much, in her opinion, but Robin accepted it as his due.

Still, L.J. was harmless. It was why Marion had deliberately left Little John's name off the list of Robin's men, when she gave it to Nicholas. L.J. wasn't the murderer. If her groom got a bit gallows-happy with Robin's men, she didn't want the poor kid to get accidently hanged.

"Are you okay?" She crouched down next to L.J., brushing back his blond hair to survey the damage to his head, ignoring the dirt and grime. The Merry Men weren't known for their hygiene. "I'm sorry. I didn't know it was you breaking in."

"I'm not 'breaking in'. I'm fleeing Nottingham. Just as soon as I can stand." He winced, as she prodded his wound. "You can come, too. Do you have any money for our passage, maybe?"

"I'm touched by your thoughtfulness." Marion said dryly. "But, I'm not going anywhere until Friday." No way was she skipping town without knowing who'd stolen Nicholas' life.

"You don't understand..."

"Marion!" The bedroom door slammed open and Nicholas stood there, sword in hand. "Are you alright?" He must've heard the commotion and come running. He probably thought Robin had come for her and he could kill him. He was in for a disappointment.

"I'm fine, love bug. This is Little John."

Nicholas' gaze switched to the unwashed teenager and she saw him sigh. "Oh, for Christ's sake..."

L.J. somehow paled even more at the sight of the sheriff, but he staggered to his feet. "I know archery! I won't let you take me alive. I'll..." He stopped short, processing Marion's words. His head whipped around to gape at her. "Did you just call him 'love bug'?"

"She did." Nicholas' said in a long-suffering tone and looked back at Marion. "The child is a Merry Man, I take it?" There was no hiding the fact Little John was dressed in green tights and a bunch of twigs. "This is the best rescuer Hood could send for you, duchess?"

"Robin didn't send him." Marion was sure of that.

"Robin didn't send me!" L.J. interjected hotly. "I'm not even following him, anymore!"

Marion's head tilted at that news. Nicholas was opening his mouth, no doubt to call L.J. a liar, but she shot him a quick "shut up" look. To her surprise, Nicholas actually complied. He sent her an exasperated glance, but he put his sword away and refrained from displaying any more of his charming conversational skills.

"You're not following Robin?" She asked Little John in her most innocent voice. "Why not, L.J.?"

L.J. sent Nicholas a suspicious look and stayed quiet. Clearly, he wasn't going to say anything interesting while the Sheriff of Nottingham lurked in the doorway like an executioner waiting for his next victim.

"Nick, step outside for a sec."

He outright scoffed at that idea.

Marion smiled sweetly at L.J. and held up a "wait just a teeny, tiny minute" finger at him. Crossing the room, she stopped in front of Nicholas and stood on tiptoe to speak into his (shockingly attractive) ear. "Get the fuck out of here, baby doll, so I can question this smelly kid."

"Question him about what?" Nicholas whispered back. "The boy can barely shave and lives in the woods. What information do you think he might possess, beyond which forest plants will get you high?"

Marion sent Little John a reassuring smile over her shoulder, signaling that everything was a-okay and then turned back to Nicholas, her friendly expression fading. "Something weird is happening, if L.J. is quitting the Merry Men. It could have to do with your murder. Let me handle this. *Alone.*"

Nicholas was not a particularly cooperative guy, under

the best of circumstances. Circumstances directly related to Robin tended to bring out the very worst in him, though. "No."

"Yes!" She shot back, forgetting to lower her voice.

He shook his head, like it wasn't even up for debate. "I don't like this boy just showing up in your bedroom."

"He's a teenager. He's harmless."

"I was a teenager once. I wasn't harmless."

No, he'd been big and defiant, as a kid. In retrospect, Robin had distracted her from having some really fun times with the kingdom's brooding delinquent. It was a tragedy, really. Marion fully intended to make up for it now.

"I think I can handle L.J. A barbarian taught me how to break bones. Did I ever tell you that? I'm amazing at it."

Nicholas ignored that. "I don't like this boy." He muttered, glowering at L.J. over her shoulder.

"You don't like anyone."

He met her gaze and then quickly glanced away. He'd almost said he liked *her*. She could tell.

Marion smiled at him. "Wanna go on a walk later?"

Smoke-colored eyes jumped back to hers and stayed there. "A walk?"

"Yeah. Like a date."

His brows compressed in suspicion. "Why?"

"Because I like you, too."

Silence.

Marion pulled out the big guns. "But, if you want any kind of future for us, you need to *listen* to me. Robin never listened to me. I need you to do better."

A quick double-blink.

"*I* see a future for us." She promised. "It scares the crap out of me, but I see it. So, be my partner in this and I will not let you down." Inside the pocket of her pants, she gripped the ugly talisman Tansy had given her, hoping for some luck. Willing him to take a leap. If she could risk it, so could he. "Let me talk to the kid alone."

Nicholas remained quiet for a long moment, weighing the odds she was tricking him. Wondering if she was secretly plotting with Robin Hood. Wanting to believe her.

"Trust me." Marion repeated his own words back at him. "Just this once."

Nicholas muttered a curse and gave up. It was flatteringly easy to convince him, really. "Two minutes." He held up two fingers for her to count. "You have two goddamn minutes to break this mastermind in questioning. Then, I'm coming back in here and I may or may not kill him. I mean it."

Elation filled Marion. Not because Nicholas had agreed to go away, although that was nice. But because he had decided to trust her, a little. That was a huge step! Marion beamed up at his stony face. "Thank you, Nick."

He grunted and the grouchy sound somehow had her body clenching in desire. The man was so damn attractive.

And he was a hell of a kisser.

Robin's kisses had always just been... wet. Marion's only lasting memory of them was a lot of tongue and a futile hope that her lipstick wasn't getting too smudged. With Nicholas, though, her only thought had been getting closer to him. ...And --fine-- a brief worry that her inexperience was going to screw up the moment. Why did she still have to worry about being inexperienced, at her age? God, it was so dumb. Luckily, her awkwardness had faded, when Nicholas surrounded her with his huge body, again. She'd gotten butterflies and Marion wasn't a girl who got butterflies.

Except around the Sheriff of Nottingham.

They'd fluttered around inside of her the last time he'd kissed her, too. Of course, he didn't remember that kiss, since it hadn't happened yet. Marion clearly recalled the feel of his lips against hers, though. The sudden punch of heat had shocked her to her core and jolted her back to awareness. For the past decade, she'd been wondering if it was a fluke. Nope. It was just Nicholas.

Her normally taciturn groom had enjoyed the kiss downstairs, too. The man had held her like his entire life depended on keeping her close. That was an extremely hopeful sign. And he swore he was interested in her for *her* and not just as revenge on Robin. Marion had been mostly sure that she was right about everything, but now she was *really* mostly sure.

Within a couple days, she'd convince her sweet, surly sheriff to take the kissing a little bit farther.

A lot bit farther, actually.

Marion was damn sick of being a thirty-six year old virgin.

"Bye, then." She made a "shoo!" sweep of her hand, herding him out of the bedroom.

Nicholas wasn't happy. "Two minutes." He warned again, trudging into the hall. "I'm going to stand right here and time it."

Marion slammed the door in his disgruntled face and turned her attention back to Little John. "Alone at last."

The kid looked baffled as to what was happening. He'd never been the fastest arrow in the quiver. "The sheriff once sent a horse to jail, because it pissed him off. How come he's being so nice to you?"

"I'm his favorite person in the world." Marion said cheerfully.

"Oh." L.J. thought for a beat. "Is that why you agreed to marry him?"

"It's one of the reasons. Nicholas is not going to hurt me. I promise. I'm staying with him of my own freewill."

"You and Robin are broken-up, then?"

"Yep."

L.J. let out a relieved breath. "Good. I think that's really smart."

Interesting.

"Why do you say that?" Hopefully, she sounded curious, compassionate, and not at all like an interrogator.

L.J. looked left and right, as if spies were lurking. "Some stuff is happening, Marion. Robin is super upset that you agreed to marry the sheriff. I've never seen him so mad."

Marion snorted and sat on the edge of her bed. "He'll get over it." Robin's colossal ego could withstand a bomb-blast. Her dumping him for a better, kinder, handsomer man wouldn't even leave a dent.

"No, listen! I'm not sure *what* he's going to do." The kid paused, like he was working up the courage to tell her something bad. "And then I heard him talking on a secret phone and it was really weird."

That caught her attention. "A secret phone?" Robin using a cellphone in Sherwood Forest *was* weird. Like televisions, cellphones weren't very common in Nottingham. Alan A. Dale might use one to write his trashy tabloid stories, but his embrace of technology was *way* ahead of his time. They seemed expensive and newfangled to most Nottinghamers, two things the backwards citizenry tended to side-eye. "Who was Robin talking to?"

"Richard." L.J. fairly spat out the name. Like all young men of draftable age, he hated King Richard. "I thought we were fighting Nottingham's oppression! How can we fight oppression, if we're helping the king!? He's the one who makes all the oppressive laws!"

Fair point.

The Looking Glass Campaigns were increasingly unpopular with everyone in the kingdom, but they were especially unpopular with the underprivileged kids who were supposed to go fight them. There was only so much a patriotic radio campaign could do after years and years of watching your friends return home dead.

"Richard is a dick." Marion agreed, because Richard *was* a dick.

There were a thousand reasons why she detested him, one of them being the way he'd relegated the gargoyles to second-class citizens. She'd been thinking about that issue a lot lately and it sucked ass that the law said they weren't really *real* or whatever. Fuck that shit. And now her asshole royal cousin and her asshole outlaw ex were phone pals? Nope. That seemed sketchy as hell.

"Did you hear what Richard and Robin talked about?" Marion asked, perplexed as to why the king was communicating with a rebel, who publically defied his duly-appointed sheriff. She'd never known Robin to casually chat with the king. He had a bounty on his head, courtesy of the palace.

"Oh, Richard wants some staff doohickey." L.J. continued, making a vague gesture. "Like a gold stick, with a lion head on it. Robin promised to get it for him."

"*Steal* it for him, you mean?"

The semantics of the matter didn't interest the kid. "But it's not even his! It belonged to King Jonathan!" L.J. shook his head, pacing around in agitation. "I love Robin, but no *way* am I giving that scepter to Richard. No way!"

Marion thought back to that morning, when Nicholas had been complaining about a missing lion-headed scepter. He'd been selling it for castle funds and it got cart-jacked, right? Had Robin stolen it on King Richard's orders? Why would Richard have to steal treasure Nottingham already owned?

Marion missed cigarettes. Thinking was easier, when you were smoking. She made do with folding another piece of gum into her mouth. It was caramel-and-whey flavor, which tasted so much better than it sounded.

"Nick is going to be pissed if Robin has that thing." She muttered, because at least that much was clear. Nicholas never needed much of a reason to be pissed at Robin.

"Robin *doesn't* have the lion stick. I took it from the Merry Men's storeroom." L.J. swallowed hard, his brown eyes wide. "I stole it."

Marion perked up. "You did?" See, she *knew* she liked the kid.

"Yeah. Now, I'm on the run. I can't ever go back to the Merry Men."

No, he couldn't go back. Robin might rob everyone else blind, but he'd clutch his pearls about someone stealing from him. Hypocritical jackass.

"Okay." She got to her feet, her mind trying to make sense of this mess. Bottom line: Robin and Richard were up to something shady and she needed to find out what. But first, she needed to make sure L.J. didn't get a quarterstaff stabbed into his back. "You can stay here at my house, until we decide what to do next."

"Really?" L.J. sounded like a hopeful child. "You mean it?"

"Absolutely." It wasn't like Marion would be staying there ever again. Nottingham was the last place she wanted to live the rest of her life. Well, aside from prison. "Make yourself at home, kid."

L.J. shined a trusting grin her way. "Thanks, Marion. You're the best."

She smiled back, projecting nothing but Good-natured helpfulness. "So, where did you say you hid that scepter again?" She prompted, focusing on the bigger issue. "I'll just pop over and get it, so it doesn't get... misplaced."

"Oh, I didn't hide it." L.J. assured her with radiating satisfaction. "I melted that golden thing-y in the community forge. Now, Richard will *never* get his greedy hands on it."

Well shit.

Chapter Ten

WHERE IS "KING" KONG?

Alan A. Dale- "Nottingham's Naughtiest News"

"You're not hanging L.J.!" Marion yelped.

"Yes, I am."

"Absolutely not, Nick." The sun was setting, providing a nice backdrop for an impromptu date with her handsome groom, while she plotted revenge on her enemies. Marion was not going to end their relaxing walk with a dead teenager. "Why do you keep saying you're going to hang poor L.J.?"

"Because he stole the royal scepter." Nicholas leaned against the wall next to her, not paying any attention to the people going in and out of the innocuous looking house across the road. All his attention was on her. "The kid confessed to it. I don't like thieves."

"Little John stole it from Robin, though. Not from you."

"And Hood stole it from *me*." Nicholas countered. The man could be a bit possessive.

"Technically, the scepter belonged to King Jonathan. And L.J. has always revered the memory of King Jonathan. He has a poster of the guy's face on the wall of his hut." She shrugged expansively. "He's young and idealistic. We all were once."

"I wasn't."

Well, that was true enough. Nicholas had never been a carefree kid. Until Marion was sixteen, though, he'd at least been approachable. He'd never approached *her*, of course. She'd been pretty sure she was a pest to him, in fact. But, whenever their paths crossed, she'd felt drawn to Nicholas and so she'd find herself wandering over to his side. He'd always mutter back quiet responses to her cheerful chatter, his unreadable gaze lingering on her face. Looking back, he'd talked to her more than anyone else, even then.

That all changed when she started dating Robin, though. After that, Nicholas had just watched her with angry smoke-colored eyes. He still didn't approach her, but the feel of his gaze tracking her movements had felt like a physical touch. It had affected her on some primal level that Maid's weren't supposed to feel. She'd tried to fix whatever was upsetting him, but by then he'd stopped talking to her, at all. Except to occasionally snap out something short and discouraging.

At the time, his hostility had hurt her feelings and made her question what she'd done wrong. Maid-ly Marion had never been especially confident. In reaction to Nicholas' attitude, she'd started nervously avoiding him, positive that he hated her.

She'd been such an idiot.

"You were always the mysterious brooding type, Nick. I like that in a man."

He snorted. "Since when?"

"Since about a decade ago. When I was a girl, I went for the charming, popular boy, sure." Marion glanced up at the least charming, most unpopular man in the kingdom. "Luckily, my tastes have matured in my thirties."

"You're twenty-six."

"Only on the outside." Marion quickly looked back at the house across the way, in case she missed something. "Anyway, like I was saying, L.J. likes to go off about Richard being a false ruler. I'm not shocked that he'd turn on Robin, if Robin sided with the king."

"So, he's a thief, a dumbass, *and* a traitor to the crown. Remind me again why I can't hang him?"

"Lots of people hate Richard. It's not traitorous to notice that he's a dipshit." Her cousin had gotten a generation of young men slaughtered in a war few people cared about. It really would've been better if he'd died at Kirklees, like everyone had initially thought. "You can't hang L.J. for his political leanings or stealing what Robin stole."

Well, he *could,* but hopefully her gallows-addict of a groom would rise above the impulse.

"How about I just hang him for being a vandal, then?" Nicholas challenged. "I'll forget he stole from me and I don't care about his political leanings. But that still leaves us with the fact he melted a lion-headed scepter worth a goddamn fortune."

"I think L.J. is just acting out."

"I think he should be executed." But that grouchy opinion was delivered with less acrimony and more resigned muttering. Nicholas already knew he wasn't going to get his way.

Marion patted his arm in commiseration. "We need to look on the bright side: Robin doesn't have the scepter and he *really* wanted it. Doesn't that make you just a tiny bit happy?"

Nicholas grunted.

Marion decided to take that as a "yes." She was opening her mouth to continue winning the discussion, but then something moved in the gathering twilight. Just for a second, she'd seen... something. A shape in the shadows. Felt eyes watching her. The next instant it was gone. There was nothing there, except swaying bushes.

Maybe it had *always* been swaying bushes.

Marion frowned, scanning the darkened landscape. Had she imagined the other presence? A decade in prison had possibly made her paranoid. ...Only a decade in prison had also taught her that it was impossible to be *too* paranoid. Right when you got comfortable, Miss Muffet, the Arachnid Queen, came at you in the exercise yard with her eight-legged horde.

Speaking of which... All the crickets had stopped chirping.

Two minutes ago, the evening had been alive with the sound of insect songs. Now it was eerily quiet, like the crickets had been scared into silence. Like they felt the presence of something bigger and deadlier in their territory.

"Okay?" Nicholas asked, sensing her distraction.

Marion continued watching the swaying foliage, not

spotting anything suspicious. She shook off the uneasy feeling. "Yeah. I'm fine."

If someone *had* been there, they seemed to be gone, now. It was probably Robin hiding in the shrubs, pissed off that he wasn't the center of attention. That made sense. When she and Nicholas had gone back to the castle for lunch, there had been a note from her imbecilic ex-boyfriend, pinned to the pillow in her room.

What the hell are you doing, Marion?
You can't dump me! No one would dump me for a rock-monster. It's insane!
Why did you give him the names of my men? What the fuck letters are you talking about? Why is Tuck in the dungeon? Are you trying to make me jealous? Are you losing your mind?
Break this stupid engagement before you ruin EVERYTHING!!!

Such beautiful, heartfelt words of romance. No wonder he was now her ex. It cost her precious brain-cells to even read his whining rant, so she'd tossed the note right into the fire. Only later did it occur to her that she could have used it as evidence in her own investigation, but she hadn't paid enough attention. Whatever. Robin wasn't worth thinking about, so she wasn't thinking about him. If he was skulking around, he could just stay in the shadows.

Overhead, the stars were beginning to come out. Nicholas glanced up and focused on the brightest one for a beat.

Marion knew what he was doing. "You once told me your mother taught you to wish on stars."

His brows drew together. "I never told you that."

Marion arched a brow, confident she was right. She'd had a decade to recall every word the man ever spoke to her. "Sure you did. You just haven't told me *yet.*"

Silence.

Marion tilted her head back to look up at the sky. "So, what did you wish for?"

He was quiet for a long time. "I want to be really *real*. Until I was a teenager, it was all I ever wished for."

That didn't exactly answer her question, but at least it was a response.

"All gargoyles wish to be human." Nicholas continued, in a distant voice. "All of us know it's the dream."

"You want to be *human?*" She wrinkled her nose. "Why?" If Marion had a choice, she'd be a witch. No doubt about it. They had amazing skin and could cast spells. Who wouldn't want that?

"Being human would be... helpful." Every word seemed to be carefully chosen, like he was trying to find the exact ones to convey his meaning and not reveal anything he didn't want to reveal. "It would create opportunities for me. I might be able to..." He cleared his throat and restarted the sentence. "Things I *need* would be more... open to me, as a human man. Magic could make so much happen."

"If that's what you really want, I can help you get it." Marion promised. "I met a lot of magical creatures in prison." Although she had no idea why he'd want something so frigging dumb. Taking away his gargoyle-ness would be a total waste, to her way of thinking. His dollop of roughness cut through the storybook handsomeness of his face and created something unique. Special.

Hers.

Nicholas shook his head. "I'll never be human. The spell to make me really *real* is dark and the price of it is too high."

"What's the price?"

"It varies, from being to being."

"What would it be for you?"

"More than I'd ever want to pay." He murmured and there was a note of finality about it.

"Well, it seems like a waste of a wish, anyway." Marion mused, relieved he wasn't going to change himself into a boring human. "You're already really real."

His gaze snapped back to her face.

Marion shrugged. "Being human doesn't give you

anything you don't already have. A heart and soul. Thoughts and emotions. Also, you're *very* attractive. You should stay exactly as you are. You're perfect, Nick."

He stared down at her.

A man suddenly turned down the walk to the house across the street, whistling a carefree tune. Marion's attention swung around, her heartbeat accelerating.

Bingo!

The newcomer was huge and covered in dense fur, no surprise since Judge Louis Kong was an anthropomorphized gorilla. Marion hated him. She didn't hate him because he was a gorilla, obviously. Marion had nothing against gorillas and she was used to being around people who didn't look like her. In jail, she'd been assigned to a craft time table with two lions, an evil sea captain, and a very big, very drugged barbarian. Marion had helped that huge jackass with his projects, because she didn't judge people on their looks, or arts and crafts abilities, or even being a huge jackass.

...Except Clorinda, because she was a duplicitous bitch who *never* should have won May Day Queen. Marion judged her for fucking *everything*. So what if she could play the damn piano? So could a radio. It didn't deserve a rhinestone tiara, either.

But anyway, Louis Kong was the fuck-stick who'd presided over her trial. *That* was why she hated him. He called himself "king" of his courtroom and he liked to lord his power over anyone unlucky enough to appear before him in court. Judge Kong was cruel and unfair and he'd laughed when he sentenced her to the WUB Club. That damn prison should have killed Marion. Very few Good folks entered it and even fewer survived. Sending her there was tantamount to attempted murder.

Obviously, she was holding a grudge.

Marion straightened away from the wall.

Nicholas arched a brow, as she moved up the path after Judge Kong. "You don't want to go in there, duchess."

"Wanna bet?"

Nicholas cleared his throat. He'd been weirdly

accommodating, so far. All afternoon, he'd been content to follow her around, up and down streets, while she searched for this damn house. He hadn't even asked what she was looking for.

Or maybe he *knew* what she was looking for.

"They're not going to *let* a Maid in there." He rephrased, with a shake of his head.

Yeah, he knew what she'd been looking for. Which meant he could've saved her at least two hours of walking, if he'd been a little more forthcoming. The man was perfect, but his communication skills drove her crazy at times.

She turned to send him a glower. "They'll let me in, if you *tell* them to let me in. You're the Sheriff of Nottingham."

"Why would I tell them to let you into a brothel?"

"Because, I'm asking you nicely?"

He arched an unimpressed brow.

"Because you like frightening the shit out of people and there's a whole bunch of them in there you can terrify?"

He grunted, still not convinced.

"Because, you want me to have an enjoyable first date with you?"

Nicholas frowned, like that argument sort of worked on him. "It's a *brothel*." He repeated. "No one goes on a date to a brothel. And I don't even believe we're *on* a date. I think you're up to something."

"*We're* up to something, gingersnap. You and me. All you have to do is agree to be partners in crime." She grinned. "Literally."

He watched her through his lashes.

"And we *are* on a date. At least, I am." She tilted her head. "Are you not on a date with me, Nick?"

He shifted away from the wall. Not following her, but also not liking the distance between them. Instinctively trying to close it, but unsure how to proceed. He was so used to isolation, he'd become stuck inside himself.

Whether he intended to or not, though, Nicholas was showing her pieces of himself that he kept hidden from everyone else. He was clearly meant for creative villainy, just like her. His plan to kidnap her had been a great first step towards Badness. He was on the right track. She needed to help him out of his shell and into the bright light of evil-doing.

With her.

Marion took another step backwards --towards the house, but with her eyes on Nicholas-- knowing she almost had him. "I'll be very, veeeerrrry Good for you." She drawled out, mischief in her tone.

His eyes grew hotter as she elongated the words, making them sensual.

"Cross my heart." She drew an X over one breast with the tip of her finger. Directly over her nipple. "I won't cause any trouble, at all."

"All you ever do is cause trouble."

She grinned, enjoying this. Flirting wasn't something Marion had practiced a lot, but she was clearly a genius at it. "What if I promise to kiss you, again? Not tonight, of course. Maids don't kiss on the first date. But tomorrow, you can pick the time and place. That sounds fair, right?"

He hesitated and she could see the longing inside of him.

She winked. "Come on. You know you want to play with me."

Nicholas' lips parted, mesmerized by the invitation to Badness. Wanting to be a part of the fun. Wanting her to lead him astray. Wanting *her*.

Marion's confidence soared.

One... Two...

"You're such a tease, Marion." He stalked away from the wall. "You always have been." He fell into step beside her.

She beamed up at him. "I think you're just a little bit wicked." That was great news! Her hand threaded through his arm, holding tight.

"Are you at least going to tell me why we're about to do something terrible to Judge Kong?"

"He oversaw my trial." The Sheriff of Nottingham passed judgement on the peasants, but the nobles had a more elaborate system of justice. "He's a dirt bag and I want revenge."

"Are we going to kill him?" Nicholas didn't sound worried about the possibility, just resigned to the bloodshed.

"No, *we're* not." She smiled with total innocence.

He made a skeptical sound. "Stay behind me, when things go to hell. I mean it."

"Nope. I don't wait to get rescued. Not ever again."

A trio of wolf bouncers intercepted them, as Nicholas and Marion neared the entrance. "Members only." One of them announced, his wary eyes on the sheriff.

"Move or I'll hang you." Nicholas retorted, not even slowing down.

The wolves moved.

"You are just the best partner in crime a girl could ask for." Marion enthused as he held open the door for her. "Seriously, things are just easier when you're hooking-up with a giant gargoyle. Why in the world would you ever want to be a human? It would completely spoil the effect."

Nicholas ignored that, glancing around the interior of the Catchfools Casino. She saw him wince at the volume of the place. The man hated noise. He really had gotten himself the wrong fiancée for peace and quiet. Too late for him to change his mind now, though.

There were card games and roulette wheels set up on the ground floor, along with a bar against the wall. Upstairs was where the real entertainment was located, though. The Catchfools employed the most accommodating prostitutes in Nottingham. It was all part of the kingdom's unhealthy fusion of sex and money.

Marion's father had visited the brothel every Sunday night, for as far back as she could remember. "Garden club meetings," he'd claimed. All organized by Judge Kong. She wasn't supposed to know what they were *actually* doing, of course. She was supposed to ignore the casual chatting between the old duke and his influential garden club pals. Maids stayed virginal and oblivious, while noblemen bought sex from girls born into poverty.

She didn't begrudge her father companionship. Losing

your True Love was a free pass to mourn however you chose, in Marion's book. But she definitely resented the double standard.

The eyes of her father's oldest friends and acquaintances did double-takes when they spotted her standing there. They weren't ashamed of their own actions, but they were visibly appalled to see Marion stroll into the brothel on the arm of a gargoyle. Useless bigots. All of them.

"Hey, gardeners." She called casually. "Chatting about bushes?"

Jaws dropped.

An orangutan maître d' came scurrying over, seeing conflict on the horizon.

Nicholas' muscles tightened, ready for a confrontation.

"Table for two." Marion called out cheerily. Not waiting for him to show them to a seat, she just appropriated one near the bar. In prison, you took the seat you wanted and dared weaker inmates to move you. Trevelyan had taught her that. "I'll take a scotch. Nick, what'll you have?"

Nicholas watched the ape in the suitcoat. "I will shut this whole fucking place down." He warned quietly.

"Two scotches." Marion decided. "I've never had scotch, actually." Maids weren't allowed to have anything stronger than wine. "I think it's gonna be great."

Nicholas stared at the maître d', saying nothing.

The maître d' wasn't a moron. He chose the path of least resistance and gargoyle-y threats. He swallowed hard and raced off to get the drinks. He just wanted to get them out of there as quickly as possible. Too bad for him Marion wasn't leaving until she saw Kong's suffering for herself. Half the fun of payback was watching your victims cry.

Nicholas sat down next to Marion, his large body shaking the table. His eyes fixed on the other patrons. "If any of them ask, I made you come here." He warned. "It's the only way your reputation will survive this."

Marion rolled her eyes and ate some pretzels from the bowl in the middle of the table. "Fuck 'em all." She settled back to wait for the show to start. "My father knew all these dipshits."

Several said dipshits were trying to sneak out the door, now that she was staying put. Others were red-faced and pretending they didn't see her. Most of them were grumbling and scowling in disapproval. All of them looked unhappy.

Excellent.

The casino was filled with laughter, music, gambling contraptions jangling, glasses being filled, plates being stacked, and a thousand other sounds. Nicholas rubbed at his temple, like he was listening to them all at maximum volume.

She felt a sudden stab of guilt. "I'm sorry. I should have thought about the noise."

He glanced her way, surprised that she understood the problem.

"You once told me you were very aware of sounds. They bother you, right?"

He stared at her, like he was trying to decide how much he should reveal about his issue.

Marion kept talking. "You can wait outside, if it's too much for..."

Nicholas cut her off. "No."

"Really, I don't need your protection in here, if that's..."

"I deal with noise, all the time. I'm fine." His tone was inflexible. "Just tell me why we're here."

Marion hesitated. "Well, these dipshits belong to the Nottingham Garden Club." She gestured around the casino. "All the social-climbers do. Daddy was chairperson, because we had the best gardens, of course. You see how much they *really* care about flowers." She waved a sarcastic hand towards the debauchery. "Oh, there were cute little fundraisers and lectures on rare plants for the ladies' benefit, but it's mostly a cover for drinking and sex."

"These men will ruin you in polite society, Marion."

"They're not so polite." She scoffed. "*That's* why we're here. Judge Kong offered me a lesser sentence. Said all I had to do was give him my virginity, right there in his office. Douchebag."

Nicholas turned to look at her, his attention focused like a spotlight.

"He said Richard wanted me in jail, but I could plead guilty to your murder and Kong would let me off with eight years, in a minimum security prison. I would've been out already, back in my timeline." Marion frowned at the memory. "He didn't even care about who really killed you. He just wanted to have sex with me. Can you imagine?"

"Yes. I can imagine that." Something about his very controlled tone had the hairs on her arm standing up.

"I said no." Marion rushed to assure him, in case he thought otherwise. "He didn't take the rejection well, but nothing more came of it."

Nicholas' head tilted to one side. "He put his hands on you?" The question was quiet.

"Kind of." *Yes.* "I think he might have tried to force the issue, but then his wife came in and he had to back down. Bagheera is jealous and scary. I can just imagine how many other girls he's pulled that trick with, who *didn't* get away."

Nicholas grunted and scanned the room, his eyes intent.

Marion made a face, thinking it over. "All these rich scumbags are creepily into virgins, right? Have you noticed that? I think it's a power trip. And Kong was at my *fourth birthday party*, the pervert. I use to call him "uncle." I mean, when the hell did he first come up with the idea of sleeping with me?" She didn't even want to speculate. "Anyway, I'm not sorry at all for wrecking his life." She smirked. "...Which I'm about to do."

Nicholas got to his feet, like he'd suddenly spotted what he was looking for.

Marion blinked. "Where are you going? We can't go, yet. I haven't even tried scotch. And I want to watch..."

Instead of heading for the exit, Nicholas went stalking off in the direction of Judge Kong.

What the hell?

"Nick!" Marion hurried after him, surprised by his reaction. "You really don't need to do anything here. I have it all handled."

The judge was sitting by the baccarat table with two very young girls on his lap. He glanced up as Nicholas approached, astonishment etched on his face. "Sheriff, what are you...?"

Nicholas kicked the chair right out from under him. The girls jumped out of the way, as the wooden seat skidded backwards into the wall and the huge gorilla went slamming into the floor.

Holy crap! Her introverted, law-keeping groom was starting a bar fight

That was both very cool and very worrisome. Nicholas wasn't the most popular man and everyone in here was Good and powerful. This was not going to help his career. Dead silence filled the casino, as the other patrons tried to figure out what to do when the Sheriff of Nottingham attacked a judge in a brothel.

"Have you lost your mind, rock-monster?!" Kong started to his feet, with an outraged expression. "You can't just come in here and..."

Nicholas shoved him back down, flipping him onto his stomach, and crouching over his prone body. Considering the gorilla was frigging massive, it was all done with very little effort and a whole lot of unnecessary force.

Marion's eyebrows soared.

Nicholas slapped handcuffs on Kong, keeping him flat on the ground. "You touched my fiancée." It wasn't an accusation. It was a verdict.

Heads swiveled in Marion's direction.

Okay... well this was *one* way to go with the plan.

"No!" Kong's eyes nearly bulged out of his head. Touching a Maid was a big damn deal in Nottingham society. "I never laid a finger on that girl. I swear!"

"Marion?" Nicholas didn't even glance her way, his knee on Kong's back. "Would you like to press charges against the judge?"

She crossed her arms over her chest. It wasn't the payback she'd been aiming for, but... whatever. Just so Kong suffered. "I think under this kingdom's ass-backwards rules, *you* would get to press charges, Nick." *Such* a stupid custom. There had seriously been more gender equality in prison. Leaving this sexist hellhole behind, once and for all, would be a colossal relief. "I'm a Maid and you're my big, strong groom. Under the law he touched what belongs to you."

"You weren't mine at the time it happened."

"Wasn't I?"

Smoke-colored eyes flicked over to her, burning hot.

"You can't do this!" Kong screeched. "I'm a judge!"

"You're not a nobleman, though. I have jurisdiction. So, shut the fuck up." Nicholas snapped at him, but his fiery gaze stayed on Marion.

She had no idea what he was thinking, now. The man was so unpredictable. "I'll press charges, if you don't want...."

"No. I'm claiming *everything* that's mine." He promised darkly.

She arched a brow at him. That sounded like a challenge. God knew why. Marion had been pretty damn accommodating, so far. What was there to argue about? The man just invented problems.

"I haven't *done* anything!" Kong wailed. "She's lying!"

Nicholas absently slammed his head into the ground and then lugged him to his feet by his hair. It was all one smooth movement, as inescapable and flowing as a rockslide. "You're under arrest."

"You believe her over me?!"

"I believe her over *everyone*, asshole."

Marion's heart positively flipped.

Kong tried a different tactic, blood streaming from his nose as he fought to get free. "I've thought about fucking Marion, sure. Everyone in the room has, including you, Sheriff."

Nicholas didn't bother to deny that. He just bent Kong's wrist the wrong way. The judge might've been a gorilla, but Nicholas' grip was stone-hard. Marion winced at the sound of something wet and breakable crunching in Kong's hand. She really did know a little something about snapping bones, thanks to her take-no-prisoners self-defense lessons. It sounded like two or three carpal bones and maybe his ulna just got pulverized.

Kong bellowed in pain and stopped struggling. He kept jabbering, his voice getting more and more frantic. "You dangle a ripe banana in front of a man and he's going to reach for it. Of *course* I want a ride on the kingdom's purest Maid. But I didn't actually do the actual *riding,* yet. I knew to wait until she was married, before I moved..."

An outraged roar echoed through the Catchfools. A feline scream of primitive wrath and fury than nearly shattered the chandeliers

Marion grinned. Oh good! Her plan was going to work, after all.

Kong paled like he'd seen his own ghost.

The other patrons scrambled away in terrified panic.

Nicholas' head whipped around to the casino's entrance.

Bagheera Kong stood there, breathing hard, her glowing yellow eyes pinning her husband like a bug.

Yeah, she'd definitely read the anonymous note Marion had sent, telling her all about these Sunday night "meetings." Marion was amazing at notes.

It was a well-known fact that Bagheera saw the garden club as her way into blue-blooded society and she wasn't going to take kindly to her husband sullying her plans. What if the other wives found out? Judge Kong really should've been more careful about covering his tracks. His wife was jealous, scary, utterly committed to being accepted into Nottingham society, and could transform into a panther.

"Told you I had a plan, poodle-scone." Marion chirped.

Nicholas' gaze cut over to her in sudden understanding.

She winked at him, again.

He got that vaguely hypnotized look he always got when she included him in the game.

"It wasn't my fault!" Kong yelled at his wife. "She's lying! They're all lying! I swear, I..." He didn't get to finish that frantic denial.

Bagheera charged at him, her body shifting into a massive, deadly cat.

Nicholas let go of Kong and took a step backwards, watching with professional interest as Bagheera sent her husband right through the side of the building. The not-so-happy couple went skidding out into the casino's yard, in an explosion of siding, contusions, and primate-y shrieks. Kong began crying in agony and that was *before* Bagheera started tearing off his lying, cheating head.

The woman was a fucking psycho.

"See? *We* didn't kill him." Marion waltzed over to stand next to Nicholas, watching the drama play out through the monkey-shaped hole in the wall. "Oh, having him in handcuffs just makes my plan even more fun." She decided with a laugh.

Nicholas glanced down at her. "*She's* going to kill him, you know."

"Probably." Marion agreed with a shrug.

"Certainly." Nicholas corrected. "I'm not going to bother arresting her for it. Turns out, I don't care what happens to scumbags who are creepily into virgins."

Marion looked up at his handsome profile. "You're *such* a good sheriff." She told him sincerely.

"I'm not Good or Bad. Gargoyles exist in a gray area."

"Everything in Nottingham is gray." From the dour expressions of its backwards citizens, to its crumbling stone buildings, to its sketchy concepts of chivalry. "I think maybe gargoyles can choose to be Good *or* Bad. That's not a disadvantage."

He didn't look convinced.

"I'm Bad." It was only fair to warn him. "I was born Good, but it didn't take. This isn't one of those deals where I emerge from the darkness, and stop being a vengeful bitch, and forgive all my enemies." She shook her head. "I *like* being Bad. You're going to have to get used to my criminal leanings, because I can't change back. I don't even want to."

He lifted an unconcerned shoulder. "I love it when

you're Bad."

Marion went still. For a man who always struggled with words, he'd just said the perfect ones.

In the short time she'd been redoing her life, she'd been pushing full-speed ahead, gulping down freedom like she might never have another sip. She wanted to do everything and do it *fast*. The longer she was back, though, the easier it was to accept that she was in the past to stay.

This really was her life, now.

It was astonishing. Maybe a Hatter's magic kind of eased you into the reality of time travel, because it was hard to process all at once. It did something to ease the transition, until you fully adjusted. Fortunately, you learned to adjust quickly in the WUB Club. It was the only way to survive. When a dragon sat down at your lunch table, you figured out how to handle him or he'd eat *you* instead of the lukewarm porridge. Marion could roll with all kinds of weird shit. Time travel was at least a positive change, so the truth took hold and she accepted it.

A kind of certainty began inside of her.

"You don't believe me about coming back ten years." She heard herself say. "Why did you believe me about Kong?"

"I don't *not* believe you. I don't know how you know what you know. I just know that you know it."

Marion squinted slightly at that confusing explanation.

Nicholas shook his head in self-disgust, like his inarticulate tendencies were a never-ending source of frustration. "My mind doesn't work like yours." He tried. "Gargoyles are predictable, passionless, and purposeless. Hatters and time travel are beyond our thinking."

She scoffed at that pack of lies.

"But," he hesitated, searching for words, "I will *always* be on your side, Marion. No matter what. I will *always* back you, over anybody else. Even when I have no damn idea what you're up to."

The feeling of certainty solidified.

It was one thing to fantasize about the life you'd missed, when you were rotting in prison. It was quite another to live it. Twenty-four hours after she was sent back --give or take a decade-- it suddenly dawned on Marion that she really had a future, again. Not just a past. A *future*. And this man was it. She was pretty damn sure.

Marion caught hold of his hand, just like she'd done the first time they'd met. "You willing to join forces, yet?"

Nicholas stayed quiet. But the rocky surface of his finger slowly closed around hers, linking them together. Making them partners.

Marion laid her head on his shoulder, satisfied. "Team Creative Villainy." She decided. "You and me, Nick."

Nicholas gave up. "Shit." He muttered in resignation, like he knew the battle was lost.

Marion smirked. Day Two of her new life and she already owned the Sheriff of Nottingham. It was a great start to their new future.

Watching the horrific violence on the lawn, Marion was content for the first time in ten years. The brawling spouses were silhouetted in the twilight, a picturesque sight for any vendetta-seeking felon. She was holding hands with her groom, on a summer evening. Next, she'd save his life and destroy Nottingham. She'd make this future everything she'd dreamed of all those lonely nights in her cell. This time through, she was going to win.

The *something* in the shadows moved, again.

There one minute, gone the next. A jarring wrongness that caught her attention. It reminded Marion of a cockroach you saw from the corner of your eye, skittering across a wall. In the WUB Club, that happened a lot. This felt a lot more menacing than a simple bug, though.

She jolted, straightening away from Nicholas. "Did you see that?"

"See Bagheera ripping off his…?"

"No, not *that*." She interrupted impatiently. "I saw something else. By the edge of the yard. Something was looking at us. I could sense it."

"I'll go check."

"No!" Marion tightened her grip on his hand,

inexplicably worried over Nicholas getting near the something. "No, just stay here with me." She turned towards his body, cuddling closer to his warmth. Wanting to protect him from the world. "Whatever it was, it's gone now, anyway."

His arm hesitantly slipped around her waist, testing his welcome. His breathing got rougher when she didn't shift away. "Hood is sure to be following us, waiting for an opportunity to grab you. It was probably him you saw."

Marion's eyes stayed on the darkness, searching for another glimpse. "I thought it might be Robin earlier, but..." She shook her head. "I don't think so. I think it was something else."

"What?"

"I don't know."

And that's what worried her.

Chapter Eleven

Merry Men say final good-byes!
Heartbroken children gathered outside the palace dungeons today, begging for the safe return of their beloved fathers. The political persecution of Robin Hood's loyal followers has torn apart families throughout Nottingham. Will they be executed or merely imprisoned forever? Only time will tell...

Alan A. Dale- "Nottingham's Naughtiest News"

"We've arrested the humans on Maid Marion's list." Rockwell informed Nicholas, at the weekly gargoyles' meeting later that night. "They all admit to being Merry Men. The woman was telling the truth."

Grunting and nods resounded among the other guards, as if they'd suspected as much. The gargoyles liked Marion. They always had. *Everyone* liked Marion, because she treated everyone with kindness.

Unless she was gleefully ratting them out to the Sheriff of Nottingham.

"Do you want me to hang Robin Hood's minions one-by-one or in a mass-execution?" Rockwell asked, in a casual tone.

"Let's do a big one!" Oore, a guard with ram's horns carved into his skull, chimed in. He was always full of enthusiasm and violent ideas. "Multiple scumbags swinging at once is more fun to watch. The singles get dull, after a while."

There was a general murmur of agreement.

Nicholas shook his head. "Just keep them locked up, for now."

Dead silence filled the room.

"Let the Merry Men live, you mean?" Rockwell seemed puzzled by that idea. Like maybe it was part of some bigger scheme that no one had filled him in on. "Why?"

"Marion says some of them have families."

Rockwell still seemed puzzled. "So?"

"So, she asked me not to hang them."

Rockwell's cracked stone eyebrows soared, sending tiny bits of debris raining down. "So?" He repeated.

"So, we're not hanging them." The words were final.

Half the room exchanged meaningful sideways looks with the other half.

Nicholas pretended not to notice.

Sunday nights, he met with all the palace guards, to discuss any issues that had arisen and plan the coming week. Usually, that meant updating the list of treasures Robin Hood stole, the number of hangings they'd conducted, and sometimes a report of a missing horse. Typically, the meetings took fifteen minutes. This one already promised to drag on for hours.

They'd gathered in the palace throne room, because it was large enough to fit dozens of armed men. Everything in the space was built at a scale to impress and intimidate, from the gigantic mirrors on the walls, to the massive chandelier on the gilded ceiling, to the colossal fireplace.

To be fair, every fireplace in the palace was colossal. It cost a fortune to keep the drafty place above freezing. They really needed to upgrade the heating, but there was no money for it, thanks to Hood's thievery. Poorly insulated or not, though, the bluebloods of Nottingham would shriek in horror to see so many gargoyles packed into their elaborately decorated space.

None of the gargoyles cared.

"I guess we can let those Merry Morons live, if it makes your girl happy, Commander." Oore generously allowed.

"She's not my girl. She's Hood's girl."

In the war, every soldier had wanted a girl. The term was sacred to Nottingham's troops. To them, "your girl" was typically your wife, or your True Love, or your girlfriend, or your fiancée. The exact relationship didn't matter, though. She was the one who wrote you letters. The vision in your mind, when you looked at the stars and made a wish. The reason a man fought to survive in the midst of battle.

She was home.

"Maid Marion's always been alright." Oore went on, not listening to Nicholas' muttered correction. "She talks a lot, but she doesn't talk down to us. She never has. And she put up a hell of a fight, when we took her from her house."

More nods.

All the men were allowed to speak freely, although they generally let the lieutenants do most of the talking. The five of them *loved* to talk. Nicholas was usually worn out by the end of the meeting. Still, no gargoyle had mentioned a single instance when Marion Huntingdon had treated them with disrespect. There wasn't another citizen of Nottingham with that record of kindness. Just Marion. In turn, the gargoyles had responded to her decades of courtesy by abducting her from her home and plotting to kill her True Love.

No.

Nicholas had been the one to come up with the plan to abduct Marion and disrupt her life. This was all on him. He pinched the bridge of his nose, guilt mixing with his inflexible resolve to keep the woman for himself. It came as no shock to him which side of the debate won.

I stole her, so now she's mine.

His reverse conscience rumbled in satisfaction at that logic.

Hell, he really *was* a little bit wicked, wasn't he?

"Nottingham will explode, if you keep her." Quarry interjected quietly.

Quarry was the man Nicholas listened to the closest. He was clever. Maybe too clever, at times. His cynical mind easily picked up on Nicholas' true intentions. He'd been right by Nicholas' side at the Battle of Kirklees, so he knew what it looked like when Nicholas was about to do something outside the lines.

And Quarry wasn't wrong about Nottingham's reaction to a gargoyle claiming a Maid.

Holding Marion under house arrest wasn't an issue for most citizens, so long as she was a prisoner. Her reputation would survive intact, because nearly everyone expected Hood to soon save her. If Marion started acting like Nicholas' actual fiancée, though, the shit would hit the fan. It was already going too far to stop the rumors completely.

Nottingham would never accept their poster-girl for flawless Maidenhood consorting with a gargoyle. That truth didn't do a damn thing to improve Nicholas' mood.

He glared at Quarry, saying nothing.

Quarry arched a brow, refusing to back down. "Marion's always had a connection to you. I've seen it. But is she up for the never-ending blowback of this? A really *real* engagement will ruin her reputation and make her a target. Will she risk that for a gargoyle? No other human would. Certainly not a Maid."

It occurred to Nicholas that allowing the other gargoyles to have a voice in these meetings was a lousy idea. He'd started the tradition during the war. Although he hated conversations, listening to his men was the only way he knew how to command. They got input and clarification on his orders. He got new ideas and information to devise better orders. It was win/win.

Also, the meetings lumped all the talking he was expected to do in a week onto one single day, which was better than spreading it out. It seemed to work well. Most of the time. When the other men told him shit he didn't want to hear, it became a real pain in the ass, however.

Quarry kept going, heedless of Nicholas' dark glower. "And then there's her boyfriend, who's always smirked about your feelings for Marion. Hood knows that you want her. But it's never worried him, because he thought you were just a gargoyle and that Marion was under control. He enjoys that he won the prize and you never even had a shot."

Robin Hood's name brought grumbles and scowls from everyone present. Hood had been in charge of the gargoyles' division in the Looking Glass Campaigns. His leadership style had done nothing to gain loyalty from his troops. As much as the palace guards approved of Marion, they *hated* Hood.

"Hood will come for Marion. Before, I wasn't so sure.

He's a selfish bastard. I could see him leaving her to her fate to protect his own skin." Quarry was talented at predicting human behavior, probably because he'd spent so much time with so many horrible ones. "But not if Marion acts like she was today. Not if she's smiling at you and holding your arm. That's going to force him into action."

Goading Hood into action had once been the point of this plan. Now, a huge part of Nicholas hoped the bastard just stayed hidden in the shrubbery.

Quarry slowly shook his head, like he was reading Nicholas' mind. "If Hood thinks you actually have a chance of claiming the woman? Of winning her away from him? He'll fight to get Marion back. He won't be able to stop himself. He'll never share something that another man values."

"I have no intention of sharing, either." Nicholas assured him quietly.

That remark brought snorts of amusement from the other gargoyles. Sometimes he got the feeling they… liked him. Maybe. He wasn't sure why. He didn't do anything particular to bond with them. He barely even talked.

Of course, that was pre-Marion moving in and changing things inside of him. Now, it felt like Nicholas never shut up. And half the shit he said contradicted all the other shit he said. Possibly because nothing in his life made sense anymore, so it was impossible to keep his thoughts and feelings in synch.

"I thought the whole point of this plan was for Hood to try and rescue Maid Marion." Gravol loudly whispered to Rockwell. "Is he not coming, now?"

He was a lieutenant, because Nicholas wasn't exactly sure what else to do with him. Gravol's carver had been new to creating gargoyles and had left large parts of him woefully unfinished. As a result, Gravol was covered in more stone than a typical gargoyle and his body was twice the normal size. He also wasn't the brightest man, so the rest of the guards were protective of him.

"Of course Hood will come for Marion!" Rockwell had an optimistic heart. He patted Gravol's arm reassuringly.

"Maid Marion is his True Love. If you had a True Love, wouldn't you do *anything* to get her back?"

Silence, as all the men considered that notion. True Love was such a foreign idea to gargoyles that it never seemed to have even occurred to most of them.

For some reason, that depressed Nicholas.

"Is Maid Marion going to make the commander pay, if he touches her?" Oore wondered to no one in particular. "Because we could start a pool to raise the gold for him."

The men started reaching for their money pouches.

"No." Nicholas said flatly.

"'No' to which part? 'No' she won't charge you or 'no' to the pool?"

"Both."

"She doesn't charge you?" Even Quarry seemed surprised by that fact. "But they always charge, when you want them. It's when you *don't* that…"

"*No.*" Nicholas interrupted and let the word speak for itself.

He couldn't explain Marion's behavior and he sure as hell didn't plan to discuss it. Earlier Marion had said she saw some kind of future for them, but that was so utterly insane that Nicholas couldn't bring himself to believe she was serious. It was exactly what he wanted to hear, but why would she say it? Why would she want to be with him instead of a thousand other, more worthy men? Something was happening with Marion and he didn't trust it to last.

Maybe she was under a spell.

Rockwell cleared his throat. "Today in the church, Maid Marion said she didn't want to marry Robin Hood. She said she wants to marry the commander."

Nicholas' heart clenched, remembering that moment.

"What if Hood shows up to save her and she doesn't *want* to be saved?" Rockwell persisted, looking around for opinions about that unlikely scenario. "We should try some visualization exercises, to quiet our anxieties and will our desires into being." He was very into visualization techniques, lately. God only knew which nutty paperback the idea had come from. "Maybe we'll find a way to keep Maid Marion."

"We're going to kill Hood, anyway." Oore flopped down on the huge royal throne, because it was the only chair in the room. "She belongs to the commander, now. She doesn't even charge him! There's nothing to fucking 'visualize.' Of *course* we're keeping her."

Nicholas said nothing, because he agreed with Oore and that was usually a bad sign.

"She could be lying, about breaking up with Hood." Boulder muttered. He had a goat-like beard carved into his chin and a pessimistic attitude. No matter what the plan was, he was sure it would fail. But he'd been the one to bash Friar Tuck's skull for screaming insults at Marion, so Nicholas didn't doubt his loyalty. "This whole thing could be a trick she and Hood cooked up."

"Then the woman is the greatest fucking actress in the world." Oore snapped back. "She looks at the commander like he invented orgasms."

"That's her plan, maybe." Boulder shot back. "She's playing him, because everyone knows he's obsessed with her. Always has been. I once saw him wait three hours in the rain, because she'd been gone for two weeks and he was desperate to see her again. She walked by, and the commander watched her walk by, and that was it. *Three hours.*"

"So what? He's in love with the girl. He can stalk her if he wants."

Dear God… Nicholas pinched the bridge of his nose.

"Do any of you believe she's been transported back through time?" Boulder continued, because Marion's story was already spreading through the palace. The damn housekeeper had probably overheard it and that meant *everyone* knew. "We don't have any proof of that, except she said it."

"Hatters can control time." Nicholas wasn't sure why he defended Marion's tale, since he wasn't convinced of it either. The words were out before he could stop them.

Boulder glanced his way. "Or she's lying. Which story seems more likely?"

Nicholas glared at him. "Marion's not lying. She

believes what she says."

"What if it's true?" Oore challenged. "What if she came back to save the commander from being killed?"

"Why would she stick around, after she warned him?" Boulder leaned against the wall, keeping his eyes on the door. Marion stood the same way. So did anyone who'd ever lived surrounded by danger. "She could be halfway to Oz, by now, safely out of the line of fire."

"Maybe she stayed because she's fallen for the commander for really *real*." Rockwell speculated, with a romantic sigh. He paused. "...And --I mean-- we also have her kidnapped, so she kind of *has to* stay. That, too."

The summation was met with wise nods.

"No woman will *ever* want one of us for really *real*." Boulder insisted sourly, crossing his arms over his massive chest. "You're a fool if you think otherwise."

Absolutely no one argued with that assessment.

Not even Nicholas.

Instead, he moved to stare out the window, absently rubbing his temple with his rough, right hand. The texture of his rocky skin felt like sandpaper, even to him. Touching Marion with his thick, misshapen fingers would probably leave bruises.

So use your other *hand to touch her, idiot. Not touching her at all isn't an option.*

Actually, it *was* an option. Marion had mentioned a desire to leave Nottingham. After he killed Hood, Nicholas could help her restart her life in some nicer kingdom, far from all the gossip and gargoyles. He could ensure she was safe. Then, he could walk away and leave her to a better life.

The very thought had him wincing.

No. That wasn't going to happen. *Ever.* Losing Marion would sent him straight past that 'brink of madness,' she'd been talking about. And he'd never find his way back, again. He needed to be able to see her and hear her voice, or he'd have nothing, at all. She could *not* leave this kingdom.

Rockwell seemed to notice his pensive mood and attempted to shift the focus of the conversation. "Nothing needs to be decided tonight about Maid Marion." He was usually a calming presence at the meetings. "We do need to discuss Friar Tuck's punishment, though."

"*Him* you can hang." Nicholas decided.

The majority of the gargoyles grunted in approval at the verdict.

"Yes, but, he *is* a friar." Bits of debris fell from his eroding fingers, as Rockwell anxiously rubbed his hands together. He didn't like to disagree with Nicholas, but he obviously felt like Tuck should live to whine another day. "Nottingham won't like it if we execute a friar and they're already restless about the… uh… stolen bride situation."

"Tuck tried to attack my fiancée, while we planned our wedding." Nicholas turned to scowl at Rockwell over his shoulder. "You think I should let that pass with just a fine?"

Quarry arched a brow. "Maybe you should ask Tuck to marry you, Commander. Robin Hood might show up to save him."

That remark elicited some chuckles.

"The commander is marrying Friar Tuck, now?" Gravol asked innocently. "Can Friars get married?"

"Can *we* get married?" Boulder asked the room at large. "Tuck might've had a point today. I never heard of a gargoyle marrying anyone."

"No law says we can't!" Oore snapped back.

That led to a heated argument on all sides.

Nicholas closed his eyes, praying for blessed silence.

"Can't we just give the friar life in prison, instead of an execution?" Rockwell tried sounding a bit desperate.

"That'll blow the weekly food budget." Oore complained, swinging his leg over the arm of Richard's throne. "Have you seen how much that man eats?"

And suddenly Nicholas thought of a solution to his Friar Tuck problem. One that his partner on "Team Creative Villainy" was sure to appreciate. "Send Tuck to the Wicked, Ugly, and Bad Prison." Even he was surprised by his words, but they were out of his mouth before he could stop them.

Rockwell blinked, both at the strange idea and at the

fact Nicholas had changed his mind so quickly. Typically, he didn't change his mind, at all. "The Friar is Good. Will they even take him?"

"I have a feeling they take a lot of people they're not supposed to take."

Oore gave a dramatic shudder. "The WUB Club is a pit. The Four Kingdoms should be ashamed it's even called a prison. I'd rather be hanged than go there."

Nicholas was perversely pleased with that glowing endorsement. "Do it." He ordered. Marion would like this plan and he liked doing things that Marion would like. ...Even when a simple hanging would be far easier.

"Where is Maid Marion, anyway?" Boulder asked suspiciously. "Someone's watching her right? She could escape."

"Cragg's watching her." Gravol volunteered cheerfully. "He's super happy that the commander promoted him. Watching Maid Marion will be way easier than patrolling the castle walls."

Nicholas scoffed at the idea that corralling Marion would ever be "easy."

"Cragg, huh?" Quarry's quiet voice was dry as the Lyonesse desert. "Interesting choice of a man to be stationed in your girl's bedroom, Commander."

This time, Nicholas didn't bother to deny Marion was his girl. Quarry wouldn't believe him and it felt like a lie. Marion *was* his home. She always had been.

"Cragg's an excellent soldier." He said instead and it was true. Cragg was young, but he was hard-working, learned quickly, and was easily the most likable of all the gargoyles. Marion would be protected and happy with him around. "He's earned the promotion to lieutenant."

"And he's only attracted to men."

"That fact barely even crossed my mind."

Chapter Twelve

**Local blacksmith is shirtless horseshoeing phenom!
Shirtless photos inside!**

Alan A. Dale- "Nottingham's Naughtiest News"

Cragg had jagged spikes surrounding his skull, like a crown of stone. He loved black nail polish and hearing spoilers about every celebrity divorce scheduled to happen over the next decade. His favorite flavor of ice cream was strawberry, with vanilla kind of mixed in and then chocolate sauce drizzled on top. With sprinkles.

In short, he was *awesome*.

Marion had hoped to sneak up stairs and search Nicholas' room tonight. But Cragg was hard to ditch, unless maybe she knocked him over the head or something. And it would be a crime to hit such an awesome person over the head, even though the stony spines would probably protect him from serious damage. So instead, the two of them were sitting side-by-side on her bed, waiting for their pedicures to dry.

"Where could I get a gun around here?" She asked her new BFF, wiggling her toes to admire their ebony paint.

"Nottingham doesn't do guns. They do *arrows*." Cragg was clearly bitter over the fact gargoyles had so much trouble with bows. The choice of weapon really did seem to be designed just to exclude them.

"But if I wanted to buy a gun on the black market, it could be done, right? Who would I talk to about that?"

"I don't know. Pinocchio maybe?"

"Who's that?"

"Guy in town, with a magical relics shop and a big nose. Nobody smart goes near him, though. He's a liar and he's done shit that nobody will ever..." Cragg broke off, getting suspicious at all the questions. "Hey, how come you want a gun? You're not planning to shoot the commander, are you?"

"No! I'd never shoot Nick." Regardless of what the damn jury had said. "I'm protecting him." She smiled. "I'm also open to suggestions on how to seduce him, if you have any thoughts."

Cragg relaxed. "I don't think it needs to be much of a seduction." He adjusted the pillows behind his head. It must've been hard to get comfortable with those spikes jutting out of his skull. "Basically, you just have to breathe and he's ready to rip your clothes off."

"You think?"

"I *know*. He watches you, like his eyeballs are attached to your body with invisible strings. The commander's a little bit obsessed with you. We all see it."

Marion smirked, pleased with that news. "I'm a little bit fixated on him." A lot fixated. "So, I get how he feels about me. ...I think."

"I *know*." Cragg repeated and his eyes grew serious. "His feelings are obvious to all the men. They have been for years. He can't hide them. They're too big." He hesitated. "The whole plan to use you as bait for Hood was a shit thing to do. But, you're in no danger from us. No danger from him. *Ever*." He uneasily rubbed at his spiky head. "If you're not serious about this engagement, you could hurt the commander in ways he won't come back from."

"I won't hurt Nick." Marion promised. Not again. "I'm *very* serious about him."

"That's what the rest of us are counting on. We talked about it. The commander deserves to be happy and so we're going to give you a chance. You've always been kind to the gargoyles. Even Boulder admits that. None of us can imagine you doing something cruel, even if the commander has been... um..."

"He's been a kidnapping, lying, stealing jerk." Marion finished for him. "But that's okay. I'm gonna keep him, anyway."

Cragg was instantly on the defensive. "The

commander doesn't lie and steal. When did he lie and steal?"

"He literally stole *me*, for one thing." Marion felt like the whole "kidnapping" episode wasn't registering with the gargoyles as a very big deal.

"Okay maybe. But he doesn't lie."

"He lies by omission." And since Nicholas did it, Marion justified her own decisions not to tell him things that he didn't need to know, right now.

"That's not the same as really *real* lying." Cragg was ready to go to the mat to protect the honor of his commanding officer. The loyalty the men had towards Nicholas was heartening, really. Everyone *should* see how great he was. "And that doesn't mean you shouldn't give him a genuine shot. The commander is so much better than Hood! You'd see that, if you got to know him."

"I see it, right now."

Cragg hesitated. "You do? You swear?"

"On my life." Marion felt like she was being interrogated by her boyfriend's family to see if she measured up. ...Her boyfriend's armed, gigantic, kidnapping family.

Cragg's spiked head tilted. "I believe you." He decided, after a beat.

Marion shrugged, because why shouldn't he? It was the truth.

"It's a hopeful sign, you being here." Cragg went on. "For all the rest of us, I mean. If the commander can find a mate, maybe we can, too."

"I'm pretty sure *I* found *him*." Marion wasn't about to let Nicholas take the credit, when she was the one who'd traveled through frigging time.

Cragg ignored her correction. "I saw the commander almost smile earlier, when he was looking at you." He confided, cheerily. "I've *never* seen him almost smile."

"Before lunch, I made out with him in my father's study. That made him real happy, I think."

"Yeah, that would probably cheer him up, alright."

"That's why I'm sure my seduction is off to a good start. If I can just get past the virgin thing, it's all going to go great."

"Virgin thing?"

She blinked up at him. "Maids are virgins." She said, in case he didn't know.

Cragg looked skeptical. "I'm sure they *tell* people that."

It took Marion a second to interpret those dry words. "You think other Maids are having sex and lying about it?" That idea had never even occurred to her. Why had that not occurred to her? It was so obvious! She gasped in outrage, at all the scandals that must've happened beneath the chaste veneer of Maidenhood. "My God, was I the only one following the rules, do you think?"

"I *know*." Cragg gave a sympathetic nod.

Marion made an aggravated sound. She'd been so naive to blindly accept all the lies Nottingham told her. If she's stayed in this dump, she might've spent her whole life never understanding anything that was going on around her. In some ways, being sent to prison had been a lucky escape from an even worse fate.

Every valuable skill Marion possessed, she'd learned behind bars. People there were so bored and isolated, they shared all kinds of shit with anyone who would listen. Thanks to her fellow prisoners, Marion could speak the Green Dragon dialect, recite the lineage of the siren's complicated aristocracy, knew the best method for tiling a bathroom floor, could name every star in the sky, could draw three kinds of pirate maps, knew all the best strategies for offensive plays in Wolfball games, knew how to assemble a crossbow blindfolded, and had memorized every bone in the human body and how to break it like a barbarian.

Nottingham had kept Marion stifled for twenty-six years. At least in jail, she'd gotten a quality education.

"The commander isn't going to be upset about 'the virgin thing.'" Cragg went on, amusement in his voice. "I *promise* you. He'll be fine with the news that Hood never fucked you."

"Well, I'm not fine with it." Marion waved a hand

through the air, correcting herself. "I'm fine with the not-sleeping-with-Robin part, obviously. The guy's a waste of tights. But, *in general*, I'm not fine with being the only awkward, inexperience idiot left in Nottingham."

"There are a lot of idiots in Nottingham." Cragg assured her.

Marion barely heard him. "I want to be a badass at sex, but the stupid Maid shit they taught me gets in the way. And now I find out all that brainwashing just worked on *me!*" The more she considered it, the more she grew disappointed in herself. "I can't *believe* everybody else was having sex. I could've been an expert by now, if I'd known I had a quarter century to practice."

"I'm not sure the commander is much of an expert, either. I can't recall him paying particular attention to any girl. Besides you, of course."

That was gratifying to hear. Marion calmed a bit. "No one?"

Cragg hesitated. His stony brow furrowed, like he wanted to be completely honest. "Well... during the war, I got the feeling he might have a girl. But I'm sure he's over that, by now."

Marion made a face.

The door to her bedroom slammed open and the dour housekeeper came in, balancing a tray of snacks. Guyla Gisborn was middle-aged, but her perpetual misery made her seem older. The only joy in her life came from making other people just as unhappy as she was. Guyla seemed disappointed that she hadn't caught Marion and Cragg in a more compromising position. No doubt, she'd hoped she could run off to tell some salacious new gossip.

"Come on in." Marion told her sarcastically.

Guyla Gisborn slammed the tray down on the mattress and glowered at Marion.

Marion glowered back.

There was a moment of silent antipathy between them.

"Why do you hate me so much?" Marion asked,

breaking the standoff.

Gulya blinked, like she hadn't been expecting to be confronted so directly. "Your mother ruined my life." She blurted out. "She stole away the man I loved. And now you're trying to do the same. You're exactly like her."

Marion's head tilted. "You loved my father? ...And now you love Nick?"

"What the fuck...?" Cragg muttered in bafflement.

Guyla gave a "humph" of disgust and marched out again, without saying a word. The door crashed closed behind her.

"That was weird." Cragg opined. "Like, you don't need to worry *at all.* The commander is not gonna sleep with that creepy lady."

"No kidding." Marion would see the woman dead first.

Guyla's rationale made no sense. From time to time, you could kind of see the attractive girl she'd once been peeking out from under her pinched, gray features. Her eyes were blue and her graying hair had once been red curls. But, no matter how pretty she'd been in her youth, Marion's father would never have chosen Gulya over his True Love. He'd adored the duchess! Everyone said so. And Nicholas certainly didn't seem romantically interested in the gloomy housekeeper. Marion would've noticed that and dealt with it already. The woman was either crazy or...

Actually, there didn't seem to be an "or." She was just crazy.

Whatever her deluded reasons, Guyla was consistent about despising Marion in every timeline, though. She'd lied at the trial, saying that she'd seen Marion come back to Nicholas' room on the night he'd died. Marion wasn't sure *why* the bitter crone made up the story, but her elaborate tale of Marion sneaking up the stairs to Nicholas' tower, wearing a dark cloak "with probably nothing under it," had riveted the court.

"Why did Nick even hire her?" Marion asked, with a shake of her head.

"He didn't. She's been here since the dark ages." Cragg reached for his third bowl of ice cream. "It's not like we can replace her. Not many people want to work for gargoyles, even if it means living in the castle."

Marion rolled her eyes. "This kingdom really is the worst." She settled back with her own massive scoop of frozen strawberries and fudge, dismissing Gulya from her mind. "We should all get out of here."

"And go where?"

"Someone told me Neverland Beach is the best place to start over. Umbrella drinks and shirtless boys, as far as the eye can see."

"Sounds good to me."

"Me too."

It *did* sound good, dammit. But, she couldn't just leave Nottingham yet, no matter how enticing the idea of blue water and palm trees sounded. First of all, she had a murderer to catch. Secondly, this rat-hole kingdom had wrecked her life and it was going to pay. Marion intended to stay right where she was and burn Nottingham down around her.

...Except she also needed to ensure Nicholas didn't get caught in the crossfire. Crap. That might be tricky, considering he was kinda in charge of the dump. He might feel obliged to stop her campaign of terror.

"I need a cigarette." She muttered, her brain hurting from thinking so much.

"Have some potato chips, instead." Cragg nudged the bowl at her.

Marion shot them a quick frown. "Do we have any Gala-Chips, instead of these plain ones? I like the caramel-and-whey flavor best."

"What are Gala-Chips?" He asked, with his mouth full.

Marion blinked in surprise. He might as well have asked her what peanut butter was. "Candy-coated potato chips, of course." The damn things were more addictive than nicotine. "Wait. Have Gala-Chips not been invented, yet?"

It was hard to remember a time when Sir Galahad's calorie-laden creation hadn't been the number one snack food in every grocery store. People in jail traded them like currency.

Honestly, everything Camelot's best knight ever

invented was successful, according to all the newspapers, and magazines, and commercials, and award shows. She'd never met the man, but literally everyone in the universe had heard of Galahad's splendorously splendid splendor.

Cragg shrugged and crushed up a handful of ordinary, bland potato chips to sprinkle over his ice cream. "I don't think so. I never heard of them."

"Huh." Marion murmured thoughtfully.

"Something wrong?"

"Nope." Marion pursed her lips. "Hey, do you know a real estate agent?"

"Sure. Why?"

"I'm selling my house."

He blinked. "Really? The whole Huntingdon estate?"

"Every stick and stone and heirloom rug." She settled back on the pillows. "I need cash and I feel like Nottingham's housing market is about to take a sharp downward turn."

The gardens alone would guarantee her a good price, even with a rushed sale. Not many people grew flowers in Nottingham's gray landscape. The sour townsfolk were bitterly opposed to anything difficult or different, just on principle. But, the ostentatious showiness of the rare flowers was the envy of the elite. The old duke had loved the status symbol of the gardens. Marion had funneled money into their care to assuage his need to keep up appearances.

More importantly, the gardens had been granted a tax exemption from the palace for their "cultural contributions to Nottingham." All the nobles coveted that piece of paper. The Huntingdons' cultural tax exemption was the only one in Nottingham and it was worth a fortune. Marion had cried the day that unexpected news arrived. It had saved her family's home from being seized and kept her ailing father safe in his own bed. Without King Richard giving her the exemption, she had no idea what she would have done.

That thought made her pause.

Wait. Why had Richard given her that exemption? She hadn't asked for it. He didn't even like her. Marion had been so overcome with gratitude that she'd never questioned how it all came about. Now, she questioned everything.

Cragg still wasn't convinced of her plan to liquidate five-hundred years of Huntingdon flowers and history. "Where are you going to live without a house, though?"

Marion shook aside the tax issue. "With my handsome husband, of course."

"Oh." Cragg paused. "...With the commander, you mean?" He hazarded warily, like he wanted to be sure of which handsome husband she planned to move in with.

"With Nick." Marion confirmed and ate an uninspired, uncandied potato chip. "So, who are you dating?" She asked in a more conversational tone. It was a far safer topic than her stubborn groom, Guyla's lunacy, leveling kingdoms, or money problems. Besides, she'd talked enough. It was Cragg's turn to share.

Cragg lifted a shoulder. "No one. At least, not in public. I sometimes sleep with Lampwick, the local blacksmith, but he doesn't want anyone else to know about us."

"Fuck him, then. You can do better."

"Humans don't get in really *real* relationships with gargoyles. We have to pay, afterwards. It's expected."

Marion frowned at that news. Even for Nottingham that arrangement was unwholesome. It really was a terrible place to live, no matter your station, gender or species.

"Lampwick is willing to see me for free! That must mean he likes me, right?" Cragg sighed. "And he's so pretty. He's sure to be named May Day King this year."

Marion resisted the urge to scoff. "He'll probably cheat to win, like that hag Clorinda does."

The King and Queen of May Day were crowned at the Maypole Ball, after everyone danced around and drank a lot. It was nothing but a talent contest and literally didn't matter, at all. Marion barely even cared about the plastic rhinestone tiara. Hardly even thought about the unfairness of Clorinda taking home the title, instead of her.

Bitch.

"Lampwick is big, too." Cragg went on, halfheartedly poking at his ice cream. "I want someone at least as big as I am, ya know? Otherwise, I feel like I'm going to crush him." He held up his gigantic stony arms to illustrate the problem.

Poor Cragg.

"If you're willing to wait ten years, I can hook you up with a bridge ogre named Benji." She offered. "He's furry, but he's a sweetheart." If you discounted the fact that he was a Red level felon at the WUB Club. "He does have some legal problems, now and then, though."

Cragg pondered that description, intrigued by the notion of dating a Bad boy. "How big is he?"

"He once lifted up the entire Eastlands' bridge."

Cragg made a considering face, looking more encouraged. "I'll think about it."

Chapter Thirteen

King Jonathan's Secret Lovechild Confirmed!
Records show that the playboy prince had an illegitimate offspring,
before he became king.
Where is this missing heir to the throne?
And was its mother an alien?

Alan A. Dale- "Nottingham's Naughtiest News"

Nicholas might've been the least popular man in Nottingham among the humans, but among the gargoyles, he was a superstar. Marion spent her breakfast watching his men stumble all over themselves to win his approval. Nicholas didn't notice how much they adored him, which made the whole spectacle even more endearing.

Within twenty minutes, she'd realized she'd have to change all her plans. Again. Nicholas' gargoyle family would be heartbroken if they got left behind in this shithole kingdom, when she destroyed it. And Nick would be sad if they died in the flames of destruction. She'd have to save them.

No biggie. Marion liked making plans, now that she had the opportunity.

She watched her groom writing some quick thoughts on the economic report he was half-reading. "Have you ever heard of Gala-Chips?"

"No.

"Gala-Gum?"

"No."

"Gala-Shoes?"

"No." He glanced at her. "Why?"

"No reason. More coffee?"

"I haven't had *any* yet. You drank all mine and none of yours."

"I like yours better."

Nicholas grunted, but he didn't tell her to stop. Instead, his mouth curved slightly, watching her drink from his mug.

Marion surreptitiously eyed the paper covered in Nicholas' notes, trying to get a clear look at the words. Unfortunately, it was at the wrong angle. Too bad she couldn't grab it without him seeing.

No biggie. She'd just have to search his room later. Flexibility was the key to any successful plan.

A particularly rocky-looking gargoyle came hustling in and silently laid a folder by Nicholas' elbow. Whoever had carved him had been incredibly untalented. He was by far the biggest man she'd ever seen, with large chunks of unfinished stone protruding from his massive body.

He gave Marion a shy wave and set a borogrove blossom, by her plate. It was displayed in a half-cleaned mason jar, the roots still attached. Someone had ripped the plant right out of a garden. *Her* garden, by the look of it. In Nottingham, only the Huntingdon estate grew borogroves. They were incredibly delicate and expensive, so seeing it murdered like this was a real tragedy.

"What a nice gesture!" She enthused, anyway.

Nicholas didn't think so. His expression darkened, his eyes on the fragile pedals, like he might just incinerate them with his stare. His gaze slowly switched to Gravol. "Who sent my fiancée flowers?" He asked in a very calm voice.

"*You* did." Gravol told him proudly.

Nicholas was confused. "No, I didn't."

Marion wasn't going to laugh. She *wasn't*. She quickly covered her mouth, to hide her grin.

Gravol leaned closer to Marion. "I'm supposed to say it's from him." He told her in a confidential tone. "The others said so. But *I* picked it for you."

"I see." She nodded gravely. "Thank you, Gravol. I'm very touched."

He beamed at her and she felt her heart melt. She couldn't recall exactly which gargoyles had escorted her from her home at the beginning of this kidnapping/engagement. It had been ten years ago, for her. But she was suddenly sure Gravol had been there. She remembered him patting her back, with one baseball-mitt-sized hand, as she unsuccessfully tried to evade the abduction. It stuck in her mind, because Gravol had nearly knocked her over with his overly enthusiastic commiseration. The man was massive and had no clue about his own strength.

Clearly, he was also a sweetheart.

Gravol looked back at Nicholas, like a desperate first-grader wanting a smiley-face sticker on his arithmetic test.

"Nick, tell Gravol what a good job he did." She urged.

"Nice work, Gravol." Nicholas muttered absently, giving up on understanding the flower debacle and already flipping through the folder.

Those three words were apparently more praise than he usually lavished on the gargoyles, because the other man honest-to-God gasped in wonder. Taking the extravagant response as a mark of high favor, Gravol saluted in grateful respect, his eyes shimmering with emotion, and he all but floated from the room. It was an interesting thing, watching a guy who weighed close to a ton float.

Marion glanced back to her oblivious groom. "Your men like you." Enough to try and play matchmaker for him, it seemed. First Cragg and now Gravol.

Nicholas shrugged, his eyes still on the papers Gravol had delivered.

"Do gargoyles treat every commander with such glowing admiration?"

He glanced up at her with a slight frown. "They don't treat me like that."

"They do. They worship you. It's highly entertaining to witness."

Nicholas looked nonplussed by that news. "I barely even speak to them."

"I guess you say enough."

He shook his head. "I just ask them to be fair about enforcing the law, follow orders, protect each other, and to tell me if they think I'm screwing up." He paused. "But not to talk to me at breakfast. I like to eat in peace and quiet." He paused again. "Unless you're here. I always like to hear you. Your voice is very soothing."

"Sweet talker." She rested her chin in her palm, elbow on the table in a way her decorum tutor would have fainted at seeing. "Why did the other gargoyles choose you to be their commander? You're young for the job."

She would've expected them to resent Nicholas. Unlike most of the gargoyles, his face was beautiful, he had an education, and he'd been raised by a loving parent. By their standards, he must seem quite favored. It was logical that the less fortunate gargoyles would blame Nicholas for his advantages. Instead, they all followed him with unquestioned loyalty.

"They chose me for the job, because they thought I'd be a good leader."

"Why did they think that?"

"Because I told them I would be a good leader." He made it sound obvious.

"And that was enough to earn the other gargoyles' respect? Just telling them?"

He shrugged again.

Marion resisted the urge to pull out her hair. "What did you do to *show* them you were a good leader? Give me some details."

Tension began to creep into Nicholas' shoulders, but he gave her what she wanted. "During the war, I was head of a gargoyle squadron. Hood oversaw the division, but most of the gargoyles here in the castle served directly under me. At the Battle of Kirklees, we were in the middle of the line. The first ones ordered in. We were supposed to protect the noblemen, coming in behind us. Soften the enemy for the more important troops."

Marion's jaw tightened. Assholes.

"You don't 'soften' Nessus Theomaddox's forces." Nicholas went on. "The man is a savage warlord."

Marion nodded at that analysis.

"The centaurs would have wiped us out." Nicholas

seemed like he was trying to convince her. "They had emplaced weapons that catapulted fireballs. There were simply too many of them, and they knew the terrain, and they knew we were coming. The gargoyles all would have died, so rich humans could have an easier fight. And the rich humans would've lost *anyway*. I couldn't go through with it. I *wouldn't*."

"So what did you do?"

He met her eyes. "I moved my men down the line and let the noblemen die, instead."

Marion slowly smiled at that news. "Fuck 'em all, Nick."

He relaxed at her approving words. "I mean, it was fairly easy to do, since Hood and the other nobles were *way* the hell back from the front. Who was going to stop me?" He paused, like he was recalling the day. "I think Nessus Theomaddox knew what I was doing. I can't prove that, but he lessened the attack on the gargoyles. I *know* he did. Just enough to get us to cover, so he could focus fire on the humans."

Yep, that sounded like a centaur tactic.

Nicholas' eyes were focused on something far away. "Then, King Richard charged in, with Hood and the other humans. ...And it was just a fucking slaughter. The loudest battle I ever remember and they were all ungodly cacophonies of sound."

War must have been uniquely hellish for Nicholas, surrounded by explosions and screaming and crowds of men.

"After we retreated, everyone was initially blaming Hood for the loss. As they should've. It was his idiotic plan to attack the centaurs head-on. Richard was presumed dead for six hours afterwards, because we couldn't sort through all the bodies. But, he eventually came stumbling back into camp, bloody and thanking Hood for his great leadership. Then, all the blame switched to the gargoyles."

Yep, that sounded like a Nottingham tactic.

"Other people think gargoyles are dumb, so no one accused me of disobeying orders deliberately." Nicholas summed up. "Not even Hood. They all assumed I was too stupid to know left from right, and I just went the wrong way in the confusion of battle. They demoted us all back to Nottingham. But, the gargoyles knew what really happened. Even the ones who never served with me, heard the story of me choosing the gargoyles over the nobles."

"And now they like you." She concluded with a nod. "A lot."

"They respect the fact that I valued them and their lives." He paused. "My mother was human, but she thought differently than most. She believed gargoyles have a purpose, beyond serving Nottingham. In my head, I know she was mistaken, but her words stay with me. I won't..."

"Of course, you have a purpose." Marion interrupted casually. "You told me so yourself."

Nicholas looked at her like she should audition for the town idiot. "I told you I had a *purpose?* When?"

"A couple days from now. In your bedroom."

His brow furrowed. "Did I tell you what it is?"

"No. You're not the most 'sharing' guy, Nick."

He grunted, disappointed in that news. Maybe he forgot he didn't believe her time travel story, anyway. "My mother told me, if you commit yourself to something with your whole heart and soul, you inevitably find your purpose." He muttered. "So far that hasn't happened for me. And I've been pretty consistent about hitting my goals. I'm in charge of the whole kingdom and still no purpose."

"Is being in charge of the kingdom what you're committed to, in your heart and soul?"

"No." He scoffed.

"Well, there's your answer, then. A purpose is bigger than just reaching a goal. It's *why* you're reaching for it."

Nicholas wasn't thrilled with that news. "Well, maybe my purpose is hunting down organized crime, pretending to be toymakers." He tossed her the manila folder Gravol had brought, ready to change the subject. "There is no Doncaster Toys and Games. It's not a factory. It's just an empty building."

Marion picked up the pages, flipping through them. "What does that mean?"

A long hesitation. "I can't be sure without more investigation..."

She cut off his carefully worded equivocation. "I don't care what you can prove as sheriff, right now. What do you *think*? That's good enough for me."

"Hood stole your money." Nicholas said instantly. "Probably with the help of someone else. And for some reason, they wanted that lion scepter. Which probably means it was somehow evidence against them."

Marion nodded. "I think so, too. We need to get that scepter back."

Nicholas looked dubious. "You're going to... what? Unmelt it?

"I'm going to hire somebody to help us magically restore it." Marion was pretty pleased with her plan. "It will be *exactly* as it was when L.J. found it, by the time it's whammy-ed back into existence."

"There's no one in Nottingham with a magic level high enough to accomplish that."

She drank more of Nicholas' coffee. "I'm outsourcing the labor." She'd already sent a message to her new employee, as a matter of fact. Hopefully, he'd actually show up. And, if he *did* show up, hopefully he wouldn't kill everyone. "I did time with a dragon."

"Dragons are extinct. Other races tried to enslave them and a lot of shit got burned. Then, they all died."

Marion hid another smile. The man should write history books. His descriptions and details were so vivid. It came from caring so much about others. "There are a few dragons left." She assured him dryly. "They're just selfish dicks, who only help when there's something in it for them."

"Wonderful."

The door opened again and another gargoyle marched in, his face grim. Honestly, the palace guard needed to learn how to take a break. They were constantly rushing around.

Something about the way this one entered the room had Nicholas going still. "What is it, Quarry?" He demanded, as if he knew something was seriously wrong.

Marion didn't recognize this man. Like Nicholas, Quarry had been carved with traditionally handsome features. There was something not quite right about how his pants fit, though. Like they were too tight or not proportioned correctly...?

Oh.

Marion's eyes went wide, suddenly realizing it was the huge bulge of his manhood creating the issue. She'd heard of gargoyles carved for "entertainment" purposes. They were given massive endowments to shock and sexually delight palace guests. She'd just never actually seen one before, because they weren't exactly encouraged to keep company with virgins.

Shit.

Her eyes hastily jumped back to Quarry's face, hoping she hadn't embarrassed him.

Luckily, he and Nicholas were focused on their newest castle emergency, talking in hushed tones. It wouldn't do them any good. Marion was going to eavesdrop anyway.

"He came over the west wall." Quarry was saying quietly, handing Nicholas a stack of printouts. "He had rope. A knife. Duct tape. Various," a quick look in Marion's direction and then back at Nicholas, "*things* that leave little doubt what he intended to do, once he had her."

Nicholas' jaw ticked, flipping through the pages.

"Someone tried to break in and kill me?" Marion interpreted. Huh. She was a little gratified to hear that, considering she'd only been back in town for a couple days. She must be making an impression.

"A local human barber, named Arthur Bland, is upset you've agreed to marry the commander." Quarry told her, when Nicholas remained eerily silent. "Do you know him?"

"Nope." At least, she didn't think she did. Clearly, they weren't great friends, if he came visiting with duct tape and a knife.

"Well, he's presently in the castle dungeon, loudly proclaiming you're a whore, who just needs," Quarry tilted his head to get an exact quote off the report, "'a human dick to suck, instead of letting some rock-monster pollute her pussy.'"

Quarry's tone was expressionless, but still full of disgust. "Mr. Bland has decided that, since no other Good male will want you now, you should be very grateful for his armed courtship."

Marion made a face. "I hate this town."

Nicholas handed the pages back to Quarry. "Hang him." He said succinctly.

Marion wasn't *against* that idea, but still... "Shouldn't we have a trial, first?"

"We just had one. He's guilty."

Quarry nodded at that legal wisdom.

"I meant a trial with like a jury." Marion pressed.

Nicholas looked pointedly at Quarry.

"Guilty." Quarry, the duly appointed foreman, decreed after a lengthy deliberation of approximately one second.

Marion gave up.

"If more of Marion's admirers come calling, don't concern yourself with capturing them alive." Nicholas told Quarry. "We don't want to clog up the court's docket."

"Right." Quarry agreed. But he didn't leave. He stood there, glancing from Marion to Nicholas and then back again. "What are you... uh... doing today?" He didn't wait for a response. "Because, some of the men were saying you two could... Maybe... go on a picnic. As a date."

Nicholas looked over at him, clearly thinking the other man had lost his mind.

Marion bit the inside of her lip to keep from breaking down in helpless amusement. "We're going to the May Day Festival." She volunteered when she was sure she could keep it together. "You can come along, if you'd like, Quarry. We're going to catch Robin in a trap. It should be fun."

Gargoyles needed to have more fun. It occurred to her that maybe humans proclaimed the gargoyles "passionless," because they forced them into servitude and were then surprised when they resisted their commands. No one ever *asked* the gargoyles what they actually wanted from life. No one cared about their opinions, at all.

Just like with Maids.

Nicholas frowned. "The men don't need to go to

the..."

"We'd love to go." Quarry interrupted. "Sounds great. I'll tell the others."

Nicholas blinked, baffled as to what was happening.

Quarry leaned closer to him, lowering his voice to a stage-whisper. "We'll have your back on the date. Don't fuck it up." He slapped Nicholas on the shoulder, saluted, and then marched out of the room.

Nicholas squinted after him, like maybe he should start randomly drug testing his guards.

"Your men *like* you." Marion reiterated.

"They're driving me crazy with all the damn talking today."

Nicholas had spoken *maybe* five sentences to the other gargoyles this morning. Apparently that was his limit. "You should be nice to them."

He snorted. "Why?"

"They're trying to get you laid, for one thing."

His head swung back around to look at her, his eyes tracing over her face.

She arched a brow.

Wheels turned in his brain, realization dawning. "Oh." He said mildly and he stopped complaining about his men. He picked up his mug and drank from it, his lips covering the same spot hers had. "Okay."

Marion smiled. But, then she thought about Quarry again and a pensive feeling came over her. "Nick?"

"I'm hanging that damn barber, Marion." He declared, hearing her tone go serious and expecting a complaint about his newest judicial ruling. "I sent Friar Tuck to the Wicked, Ugly, and Bad Prison to make you happy, but I'm not going to..."

Marion cut him off in surprise. "You sent Tuck to the WUB Club? For me?"

"Of course for you. Why would I work to make anyone else happy?" He shook his head, as if her question was crazy. "But this Bland person is a rapist in training. So, I don't want to argue about killing him."

"I'm not arguing." She promised. "I don't care about

this new duct-tape scumbag, at all. It's just," she hunted for the right words and found a segue, "there was a lot of abuse in the WUB Club."

A savage light ignited in his eyes.

"Not to me!" Marion rushed to assure him, splaying a palm over her chest. "Not ever."

Maybe he *did* believe her about traveling back in time, because he relaxed at her hasty assurance.

"It was mostly the male prisoners who suffered. Dr. White --the warden-- was a woman and she was a maniac. She took people's choices away, just because she could. It wasn't right."

Nicholas was listening.

Marion leaned closer to him. "Don't let that happen to Quarry or any of the other gargoyles. I know some of them were created to be royal... um... entertainment." She wrinkled her nose in distaste at the idea. "But, that doesn't make it *right*. They have thoughts and feelings and passions. They should get to choose."

Something softened in Nicholas' face. "As long as I'm sheriff, no one is touching my men without their permission." He promised. "They know that. Don't worry."

Marion smiled in relief. She'd known he was a good leader. "Okay. I'm glad you're protecting them." Satisfied, she settled back in her chair. "And thank you for sending Tuck to prison. I know you would've rather just hang him. It was very sweet of you to extend his torture for me."

"You're welcome, duchess."

Marion beamed. She couldn't have been more pleased with the way breakfast was going. She took the coffee back from him.

Nicholas watched her sip from his pilfered mug, enjoying himself, too. "Hiring a dragon to reconstitute the scepter will cost a fortune, you know." He said, picking up their earlier conversation like they'd never stopped talking. "We don't have a fortune. Hood stole it all."

"Oh, *this* dragon's going to do it for free. He just doesn't know it, yet." Marion waved that concern aside. She was already onto new ideas. Once she started coming up with plans, the creative villainy just flowed out. "In the meantime, we can't put all our eggs in that basket. We don't even know for sure the scepter means anything important."

"It means paying for a month's worth of grain for the castle."

She made an annoyed sound, slamming his mug back down. "I don't give a shit about grain, Nick! I'm trying to find out who kills you."

He grunted, not overly worried. "The festival is today. Tonight is the May Day Queen Pageant. Tomorrow is the Maypole Dance. Our wedding is Wednesday. And on Thursday, I'm planning to hang Robin Hood. Anyone who wants to kill me had better make an appointment for Friday afternoon, because my schedule is packed this week."

"On Thursday you'll be dead." She summarized flatly. "You're killed in your bedroom, sometime between one and two in the morning. Shot in the chest. I was at the crime scene earlier and we'd had a very loud argument. I left around ten and I spent the next five hours sitting in my gardens. In the dark. Alone and furious at you." She'd needed time to think, away from everyone and everything. Reasonable enough, under the circumstances, but it was a terrible alibi.

A slight frown tugged at Nicholas' brow.

"Guyla Gisborn says she saw me entering your bedroom, again, later that night. It was a lie. I never came back to the castle. I swear it. But, *I* will be instantly blamed and no one else will ever be investigated. They never find the gun. They just declared I had motive and opportunity and have me arrested." She paused. "And you let whoever killed you into your room. You unlocked the door."

He shook his head. "I wouldn't have done that."

"Except you *did*. It's all *fact,* Nick. Or at least it was, until I got here to fix it." She leaned closer to him, her gaze intent. "I'm not sure the scepter is going to solve *anything*. I don't know how it's mixed up in this. We need to keep searching for who might want you dead, because that's all that really matters."

Nicholas stared at her with a strange expression. Maybe he was finally taking his impending homicide seriously. "How in the hell did I get you into my bedroom, in the first place?"

Or maybe not.

"Oh for God's sake, *that's* what you focus on?!" Marion reached over to whack him on the shoulder and only succeeded in hurting her palm on his stony flesh. "Ow!"

Nicholas' eyes widened in alarm. He caught hold of her wrist, turning it to examine her hand. His brow furrowed in concern. "Did you break anything?" He gently prodded at her fingers, searching for damage.

"I'm fine." She liked the feel of his large hand holding hers. It felt right. "But you're *so* hard, Nick."

His gaze slowly rose to her face and Marion belatedly picked up on the suggestive double-meaning to her words.

Whoops.

She cleared her throat, feeling like an idiot. Sexual innuendos were out of her league, for the most part. Anything sexual kind of flummoxed her, really. She could brazen through, but only when she worked herself up to it. This had come out of nowhere.

"Sorry." She tried to pull back her hand.

Nicholas didn't let go. Instead, his expression lit with some new predatory glow and he held her tighter. Marion's heartbeat sped up, but she stopped trying to get away. Unsure what he wanted, she just gazed up at him and waited. He felt her small resistance fade, accepting him, and his breathing got rougher. His thumb touched the pulse in her wrist and she jolted in sudden arousal. He made a low sound, part soothing and part *not*.

Oooohhh... Hang on. This was very promising.

The door of the banquet hall opened and Rockwell came in, carefully carrying a spray-painted golden arrow. "Sir, the... um... *prize* for the May Day Festival is ready. It's still a bit wet and drippy in places, but..."

Nicholas cut him off. "Get out." He commanded, without looking away from Marion. "And lock the door behind you."

Marion blinked.

Rockwell hurried to comply with the order, beaming with the smug happiness only a successful matchmaker could feel. "The commander's doing great in there!" He enthused to one of the others. "He must be using my visualization techniques. I don't think she's even noticed that he's obsessively obsessed with her." The door slammed so hard the chandelier shook.

Oh, Marion *had* noticed. And she liked it.

Nicholas settled back in his chair, ignoring Rockwell's enthusiasm for gargoyle-y stalking. He took a deep breath, his gaze still fixed on Marion. "So, tell me about betrothal rights."

Chapter Fourteen

**Sheriff holds Maid Marion as sex slave! Maid Marion refuses to escape!
Instead plans most expensive wedding in Nottingham history!
Which designer will she be wearing to her virgin sacrifice?**

Alan A. Dale- "Nottingham's Naughtiest News"

Marion frowned, thrown off guard by the question. It was hard to think of anything, when he was holding her wrist and his thumb was rubbing against her pulse. He'd caught her with his more human-looking left hand. It wasn't his dominant side. That meant something, but the feel of his skin on hers was so distracting it made it hard to pay attention to what. "Betrothal rights?"

"Yes. I wasn't allowed to attend your fancy schools. I don't know the specifics of this courtly tradition. Explain it."

"It's just a ceremonial thing. I told you last night, Maids are considered enfeebled, so we need some big, strong man to take care of us. When we accept a proposal, our new fiancé becomes like... our bodyguard, I guess. In return, he gets access to the body he's guarding."

All sexual activity in Nottingham had some calculation of exchange involved and virginity was one of the most valuable commodities on the market. Noblemen had tons of rituals about "protecting" it. It was all *so* unhealthy.

"What kind of access?" His touch slid down to caress the inside of her palm. "Be specific."

"Theoretically, the groom is entitled to make certain demands." This was all boring and backwards chivalry nonsense. She tilted her hand, so he could brush between her fingers and butterflies took off in her stomach. "He can touch his new bride. But, she doesn't have to touch him and they can't have intercourse. Not until after the wedding."

"Define 'touch.' What parts and for how long?" Once he started talking, the man loved asking questions.

"This is a ceremonial thing." She repeated a little baffled by his interest in arcane laws. Couldn't he concentrate on hand holding? It was certainly all she could focus on. Was she too old to hold hands? Hopefully not, because she loved it. "Men don't really make the demands. It's just some sexist remnant of..."

He cut her off. "It's still the law, isn't it?"

Marion's heartbeat sped up, finally realizing where this was headed. "Technically."

"So, as your fiancé, where am I technically allowed to touch you, Marion?"

"Everywhere." She heard herself whisper. "You're allowed to touch me everywhere."

Satisfaction glinted in his eyes. "Whenever I want?"

She bobbed her head, her blood thickening in her veins. "According to the law, my body is under your protection. You can touch it for as long as you want. Just so you pledge to take care of me."

He very slowly smiled. The first real smile she'd ever seen from him and it was beautiful. It lit up his handsome face, softening the menacing angles and making him look almost boyish. "Deal."

Uh-oh...

Marion yanked her hand back, trying to rally her thoughts. "I'm telling you, *no one* actually demands their betrothal rights. It's all symbolic, Nick. Like how honor guards wear swords, with their snazzy uniforms. They're not going to *use* them. They're just for show. Some outdated, formal ritual."

Nicholas crooked a finger at her. "Come here, Marion."

She gaped at him.

"I don't care what those pasty highborn assholes do. I'm demanding everything I'm entitled to." He paused meaningfully. "...Or you can run." It was a dare.

Marion swallowed. Her gaze flashed towards the door,

thinking. Nicholas would never force her to do anything. She could walk out and he wouldn't stop her.

But why in the world would she want to leave?

Her eyes flicked back to Nicholas.

"I will take care of you." He promised quietly.

The intensity of his voice washed away the last bit of her hesitation. The vow sounded very, very serious when he gave it. When the chips were down, Marion knew she could only really count on herself, but still... her insides fluttered when he gave her the pledge of protection.

She slowly stood up, so she was directly in front of him. She was close enough to see the pulse in his neck hammering, just as hers was. The small tell gave Marion more confidence. Despite his demands, Nicholas wasn't so sure this new plan of his was going to work. She liked that he was vulnerable, too.

"Now what?" She asked, her gaze on his.

He hesitated a beat, then his left palm reached out to settle on her waist. Two seconds ticked by. Then, his other hand slowly moved, as well. Big, thick fingers gently settled on the opposite side of her body, giving her time to retreat. Nicholas watched his rough palm curl around her waist and his chest expanded in a deep breath.

And Marion finally processed why he always tried to hide his right hand from her. It was the stoniest part of his body. He thought she would cringe away from it. Gray eyes flicked up to her face. He searched her expression, as if he expected rejection.

Marion arched a brow in flirtatious challenge. "Is this *all* we're going to do, dumpling?"

Nicholas heard all the permission he needed in those playful words. Both hands tightened, dragging her down onto his lap.

Marion jolted in surprise. She hadn't expected him to gain so much confidence so fast. She should have. Nicholas never missed an opportunity.

Her legs ended up on either side of his hips, her knees on the seat cushion. Even through the fabric of her stolen pants, she could feel the heat of him pressing against her core. It felt exotic and... nice. Really nice.

More than nice.

His right hand slid under the hem of her shirt, the textured skin of his thumb barely brushing over the flesh of her ribcage. Marion's body got so wet so fast it was a wonder she didn't come right then. Holy *shit*. She scrambled to think through the sudden heat, wanting to do everything right. Only she had no idea how she was supposed to think, when her body was on fire.

She seriously *hated* being a virgin.

Okay. She tried to rally. So Nicholas was amazing at this. No surprise. She needed to figure out her part, before he noticed she was an idiot. Marion bit her lower lip, trying to decide where her own hands should go. Fuck. Was he going to get annoyed because she didn't know where her hands should go?

Nicholas felt her stiffen. "Alright?"

"Robin would be annoyed." She blurted out.

Nicholas stilled.

Fuck.

Had any other Maid ever had a moment like this? She doubted it. None of the boring blue-blooded Nottingham men cared about their betrothal rights. To them, a Maid was just a trophy to win. If they wanted to get laid, they went to some pretty serving girl. Maids were supposed to be sexless and pure. Her whole value was in her virginity. Only Nicholas wanted to touch his untouched prize. It was sheer luck that she'd gotten this guy right where she wanted him and she was not about to screw it up.

"Hood will be very, *very* annoyed that I have my hands on you. Yes." Nicholas said quietly, misunderstanding her nerves. He didn't offer to let her go, though.

"No." She waved Robin aside, with a dismissive laugh. "He wouldn't be *jealous*. Not of me."

Nicholas arched a skeptical brow.

"I meant, if he and I were doing this... And he was *you*...?" She cleared her throat. "Robin would be annoyed that

I have no idea where my hands should go." She held the awkward appendages up for him to see. "And I don't want you to be annoyed."

Nicholas stared at her.

Marion took a deep breath, trying to regain her normal, prison-learned bravado. You couldn't show weakness or you'd be crushed. "I'm fine. Just give me a second. I'll figure it out." Weighing her options, she settled for reaching up to grasp the front of his uniform. "There." See, she was getting the hang of this already.

Nicholas' mouth curved in tenderness, the tension seeping from his muscles.

"I'm just not used to anyone touching me." Marion told him defensively.

"Get used to it." He advised. "As long as I have the right to do it, my hands will be all over you. At least, in private."

Yes, that sounded *very* promising. Except... "Why just in private?"

His brows tugged together, not meeting her eyes. "It will ruin your reputation, if it seems like you want to be with me. Even a little." He watched, seemingly fascinated, as his stony fingers grazed along the length of her neck. His coarse thumb traced the tender valley at the base of her throat. When she didn't recoil, he gave a sigh of masculine possession.

She refused to be distracted. "Nick, I don't want to be with you a 'little.' I want to be with you *a lot*. My reputation in this kingdom is meaningless to me, because the people passing judgement on me are meaningless. I don't care what they think. I'm very happy here with you."

He shook his head, like he didn't believe that.

"It's true!"

"I kidnapped you."

"I'm not holding a grudge. It was years ago."

"It was a couple days ago." He retorted. "You're not thinking clearly. Which is why I *really* shouldn't be doing this." Even as he said it, though, his palm smoothed over her hair and he gave a low groan at the feel of the strands sliding between his coarse fingers.

"I'll make you a deal." Marion promised in her most I'm-taking-this-ridiculous-conversation-seriously voice. "If anyone asks, I'll claim I'm an innocent hostage, held in your granite clutches."

"You *are* an innocent hostage, but you're still going to bear the brunt of this, if it goes on. You heard Quarry this morning. Some asshole tried to break in to take you for himself, because he thought I'd soiled you. Shit like that will keep happening, Marion."

"Well, maybe it's not so terrible that you're claiming your betrothal rights, then. It's your job to guard my body." Marion leaned closer to his ear, getting into this game. "You can just hang anyone who wants to steal me away from you."

"I'll end up killing half the kingdom."

"They all suck, anyway." She settled down more comfortably on his lap, gaining confidence. This was actually fun!

Nicholas was breathing faster, watching as her body relaxed under his touch. "If we kept this private, it would be a lot safer." He tried, wanting to convince her of his stupid idea, but too turned on to think it all through.

"If I wanted safety, I'd already be on Neverland Beach." She grinned. "Instead, I'm here with you."

The smile was all it took.

Since she didn't shove him away and run for her life, Nicholas was done hesitating. Massive hands swept upward to cover her breasts, like he owned them. Which according to the law, he kind of *did*. Marion didn't care about the stupid betrothal rights rules, but the idea of Nicholas having erotic ownership of her body was weirdly hot. Like a dirty fantasy, where she could do nothing but let the dastardly sheriff have his wicked way with her.

Thanks to Nottingham's chauvinist brainwashing, there was a lot of guilt tied into her sexuality. There always had been. Even in prison, Marion had shied away from sexual discussions. And she'd never let anyone touch her, although she'd had offers. Some of them more forceful that others. On the rare occasions she'd masturbated in her cell, she'd pictured Nicholas and then felt even lonelier afterwards.

All that baggage was bullshit and she *knew* it was bullshit, but it still messed with her head. The betrothal rights gave her an off ramp. They were just a silly tradition that nobody ever took seriously, so she didn't have to worry. If Nicholas wanted to play, she was happy to let him navigate this whole encounter. She just had to sit there and enjoy the game.

And --holy crap!-- was she enjoying it.

Nicholas' eyes nearly glowed, as he squeezed her breasts through the fabric of her shirt. "Oh I will *definitely* be guarding these." He murmured.

His rock-hard hands massaged her delicate flesh and Marion gasped in pleasure. She had no idea that her breasts were so sensitive. So starved for attention. Inside her bra, her nipples grew even harder, wanting more of his touch.

Nicholas noticed their pleas. His gaze sharpened at the evidence of Marion's own desire. "Take your shirt off." He rasped. "Show me what I'm pledging to guard."

That was a *great* idea. Possibly the greatest idea in the history of ideas. She hastily yanked her shirt over her head and tossed it aside.

Nicholas' gaze was riveted on the lacy cups of her bra. He blinked rapidly, as if he was shocked she'd actually complied with his demand. "Betrothal rights are the greatest idea Nottingham's ever come up with." He decided in a strained voice, echoing her own thoughts. They were so in synch. "I've never been so happy to represent our legal system."

"I guarantee, you're the only groom who's ever pushed the law this far." Marion got out breathlessly. "I think you might just be the wickedest man in Nottingham." It was a revelation!

"Are you sure you want to do this with a wicked gargoyle?" He asked, like he didn't fully understand what was happening.

"I'm sure I want to do it with *you*."

Nicholas' thumbs brushed her aching nipples through the fabric of the bra. He seemed fascinated with the contrast of the black lace against her skin. Marion's sharp, indrawn breath made his eyes glow. "Hood never saw these?"

Marion licked her lower lip. "Robin never had any betrothal rights. We were never really engaged."

He glanced at her, hearing the evasion.

She made a face, relenting to the silent question, even though it was none of his business. She understood his insecurities. If Nicholas had been dating someone else for ten years, Marion would've shanked the bitch, by now. She was a bit *over* the brink of madness about the guy. "Robin did want to see me naked, before he went to war. Happy?"

"Thrilled." Nicholas didn't sound thrilled. He caught her in a firmer grip, like he was afraid she might slip away. His hatred of Robin was a live current in their relationship that could still burn everything.

Marion navigated carefully. "Robin insisted that he needed the mental image of me to remember what he was fighting for."

"Richard's greed?"

She ignored that snarky comment. "Well, we got to about this point, where I was in my underwear, but then I called it off. Robin had some... *ideas* about how we could get around the betrothal rights rules and that upset me. He shouldn't have suggested that without a legitimate marriage proposal. I think it was a test of my chastity. He used to do stuff like that."

"What kind of ideas did he suggest?" The question was deceptively calm.

She wrinkled her nose. "He wasn't supposed to touch me. So, he said he didn't *have* to touch me to enjoy himself and I said that wasn't going to just sit there in the nude, while he..." She trailed off with a sigh. "Anyway, he apologized. Said that he liked that I refused him. That my 'low sex drive' proved I was virtuous and Good and that he'd always wait for me."

Nicholas scoffed at that promise.

Marion kept going, embarrassed by how small her life had once been. "He said we would be married, one day. That he'd speak to my father about arranging a formal betrothal, when he returned. I believed him, because I *always* believed him. And... that's it." She shrugged, because it wasn't a very interesting story.

Nicholas thought that over. "So, Hood wanted to jerkoff and come all over your breasts?" He translated. "And you shut him down? And then he claimed you had a low-sex drive?"

"Yes. If you want to put it bluntly." She rolled her eyes. "Which of course you *do*."

Nicholas grunted. His hands slipped under the band of her bra to cup her breasts beneath the cups. The feel of his hot skin against her bare flesh had Marion's back arching in pleasure. Everywhere he touched he left a burning path. His right hand was especially turning her on. She hadn't expected that. Hadn't thought much about it, one way or another. But the rough texture was enflaming her hyper-sensitive skin.

She pressed closer to him, demanding more. It was absolutely shameless behavior for a Maid. Marion didn't care. With Robin, she'd always been second-guessing her actions and his responses. With Nicholas, Marion just wanted... *more*.

She wanted everything.

She reached behind her back to unclasp her bra.

Nicholas' chest heaved, as she carelessly dropped the black lace to the floor. His eyes stayed riveted on the soft globes, displayed before him. "You didn't show Hood, but you're showing *me?*" He got out in confusion.

"Seems that way." Marion felt powerful.

"Why?" It was a whisper.

"I trust you. Just this once." That was one reason anyway.

He blinked, his eyes flashing up to her face. "Thank you, Marion."

It was a cute thing to say and Marion smiled. "You're welcome."

His gaze traveled back down to her naked breasts. "You'll really let me...?" He reached out, without finishing the question. His inhuman fingers carefully encircled her straining nipple and Marion didn't stop him. Nicholas pinched her straining flesh and a shudder of lust went through him, as she jerked and whimpered for more. "All of you is so beautiful.

Inside and out."

Under his unwavering focus, she *felt* beautiful.

"I've never... With anyone who didn't..." He trailed off with a shake of his head, watching his textured hands explore her smooth skin.

Marion recalled what Cragg had said the night before. "Gargoyles usually have to pay for sex?"

Nottingham mixed sex and money and power-dynamics in so many creepy ways. It was a wonder any of them managed to be halfway functional. She couldn't wait to destroy the whole misogynistic, bigoted place.

He winced, muscles tensing. "Gargoyles *always* have to pay. It's expected, no matter who we're with." There was an uneasy pause. "Most women would be insulted, if I didn't offer some kind of compensation for this."

Marion heard his internal conflict. "If you offer me money, I'll be pissed, pudding-fish."

His mouth twitched at the reassurance that she welcomed his touch and at the ridiculous endearment.

"Besides, you already own every inch of me, under the law. Why should you pay for what's already yours?"

That reasoning appealed to him. "You said 'yes,' when I proposed." He reminded her, like it was somehow in doubt.

"I always say 'yes' to you."

"So, I'll take care of you... and then I can touch you however I want." That rationale still sounded a bit too transactional, but he seemed pleased. "That's what I've been dreaming of, Marion. Touching you." His fingers were back at her nipples. "Gargoyles are expected to hurry through the process. I've never been with a woman who just let me touch her for the sake of touching."

"Do you like it?"

"Oh God..." It came out as a prayer, his eyes finding hers, again. "I like you better than *anyone*."

That was exactly what she wanted to hear. Marion fell into a timeless, pliable trance, lulled by the erotic pressure of his palms. She *knew* being a Maid was lousy, but she'd had no idea the full scope of what she'd been missing out on, until now. Nicholas was onto something with his love of touching. Being touched was *so* much better than being untouched.

"More." She whispered. "Please."

"If you were ever in my bedroom, you wouldn't have left." He assured her and it sounded like a vow. "Kiss me, again. Right now."

The man was a genius. Marion leaned up to accept his lips, her mouth opening beneath his. It was lucky that she was still holding on to his shirtfront. Her body went lax at the relentless invasion of his tongue and the incredible feeling of his hands. It was almost too much, but it still wasn't enough.

Inside her pants, her core grew wetter, wanting more of what he was promising. Knowing she wasn't going to get it today, but needing it. Needing him. "*Nick.*" If anyone was listening at the door (and Guyla Gisborn surely was, the nosy bitch) they would have heard her passionate wail. Marion couldn't care less.

Nicholas gave a primitive snarl, as she broke the kiss to call out his name. "Exactly. *Me*, Marion." It was somewhere between a demand and a plea. "For once, see *me*. Please."

Marion tried to breathe, as his dominant hands claimed her body. She made a languid sound. Her forehead came to rest on his shoulder, giving herself fully over to his possession.

Nicholas kissed the top of her head in approval. "That's it. You belong right here with me. I can give you more than Hood can. I swear it."

He was waking up nerve-ending she hadn't even known existed. Thick, syrupy pleasure enveloped her, making it hard to think. "You don't have to give me anything, but *you*." She got out.

"You already have me. You always have." His voice was sure and hot in her ear. "It was *always* supposed to be me, Marion."

The familiar words jolted Marion out of her fluffy pink cloud of desire. She reluctantly pulled back, looking up at his hard, perfect face and remembering what he didn't.

Nicholas had told that to her, once before.

It was why he'd died alone.

Chapter Fifteen

How It Happened the First Time...

Robin Hood hadn't come to save her.
Marion knew he wouldn't, but living with the reality of being forsaken by her True Love was even worse than imagining it. Her tears had dried up and now she was in a numb state of shock. Large parts of the evening were a blur.
Presently, she was lying in a bed, acutely aware that it belonged to Nicholas. She'd been dozing there for hours. Nicholas' room didn't have a fireplace, but it was still the warmest spot in the castle. Marion was comfortable in her misery.
Nicholas hadn't been more than five feet from the edge of the mattress, as far as she knew. It seemed that the sheriff had no idea what to do with her now, so he was keeping her close. She was apathetically confused as to why. Caring for a jilted True Love wasn't really in an evil-doers repertoire. So far, though, Nicholas had done everything a well-brought up young man would do to comfort a distraught Maid. More in fact.
She'd fallen asleep without the slightest doubt that he'd watch over her. Maybe he was afraid she'd throw herself out the window. Maybe that was why he was standing right in front of it, staring out at the night with an expressionless expression on his face.
Marion wasn't going to kill herself over Robin, but she also wasn't sure what she *would* do next. Her entire reality had been upended. Still in her ugly, fake wedding dress and with no real plan for the future, Marion didn't care about anything.
At some point, she would have to face the outside world, but for now she was hiding under the covers and she intended to stay there indefinitely. Tucked away in Nicholas' impenetrable tower, she felt safe. No one could reach her

here. Nicholas would never allow it. The man was huge and scary. He'd keep them all away, while she figured things out. He owed it to her.

"Would you like something to eat, duchess?"

Her swollen eyes swung over to Nicholas' broad shoulders. He hadn't turned to ask the question. Somehow he'd just sensed her waking up. She wasn't surprised. She could always feel how his attention focused on her, whenever he was close by. Angrily cataloging all her flaws and committing them to some mental list, no doubt. At the May Day Queen contest, she'd almost thought she *liked* how his eyes never strayed from her, but she'd clearly been hallucinating.

Right now, Nicholas seemed to have trouble looking at her, at all. Maybe he felt Bad for all the trouble he'd caused her.

Good.

She might be safe in his sparsely decorated, deadbolted bedroom and Nicholas might be behaving like a perfect gentleman, but she also blamed him for everything that had happened. Robin was to blame, too, of course. She would never forgive him for abandoning her. Nicholas was the one who made a public spectacle of her undesirability, though. His stupid kidnapping stunt had set all this into motion.

What had she ever done to him to make him hate her so much?

"You really should eat." He urged, when she didn't respond. "Starving yourself won't solve anything."

Nothing would solve this mess.

"Why do you think it called you 'Nick'?" She asked dully. It didn't much matter, but she'd noticed that detail.

"It's my name."

"You're also Nicholas Greystone, Sheriff of Nottingham. It could've called you that."

"That name doesn't matter as much to me."

Nothing much mattered to her, anymore. Wallowing in self-pity seemed the only way forward.

Marion groped towards Nicholas' nightstand, feeling the tears welling in her eyes, again. She missed the box of tissues and ended up with her hand in the partially-opened drawer. Her groping fingers landed on a small round box. For no reason, she pulled it out and flipped it open. A sparkling ruby winked up at her.

"Was this ring supposed to be part of your big wedding plan?"

Nicholas busied himself crossing the room. He unlocked the million locks and opened the large, curved-top door. "Mrs. Gisborn, bring the duchess some food!" He bellowed down the curving stairs.

There was a rush of footsteps as the ever-skulking housekeeper hurried to comply.

Marion's attention stayed on the ring. Sitting up on the bed, she turned the ruby back and forth in her hand, watching the light catch the stone. It reminded her of her mother's necklace. Seeing the deep red color of the gem soothed her and took her mind off Robin for a moment. "This is so pretty." She murmured, feeling better than she had all day. "Where did you get it?"

Nicholas was silent for a long beat. "It was my mother's." He finally said. "The one piece of jewelry she ever kept. She died when I was a boy."

Marion's gaze jumped to his. "Really?"

Nicholas nodded.

"My mother died when I was born." Marion felt a strange sense of connection with him over that. She'd always felt a connection with Nicholas, even though he was an asshole who despised her. It just went to show she had consistently terrible judgement.

Nicholas met her eyes and then quickly looked away. "When I was young, I wore the ring around my neck, on a chain. I didn't want to take it to war, though. It seemed wrong. So, I left it home." He gestured towards the drawer. "Now, it lives here."

"You aren't afraid someone will steal it?" It looked valuable.

"No. I would kill anyone who came into this room and everybody knows it. I don't like people in my space." He must have missed the part where he'd carted her up here and nestled her against his pillow, just a few hours before. "Also, the ring is enspelled. It has to be given straight from my heart and soul, and accepted by the other person, in the same way. I suspect that will never happen, so it's safe."

"I wouldn't give it away, either. It's beautiful."

Nicholas came close to smiling. "It *is* beautiful. When I took it off, I missed it. I hate that it's hidden away in a drawer. But I don't want its legacy to have blood attached. Stones can absorb emotions from the people who wear them. All the fighting and plotting in my life might change its energy."

"I didn't realize gem stones felt things."

"I'm part stone. I feel things, Marion."

She wasn't sure what to make of that or of his defensive tone. "I know you do." She agreed, because Nicholas did feel things. He hated Robin. That was an emotion.

Nicholas cleared his throat. "My mother had big plans for that ring. She was a human, but she cared about the future of the gargoyles. She wanted us to have real families. I *was* her family. It's why she chose my name with such care." He met Marion's eyes, again. "A name *means* something. When someone gives you one and you accept it, it's important."

Marion nodded, although she wasn't sure what he meant by that. She'd never heard the man talk so much. Or so eloquently. His mother had been important to him. He'd loved her. That was an emotion, too. He was capable of experiencing more complex feelings than he ever showed on his inscrutable face. Somehow, that idea didn't surprise her, at all.

"My mother wanted me to be more than just a predictable, passionless follower of Nottingham." Nicholas went on. "She would point up at the stars and tell me to wish on them every night. To always focus on my dreams. She wanted me to have something really *real* in my life. A purpose."

"And did you do it? Find a purpose?"

"Yes." He said simply.

Marion wasn't surprised, by that either. Gargoyles were supposed to be purposeless, but Nicholas had never seemed that way to her. He was always driving towards something. She admired that. She'd never been allowed to make any real plans of her own and now all her tomorrows were blank.

Nicholas nodded towards the ring, which was still clutched in Marion's hand. "My mother was a very independent and talented woman. Like you."

Marion frowned. He saw her as independent and talented?

"Mother designed that ring herself." He paused uncomfortably. "She believed gargoyles should marry and have families. She meant for the ruby to belong to my wife, one day."

"Oh." Marion put the ring back in the drawer like it burned her, feeling foolish and recalling the damn wedding, again. What was wrong with her? Why in the world had she been talking to him, in the first place? The man had wrecked *everything* for her! "I'm sorry for asking. I shouldn't have..." Her voice trailed off, getting a look at the drawer's interior for the first time.

Letters.

Her letters.

Dozens and dozens of them. All of them tattered from reading and rereading. All of them neatly stacked, stored alongside his mother's treasured ring. In the large and impersonal room, no other items had been preserved with such care.

Nicholas made a sound of horror, realizing what she'd just uncovered. "Marion, don't!"

Too late. Marion grabbed a stack of stained and crumpled envelopes. The first three in the pile were passionlessly slit open on one end. The others were *ripped* open. The envelopes torn, like someone had been desperate to get to the letter inside. There was no mistaking her own handwriting. These were the letters she'd written to Robin when he was fighting in the Looking Glass Campaign.

Her amazed eyes went up to Nicholas.

Nicholas stared back at her, going deathly pale.

"How do you have these?" Marion asked, too shocked to even be upset.

He said nothing, but his eyes darted towards the door, again. Instead of gloating about his theft, she had the distinct impression he was gauging the wisdom of fleeing into the night. The next second, he was staring at the floor. Two seconds later, a spot somewhere to the left of her. It was like he felt trapped and didn't know what to do. She'd known Nicholas for so long, but this was the first time she'd ever seen him nervous.

Maybe this was the first time she'd ever seen him, at all.

"Answer me." Marion snapped. *Now* the anger was coming. "Did you steal these from Robin?"

"No." Nicholas stopped contemplating retreat and drew himself up. She saw him take a deep breath, like he anticipated a battle. Which was a real good guess. "Hood never even read them."

Her head tilted, her heart beating too fast. "*When* did you get them?" Asking him "why" he got them would've been more logical, but "when" would tell her so much more.

He seemed to know it, too, because he didn't want to answer. "What does it matter...?"

"When, Nick?"

His jaw clenched at the nickname. "During the war." He admitted reluctantly. "When they arrived at whatever camp we were stationed at."

He'd had them all this time? He'd kept them right beside his bed? Marion's mind was whirling. "I poured my heart and soul out in these letters." She pointed to her chest. "They were meant for my True Love."

"I know."

"Thoughts and dreams and things I told *no one else*, I wrote in them." Embarrassment and confusion were filling her, now. "And you read them all? You're the one who opened them?"

"Most of them."

All but the first three. She knew that instinctively. "But you didn't steal them?"

"No."

She thought for a beat. In conversations with Nicholas, you had to fill-in-the-blanks a lot. "Robin threw them away." It wasn't a guess.

Nicholas ran a hand through his hair and stayed silent. Clearly, he'd rather eat rat poison than discuss this.

"*Tell me!*" It was the first time she'd truly raged at anyone. It didn't feel half as bad as she'd expected, so she decided to keep going. She got to her feet, grabbing a porcelain lamp off the nightstand and pegged it at his huge body. "Tell me, right now, damn it!"

Nicholas shifted out of the lamp's path with no difficulty, so she decided to heave the matching one at him, too.

Unfortunately, the housekeeper had just been coming in with a tray of food. She yelped as the lamp crashed into the doorframe, right next to her. The tray fell to the floor in a cacophony of cups and saucers, and Mrs. Gisborn retreated in a flurry of gray skirts. Crap. Guyla Gisborn was a notorious gossip and she'd never liked Marion. Soon, everyone in the kingdom would hear that Marion was a loud, violent shrew and Robin was lucky to be free of her.

Marion didn't care.

She suddenly didn't care what anyone said about her. Let them all talk. What was the worst that could happen? She didn't need to worry about being a pristine Maid, or Robin's destined bride, or hosting civilized luncheons for the Nottingham Garden Club. There was no going back to that destiny, now.

The revelation brought a strange sense of freedom.

She headed for Nicholas' desk, in search of more projectiles.

"Hood wasn't interested in reading your mail." Nicholas admitted, also ignoring the housekeeper and the inevitable tales she'd spread. "He was too busy with other… pursuits."

Marion paused, a reading lamp aimed and ready. "Robin cheated on me?" If her heart hadn't already been shattered, that probably would have hurt.

He said nothing, which meant "yes."

Sadly, Marion *wasn't* surprised to learn that news. Robin had only answered one of her letters, in all the time he'd been away. She'd been touched by his poetic note. Truly moved. But, on some level, Marion had still suspected that Robin wasn't fully devoted to her. She just hadn't been able to admit it, because she'd been blinded by her childish love for the jackass.

"I saw Hood dispose of some of your letters." Nicholas went on. He sent the reading lamp a wary look, ready to dodge if she hurled it at him. "I started fishing them out of the trash and opening them, just to see what you wrote to the man you loved. I wanted to know what it was like to have someone like you... care."

Marion set the lamp down. For now. "No one wrote to you?"

"Of course not. Who would write to a gargoyle? We aren't even really *real*."

She refused to be distracted by that nonsense. "Even if you were lonely, it didn't give you the right to take *my* letters, Nick." It embarrassed her to know that he'd read things she'd never even said out loud. Things about her mother. Things about her hopes for the future. Things about her frustrations with her place in the world. Even innocuous things, like her love of strawberries and ideas for her birthday party. All of her thoughts and dreams and secrets were on those pages and he'd stolen them. "Did you steal *other* people's mail?"

"No." Nicholas scoffed, like that idea was insane. "Fuck other people. Fuck 'em all."

"Wonderful attitude."

"Glad you like it, since it's my family motto. Invented by me, because it's true. They told me I had no *purpose*, Marion. No place to belong. But I *do*." He sounded sure of that, in the way only Nicholas could. Rock-hard, inflexible, and ready to fight. "So, I don't care what anyone else has to say, in person or on paper." He began to pace, restless with her questions. "It's always just been *you*."

"So, you did all this just to laugh at me, then?" She surmised. "Fuck me, too, I guess. Along with all the rest of them. Is that it?"

That accusation caught him off guard, as did her swearing. "No! I would never laugh at you. I'm trying to tell you... I've always thought..." He trailed off with a sigh, looking frustrated with himself for not being more articulate. "You're my favorite person in the world."

Marion barely processed his words. "It's because I'm dating your nemesis, right? That's why you targeted me for this plot? To get at him?"

"It had nothing to do with Robin Hood." Nicholas sounded defiant, now. "It was just about *me*. I needed your letters too much to stop reading them. I was trekking through some godforsaken desert, to fight some godforsaken war, while Hood drank all the water with the rest of the idiot nobles. Everything was *loud* and hot and made no sense."

Marion rubbed at her forehead, trying to think.

Nicholas kept talking. "None of us wanted to be there, except the men who didn't fucking fight! The humans came up with plans that were doomed to fail and ordered the gargoyles to carry them out." An uncharacteristic torrent of words poured out, as if a dam had burst inside of him. "The Battle of Kirklees was *Hood's* fault. I told him it was a trap, but he didn't listen. Men died by the hundreds and he didn't even *notice*."

Was that true? Probably. Robin would never admit it if his plan had gone wrong...

Wait.

Had Nicholas just said she was his favorite person in the world?

Her head popped back up to blink at him.

"I *needed* the letters." Nicholas persisted, not noticing her surprise. "I needed them to survive. The war was killing me. That's the truth, Marion. I couldn't go on without... I needed..." He broke off and muttered a curse.

Her.

This time she understood the missing parts of his awkward stumbling. He was going to say he needed *her*. That he couldn't go on without *her*.

Nicholas scrubbed a palm over the back of his neck, but he wasn't done talking. Once he got started, it seemed like he had a lot of bottled-up stuff to say. "Damn it, you sent Hood a letter every day. Every. Fucking. *Day*." He sounded pissed about that, for some reason. Like he was blaming her for being devoted to another man. "You wrote him such beautiful things. Everything in your heart and soul. Why should Hood have all that, when he didn't even want to hear it?" He pounded a fist against his chest. "When *I* needed it."

"Is this why you really kidnapped me? Because you were jealous that Robin had a True Love and you didn't?"

"No!" Nicholas roared, his voice carrying through the castle. Anyone who claimed gargoyles were passionless had clearly never met this one. Passion glowed from his eyes and radiated from his expression as he loomed over her. "I was jealous that he had *you*."

Marion drew in a breath at that revelation.

"It had *nothing* to do with Hood!" Nicholas went on. "Not the way you mean. I wanted to capture Hood today, because I hate him. Yes. But mostly I was just *angry*. And I know it doesn't make sense. I *know* that. But I *hated* that you chose him. That you trusted him. That you never saw me…" He paused for a beat, his gaze roaming over her face and his tone became softer. "And all I *ever* saw was you, Marion."

"You barely know me." She whispered.

"I know you better than anyone." He gestured towards all the letters she'd written. All the secrets she'd shared. "I know you inside and out. I know that we *fit*. We always have. It was always supposed to be *me*."

Marion felt like she'd been dropped through a rabbit hole and everything was topsy-turvy. If he read those letters, he knew absolutely everything about her. It made her feel exposed and confused.

"I thought that maybe with this damn wedding I could…" Nicholas swallowed. "I don't know. Make you notice me? Have you to myself for a little while? I wasn't even admitting it to myself, but I know that was my real plan." He made a self-deprecating sound. "I was an idiot. *Yes*. But, I didn't intend for *this* to happen. I didn't intend to hurt you. That's the last thing I want. Hood was supposed to come to the church. I thought he would. I swear, I did."

"You really thought that Robin would risk his life for me? He didn't even open my letters!"

Nicholas frowned, as if he was belatedly considering the flaws in his plan.

Marion laughed with no humor at all, incredulous at how badly he'd screwed this up. "You could have just *talked* to me. Did that even occur to you?"

"I didn't know how. I never have. You see what a damn mess I make of it, when I say more than two words." He seemed to deflate. "What good would it have done, anyway? He's your True Love. Nothing I say will compete with that."

"You could have tried! *Trying* to talk to me would've been better than ruining my whole life!"

"I know." He whispered hollowly.

Marion had so many thoughts and feelings filling her that she couldn't sort through them. In that moment, she didn't even want to. Since childhood, she'd been nothing but a pawn or a prize. No one ever asked her permission or wanted her advice or listened to her plans. She wasn't even allowed to *make* plans. No one ever thought about her feelings, just about their own. The frustration exploded out of her and Nicholas was the target for her rage.

"*You and Robin have ruined my whole life!*"

Gray eyes met hers and he didn't say a word.

She stabbed a finger at him. "Just... stay away from me. Both of you." She headed for the door, throwing it open, so it slammed into the wall. Words were flying out of Marion without her even considering them first. Everything was just red-fury and betrayal. "I'm going home and you can go to hell.

He shook his head, still not ready to quit. He really was the most determined bastard in the kingdom. "You can't just leave, Marion."

"I can and I *will!*"

"You *can't*. Not now. You know that."

He had a point, but Marion didn't care. "I'm *leaving!*" She screamed back at him, already heading down the stairs and away from all the emotions roiling inside of her. "I never want to see you, again, Nicholas! I mean it."

"Marion!" He called after her, but she'd started running and she didn't look back.

She wasn't sure what she might have done the next day, once she'd calmed down. She probably would have thrown more lamps at his big, dumb head. But maybe --*maybe*-- she would have thought through all the things he'd said. Maybe she would've started realizing what it eventually took her years in prison to piece together. Maybe it all would've been different.

Sadly, she never got a chance to find out.

Seven hours later, Nicholas was found dead.

Chapter Sixteen

President of the Peasants' Guild has a lot to say... Again.

Alan A. Dale- "Nottingham's Naughtiest News"

Marion looked adorable in a hennin, but Nicholas wasn't dumb enough to tell her that. Her tall, princess-y hat was blue, with a gauzy gold scarf fluttering from the point. Nottingham's colors.

Nicholas' colors.

The sheriff's uniform was blue and gold, and he wore it every day. He wasn't sure if her choice was intentional or not, but he liked that she'd aligned herself with him, even if it was an accident.

Nearly everyone at the May Day Festival was dressed in colorful, sparkly, sometimes outrageous clothing, but Marion was one of the few who looked good in a crazy outfit. Marion *always* looked good. Brunette hair cascaded in waves over her shoulders and down her back. There were hints of red in it, when the sunlight hit the curls. Fire and softness, all mixed together in wild perfection. *That* was Marion Huntingdon.

"Are you sure all the fair noise isn't too much for you?" She asked for the third time.

"I'm sure." Nicholas vaguely realized he was gazing down at her, like a lovesick idiot. He couldn't make himself stop, though. He didn't even *want* to stop, because he *was* a lovesick idiot.

God, he was so in love with her.

Nicholas carried a broadsword every day, but the woman could drive him to his knees with nothing more than a smile. Marion casually walked beside him, through the crowded fairgrounds. People were shooting scandalized looks her way, but she didn't seem to notice.

Nicholas noticed, though. He might be a lovesick idiot, but he wasn't blind.

"You shouldn't stand so close to me." He cautioned, even though distance from her was the last thing he wanted. "It really will damage your reputation."

She responded by taking hold of his arm.

Logic told him to pull away for her own good. It was swiftly drowned out by every other thought and feeling inside of him. Nicholas excelled at prioritizing rationality over emotion... except when it came to Marion. There had been moments of his life when Nicholas would have willingly died to have her hand on his arm. This might just be one of them.

"I don't get why I have to wear this stupid hat and you don't." Marion complained, like nothing else was going on around them. She ignored the surrounding stares, unbothered by all the attention they drew. "It doesn't seem fair."

"It would have messed up my hair."

It took her a beat to realize he was joking with her. It really wasn't much of a joke. Nicholas wasn't great with words. And gargoyles weren't a funny group as a whole, so maybe he hadn't done it right. Maybe he should have...

Marion's slow grin cut off his thoughts. "You *do* have pretty hair." She agreed, liking his small bit of humor. She reached up to brush the long strands back from his forehead. "All the colors of granite, shiny and mixed together. If we could find a way to magically bottle it, we'd make a killing in beauty salons."

Nicholas' eyes closed briefly, luxuriating in the feel of her.

He would never get used to the sensation of her smooth skin against his. Everything was quiet and peaceful, when she touched him. The betrothal rights were *spectacular*. Her glorious breasts beneath his hands and the soft sounds she'd made when he explored her curves... The intimacy of it had been more than he'd ever dreamed.

Never had he been so grateful for Nottingham's abysmal record on gender equality. That asinine law Marion had been taught to follow was the stuff of his wildest fantasies.

Promising to care for her, in exchange for having rights over her body? That was the greatest fucking trade in history! He had no clue half of the things he'd said during their encounter, because he'd been drugged on sensation. The scent of her hair, and sight of her grin, and the feel of her willingly yielding to his touch.

"You know, in traditional Nottingham weddings, the groom is supposed to wear a bycocket." Marion told him. "That will *definitely* mess up your hairstyle."

"I have no idea what a 'bycocket' is."

"A green hat with a pointed front and a red feather on the side."

"Is that what that dumb-ass thing's called?" He snorted. "How do you know all the names for these weird hats?"

"Nottingham provides Maids with a very useless education." She assured him. "And bycockets are not ugly. You're going to need to wear one to our wedding."

"Is that what I wore the last time?"

She shot him an arch look. "Do you really want things to happen like they did the last time, Nick?"

"No." He said honestly. "I want something else."

I want you.

At the casino, Marion had said that gargoyles might be able to choose whether they were Good or Bad. If that was true, the decision was long over for him.

He was wicked, through and through.

Nicholas could only summon up so many ethics, at any given time. And he had no desire, *at all*, to go digging for them if it meant talking himself out of possessing Marion. He didn't care if he was stealing something that wasn't his. He didn't care if his choices made him a villain. He didn't care about much of anything if it gave him Marion.

For the first time ever, his obsession with the woman was being satiated. It was like being able to drink water after decades in the desert sun. Even better, Marion seemed to enjoy his company and his touch. To his shock and delight, she'd cuddled against him like a contented kitten, that morning.

Even his hideous right hand didn't seem to upset her. She'd eventually halted their betrothal-rights session looking a little shaken, but up until the very end, she'd been consenting. Nicholas was certain of that much or he would've stopped.

Watching her slip away from him afterwards had been wrenching, but he'd let her go without uttering a word of protest. Her withdrawal was understandable. She probably felt guilty, because she was letting someone other than her True Love put his rough, greedy hands all over her pristine body. Marion was kind, and loyal, and in love with Robin Hood.

That thought darkened his mood.

The thought of Hood *always* darkened his mood, but imagining that asshole touching Marion seriously pissed him off. She'd apparently shut down that tree-hugger's clumsy attempts at seduction, at least once before. That cheered him some. But, Hood still had a bond to her that Nicholas couldn't match. Nicholas knew that and he *hated* it.

As always, his not-Good instincts told him to do everything possible to erase Hood from Marion's heart and soul. "What about kissing?" Nicholas asked her, out of the blue.

"What *about* kissing?"

"Am I allowed to demand that, as part of my betrothal rights?"

"I'm not sure." Her eyes gleamed with secrets and mischief, like she saw the betrothal rights as a fun new game they were playing. "No one ever explained all the footnotes and addendums of the law to me, sheriff. I guess you'll have to kiss me again and see what happens." She stopped walking, like she expected him to test the idea, right then and there.

Nicholas hesitated, searching her face, as questions swirled in his mind. He'd meant *later*, when they were alone. She was going to let him kiss her in public? Did she not understand him earlier, when he'd said they needed to keep things private? There would be no coming back, if Nottingham saw his hands on her. No explaining it away. Hood would hear about it.

Why was she really doing this? Was she under a spell?

Do you care if she's under a spell? Stop questioning it. You have everything you want.

Nicholas tried to think.

Marion shifted closer to him, her magnificent breasts brushing up against his shirt, and all rational thought left his mind. She always fit against him so perfectly. Nicholas dipped his head, intent on reaching her lips, suddenly not giving a damn who saw them. And Marion didn't retreat. He was being accepted by the woman and she was the only one who mattered...

"Maid Marion, I would like to talk to you." A new voice interrupted.

Marion jolted, turning to look at the intruder, and Nicholas seriously, *seriously* considered livening the May Day Festival up with a hanging. He let out a sound of furious frustration, his eyes pinning the asshole who was about to die.

Much-the-Miller stood there, dressed in his flour-covered apron and work boots. He was young, handsome, and outspoken, three qualities that got him quoted in the newspaper just about every day. He was also an arrogant jackass, who thought his every utterance was important.

"It's important." Much-the-Miller declared importantly.

Marion blinked. "Okay. Uh..." She seemed to rack her brain for a beat and then sighed. "Yeah... I completely forget who you are."

That was strange, because these days everyone in Nottingham knew Much-the-Miller. He was a miller by trade and his "working man's" status was a source of much pride for him. Hence, the ridiculous hyphens in his ridiculous name. Nicholas took names seriously and Much-the-Miller's was not serious, at all.

The moron wasn't part of Marion's social circle, so perhaps that explained why she didn't know him. The man was unquestionably the most famous commoner in the land. Much-the-Miller was a bold opponent of the war and Richard, *and* of Robin Hood and the Merry Men. He always had some naysaying quote for Alan A. Dale and the other reporters, which kept his opinions front and center.

Basically, Much-the-Miller disapproved of everyone except King Jonathan. The vanished ruler's vague statements about changing Nottingham for the betterment of the people were exaggerated in Much-the-Miller's mind. He, and most of the kingdom's youth, had seized upon Jonathan's memory as a mascot for their ideals of democracy and freedom.

Nicholas thought they were all pitifully naïve. So long as they didn't break any laws, he left them alone, though. He generally had bigger problems to deal with then a bunch of malcontented yeoman.

Obviously, that was about to change, since the leader of the malcontented yeoman had just screwed up his kiss with Marion. Now, Nicholas wanted the man dead.

"I'm Much-the-Miller." Much-the-Miller told Marion, a little offended by her lack of recognition.

"Much-the-Miller? Like it's all one word?"

"Precisely! I'm President of the Peasants' Freedom Guild and a strong advocate for commoners everywhere embracing their roots with pride. As our ancestors did." He smiled, as if that might work to remind her of his identity. His wholesome blond looks reminded Nicholas of Robin Hood and that didn't bode well for the Peasant President's lifespan.

"Your ancestors also lived in servitude, with no running water and dirt floors." Nicholas heard himself say. "Should you embrace that, as well?"

Marion snorted in amusement, liking that remark. She had always had a troublemaking streak down deep, but since he'd kidnapped her it was front and center. Every sarcastic remark Nicholas made earned him a smile. So he kept making them, even though it meant he had to talk to morons.

Much-the-Miller shot him an annoyed scowl. "Our ancestors rose above their humble circumstances to build this kingdom! Now we're reclaiming it for commoners everywhere."

"Oh, *that's* who you are!" Marion snapped her fingers. "You're the guy who was always protesting stuff." She leaned backwards, so she was resting against Nicholas' chest, and frowned at Much-the-Miller. "Shit. I was totally blanking there. You don't really stick out in my memories." She waved a hand. "Yeah, go ahead and talk."

Nicholas smirked at her blasé response to the other man, his arms folding around her lush body. It was a mistake to touch her so openly. He *knew* that. But, the woman destroyed all his noble intentions. Nicholas forgot about slaughtering Much-the-Miller right there on the grass. Holding Marion didn't allow for negative thoughts. He'd just execute the asshole later.

Much-the-Miller seemed baffled as to what was happening, but he quickly rallied. "I need to speak with you *alone*, Maid Marion."

"No." Nicholas said flatly.

Marion shrugged at Much-the-Miller, like there was nothing she could do. "I'm just an innocent hostage," she reported cheerily, as she'd promised she would, "held in the sheriff's granite clutches."

Oh, Nicholas *loved* that image.

Much-the-Miller scowled, trying to decide what to do next. "We can't speak with the sheriff around. He's part of the authoritarian regime that we righteous citizens are fighting against."

"Okay." Marion agreed. "Bye, then." Her attention had already strayed to a booth selling carnival snacks. "Holy crap! They've got Carbonated Magic Bean Juice here, Nick!" Excitement echoed in her voice. "I *loved* Carbonated Magic Bean Juice. It's going to get discontinued in a couple years, because a bunch of people die from it or something. I need some." She held out her palm. "Gimme money."

He fished into his pocket for some gold. "People die from it?" He repeated warily, dropping the coin into her hand.

"Only because of the chemicals. It's fine."

"Let's get nice, healthy Wishing Well Water, instead."

"No! Are you crazy? Carbonated Magic Bean Juice is the one good thing this shithole kingdom ever invents. I'm not..." She broke off suddenly, her eyes on some indeterminate spot in the crowd.

"Something wrong?" Nicholas turned to see what she was looking at.

Marion shook her head. "I felt like something was watching us, again."

"Hood?"

"I don't think so. I just…"

Much-the-Miller cut her off. "Oh very well, I'll talk to you here." He declared, as if Marion had been begging him to reconsider.

She blinked and glanced his way, like she'd already forgotten about him. "Really?" She sounded disappointed that he was still standing there.

"It's for the Good of the kingdom, so I must take the chance that the sheriff is truly as smitten with you as Little John says."

Nicholas mentally sighed. The noise of the fair made it hard for him to think, and Much-the-Miller was irritating as hell, and he didn't like the idea of Hood being close to Marion. At all. The whole point of this plan was to lure Hood in, so Nicholas couldn't go searching for the little fuck. Still, he *hated* staying still, while Hood was lurking.

"You talked to L.J.?" Marion was paying attention to Much-the-Miller, now. "Damn it, I told him to lay low, until I figured out a plan."

"L.J. is a member of the Peasants' Freedom Guild." Much assured her, as if that explained everything. "He knows he can trust me. He tells me that you've opened your eyes to Robin Hood's pointless violence *and* to Richard's tyranny."

"Neither one of them is my favorite person." Marion agreed.

"That's a good start." Much-the-Miller praised, in a condescending tone. "Especially, for a Maid. I know you're not the smartest group, so it speaks well of you that you were able to piece together the truth."

Marion's brow arched.

Nicholas stirred, back to measuring the miller for a rope.

Much-the-Miller kept talking, unaware of the danger.

"My mother was a Maid, you know. But, my father was her True Love, so she settled for becoming a miller's wife. She wanted me to become a pianist, instead of following in his footsteps. Father told her it was impractical and crazy, but mother was always dreamy. It's hard for a noblewoman to become a peasant. Working people are mentally tougher than the bluebloods."

"What did you *want* to do?" Marion asked, quietly. "Play the piano or become a miller?" The woman always asked questions like that. She saw right to the heart of things.

Much-the-Miller paused. "I wanted to play the piano." He admitted in a more subdued tone. "But, that wasn't my calling. Everyone knew I had to become a miller, like my father. That's the way of things, in Nottingham. We all have a role."

"I always wanted to sing." Marion told him. "But, I was too afraid to get on stage. Maid's aren't supposed to seek the spotlight."

Nicholas glanced down at her in surprise. He'd had no idea she liked singing.

"Well, we both saw reason, I suppose, and embraced our place in the world. I celebrate my humble wages and hard work. It builds character." Much-the-Miller cleared his throat, back to business. "When King Jonathan returns, I'll tell him of your good-sense and loyalty."

"Jonathan's dead." Nicholas intoned. How could anyone think otherwise? "Like you will be, if you don't get out of my sight, soon."

"The true king is *not* dead!" Much-the-Miller gasped, like Nicholas spoke treason. "They never found his body. He'll return and reclaim his throne, any day now."

Nicholas rolled his eyes at that ludicrous idea.

"Why do you think Jonathan is still alive?" Marion asked, inexplicably interested in Much-the-Miller's fairytale.

Much-the-Miller leaned closer, eager to impart some grand secret. "Richard's royal enchantress warned him that King Jonathan will return. L.J. overheard Hood talking about it."

"There are no enchantresses in Nottingham." Nicholas certainly would've met them by now. Those beings were colossally powerful and universally evil. Evilly powerful beings tended to pop up on a sheriff's radar, because of all the corpses they left in their wake.

"Richard has a private enchantress." Much-the-Miller wasn't ready to give up on his nonsense. "The woman has fathomless magic. She can travel to spots that are miles apart in an instant and she knows our deepest thoughts. He keeps her identity secret, but he relies on her prophesies to guide him, because she can see the future."

"Yeah, there's a lot of that going around." Marion sounded amused.

Much-the-Miller wasn't laughing. "Whoever the enchantress is, she'll be coming after all of us." He warned. "She already senses we're plotting against her."

"I'm not plotting against her." Nicholas interjected. "First of all, I don't think she exists. Secondly, even if she *did* exist, I wouldn't care, unless she broke the law."

Much-the-Miller's mouth thinned. "Just be on guard." He warned Marion, pointedly ignoring Nicholas' input. "We're on the side of Good and the forces of Badness will do *anything* to stop our quest to save the kingdom."

Nicholas snorted at the extravagantly worded nonsense. Since he *wasn't* on the side of Good, he supposed he didn't have to worry.

Much-the-Miller thumped a fist against his chest. "Long live King Jonathan!" He cried and went marching off to spread more bullshit to brainwashed peasants.

Marion stared after him, a thoughtful expression on her face.

"King Jonathan is *not* alive." Nicholas told her with a firm shake of his head. She had the sharpest mind in the kingdom, so she was surely bright enough to know that. "The man went on a hunting trip in Sherwood and vanished. With Richard. The same Richard who now sits on Jonathan's throne and wears his crown. There's no need for an enchantress to psychically intuit what happened. It couldn't be clearer."

Marion turned to look at him in shock, as she realized what he was implying.

Nicholas shrugged and said it anyway. "Richard killed him."

Brown eyes blinked up at him, like that possibility had never occurred to her. The woman enjoyed being Bad, but inside she was surprisingly innocent. "You think Richard murdered his own brother?"

"Of *course* he did." Was Nicholas the only one paying attention? How was this even a question?

"He's the king!"

"So?"

"So, you can't just say stuff like that. ...Even if it might be true." Marion frowned off into space for a long moment. "Have you told anyone else this theory?"

"No." Who would he tell *anything* to, except her? She was the only one he'd ever wanted to share ideas with. The other gargoyles had no doubt reasoned it out for themselves, though. Things always looked clearer from the outside.

"Good. Don't." She chewed on her lower lips, probably just to torture him. He nearly groaned as the pink flesh disappeared between her white teeth. "Your suspicions could be why you're murdered, Nick. Someone could be trying to shut you up."

Nobody had ever said such a crazy thing to him before. He wanted to smile. "Because I talk so damn much?"

"Well, you're definitely talking *more*."

That was true. Words were coming quicker and easier than ever, now. He felt himself communicating openly, when he'd ordinarily stay silent and disengaged. That was Marion's influence. He couldn't remain quiet when there was so much he wanted to say to her.

"Whoever the king is, it doesn't much matter to me." Nicholas reached out to fix her listing hat, just because he could. "Even if it *did*, no one cares about a gargoyle's opinion on the royal line. Or on anything else. They'd just ignore me, not have me killed."

"Well, *somebody* cared, obviously, because you'll be dead in a matter of days." Marion readjusted herself in his arms, resting her forehead against his chest. "I don't want you to die, Nick."

His heart flipped at her soft words. "I'm not going to die." He moved her hat so the point didn't blind him, unaccountably touched that she'd give a damn.

"You did the last time." She insisted. "We need to *focus* here."

"I'm incredibly focused." His thumb absently rubbed up and down her back, feeling the ridge of her bra. Remembering the black lace against her flawless skin.

"We have to catch Robin *today*."

Nicholas made an "ummm" sound, wondering what the rest of her underwear looked like and if it was as transparent as her bra had been.

"Nick!"

He snapped out of his pleasant musings. Forcing himself to concentrate on her words, he mentally rewound the last bit. "You think Hood colluded with Richard to kill King Jonathan?" Nicholas considered that idea and nodded. He didn't like to convict without evidence, but in this case... "Yes. I could see that happening."

Marion's head popped up. "No! I'm not saying Robin was involved. I mean, he was only --what?-- seventeen when Jonathan vanished."

"Plenty old enough to shoot an arrow and dig a hole." Half the foot-soldiers in the Looking Glass Campaign were teenagers.

Marion shook her head, refusing to believe that her precious True Love could've done anything wrong. "I seriously doubt Robin killed Jonathan. I'm not sure *how* he fits into everything, honestly. That's why we need to question him. You still with me on that plan?"

"Of course." Nicholas had no issue with capturing Hood, dead or alive. Preferably dead. No... maybe alive would be best. Then he could kill the bastard himself and make sure the job was done right. Nicholas mulled it over, savoring both possibilities.

"Good." She nodded, oblivious to his murderous contemplations. "So, let's go over that part, one more time.

The archery tournament is at three. I'm *positive* Robin will show up for it. And he'll win, of course."

Nicholas grunted. Hood's skill with a bow irritated him. It made him morbidly aware of his malformed right hand and how Marion must view it.

Marion kept going, still not noticing his displeasure. "Then, Robin will try to claim his prize…"

"That priceless arrow with the dripping spray paint."

She sent him a repressive frown. "It's *solid gold*. It says so right on its specially engraved sign."

"Which you made from tinfoil and a toothpick."

"I needed it for the front of the magically-imbued, laser-guarded, custom-made arrow case."

"The fishbowl you turned upside down."

"That's the one." Marion agreed. "So, as soon as Robin steps up. *Bam!*" She made a mini explosion motion by moving her fingers in a quick outward expansion to signify the power of the moment.

Despite himself, Nicholas was charmed by Marion's storytelling. He had been since childhood. The hand gestures and added sounds were always entertaining.

"Your guards will swoop in and nab him." She went on. "We'll toss Robin in the dungeon for an interrogation. Hopefully, he'll tell us who wants you dead and everyone lives happily ever after. I didn't believe in them three days ago, but that was pre-time travel. I can *make* our ever-afters happy, this time through." She paused her mile-a-minute strategy session. "Oh and be sure to send *a lot* of guards when it's time to nab Robin, because he'll be suspecting a trap. He's smarter than he looks."

Nicholas' jaw tightened, irritated by the oblique praise of her boyfriend. Why was everything always about Hood's amazingness? "What kind of happily-ever-afters are you making?" He demanded.

She blinked at the harsh question, still caught up in her arts and crafts projects and scheming. "Huh?"

"What *kind* of happily-ever-afters?" He repeated more slowly. "Who *gets* them? Because our goals are in direct conflict, so someone is going to walk away *un*happily ever after."

And it sure as fuck won't be me.

She looked confused. "Which of our goals are in conflict?"

Was she kidding? "My goal is to hang Hood. Yours is to marry him. So, unless you're planning a very short honeymoon…"

"Oh my holy God, *tell* me you're not back to that shit!" Marion scrambled out of Nicholas' embrace, her brown eyes alight with indignation. "Are you kidding me, right now?"

His arms felt empty without her in them. That just aggravated him more.

"Robin stole from my father!" Marion snapped. "Not to mention robbing the rest of Nottingham blind. I'm not going to marry that dirtbag." Her brows furrowed, her fascinating mind off on a new tangent. "And where does all that stolen money *go?* I've been wondering about it for years. We're talking about millions of gold coins supposedly 'given to the poor' and the peasants *still* can't buy bread. It makes no sense."

It made perfect sense. "Hood keeps the money."

"And spends it on what? Crossbows?"

Nicholas shrugged. "And bottles of mead." Probably some prostitutes, as well, knowing Hood. "Maybe he gives some of it to Richard." The two men seemed to be working together, so it seemed likely. God only knew why Richard wanted to work with the jackass who'd nearly gotten him killed at Kirklees, but Nicholas didn't understand why most people did the stupid things they did.

"Why would the king steal from the treasury? It's Richard's money to begin with."

"No, it's *Nottingham's* money to begin with." Nicholas refused to get sidetracked. Marion's mind worked faster than his and she'd take them off in fifty directions at once, if he wasn't careful. "The point is, you haven't heard Hood's side of things, yet. Once you do…"

"He doesn't *have* a side! He's just my dipshit ex! Jesus

Christ, why are you so hung up on me reconciling with him?"

Nicholas had no idea. His mind just kept circling back to it, because it had always been a bedrock truth in his life. Marion loved Robin Hood. She seemed to have forgotten it and Nicholas sure as hell *wanted* to, but it was impossible. Why did he want to try and remind her of something that would gain him nothing but heartache?

Because it's wrong to take advantage of Marion.

He wasn't Good, but it didn't matter. *All* parts of Nicholas knew that.

So, he kept talking. "...You will forgive him, because he's your True Love." Hood was sure to have some bullshit excuse for everything. Nicholas had no doubt it was an epic tale of woe that would bring tears to any Maid's eyes. "You'll want to marry him, again." And Nicholas would die before he let that happen. He should probably skip that part, for now.

"I'm not sure I *ever* wanted to marry Robin. Not really." Marion shook her head. "I wasn't allowed to make my own plans, back then. I think I convinced myself of things that weren't really... real."

Nicholas scoffed at that revisionist history. "There's a wedding dress hanging in your room." He pointed back towards the castle, where she'd carted her precious gown. "Which you bought to wear as that forest-dweller's bride, so don't pretend..."

"Robin has nothing to do with *my* dress!" She interrupted hotly. "It's *mine*. Grooms are changeable. Perfect tulle dresses are *not*."

"You have spent the past *ten years* loving Hood." Nicholas could name the exact date she'd begun her grand love affair with that pretentious son of a bitch. "And now you've suddenly stopped caring about him over the weekend? Is that what you seriously believe?"

"You *know* what I seriously believe, Nicholas. I've told you, over and over."

She was calling him by his full name. He *hated* that. Marion only switched to "Nicholas" when she was good and pissed, so maybe she knew how much he hated it. In his own head, he was "Nick." He had been since he was thirteen. It was the only name, title, or rank that meant a damn thing to him and she was the only one who used it.

Taking a deep breath, he struggled to lower his voice and regain control of the situation. "You could be under a spell." He gritted out. The thought had been lurking in his mind, but now it blossomed into near certainty. Someone had enspelled Marion. Nothing else made sense. "Have you considered that?"

"A spell?"

"Yes. Some kind of memory spell. Something that makes you blind to what's true and replaces reality with this convoluted idea that you've traveled back in time."

Marion crossed her arms over her chest. "Wow. It's so lucky you're here to explain this all to me, then." She didn't sound grateful. She sounded sarcastic.

"There are spells that make a person forget their True Love." He insisted. "I've researched them."

Marion tilted her head, her attention shifting right where he didn't want it. Her razor-sharp brain could be damn inconvenient at times. "Why would you research that?"

Nicholas hesitated. When he was a heartbroken kid, he'd been desperate to remove Marion's connection to Robin Hood, so he could have her for his own. He'd had all kinds of wicked ideas. It had been part of his ongoing obsession. He'd looked into ways to make it happen, but it didn't go farther than his fevered imagination. He'd never actually *done* anything.

...Well, not until he'd kidnapped Marion from the safety of her house, locked her in a castle, and told her she had to marry him instead of the man she actually loved. The man who would soon come and try to save her from Nicholas. The man who didn't need to use obsolete laws to have her in his arms.

Robin Hood: The most heroic bastard in Nottingham.

Nicholas pinched the bridge of his nose, despising himself. "I was young, when I read about the spells. I wanted someone who wanted someone else." He still did. He always would. He would die wanting Marion. "Nothing came of the research, though. I stopped, because I would never hurt her. Him? Absolutely. But *never* her." He lifted a shoulder. "And she was happy."

Marion watched him. "I'm not under a spell." She finally told him in a much calmer voice. "I've never felt clearer in my life."

"You can't be sure without a test."

Yes, he *did* care if this was all a spell. That was the answer to his earlier question to himself. Of course he cared. Maybe it was giving him everything he'd ever wanted, but at what cost? What about Marion? He cared *very fucking much* if someone had used magic to drug her. That person would hang. Repeatedly. No one harmed Marion Huntingdon and kept their neck intact.

She pursed her lips in deep thought. "If I *was* under the influence of magic, you and I wouldn't legally be engaged, right? Because, I wouldn't be responsible for anything I've said or done." She paused. "So, you wouldn't have any betrothal rights, after all. Did you think of that?"

Nicholas' new theory hit a stone wall.

"Still want the test?" She asked sweetly.

No, he didn't *want* it... but he also didn't want Marion hating herself later for forsaking her True Love. Nicholas's teeth ground together in frustration. As much as he detested Hood, if Marion was being controlled by some spell, he needed to help free her from it.

He'd taken a vow to care for her, when he demanded his betrothal rights. He'd said the words and he'd meant them. *That* much was really real. He'd keep her safe, no matter the cost.

You're such an idiot.

"You should have the test." He ran a hand through his hair. "It'll take fifteen minutes and then we'll be sure. I'll find a witch-practitioner and she can check you out."

Marion rolled her eyes. "You're such an idiot."

Chapter Seventeen

It's official! Sheriff voted Nottingham's most unpopular man!

Alan A. Dale- "Nottingham's Naughtiest News"

Nicholas was used to being the most unpopular man in Nottingham, but not even he had ever been *this* unpopular before.

While he waited for Marion outside the medical tent, scores of angry townsfolk walked by. Most paused to glare at him. Their eyes were filled with some combination of fear, resentment, condemnation, and/or licentious speculation. Clearly, word was getting around that Marion's kidnapping wasn't going according to plan. Now, Nottingham was wondering just what he was doing to their virginal duchess behind closed doors.

Fuck 'em all.

Until Richard returned from war or King Jonathan came back from the dead, Nicholas was in charge of the kingdom. Nothing could change that and no one had the strength to take Marion from him. Certainly not the perpetually disgruntled populous. Let them stay on Robin Hood's side of the love triangle and cry, because Nicholas wasn't backing down.

The only way he'd let Marion leave was if she *asked* to leave. And so far she hadn't asked. Unless that fateful day occurred, Nottingham's precious jewel was staying locked in his granite clutches.

Nicholas had everything he wanted --somehow or other-- and he wasn't going to lose it. If Marion wasn't under a spell, then she was staying right where she was. With him. Like it was always supposed to be. His obsession with the woman wouldn't allow anything else.

"Sheriff." Alan A. Dale, reporter and pain in the ass, made a beeline for him. "Just the man I was looking for. Do you have an update on your engagement to Maid Marion, for my readers?" The weasel dug a phone out of his tweed-coat, ready to take notes.

Nicholas stared at him, not bothering to answer.

Alan wasn't deterred. "Any comment on the disturbance at the Catchafool Casino, last night? Not that we admit that there *is* such a place, you understand. But I heard you were there, with your lovely fiancée."

Nicholas lazily checked the position of the sun.

"There was a report of another robbery in Sherwood, two days back." Alan tried. "People are saying Robin Hood stole some very interesting items from you. Something about a magical scepter...?" He let his voice trail off, leaving plenty of time for Nicholas to fill in the blanks with all sorts of print-worthy news.

Nicholas stayed quiet.

Alan frowned. He tried to interview Nicholas several times a week and always ended up annoyed by the resounding silence. He lived in hope that he'd one day get some kind of quotable response.

"What about King Jonathan's secret lovechild?" He blurted out suddenly.

Nicholas frowned and glanced his way, because that question was... bizarre.

Alan brightened, seeing he'd caught Nicholas' attention. "There are new reports that King Jonathan had an heir, before he died."

Maybe, but Nicholas couldn't imagine what that had to do with him.

"Illegitimacy wouldn't impede the line of succession, according to the revised royal charter. So, that child would be the rightful ruler of Nottingham." Alan arched a brow. "*Not* Richard."

Nicholas shrugged. Under the pageantry and catchy slogans, one king was the same as another. It didn't matter which of them was in charge, because they were all selfish assholes.

"Have you heard anything about a long-lost heir, over the years?" Alan persisted. "Any confessions from Richard, when he was drunk or in the throes of war? Like maybe admitting he murdered a baby to keep his crown?"

Nicholas arched a brow at that idea. He didn't know if King Jonathan had ever had a kid and he doubted anyone else did either. Alan was fishing. But, hypothetically speaking... It wasn't the most farfetched story Alan had ever asked him about. Richard surely would've killed any child that stood between him and the throne.

"A deep-dark castle secret, maybe? Or maybe Richard hid it away in a dungeon!" Alan kept weaving his elaborate fantasies, desperate for one to be right. "Or maybe he's searching for the child, because *Jonathan* hid it away to keep it safe from his power-hungry brother."

Nicholas was getting bored. He'd never been a lover of fiction. He read true crime and newspapers.

...And whatever arts-and-crafts tomes Marion was checking out of the library. He always tried to read the same books she did. The past few weeks, she'd been fascinated with pottery, which wasn't so bad. For several months last year she'd been very into quilting, though. Jesus, that had been a tough time. Literally, no one on the planet could write an interesting article on quilting. Nicholas had been struggling to stay awake, as he learned the difference between a four-patch star block and a pinwheel flower pattern.

Being an obsessed stalker was hard work, at times.

Several stalls away, Nicholas spotted someone selling Carbonated Magic Bean Juice. Since Marion wanted some of that incredibly unhealthy swill, he headed over to buy her a can. He didn't bother to say good-bye to Alan.

"Sheriff, wait! Could you confirm that Maid Marion has commissioned a fireworks show made from liquefied rainbows and actual stardust for your wedding reception? Who's paying for something that expensive?

Nicholas kept walking. Jesus, the tabloid stories just got weirder and weirder.

"I was hoping Maid Marion would be a Good influence on you!" Alan shouted after him.

Nicholas snorted at that idea. If anything, *he* was the one being influenced towards evil. Marion wielded her bewitching Badness like a superpower.

The line at the Carbonated Magic Bean Juice stall quickly dissipated as he approached. Unpopularity had its privileges. He'd told Marion that he could deal with the festival noise and that was true. It was torturous, but Nicholas was used to filtering out chaos in order to function. Still, the fewer people near him the better.

He bought a can of the gunk from the unsmiling vendor, wondering if he should arrest the man for even selling it. It couldn't possibly be legal to call Carbonated Magic Bean Juice "juice." Scanning the label, it contained nothing but numbered compounds he couldn't pronounce, caffeine, and sugared magic.

He wanted to get Marion every single thing she desired, but he didn't want to kill her in the process. What the hell was in this shit, if water wasn't even listed as an ingredient? He could be poisoning her with a single sip of...

Dark hair moved in his peripheral vision. The way the soft curls bounced and caught the light, instantly grabbed his attention. Nicholas could've identified one strand of it, mixed into a tangle of a million others. Also, there was the distinctive pointy, princess hat.

Marion.

She was headed away from him, towards the midway. His eyebrows drew together in confusion. Was she done with the witch-practitioner already? How? And where was she going?

"Marion!" Sticking the can of Carbonated Magic Bean Juice into his pocket, he went after her. She was only a few yards ahead, but she didn't turn around. She *had* to have heard him.

Was she ignoring him?

"Marion?" He shoved aside fairgoers who got in his path, his eyes fixed on the back of her head. "Marion, wait!"

She didn't wait.

Yes, she was *definitely* ignoring him. Why? All the insecurities of Nicholas' life came rushing back. All the slights and barriers against gargoyles. All the times he'd watched Marion from afar, knowing she was beyond his reach.

She'd only been gone ten minutes!

What the hell was going on? All day, they'd been walking arm-in-arm and now she was avoiding him. Not even looking at him, when he called to her. What had he done to…?

Oh God.

His eyes widened and realization dawned. She *had* been under a spell.

A sick feeling hit Nicholas, right in the chest. It was suddenly hard to breathe. The witch-practitioner had cured her and now Marion was free from the illusions that had been clouding her mind. She no longer wanted to be engaged to Nicholas. She no longer even *liked* him.

Her memories had been fixed and now everything was back to normal.

Marion was back to loving Robin Hood.

***

"There's no evidence of an amnesia spell or a True Love spell." The witch practitioner told Marion. She looped a stethoscope around her neck importantly.

It had taken the woman *eighteen minutes* to come to that obvious conclusion.

Marion restrained herself from rolling her eyes. "No kidding."

The witch-practitioner wasn't technically a witch, because Nottingham couldn't afford one. She was a fairy, just out of school. She seemed to know what she was doing, but she was incredibly *slow* at it. Marion was getting antsy.

The two of them were alone in the May Day Festival's medical tent, conducting a totally useless examination. Nicholas had insisted on it. Her groom really was tragically honorable for someone who was neither Good nor Bad.

Thankfully, Marion was here to guide him onto the wrong path.

Living with criminals for a decade meant she self-identified as a villain, now. She'd learned from them. Adjusted to their way of thinking. Assimilated into their evil club. For whatever reason, that had done wonders for her confidence. Marion knew exactly what she wanted and she had a plan to achieve her wicked goals.

She wanted Nicholas. To the brink of madness.

She really was "unhealthily fixated" on the man. She'd spent the past ten years remembering every word he had ever said to her. Reliving their every interaction. Piecing together what kind of person he really was behind the surly exterior.

Suddenly encountering a living, breathing Nicholas was overwhelming, at times. Even when she'd been pretty sure what she'd discover, spending time with him felt a little dazzling. It was shocking to her how *clear* things were, this time around.

Being a cynical, creatively villainous, evil-doer, Marion wasn't ready to buy into *all* her happiest fantasies, just yet. Life had kicked her ass too many times to blindly believe. She needed to search Nicholas' room and prove to herself that she wasn't imagining it all.

But she *wasn't* imagining it all.

"There is some magical residue around you." The fairy went on, with a puzzled frown. Her name was Tilda and she had bright turquoise hair. "A lot of it. Some kind of spell was cast, recently. It doesn't seem to be harming you, though. It's very unique magic, so I'm not sure where it came from."

A Hatter doing hard time.

"Don't worry. I've got a pretty good idea." Marion smiled her Maidy-est smile. "Hey, are there any enchantresses around here?"

Tilda seemed startled by the non sequitur. "This isn't an enchantress' spell. The colors of it are all wrong."

"No, but do any enchantresses live in Nottingham?"

"Of course not." It was a scoff. "The only specialized magic Nottingham has ever been able to produce is the gargoyle spell. And that's so old, no one alive had a hand in crafting it. Any enchantress born here would have long ago moved to some more progressive, prosperous kingdom, with better career options. Who could blame them? Nobody in Nottingham has their kind of power. Few people *anywhere* have their kind of power."

Marion wasn't convinced. Much-the-Miller was a doofus, but he clearly believed Richard had an enchantress helping him out. It was worth looking into, given all the weird shit happening. "What if an enchantress wanted to work undercover? Could she do that?"

"I doubt it. The power an enchantress gives off is incredible. It would be impossible to overlook."

Shit.

"Could someone... *pretend* to be an enchantress?" Marion asked, trying to think of possibilities. "Like maybe do small spells that would convince a very stupid man that she could predict the future?"

"Well, other types of beings can see events coming." Tilda explained. "Cheshire Cats, for instance. Some wizards. It's rare, but not unheard of. An enchantress' abilities are much bigger than the others can muster, though. Think a campfire versus a spotlight." She pursed her lips, in deep thought. "For somebody to fake even *part* of their powers, they'd have to be at least a level four."

"That's high?" Tansy had said she was a level four, so it was probably high.

Tilda rolled her eyes, like Marion's question was just silly. "The scale only goes to six. And basically *no one* is a six. Level four would be *huge* for a magical backwater like Nottingham. I'm a level three and people around here are impressed."

Marion thought that over. "Is there any way to track higher levels of magic, then?"

"I'm not sure. *I* certainly can't. But I could enspell a talisman, perhaps? So it would signal when someone with strong powers gets near you." She paused. "For a price."

Marion reached into her pocket and pulled out the hideous necklace Tansy had given her in prison. "Do I get a discount if I provide my own creepy talisman?"

Ten minutes later, Marion had traded the gold coin Nicholas had lent her for a magic detection spell. More power had been uploaded into Tansy's icky pendant. Now, it was recharged and ready to signal whenever anyone with level four and above magic got close.

"Thanks." She told Tilda, dropping the pendant into her pocket and getting to her feet. "You've been a huge help."

"Maid Marion?" Tilda called, as Marion turned to leave. "Can I ask you...? Are the newspapers right? Did you really *agree* to marry the sheriff?"

"Yes."

"Why?" The woman shook her head in bafflement and disapproval. "You had *Robin Hood!*" She made it sound like Marion had been dating Sir Galahad. "Why would you want a gargoyle, instead?"

"Because, Nick's my favorite person in the world." Marion said truthfully and headed out the flap of the tent.

All around her, the May Day Festival was in full swing. Fairgoers in tie dyed outfits and face paint danced around to electric lute music. Drinking grog from large souvenir cups and pleasantly buzzed on hallucinogenic hand-pies, the kingdom threw itself into revelry. Colorful banners were draped between the rows of tents, hanging over the walkways and creating a claustrophobic atmosphere. Nearby a bell rang, signaling that someone had hit the top of the strongman high-striker game.

And every one of the revelers glowered at Marion like she was a fallen woman.

Seemed like Nicholas was right about the upright, do-right citizens of Nottingham. Maybe they were displeased about Marion's PDAs with her smoking-hot kidnapper. Or maybe they were upset because she'd ratted out the Merry Men. Or because she'd gotten Tuck arrested. Or because she'd instigated that fight in the brothel. Or because she'd publically dumped Robin. Or because she'd said 'yes' to a gargoyle's proposal.

Or all of the above.

Bagheera Kong sent her a scowl, silently blaming Marion for Judge Kong's lascivious behavior and resulting "disappearance." Clearly, the panther thought it was outrageous that Marion was attending the May Day Festival without wearing a scarlet A. ...But murdering your husband on the lawn of a brothel was *fine*, so long as everyone pretended they didn't know about it.

Marion grinned back, darkly amused, and mentally added Bagheera to her list of people who needed their dreams destroyed.

She had no desire to cavort through a field with a bunch of idiots, so she didn't give a damn if these mouth-breathers wanted her at their dreary fair. To her eyes, there was a sense of desperation to the May Day frolics. As the kingdom decayed around them, the citizens' gaiety took on a bitter edge. They were hanging onto the past too tight. Trying too hard to laugh and have fun. Eating and drinking too fast to actually enjoy anything. The kingdom was dying and this was its wake.

Marion couldn't wait to bury it, once and for all.

In the meantime, she scanned around for Nicholas' muscular form. He wouldn't have gone far and she still wanted that can of Carbonated Magic Bean Juice. The chemical-ly goodness of the drink was worth all the chemical-ly badness, she didn't care what the food safety wizards said. It wasn't like the manufactures could use *real* magic beans in the formula, after all. The damn things were rare and expensive and sometimes grew beanstalks inside the people who ate them. No one wanted...

An arrow came flying out of nowhere, nearly hitting her in the head.

Marion scrambled backwards, as the quivering tip embedded itself in a wall of the temporary building beside her. Cheap wood splintered.

Marion stared at the deadly projectile, her frantic heartrate slowing. Robin always did shit like this. There was a message wrapped around the arrow shaft, because of *course* there was. Her man-child of an ex-boyfriend was apparently one of the few people in Nottingham with a phone, but he still resorted to archery tricks instead of texting. What had she ever seen in that nimrod?

Her lips firmed together in annoyance and she ripped the parchment down:

Meet me at the puppet show. Don't worry about the sheriff.

Marion's eyes narrowed, rereading the short note. Why would Robin want to meet her? Could the jackass not take a hint? She expected Robin to show up to win the golden arrow. She hadn't expected him to demand a chat, after she'd ignored his last missive and continued on with her engagement to Nicholas. She certainly didn't *want* him to seek her out.

And what was this shit about not "worrying about" Nicholas? What did that mean? Wait. Where *was* Nicholas? She'd been gone half-an-hour, but she couldn't imagine he'd just *leave* when she ran a little late. He should've been waiting for her, when she left the medical tent. She was supposed to be his hostage, damn it. He needed to be attentive.

Marion looked around for his big, familiar figure, more urgently this time. "Nick?" She turned in a circle, worry consuming her when she still didn't spot him. "Nick!"

Nothing. No Nicholas. Just an endless parade of dimwits eating mutton legs, painting their faces with glitter, and passing judgement on her new sexual freedom.

Marion suddenly found it hard to breathe. What if Robin was the one who murdered Nicholas? What if he'd moved up the date of Nicholas' assassination and decided to carry it out today?

Just by being back here, she was messing up history. Things could have already changed. Robin wouldn't want to fight Nicholas head-on. She *knew* she was right about that. He always hit his targets when their backs were turned. What if "don't worry about the sheriff" meant Robin was murdering him, right that minute?

Genuine panic set in. Marion took off running towards

the nearest palace guards. Rockwell was stationed by the golden arrow case, along with Oore, the gargoyle who never shut up.

"Where's Nick?" She demanded, gasping for breath.

Both men stared at her in confusion. "With you?" Rockwell guessed. "The commander's been right beside you, ever since we brought you to the castle. Even longer than that, but he was kind of lurking in the shadows, so you probably didn't notice."

"He's *not* with me!"

Oore seemed blasé about that news. He scratched at one of the stone ram's horns carved where his ear should've been. "Maybe he's just worn out of being with you and needs a break, Maid Marion. You talk a lot. It's tiring."

Rockwell scoffed. "The commander kicked me out of the room at breakfast, because he was so *not* worn out of this girl. He's crazy about her. And she doesn't even charge him!"

Oore grunted. "If I was her, I'd be charging. He'll pay whatever she wants. Guaranteed. She'd be rich."

"Focus!" Marion snapped. "Nicholas is *missing*."

"The commander never goes missing. He's probably off buying more flowers for the wedding." Rockwell speculated, refusing to listen to reality. "I had to track down every red tulip in Nottingham, for him yesterday." He paused. "Or maybe he's killing your other potential groom. Hanging Hood, so the human can never steal you back." Huge hands clapped together in dreamy speculation. "That would be so romantic!"

Oore nodded, like the theory made a lot of sense.

Marion squeezed her eyes shut in frustration. Nicholas' men weren't worried about his safety. They thought he was invincible. She knew better. "Lock down this fucking fair. No one comes in and no one goes out, until I find him. Do it. *Now*."

The men saluted at the bellowed order, but Marion barely noticed. All she cared about was getting Nicholas back. Robin must have done something to him, so her ex seemed like the best place to start looking. She began scouring the rows of gaudily striped tents, searching for wherever the damn puppet show was set-up. It wasn't like she'd memorized a map of this psychedelic shithole.

Intent on her search, she plowed into someone outside the corndog booth. Clorinda, her former lady-in-waiting, hit the ground, spilling mustard all over her pink chiffon dress.

She let out an enraged sound, when she saw Marion was the one who'd knocked her down. "Look what you did now, you idiot!" Anger and something else flashed in her eyes, as she ineffectually swiped at her ruined dress. "Why are you doing this to me?"

"I'm not doing anything to you! *You're* the one who..." Marion stopped short. Up ahead, she spotted a dilapidated red awning that advertised "Mangiafuoco's Magnificent Marionettes! Free Admission!"

Bingo.

"Is this all about me being a shoo-in for May Day Queen?" Clorinda pressed. "Is that it? Are you *that* jealous and petty?"

Marion didn't even bother to answer her. She stepped right over Clorinda's splayed body to reach the tent faster. Clorinda squawked, but Marion kept going.

Bursting through the flap of the dirty tent, Marion dashed into the darkened interior. "Robin? Where are you?"

Inside, she didn't see anyone, at all. Puppets were shockingly not a huge draw to festival-goers, even for free. It was still and empty inside the tent. Nothing but rickety bleachers along the walls and a garishly decorated stage in the center.

And puppets.

Marionettes of all sizes hung from the ceiling. Some were human-shaped. Some looked like animals. Some seemed to have been created straight from nightmares. Their limp limbs all swung gently, as the canvas roof rippled with the wind outside, giving the impression the puppets were moving on their own. Their wooden heads were skewed to odd and unsettling angles. Their sightless eyes stared at everything and nothing.

And that's when Marion realized the enspelled necklace in her pocket was vibrating. A lot. Like a cellphone set to silent mode it insistently buzzed against her leg. Someone close by was using tons of magic.

Why?

"Marion?" Robin's voice shouted from somewhere in the blackened depths of the tent. "Thank God you're here! Come quick!"

The hairs on the back of her neck rose up. It was just like the eerie feeling she'd experienced outside the casino, only more extreme. Marion unconsciously shook her head. There was no way this was right.

"Marion! Please! I need you."

Robin never needed her for anything. Even if he did, she wouldn't help his worthless ass. No. Something about this situation was very, very wrong. She wasn't taking a single step in that direction. Not a chance.

Marion had done time with a stately old Mock Turtle, who wore thick glasses and an ancient bowtie, even with his prison-issued "EVIL" sweatshirt. He'd been over two-hundred years old, most of them spent behind bars, because he was a mean son of a bitch. When she asked him how he'd survived so long, he'd leaned in close to her and whispered in a voice full of elongated Ss, "Instincts, child. Always listen to your instincts."

Her instincts told her this was a trap.

As usual, her WUB Club education was invaluable.

She glanced over her shoulder, but the door to the tent had vanished. Where the flap had once been, there was now just solid canvas.

Magic. *Shit*.

Edging sideways, Marion used the darkness to stay out of sight and didn't say a word to Robin. She needed another exit, but first she needed to make sure Nicholas wasn't trapped somewhere in this puppet-y hell-scape. Marion began peering under the bleachers, in case Nicholas had been tied up in marionette strings and stuffed underneath of them.

"I have a plan to rescue you, but we have to hurry." Robin called. "I'm right over here, darling!"

Something wasn't quite right with his voice. The cajoling tone and flowery words weren't how she remembered him sounding. Ever. She mostly recalled empty promises, whiny complaints about how unfair everything was, and long lectures on different kinds of arrows.

The puppets kept swaying.

The necklace kept jangling.

Marion tried not to freak out, but it was hard. Robin didn't have any magic, so there must be someone else in here with him. It could only be the creature pretending to be the enchantress. That was probably really, really Bad.

"Marion!" Robin sounded desperate. "We have to get out of here, *now!* Don't you trust your own True Love?"

She very nearly scoffed at that question and kept looking for Nicholas. She wasn't sure whether to be relieved or not when he wasn't anywhere in the tent.

"Fine." Robin's voice went hard, seeing that she wasn't going to rush into his arms. "If you're not going to cooperate, we'll do this the hard way."

Above her head, the marionettes danced wildly in some unseen gale.

Oh crap…

Marion jolted at the sound of a twirling puppet abruptly falling to the ground. Then another one fell. Then more and more. Nothing was cutting their strings, but she could see the thin wires snapping. It was like they were *escaping.* Like they were alive.

No, no, no, no, no.

Ten years in prison gave Marion some real good insight as to when something extremely fucked-up was about to happen and a checklist of what to do when it inevitably did. When a pack of wolves came prowling into the TV room, sniffing for prey, you created a distraction. When a pissed off fire imp began incinerating everyone in sight, you ran. When a dwarf guard was scanning for rule-breakers to punish to make himself feel big, you hid.

When zombie puppets started stirring, you did all three.

Thinking fast, Marion took off her dumb princess hat and propped it up on one of the empty bleachers. Then, she slipped sideways in the opposite direction, keeping low and already scanning for a way out. She didn't see one.

God*damn* it.

On the floor, the puppets began to rise. Jointed arms twisted, pushing up their brightly painted bodies so they stood on wobbly legs. Large eyes blinked, as if they were coming awake after a long rest. Wooden heads tilted, listening for movement. Listening for Marion.

She froze, crouched down against the canvas wall of the tent. Afraid to breathe.

Five years in the future, the WUB Club would be filled with barbarian slaughter. Screaming and death had filled the halls, that night. Marion had been huddled behind her prison cot, when black eyes had suddenly fixed on her through the bars. Blood dripping down an angry face. That was the last time she was this scared.

Half-convinced she'd never escape her darken cell alive, her only thoughts had been of Nicholas. She'd known right then that if she had a chance to redo her life, she'd make so many different choices. Well now she had her second chance. No way was she going to waste it.

Her lips firmed together, determined to survive.

There was a chittering sound, as the puppets' boxy mouths clacked up and down. It must have been some kind of communication, because others bobbed their heads. They began to move in unnatural, bouncy, bobbing movements.

Searching.

For her.

One of them raised a teeny hand, pointing to the hennin that Marion had left as a decoy. The breezy gold scarf was barely visible, tucked away in the bleachers.

In a wave of tiny wooden legs, the marionettes surged towards it. It was a feeding frenzy. They descended on the hat, ripping it apart. Fabric flew into the air. Frustrated that Marion wasn't attached to the hennin, some of the puppets then turned on each other. Eating their own.

Their bodies were wooden, but their teeth were razor sharp. She could see their fangs flashing and snapping. The marionettes were hungry. Rabid. If they found her, she was dead. Even if she could fight one or two, there was no way she could stop them all. There were too many. They were too fast. And they were laughing.

Marion cringed and covered her ears, trying to block it all out. Shrill, chittering screams and broken doll parts raining down. And Robin's crazed laughter, as he delighted in the carnage. It was *his* laughter she heard.

Only that wasn't Robin's laugh.

It wasn't Robin.

"Find her!" The being pretending to be Robin called to the puppets. "She's in here somewhere. Tear her apart."

Holy *fuck*.

Marion was out of time. She looked around and her gaze fell on the side of the tent. That was her only option. She tried to lift up the heavy canvas, so she could crawl beneath it, but spikes were holding it to the ground and she couldn't pull them free. She wasn't strong enough.

The puppets were swarming closer, spreading out to cover more ground.

She let out a panicked sound, tugging desperately on the fabric of the tent. She managed to get her arm through a small section, but it was so heavy. How was she going to lift it high enough to squeeze through? There had to be a way. Maybe she could…

Suddenly, a rock-hard palm grasped her wrist from outside the tent. Marion gasped, recognizing the touch. The feel of his hand on her skin was burned into her brain. She would've known it anywhere.

"Nick!" She instinctively called for him. Small wooden footsteps raced towards her, fixing on her position. "I can't get out!"

"Hold on." Not letting her go, Nicholas used his other hand to yank the canvas up with relentless strength. His stony grip ripped the tent spikes straight out of the ground. "I've got you." He pulled Marion up and into the sunlight.

Marion's whole body was shaking, as he lifted her into his arms. She clung to him, thrilled he was alive. Thrilled that *she* was alive.

"I've got you." Nicholas said, again. He carried her away from the tent, like he knew she wasn't comfortable being so close to it. "Are you alright?"

She nodded, a little frantically. Someone had tried to kill her.

Some*thing* had tried to kill her.

"What happened?" Nicholas wasn't putting her down, but he also wasn't holding her as tight as she'd expect. Like he wasn't sure how close she wanted him to get.

Suddenly, she wasn't sure either.

Not only was Marion still frightened of the deadly wooden dolls, she was also a little bit unnerved by how quickly she'd accepted Nicholas' help. Marion wasn't a girl who needed a rescue. Not ever again. The betrothal rights were just a game. The idea of him protecting her for really *real* made her nervous. When the chips were down, she only counted on herself.

Her eyes stayed still fixed on the tent, just in case any maniacal marionettes sprang out after her. "I could have handled that. I was just…"

Nicholas cut her off. "What happened?" He repeated harshly.

Marion looked up at him, trying to catch her breath. "Puppets just tried to eat me."

Chapter Eighteen

Trouble in paradise!
Maid Marion and Sheriff seen in a lovers' quarrel.
Will he hang her before or after their lavish wedding?
Our expert odds-makers weigh in.

Alan A. Dale- "Nottingham's Naughtiest News"

"I didn't 'sneak off to meet Robin Hood.'" Marion snapped, adding air quotes around his very reasonable accusation. "How many times do we have to go over this, Nick?"

"Until you explain why you snuck off to meet Robin Hood."

"I was looking for *you*, jackass. I *told* you that."

The two of them were sitting side-by-side in the royal box at the tournament field. The May Day games were going full blast, in front of them. In order to hide the real intent of her fake archery contest, Marion had cobbled together some lesser events. Presently, peasants were juggling. Nicholas couldn't even pretend to care why.

He shook his head, wholly unsatisfied with Marion's explanations. "I don't even know how you got into that tent. There wasn't a door on it."

"There was when I went in. You want me to explain how evil magic works now? Because I can't." She crossed her arms over her chest. "Where the hell where *you*, anyway? That's the real question."

"I followed you out of the medical tent. I called your name, but you ignored me and kept walking."

"That's ridiculous. I have never ignored you in my life."

"Well, you did today." Nicholas could admit that it was unusual behavior, though. Even when he'd been a bastard to her, Marion had always been kind to him. And since he'd taken her hostage, she'd been acting like he was her very best friend. He'd always, *always* dreamed of that. The thought of losing the connection ripped him apart and drove his own anger. "Once the witch-practitioner lifted that spell from you, you ran off to be in Hood's arms. You somehow vanished on me, over by the midway, but I was…"

"I was never near the midway!" She interrupted at a yell. People in the neighboring boxes sent them worried glances. "I was never under a spell! I did not run into Robin's arms! Are you stoned on that mushroom funnel cake?"

"I know what you look like, Marion. It was you." She'd publically avoided him. Moving ahead of him. Not stopping when he called her name. Pretending he didn't even exist. Which he no doubt deserved and he'd literally told her to do to save her reputation, but it still hurt like hell.

And the fact that she'd done it, so she could meet with her own True Love just pissed him off more.

Marion made an expansive gesture with her hands. "Ask Oore and Rockwell, if you don't believe me. I was with them for part of the time. How could I be with them *and* on the midway?"

"I did ask them. I was looking for you --*after* the midway-- and I asked if they'd seen you go by. Oore pointed me in the direction of the damn tent." Nicholas glowered at her. "Where you were apparently chatting with your vine-swinging boyfriend."

"Robin wasn't even there! Even if he *had* been, I wouldn't have 'rushed into his arms.'" More air quotes. "Why would I?"

"Because you're devoted to him. You always have been."

"*Devoted?*" Marion made a repulsed face. "After I was sent to the WUB Club, gold appeared in my commissary account. I assume it was from Robin. It would've been much harder to survive in that hellhole without money, so I was grateful. Aside from that *one* lapse in assholery, though, the man has been a total shit-nugget for decades. If I never see his smirking face again, it would be too…" She stopped and blinked, like a new thought had just occurred to her. "Wait, why would *Robin* give me money? He's a thief! Huh. It must've been someone else who funded my account."

Nicholas refused to be sidetracked on one of her tangents. "You went to the puppet tent to see Hood, so he'd rescue you from the Sheriff of Nottingham." He decided grimly. "But, too bad. I've got you back in my granite clutches. You're kidnapped. Deal with it."

She scoffed, refocusing on him. "I don't need anyone to rescue me. Not from anything."

"Really? You needed *me* earlier. I'm the one who pulled you out of the damn tent, after your beloved boyfriend led you to it."

Marion's face changed, going cold. He hadn't seen it look that way before. "No." She said very clearly. "I don't need *anyone*. You taught me that, Nick."

Nicholas hesitated, momentarily surprised out of his jealousy. "I did?"

"At the wedding. Robin didn't come for me. You told me, 'When the chips are down, you can't count on True Love to save you, Marion.'" She quoted it so quickly, he suspected the sentence was burned into her brain. "And it's true." She nodded. "I can only count on myself. I didn't understand it then, but I do now. You were right."

Was he?

Hearing Marion say it sounded… wrong.

Nicholas didn't disagree with the general philosophy. The very fact True Loves existed annoyed him. The mystio-physiological bond was unbreakable. Part of a person's blood and bone, heart and soul. Marion wanted that kind of destined pairing and Nicholas couldn't offer it, because some stupid, arbitrary quirk of fate had given her to Hood, instead. That was all horseshit and he *hated* it.

But, contradictorily, Marion refusing to count on her True Love also annoyed him. He had no idea why, considering her True Love was Robin Hood. The woman was smart to doubt that dumbass. She'd do better relying on any random frog that hopped by to somehow morph into a prince.

Still, for some reason, Nicholas found himself wanting to argue about her lonely assertions that she could only depend on herself. He wanted to say that *he* would come for her, if she needed him. That she could always count on him to save her.

But what good would it do?

He wasn't her True Love, so she wouldn't want to hear it. Nicholas' words were sure to be wrong and she wouldn't believe them anyway. So, he didn't say anything, at all.

Boulder came up beside him, leaning close to Nicholas' shoulder to speak into his ear. "We tore the tent apart. No puppets. No Hood. Just this." He handed over Marion's pointy princess hat. There was an underlying suggestion that maybe Marion had imagined the whole thing, because Boulder always thought the worst about everything.

Marion frowned when she saw the hennin still in one piece.

Nicholas shook his head, his attention on Boulder. "Something was inside that tent." He said quietly.

It wasn't just Marion's fear that had convinced him, although that would have been enough. He'd seen the desperate relief in her eyes, when he'd pulled her under the canvas side and into the sunlight. But, Nicholas had also felt the presence of something behind the canvas walls. Something that made the hairs on his arms stand up.

Boulder still didn't look convinced.

In the festival ring, the juggling event was over. Nicholas wasn't sure if there was a winner. Hopefully not, because they'd all been terrible. Next up was something to do with chickens. Nicholas was supposed to give a ribbon to the fastest one, according to the announcer he was half-listening to. The very, very *loud* announcer.

God, he hated his job sometimes.

Nicholas scowled at Boulder, ignoring the chickens. "Make sure somebody stays close to her." He nodded towards Marion. Whatever had been in that puppet show, it could come back. Nicholas had made a vow to protect Marion, when he claimed his betrothal rights. Even without the vow, though, keeping her safe would always be his number one priority.

"Nothing comes near my bride."

"Afraid Robin's going to come and save me?" Marion taunted, overhearing that remark and misunderstanding it. "Hold your breath for him to arrive. I dare you."

"You already *admitted* he came for you." Nicholas retorted, craning his neck around Boulder to glower at her. If she wanted to continue this argument, he was ready. Fury was still beating in his veins. It made no sense to feel betrayed. He *knew* that. But he felt it anyway and he couldn't contain his reaction.

"Robin wasn't there! I *told* you that."

"You also said he was the reason you were in the tent to begin with. He *was* there. He was just late, for some reason. That's all." Hopefully, Hood was dead. Another tragic victim of puppet-cide.

"Nooo." Marion corrected slowly, like maybe Nicholas had the IQ of one of the chickens. "I said I got a note, signed by Robin, to meet him at the puppet show. *That's* all."

"And how is that any different than what *I* just said?"

"Because you're adding shit that didn't happen! He wasn't 'late.' He just wasn't *there*. Do we really have to rehash this, again and again and again?" Her palm made circles in the air, representing a conversation on repeat.

Nicholas wasn't budging. "Someone shot an arrow with a note on it, yes? Was that Hood? Or do *other* archers send you secret messages?"

"It was probably Robin," she admitted grudgingly, "but we can't be positive. I'm pretty sure I burned my only sample of his handwriting."

Nicholas wasn't willing to wait on forensics. "Hood was there." There didn't seem to be another explanation. "You just didn't see him." He arched a meaningful brow. "Is that why you're upset? Do you think he's avoiding you? Maybe he's heard you had my hands all over you earlier and now he's wondering what *else* you've been doing with me."

Brown eyes narrowed. "I have never disliked you as much as I dislike you right now, Nicholas. Including the time I told you I'd hate you forever-after." Marion crossed her arms over her chest and did her very best to ignore him all together.

Nicholas stifled a wince.

Boulder's gaze slid over to Marion's furious face and then back to Nicholas. "What are you doing?" He whispered fiercely. "Why are you deliberately pissing off your girl?"

Nicholas had no answer for that, so he went with something simpler. "She's not my girl. She's *Hood's* girl."

"Bullshit."

What the hell was happening to his life? The other gargoyles were getting involved in his relationship? *Boulder*, of all people, wanted to lecture him on being more thoughtful? Why were they suddenly talking to him, like they expected him to talk back? He'd established the damn weekly gargoyle meeting, so he'd only have to communicate every seven days. Was his leadership growing more lax or were the men all going crazy?

Nicholas shot him a menacing glare. "Leave." It was a warning.

In the festival ring, chickens raced around in mindless circles, while Nottinghamers cheered them on. Even focusing on that pitiful spectacle was a step up from listening to Boulder give advice on women.

Boulder kept talking, his voice low. "You don't want to do this, Commander. You worked too hard to get Maid Marion smiling at you. Every one of us has seen it. Don't fuck it up, now."

"You've been saying she was lying, since she got here." Nicholas snapped, although he had no clue why he was bothering to respond, at all. "Now you're suddenly changing your mind?"

"I didn't change my mind, exactly. I just know you're fucking up."

Nicholas was done. "Find Hood and kill him." He ordered. If that arrow-shooting son of a bitch was dead, all of Nicholas' problems would be solved.

Muttering under his breath, Boulder turned away. He started to stomp off, only to stop short when Marion laid a hand on his arm.

"Boulder, wait."

Boulder waited. His gaze slashed down to her manicured palm on his rocky-skin, as if he'd never seen anything like it. He probably hadn't. No other Maid would touch a gargoyle. Not in public. His astonished eyes jumped back to Marion's face.

"When we had the trial, you were the only one who testified on my behalf." She said, missing his amazement. "You won't remember, because it hasn't happened yet. But you were on guard duty by the castle gate, when Nick was murdered."

"Thursday." Boulder's voice was uncharacteristically soft. "My shift on the castle gate starts at midnight on Thursday."

Nicholas felt a chill.

Marion nodded. "You said that no one could have slipped past you, that night. You said I couldn't have gotten through the castle gate, without being seen."

Nicholas frowned, thinking that over.

"You said Nick was too well trained for me to take him down, anyway." Marion went on, her eyes on Boulder. "You said that there was no real motive for me to do it, since I knew he wouldn't hurt me. That *everyone* knew it. You said I was innocent and the real killer was still free."

Boulder stared at her.

She gave a small shrug. "Nobody believed you, of course. The prosecution accused you of vile things, because you were a gargoyle. But, you stood there and said it all, anyway." She patted his arm in gratitude and withdrew her hand. "I want you to know, I have always appreciated that. Thank you."

Boulder swallowed and then gave a curt nod. He left without giving a response, but Nicholas knew Marion had just made another conquest. She didn't even have to try. The woman was just irresistible.

And she was so damn pissed at Nicholas that she'd probably hate him forever-after.

He closed his eyes, knowing Boulder was right. He was

fucking up. He might've *already* fucked things up beyond repair. And for what? Was it any wonder Hood was trying to steal her back? Was Nicholas even surprised? What would Nicholas do, in Hood's place? If some obsessed, stalking, gargoyle asshole took Marion from him and tried to force her into an unwanted marriage?

Granted, he wouldn't enter May Day tournaments or hire puppeteers. (What the *hell* was Hood thinking with that shit?) But, Nicholas would do other dangerous, foolish, desperate things, if that's what it took to save her. All of Nottingham would bleed, until Marion was back in his arms.

Nicholas scraped a hand through his hair, trying to get his raging emotions under control. Whatever was happening, Marion was at the center of it. She was a target. His anger paled beside his need to protect this small, exasperating woman. Nothing mattered except her.

"I will find out who owns that marionette tent." He promised, in a calmer tone than he'd used in an hour. "I will make sure they pay for frightening you."

Marion glanced his way. "Why? You don't even believe me about what happened today." It wasn't a question.

"That's not true." He shook his head, feeling defensive. "I believe Hood wrote you a note, in some harebrained scheme to rescue you. I'm not sure why he involved the deranged puppets, but the man is always absurd, so I can't say I'm surprised, either." Nicholas rolled his eyes in disgust, remembering the slaughter at Kirklees. "Hood makes poor choices."

Her gaze was intense, like she wasn't sure how to make him understand what she needed him to understand. "There was something *evil* inside that tent, Nick. It wasn't Robin. I swear it."

"I know something was in the tent. I'll find it and kill it. You have my promise." He hesitated, her earlier words still preying on his mind. Even though it made no sense and might not even have happened. "Why did you once tell me you hated me? What did I do?"

"You tricked me."

He seriously doubted that. Marion was so much smarter than him, he didn't see any way he could've successfully fooled her. "I'm a big, blunt hammer, remember? Predictable. If I tricked you, you must've wanted to be tricked."

To his surprise, Marion seemed to consider his words. She turned and studied him in an appraising way, as if she had some thought to share. He waited, because Marion had been telling him all her ideas for days. He fully expected her to explain what was going on in her razor-sharp mind.

This time she decided not to include him, though. Instead, Marion pressed her lips together and turned away to watch the end of the chicken melee.

Nicholas felt like he'd been slapped. He'd liked being in her confidence. Even when he disagreed with her, he really did feel like they were a team. Losing that privilege was worse than the public snubbing had been. He slumped back in his chair.

For a very long time, there was only quiet between them.

It ate at him.

He got up and grudgingly handed out a blue ribbon to which ever random chicken owner approached the box, but all his thoughts were on Marion. Nicholas had always been fine with silence before, but now it felt different. Marion *wasn't* silent. Not really. Her mind was filled with words. He just didn't know what they were, because she was keeping them secret.

He slammed back into his seat, the inhuman weight of his body shaking the entire royal box. Marion didn't seem to notice. "The witch-practitioner really said you were free from any spells?" He asked, just for something to say.

"Yes. I'm fine." Marion assured him distractedly. She hadn't even made any snarky comment about the chicken race winner crying with joy over his bird's performance, which didn't seem like her, at all. Maybe she was saving all her wittiest remarks for Hood.

You can hold the woman captive, but you can't make her talk to you.

Nicholas drummed his fingers on the arm of his chair.

He'd always known this would happen. Marion wasn't truly his fiancée, no matter how much he wished otherwise. He'd abducted her from her home. *That's* why she was here with him. *That's* why she didn't want to spend the day chatting. That was normal. It was her behavior up *until* this point that had been strange. It was why he'd thought she was under a spell. This new aloofness was exactly what he'd expected, in the first place. It would be best to accept reality and allow the distance to grow.

But Nicholas never accepted that a barrier couldn't be toppled, if he pushed hard enough.

"Puppets are toys." He heard himself say.

Marion looked his way, again.

"That supposed factory you supposedly own with the supposed David Doncaster supposedly makes toys." Nicholas lifted a shoulder. "It's an odd coincidence. Or it's not a coincidence, at all."

Brown eyes blinked, a faraway expression falling over her face. "It's toying with everyone. We're all just puppets. *That's* what its saying." She murmured and then she was quiet again.

This time the silence wasn't about keeping him away, though. It was Marion trying to figure out a puzzle. Nicholas could accept that. He enjoyed watching her mind work.

Feeling slightly encouraged, he reached into the pocket of his uniform. He pulled out the Carbonated Magic Bean Juice he'd bought for her, while she was with the witch-practitioner. Reaching over, he placed it on the wooden railing of the royal viewing box, directly in front of her. Then, he withdrew his hand, leaving it like bait in a trap.

Marion glanced up at him with an unreadable expression.

Nicholas stayed still and waited.

Suspicious and wary, she slowly took the can and then settled back in her seat.

Satisfaction filled Nicholas. He still thought that "juice" was unhealthy and possibly unnatural, but at least she seemed content with it. He grunted, afraid to say anything for fear it would be wrong. He didn't want to fuck up even worse.

Marion busied herself with opening her drink. "How close did you get?"

"To what?"

"To the woman on the midway. How close were you?"

"A few yards."

She gave another nod and drank some of her syrupy beverage.

Trumpets sounded, signaling the start of the main event, and Nicholas literally cringed at the noise. The announcer's excited voice proclaimed that the wonderful, fabulous, oh-so-thrilling archery contest was about to begin. Nottinghamers clapped in breathless anticipation. Target shooting was the height of sophistication and sport, after all. Only jousting could rival it in the hearts of the kingdom. There was nothing more thrilling to the citizens of Nottingham then morons with perfectly-formed fingers firing arrows at a bullseye.

Nicholas crossed his arms over his chest and hated the world.

A woman in a low-cut dress walked around the interior of the arena, proudly holding up the spray-painted arrow for the crowd to see. "Oohs" and "ahhs" abounded. Sunlight glinted off the golden surface and Nicholas had to admit that Marion's arts and crafts project looked pretty damn convincing, from a distance. Everyone was impressed with the glistening prize.

Marion was right. Hood would want to win it, just to prove he could. Nicholas was suddenly sure of that. ...And he was sure he'd been an idiot.

"This is a good plan." He muttered grudgingly.

Marion looked his way.

Nicholas cleared his throat and tried to fix what he broke. "I'm sorry."

"For?"

"Everything."

"Well, that's a start."

Her tone still wasn't happy. She was listening, though, and she was drinking the soda he'd bought for her. So, Nicholas kept going.

"I shouldn't have reacted the way I did."

"Nope."

"When I heard you got the note from Hood and went to see him, I was…." he struggled to describe the rage and fear and loneliness and desperation and possession that had washed over him, "troubled."

"Troubled?"

"Yes. But, I was wrong. If you wanted Hood to save you, you wouldn't be trying to catch him with this contest."

"No shit."

His tension eased a bit, because now she sounded like Marion, again. "If you planned to secretly run off with him today, your plan would've *worked*. You're good at creatively villainous plans."

Her mouth tipped up at one corner, liking that compliment. She made a "gimme more" grabby gesture by quickly folding her fingers against her raised palm. "Keep going, big guy."

"If you were pining to see Hood at this festival, you'd never sit on my lap and let me touch you this morning. I know that, because I know *you*."

"Doing better."

"But, I just can't… I don't…"

"Yes?" She prompted, when he stopped.

He tried to articulate his feelings, but, as always, the right words eluded him. "You have *always* been his girl. Changing that perception in my head is hard. I keep going back to it, because… it just doesn't make sense."

Marion's brows furrowed. "What doesn't make sense?"

"All of it." Nicholas wished he'd never started this part. It was all coming out garbled. "And picturing Hood's hands on your body makes me… irrational. Picturing anyone but *me* having your attention or affection… I don't want to go back to that. I *can't*. Not when I know what it feels like to really have you with me."

Now, he had her total focus.

"You're... And I'm not... *Fuck*." He ground his teeth in self-disgust, trying to find words that weren't ridiculous.

Marion waited.

Nicholas gave up trying to be even halfway eloquent and just went with bald facts. "I want you for myself, Marion."

Her lips parted.

"That's the truth." He admitted helplessly. "It just *is*. I am obsessed with you. It's wrong and I don't care. You are all I think about. All I see."

Her head tilted, considering that crazy declaration. Probably wondering if he'd lost his damn mind. Maybe he had. No sane gargoyle would ask a Maid to choose him over the most heroic bastard in Nottingham. It was the very definition of insanity.

Nicholas turned back towards the tournament field and wished someone would just shoot an arrow through his brain to put him out of his misery.

"Okay."

He frowned at her casual response to his awkward confession. "Okay?"

"Okay. You can have me for yourself." She shrugged, like it was obvious. "It's what I want, too."

That's impossible and you know it, Greystone. She's kidding herself.

Nicholas shook his head, listening to his own dark thoughts, because what else made sense? "You don't mean that."

"Yes, I do. There are no issues keeping us apart, Nick. Not anymore. You just have to stop inventing problems and *communicate* with me."

It wasn't as simple as Marion made it seem. It couldn't be. Why would she just give up on Robin Hood forever? Marion said she wanted the kind of marriage her parents had. That meant True Love. That meant *Hood*. She might believe what she was saying right now, but she'd change her mind eventually. It was inevitable.

Marion sighed, seeing his doubt. "Sometimes, I feel unsure of you, too, you know. About why you want me, in the first place."

Nicholas scoffed at that nonsense. Anyone with eyes knew how he felt about Marion. She couldn't possibly doubt it. He'd been staring at her nonstop for almost fifteen years.

"We both need to be better at trusting." She decided, relenting in the face of his misery. "We'll get there. We're already *almost* there. Just give me until the wedding and it'll all come together. I know it."

"By Wednesday you'll know if you trust me?"

"Yes. And you'll know if you can trust me. If I don't show up in my perfect dress, you'll know I'm lying about everything and can feel very vindicated. If I *do* show up, you just smile pretty and say 'I do.' ...And I never have to hear you say Robin's name, again. Deal?"

He nodded, pathetically hopeful and deeply skeptical at the same time. "Deal."

No matter what happens on Wednesday, don't let her go.

On the field, the contestants were lining up to vie for the prize. There were six of them, all dressed in Nottingham's traditional archery garb of elaborate capes. None of them looked like Robin Hood. Good. Nicholas hoped the other man stayed far away. He no longer cared if the outlaw was caught, just so Hood was nowhere near Marion.

"Someone in the puppet tent sounded like Robin." Marion told him abruptly.

Nicholas frowned, his gaze snapping back to her face. "You said Hood wasn't there."

"He wasn't. I heard what I thought was his voice, but it wasn't... right. It wasn't him. It was just someone who sounded like him." She met his eyes. "Some*thing* that sounded like him. I think it was the same something I saw outside the brothel."

Nicholas understood where this was headed. "The woman on the midway looked *exactly* like you, Marion. At least, from ten feet or so. If she wasn't you, she was an incredible imitation."

Marion stared at him, saying nothing.

"Shit." Nicholas muttered, searching the depths of her incredible eyes. "It wasn't you."

Her mouth curved at his capitulation. "It wasn't me. I've never been able to ignore you, Nick. Even when I hate you."

His mind raced. "It lured me away from the medical tent, so it could target you."

"I have no idea *why* it would do that, though. It doesn't make sense." Despite the circumstances, he was grateful to have Marion sharing ideas with him again. "You were the victim, last time. Not me. You're the one who ended up dead."

Nicholas shook his head, unable to accept that was even a possibility.

"I think the enchantress was tricking both of us today." Marion continued. "Or some being pretending to be an enchantress, anyway. Some kind of... *thing* that can make people think it's something else. It's tied to King Richard and Robin and whatever the hell they're up to."

Nicholas' jaw clenched. "A Wraith." That was the only explanation. "It's a Wraith."

Chapter Nineteen

**Countdown of the biggest scandals I've ever covered, as a seasoned and impartial reporter of truth:
Number 4: Magical shapeshifting deer are illegally hunting the Merry Men!**

Alan A. Dale- "Nottingham's Naughtiest News"

Marion had done time with just about every type of creature under the sun, but she'd never heard of a Wraith. "What's that?"

"A monster."

"Like an *actual* monster or a regular-criminal-scumbag kind of monster?"

"The first one." He sounded grim. "I don't know *what* they are, really. What they're born looking like or where they come from. Wraiths can change their appearance, so they can be... anything."

"Like a glamour?" Witches used those to transform their looks, all the time.

"No. Wraiths are..." He frowned, trying to explain it. "They can mimic other beings voices and forms. Like a glamour, yes. But they can do *more* than that. They're powerful, because they get in your mind."

"Have you ever seen one?"

"During the war, we fought in some desolate places. Near the Pellinore Mountains, deep in the Wilds, there was... something." He gave his head a shake. "Monsters live in those mountains. Old creatures, rare, better off isolated. But the war riled them up. Disrupted their homes and feeding grounds. Drove them down, towards the fighting."

Marion didn't like to picture Nicholas in the war. She didn't like to picture him anyplace dangerous, where she wasn't there to keep an eye on him. It was why she needed to stalk him forever.

"We'd set up camp, one night, and I was keeping watch." He stared at something only he could see. "It was miserable. Cold. But the stars out there are… endless. So bright you could read by them. They reminded me of my mother."

"Were you wishing on them?"

Nicholas glanced at her. "Yes." He said quietly. "I was wishing on the stars that night, like I always did when I was reading one of the letters…" He stopped, his jaw tightening.

"You were reading a letter?" Marion prompted, when he suddenly broke off.

She didn't need to ask who it was from. It warmed her to know he'd been carrying her letters around with him, reading them for solace on cold and miserable nights. That's why she'd written them, in the first place. So her future husband would feel less alone, even when they were so far apart. She hadn't set out to write Nicholas, but, in every way that mattered, the letters were always his.

Nicholas cleared his throat, not meeting her eyes. "A letter. Yes. And as I sat there, alone and missing my home… Reynold Greenleaf walks by."

"That was unusual?"

"Somewhat. He'd been dead for six days."

Marion winced. "The Wraith was impersonating soldiers?"

"Yes. It was sneaking into camp. I don't know why or how long it had been doing it. But I know that the resulting fight to kill it nearly destroyed the camp and cost dozens of men." He shook his head. "Not even Nessus Theomaddox did more damage to us, that day. And *every day* with him around was a barbarous slaughter."

"Do Wraiths have claws or something?"

"No, *the soldiers* were the ones killing each other, because of what it made us see. I didn't know what was real and what wasn't. No one did. We were fighting amongst ourselves, panicked and confused, while it sat back and watched."

Marion swallowed.

"Wraiths can get inside your head and they know things about the people their pretending to be." Nicholas continued. "The one pretending to be Reynold knew my name. Knew Reynold had sons. How did it know that?"

"Can they predict the future?"

"I don't know. They can create these..." he made a vague gesture, "illusions, though. Images of people and creatures and things. Multiple images. All at once. All moving in different directions. But they're just... projections, I guess? They move, but you can't interact with them. A bear came at me, during the fight. Raced at me and it was as real as anything I've ever seen. I rolled out of the way, but it vanished just as quick as it came." He met her eyes. "*That's* what I saw on the midway. A projection of you."

Marion didn't like the idea of a monster copying her face. At all.

"I'm sorry." Nicholas said simply. "I shouldn't have doubted you."

"I heard Robin's voice. I didn't doubt it was him, until the very end." Marion reached over to touch Nicholas' arm. "Do you think the puppets were an illusion, then? That's why my hat wasn't really shredded."

"And that's why Boulder and the others couldn't find any trace of them."

"They were so *real*, Nick."

"I know."

Marion frowned considering everything he'd said. "You're sure the soldiers stopped the Wraith, during the war? You're sure it's not the same one? Maybe it could've followed you guys home to Nottingham."

"Whatever was disguised as Reynold Greenleaf died in a hale of fiery arrows. I saw the crispy remains myself. I don't know what the Wraith looked like when it was alive, but I know that pile of blackened ash sure as shit wasn't breathing."

"How many of these damn monsters are there?"

"According to Richard, *none*. He called in wizards and rare-species experts, who gave us a slideshow presentation after the encounter to help calm nerves. They said Wraiths always traveled alone, and were exceptionally rare, and there weren't any more of them to worry about." He lifted a shoulder. "The Battle of Kirklees happened not long after that, so no one ever talked about the Wraith again. There's only so much you can hold onto in war. If you try to deal with everything, you'd go crazy."

"Richard's a politician." Marion said flatly. "He'd tell the men anything, if it meant getting on with his beloved crusade. There could've been fifty Wraiths and he wouldn't have warned you."

"Yes." Nicholas agreed and then he was silent for a long moment. "It wasn't just that Reynold Greenleaf was dead, and now he was suddenly walking around, that had the hair on my arms standing up. I knew it wasn't him, because of the eyes."

"The eyes?"

"They weren't... right. I think the Wraith can impersonate people, but it can't make them perfect. If you really know the original, you can spot the fake. I wasn't close with Reynold Greenleaf, but I realized it couldn't truly be him, because the man was dead. So, I looked closer and deeper. And when I did, I could see the eyes were wrong."

"I never saw Robin in the tent. I just heard him calling me and telling me he was there to save me."

Nicholas nodded. "The Wraith knew you'd be able to spot the ruse. When you love someone, it's impossible to mistake them for long, I imagine."

"I don't love Robin."

He ignored that. "It was trying to trick you closer and then grab you before..." He hesitated, catching up with what she'd said. "Hood was calling to you?"

"No, *the Wraith* was calling to me."

"But, you thought it was Hood. Right up until the end, you said."

"Yes. The voice was wrong, during the puppet attack. Maybe it was running out of power. Or maybe it just didn't care." She chewed on her thumbnail and wished it was a cigarette. "I think you're right. It can't make a perfect copy. It can just get really frigging close."

Silence.

Marion glanced his way and saw that Nicholas was staring at her. "What?"

He had a strange expression on his face. "You didn't go to him. You thought it was Hood calling your name and promising to protect you. ...But you stayed."

She met his eyes. "I stayed."

His mouth curved.

Marion found herself smiling back.

Nicholas eventually glanced away, like he was worried she'd see too much. "So... yes. There must be a Wraith in Nottingham." He decided, as if that random summation was just the first thing he could think to say. His conversational skills were truly awful. But in a cute way.

Marion went along with his awkward topic shift. "And of course Robin's now made friends with the damn thing." She hesitated. "He might not *know* it's a Wraith, I guess. He might think it's someone helpful or Good. For all we know, it appears to him like a baby forest elf, with big eyes and braids in its hair."

"Don't defend that idiot!"

"I'm not defending him. You're the one always saying we have to be sure, during an investigation, though. I'm just..."

"Hood almost got you killed by a monster. Fuck investigating. I'm just going to hang him without a trial."

That made her blink. "You were going to give him an actual trial?"

"Of course. Everyone gets a fair trial in Nottingham. Just like that man who broke into the castle got one this morning. Quarry considered the evidence and impartially rendered a verdict." Nicholas nodded righteously. "It was very fair."

"Yeah, the 'very fairness' of it reminded me a lot of *my* trial." Marion deadpanned and then waved it aside. "Whatever. Robin can blow himself. We need to focus on finding this Wraith thing, before it..." She trailed off, her eyes on the tournament field, where the first contestant was approaching the firing line. "Hold on. I need to watch this."

The announcer gave a vivid play-by-play as the archer notched his arrow. Marion tuned out the noise and focused on the guy's body. He was built like Robin, right? But maybe too short? It was hard to be sure. Dammit, this was harder than she'd thought it would be.

Nicholas switched his attention to the field. "Do you see Hood?"

"I haven't laid eyes on him in ten years. Give me a second." Marion squinted down the row of men waiting their turn to shoot, trying to look through the over-the-top, caped getups that all archers wore in Nottingham. The whole kingdom was seriously a fashion desert.

Was one of these guys Robin in disguise? Shit. Why was it so hard to recall the exact shape of his body or how tall he was? Oh. Right. Because her mind had been filled with a big, grouchy gargoyle for the past decade.

She sent Nicholas a sideways look, blaming him for her memory issues.

"I can just arrest everyone who entered this contest." Nicholas offered, missing her accusatory glare. "That would be simpler."

Huh. That *would* be simpler. Marion hesitated. "Would you hang them all?"

"Yes. But, only after their trials."

She rolled her eyes. "Let's just do this my way, for now."

The first contestant shot his arrow. It hit one of the outer rings of the target. Disappointed, the crowd half-heartedly clapped and the man stepped back from the firing line, cursing in frustration.

"Nope." Marion shook her head. "If it's not a bullseye, it's not Robin."

"Hood might suspect this is a trap. He could have deliberately aimed wide to allay our suspicion."

She snorted. "No. He only wants to win. If he can't win, he won't play. It's why he didn't come to the church to rescue me, that day. You'd outmaneuvered him in front of the whole kingdom. He knew it. So, he refused to show up, at all."

Nicholas' brows tugged together. "You think I'm going to beat Hood that badly?"

Marion looked up at him, surprised by his surprise. "You already *did*. You outsmarted us all, Nick. You got everything you wanted and the rest of us were helpless against you."

He made an arrogant sound of approval and settled back in his seat, pleased by that news.

The second archer got ready to fire. He was dressed in yellow. Robin wouldn't wear yellow. He thought it clashed with his reddish-blond hair. Marion wasn't even mildly shocked when he missed the bullseye all together.

"You notice how there aren't any female archers?" She asked with a sad shake of her head. "God forbid Nottingham teach girls how to shoot."

"No gargoyles entered, either." Nicholas kept his eyes on the arena. "Our hands are too big for the bows."

"They make the bows too small for your hands." Marion countered. "Probably on purpose, to help keep you subjugated. Maids and gargoyles," she crossed her fingers to show interconnectedness, "we're the same. Second-class citizens of a third-rate kingdom."

Nicholas said nothing, but his right palm was now tucked out of sight, like he didn't want her to see it.

The third contestant swanned up to the firing-line, giving the crowd a "look at me" wave. The cheers for him were much louder than they'd been for the first two.

"I know him." Marion snapped her fingers, trying to recall his name. "Something with a 'G'. Gifford, maybe? He's kind of famous. I remember that much. All the local girls wanted to sleep with him."

Nicholas didn't look thrilled with that news. He got up from his seat, restlessly moving to the railing of the box. Sitting still and waiting for something to happen went against his nature. He liked to drive forward.

"Gilbert Whitehand is up next!" The announcer proclaimed loudly, breathless with excitement. "We should be in for quite a show, folks!"

"Gilbert! That's it." Marion nodded. "I *knew* he looked familiar." She gave herself a mental pat on the back. "Anyhow, he's not Robin. Gilbert is Nottingham's second-best archer. Robin wouldn't even *pretend* to be him."

Nicholas grunted, his eyes on Gilbert. "Did you?"

Marion watched as Gilbert slammed an arrow into the bullseye. The crowd went wild. "Did I what?"

"Want to sleep with Gilbert?"

She made a face. "No. Archery's never really been my thing."

Nicholas snorted. "Did you ever tell Hood that? Because I've watched you sitting front row at all his matches, since you were sixteen. Clapping for him."

"Robin never asked if I liked archery. No one ever asked what I was interested in, actually. They just thought I should be interested in Robin and what *he* was interested in." She shrugged. "I went to his matches, because I was expected to go. Because, I thought it was my duty as his girlfriend to support him. Not because I wanted to watch dumb sticks fly through the air."

Nicholas turned to stare down at her, for a long minute. "What are you interested in, Marion?" He finally asked.

He knew most of her interests. They'd all been in her letters. But, there was one new thing... "At the moment? Planning our dream wedding."

His head tilted, paying close attention.

Encouraged by his interest, Marion smiled. Discussing the elaborate ceremony she envisioned lightened her mood. "I know it's a little clichéd, but I am really getting into it. I'm sparing no expense, since Richard's paying for it all."

"He is?"

"Of course! He's my nearest male relation, so tradition says he foots the bill. He can't get out of it without looking like a stingy asshole."

"I can afford anything you want, Marion. Gargoyles aren't paid much, but my mother left me a trust fund from her jewelry business."

"Don't be silly. We need all our money for Gala-gum."

"What?"

She kept talking. "Besides, this is the only time Nottingham's sexist bullshit has ever worked in my favor. Nope, I'm charging it all to our glorious, generous king. The vendors are happy to agree."

And there were *a lot* of zeros on her running tabs. Marion was ordering the best of everything. *Two* of the best of everything. It was amazing how fast you could spend money when you really applied yourself. Her glitzy, gilded, flower-bombed wedding was like a money pit of glitter. Expensive shit was being invented just so she could buy it on Nottingham's credit. Hopefully, it would bankrupt Richard's entire reign. Since her cousin was in Lyonesse, she couldn't get revenge face-to-face, but this was just as fun.

Nicholas' mouth curved, as if he was reading her diabolical intentions. "Alan A. Dale mentioned something about fireworks made from liquid rainbows. He's not sure it's such a great idea."

"Oh, it's a *wonderful* idea! Multicolored fireworks are going to spell our sparkling names in the sky, as a pegasus-driven coach ushers us off to our honeymoon."

Nicholas blinked at the word honeymoon. "Wonderful idea." He agreed instantly. "Yes. Let's do *that*."

"Right? Now, for the reception, Cragg and I were looking at bridal magazines and I decided I want ice statues the size of glaciers." Marion continued. "In fact, they'll be *made* of glaciers, from some frozen lake in the Club Kingdom that hasn't even been discovered yet. I've hired explorers to go find it."

Nicholas' smile grew.

"And our wedding cake is going to be *huge*. I've got workmen building a barn-sized oven, just to bake it in. Each layer will be a different variety of rare strawberry. We're importing them from every known land."

"How many known lands are there exactly?"

"Fifty-six hundred." Her eyes gleamed. "We've had to commission an armada of ships to go fetch the berries from all those distant shores, of course. But, I'm *sure* that's what dear cousin Richard would want. Oh and there will be a thirty piece orchestra! All their instruments are made of magic. Literally."

"Make it fifty magic instruments." He murmured. "Why be subtle?"

"Exactly! I really want everyone in this whole damn kingdom to look at our wedding and positively *hate* how flashy it is. I want them to hate us for being so happy and hate themselves for being losers with no gigantic ice sculptures, magical instruments, or strawberry cake." She sighed in delight, her face shining with evil ideas. "It's going to be great."

Nicholas kissed her.

She hadn't been expecting that. The man had spent all morning telling her not to touch him, for fear of social backlash. Then, he goes and kisses her in front of everyone? He was so unpredictable. It was no wonder she didn't listen to half the crazy stuff he said. Did he even listen to himself?

She drew in a quick gasp of surprise, as he stepped forward and lifted her from her seat, his mouth on hers. Nicholas took her parted lips as an invitation. His tongue slipped between them, slowly tasting her. Taking his time. Not caring who saw them.

Marion hadn't cared who saw them in the first place, so she was fine with making out in public. She'd kiss Nicholas anytime, anywhere. And he seemed to need reassurance of that. Her arms twined around his neck, accepting him.

He groaned at her eager response. "Thank you." He whispered, his large palms stroking her hair and back.

He always said "thank you" when she gave herself over to him. It was very sweet. In fact, this entire kiss was sweeter than his usual dominant possession. Gentler. Slower. As if he was savoring her. She was *seriously* into it. Her body melted into his grasp, letting him take his time. She felt her nipples tightening, pressing against his big chest. Her breasts were hyper-sensitive to him, now. Remembering his touch. Responding to the pheromones he gave off. Jutting out, craving more.

Nicholas made an approving sound, feeling her desire

build. "You're so pretty when you're being Bad, Marion. I love to see your mind work."

Marion barely noticed as he maneuvered her up against the balcony of the royal box. He didn't put his hands anywhere shocking, but her body was still on fire. Nicholas kissed her with unhurried authority. Like he had every right in the world to have her in his arms and nobody could stop him. It was *such* a turn on.

Somebody was for certain going to get a picture of it for the tabloids, though. They were surrounded by hundreds of spectators and there was plenty of time to reach for cameras. Maybe that was his intent. Nicholas was always up to something. It was one of the qualities she admired most about him.

"Are you trying to become even more unpopular with the townsfolk?" She casually inquired, as he took a detour to nuzzle her neck. "Or block out all the tournament noise that's bugging the hell out of you? Or are you attempting to piss off Robin?"

"Choice 'D': I'm just helplessly and psychotically obsessed with you. And you promised me last night I could kiss you whenever I wanted, today."

"You already kissed me at breakfast."

"We'll count this as part of my betrothal rights, then."

The man did love claiming those. "I told you, I'm not sure you can demand kisses under the rules." Marion said, just to tease him.

His teeth grazed her neck, like he wanted to mark her. "I've also been considering my earlier worries about your reputation and it occurs to me I was thinking about it all wrong. If you're *me*... what's the downside in publically compromising you?"

"Well," Marion drawled out, suddenly seeing his grand plan. "If you ruin a Maid, you have to marry her. It's only gentlemanly."

"Exactly. So, I think I'm going to ruin you. Thoroughly. Then, all the noble idiots will stay away. No one else will come riding to your rescue, duchess. You'll be stuck with just me."

He smirked at his own genius. "Once you're a fallen woman... I'll be the only one who can catch you."

"Team Creative Villainy."

"I thought you'd appreciate my wicked scheme." His tongue returned to touch the corner of her mouth. "God, I have wanted to taste that strawberry lip gloss you're wearing, ever since I watched you buy it at the store two weeks ago."

She bit back a whimper of lust. "You watched me buy lip gloss?"

"I watch you constantly. It's bordering on illegal."

Personally, Marion was okay with going fully illegal. She couldn't stand it when he was out of her sight, so she was already considering GPS trackers for her groom. Who knew what might happen to him, if he wandered away?

"So, is the lip gloss living up to the hype?" She whispered seductively.

His mouth went to her ear. "I want to smear it all over your body and then lick it off." He nipped at her skin.

Marion shivered and laughed at the same time. "Holy *shit*, I love it when you're Bad, too." She really, really did. A decade spent fixating on the man had not been wasted, because he'd been just as fixated on her. "Let's go home and you can demand some betrothal rights, tiger."

His eyes softened and Marion realized she'd just called the castle "home." It wasn't, of course. She didn't even like the castle. "Home" was just anyplace Nicholas was.

"We can't go home, yet." He braced his hands on the railing, one on each side of her. It was the predatory posture of a male animal cornering his mate. Marion's back was to the tournament field, which ordinarily would've bothered her. Prison had taught her to stand with her back against walls. But, she just *adored* it when he captured her. "We have to watch the rest of the archery contest."

Marion blinked. She'd forgotten that was even a thing. "Oh." She said blankly. "That."

Nicholas seemed amused by her response. "Oh, *that*." He agreed and pressed a kiss to her temple. "Jesus, you smell so good, Marion. I can't breathe without wanting you. You have no idea how many times..."

He didn't get to finish that very nice compliment, unfortunately. He was distracted by the arrow flying at his head.

Chapter Twenty

Editorial: Nottingham was wrong to ban guns. Arrows are the *true* danger.

Alan A. Dale- "Nottingham's Naughtiest News"

When Robin shot an arrow, it never missed.

The deadly projectile wasn't aimed at Marion --It was aimed at Nicholas-- but he still moved to protect her, rather than himself. She was too shocked to even process it. Nicholas grabbed Marion and shielded her body, before she even knew what was happening. His huge form curved around hers like a force field, so only he was exposed to the attack.

Marion cried out in fear, as the arrow struck him in the back. It was meant to kill him. It *should've* killed him. She expected an explosion of blood, but instead the arrow bounced off his right shoulder and fell harmlessly to the wooden floor of the box.

Her huge eyes met his. "Nick." She breathed, still irrationally sure he was somehow mortally wounded and that her brand new life was already over. "Don't die, again. *Please* don't die, again!" Her voice bordered on hysteria by the final word.

Nicholas half-carried her backwards, so they were sheltered by the box's wooden enclosure. "I won't die." He didn't let her go, his voice soothing and alive in her ear. Trying to keep her calm. "The arrow hit stone. The stone goes down my right side. It didn't penetrate my skin. It's alright."

Marion nodded somewhat wildly and tried to search his body to be sure.

He kissed her forehead, even as his eyes scanned the tournament field. She felt him still. Marion moved her head to peer around his gigantic body, wanting to see what had captured his attention.

Instantly, her eyes fell on an archer dressed in solid tree-frog green. He was standing alone in the middle of the arena, the bow he'd used to fire at Nicholas still clutched in his hand. He'd been waiting his turn to compete. The last man in line. From under the hood of his heavy cloak she could feel his angry blue eyes burning into hers. Blaming her for all of this.

"Robin's here." She whispered.

It was really him, not one of the Wraith's illusions. No monster could reproduce that familiar look of hypocritical judgement and entitled superiority.

"That miserable little fuck." Nicholas' words were dark and low. "That's the second time today he shot an arrow at you."

"He was trying to kill *you*, not me!" This was wrong. This was all wrong. "Nick, this isn't the plan!"

Nicholas grasped her chin between his thumb and forefinger, forcing her to meet his relentless gaze. "A confrontation *will* come, Marion. It might as well be now. Hood and I have been on this path, ever since he first approached you and said you were his."

She gaped up at him. "No, that's not what this is about!"

"You are *all* that this is about."

"*No.* There has to be some other..."

He was already moving. Nicholas vaulted over the railing and landed on the grass. Despite their size, gargoyles were surprisingly agile. In less than two seconds, he was stalking towards Robin.

Marion had the impression of the other gargoyles moving through the crowd. Reacting to the shooting far faster than she did.

"Quarry! Protect Marion!" Nicholas bellowed to the closest guard.

"I don't need to be protected!" Marion screamed after him. "Get back here!"

He kept moving towards his nemesis. Nicholas always fought head-on.

Robin didn't.

Panic consumed her. If she jumped over the railing, like he had, she'd probably fracture her skull. Unlike Nicholas, she wasn't particularly athletic. She also didn't want to take her eyes off Robin and Nicholas, though, so that meant turning towards the stairs was out.

She was stuck.

Quarry climbed up the side of the royal box, before she could come up with a solution. Literally *climbed* it, like the elaborate woodwork was a ladder, and pulled himself inside.

Could she do that? Maybe. She might break a leg, but no one died of a broken leg.

"No, Maid Marion." Quarry moved into her path, anticipating her intention to try his route down to the ground. "Let them fight."

Was everyone insane?

"Robin shot Nick. He never did that before!" She shifted to get around Quarry's large body. "I've changed something, by being here. If Nick confronts him like this, I don't know what will happen. I don't *know* and I won't risk it. I have to make Nick stop!"

"Nothing will make him stop." Quarry's arm blocked her path without actually touching her skin. "Gargoyles are primitive."

"What?" Marion was distracted for half a second. "You guys aren't primitive. You're every bit as civilized as..."

Quarry cut her off. "We are about *this*. Hood wants to take you. The commander will die before that happens. There is no arguing with him. There never has been about you."

"I don't want Nick to die! That's the whole *point*."

"He won't. There isn't a contest between the commander and that human boy." Quarry made a dismissive face. Robin had been born before Nicholas, but Nicholas was so much older. Everyone saw it. "Just stay here and enjoy the show."

Marion shook her head. The tournament field had gone quiet. She could hear Robin shouting nonsense, but Nicholas' responses were too low to carry. What was Robin thinking, shooting at such a sweet, soft-spoken man? Aside from the hangings, and the war, and probably a bunch of other stuff she didn't know about, Nicholas had never hurt anyone!

Robin was supposed to be the Good guy, but he'd clearly missed the fucking memo.

She told Nicholas that her ex was calculating and distant, but even she hadn't anticipated her breezily self-involved former boyfriend turning into a goddamn sniper. He'd just tried to straight-up murder Nicholas! It shocked her.

It scared her.

Marion had survived prison without a total freak-out, but now she was on the verge of tears. Fine tremors ran through her body, a reaction to how close she'd come to losing Nicholas. His vulnerability suddenly struck her. He'd died once. He could die again, at any moment.

Marion couldn't let that happen.

"Robin's acting crazy." She whispered.

"Your plan worked." Quarry made it all sound simple. "He came to this archery contest, thinking it would be an easy way to thumb his nose at the commander. Then, he saw you two kissing, got enraged, and decided to kill his rival. Gargoyles might be primitive, but humans are even simpler to understand."

Down below, Robin was screaming some gibberish about blowjobs, but she didn't even care enough to listen. All she cared about was Nicholas. She had to reach him. She had to *save* him.

Marion wasn't just "unhealthily fixated" on Nick Greystone.

She was madly in love with the man.

Her eyes went to the balcony again, deciding on the best place to climb down. She would beat the shit out of Robin and reclaim her happily-ever-after. Nothing would stop her from protecting Nicholas.

...And right about then her sweet, vulnerable, soft-spoken groom punched Robin Hood right in the face.

***

The Sheriff of Nottingham stalked towards Robin Hood.

It was the showdown the entire kingdom had been waiting for. In the stands, people grew quiet. (Fucking *finally*.) They were waiting to see what would happen next. Hoping that Hood triumphed against his evil gargoyle foe.

Nicholas didn't give a shit about the audience's opinion. His eyes were focused on Hood's boyishly handsome face. Hating him. Somewhere along the line his thinking had switched. He no longer saw himself as the villain, out to steal Marion from Hood. He now saw Hood as the asshole trying to steal Marion from *him*.

And no one was stealing Marion from him.

If you kill Hood, Marion might not forgive you.

That was a rational, quasi-moral thought, very unlike his reverse conscience. Perhaps even the deepest, darkest parts of him knew he was wading into dangerous waters. But still he went, because his obsession with the woman was too deep for logic. There was only the primal knowledge that another man was threatening to take the one person who mattered to him most.

"You're an inhuman *thing*." Robin shouted, his voice carrying across the field. He hadn't liked gargoyles as a boy and he didn't like them now. "You're not even really *real*. You think I'll let you get away with defiling a virtuous Maiden?"

Nicholas kept walking.

Robin took an instinctive step back. He still had the bow in his hand, but he wasn't going to shoot. His own vanity wouldn't let him. Everyone was watching. Firing that arrow at Nicholas before had been an explosion of anger and shock, from a True Love whose innocent bride was being pawed by a nefarious rock-monster. Nottingham would wave it away. But, if he assassinated the duly-appointed sheriff, with the entire May Day Festival watching, it would be a lot harder to explain. He'd never be able to play noble hero again and he knew it.

"Allow Maid Marion to return home." Robin tried, his voice rising for the crowd's benefit. "Free my men from the dungeon. Return Friar Tuck to the church. Otherwise, I'll make you pay, Sheriff. And all these Good people are with me!"

Nicholas stopped directly in front of him.

And waited.

Robin stood there, breathing hard. His eyes darted to the stands of people, to Nicholas, back to the people, back to Nicholas.

No one was rushing forward to help him.

Obviously.

Nottinghamers weren't dumb enough to get involved in this fight. The gloomy populous had their own problems. Not to mention gargoyles were moving through the crowd, watching for any dissenters. No. This was just Nicholas and Hood. As it was always meant to be.

Robin saw he was alone. His mouth thinned, his mind racing for a new plan. He'd trapped himself over a spray-painted arrow, just as Marion intended. Ordinarily, the Merry Men could be counted on for backup, but thanks to Marion, Nicholas had captured them all. Robin's ego had thoroughly boxed him in, as Marion predicted it would.

She'd been right about everything.

The woman's creative villainy was such a turn on.

Nicholas crossed his arms over his chest. "I can arrest you now." He told Robin quietly. "Or you can talk shit for a while. Then, I'll break your jaw. *Then,* I'll arrest you. Choose."

Celestial blue eyes met his, wild and furious. Clearly, Hood was going for the shit-talking option. "Marion's only with you because she's pissed at me, for some reason. I could have her back anytime I wanted."

"Maybe. But your reunion will be short, since I'm going to hang you in about ten minutes."

Robin's temper exploded. "Marion is *my* girl! *My* True Love!" He pounded a fist against his chest. "Not yours! Mine!"

Nicholas said nothing, because that was true.

"I always saw the way you'd watch her." Robin ranted. "Your soulless eyes looking at what's mine. I thought it was funny that a gargoyle wanted a Maid. Destiny gave her to *me*. I'm going to make her my forest queen. You think you can just steal her away?"

Nicholas' head tilted. Hood didn't mention Marion's wishes. Not even once. Just his own. Like she was a doll he'd won in some carnival game.

And are you much better? Did you ask her what she wanted, before you kidnapped her?

Nicholas stifled a wince. His reverse conscience was behaving like a regular conscience today and he didn't like it.

"And do you really think I'm stupid enough to fall for this wedding scheme you've cooked up?" Robin went on, with a harsh laugh. "Nothing is going to happen in that cathedral. You'll drag her to the altar, she'll say 'no' and then what? Huh?" He lifted his hands and dropped them again in an expansive shrug. "You're not going to hurt her. We both know that. Your big dumb self is in love with her, right? So, this wedding you've planned to capture *me*…? It's really just going to make *you* look like a pussy-whipped fool."

The wedding was a bit of a moot point, considering Hood was already trapped. Hood didn't seem to care about that.

Neither did Nicholas.

"Marion's going to say 'yes' at the altar." Despite her reassurances, Nicholas wasn't so sure about that, but he sounded sure and that was enough. "I'll either capture you or I'll have a wife. I'd say the plan is sound."

"Bullshit! The woman's blood is the purest in Nottingham. She'll never say 'yes' to a gargoyle."

"She's said 'yes' to me, so far."

Nicholas was awkward with words. He'd been thinking of Marion accepting his proposal when he'd made that taunt. But the second the sentence left his mouth, he knew Hood would interpret it in the most lascivious way possible.

He mentally swore at his own stupidity. Marion would probably not be happy, when she heard about this, and Nicholas didn't like doing anything that made Marion unhappy.

Hood's nostrils flared. "Well, if she's fucking a rock-monster like you, she's obviously no Maid." He screamed. "You haven't claimed anything special. She's probably giving blowjobs to every millers' son!"

The entirety of the festival stands turned to look at Much-the-Miller.

"No!" He surged to his feet, beet red in the face. "I swear, I never..."

Nicholas slammed his fist into Robin's jaw. The stony surface crashed into flesh, bone and teeth breaking. He didn't think about it before it happened. He just hauled off and punched that smug bastard, the way he'd been imagining for fourteen years. Ever since that fucking little punk hit Marion with that rock, he'd wanted to beat the shit out of him. It felt fantastic to live his dream.

Robin Hood had not been expecting the punch.

God only knew why. Nicholas had warned him. Maybe he was just used to battling with quarterstaffs and quivers, instead of fists. The outlaw gave one desperate squawk of surprise and then his eyes rolled up in his head. He tumbled backwards, hitting the ground with a thud. Unconscious.

Nicholas grunted. One punch? Really? That was so... unsatisfying.

He sighed and glanced towards the closest gargoyle. "Arrest him." He ordered, a bit disappointed it was done so fast.

Gravol was standing there, his wide, guileless eyes on Hood's splayed form. "Should we hang him, right now, Commander?"

Nicholas absolutely wanted to string him up right then and there. He wanted Hood gone for good, but he needed answers about the Wraith. Also, Marion might be upset if he hanged an unconscious man. Especially, *this* unconscious man. She was talking to Nicholas again, and kissing him, and smiling at him. He wasn't about to screw that up or risk her safety, because of his impatience to get rid of this arrogant ass.

"Wait for him to wake up. Then, we'll torture him for information. *Then*, we'll hang him." Hopefully, Marion would appreciate his mercy.

Gravol saluted his order and began carting Hood off to

the dungeon. The gargoyle was so massive, it didn't take much effort. Hood's stupid green shoes left long marks in the dirt, as he was dragged along. All around the arena, the citizens of Nottingham silently watched their hero's comatose body lugged off like baggage. There were some gasps and crying, but no one moved to intercede. Marion was right. Nottinghamers were pretty useless.

"So... we can continue on with the contest, then?" Gilbert Whitehand asked no one in particular. The kingdom's second-best archer suddenly had an opportunity to take first-place and he wanted to grab for it.

Yep. Nottinghamers really were the worst.

Nicholas ignored the man's arrow-shooting ambitions. His eyes went up to the royal box, where Marion was gazing down at him. He wasn't sure what he expected her to do or say, now that he'd defeated her True Love. Maybe she'd be conflicted. Or upset. Or pissed at him.

His gaze locked with her wide brown eyes. She looked shocked.

He sighed and headed for her. Of course he did. Marion was the only direction he'd ever go.

Using the same method Quarry had used, he easily climbed up to the royal box. When he reached the top, Marion was standing on one side of the balcony and he was on the other. He paused there, the railing between them, waiting for her to say something. Braced for her to tell him all the things he didn't want to hear.

She could leave now.

How could Nicholas possibly justify kidnapping her, if Hood was in jail? How could he rationalize the wedding as a trap, when Hood was already caught? Nicholas really should have thought this out more, because it seemed like he'd just screwed himself over.

He watched Marion warily, his predictable mind trying to come up with some creative villainy of his own that would keep her safely captured.

"One punch?" She finally whispered.

Nicholas lifted a shoulder, not sure if she was

complaining or just surprised. He waved a hand at Quarry, dismissing him.

Quarry took the hint and loped off to help the others, smiling cheerily. At least someone was happy.

Marion's eyes continued to roam all over Nicholas' face. "No one *ever* beats Robin… And you knocked him out without even trying. You captured him. You really did it. With *one punch.*"

That sounded… okay? She wasn't yelling. "Hood deserved it. He insulted you. I'll break the jaw of anyone who does that."

Marion's pupils literally dilated. "I have never been more attracted to you than I am right now." She swallowed hard. "Let's go home and make babies. *Right now.*"

Of all the possible reactions she could have given him that one wasn't even on his list. Nicholas' eyebrows soared. He grappled for a response. "I'm a gargoyle. We can't procreate."

"Even better. We'll just have sex for fun." She leaned over the balcony to kiss him lavishly.

He groaned and chuckled at the same time, loving her enthusiasm. "Well, there's also the matter of you losing our bet. You did wager me your virtue that Hood wouldn't explode over our engagement. …Seems like I won."

"It's all yours." She half-dragged him over the railing, closer to her. "Take me now, Nick. I am totally fucking serious."

Overwhelming relief swept through him. Marion wasn't turning him away. She wasn't mad he'd captured Robin Hood. She was proud of him. That was so much better than winning an anticlimactic fight with his mortal enemy. Just so she was at his side, Nicholas didn't much care what else happened.

Except right about then, everything caught fire.

Chapter Twenty-One

Robin Hood's shocking arrest leaves Nottingham crippled with grief.
All hope is now lost.
What the triumph of evil means for your horoscope!

Alan A. Dale- "Nottingham's Naughtiest News"

The Nottinghamers screamed in terror.

Flames erupted from the ground, tall and sparking with magical energy. They zigzagged in intricate, impossible patterns, spiraling out in all directions

Nicholas broke off the kiss, shielding Marion from the unrelenting heat. He didn't need to do that, but she was too preoccupied by the inferno to tell him so.

For a second, she thought the spectacle was the Wraith's doing. Some new trick the mysterious, puppet-wielding monster had cooked up to roast them alive. She expected the inferno to spread rapidly through the wooden buildings of the fair, destroying everything it touched.

But, it didn't.

Something else was happening here. The necklace in her pocket vibrated at a far greater frequency than it had before, indicating more magic than the Wraith had given off. *Lots* more magic. The terrifying fire stayed contained. And in the center of it all, there were two rows of parallel flames, clearing a walkway. Perfect and precise. Controlled by some unseen force. The strength of the power was astonishing. Impossible.

And pointlessly, annoyingly showy.

Her eyes narrowed.

Around Marion, the May Day Festival emptied out in record time. The gargoyles were stretched thin trying to keep the citizens from killing each other in the stampede. Marion wondered why they even bothered. Nottingham didn't have anyone worth saving, anyway.

Nicholas stared at the roiling flames with dark suspicion. "Is this the Wraith?"

"No, this one is my doing." Marion muttered. "I invited the guy."

"What guy?"

"The arrogant dickhead who's about to make this day even lousier." She exhaled in annoyance. "For real, this is the worst May Day Festival ever and they *all* fucking sucked. You should have taken me home to have sex, like I wanted."

Nicholas ignored that truth. "Who's coming, Marion?" He sounded impatient with the lack of a straight answer.

"A friend. Kinda-sorta. Just let me handle him, alright?" She patted his arm. "Do that thing where you don't talk and maybe he'll cooperate quicker than usual."

Nicholas was visibly unhappy with the universe.

A tall, powerfully-built man appeared. He calmly walked between the lines of raging fire, like they were the edges of a red carpet welcoming him to town. He was younger than when she'd known him. Less hardened. His hair was the same, long and black and studded with beads. He wore a trench coat embroidered with flames along its hem and a bored expression on his exotically beautiful face, as people fled for their lives.

Creating abject terror was all in a day's work for Trevelyan, Last of the Green Dragons.

Marion shook her head in exasperation. She was happy to see him alive again, but she'd nearly forgotten how much trouble he could be. "Goddamn it, Trev! You just screwed-up a really great kiss with your damn theatrics."

Trevelyan didn't look very repentant. No surprise. He'd never repented for anything in his whole nefarious life. Like all dragons, Trevelyan was unceasingly dramatic, uncaring to the point of cruelty, and unwilling to help another living soul without payment. He also killed a lot of people.

Beside her, Nicholas stiffened, getting a good look at their guest and knowing he was the sauntering personification of Bad news. How could you miss it?

"You must be the woman who sent me the note." Trevelyan stopped beneath the royal box and stared up at Marion with a slight frown. "My, you're quite ordinary, aren't you? I expected someone far more interesting."

Nicholas made a low sound.

Marion put a restraining hand on his arm. "Sorry to disappoint you." She told Trevelyan, not taking the bait. "I'm Marion. The one-and-fucking-only. Good to see you, again." A pause. "Well, *slightly* good."

"I'm never Good." He arched a brow. "We've met, I take it?"

"We will."

"And I let you survive?"

"So far." She mockingly knocked on the wooden railing. "The real question is: Will I let *you* survive? Right now, it's sixty/forty 'no more green dragons,' dickhead."

His mouth curved into a grin that was nothing but demonic intentions and glinting teeth. "Ah... Now, I see the spark." He murmured, almost to himself.

Marion wasn't sure what that meant.

Nicholas seemed to understand it just fine. He shifted so his body was partially in front of her. He didn't say anything. He just stood there, watching Trevelyan. From the outside, he looked calm, but she could feel his tension. She'd never seen him quite so focused before. Not even with Robin. It must've been how he acted when he was braced for an actual battle.

Shit.

Trevelyan arched a dark brow, viewing Nicholas' move as aggressive. That just reinforced Marion's idea that Nicholas was ready to go to war with a guy who could transform into a fifteen-foot rampaging dragon. He was too smart for that, right? And Trevelyan saw most *everything* as aggressive, so maybe he was just overreacting, right?

."You have a pet gargoyle, Marion dear?" Brilliant green eyes stayed on Nicholas. "Now *that's* interesting. Beings made from magic are always interesting." Trevelyan hesitated for effect. "I'm made *of* magic, though. Very different. Very much... better."

"Not to me." Marion said easily, trying to ratchet down the brewing conflict. "And Nick isn't my pet. I'm marrying him on Wednesday, dumbass. You can come if you want. We'll use you to brûlée the three-hundred strawberry crème brûlées I ordered."

Nicholas stayed quiet and didn't move. She could see him plotting how he was going to hang Trevelyan. Yeah... this wasn't going well. And before it got any worse, she'd better head off Trevelyan's next move.

Marion leaned in closer to Nicholas. "I never let him touch me." She assured him softly, because that was bound to be an issue real soon. With Trevelyan it was inevitable. He was an intensely sexual being and also a total ass-hat. "I never let anyone but you touch me, Nick. And Trev never pushed it. He offered. I said no. End of story."

Sex was nothing personal to Trevelyan. He casually propositioned half the people he met. As far as she could tell, very few turned him down. The fact that Marion wouldn't sleep with him was probably the reason he'd initially hung around with her. The novelty of it seemed to entertain him.

"How many times did he offer?" Nicholas' words were so low that only she could hear them.

Marion hesitated a beat too long.

Nicholas grunted, correctly interpreting that pause to mean "*so* many times." His expression didn't change, but she still felt his hostility building towards the dragon. He for sure thought that it was a rotten idea to invite fire-breathing, sexually uninhibited, magical criminals over for a friendly visit.

Marion felt the need to defend herself from all the silent ranting. "He's the only dragon I know and we need that scepter back." She reminded Nicholas, while keeping her attention on the evil-doer she'd summoned. It wasn't safe to take your eyes off of Trevelyan for long. "By the way, I had to sell Richard's coronation robes to afford the enchanted delivery charges for that note. I forgot to tell you, I stole them earlier."

Nicholas snorted, like he didn't believe she "forgot" and also didn't much care about the robes. It was amazing how much he could say, while saying so little.

Marion returned to the cause of her burgeoning migraine and raised her voice, so he could hear her. "I didn't expect you to get here so fast, Trev."

"Yes, I'm sure it's a shock." Trevelyan drawled sarcastically and reached into the pocket of his dumb leather coat. It was May, for God's sake. He extracted a folded sheet of paper and shook it open, so he could read her letter verbatim. "'Dear Trevelyan, I'm from the future and I know how you die. Stop by Nottingham, if you want to chat. Best Wishes, Maid Marion." He paused. "See, that message struck me as somewhat urgent."

Marion nodded, still pleased with her poetic turn-of-phrase. "I really am *incredible* at correspondence. Right, Nick?"

He sent her a quick, slightly worried, look, trying to decipher what she knew about the letters he'd stolen from her.

Marion smiled back innocently.

Trevelyan didn't seem impressed with her literary skills. "Remind me how we'll know each other, again. Remembering the future is one skill I don't possess. ...Yet."

"We'll meet in prison, years from now. I traveled back and thought I'd say 'hi.'"

The news that she'd jumped through time didn't seem to faze him. Trevelyan knew more about magic than anyone she'd ever met. She wasn't sure if he was made from magic, as he'd claimed, but she knew it was part of a dragon's DNA. All of them were magically gifted. If the witch-practitioner could identify Tansy's residual magic lingering around her, Trevelyan would be able to scent it like perfume.

"Hatter?" He guessed, right on cue.

"Hatter." She agreed.

Trevelyan made a considering face. "You're becoming more interesting." He allowed.

"Impressing you is my life's goal, ass-wipe."

His head tilted, the beads in his long hair melodiously shifting. "Oh, yes... I *definitely* see the spark, now. I knew you must have it or I never would have paid attention, in the first place."

Marion wasn't going to let that remark pass again. "What spark?"

"The one Good girls sometimes have. Not many of them, sad to say. Only the most delectable seem to light up with it. Life and purity and *ideas*, shining in your pretty eyes." He made an appreciative sound. "Yours is *bright*, Marion. No wonder we're destined to be such grand... friends." The word was full of all kinds of sleazy implications.

Nicholas' smoky gaze narrowed like death.

Trevelyan smirked, loving that he'd provoked a reaction.

Nicholas shifted, as if he was about to start forward.

"Trev saved my life." Marion blurted out, knowing that might be the only thing she could say that would prevent a fight. Not a one-punch knockout, like with Robin, but a brawl that left both men bleeding on the ground.

Nicholas and Trevelyan jerked their attention away from each other to stare at her with various degrees of surprise.

Marion ignored the dragon, her eyes on Nicholas. "Don't." She whispered. "He's a jerkoff, but he won't hurt me. This is all just a game for him." Trevelyan loved to play games.

His gaze flicked back to the dragon, but he remained still.

Marion refocused on Trevelyan. "And you're a colossal dickhead, but we're kinda-sorta friends."

"Are we?"

"Yep. And you did help me, once. I'm about to return the favor."

Marion and Trevelyan had always been unaccountably loyal to each other in jail, despite the fact he was the worst-of-the-worst, while she was seen as an easy target for every villain in the place. Being Good in a prison full of Bad folk meant Marion had been an outcast from the day she arrived.

During her first months of incarceration, she'd survived

by thinking, "What would Clorinda say?" and then doing her very best to channel her former lady-in-waiting's off-the-charts spitefulness during all confrontations. That had helped some, because Clorinda was a scary, psychotic bitch. Still, Marion had to get tough *fast* and stay alert every minute. As a result, she'd grown more in touch with her own Badness, less afraid (because what did she really have to lose?) and she'd always been ready to throw down with maniacs twice her size.

She thought maybe her do-or-die intensity entertained Trevelyan.

"I don't help anyone, but myself." He told her, like she'd insulted him by even suggesting otherwise. "And I'd certainly never *save* anyone." He made a vaguely repulsed sound.

"It was a spur-of-the-moment impulse." Marion assured him.

She hadn't been paying enough attention, that day. She'd been "unhealthily fixating" on Nicholas. An orc with a body-odor problem had grabbed her from behind and tried to drag her into a closet. It was the nearest she ever came to disaster, in the WUB Club. And it had been *very* close. She'd been fighting, but the guy outweighed her by two-hundred pounds. She would've lost.

Except right at that moment, Trevelyan was on his way to group therapy. He'd strolled past the struggle on his route, wearing his red level "EVIL" sweatshirt and a bored expression. He'd casually come up behind the orc, broken the guy's neck with a negligent twist of his wrist, and just... kept walking. Not a word to Marion. She'd been left gasping for oxygen, with a dead orc carcass beside her, and very few plausible explanations for how it happened.

But no one bothered her much after that.

That was another reason she'd written Trevelyan the note. *Kodamara vadu.*

Trevelyan studied her without blinking. "I need proof we'll meet in the future. I never believe anything I can't see for myself." He'd always been a mistrustful bastard.

"What do you want? Some kind of time-travel

passport, stamped ten years from now?" Marion shot back. "Use your head. I can't show you what hasn't happened yet."

"Paint me a convincing scene, then." He demanded, ready to look for flaws in her story. "First time I ever saw you, what happened?"

Nicholas made a low sound of warning at the challenge in his tone.

Trevelyan slanted him a dark look in return.

The dragon was beginning to view Nicholas as an opponent. Nicholas' silence annoyed him. Trevelyan liked to talk. And Nicholas was already seeing Trevelyan as a threat. The two of them were going to be a problem if she didn't defuse the situation.

Luckily, she knew the answer to Trevelyan's dragon-y test question. She vividly remembered the moment they met, because it was another one of the times she'd felt closest to death. "First time I ever saw you, I put a cigarette out on your hand, because you cut in line in the cafeteria."

Nicholas winced a bit, like he was imagining that scene and wondering how she'd survived. Marion wondered that herself.

Trevelyan's attention sharpened.

"It was lukewarm porridge." Marion went on. "It was *always* lukewarm porridge. I have no damn clue why you wanted to hurry for it, Trev. I lost twenty pounds on that godawful food."

"Oh, Lord. That would be tragic." He lamented with a heartfelt *tsk*.

Nicholas scowled at him, even though his earlier fascination with her breast size indicated that he agreed with the overall sentiment.

Marion kept talking to Trevelyan. "You turned and super-calmly asked how I wanted to die. I responded," she cleared her throat, because it really wasn't her Maidly-est moment, "'in bed, fucking your mother.'"

Trevelyan made a considering face. "Mother would have liked that."

"Last time you said 'father.'"

"Both are true."

"So then, you seemed kind of... amused, I guess? You didn't kill me, anyway. I walked off, thinking that was the end of it. But, you came over and sat down at my lunch table. You spent the whole meal telling me about some new magic spell you were working on. And how nobody understood it, except you, because you were just *so* smart. And there was a typo. Something about..." She thought for a second, searching her memory. "Sealing wax?"

Green eyes widened and his mocking expression changed to one of surprise.

"Anyway, I tried to switch tables and you followed me." She went on. "I threatened to poison your gruel and you went off on a tangent about your favorite poisons to use on people and how funny it was when they bled-out through their eyes. *That* was great for the appetite."

At the time, it had bugged the crap out of her that Trevelyan wouldn't go away, but it did weirdly ensure that most of the random scumbags who propositioned her on a daily basis permanently backed off. Far, *far* off. With Trevelyan circling Marion, every other male fled. Maybe that was why he'd killed the orc, come to think of it. Dragons didn't share well with others.

Neither did gargoyles.

Nicholas *hated* this story. Hated that she had any kind of history with Trevelyan, no matter how platonic. She could see the muscles in his jaw clenching. He wasn't going to back off, regardless of what Trevelyan did. The sexy possessiveness was kind of flattering. Not many men would fight a dragon for a girl. And he looked incredibly handsome when he was brooding.

Still, she didn't want him to worry over nothing, so she shifted closer to him. Clearing her throat, she wrapped up her recollections. "After that, you ate lunch with me every day, Trev. I asked you why and you just... smiled."

Trevelyan smiled the same damn smile he'd smiled at her in the cafeteria. "Dragons appreciate a woman with fire." He murmured, convinced by her crazy tale. He looked her over appraisingly, his voice a purr. "And I must have appreciated you *very* much, Marion dear."

Dickhead.

"Enough." Nicholas intoned. It was a warning.

Trevelyan's head tilted in a way that hinted at violence, not playing dumb about what Nicholas' flat "enough" meant. He mulled over whether he should start a fight, just for the hell of it. Because he was Trevelyan, he --of course-- went with "yes."

"She's yours in *this* timeline, gargoyle." He gave a lazy shrug, but his eyes were watchful. "Maybe in the other one, she's mine."

Nicholas took a step towards the railing, done talking. One word was apparently plenty.

"No." Marion grabbed his arm and sent an aggravated glower towards Trevelyan. "Jesus, you always have to cause pointless trouble. "I never touched you in any timeline."

She'd never even considered it. Twenty-six years of Nottingham's indoctrination meant it was hard for Marion to seriously contemplate sex outside of marriage. Even when she knew it was mostly chauvinist horseshit, the idea of anyone other than her husband touching her still felt wrong on an instinctive level.

Unless it was Nicholas. She would've happily slept with him, vows or no.

Trevelyan's gaze cut between Nicholas and Marion, as if they were the ones causing drama. "So, you'd fuck *him* and not me?"

"Yes! *Of course,* I'm going to fuck him and not you. I'm marrying him in two days. Which means, I'm going to fuck *just* Nick, and nobody else, *forever*."

Too bad those eloquent words couldn't be her wedding vows, because Nicholas seemed genuinely moved by them. His whole body jolted, his attention riveted on her face.

Trevelyan frowned at her, pityingly. "Just the gargoyle forever? Dear God... *Why?*" He seemed honestly baffled.

Rather than become more pissed at the dragon, Nicholas looked like he wanted to hear her answer, too.

"Well, I mean," Marion shrugged, because at least one reason was obvious to everyone with eyes, "*look* at him. Who else can compare to my handsome groom?"

Nicholas' mouth curved and she felt some of his tension ease.

Trevelyan scoffed. "Are humans even *allowed* to marry gargoyles? They're not really *real*, according to the rumors." He didn't wait for an answer, already losing interest. His attention span could be measured in nanoseconds and everyone else was meaningless to him. "Never mind. I don't care. Just tell me why I'm in this backwater."

"I want to hire you for some magical assistance." The dragon bought and sold all kinds of spells. That was one reason he'd been locked up. "I need you to unmelt a lion-headed scepter."

Trevelyan didn't appear particularly interested in lending a hand. "And what are you going to pay me with?" He waved an elegant palm towards their rustic surroundings. "Goats?"

"No. I'm going to save your life, like you saved mine."

Nicholas muttered a curse. "Do you have to?"

Trevelyan silently mulled over Marion's words. It was impossible to know what he was really thinking. It always had been.

"I wasn't lying in that note." She persisted. "I know exactly how you die, Trev. Not even your magic can tell you that."

"My magic is level five. There's not much I can't do."

Five was pretty much at the top of the scale, if Tilda, the witch-practitioner, was to be believed. "If your magic could do what *I* can do, then you wouldn't be here. Would you?" Marion bluffed. She wasn't sure what his powers could accomplish, but it seemed like a safe bet she was right.

He considered that claim, searching her face for some trace of deceit.

Marion stared back at him, not looking away from his brilliant green gaze. "I'm rewriting my future. Rewrite yours, too. What do you have to lose by hearing me out?"

"Brain cells?"

"But you have so many to spare." Marion flattered. Trevelyan was an egomaniac, so it always paid to tell him that he was the prettiest one at the ball. "You were the smartest prisoner in the WUB Club."

His dark brows slammed together. "I get sent to *that* hellhole? For what?" He sounded incredulous and insulted. Like he couldn't imagine why anyone would complain about his numerous felonies.

She pursed her lips, trying to recall some parts of his phonebook-sized rap-sheet. "Off the top of my head...? You were convicted of misuse of magic, blackmail, inciting mayhem, like eighty counts of arson, stealing some enchanted harp thing, and --I think-- a bunch of murders."

He rolled his eyes dismissively. "Are those even crimes?"

"Yes." Nicholas told him.

Trevelyan sighed, the most mistreated villain in the whole wide world.

"This job won't take long." Marion assured him. "Not for someone with *level five* magic." She infused her voice with as much awe as she could fake. "Let's just go talk and we'll see if we can't make a deal."

"Fine. I'll listen to what you have to say. But, I'm not staying in this squalid kingdom even one second more than I have to. I'm *sure* there are bugs here. And plague. And very dirty peasants. Nottingham is the worst possible place a person can get stuck."

Marion snorted. "Wait until you get to prison."

Chapter Twenty-Two

Celebrity watchers were dazzled today, when an actual dragon came to the May Day Festival!

It's not often our small kingdom is graced by such a rare and powerful species. Attracting such well-connected tourists has long been the dream of the event's planners. Damages from his visit are already estimated to be enormous, but it's all worth it for the social cache such an esteemed guest brings.

Everyone who loves Nottingham welcomes Trevelyan, Last of the Green Dragons for a long stay!

Alan A. Dale- "Nottingham's Naughtiest News"

"Would you be upset if I burned down this kingdom?" Marion asked seriously. "I need to know, because I'd *love* to destroy it, but I don't want to make you sad."

"You'd spare Nottingham, for my sake?" Nicholas sounded touched.

"Maybe. If you made it worth my while." A mischievous glint lit her face.

His mouth curved. The man loved it when she teased him.

Nicholas, Marion, Little John, and Trevelyan were in the palace's excruciatingly formal living room. Trevelyan was closest to the fire, because he'd been whining about how drafty the castle was. Dragons hated to be cold. Even right up against the hearth, he seemed disgruntled.

Marion didn't care, just so Little John was happily working. With Robin Hood caught and most of the Merry Men in the dungeon, it was safe for L.J. to leave the Huntingdon estate. Marion had brought him to the palace to help them get the scepter back. She was sure it somehow tied in with Nicholas' murder.

She still wasn't putting *all* her eggs in that basket, though. Marion had to go see Pinocchio about a gun, but that moron's magical relics shop was shut down for the fair, so that would have to wait. Even with Trevelyan's antics, the May Day Festival was still going strong, down on the village green. Dragon fire and Robin Hood's arrest couldn't stop Nottinghamers from their drunken revelry.

They really were a useless group.

Since Marion was waiting for Pinocchio's shop to open tomorrow and for L.J. to finish his damn drawing, she might as well tick another item off her "redoing her life" list: Revenge on Nottingham.

"I mean, I'd spare the lives of the innocent, and try not to kill all the old-growth trees, blah, blah, blah..." Marion went on, with a dismissive wave of her hand. "But, I want to *flatten* this fucking kingdom to rubble. I've made a deal to sell my father's house to a really scummy viscount, who deserves everything he's about to get. So, we've got nothing to lose, when the flames start."

"You're selling the Huntingdon estate?"

"It's already sold. Cragg helped me. I asked a rock-bottom price, so it only took like an hour. I didn't need anything in the whole place, except some maps and my parents' portraits."

Nicholas looked unsettled.

She frowned. "Wait, you didn't want to *live* there, did you? You said you didn't, Nick. We had a discussion about it. It's kind of dismal, aside from the gardens." She paused, recalling the question she'd had the night before. "Hey, do you know why Richard gave me that tax exemption for the...?"

Nicholas cut her off. "No, I don't want to live in your parents' house. I would think *you'd* want to live there."

"Why? We'll need our own place."

Nicholas blinked and the tension eased from his shoulders.

"So, there's no problem with my plan to level

Nottingham and dance in its ashes." She sent him a bright smile. "Right, wuffles?"

He considered that idea. "Well, I would like the gargoyles to survive your onslaught, obviously."

"Of course! I'll always protect your men." She knew what they meant to him, even if he didn't like to admit it.

Nicholas looked briefly amused by her promise to guard a legion of gigantic soldiers. "I'm sure they'll be thrilled to hear that."

"They should be. You guys are the only ones around here that I like." She bit down on her lower lip. "Nick?" She lowered her voice, so only he could hear.

"Yes?" He obligingly lowered his own voice to match hers, his attention riveted on her mouth.

"Would you run away with me, if I asked?"

"Yes." The answer was immediate.

"Are you sure? Because, I *hate* Nottingham. I know you're kind of in charge of the place, though. So, if you want to stay here in the castle," she cringed at what she was about to say, "...I'll stay. For you." She poked a finger at him. "I wouldn't make that kind of sacrifice for anyone else. So be *sure* about this, because we don't want to be stuck in Nottingham, after I destroy it."

"Nottingham means nothing to me. Use your creative villainy to burn it all, if it makes you happy. I would never stand in your way, Marion." His attention stayed right on her face. "But take me with you, if you go. ...Otherwise, I'll just follow you."

"Good answer." She leaned over to press her lips to his, pleased he was always so supportive of her Badness. "Thank you, Nick."

Trevelyan's brilliant green gaze cut back-and-forth between them, watching them kiss. "My God... Relationship goals." He mocked.

Marion flipped him off, her mouth still on Nicholas'.

The dragon chuckled.

L.J. ignored them all. "Okay." He was laboring over a sketchpad, his hair falling over his eyes. He kept brushing it back, as he worked. "So, the scepter kind of looked like *this*." He held up the paper, so Trevelyan could see his masterpiece.

Trevelyan reluctantly took the pad from him, staring down at the drawing. "It's a stick." He reported without inflection. "With a smiley face on top."

"That's a lion head." L.J. told him. "See? I wrote a little 'Roar!' in the bubble coming out of its mouth, so you could tell it's a lion." He helpfully pointed to the bubble. "See?"

Trevelyan looked at the kid through his lashes. Possibly deciding whether or not to fry him for the greater sake of art.

"Trev." Marion drew his attention back to her. "Is that picture good enough to recreate the scepter or not?"

"For anyone but me...? No. It would be laughable to even suggest it." He shrugged with arrogant ease. "Luckily, I *am* me, so I can get it back for you."

"When?"

"I'm working on it." He lounged in his chair and moved his hand. "Working *so* hard." A glass of bourbon instantly appeared in his grasp. "There *are* bugs in this kingdom, by the way. I told you there were. I can smell them."

"Oh, that's just L.J." The Merry Men weren't the greatest at showering. It wasn't like the forest had indoor plumbing. Or any *indoors* at all, really. The boy reeked. "Sherwood is crawling with bugs."

Trevelyan shot Little John an irritated look.

L.J. frowned in concern and inched back from him.

Satisfied, Trevelyan turned back to Marion. "So... did someone say there's a party tonight?"

"That's tomorrow night. The Maypole Ball. Tonight is the May Day Queen Pageant."

"Well, that sounds... wholesome." His exotic face creased in distaste.

"It's a crinoline-filled nightmare. I never won 'May Day Queen' and I totally should've been crowned instead of that bitch Clorinda." Marion crossed her arms over her chest. "It was the fucking talent show part that stymied me."

Trevelyan couldn't have cared less about the

catastrophic unfairness of the scoring system. "There will be *actual* women at the Maypole Ball, though? Not just virgins?"

Marion saw where this was headed. Her temper sparked, because Trevelyan's pointless, rebellious insubordination always got on her last damn nerve. He just *had* to create conflict. Sometimes that conflict ended with a hundred and eight people dead.

> As an instrument of destruction, Marion was a match.
> Nicholas was a hammer.
> Robin was an arrow.
> Trevelyan was a bomb.

The dragon had massive power, he was easy to set off, and he had little regard for fall out. The older-him had never turned his explosive impulses towards her, though, so Marion wasn't worried this version would either. She just resumed their relationship where they'd left it and expected him to catch up. And he seemed to be accepting that, so far. She could see him trying to get an exact read on her, but he hadn't unfurled his claws.

This younger-Trevelyan was more lighthearted than the dragon she'd known in prison, in a lot of ways. More relaxed. Less scornful. He hadn't yet developed the blatant, jagged edges of impending violence. Still, he was just as unruly to deal with. She felt like she was babysitting some wayward little brother with superpowers and an attitude problem.

"No, you don't need to go to the Maypole Ball!" She jabbed a finger at him. "Absolutely not. It can't possibly take you a day and a half to get the scepter back."

"Now you're an expert on how long magic takes?"

"I'm an expert on your lies."

Trevelyan *tsk*ed. "You can't rush powerful spells, Marion dear. No matter how much we both want to accomplish..." He paused, trying to recall what they were doing. "Well, *whatever* it is we're accomplishing, with this smelly boy and his crayons."

"We're saving Nick's life!"

"And I'm *incredibly* invested in that." Trevelyan assured her, honesty oozing from his very pores. "It's going to take long hours and expert dedication, but there's no other choice. I'll stay right here, until it's finished." He laid a heroic palm against his wide chest, nefarious delight in his eyes. "...But it won't be finished until after the ball."

Marion debated murdering him and risking another prison sentence. What jury in the world would blame her? "Is this about your birthday?"

His dragon-green gaze snapped to hers in surprise.

"I know more about you than anyone else alive, because you never shut up about yourself." She assured him, answering his unasked question.

Like Hatters, dragons valued birthdays, because personal magic was stronger or something. Trevelyan especially liked *his* birthday. In the WUB Club, Marion had taken to stealing him a bag of Gala-chips as an annual present, just to mark the date. It was one of the few occasions he'd smile at her with no snarkiness, at all.

Trevelyan studied her, his head tilting ever so slightly.

Marion arched a brow. "You want me to prove how well I know you?" She switched to the Green Dragon dialect, which this dummy had once been bored enough to teach her. "How many *other* people have you told about your dead uncle's nymph girlfriend and the invisibility spell?"

He watched her, almost convinced. "What was her name?" He asked in the same language.

"You have no damn idea."

That did it.

Trevelyan finally accepted they'd been close. Magic was commonplace to dragons. He'd allowed that Marion knew him in the future, without much difficulty. But he hadn't been sold on the kinda-sorta-friends part. That idea seemed more unlikely to the suspicious bastard than time travel.

Now, he believed her, though. She could see it in the softening of his angular features. He seemed pleased by the realization that Marion was inexplicably fond of his irritating ass. Unfortunately, it didn't change his lousy attitude one bit. In Trevelyan's head, friendship meant you doing stuff for him, while he was a huge jerk.

"If you know me so well, then you know I couldn't care less about my birthday." He lied, just to be difficult. "*Every* day of the year is a celebration of me."

"Well, why do you want to celebrate any of those wonderful Trevelyan Days *here?*" She went back to speaking the universal language. "I thought you were desperate to leave Nottingham."

"Oh, I am. That's why I'm slaving away on this spell for you."

"Bullshit. You're just on a power trip."

He sipped his drink, loving his newest game. "Well, unless you know another dragon to extort, I'm afraid you're stuck on my schedule."

"I'm not extorting you, dingus. I'm saving you from a horrible death. I'd think you'd want to hear about that as soon as possible."

"I have time. I doubt my horrible death happens before the ball."

"I wouldn't count on it."

That threat earned her another dark chuckle. Trevelyan's focus flicked to Nicholas. "You should thank me for not killing her back in that future-prison, gargoyle. It would be such a pity to lose a woman with fire, wouldn't it?"

Nicholas grunted, looking bored.

He was barely paying attention to their bickering. It occurred to Marion that he hadn't been sexy and possessive since the festival. Not that he *should* be, since she'd rather sleep with a live snake than Trevelyan, but it wasn't like Nicholas to ignore other men when they got close to her.

She shot him a vaguely concerned look. Was he sick?

Trevelyan looked back at Marion, but he was clearly trying to get a rise out of Nicholas. He'd notice the other man's lack of response too and he didn't like it. Trevelyan hated not being the center of everyone's attention.

"You know, Marion dear... I heard some of what you were saying earlier. If you really want to burn Nottingham to ashes, I would be thrilled to help with that little job, as well. I *am* a dragon, after all. I'm sure we can make a deal." The offer was a suggestive purr.

Marion cut that shit off before it even began. "I don't need you to destroy this kingdom and I'm *certainly* not having sex with you, Trev."

His unwholesome grin gleamed with all the Badness in the world. "Why, I didn't even get to *that* part, yet. Interesting how you just came up with the idea, all on your own." He looked over at Nicholas, waiting for a reaction.

Nicholas rolled his eyes. Literally *rolled his eyes*, like he was totally uninterested in the entire conversation.

Trevelyan frowned.

L.J. looked confused. "Want me to draw another picture of something?" He offered.

Marion ignored him, watching Nicholas and wondering what he was up to. The man was so unpredictable.

Nicholas checked the time.

L.J. started sketching Robin Hood prancing around the forest with smiling bugs.

Trevelyan sighed and went back to drinking. "Do you have TV here, at least?" He asked in a long-suffering tone.

Oh!

Now, she got it. Who better than a gargoyle to perfect the gray-rock technique of just not reacting to a narcissist? Without an opponent, Trevelyan quickly lost interest in the game. He really did have the attention span of a gnat. Nicholas had just beaten him by saying nothing. That was awesome!

She sent her taciturn groom a grin.

He arched a brow and she read the smugness in his expression. "Would you like to go question Hood with me, duchess? I'm eager to interrogate him quickly, so we can get onto the hanging."

"Hell yes." Marion bounded to her feet. "Tilda *must* have his jaw working, by now."

It was hard to force Robin to explain his insidious plans, when he had multiple facial fractures. At the moment, her ex literally couldn't talk. Usually, that would be a blessing, but not when Marion needed answers. The turquoise-haired witch-practitioner was healing Robin, but it was taking *forever*.

Marion looped her arm through Nicholas' elbow and yanked him out the door. "Do you really think we'll have to torture him to get information? I hope we get to torture him."

"Who are we torturing for information?" Trevelyan called. "I want to torture whoever it is, too. That would be much more fun than this."

"You torture everyone already." Marion shut the door behind her, leaving him alone with L.J. Hopefully Trevelyan wouldn't eat him.

"I hate that dragon." Nicholas informed her gravely.

"Everyone hates Trev. I'm the only friend he kinda-sorta has and even I can't stand him, most of the time. Don't worry. He'll be gone soon. He's easily distracted." She dismissed Trevelyan from her mind. "We need to focus on Robin."

"I hate him, too."

"No shit." Marion scoffed. "But I have a theory and I need him to confirm it all."

"What theory?"

"I think Robin's an idiot."

He grunted. "It's a good theory, so far."

Marion led him towards the stairs, eager to share all her thoughts with Nicholas. The foyer of the palace soared three stories high, with open staircases in between. The landings were exposed to the floors below to impress visitors with the castle's scale. On the ceiling, high above, a domed skylight gleamed. In her opinion, the grand entrance was the nicest part of the whole palace.

"I think you were right before and Robin trusted the Wraith." She told Nicholas. "I think you were right and Robin and Richard killed King Jonathan. I think you were right and they're stealing my money, and Nottingham's money, and *everybody's* money, washing it through fake toy factories and who knows how many other phony businesses."

"I enjoy hearing how right I am." Nicholas deadpanned. "This theory makes more and more sense."

"But I don't think King Richard has anything to do with robbing the kingdom blind."

Nicholas shook his head. "No. Richard would have to be involved if..."

"I think Richard is dead."

Nicholas looked at her sharply and stopped walking.

Marion halted as well, her hand resting on the railing of the staircase. "You said yourself, he was gone for six hours after the Battle of Kirklees. That everyone began to blame Robin for his death. And then 'Richard' comes stumbling back into camp, praising Robin's leadership? Robin gets to leave the war and come home to play in the forest, all day?" Marion snorted. "Fuck that. The two of them made a deal. Robin would help the Wraith be Richard. The Wraith would help Robin become rich and famous."

Nicholas thought for a long moment, examining the theory in his head. "Richard's probably dead."

Marion beamed, happy he was agreeing with her logic. "So then, the Wraith took his place as king. It invented some rumors about an 'enchantress' to explain away the random stuff it knew from impersonating people. And then it and Robin stole everything that wasn't nailed down."

"We don't have enough evidence to support the fake-enchantress part." Nicholas told her with sheriff-y precision. "Maybe Wraiths *can* see the future."

"When I catch the damn thing, I'll ask it." Marion wasn't worried about reasonable doubt. "I *know* I'm right about most of it, though. Only I have no idea why *we're* involved, at all. What the hell do I care if Richard is dead? I never liked him anyway, even if he is paying for our wedding. If the Wraith left me alone, I'd leave it alone. I don't start shit."

Nicholas looked amused by that claim. "Isn't that exactly what you're doing, all around Nottingham? Starting shit."

"Well, sure. But I didn't start shit with the Wraith. So why is it after you?"

"It's not. Last time it killed me. ...But it came right at *you*, with that puppet show."

Marion gasped in wonder at his casual words. He'd accepted that there was a "last time." Nicholas was finally coming to see she was telling the truth about time travel. That was huge!

Nicholas didn't notice her excitement, lost in his own head. "Unless the Wraith was *always* targeting you." He mused.

"It shot *you*, Nick."

"And framed you for it. That got you locked away, far from Nottingham." He slowly nodded, liking his addition to the theory. "This has always been about you, Marion."

"Commander." Quarry came in from outside, papers in his hands. "We looked into the puppet tent and it seems like it's owned by someone named David Doncaster... and Maid Marion."

Marion groaned. "If I owned half the shit I'm *supposed* to own, I wouldn't need to worry about money, ever again."

Nicholas sighed in exasperation. "Get Hood down here." He told Quarry. "We're about to politely ask him what the fuck is going on. Then, we'll hang him."

Quarry shot Marion a quick look, as if gauging her reaction to the pending execution.

"You know the last thing Robin said to me, as I was being dragged off to jail?" She shrugged. "'Good luck, Marion. ...But I think we should see other people.'" She leaned against Nicholas' side and smirked. "I'm just taking his advice."

Quarry's mouth curved slightly.

"Now that I'm pretty damn sure he didn't even put that money in my prison commissary account, I'm even less disposed to care whether or not he's breathing. Plus, Robin stole from my dying father. I've vowed to destroy his dreams and I think hanging qualifies." Accomplishing so much justified vengeance in one fell swoop was glorious. "Screw that bastard sideways." She looked at Nicholas and smiled sweetly. "Right, donut hole?"

"I'd prefer you not screw that bastard, in any direction, actually." Nicholas said, flipping through the papers Quarry had handed him.

The very calm comment made her laugh. His sense of humor was so dry it often took a moment to even realize he was joking. She loved that! It kept her on her toes.

Nicholas' eyes gleamed, liking the sound of her amusement echoing in the vast foyer.

Quarry's gaze cut back and forth between them and he seemed to nod to himself, as if he'd been right about something. "Alright. I'll go get Hood and..."

The deadly sound of a repeating crossbow cut him off. A rapid succession of steel-tipped arrows impacted the wall behind them, hitting with enough force to propel the projectiles straight into the stone.

Holy *crap!*

Someone had just shot at them from the third floor landing.

"Down!" Nicholas shoved Marion to the foyer floor, as the red dot of a laser scope swept past them, looking for targets.

Footsteps and shouting sounded from up above.

"Stop!" Tilda's voice cried. "I just healed you! You'll reinjure yourself!"

More arrows were fired, whooshing through the air at incredible speed. This time they hit the railing, blowing out a huge chunk of wood. Nicholas' body shielded Marion from the splintered debris raining down.

Thanks to doing time with the Black Knight, she quickly identified the crossbow as an Oak Major 1000. The former soldier had loved chatting about weapons, so she even knew about the obscure ones. It didn't take a skilled archer to kill a ton of people with a crossbow like that, but they were banned in most lands. It automatically readied the projectiles and rapidly fired them, one after another. All you had to do was pull the huge trigger.

The Oak Major 1000 was illegal for good reason. It was the closest Nottingham came to a machine gun. That didn't really answer the most pressing question, though.

"Who's shooting at us?"

Quarry snorted. He'd taken cover by the newel post. "Given how popular you two are, it could be anyone in Nottingham."

That was fair.

"It's Hood." Nicholas' said grimly.

"No, Robin wouldn't…" Marion stopped talking, because the arrows stopped firing. The shooter was trying to figure out how to reload. "Let's get out of here."

Nicholas seemed to concur. He stood up, grabbed Marion, and carted her out the front door. "Wait here." He ordered and dropped her onto the steps. Then, he headed back inside.

Was he insane?

"No! We're not doing *that,* again." Marion went after him, back into the foyer. "Stop trying to protect me, all the time."

"I swore a *vow* to protect you, when I claimed the betrothal rights." The words were inflexible as rock. "If you had an issue with it, you shouldn't have taken your top off."

Quarry glanced over at them, his eyebrows soaring.

Marion was not about to argue about the silly betrothal rights, during an assassination attempt. "Come out *with* me, until we figure out what's happening, Nick!"

"I know what's happening. It's Hood." Nicholas prepared to head up the stairs.

Marion seized hold of his sleeve, before he could go marching off to fight a maniac with automatic arrows. "I don't want you to die again! How many times do I have to say it?"

"I'm not about to let Hood escape!"

"It can't be him!"

"Don't defend that bastard!"

"I'm *not.* But Robin wouldn't use an Oak Major. They're too heavy. He likes longbows, because they're more portable for running through the foliage…"

"I'll never surrender!" Robin screamed from the top of the stairs.

"Oh." Marion frowned. "Huh. Okay, never mind, I guess."

The three of them looked upward, just in time to see her moronic ex jump from the third floor landing onto a rope that dangled from the skylight.

A rope? Where had *that* come from?

Tilda, the witch-practitioner, chased after him. "He escaped!" She called to Marion, which was honestly kind of obvious. "He's just *so* brilliant." She stood by the railing, her hands clasped over her chest, as she watched her favorite patient make a scramble for freedom. "And *strong*." Clearly, the woman was awed by his heroics.

Marion wasn't nearly so impressed with the spectacle Sherwood's biggest shithead was creating. If he was clinging to a rope, then he couldn't shoot the Oak Major 1000, which meant he couldn't escape. The gargoyles would just catch him, again. Did he even *have* the crossbow? She didn't see the immense thing anywhere on him.

Was she missing something or was this a terrible plan?

"Marion, I forgive you for everything!" Robin shouted down at her, climbing around like a kid on a jungle-gym. "We'll be together soon!"

Unbelievable! "What do you mean you forgive *me?* You were in on a plot to kill me this afternoon!" Marion wasn't over getting attacked by puppets. She would *never* be over getting attacked by puppets.

"I didn't try to kill you!" Robin sounded genuinely outraged by the accusation. "I would never do that! Our love is fated in the stars! The sheriff is trying to turn you against me, because he knows you'll *always* come back to me in the end!"

Nicholas was plotting ways to kill him. She could see it on his face. Gray eyes flicked up to the glass of the skylight, like he was wondering if he could somehow break it from this distance and stab Robin with falling glass.

"You'll end up shredded to pieces, too, coo-berry. You'd be right under it when it collapsed." Marion ran a consoling hand up and down his arm. It was always tough on Nicholas when he couldn't murder Robin.

"Get away from my girl, rock-monster!" Robin shouted, seeing Marion's touch.

Nicholas' expression went even darker. "She is *my* girl." The claim was an absolute roar.

Marion appreciated his sexy possessiveness, but that

particular phrasing was a wartime colloquialism. A soldier's girl was almost mythical in Nottingham. In all the most-popular ballads, brave men went into battle to protect their helpless beloved girls back home. Marion wasn't helpless! She'd once been some drippy damsel, waiting for rescue, but not ever again.

"Did I agree you could call me 'your girl'?" She asked pointedly.

"Did I agree you could call me 'coo-berry?'" Nicholas' scowl stayed fixed on Robin.

That was totally different! "Marion belongs to *Marion.*" She informed all interested parties. "Nick *also* belongs to Marion. Nobody gives a shit what happens to Robin or who he belongs to." She flicked an indifferent hand towards her former flame. "That is how this *actually* goes."

Nicholas glanced her way and didn't argue.

Robin did. "You've been my girl for years! You can't just change that! Why would you even want to? You're just trying to prove a point with this fake engagement..."

"It's not fake! I've *dumped* you, Robin."

Robin didn't want to hear that, so he didn't. "...but don't worry your little head about the trials of men! I'll soon defeat the sheriff, save you from this hellish castle, and make you my forest bride! We'll rule over my woodland utopia, arm-in-arm!"

Marion threw her hands up in exasperation.

Nicholas's jaw clenched. "I'm going to go upstairs, get him off that damn thing, and then hang him." He turned to Quarry. "Take Marion outside, again. Then, go up on the roof and cut the rope from that end. If Hood won't swing one way, he'll swing another."

Quarry nodded and went dashing towards the door, seizing Marion by the waist as he past. She gave a yelp of protest, as he carted her out to the front step and casually put her back on her feet. He gave a salute and went loping off. Since she couldn't yell at him, she settled for yelling at the mastermind of her newest abduction.

"Damn it, Nick!" See, this was *exactly* what she meant!

And why was Nicholas always so intent on sheltering her, when the other him had been the one to tell her she could only count on herself? "I just told you..."

He cut her off. "Stay there, until I'm sure you won't be shot. Please."

Marion sighed loudly. Since he'd said "please," she compromised on standing in the doorway. "I hope he falls on your kidnapping head." She muttered.

Despite the situation, Nicholas' mouth curved. He started up the stairs.

"What's all the noise?" Trevelyan came wandering into the foyer at a leisurely stroll. "When I torture people, it's never so shrill."

Marion's eyes widened. "Where's L.J.?" She didn't want the boy inadvertently harmed by the attack.

"How should I know?" Trevelyan asked, like he hadn't just been with the kid twenty seconds before. Other people were never very important to him. Presumably, L.J. was still drawing by the fire and Trevelyan didn't even notice he existed. His gaze went up to the ceiling. "And who's that?"

Robin continued to flail around on the rope. With any luck, he'd break his neck. "My dumbass ex."

"You dated a murderous housekeeper?"

She glanced at him in confusion. "What...?"

"Get back!" Nicholas roared.

He came down the stairs so fast he was a blur. Marion didn't have time to react, before he was in front of her. An arrow bounced off the rocky skin of his right arm and he didn't even notice.

"Nick, my God...!"

More arrows flew from the third floor landing, peppering the walls. Who in the hell was firing? It couldn't be Robin. He was still on the rope.

"Marion, get *back!*" Nicholas headed across the foyer, ignoring the deadly projectiles. All he saw was her. Big arms grabbed her up, scanning for injuries and pushing her behind the relative safety of the doorframe. "Are you alright?"

"I'm fine! *You* were the one who got shot!"

He didn't bother to check for a wound. "The arrow bounced off the stone."

"Are you sure?" She tried to examine his arm, but an arrow hit the door exactly where her head had been twenty seconds before. That was all he seemed capable of focusing on. Nicholas dragged her farther back from the open doorway.

"I'm *fine*." She assured him again, her heart pounding.

Trevelyan stood alone in the foyer, casually keeping score. "Your ex hates you, I think." He reported to Marion. "She's got a crossbow."

"Stop!" Robin bellowed to the murderous housekeeper who'd sighted on Marion. "Don't shoot her! Marion is going to be my wife!"

"She's just like her whore of a mother!" Guyla Gisborn shrieked back. Dressed in her gray uniform, her graying hair askew, her usually gray face was lit with triumph. She'd braced the gigantic crossbow against the third floor railing and was letting loose. "You can do better, Robin!"

Tilda nodded like that was a great point. "You really, really can." She loyally fan-girled.

Guyla shot at Marion, again. Then, she fired at Tilda, too. "Get your eyes off of him, tramp!"

Tilda cried out in terror and fled. You'd think the fairy would've tried some magic against Guyla, but nope. Like everyone else in Nottingham, she was useless. And in love with Robin. Even the damn housekeeper was willing to commit homicide for that idiot. It was nauseating.

"I cannot *wait* to get out of this horrible place." Marion told Nicholas sincerely, double-checking to make sure the arrow that hit his arm hadn't injured him. Luckily, the lovely stone sections of his skin had kept him safe.

Nicholas kissed her hair. "Wait here." He stepped back and scanned the outside of the castle. Two seconds later, he was scaling the stone edifice.

Marion's eyebrows soared. "Where are you going?"

"Up."

Marion frowned in frustration and knew she couldn't possibly follow him. Being pudgy and un-athletic was definitely a drawback in combat situations. At least the view was nice, though. When Robin climbed around, it was juvenile and stupid. When Nicholas did it, it was hot as hell. The muscles in his arms were *massive*.

Trevelyan continued to watch the chaos inside. Dragons loved chaos.

Speaking of which... Marion backtracked to peer through the door. "You know, you could turn into a dragon and incinerate her." She reminded him.

He lazily shrugged, not taking the situation seriously. "What'll you pay me, if I do?"

Marion wished she was close enough to hit him. "I'm not paying you for help, when someone is legit trying to kill me, Trev!"

"When someone's trying to kill you, you should pay me *more*."

"God, you are the worst kinda-sorta friend I have ever had!"

Trevelyan looked offended. "I saved your life in prison."

"That was the *other*-you!"

Trevelyan frowned, not appreciating the former-him getting any credit. He was competitive about everything, even against a dead version of himself.

Robin made it to the ceiling, while Guyla laid down cover-fire. The glass access panel to the skylight was suddenly open to aid Robin's escape. No way could Guyla have done that. It must have been the Wraith's contribution to the plan.

Robin heaved himself through the opening. "Believe in our destiny!" He called to Marion and vanished from sight.

Quarry wasn't going to get up there in time to stop his escape.

Fuck.

"Did I miss the part where you explained who that is?" Trevelyan wanted to know.

"I told you, he's my ex."

"You dated him, *too?*"

"Run, my love!" Guyla screamed after Robin,

frantically shooting down into the foyer. Arrows went everywhere.

Trevelyan made a face, as one nearly hit his leg. "I can't believe you were ever involved with that terrible assassin, Marion dear. Not to mention that cowardly blond gymnast. *And* the dull gargoyle, as well." He *tsk*ed at her. "You have *abysmal* taste in lovers."

Marion ignored him and stepped back to check on Nicholas. He'd made it to the third floor. Slamming his impervious stony fist through a pane of glass, he unlocked a window and made his way inside. He'd reached the top level, without using the stairs, and now he was closing in on his target.

Guyla screeched in panic, when she spotted him coming. She was clearly terrified of Nicholas. "Get back! Get back or I'll shoot your slut!" She kept firing as she retreated, but the shots went increasingly wild, because the crossbow weighed nearly as much as she did.

Another arrow imbedded itself in the doorframe, three inches from Marion's chest. Thankfully, Nicholas was too far away to see how close it had come.

Trevelyan wasn't. He arched a brow and finally bestirred himself. "Oh, *fine*." He lifted a palm and gave his wrist a quick twist. The Oak Major 1000 jerked from Guyla's grasp and somehow ended up in the dragon's elegant palm. "Level five powers." He told Marion smugly, waggling the bulky crossbow at her. "Who's the best Trevelyan, now?"

"Shut up and give me that thing." She marched over to snatch it out of his hand.

She was grudgingly impressed that Guyla had been able to heft it, at all. It was massive. The trigger on it was gigantic and the bow itself was heavy as hell. That was another reason they were so obscure. The Oak Major 1000 was simply too big for soldiers to carry.

Nicholas kept heading for Guyla. "You're under arrest." His quiet voice echoed throughout the foyer. "Also, you're fired."

She gave an eerie wail of fury and loss, backing

towards the railing. "You can't fire me! I serve the *true* king. The *real* king!" She hoisted herself up onto the banister. "He's going to reclaim everything that was stolen by Richard!"

"Jonathan is *dead*." Nicholas told her, slowing his approach. "Come down from there and we can talk."

"And then what? You'll send me to prison, like Friar Tuck? Lock me in the dungeon, like the Merry Men? *Hang me*, like all the rest of the people you've arrested?! It doesn't matter that you and Marion weren't born Bad. You're still the wickedest villains in the kingdom and everyone knows it!"

Trevelyan scoffed, like he should have won that title.

Marion ignored him, struggling to aim the Oak Major 1000 at Guyla, just in case the housekeeper had some new trick up her sleeve. She didn't love the idea of shooting the woman in the back, but she also didn't hate it. She'd never liked that bitch, in any timeline.

"Guyla," Nicholas held out his left hand to her, as if he thought the sight of his gargoyle-y right palm might freak her out even more, "get away from the..."

Guyla jumped.

Marion cringed and turned away, not wanting to watch the housekeeper plummet to the floor. Whatever lunacy had driven Guyla to try and kill them, she took it to her grave. She impacted the marble with a sickening thud and lay ominously still.

Trevelyan made a considering type of sound. "Well, that was interesting."

Chapter Twenty-Three

Bagheera Kong speaks out:
"Maid Marion is an evil siren and a Bad influence on Good children. She once tried to seduce my dear husband. Also, she framed poor Friar Tuck!"
Plus, more on Bagheera's heroic quest to find the missing judge, her must-have makeup for panthers on the go, and her campaign to become this year's garden club chairperson.

Alan A. Dale- "Nottingham's Naughtiest News"

Clorinda's broken nose did not distract from her virtuosity on the piano.

Marion leaned against the wall of the Nottingham Assembly Hall. Like every other building in the kingdom, it was a pile of decrepit stones and peeling paint. Some brave souls had tried to fancy it up with blue crepe paper streamers and gold bunting, but it didn't hide the water stains on the ceiling or the moldy wallpaper.

It was a travesty that she was back here, again, wearing the same stupid white dress she'd worn the last time and feeling most of the same stupid emotions: Inadequacy, sadness, and a vague sense of missing something... more.

Redoing her life was supposed to be way easier than this.

Quarry had done more digging and found out Guyla's Maiden name was "Doncaster." As in "David Doncaster." As in "The fake owner of the fake toy factory." Clearly, the housekeeper had been a part of whatever plan Robin and the Wraith were hatching, but Guyla was inconveniently dead and thus hard to interrogate about it. That pissed Marion off. What were the three of them up to? Why were they stealing so much money?

The rest of Nottingham barely noticed Guyla's demise. Instead, the citizens focused on the bright side: Robin had escaped and was free again, presumably romping through the woods. All the townsfolk were in uncharacteristically jolly moods.

It was so damn annoying.

Marion glowered, as Clorinda finished playing some complicated classical piece, complete with an artistic flourish and a modest curtsy at the end. Clorinda would win May Day Queen. Again. She probably wouldn't even have to cheat.

Not only was her talent annoyingly adequate, but she looked even more gorgeous than usual. Her long, golden hair glistened. Her body was all graceful curves in her signature pink dress. She'd even managed to disguise the bandage on her nose with a sparkly masquerade mask. And she could simper out a smile as simpering as any Maid's.

The judges would love that.

Lampwick had already been awarded the title of May Day King. Cragg's secret boyfriend was handsome, muscular, and did an impressive scene-reading from some famous play about King Jonathan's glorious reign. For the males' talent component, orations were scored the highest. Marion wasn't at all surprised when Lampwick won the crown. Something about the redheaded human's smug smile annoyed her, but Cragg had seemed overjoyed, so she guessed Lampwick's victory was positive news.

Unfortunately, the May Day *Queen* competition was going terribly.

Marion had many, many pressing problems she could be focusing on, back at the castle. Robin's escape. The Wraith lurking around. Plotting the destruction of her homeland. Winning her groom's love and preventing his murder. The list went on and on. But that damn rhinestone tiara had come to represent every failing of her life. If only she had it, everything else would fall into place. She was weirdly sure of it.

Clorinda left the stage in a triumphant swirl of pink chiffon.

It was Trevelyan's fault she'd performed, at all. Marion had very nicely asked the dragon to seduce that bitch away for a couple hours, so she'd miss the contest. He'd slept with far uglier girls. He slept with everyone!

Instead, his green eyes had swept up and down Clorinda and he'd snorted in derision. "No." He'd said simply and turned his attention to some average-looking matron with a streak of gray in her hair. The woman was thirty years older than him, but she'd just about swooned when he smiled at her. You could never tell who Trevelyan was going to proposition. Half of it was based on scent and half was just fucking randomness.

And another half was just him being a jackass.

For whatever reason, Clorinda didn't meet his exacting standards. Presently, Trevelyan was off someplace with the older lady, no doubt doing lascivious things to her, while her ancient husband droned on about hunting dogs in the corner and Clorinda prepared to win Marion's crown.

It was so unfair.

On stage, the announcer announced some new contestant in crinoline. She sat at the piano and began plunking out an interchangeable classical melody, just like every other girl had done before her. The contestants didn't *have* to play the piano, but it was the talent that scored the highest. Any other acceptably ladylike skill, like flute-playing, singing, or even baton twirls, was technically allowed, but they wouldn't be able to make up the difference in points. So, everyone played the piano, even though it wasn't a particular talent of most of them. The new girl had already hit the wrong key twice.

She wasn't going to win. No one was going to win except Clorinda.

Marion shook her head in frustration.

Ten years before, she'd entered the contest herself. She wasn't sure why. Marion was competitive, sure. She wasn't an idiot, though. She was pretty, in an average, girl-next-door kind of way, but her shape was unfashionably rounded and she had no talent for instruments.

After several days of being kidnapped, the former-Marion had been going stir crazy in her bedroom, though. Nothing terrifying had happened to her. Nothing even particularly upsetting. Food had been brought to her and was then taken away. Clorinda showed up to keep her company, chaperone her abduction, and/or look for gossip. Twice a day, Nicholas would check on her and she'd mostly ignore him. At the time, she'd been sure he was just trying to see if Robin had saved her, yet.

Which he never had.

Marion had grown tired of sitting there, waiting for Robin to finish his exciting escapades, before he finally got around to her. May Day Queen was at least something she could focus on in the meantime.

And she'd just really, really wanted the plastic crown.

The last time around, she'd been standing in this very spot for most of the night. Then Nicholas had come up beside her and everything had gone all wonky.

"I agreed to let you attend tonight, because you said you planned to enter the May Day Queen pageant." His voice was emotionless, but his gray eyes were intently fixed on her. *"And yet here you are, Maid Marion. Hugging the wall, instead of getting up on stage."*

Marion winced a bit and wished she'd never had this dumb idea. "I changed my mind." She muttered.

One of Nicholas' shoulders braced on the wall, so he was facing her. His stance was oddly intimate, blocking the two of them off from the rest of the large open space. "Why?"

Marion blinked at the question, her eyes flicking up to Nicholas.

He arched a brow, waiting for her to answer.

Marion frowned. No one else would have asked her to explain her reasoning. No one else would have cared. Robin just would've been relieved that she wasn't about to embarrass him by losing. That random thought made Marion feel guilty, because it seemed like she was finding Robin lacking in some way. She instantly made up her mind to tell Nicholas it was none of his business why she didn't want to participate in the contest.

Only those weren't the words that came out of her mouth.

"I don't feel confident in my piano playing." She admitted instead.

"I've heard you play the piano. You're very good."

She had no idea where he'd heard her play the piano. She'd only ever preformed at home. Maybe he'd been walking by the estate and happened to catch a few bars through an open window or something. She made a face. "If you've heard me, then you know I'm not as good as Clorinda."

"Who?"

"Clorinda! The girl who's playing, right now."

He didn't even glance towards the stage. "Oh, you're much better than her." He sounded utterly sure of that lie. "Trust me. I'm very aware of sound."

She didn't *trust him, actually.* "I'm not better than her." Marion's lips pressed together in annoyance. "I think she's cheating. I think she's using a spell or something. That's against the rules."

"I can arrest her, if you'd like."

That grave offer amused her. He actually sounded serious! Before she could stop herself, Marion grinned up at him.

Something ignited deep within Nicholas' eyes. Something soft and intent, which made him seem less intimidating and more... attractive. His eyes were very attractive, actually. The color of them and the way they focused on her, like she was the only one in the room.

Marion quickly glanced away, confused that she'd noticed the color of another man's eyes. She'd always belonged to Robin. He was the only one she was supposed to find attractive.

It felt suddenly warm in the assembly hall. Very warm.

She cleared her throat. "Anyway, I'm not going to go up on stage, just to make a fool of myself." She declared, mostly just for something to say.

"Pick a different talent, if you're worried about the piano."

It occurred to Marion that this conversation was the longest one they'd shared in years. Usually, Nicholas just silently watched her and brooded. His hatred of Robin had bled over onto Marion. She was sure of that. It was the only explanation she'd been able to come up with for why he'd pulled back from her so completely, when they'd always gotten along as children.

She looked up at him again, unable to help herself. "Why are you talking to me?"

Nicholas somehow shifted even closer to her, without really moving. "Why are *you* talking to *me*?"

Marion had no damn clue. "I'll lose if I choose a different talent." She said, because the contest seemed like the safest thing to focus on.

"No, you won't."

"Yes, I will! I'm better at singing, sure. But piano is scored the highest."

"You're good at singing?" He sounded intrigued. "I didn't know that. I've never heard you sing."

No one had. She could hit notes in the shower, but doing it in public scared her. She'd never had lessons or anything. Marion chewed her lower lip, wishing she had the nerve to get on stage and try, anyway. Maids were supposed to be modest and eschew the spotlight, but a part of her was tired of always worrying about everyone else's opinion.

And she wanted that tiara.

"What do you sing?" He persisted, like he was genuinely interested.

Marion cleared her throat. "Doesn't matter. I'm not doing it. It wouldn't be proper. And what if I'm terrible?"

"If you go up there, you'll win, Marion. I'll make sure of it."

The calm promise surprised her. He wasn't reassuring her just to be nice. The Sheriff of Nottingham was never nice. He must be offering her a bribe! He wanted to pretend they were still friends and wheedle secrets out of her, so he could *weaponize them against Robin. Marion didn't know any secrets, but it pissed her off that Nicholas was trying to use her.*

"You'll cheat, you mean?" She demanded. "That would be wrong."

He lifted his shoulder, like he didn't much care.

Marion's brows tugged together, because a part of her didn't care about right and wrong, either. She just wanted to win.

Nicholas' mouth curved the tiniest bit, like he saw the secret Badness lurking in her thoughts.

That pissed her off even more. "What do you want from me? Tell me the truth."

Nicholas never did well when he had to answer emotionally charged questions without preparation. "I want what I've always wanted…" *His gaze traced over her face and he hunted for words.* "You and I… Kidnapping you was…" *He sighed and started again.* "You've been nothing but kind to me, your whole life, Marion. I know that. But, this obsession I have is too…" *He trailed off with a low curse.*

"Yes!" *She was able to interpret the bullet-points of that explanation and he was right.* "You're obsession with Robin has to end!" *Finally, he made some sense.* "Nick, will you stop this crazy plan, then?"

His whole body jolted at the shortened form of his name. She hadn't called him that in years. She'd barely spoken to him, at all, because he'd been glowering at her, and then off at war, and then back in Nottingham and glowering at her, again. "No."

Marion threw her hands up in aggravation. "No?! Really?"

"I'm not stopping." *It was a vow.* "I can't. The wedding will go on, and I'll arrest Hood, and then…." *He paused, like he wasn't sure what would happen next.*

"I don't like being used as a tool to hurt Robin." *Marion stated flatly.* "It's not fair to me, Nicholas."

He winced a bit. "Don't call me that."

"Don't use me as a pawn in this never-ending fight!"

"You're not a pawn." *He scoffed, like it was obvious.*

"You're at the center of everything."

All Marion heard was blame in those words. "How is this my fault? I barely even rate a mention, in your big feud! In anything! I get no say. No adventures. No plans. No one ever wants to hear what I think..."

"Tell me what you think, then." *He interrupted.* "Of course, I want to hear that. I like talking to you."

Marion hesitated. "You... do?" *Then why did he never do it?*

"*Of* course. And I would truly like to hear you sing, right now." *All of that had been delivered in a sincere tone.* "Please, duchess. Go on stage and sing for me."

Robin had never wanted to hear her sing. He'd even complained when she hummed.

That fissure of guilt snaked through Marion, again. She'd technically done nothing but stand there. No one in Nottingham could say that she'd broken any rules of decorum. But something about this whole conversation felt like a betrayal to Robin, just the same.

There was an undercurrent of heat inside of her, when she looked into Nicholas' eyes. It struck her as dangerous. Disloyal. Standing so close to him, she felt warm all over. Her breathing felt rushed and her heart was going fast.

Panic filled her.

Nicholas' gaze hadn't strayed from her even once. Like she was the only thing he saw.

Marion stared back, half-hypnotized. Trying to think of what to do. This had never happened before. Not ever. *Not even with Robin.*

"Marion..."

"I'm going back to the castle." *She blurted out, at the same time he began to speak.*

Nicholas had kidnapped her, for crying out loud. He was her True Love's mortal enemy. She didn't know what was happening exactly, but it frightened her how right *it felt to talk to him and let him look at her.*

But it wasn't right. It was all wrong.

"You want to go back now?"

"Yes. Right now." She decided a little defiantly. "I'll sing Robin a song, when he finally gets here to save me." No, she wouldn't. He'd hate that and it would make her feel awkward... and why the hell was it so warm?

Nicholas' expression went shuttered. "Better make it a funeral dirge. When Hood gets here, I'm going to hang him."

Turning on her heel, Marion retreated towards the door.

Ten years before, she'd left Nicholas' side and forfeited her chance at the May Day Queen title, because she was too worried about all the wrong things. In retrospect, Marion should've just taken Nicholas up on his offer and cheated to win the crown. She *still* wanted that damn tiara. It was currently displayed on a satin pillow, up on the stage. All the arts-and-craftiness in her soul longed for the stupid rhinestones.

Whatever.

Marion made a face. She wasn't competing this time around, either. She hadn't touched a piano in ten years, so she'd be even worse at playing, now. She'd lose, and still have no crown, and embarrass herself, and she had way more important things to focus on.

Speaking of which... Nicholas came up beside her and Clorinda was forgotten. Marion's mood improved, just looking at him. "Hello, my darling boopsy-woo."

He flashed her a put-upon look at the endearment. "Definitely not that one."

"'Sugar-face?' 'Sir Kiss-a-lot?'"

Nothing.

Marion rolled her eyes at him. "There has to be *some* pet name you like?"

"Not so far." Nicholas leaned a shoulder against the wall next to her, exactly like he'd done ten years before. Creating a small private space, for just the two of them. "Why are you standing over here, hiding in the corner, duchess?"

"I'm not hiding. I'm *thinking*."

"About?"

"Last time we were here." She sent him a sideways look. "I think you were trying to flirt with me."

"My God. That must have been terrifying."

His horrified tone made her grin. "Actually, you did a super good job. Too good a job, because you scared me."

"You never have to be afraid of me, Marion. Not any version, in any timeline."

"No. See," she wrinkled her nose, still feeling stupid, "I was in love with Robin. I believed I was, anyway. But, you made me feel all... *warm*. And I liked how your eyes stayed on me."

Nicholas began to smile. "Where else would they be?"

"Well, it made me afraid, because I was drawn to you. And I felt disloyal to Robin. And so I hid in my room and thought about how much I hated you. And then I possibly had a dream about you and refused to see you again until the wedding."

The smile was wider now. "What kind of dream?"

Marion sniffed loftily and refused to answer.

"You had a sex dream about me? While you were still with Hood?" Nicholas was unapologetically delighted with that news.

Marion made a face at him. "You offered to rig the May Day Queen contest for me, and I was a tiny bit intrigued."

"You were, huh?" His big hand toyed with her hair, rolling one of the curls between his stony fingers.

"*Yes.* Alright? But, overall, it was not my finest moment. Like I said, it felt disloyal to even notice another man, when I was supposed to be dating Robin."

"Disloyal to Hood? The jackass who's run off and abandoned you in my granite clutches? I could be doing very, *very* Bad things to you, up at that palace, Marion. He *knows* that and still he's hiding."

Marion considered his words. "Fair points." Why *was* she feeling guilty? Of course she was attracted to Nicholas! The May Day Queen Contest was the first time she'd consciously noticed it, but it was bound to come out sooner or later. Who else could even compare to him?

"Did you ever stand outside my house and listen to me play the piano?" She asked.

He hesitated at the random question. "Only sometimes."

"How many sometimes?"

"Seven hundred-ish."

She loved it when he was obsessive. "The noise of it didn't bother you?"

"Noise never bothers me, when you're the one making it."

He was *such* a sweet-talker.

Marion stood on tiptoe, closer to his ear, feeling better about everything. Nicholas always made her feel better. "In my sex dream, I was in a wedding dress and you were pinning me against a stone wall. Your hand fisted in my hair. Marking me with your teeth. Making me say I was yours, over and over and over. I came so hard, it woke me up."

Nicholas gave a choked sound, like his oxygen supply had been cut off.

Marion shined a mischievous smile.

"Such a little tease." He got out and he had to adjust his uniform to hide his erection.

Marion snickered.

The latest girl finished her piano solo and then it was time for the next one. It was hard to tell where one stopped and the next started, since they were identical, so the balding guy was mostly needed as a place marker. "Our final contestant tonight is... uh," the announcer cleared his throat, "Marion Huntingdon."

A shocked silence filled the ballroom.

No one was more shocked silent than Marion. It took her a second to realize the announcer meant *her*. She hardly recognized the name as her own. But then everyone was looking at her, with hostility and expectation, like they actually expected her to perform. That couldn't be right. What was happening?

Instinctively, her eyes jumped to Nicholas' face.

He looked back at her with contrived innocence.

"*You* did this?" She hissed, quickly putting it together. "What the hell were you thinking?!"

"I'm thinking you want the tiara. You've been talking about it for days." He gestured towards the stage. "Go get it."

"I can't!" Why did none of the Nicholases understand? "I can't play the piano well enough and the judges only like the piano."

"I *am* the judge. And I hate the piano. I think you'll be surprised how much I favor whatever your talent is."

Marion blinked. "You're the judge?" She repeated blankly. The words made no sense. "Of the May Day Queen contest? How?"

"I appointed myself."

"Can you do that?"

He scoffed. "I'm the Sheriff of Nottingham. Who's going to stop me?"

Marion stared up at him, her mind racing. "This is how you were going to rig it the first time, too." She guessed. "I always wondered that."

"Probably. I'm pretty predictable."

No, he wasn't. "It's wrong to cheat, you know."

He didn't seem convinced. "I guess it depends on how important the prize is."

"Are you going to judge the competition fairly, Nick?" She crossed her arms over her chest. "Yes or no?"

"Hell, no."

Marion very slowly smiled.

"You still intrigued by me, duchess?"

"Hell yes." She loved it when he was wicked. "I can beat them all without cheating, though." And she suddenly believed it.

"Uh... Maid Marion?" The announcer prompted into the microphone. "Are you coming?"

"Go." Nicholas gently nudged her forward. "I'm sure you'll win through sheer talent. And if you don't...?" He shrugged, with zero concern. "You're still going to win."

Oh, she had definitely traveled through time for the right groom.

"The stage-mothers of Nottingham will *hate* you for this." Marion bounced up and down on her heels, giddy with all the impending tears and recriminations from those evil bitches. Making Nottingham suffer was always such a joy. "The mass hangings are one thing, but they will *never* forgive you for wrecking their beauty pageant."

Nicholas lounged against the wall, content with his unpopularity, as long as she was smiling at him. "Fuck 'em all."

No wonder she'd had sex dreams about this man for a decade.

Marion beamed up at him, her heart in her eyes, and then bounded off towards the stage. Shoving past a scowling Clorinda, she climbed up the wooden steps and headed straight for the microphone. "Anybody here play the piano?"

There was a general murmur that roughly translated to, "Isn't *she* supposed to be doing that part?" Marion ignored it, her eyes on Much-the-Miller, who had hesitantly raised a hand.

"Awesome!" She pointed to the President of the Peasants' Guild, whose mom had wanted him to be a musician. "Get your ass up here and accompany me."

Marion might be assured first place, but that didn't mean she wouldn't do her very best to win it fairly. ...Just to rub it in Clorinda's dumb face.

She was terrible at playing instruments, but back in the WUB Club, one of the members of the Saturday share circle had been a siren. Calliope had been happy to give singing lessons to pass the time. It was the type of one-on-one instruction you could only really get while doing hard time. Prison really did provide a quality education, if you were motivated to learn.

And Marion loved to sing.

Calliope had a twelve octave range and a real talent for teaching. She'd also been a huge fan of the country singer, Pecos Bill, so most of the lessons had been learning his endless parade of hits.

"Do you know *My Own True Love*?" Marion asked, when Much-the-Miller made his way to the stage. "Everyone knows that song, right?"

It charted at number one in every kingdom with sound. It was a huge power ballad of complicated vocals and dramatic lyrics. Lovelorn and tragic, but with a hint of eventual redemption. And it was *big*. Real big. If you were going to sing *My Own True Love*, you had to go all in or it just wouldn't work. Granted, it was going to lose a bit of drama, without the instrumental overlays, but Marion could make up for it.

Much-the-Miller shook his head. His eyes darted around like he had no idea what he was doing on the stage.

"You don't know that one? Pecos Bill sings it."

"Who?"

Holy shit. People here didn't know who Pecos Bill was, yet? Well, that would need to change. "Here." She all but shoved him onto the piano bench. "It goes like this." She remembered enough piano lessons to pick out the chorus. Or at least it was close enough. "Just play that at the *big* parts. Believe me, you'll know when we get there."

He nodded, his eyes glassy with stage fright.

"Good. Make your mom proud and play." Marion turned back to the microphone. "A very long time ago, a handsome man asked me to sing a song for him." She told the crowd. "And I said 'no'. I was feeling a little too... warm. So, I'd like to make it up to him, now."

She met Nicholas' eyes across the ballroom and very deliberately winked at him.

His lips parted, just like they had that day when he was thirteen. Like he suddenly knew she was playing a trick and he was thrilled to be a part of the fun. The man was already dazzled by her.

...And they hadn't even started the show, yet.

The song started off low, with just Marion's voice stroking up and down the lyrics. Soft tragic yearning for a True Love beyond reach. Need and desire and perfect pitch. Was it as good as Calliope could sing? No. But it crushed the May Day Queen pageant. By the end of the first verse, jaws had dropped throughout the audience. Whether they were surprised at her siren-taught skills or the debut of a monster country music single was anyone's guess. Marion didn't much care.

Her eyes stayed on Nicholas, because she was only singing to him.

And he knew it. He slowly straightened away from the wall, his expression gradually shifting from casual confidence, to disbelief, to downright reverence.

Much-the-Miller regained a bit of sense and started coming in with the piano. Apparently, he'd decided this was his chance for stardom and he actually wasn't too bad. He had enough skill to follow the song's progression, giving her some accompaniment to play off of.

Marion made the most of it. The song got faster, and lyrics became calls for the lost True Love to return. Assurances and demands and laments for all that had happened. Her voice rising and hitting higher notes. Nailing them. And all the while her gaze was locked on Nicholas. No one in the room could miss that the song was just for him.

Nicholas started for the stage, shoving people aside, without taking his eyes off Marion. The noise of this was definitely not bothering him. He was drinking it in.

"Holy *shit*." She heard Boulder mutter from somewhere off to the side. "There's going to be a riot, if he claims her for really *real*."

"Worth it." Rockwell whispered back.

Pecos Bill had sung about a female lover. Marion switched the lyrics, making it a heartfelt ode to just one man. She held onto the microphone and poured herself into the words, not worried now about hitting every nuance perfectly, just focused on her performance. Her voice reflecting the aching loss of her lost love. Her dedication to his memory. The price she'd pay to have him beside her once again.

Nicholas reached the edge of the stage and stood there, his eyes hot.

Much-the-Miller had gained confidence and was now improvising music that kind of, almost matched the song. Not too shabby.

Clorinda crossed her arms over her ample chest, her hate a palpable miasma oozing out in all directions. Marion ignored her. Well, first she mentally gloated. *Then,* she ignored her. But this was bigger than Clorinda now. This was about Nicholas.

Marion's hips moved as she entered into the finale, gliding from side-to-side behind the microphone stand. Her head began to bob along with the rhythm she heard in her head, trying to convey it without any of the drums or guitars. Throwing herself into the performance. Marion's hands rose and fell with the song, communicating as she always did: With her whole damn body.

Nicholas was transfixed. He'd even stopped blinking.

The last verse had an operatic quality of angst and passion and soaring melody. The lost man would return, wouldn't he? Or was it all the desperate dream of a woman who could never move on from her own True Love? The music got more demanding, topping out Marion's vocal range. It took her weeks of lessons to hit that show-stopping high note. And it was all worth it. Even in this body, she could sustain the echoing finale. The trick was... there was no trick.

You just had to go for it, full speed ahead, all in, no stop.

Gasps filled the assembly hall as her voice rang out clear and strong, bouncing off the hard surfaces of the floor and ceiling and walls so it sounded *big*. Huge and all-encompassing, like love itself.

Nicholas' pupils dilated, gaping up at her in absolute wonder.

The song faded away and Much-the-Miller allowed the piano to quiet along with it. Marion stepped back from the microphone, her chest heaving from exertion. Dead silence greeted her. No one even clapped. They were too bug-eyed and astonished. Marion executed a Maidenly curtsy just to fuck with her uptight audience of judgmental douchebags. Her proud grin was only for Nicholas.

"You once said you wanted to hear me sing." She told him, breathlessly.

He gave his head a dazed shake, an incredulous smile curving his mouth. Bypassing the stairs, he vaulted up onto the stage and loomed over Marion. He stared down at her, like she truly was a siren. Maybe she was. She'd lured him right to her side.

"So, did I win?" She asked sweetly.

Clorinda stormed off in a weepy huff, all her dreams destroyed.

Nottingham society was abuzz with unhappiness and disapproval.

The gargoyles were subtly moving to block the stage, in case an angry mob attacked.

Nicholas didn't seem to notice any of it. All his attention was on her. He snatched the rhinestone tiara off its white satin pillow and dropped it onto Marion's head. Then, he was sweeping her up into his arms, kissing her right in front of the entire kingdom.

There might've been some wiggle room, even after the kiss at the festival. Some doubt that Marion was with Nicholas for really *real*. Now, that was gone. Now, all of Nottingham knew the truth. Marion wasn't kidnapped, at all. The Sheriff of Nottingham was the actual prisoner here. The man was totally in her thrall and she was never letting him go.

Marion wrapped one hand around his neck to hang on and grabbed her crown with the other, laughing against Nicholas' lips. Boulder had been wrong. This wasn't about Nicholas' claiming her. This was about Marion claiming *him*.

Just like she should have ten years before.

That's why the stupid May Day Queen title had lingered in her mind for so long. She suddenly understood it. It wasn't the crown. (Although that was obviously awesome.) No, this was the moment Marion should have had the guts to listen to her instincts. She should've sung as loud as she liked, won her damn tiara, and gone home with the right groom.

Even back then, she'd felt the pull towards Nicholas. She'd looked into his eyes and experienced a connection far deeper than she'd ever had with Robin. She'd *felt* it. She'd just been too afraid to take the risk.

But not this time. This time, she was only afraid of losing the magic she'd found with this man. This time, she was fixing her mistakes and not worrying about making new ones in the process. This time, she was only listening to her heart and soul. This time, she was full speed ahead, all in, no stop about

Nick Greystone.
    And everyone knew it.

Chapter Twenty-Four

The following note arrived on my desk. It is published here in its entirety, complete with uncensored language.

Dear Alan,
Good news! I can answer the headline question from your article, "WHERE IS 'KING' KONG?"
His wife murdered him on the lawn of a brothel.

I'm happy to provide a complete list of all the noblemen who were there with him, as proof of my claim. They witnessed the whole thing, along with the prostitutes they were cavorting with. But, I have a feeling the wives and mothers of Nottingham would prefer their names not be published. It might prove embarrassing. Better to just forget the whole sordid thing and socially banish that lying murderess from polite society.

Gosh, I sure hope that doesn't wreck Bagheera's dreams of ruling over the Nottingham Garden Club, though. Such a great gal. I really enjoyed her quotes about me being a Bad influence.
Tell her I said "Hi!" and to go fuck herself.

Best wishes,
Maid Marion

Alan A. Dale- "Nottingham's Naughtiest News"

    Nicholas always kept a mental count of all the people he was going to hang.
    The disapproving citizens of Nottingham were making that list longer, by the minute.
    As Marion led him down the alleyways of

Nottingham's Barn Owl District, every moralizing asshole they past was glowering at her. A Maid's reputation was always precarious. One wrong step and she was ruined in the eyes of Nottingham society.

And Marion had been making *a lot* of risky steps lately.

Her letter to the editor in the newspaper today was just the latest in a long line of burned bridges. The Merry Men's incarceration certainly hadn't helped with her popularity. Robin Hood being on the run, in connection to a dead housekeeper, was also an issue. Then there was Marion's outspoken dismissal of Maidly-ness, her extravagant wedding plans making all the nobles' tasteful tastes look bland in comparison, and her kinda-sorta friend Trevelyan cultivating mortal enemies everywhere he went. The list went on and on and *on.*

Marion's refusal to act like a hostage was still her biggest mark of disfavor, though. Nottingham would tolerate some minor scandals, but a Maid engaged to a gargoyle for really *real* was a deal-breaker for them. Nicholas had warned Marion to stop touching him in public. He'd warned her of the dire consequences she was courting, by smiling up at him so brilliantly. He warned her not to walk beside him, like she wanted to be there.

Marion hadn't listened. When did she ever listen?

Instead, she kissed him in front of the entire May Day Queen pageant.

Nicholas should've been strong enough to make the decision easier for her, of course. For her sake, he shouldn't have reacted the way he did. Seeing her in that innocent white dress, her body swaying as she sang just to him, had short-circuited his brain. He had never in his life been so mesmerized.

For once, Nicholas hadn't been overwhelmed by loud sounds. Not when Marion was creating them, weaving them together so they transported anyone hearing them to someplace better. It had been a revelation. Like listening to colors swirl around him. Marion's voice was magical. *Marion* was magical. Staying away from her had been impossible. He might as well have fought the pull of gravity.

But his obsession with the woman had ruined her reputation, once and for all.

Good.

His reverse conscience had a point. Why *should* Nicholas hide his feelings? How would that benefit him, at all? If Marion was tossed out of Nottingham's respectable circles, she'd have nowhere to go but Nicholas. He'd known that since the festival and now it had actually come to pass. She didn't seem upset about it, so there was no real harm done.

It could even help to keep Hood away.

Granted, that jackass might still want her, even after everything. Nicholas couldn't conceive of anyone *not* wanting Marion, so it seemed likely to him that Hood would continue to try and lure her away. Nicholas would, if their positions were reversed. But maybe --*maybe*-- the threat of social ostracism would cool Hood's ardor enough that he'd give up. The man was all about adulation. The threat of losing that might just win out over his True Love. With Hood bowing out of the race, Nicholas's path would be wide open.

All in all, it was a logical plan.

Except a natural consequence of ruining Marion's reputation was Marion's reputation got ruined. Watching the hypocritical Nottinghamers silently judge her pissed him off. Marion had done nothing wrong. Nothing at all. If they wanted to see someone actually committing Badness in the world, he'd be happy to offer up-close and personal demonstrations with a rope and gallows.

As a result, his execution list just got longer and longer.

And the trials were happening faster and faster.

"I just love pissing these bastards off." Marion said gleefully. Her arm was once again looped through his, as they walked. Nicholas didn't do a thing to dissuade her. Why should he? "I think I've ruined the kingdom's whole notion of Maidenhood."

Nicholas grunted, his gaze on a cobbler who was watching Marion intently. Imagining all the things Nicholas was doing to her, up at the castle. No doubt liking the idea that she was being forced to submit to a rock-monster. It was all over his face. The cobbler rubbed at the front of his apron, where an erection was forming, watching Marion's ass in her stolen pants. Wanting what belonged to Nicholas.

The cobbler suddenly realized he was being watched by the Sheriff of Nottingham. He paled and quickly tried to dart away, down a dirty alleyway. Too late. His name was on the list.

Nicholas glanced at Quarry over his shoulder.

Twenty seconds later, the cobbler was being yanked off the street, with stone hands wrapped around his neck. Another guilty verdict.

Marion had no clue justice was happening all around her. "I don't like birds." She said with the randomness that he loved about her. She was always so unpredictable. The May Day Queen crown was perched on her head, the rhinestones twinkling. Nicholas loved that, too. She looked adorable in hats. "Well, except for the parrot sommelier I've hired for our reception. He wears a little tuxedo and picks incredible wine pairings. Isn't that cute? He's expensive, but *so* worth it."

"I'm sure King Richard would agree, if he was alive to get the bill."

Marion nodded happily. "But anyway, *ordinary* birds are not my thing. I don't get why the people of this neighborhood don't do something about all the damn owls."

She had a point. The buildings in the Barn Owl District were, unsurprisingly, covered in barn owls. The creatures nested in the damaged rooflines and the crumbling facades of the ancient structures, filling the street with feathers and droppings. The smell was rancid, even for Nottingham.

"There's no money to get rid of them." He told her. "There's no money for anything in the whole kingdom, but this is one of the poorest spots of all. All the taxes that would've been used to capture the birds went into Hood's pockets."

"Speaking of which... Did you know Richard gave the gardens at my house a special tax exemption? I wanted to ask you about it yesterday. It helped sell the estate *really* fast, but I never technically applied for that thing. I didn't even know it *was* a thing, before I got a letter telling me I didn't have to pay."

"There are a lot of arcane tax laws in Nottingham." He shrugged, watching the barn owls. "And your gardens are lovely, Marion."

"I know, but... it's strange, right?"

"Not as strange as you dragging me to this birdcage to speak to a man I hate." He'd been complaining about the trip all morning, but she wasn't listening. "Pinocchio is a liar. Anything he tells you, believe the opposite. This whole thing is a waste of time."

"What does he lie about?"

"Everything important." Nicholas shook his head, hating this whole plan. "He's a heartless, soulless beast."

"Because he was originally carved from wood? That's not fair, Nick. You were originally carved from rock, and you have a heart and a soul."

Maybe I don't. Maybe that's why I never found my purpose. Maybe I'm just rock, with no heart and soul to commit to anything, at all.

Nicholas shook aside the depressing thoughts. His reverse conscience was feeling morose now. Lately, it hadn't been sure what to tell him or how to feel. It was odd. "It's not that Pinocchio had to work to become really *real*. It's *how* he did it. That's what makes him heartless and soulless."

"What did he do that was so Bad?"

Boulder met Nicholas' eyes and he gave a small shake of his head, dissuading him from telling Marion all the details. He was right. Those images didn't need to be in her head.

What Pinocchio did was... terrible. *Beyond* terrible. The gargoyles at least partially understood why he'd done it, though, which made it even more terrible.

If there was one bedtime dream of every gargoyle child, it was to become a real boy. Nicholas had researched the idea well into adulthood, the same way he'd researched ways to break True Love bonds. With frantic desperation and false hope. For a time, he'd convinced himself that if he could only turn into a human, he'd have a shot with Marion.

It had been a doomed idea, for many reasons. Not the

least of which was the amount of distilled Badness it took to enact such a powerful spell. And the deals you had to make to acquire that kind of dark magic. And the devastation it inevitably wrought in its wake.

To get a wish that big granted, you had to give things up. Things that you couldn't get back again. The things that meant the very most to you. There was always a price. And Nicholas had instinctively known it would be far too high.

Pinocchio had willingly paid it, though.

He'd gained humanity through inhuman means. Because of that, the gargoyles were both repelled and fascinated by the man. Pinocchio went farther than any of them were prepared to go. Seeing him reminded them of why they chose to remain as they were. But it also made them question what they would be willing to trade, if they were ever offered the opportunity.

In the abstract, it was easy to say you'd never give into temptation. That you were too smart to be fooled by some evil-doer offering a bargain. That you would never risk what you loved the most. ...But, there was always that kernel of doubt.

None of the men liked to visit Pinocchio, because he made them question what choices they'd make, if they ever had the chance to choose a new destiny.

Marion's eyes traced over Nicholas' expression and whatever she saw there must have told her enough. "I see." She said quietly.

She didn't. Not fully. Nicholas hoped she never did.

Marion cleared her throat, glancing around her protective ring of gargoyles. They were all abnormally quiet, brooding about Pinocchio.

With the Wraith still on the loose, Nicholas was taking no chances with Marion's safety. He'd brought all six of his top lieutenants on this mission. Not that he *could've* left them behind, even if he'd wanted to. The gargoyles had just shown up this morning, like it was understood they were coming along.

They formed a loose circle around Marion, as they

moved through the streets. Clearing her path, without any orders being given. The townsfolk might glare and mutter, but none of them got within four yards of her. All the men knew Marion was the only priority now. Their loyalty and strength had swung behind the woman faster than Nicholas could ever have imagined. Anything that came at Marion would have to get through all of them.

She didn't seem to notice that she was shielded by a wall of living stone. "You know," she said casually, as if trying to lighten the mood, "tomorrow you're going to marry a rich woman, Nick. I have the low-down on every fad and invention coming out, for a long time. Time travel seriously helps with stock picks."

"And sports gambling. Marvin Wolf is the player to bet on, as I recall. He's very handsome and charming." Nicholas was still disgruntled over her praise of the man.

"*Marrok,* not Marvin. And yes, the Big, Bad Wolf is probably the best looking guy in the Four Kingdoms."

Nicholas grunted.

"Otherwise, Marrok's not my type, at all, though." Marion went on, wrinkling her nose. "Always smiling and talking and making people like him…" She gave a mock shudder. "It's just a nightmare. I could never be serious about a handsome man who isn't adorably antisocial and into hanging peasants as a hobby. I have standards, you know."

Against his will, Nicholas' mouth curved.

"Anyway, I was thinking that my burgeoning fortune should buy us the nicest house on Neverland Beach. We need a place of our own, right?"

Nicholas would die for just the chance of that.

"So, as long as we avoid that rabid bitch Tinkerbelle and her blood feud with Thumbelina, everything should be great." She frowned a bit, momentarily lost in thought. "Actually, we might be able to pick up property cheaper, after the massacre. Shit. When does that happen? Like two years from now?"

"Massacre?"

Marion shrugged and kept talking. "Anyway, we'll

soon be swimming in money and covered in sand, precious-pie. I have it all figured out. We just gotta catch a murderer first." She paused, looking around the Barn Owl District. "Oh, and I have to eviscerate this fucking kingdom, of course. But, that shouldn't take long."

All the gargoyles were listening, now. They didn't care about Nottingham, but they certainly cared that Nicholas might be *leaving* Nottingham. He could see it in their faces and it surprised him. He'd stayed distant from them, but they liked him anyway.

...And he was fairly sure he liked them back.

Marion casually looked around at the other men, as if their worried expressions were only to be expected. "You guys are coming with us, right?" She offered, like she already knew the answer. "It's going to be a big house. Plenty of room for Nick's family. I have it all planned."

As a chorus, the gargoyles exhaled in relief.

"We're coming." Rockwell said, happiness in his voice. "I did a visualization exercise about this and willed it into being, you know."

The others were already muttering amongst themselves about what they should pack for life in a tropical paradise.

Nicholas blinked.

"Awesome." Marion shined a smile at all of them. It was brighter than the fake gems in her beloved plastic crown. "Hey, should we get a pool? Do you need one at the beach?"

"We need one." Oore told her with total surety.

"We'll have the ocean." Boulder argued, probably just to argue. "Why do we need a pool?"

"Salt water. Fresh water." Oore retorted, weighing his hands up and down like a scale. "Do you only want to have *one?*"

Boulder frowned, as if that possibility did indeed sound like a tragic fate.

"Both." Marion nodded wisely, also persuaded by Oore's logic.

Everyone else seemed to agree.

Gravol slung an arm around Marion's shoulder, nearly crushing her with his puppy-like exuberance and sheer size. Nicholas started to push him away, but Marion just laughed and let Gravol drag her along. Cragg began expounding on the virtues of personal bowling alleys in a house. Rockwell was brainstorming landscaping options for their new island estate. Quarry grabbed some other son of a bitch who looked at Marion wrong, not even waiting for Nicholas to give the command.

This was either very Good or very Bad.

If Marion changed her mind and broke the engagement, it wouldn't just be Nicholas' heart she shattered. There would be no recovery for *any* of them. Marion gave all the gargoyles hope. Taking that away would be catastrophic and Nicholas wasn't sure he could stop it from happening.

He didn't fully understand why she was with him in the first place. So, how could he convince her to stay?

"Maid Marion!" Alan A. Dale came jogging up, trying to worm his way through the barrier of gargoyles surrounding her. Cragg shoved him back. Alan didn't let it dissuade him. Weasels were agile creatures. "Can I get a comment from you about the rumors?" He called, his beady eyes fixed on her.

"What rumors?" Marion shot him a frown.

"About your mother and King Jonathan." Alan adjusted his glasses on his furry nose, his phone at the ready to jot down notes. "Speculation about their affair has resurfaced, now that we know King Jonathan had a lovechild..."

Marion cut him off. "My mother did not have an affair with Jonathan! Are you out of your mind? She and my father were True Loves! No one sleeps with another man when they have a True Love."

Nicholas winced.

"It's well known the former duchess and King Jonathan were 'best friends.'" Alan added air quotes around the words. "She advised him about everything. I have pictures to prove how much time they spent together. Holidays. Birthdays. Picnics. He's always there at the Huntingdon estate."

"Jonathan was my father's cousin, you moron. Of

course, he was in family photos."

Nicholas didn't like the reporter bothering Marion, but he also didn't want to slaughter the weasel right in front of her. It didn't seem like something even a creatively villainous groom should do the day before the wedding. "Do you want me to arrest him for harassment?" He asked quietly. "The dungeon is getting full, but I can always make room."

One way or another.

She shook her head, because she only ever counted on herself to solve problems. The idiot other-Nicholas and his words of wisdom at the altar were apparently to blame for that. No matter the timeline, Nicholas could be relied on to say the wrong thing. "I can handle this, turnip blossom. I'll give him a quote, if it keeps him from making up lies about my mother."

"Nottingham's Naughtiest News doesn't print lies!" Alan objected, still trying to get closer to her. This time Rockwell kept him at bay. Alan darted around to the other side of the gargoyle wall. "We thoroughly vet sources and investigate every detail of our stories."

"You once did an exposé on how Cinderella was really a zombie stripper."

Alan glanced right, then left, then leaned in closer. "Off the record? I've *heard* things about Cindy and those mice." He told her meaningfully. "That stripper story is completely plausible."

Marion rolled her eyes. "Look, my mother was never pregnant with King Jonathan's secret lovechild, if that's what you're insinuating. She was faithful to my father. They were very much in love. I am her only offspring. *That's* my response to the so-called rumors. Are we done?"

Alan readied his pen. "So, you're *denying* that the old duke hid your mother's illegitimate affair-baby away? That he forged a teeny iron mask to prevent the kid from ever taking the throne?"

Marion's lips pressed together and she glanced up at the mountainous gargoyle beside her. "Gravol, would you do me a favor?"

"Sure, Marion!"

"Smoosh that annoying weasel if he ever publishes a word of that nonsense, okay?"

Gravol smiled guilelessly. "Heck, I can smoosh him right now." He took a step towards Alan and the whole sidewalk seemed to shift under his colossal weight.

Alan's gaze widened behind the lens of his glasses and he took off running.

Gravol pouted. "He got away. Want me to chase him?"

"No thanks, buddy. You dealt with him perfectly." Marion patted his arm and grinned up at Nicholas. See? Handled."

"It would be no problem to hang Alan." Nicholas assured her, because it really was a better option. "I already have the gallows."

"Nope, I believe in freedom of the press. ...So long as they're writing mean stories about *other* people." She stopped in front of Pinocchio's magical relics shop. "Ah, here we are!"

The large sign over the door read, "The Terrible Dogfish." It still shocked Nicholas that Pinocchio had chosen that name. The little wooden fucker truly was demented. The dogfish had stolen away everything that should've mattered to him. You'd think he'd want to avoid remembering it, every time he passed through the door.

Or maybe he refused to forget it, because it would mean forgetting them, too.

Nicholas suppressed a shudder.

Marion was oblivious to the sign's deeper meaning. "Cute whale." She decided easily, glancing up at the painted logo, which must have haunted Pinocchio's every waking moment. "Okay, you guy's wait here. I'll be right back." She headed into the store, like she really expected the gargoyles to leave her alone with a heartless, soulless beast who'd fed his family to a sea monster.

Nicholas glanced at the others and they instantly began encircling the building, scanning for possible threats.

"What the hell are we even doing here?" Oore muttered, eyeing the sign with palpable distaste. "Pinocchio's a liar and this place gives me the creeps."

"She was asking about buying a gun the other night." Cragg shrugged. "Said she wanted to protect the commander. Let her get one, if she wants. She's too small to carry a broadsword, like a normal person."

Not even Oore could disagree with that analysis.

Nicholas frowned and followed Marion into the shop. He'd known Marion had come to The Terrible Dogfish as part of her investigation into the other-Nicholas' death, but he hadn't realized it was related to a weapon.

What was she up to?

Unlike the others, he doubted she wanted a gun to protect him. If that was the case, she wouldn't have put the Oak Major 1000 in the armory. She'd be lugging it around, because that enormous crossbow could do more damage than a sledgehammer. No, she must want a gun for some *other* reason, related to the first-Nicholas' demise.

People generally thought Nicholas was big and dumb, but he was surprisingly good at puzzles. It was why he excelled at being the Sheriff of Nottingham. He examined the evidence and reached logical conclusions. Thinking it over, he quickly understood Marion's actual intentions.

According to her, he'd be shot early Thursday morning. Guns were rare in Nottingham. Pinocchio was one of the few black market dealers around. The killer probably bought it from him.

She was looking for the gun that killed the other-Nicholas.

Marion was serious about this. All of it. He hadn't doubted her exactly, but his practical mind also hadn't delved deep into all the meta-physical realities of time travel. Marion was trying to save his life, because she'd lived through it once before. If Nicholas didn't help her, she might live through it again.

And he *wouldn't* live through it.

Nicholas didn't want to die. He refused. He could fight this. There wasn't another option. He had Marion, now.

He wouldn't give her up. He couldn't. There *had* to be

a way.

For the first time, Nicholas began to look at his "murder" the way he would any other crime. Pieces slid into place for him, recalling all the evidence Marion had laid out. It didn't take long for him to solve the mystery. He only needed three clues:

Someone had shot the other Nicholas inside his bedroom.

He hadn't fought back against the killer.

He'd unlocked the door to let them in.

There was only one person in the world he'd allow inside his bedroom. Only one person he'd never fight against. Only one person he'd unlock that door for. Only one person could have killed Nick Greystone so easily, in any timeline.

Nicholas closed his eyes, instantly knowing who was guilty.

Fuck.

Chapter Twenty-Five

How It Happened the First Time....

Robin Hood hadn't come to save her.

Maybe that wouldn't matter to Maid Marion, though.

Maybe Hood had some passable explanation for why he'd left her in the church. Maybe Marion would forgive him for being such an unmitigated asshole. Maybe she'd vanish into Sherwood Forest, with her arrow-shooting True Love, and he'd never see her again.

The Sheriff of Nottingham muttered a resigned curse, resting his forehead against the window. He would die if he couldn't see Marion, again.

Ever since she'd found the letters and stormed out, he'd been vacillating between hope and despair. Rethinking the whole day in his mind, he looked for what he could've done differently.

Nothing.

He'd change *none* of it, because he had gained far more than he'd lost. Even if he'd had a setback at the end, he'd still moved closer to his ultimate goal. Determination returned. The rock-hard core of Nicholas switched on, refocusing on the only thing that mattered.

Marion.

He wouldn't give her up. He couldn't. There *had* to be a way.

The letters were an issue, yes. Marion was furious about them. And her tears at the wedding still bothered him. He never wanted to see her cry. But overall, today had still been a success. It hadn't been the plan he expected, but it had worked. Marion had been curled up in his bed, for God's sake! The scent of her was on his pillow and the warmth of her body had touched his sheets. That alone was worth anything.

Nicholas had more tonight than he'd started with this morning. Much more than he'd ever thought to possess. By any reading of the evidence, he was closer to Marion than ever before and Hood was farther away.

No matter what she'd said, Marion was too kindhearted to hate Nicholas forever-after. She was too Good to hate anyone, even the man she blamed for ruining her life. For several amazing minutes, she'd been calmly talking to Nicholas, asking questions about his mother. And at that damn May Day Queen contest on Monday, there had been a moment when she'd smiled at him. She'd *smiled* at him! Maybe he could get her to do that, again. After a while, maybe she'd at least accept him as a friend. He'd always wanted that. Always.

He could build on what he now held. He felt that on some elemental level.

Marion might not like what Nicholas had done, but the two of them were connected. They both knew it. He had years to persuade her to see things his way. Decades. He wasn't going anywhere. Surely, Marion could get over Hood in decades. The man wasn't *that* fucking special.

He had so much time to convince her. To fix things.

A knock sounded on his bedroom door.

Surprised, Nicholas' head whipped around. As the least popular man in Nottingham, visitors weren't usually an issue for him. No one came to his room. No one except servants used the stairs to his tower. No one even talked to him, most days. Maybe it was one of the palace guards. His men were the only one's who'd ever seek him out.

"Go away." He snapped, fully expecting his orders to be followed.

Another knock. "It's me."

His eyes widened. Her voice was clear through the heavy wooden door. He would've known it anywhere.

Marion.

She'd come back!

Nicholas crossed the room without even consciously thinking about it, unlatching the massive locks on his door and yanking it open.

Marion stood there in a black cloak, her face partially hidden. She was staring back down the curving steps, like someone might have followed her to his isolated room. He couldn't have been more shocked if Santa Claus and the eight tiny reindeer showed up at his door.

"Marion." He breathed.

"Can I come in?" She didn't wait for an answer. She already *knew* the answer.

Marion started forward and Nicholas automatically fell back. Letting her into his private space and softly shutting the door behind her.

His brain was whirling. "What are you doing here?" He asked, trying to think of one possible reason she'd seek him out. Nothing came to mind.

"I had to see you." Her face was turned away, not wanting to look at him. Who could blame her? "It's urgent."

His eyebrows drew together in concern. "Are you alright? Are you hurt?" Surely Hood wouldn't have…"

She cut off his dark thoughts, ignoring his questions. "Do you know where the scepter is?"

The words were so bizarre that he didn't even process them. He just stared at her.

"King Jonathan's scepter." She prompted, in a silken tone. The kind of voice he'd always wished Marion would use when she talked to him. "It has a lion head on the top." She paused, her dainty hands tucked in her cloak pockets. "Do you have it, Nicholas?"

Nicholas.

She never called him that unless she was angry. Only Marion didn't sound angry. She sounded honeyed and whiling. Only Marion *never* sounded honeyed and whiling. Not when she spoke to him. And she *shouldn't* be speaking to him. Not after he'd kidnapped her, and lied to her, and tricked her when she was at her most vulnerable.

Marion shouldn't be in his room.

The hairs on the back of Nicholas' neck stood up. It was a feeling he hadn't experienced since that dark night in the foothills of the Pellinore Mountains.

"You're so clever." She went on, when he didn't respond. "You know Robin is trying to find the scepter, so you're keeping it from him. You know where it's hidden, don't you?"

Nicholas didn't have the scepter.

He didn't know who did.

He still didn't say anything.

Instead, his feet edged towards the door.

"Where are you going?" She asked sharply and Nicholas stopped moving.

That seemed to please her. "You can tell me all about it, you know." She all but cooed. "I promise, I won't let Robin know you have the scepter. I only want to be with *you* now, Nicholas. Not him."

Against his will, his whole body jerked.

She giggled, seeing his reaction at her words. Her eyes were demurely lowered. Her profile a work of art. "We belong together." One graceful hand left her pocket to trail along the nightstand, where the lamp had once stood. Enticingly. As if she didn't even remember shattering it against the wall, just a few hours earlier. "If only we had money, we could run away."

Nicholas stayed quiet. That wasn't unusual for him. Everyone in Nottingham knew he was silent by nature. And choice. Marion was the only one he'd ever wanted to talk to.

"That scepter is very valuable." She sat on his bed, like she had in a million of his daydreams. "If you had it, the two of us would have enough gold to leave Nottingham tonight. ...Together."

It was everything Nicholas could ever hope to hear.

And it was all a lie.

He wouldn't have time to fix things, after all. He knew that, now. There was no way he could get out of this room fast enough to escape. And there was a very small chance he was wrong about her, so he couldn't fight, either. The element of surprise was lost, because he'd never take the risk of harming

Marion. Not even to save his own life.

"I don't have the scepter." Nicholas heard himself say, as if from a great distance.

She faltered, frustration flashing across her perfect face, before she controlled it. "Are you sure?" She prompted, straining to be sweet. "You'd tell me if you have it, right? You love me."

"No." He said quietly. "I love Marion."

Her head whipped around, her gaze slashing to his in fury and surprise. Their eyes met for the first time since she'd arrived at his door.

And Nicholas knew he'd been right.

She gave a harsh laugh and turned to look him full in the face. "I didn't expect a gargoyle to be so clever." The Wraith mocked. "I should have known you would be, after what you did to poor Jiminy. I've just never known anybody to 'see' that fast."

Nicholas didn't know who Jiminy was, but it didn't really matter. "*All* I see is Marion." He said truthfully. "And you're not her."

"I'm everyone." The voice was cold. As cold as the gun in her hand. The fake-Marion pulled it from her cloak pocket and aimed it straight at his heart. "And you're *no one*. Not anymore." She shrugged. "If you don't have the scepter, you're no good to me. But at least, I'll get rid of that bitch Marion. That's all I *really* care about, anyway."

Nicholas didn't feel the bullets impacting his chest.

He didn't feel his large body hitting the floor or his blood draining onto the cold stones.

He didn't feel his final breath rattle out.

His last seconds of life were spent far away from Nottingham's damp castle. He was thirteen years old. In Sherwood Forest. And a small brown-eyed girl playfully winked at him, like he was her very best friend.

Marion.

Chapter Twenty-Six

Countdown of the biggest scandals I've ever covered, as a seasoned and impartial reporter of truth:
Number 3: Pinocchio. Dogfish.

Alan A. Dale- "Nottingham's Naughtiest News"

The Terrible Dogfish was fascinating.

Marion's curious eyes ran all over the dusty, junk-filled interior, wondering about the weird objects crammed in around her. The tightly-packed shelves were full of exotic looking whatzits.

Statues of strange gods, carved from ancient orange stones. Shells from lands she'd never heard of and seas that didn't exist. Multi-colored bottles filled with bubbling liquids. Heavy gold chains heaped in careless piles. A painting of a woman with no eyes, who seemed to be looking right at her. A music box that endlessly played, but no music came out. Lots and lots and *lots* of crystal balls. Stacks of books, some of them locked shut with heavy keys. Knives and arrows of every description.

Magic. Everywhere. Even she could scent it in the air.

Marion turned in a circle, drinking it all in. Trevelyan would love this place. Too bad he was wasting his birthday sleeping with random kitchen-maids. At least he wasn't barbequing anyone, though. That was something. And if he *was* there, he'd just be stealing enchanted knickknacks and they'd all probably end up cursed. She already wasn't having the best morning and some weird-ass hex wouldn't make it any better.

The previous night, she'd dreamed that Nicholas was dead again and she was back in the WUB Club. The nightmare had woken her up with a stifled scream. To make matters worse, when she'd returned to her bedroom, after breakfast, there had been another note pinned to her pillow.

Robin had regrouped and was back to skulking around her. The man wrote her more now, than when he'd been in the war. *A lot* more. Elaborate cursive letters spelled out his newest inanities:

You win, Marion. I get the message.
You want to marry me. You're tired of waiting.
I know the sheriff was lying about sleeping with you, the same way he lied to you about me wanting you dead. I would never want that! I plan to make you my queen!
Greystone knows we belong together. <u>Everyone</u> knows it. Even you. You're just acting out by pulling all these crazy stunts. You want my attention... and you have it!
It won't be long before we can be together.
I was forced to leave you behind, yesterday, when I escaped the castle. I could see how you longed to come with me, back to Sherwood and our forest kingdom. But my mission to free Nottingham from the gargoyle menace is too important to wait. A gentle Maid would just slow me down. Try and understand your limitations and leave the planning to me.
We've both made mistakes, but we'll put it all behind us, now. We're destined for each other. Our blood is the purest in Nottingham. Nothing like that rock-monster's.
And stop wearing that stupid plastic crown he gave you!

The self-absorption and willful blindness of Robin's words set her teeth on edge. Why wouldn't he just accept he was dumped? Marion *hated* that the egotistical dipshit had been in her bedroom. It was just so icky.

Honestly, it seemed like Robin was waltzing in and out of the castle whenever he felt like it. Which was typical. Her ex had tunnels all over Nottingham. Sadly, she didn't know the location of most of them.

Marion wasn't going to mention the note to Nicholas, because she could handle it herself. Also, because her obsessive groom would flip the hell out. She didn't like keeping things from him, but he wasn't exactly sharing everything with her, either. This was a good lesson for him. She'd compromised by telling Boulder that he needed to check for holes in the perimeter defenses.

The grouchiest gargoyle was surprisingly receptive to her idea. He was convinced the former-him had been correct at Marion's trial. Nobody could have gotten through the gate without him seeing them. Boulder agreed to investigate the possibility of some secret entrance. Hopefully, he found something quickly.

The more she considered the evidence, the more certain she was that Robin hadn't killed Nicholas. But *someone* had. And if there was a hidden way into the castle, the killer could use it to sneak in and target Nicholas, again.

"Marion." Nicholas came striding up to her side, as she poked at a catur board carved from some kind of wobbly jelly that glowed. "Let me do this part of the investigation." His voice was strangely intent.

She blinked up at him in astonishment. "What?"

"I will question Pinocchio. You wait outside with Cragg and Quarry, alright?"

"No, it's not alright." Her eyes traced all over his face, reading his agitation. "What's going on? What's wrong?"

He frowned, not quite meeting her gaze. "I think," he seemed to be hunting for words, "you might be about to find out something that will... upset you."

That didn't sound good. "Tell me yourself, then."

"I will." He rubbed his forehead. "I promise. Later. I just don't want you hurt by the other-Nick's murder, any more than necessary."

Marion was getting worried. "Whatever you know, you need to tell me, *now*. I mean it." She thought for a beat. "Do you know who killed you? Is that it?"

"The Wraith killed the other-me." He assured her quickly, grasping her arm and guiding her back towards the exit. "I'm sure of that. There's no need for you to..."

"Hello, Marion." A boyish voice said, cutting him off.

She felt Nicholas tense and turned to look at the newcomer. Why, he was so sweet! A small, doll-like man, with button eyes and a jaunty cap. His nose was pretty long, but Marion had done time with a giant elephant-bee named Ned... until the Black Knight had swatted him. They'd had issues. Anyway, disproportionate nasal sizes weren't anything too unusual for her. She was fine with people not looking like she did. It made the world more interesting.

Marion smiled at Pinocchio. "Hi." She was a little surprised he knew her name. She'd never met the man before. Maids didn't usually frequent magical relics shops in the Barn Owl District, more's the pity. "I'm here to ask you about a gun you sold."

This was the most likely place for Nicholas' murderer to buy a weapon. If she could get a list of recent gun purchases from Pinocchio, she'd have a lead on the killer. Back in the original timeline, the gun had never been found, but the forensics expert testified it was a kf-2802 revolver.

Nicholas' grip on her arm tightened.

"Did the first one not work out for you, then?" Pinocchio's extremely long nose bobbed, as he hoisted himself up onto a stool behind the counter. "I can show you some other options, if you'd like. The kf-2802 is an older weapon, so maybe something with more firepower?"

Marion blinked. An anxious feeling twisted in her stomach.

Nicholas cursed under his breath.

Pinocchio's head tilted every which way. "Did you not come for another gun?" He asked her.

She looked up at Nicholas, like he might explain what was happening.

Nicholas slowly shook his head. "I'm so sorry." He sounded agonized.

"Is the sheriff... okay with your purchase?" Pinocchio asked, his strange eyes going back and forth between them. "I know guns are illegal in Nottingham, but how could I say no to a duchess?"

And Marion suddenly understood.

The Wraith had created an illusion of her on the midway, but this was so much worse. This was a living, breathing, exact replica of Maid Marion. Dressed in her body, the Wraith had bought a gun. It would no doubt do more. No wonder Guyla Gisborn had been so sure she'd seen Marion returning to Nicholas' room the night he died. Marion *had* been there.

She'd murdered him.

Her lips parted, but no sound came out. The Wraith had disguised itself as *her* to get close to Nicholas. It was able to kill him, because he'd trusted her. He'd been shot by someone he thought was… Marion.

She sagged against Nicholas, trying to think. Not wanting to think, at all. Wishing she could block it all out, or make it a lie, or redo it somehow. A strange sense of shock came over her, reminding her of that day in the church.

And just like that day in the church, huge arms wrapped tight around her.

"It wasn't your fault." Nicholas promised, holding her against his chest. "None of it. I will find the Wraith and I will kill it. That will end this, once and for all. Alright?"

She couldn't answer him. She would've started crying. Marion squeezed tight against the front of his uniform, trying to hold back the tears.

Nicholas hauled her even closer to his body. "Duchess, please don't. No version of me has *ever* wanted to see you cry. Not for *anything*. Certainly, not over my death, when I'm not even dead."

Yet.

But now the Wraith had the gun that had murdered him and it would be coming, again.

"Did you say a Wraith, Sheriff?" Pinocchio interjected, his boyish voice perturbed by the possibility. "Oh my… we haven't seen one of them in Nottingham for an age."

"For all you know, you're seeing them all the damn time." Nicholas shot back. "One of those bastards came in here pretending to be Marion and you sold it a gun."

"Oh my." Pinocchio repeated.

Marion closed her eyes, breathing in the scent of Nicholas and reassuring herself that he was alright. He pressed a kiss into her hair.

"You know something about Wraiths?" Nicholas demanded, his eyes on Marion, even as he spoke to Pinocchio.

"Even if I did, why would I tell you?"

"Because you sold Guyla Gisborn the Oak Major 1000 that shot up the palace, yesterday."

Pinocchio gasped. "That is simply not true! How can you even suggest…?"

Nicholas cut him off. "She kept the receipt in her room, you idiot."

Pinocchio's outraged expression vanished and he made an exasperated face. "Oh, very well. I sold the crossbow." He rolled his eyes. "I'm not the one who *used* it, though. I'm a businessman, not a criminal."

"Selling automatic crossbows *is* a crime and I'm about to find you guilty." Nicholas' voice was cold. "You're really *real*, now. So, you can die just as quick as the other criminals I hang… or you can tell me about Wraiths."

Pinocchio took the hint. "Of course! I'm always happy to help local law-enforcement." He smiled pleasantly.

"Can Wraiths see the future?"

"No. But they take on the memories of the people they duplicate. Enough of them anyway. The copies are never perfect, but they know plenty of secrets. Even when the victims they're impersonating are dead, they can remember some of what they once knew. It's very interesting, the things they can see."

Marion shivered.

"Some of their victim's personality seeps through the mask, as well, so they can be very convincing mimics. Except around the eyes." Pinocchio *tsk*ed. "Eyes are always hard to get right."

Nicholas wasn't interested in their problems with copy resolution. "What do Wraiths want?"

"Who knows if they want *anything?*" Pinocchio scoffed.

"*Everyone* wants something. Even monsters."

"Well, I'm not sure what a Wraith's desires could be, really. They can be any gender, species, color, social-rank…. so it seems like their problems would always be easy to solve. Just assume someone else's life, suck it dry and move on. Wraiths are…" He paused, as if looking for a proper description, "parasites. Large, crafty, dangerous bugs."

"Scorpions?" Nicholas guessed. Maybe anyone who'd fought in the Lyonesse desert instinctively thought of scorpions when someone said "dangerous bugs."

"More like oversized crickets. They can hop from place-to-place very fast. Teleporting perhaps?" He shrugged. "It's hard to tell."

"Teleporting crickets." Nicholas summed up. "Wonderful."

"They rarely look like the insects they are, if that helps any. They can take on the appearance of any living being they wish." Pinocchio paused again, this time with condescension. "Really *real* beings, anyway. They can't become gargoyles. But then, why would they want to?"

Nicholas ignored that taunt. "How do I kill it?"

"A hammer." Pinocchio said, as if it was obvious. "Just a small rap will do."

"A hammer?" Nicholas repeated scathingly. "The human soldiers finished off the one in Lyonesse with flaming arrows."

"No. You can stun a Wraith with other weapons, but only a hammer will kill it."

"It seemed pretty dead to me."

Pinocchio shook his head. "That's what it *wanted* you to think. It regenerated, the minute your backs were turned. Bugs are very hardy beings, you know."

"Or you're lying about this, the way you lie about most everything else. Anything you say, I believed the opposite."

"I might fib a bit, here or there, but I have no interest in hanging, Sheriff. And why would I want a Wraith to invade Nottingham? I live here, too. An infestation can cause all sorts of problems."

"So can a dogfish and you dealt with that okay."

Another --longer-- pause. "You don't like me very much do you?"

"No. I really don't."

"Because you don't approve of what I did to become real? Or because you're jealous I had the little wooden balls to do it?"

"I'm not jealous of you. You made the deal. I didn't. But, which of us is holding more?" Nicholas' arms tightened around Marion.

"For now, you're holding her." Pinocchio agreed. "But how long will it last, when she's a human and you're... not." His voice was almost pitying. "She'll want her True Love, sooner or later. They always do, in the end."

Nicholas' muscles went taut.

Marion roused herself from her agonized stupor, instinctively wanting to soothe him. "Nick?"

His attention was back on her in an instant. "Yes?"

She lifted a hand to touch his perfect face. She didn't want to hear any more of this. She wanted to go back to the castle and lock all the doors, so nothing could get to Nicholas. All that mattered was keeping him safe. "Take me home."

Chapter Twenty-Seven

Ancient vampire sect using hidden tunnels to travel around Nottingham!
Garlic sales skyrocket!
Are *you* safe from the blood-sucking monsters?

Alan A. Dale- "Nottingham's Naughtiest News"

Marion had locked herself in her room.

It was driving Nicholas crazy.

He stood across from her closed door, leaning against the wall, arms folded over his chest. His eyes stayed fixed on the wooden surface, willing it to swing open and for Marion to appear.

Half his life was spent waiting for Marion to appear. Watching out windows for her to walk by. Scanning rooms for the glint of her shiny hair. Listening for the sound of her approaching, because no one else's footsteps sounded like hers. Waiting for Marion was his main hobby. Or it *had* been until she'd moved into the castle.

For the last few days, he'd had so much more than fleeting glimpses of her. He'd had her time and attention and smiles. He didn't have to wait for them. She just *gave* them to him. He wouldn't return to cold isolation, stuck on the outside of her life.

Nicholas went *forward*, not back.

Jaw firming, he pushed away from the wall. "Marion?" He knocked on her door. "It's Nick. Open up."

Nothing.

She'd barely spoken after they'd left The Terrible

Dogfish. She'd pulled into herself and away from him. Nicholas wasn't going to allow that to go on. The idiotic former-him had told Marion that she could only count on herself. Now, Nicholas needed to say something to convince her otherwise.

Somehow.

Conversations were a struggle for him. The words always came out wrong. But, talking to Marion was worth the near certainty of making an ass of himself. He thought for a beat, trying to come up with a topic that might interest her and make her engage with him, again. She'd been asking about the damn tax exemption earlier. It wasn't something he particularly wanted to discuss, but he decided to give it a shot. Maybe he could gloss over the incriminating parts.

"The gardens at your estate are very beautiful. And very taxable. The real estate value on your property went up, because of them. A while back, I began to notice the bill was getting high."

And he'd noticed her clothes were no longer changing with the newest styles. She'd been wearing the same outfits, again and again. Nicholas knew every piece of clothing Marion owned. He obsessed over every detail of the woman, like a miser hording gold. It had been easy for him to spot that she wasn't buying new dresses. Some digging had revealed the old duke was broke and the estate was failing.

Since Nicholas had seen no way of getting Marion to take money from him directly, he'd had to think of more oblique ways of helping her. It was before he'd learned about creative villainy from his diabolical little partner-in-crime, so it had taken a lot of energy for him to come up with a workable plan. He'd never expected that Marion would ever start questioning it, though. Why was the woman so damn clever?

Nicholas cleared his throat. "Logically, tearing out the gardens would have been a smart financial move, for your family. I'm sure you were considering that, so your bill would be lower."

Actually, he was sure it had never occurred to her. Marion didn't see things as predictably as he did. Nicholas thought in straight lines. "Need money" plus "expensive gardens" equaled "get rid of gardens." Marion's mind was so much more interesting. He loved that about her. But she also needed to buy food, so he'd ensured she'd had gold to get it.

"But, the --um-- cultural impact of losing the gardens would have been... just... devastating." He tried to infuse his voice with a suitable amount of concern over a bunch of useless flowers. "Nottingham *needed* the gardens, for so many reasons. So, so many."

Please don't ask me to list any.

He rushed onward, wanting to escape this explanation, before he really had to explain anything. "So, the kingdom needed to intervene, a bit. For the greater Good of the --uh-- culture of the... you know... kingdom." That sounded pretty plausible. "I was the one who had the idea, initially. For the kingdom. But I think everyone agreed it was the best course."

Not that he'd bothered to ask anybody else for their opinion. Fuck 'em all.

"So, I put through a tax exemption, for your home. As a way of culturally preserving Nottingham's," he squinted up at the ceiling, thinking hard, "strategic wildflower supplies?" It came out sounding too much like a question. Shit. "Um... It was the best choice for the *kingdom* and..."

Marion opened the door. Her eyes were reddened and damp, like she'd been crying and crying.

Nicholas stared down at her, his heart breaking. "Oh, duchess..."

She walked into his arms, burying her face against his chest and giving a choked sob.

"No, don't do that. Please." He picked her up and carried her back into the bedroom, shutting the door with his foot. "You don't need to cry. Really." Like all the castle's fireplaces, the one in her room was the size of a walk-in closet. He sat down on a chair next to it, holding her in his lap. "I will never let anything happen to those plants. The gardens are..."

"I don't care about the damn gardens." She interrupted. "I'm upset over *you*. And how you died." Her voice broke on the last word.

This was his fault. He should never have taken her to

see that lying prick Pinocchio. "I'm not dead. I'm right here."

"You *were* dead and you must've believed the person who killed you was *me*." She held him tighter. "You thought *I'd* hurt you, Nick. At the very end. You must have felt so betrayed. I can't bear it." She started sobbing, again.

Nicholas ran a hand over her dark curls. He wasn't a fanciful man. He wasn't particularly well-versed in magic or alternate timelines. It was hard for him to conceptualize another reality, where he'd lived and died. But, he believed it had happened, because Marion said so. And he believed that she was suffering because of it. He stretched himself to try and find words that might soothe her anguish.

"I would have known the truth." He assured her, attempting to put himself in the other-him's place. "I opened the door and I let the Wraith in. So, I'm sure I thought it was you, at first." There was no one else in creation he would've allowed into his bedroom. Just her. "But, I guarantee I knew something was off very quickly, after that."

She sniffed, listening to him.

"As soon as I saw its eyes, I'm *positive* I'd know it was a trick." He was being totally honest about that. He loved her too much to be fooled for more than a few seconds, at close range. The other-him was no doubt the same. "Probably, even *before* I saw its eyes. I am obsessed with you, Marion. I know your dress size, your shoe size, your glove size... And you don't even wear gloves. See? I know that, too."

There was a muffled snort of amusement against his shoulder.

Nicholas was encouraged by her response. "I *know* you." He went on. "Inside and out. If the smell of it wasn't your smell, I would've noticed. If the words it used weren't the ones you would have chosen, or if the way it moved was off, or if one of its freckles was out of place... I would've seen it was wrong. I swear it."

She snuggled closer to him, no longer crying.

"There is no possible way that I died thinking you shot me." His lips were next to her ear, his voice sure. "I *promise* you, when that Wraith killed me, your name was the last word in my head, but it wasn't in anger. It was for comfort. In the end, you were what I reached for." He pressed a kiss into her hair. "I know that, because I know *me*, too."

She raised her head to look at his face.

He stared back, grave and certain. "You are all I see, Marion."

"I will never give you up." She said softly. "Human, gargoyle, gryphon, wizard... No matter who or what you were, I would *always* choose you, Nick. Don't listen to Pinocchio about that. You said yourself he's a liar. You're *perfect*, exactly as you are." Her lips found his, parting for him.

Nicholas kissed her back, savoring the taste of her. He had dreamed of this woman most of his life and the reality of having her in his arms was better than he'd even imagined. The kiss seemed to reassure her. Sighing with pleasure, Marion nestled back into his arms. Safe on his lap. Welcoming his touch. And Nicholas' life was exactly how it was always supposed to be.

He was *not* going to fucking die, again. Not when he had Marion.

So, obviously, he was going to have to kill the Wraith.

Pinocchio said only a hammer would slay the monster, which, Nicholas supposed, wasn't *that* farfetched. Smashing something's head in with a hammer was usually a good first step to killing it, regardless of the species. Still... He wasn't about to bet his life on Pinocchio's honesty. Whatever that wooden dickhead said, Nicholas believed the opposite.

"Did you really say 'strategic wildflower supplies' earlier?" Marion eventually asked, pulling Nicholas from his thoughts.

"It's for the Good of the kingdom."

"That should be our secret code, in case the Wraith tries to impersonate me or some other terrible thing happens. 'Strategic wildflower supplies.' Even reading memories, I don't think it will be able to guess *that*."

"Because it's ridiculous. Half of what I say is ridiculous, when I don't have time to think the words through."

"I love talking to you." Her gaze had cleared. "You

always make me feel better."

"It's not every day I hear that."

"I'll have to start telling you every day, then."

His mouth curved at that promise. Resting his chin on her head, his eyes fell on a crumple of familiar fabric on the pillow of her bed. He blinked. "Is that my shirt?"

"No, it's my new nightgown."

Which used to be his shirt. "You stole it?" Stealing from the laundry seemed to be how she acquired most of her clothes these days.

"'Stole' is such a harsh word. I'm just borrowing it forever."

"Did my men not pack you enough nightwear?"

"I have plenty. I just like your stuff better. Because it's yours."

Nicholas slowly processed that.

"I'm 'unhealthily fixated' on you." Marion went on. "I think I've mentioned it. That bitch, Dr. Ramona, was very concerned about me teetering on the brink of madness over my inability to move on." She tilted her face to look at him. "You worried about it?"

"Worried that you're wearing my shirts, while you sleep? No. I'm all for it."

She shrugged. "I also stalk you a lot. You may have noticed that part. And I'll probably steal other stuff. And there may be some video surveillance."

"Just me, right? No other men?"

"Of course, no one else. *You're* my fixation, cupcake."

He smirked, completely satisfied with that arrangement. "Then fixate away."

"I had a feeling you'd get it." She played with the buttons on his uniform, probably plotting to steal that, too. "Hey, by the way, did you tell Robin we were sleeping together?"

Nicholas winced. "No...? He might've heard it that way, though."

Marion looked amused.

"Everything I say comes out wrong." Nicholas

reiterated. "I didn't tell him that we were having sex, but it *sounded* like I did."

She bit her lower lip, trying to contain her snickering.

"I'm sorry." He shook his head in self-disgust. "If it makes you feel any better, I'm sure he's talked himself out of believing me, by now."

"I really don't care what Robin thinks, feels, or does." Brown eyes danced. "I just think you're cute, when you try to talk and it all goes so very wrong."

He sighed. "Honestly, that shit with Hood isn't my absolute dumbest conversation screw up. 'Strategic wildflower supplies' still beats it, I think."

Marion kissed his jaw. "Actions matter more than words, Nick. Thank you for helping my father to keep the estate, with your dedication to stockpiling plant life."

"I didn't do it for him."

"No?" A flirty glint entered her eye, aimed right at him, and it was all he could do not to beg for mercy. "Who did you do it for then?"

"Some girl I met in the woods."

Marion laughed and it was the most beautiful sound he'd ever heard. "An *amazingly* pretty girl? With an *amazing* sense of humor and *amazingly* brilliant plans?"

A smile tugged at the corner of his mouth. "That sounds like her."

"Why, she must be amazing!" Marion shifted on his lap and there was no way she could miss his growing erection. "You should marry her, maybe." She moved against him, instinctively seeking out a rhythm.

Nicholas' eyes drifted shut for a beat. She *definitely* hadn't missed his arousal. She just wasn't startled by it anymore. Marion was innocent, but she learned quickly.

"Oh, I'll have her for my wife." He murmured, letting her play. "And in the meantime, I have other plans for the little troublemaker. I've been thinking over some fine print on my betrothal rights. Seeing how far I could push the rules."

That earned him a mischievous smile. God, he loved it when she was Bad. "Demand every nefarious thing you're allowed. I can't wait."

"No." He shook his head. "I'm beyond analyzing what's allowed. Do betrothal rights say I *can't* touch anything? Because if it doesn't say 'no,' then I'm going to assume it means 'yes.' And I'm going forward from there."

That seemed to intrigue Marion. "I mean, they don't specifically outline any off-limit spots. I'm sure they're expecting a gentleman to just *know* the limits."

"What if I'm not a gentleman? And I don't care about the limits, just so it gets me what I want?"

She blinked, like she didn't have an answer.

Nicholas dragged her down, so she was fully seated on his lap and she felt all of him. He leaned close to her ear again. "See what happens when you tease? Sooner or later, you get caught and punished."

He felt a shiver course through her entire body and he'd never felt more powerful. Wide brown eyes met his, full of nerves and curiosity. "You said that before. Do you really think I'm a tease?"

Nicholas arched a brow. "I say it all the time, because you *are* a tease."

Marion didn't look sorry. "What if I give you everything I've been teasing you with?" She asked softly. "What if I was a Good girl? Would you still have to punish me?"

Oh... fuck... *yes*.

"Show me." He set her on her feet. "Take your clothes off, Marion. All of it this time."

Chapter Twenty-Eight

Clorinda Sets the Record Straight: "Will Scarlet and I never went all the way!"

Alan A. Dale- "Nottingham's Naughtiest News"

Nicholas held his breath after he gave the order for Marion to strip, half expecting her to refuse. She'd refused Hood and he'd wanted less.

Instead, Marion began unbuttoning her blouse, like it was just *such* a hardship. "Seducing you happens so differently in my imagination." She informed him in a haughty tone.

"Funny, this is exactly like one of the million ways *I've* visualized it. And now I've willed it into being."

"That is *not* how Rockwell's visualization exercises work, peachy-bear."

"Seems to be working just fine, to me." When she was down to her bra, he held up a hand. "Wait."

This time her underwear was white. Sweet. Innocent. For a moment, he wanted her to keep it on, just because it fit all of his fantasies so perfectly. Marion's curvy little body at his mercy. Her wide brown eyes shining just at him. Purity and warmth in her mischievous grin. Imagining her like this had gotten him through the war and now he was living it for really real.

"I like you in white." He whispered.

"Good, because my wedding gown has ten feet of white tulle and I'm not changing it." She gestured towards a large garment bag, carefully hung on the closet door.

Nicholas spared it a brief glance. "The dress you

bought for Hood to see you in." He muttered.

"No. The dress I bought for *my groom* to see me in." She tilted her head and her hair brushed her rosy nipples, barely visible through the transparent fabric of the bra. "Robin's not my groom. The dress is meant for *you*, Nick."

Nicholas had to squeeze his eyes shut for a second to control himself, undone by both the view and her words. "It's mine?" He got out. "You swear it?"

"Of course. Robin gets nothing. You get... *everything*."

Oh, he liked that sultry promise. The little tease knew he would. Nicholas slowly smiled at her. Marion smiled back and he almost came right then and there.

She stripped off her bra, without waiting for instructions. It took her two tries to unclasp the damn thing, because her fingers were shaking. "You never visualized me in a wedding dress?"

"I have visualized you in every possible position, seductive outfit, and adorable hat." Nicholas' eyes shone as he surveyed her spectacular breasts.

"You know, in traditional Nottingham weddings, the groom really does wear a bycocket. I'm visualizing *you* in *that* adorable hat, right now."

"You show up in the dress and I'll show up in whatever hat you want." Nicholas assured her absently.

"Deal."

"Deal. Take off your pants, next." His heavy gaze memorized her exposed flesh.

Marion toed off her shoes. Seeing her bare feet was oddly intimate. Nicholas hadn't expected that, even with all his imaginings. He managed to tear his eyes away from her glorious chest to stare down at her small, vulnerable feet, his pulse thudding.

Her toenails were painted a very unMaidenly black. Marion curled them against the carpet, like his intense interest embarrassed her. "Cragg and I did pedicures." She muttered.

"It suits you." And she suited him. Perfectly.

Marion's toes relaxed, as if his approval soothed her nerves. Unfastening her pants, she slid them down her legs and kicked them away. All she had on was her plain, white underwear and it was so erotic he wanted to rip it straight off her body.

"That's as far as I'm going." She decided, suddenly mutinous.

His attention flicked back to her face. Her Bad side was coming out. He loved that she couldn't be a Good girl for long. "Everything." He intoned. "It's all mine, remember?"

"You're twisting that to your advantage, Nick."

"Of course. But, I'm still within the rules. Are you going to cheat?"

She made a face, but relented. She saw this as a naughty game and she liked to play with him. Nicholas wheezed out an agonized breath when she finally stood before him completely naked.

Marion swiped her hair behind her ear. Despite her willingness to participate, she was clearly nervous about being so exposed. Nicholas had no idea why. She was stunning. Was she frightened of him? He did outweigh her by about three-hundred pounds, so it would be logical.

"Betrothal rights or no, you're in control of this, Marion." He said quietly. "I won't move, until you come to me."

Marion's confidence grew again, not so much at his words, but because his scorching gaze was running all over her. Not even a virgin could miss how enthralled he was. She grinned at him in a very feminine, very playful way that had Nicholas' control straining. "The rules say you can touch me, but not vise versa. Are you sure this is going to be fun for you, dream boat?"

"I'm sure it will be *very* fun to feel your body coming all around me, yes."

Marion's mouth parted, like she hadn't expected that graphic response. "You want to have sex? Right now?"

"The rules say I'm not allowed, until our marriage. That part is actually spelled out." And there *would* be a goddamn marriage. He'd make sure of it.

To his mind, though, he'd agreed to follow all the

boundaries of the tradition when he'd asked for his betrothal rights. He'd made a vow to always keep her safe and she'd given herself into his care. It was very straightforward. The reciprocity of it made sense to him.

But, that didn't mean there weren't loopholes he could exploit.

Nicholas' tilted his head, considering ideas. Noblemen really were idiots to think their code of chivalry could keep him from what he wanted most. "Does the touching I'm entitled to have to be on the *outside* of your body? Does it explicitly say that?"

Marion's eyes were huge. "Really?" She blurted out.

"Really." He crooked a finger at her, deciding to take her astonishment as permission. "Come here, duchess." It was another dare.

She cautiously started towards him, intrigued by this whole idea. "You're really going to demand *this?*" She asked, as if she wanted to be sure it wasn't a trick.

"Yes, I really am." He caught hold of her wrist, tugging her down, so she straddled his lap. "Get used to being naked. I stay up at night, thinking of depraved things to demand from you. And I'm pretty creatively villainous."

"We have so much in common." She whispered with great feeling.

He was still fully dressed and she was nude. That turned him on even more. His palms covered her bare breasts, desperate to feel her skin against his. The stony fingers of his right hand were rough on her tender flesh. He tried to ease his hold, but Marion pressed forward, asking for more. Nicholas let out a long sigh of satisfaction, as he felt the eagerly jutting points blossoming under his sandpaper touch.

"So pretty." He whispered, admiring the way the globes filled his palms. Nicholas made a hungry sound, playing with them. "I have always loved your breasts, Marion. Did I ever tell you that?"

"You haven't specifically mentioned it, in any timeline." She licked her lower lip. "But I could kind of tell. You stare at them, when you think I'm not looking. And sometimes when I *am* looking."

True enough. "Is it just my hands that can touch them?"

"W-what?"

"Under the rules, can I use my mouth on them, too?"

"I don't know. You're asking questions that no nobleman would ever think to..." She broke off with a gasp as his lips sealed around one of her nipples. "Nick!" She clutched at him, her head going back, as he suckled hard. "Oh my *God*."

His right hand settled at the base of her spine, holding her on his lap as she writhed against him. Keeping her breast locked against his ravenous mouth. Preventing her from accidently falling off or intentionally escaping. Not that she was in danger of doing either. The woman was actively trying to get closer to him.

Nicholas' rubbed her nipple against his tongue. Marion's fingers tangled in his hair, undulating against the granite-hard length of his erection and whimpering in need.

He wasn't about to turn down the offer.

His left hand slid between her legs, brushing against the very center of her desire. He paused, his gaze jumping to her face when he discovered just how wet she was. There was no way he could miss it. She was soaking with hot, syrupy need. Need for *him*.

In his whole life, he'd never been with anyone who genuinely wanted him back. Gargoyles always had to pay for sex, when they sought out a human. There was no genuine desire involved.

Marion *wanted* Nicholas.

She stared back at him, panting for breath. "I really like this game." She whispered. "I don't think I have a low sex drive, after all. At least, not around you."

Nicholas' lips curved and his chest swelled with emotion. "I think you're perfect."

She smiled, looking more confident than ever.

Maybe Maids and gargoyles *were* a lot alike. They both worried that they weren't desired for who they really were. They both needed reassurances, now and then.

"I've only ever wanted one girl in my whole life." Nicholas wasn't the most eloquent man, but he tried to verbalize his feelings. "*My* girl."

Marion went still.

Shit!

He'd said a dozen words and at least two of them were wrong. Calling her his girl seemed to be one of the few things that made her nervous. He'd noticed that, back in the castle foyer, when Hood was escaping. He had no idea why the phrase upset her, but it didn't matter. If she didn't like hearing it, he wouldn't say it.

"I'm sorry. A name only means something when the other person accepts it, so I won't call you..."

Marion cut him off. "Why is me being your girl so important to you?" She asked warily. "I'm just hearing it as me being helpless and in need of saving. How are *you* hearing it?"

Nicholas frowned. "No, that's not... It's not about *me* saving *you*. It's the opposite. It's..." He dug for a way to explain what the idea actually meant to Nottingham soldiers, desperate and alone in a foreign land. "Your girl is your home."

Marion blinked rapidly... and then kissed him.

Triumph swelled within Nicholas, as her lips covered his. That had been a huge victory and he knew it. She'd heard what he was really trying to say.

Words came easier, now. "You are my everything, Marion." He got out when they came up for air. "Everyone else is invisible to me. I can't look away from you."

She gave a languid sigh that sounded like goddamn music. He felt her grow even wetter and more pliant. He touched her deeper, needing everything. His explorations stopped when Marion suddenly grabbed hold of his wrist.

"Aren't you right handed?" She asked, her face glowing with all kinds of secrets.

"Yes."

"Then why are you using your left hand to touch me?"

She knew why. Nicholas unconsciously curled the hideous fingers of his stony palm against the small of her back, wishing he could hide them from her sight forever. The idea of the ugliest part of him violating the most secret, delicate part of her...?

He unconsciously shook his head, rejecting the idea. The gargoyle sections of his skin shouldn't touch Marion, at all. He'd never even considered penetrating her with his huge, inhuman finger. Any other woman in Nottingham would die before letting that happen.

Marion wasn't taking "no" for an answer. "Nick, use your other hand." She ordered in a firmer tone.

"It would be a defilement." He said and he believed it. Everyone believed it.

Marion frowned at his words, clearly *not* believing it. She studied his face, looking for some way to convince him. There wasn't one. No way in the universe was he going to squeeze the rockiest part of his body into her velvety little channel. ...Where no one had ever touched her before. ...Making her his alone.

Fuck.

Nicholas realized he was breathing too hard.

Marion noticed, too. Her mouth curved into a smug smile, sensing her impending victory.

"Hood will never forgive you, if he finds out." Nicholas tried a little desperately, because it was the only argument he could think to make. There was a roaring in his ears, blocking out the rest. "He'll blame me for most of this. He'll be right to. You still have a path back to him. But, this will *ruin* you in his eyes. Forever. And all of Nottingham will agree with him. You've already burned bridges. This will scorch them to ash."

The entire kingdom would see her as tainted. Marion *knew* that.

She just didn't seem to care.

Instead, she leaned closer to him, so she was right up against his ear. "I told you before, I'm a match. I'm going to set Nottingham ablaze and dance in the flames."

Nicholas swore he saw stars.

Her voice was a silken whisper straight out of his dreams. "Fuck 'em all, Nick. Every. Single. One." Her teeth nipped his ear.

Nicholas stopped arguing and switched hands. Once he chose a path, he didn't hesitate. Look where seizing opportunities had gotten him, so far. He had Marion, smiling and soft and asking for more.

He traced his index finger over her damp flesh, savoring the pleasure that suffused her face. The warmth of her body soaked into his stony hand, cleansing it somehow. Making it feel like an actual part of him, for the first time. It wasn't just something misshapen and ugly attached to his body. It was *part* of his body. And every single part of Nicholas worshipped this woman.

He pressed the thick digit upward with relentless intent.

Marion moaned. So did Nicholas.

Nothing had ever been so good. He watched his inhuman finger disappear inside of Marion and it looked... right. It felt right. It *was* right. It wasn't a defilement. This was exactly the way it was supposed to be.

They fit together. Opposite parts of the same whole.

He pushed and took and *needed*... and she gave, connecting them as one. Feeling her small muscles yield to his invasion was the greatest victory of his life.

Marion instinctively shifted at the unfamiliar weight of his finger inside her. She gave another tiny whimper and it was magical.

"Careful, now." He couldn't pull his eyes away from the rough skin of his hand claiming her. It was riveting to watch it vanish into her burning hot core. "Not too fast." He held her still, insisting that she slowly accept the hard length, right up until he felt her maidenhead.

He stopped, trying to think through the pulsing need. "You're a virgin."

"Did you doubt it?" She sounded happy. "That must mean I'm pretty incredible at sex, so far. I'm trying real hard to be a badass, but it's difficult to focus when you're touching me."

"You're definitely holding your own." He assured her, forcing himself to concentrate.

He'd never doubted she was a virgin. It was just that feeling the proof of it made it really *real*. Marion was innocent. She'd saved herself for someone worthy. For the most heroic bastard in Nottingham, who'd write her poetry, and slay fearsome monsters, and maybe overthrow kingdoms to win her love.

He shouldn't be doing this to her. He should walk away, before he went too far.

Are you out of your fucking mind!?

Nicholas winced at the volume of his internal denial.

"Does it matter that I'm a virgin?" Marion prompted, when Nicholas didn't continue his exploration of her skin.

"I don't know. I've never been with a virgin before."

He'd barely been with anyone, at all. He'd hated paying, so he'd only tried sex a few times. It had made him feel dirty, knowing the women didn't really want his touch. And he didn't really want to touch *them*. There had only ever been Marion in his head. Even when she was with Hood, and so far beyond his reach she might as well have been the stars, it had still felt *wrong* to be with anyone but her.

Marion made a distressed sound of thwarted desire. "Are you going to stop?"

His grip on her tightened, that small, needy sob clearing away the last of his doubts. "No." Of course, he wasn't going to stop. What kind of moron would *stop* when the woman he longed for was naked, willing, and sitting on his lap?

"Good."

Her eager expression got things back on track, because Nicholas had to have her mouth on his. Simply had to. Whenever she smiled at him, it was like winning the lottery. "Kiss me again, Marion."

She kissed him. Her lips opening to his, even as her tight channel accepted the shallow thrusts of his finger. In that moment, he really did have everything.

He just wasn't sure *why* he had it.

What did these betrothal rights really mean? Like every other relationship in Nottingham, there was a transactional element to them. Not money, but a trade nonetheless. The Maid got a bodyguard to keep her safe. The bodyguard got to touch the Maidenly body he was guarding. That made sense to Nicholas. It made sense to most people in the kingdom.

But, Marion's brain didn't work like everybody else's. It was so much more special. She panicked when Nicholas even suggested that he'd protect her. The moronic former-him had told her she could only count on herself and Marion had listened. There was no trade happening, in her mind.

Instead, she seemed to view betrothal rights as a sex game, which allowed her to divorce herself from any deeper meaning to this ritual. But, there *was* a deeper meaning or she wouldn't be playing, at all. No one stayed a virgin for thirty-six years, if they were only interested in sex games. What was really happening here? Why was she doing this with him, if not for protection or for naughty fun...?

"Nick." Marion's murmur of bliss cut through his dazed thoughts. She rested her forehead on his wide shoulder, giving her body over to his touch. Instinctively trusting him to keep her safe.

And Nicholas suddenly understood the betrothal rights.

They weren't empty, pompous pledges of devotion, as nobles believed. And they weren't just the wicked game that Marion thought she was playing with him. And they weren't a trade of affection for safety, like he'd been conceptualizing. They had *elements* of devotion and fun and safety, sure. But, like everything he shared with Marion, they were far more important and complicated than all of that.

Betrothal rights were a trust exercise.

Marion needed to trust him to care for her. Nicholas was proving that she *could* trust him to care for her. The experience was meant to be fun, and reverent, and to teach the participants how to start counting on each other.

And, whether she'd admit it or not, the betrothal rights actually seemed to be working. Marion felt safe with him. Her untouched status was being systematically shredded by a gargoyle and she seemed blissful about it. This experience was helping her get over her fear.

Nicholas pressed a kiss into her hair. "I've got you, duchess." He wanted to press another finger inside of her, but she was too small. It would take her virginity. Instead, he supported her weight, so he could hold her at the perfect angle. His jaw locked in pleasure at the sensation of her body stretching to accommodate him, as he slipped inside as far as he dared to go.

The strong pull of her body, tugging against his finger, enthralled him. Terrified him. Enflamed him. Every part of him was huge and she was so fucking *tight*.

Her lips parted, as she fully adjusted. "*Oh*." Her head went back in ecstasy, not minding his monstrous size. "Deeper."

Nicholas watched her reaction and knew he'd never see anything more dazzling. "I can't go deeper. Not yet."

"I don't care about my virginity. Take the damn thing, so we can have some real fun."

"No." He shook his head. The betrothal rights meant something to him. He wasn't abusing her trust by breaking the rules. Not even his reverse conscience complained about that call.

Marion didn't seem appreciative of his heroic self-denial. She made a sound of aggravation and lust. "I swear to God, Nicholas, if you're teasing me with all this... Holy *shit!*"

He began guiding her up and down on his roughly-surfaced finger, finding a rhythm she liked. "Don't call me 'Nicholas.'" He instructed. "You know what I want to hear."

She obediently switched to the name he liked. "Nick." She whispered and rode the most hideous part of him, bliss on her face. "A little more. Just a little more."

"Tell me exactly what you want. Tell me what you like." He was trying to figure this out, just like her. Touching a woman so she could find release was new to him.

"I," she swallowed, trying to think, "I don't *know* what I like. Sometimes I'd touch myself and I'd think about you, but no one else has ever..." She trailed off again, as he carefully rubbed the calloused heel of his palm against her soaked flesh.

"Oh... Right there! Just like that."

He quickly complied and her response was luminous.

"*Nick!*"

He loved it when she said his name. "I'm here." His teeth scraped along her neck, marking her skin. Claiming her. Others would be able to see it later. They'd all know he put it there and she belonged to him. He licked the spot, lavishing it with his tongue.

She whimpered and tilted her neck to give him better access. At the same time, she reached down and adjusted his hand so he was touching her with more force, her breath coming in pants. "I love the feel of you. This is so much better than when I did it myself. Your fingers are so *hard*."

"Too hard...?"

"Do *not* fucking stop!" She shouted when he began to ease off.

He felt himself grin. "You're a natural at making demands, duchess."

She lifted her head from his shoulder. "Only with you." Brown eyes met his, filled with a shocking amount of innocence, considering the cheerful Badness in her soul and the sheer number of curse words she let fly each day. On some level, she seemed to realize that this was more than just a game, too, because her gaze was suddenly solemn. "I would only *ever* do this with you."

Well, shit...

If there was any little bit of Nicholas that hadn't already belonged to her, it was gone. Every piece of him was handed over to Marion now and he'd never get it back.

"Before you, it wouldn't even occur to me to demand... more." She continued.

"You can demand more, whenever you need it. And I'll demand it, whenever *I* need it." He kissed her possessively. "And I'm going to need it *a lot*. You're going to forget what it feels like when you're not coming around my finger."

Her body clenched in anticipation at that idea.

He chuckled at her enthusiastic response. "You want to *obey* demands, too, huh?"

"Only when you give them." Her eyes fluttered closed in pleasure. "And only when they're *very* wicked."

Nicholas liked that answer. A lot. On so many levels. "Very soon, I want to use my mouth. I want to taste you. Can I demand that with my betrothal rights?"

Her eyes popped open. "No! Husbands don't like to..." Nicholas increased the speed of his hand and she lost her train of thought. "*Yes!*"

"Yes *who?* Say my name."

"Yes, Nick." She was barely hanging on. "*Yes.*" Marion was caught somewhere between agony and delight. She leaned forward to kiss him again, like her life depended on it. He kissed her back just as hungrily. "I can't wait, anymore." She breathed against his mouth. "Take care of me, like you promised."

Oh *fuck* yes.

Something like the first stirrings of panic fluttered across her face, when she realized what she'd just said. He felt Marion begin to pull away. Wanting to regain control. Afraid.

He pressed his thumb against her harder and made sure she stayed, soaking in her cry of desire. "I'll always take care of you. I made that vow to you and I meant it." He cupped her face with his free hand, willing her to hear him. "I mean *everything* I say to you... even the shit I don't have the right words for."

Big eyes met his, listening to him even as she hovered on the edge of completion. Wide and a little scared, because she *almost* believed him and she wasn't sure she should. Nicholas knew that, because he felt the same thing every single time she spoke to him.

He met her gaze, feeling just as hypnotized as she looked. "Gargoyles aren't supposed to feel passion, but you are the grand passion of my life, Marion."

She exploded. "*Nick!*" Her core rippled around his stony finger in waves of ecstasy.

Nicholas' lips parted in awe. He twisted his wrist, wanting to draw this out for her. Marion screamed and the sound shot straight down to his painful erection. She trembled from the force of her orgasm. Calling out *his* name and shaking from the climax *he'd* provided. No desperate midnight fantasy had ever been better.

"Perfect." Nicholas murmured reverently, watching her find release. He couldn't have been more satisfied if he'd come himself.

Marion gave a sensual sigh of surrender, totally open to his touch. He stroked the last aftershocks from her as she collapsed against him, her body lax and quivering.

He pressed another kiss to her hair, his breathing ragged. His free hand gently rubbed up and down her back. "Thank you." Nicholas whispered. He always found himself thanking her after she let him touch her. He felt grateful she chose him. Blessed to have her in his arms. He continued to stroke her silky skin, because he couldn't quite bring himself to stop.

She nuzzled her face against his chest, content to be held securely against his body. Which was excellent news, because he was in no hurry to let her go.

Don't ever let her go. Without her, there's nothing. Just take her to bed and stay there. She can't go anywhere if she's orgasming every twenty minutes.

That idea had some merit. For whatever reason, Marion was sexually attracted to him. It was... shocking. Inexplicable. But the evidence of it was pretty damn overwhelming. Could he use lust to hold her? Could he make her forget all her dreams of happily ever after with Hood? Could passion trump True Love? Nicholas wasn't sure, but he was willing to give it a try. Very, very, *very* willing.

"Nick?" Marion said after a long time. "About your betrothal rights...?"

He braced himself, expecting her to pull away. To try and establish distance, now that she'd been vulnerable. "Yes?"

She lifted her eyes to his and smiled enticingly. "Demand them all, again."

Chapter Twenty-Nine

Magical Menace Menaces Maypole!
It has long been the position of this reporter that dragons have no place in civilized society.
The Sheriff of Nottingham bringing his evil bestie Trevelyan to our glamourous party raises grave suspicions about ethical law enforcement.
What kind of vile deal have these monsters struck behind our backs?

Alan A. Dale- "Nottingham's Naughtiest News"

The Maypole Ball was a bacchanalia of privilege.

The richest, prettiest and/or most powerful people in Nottingham gathered to celebrate another year of being rich, pretty and/or powerful. There was a bonfire outside, roasting a buffet of delicacies. Guests stood around chatting and laughing, dressed in their finest clothes. In the ballroom, there was a huge maypole, which gave the party its name. It was twenty feet high and the center of all the action.

"That's quite phallic, isn't it?" Trevelyan mused from beside Nicholas. He watched the guests weave in and out, twining ribbons around the giant, erect maypole. "Do you think these rubes even notice the symbolism? Or am I the only one here who has sex?"

Nicholas hated the dragon almost as much as Robin Hood and that was quite a high bar to clear. The other man was drinking champagne and dressed in a solid black tuxedo, which somehow made all of Nottingham's elite look like unsophisticated hicks at their own celebration.

"You know, this whole trip to Nottingham has been something of a letdown, as far as vacations go." Trevelyan grumbled, when Nicholas didn't answer him. "It smells vile here. And the people are mostly very unattractive. And today is my birthday and this is a terrible party."

Is *that* why the dragon had insisted on staying for the Maypole Ball? He didn't want to spend his birthday alone? Was he lonely? Nicholas somewhat understood that, because the isolation he felt without Marion was like a cage.

"And I simply don't understand why Marion likes you better than me." Trevelyan went on, ruining any small spark of empathy Nicholas might have felt. "She *seems* intelligent, but her choices in lovers are abysmal. I mean desiring a gargoyle? Over a *dragon?*"

Nicholas didn't bother to engage. The dipshit clearly wanted to start a fight, just for the hell of it. The only way to win was to not give him the satisfaction. Trevelyan's jeering was more of a mild irritant than a genuine threat, anyway. Marion wasn't romantically interested in him and the dragon sheathed most of his claws around her. She wasn't in love with Trevelyan and she wasn't in any danger from him, therefore arguing with the dickhead wasn't worth the effort of Nicholas talking.

Across the room, Marion was dancing with Gravol. Every other Maid at the party wore white taffeta gowns, the traditional uniform of the pure and protected. Marion wore black satin that hugged all of her sinful curves.

Nicholas liked her in white, but he *loved* her in black.

He just... loved her.

His gaze lingered on the small, dark mark he'd left on her neck, that afternoon. Marion hadn't covered it up, so it was impossible to miss. Whispers and disapproving frowns abounded among Nottingham's high-society, but, there wasn't one fucking thing they could do about Nicholas' claim. He was done even trying to hide his obsession. He'd given Marion a chance to protect her reputation and she'd turned him down. Now, he was making sure *everyone* knew who she belonged to.

Nicholas' mouth curved.

Trevelyan didn't appreciate the lack of verbal response to his provocations. He quickly deduced what Nicholas was smug about. "I've slept with eight women, since I've been here. I could have marked any of them. Eight is more than one, in case they don't teach gargoyles math. Technically, I have you beat."

No, he didn't. Trevelyan didn't mark the women because they weren't *his*. They both knew it. And they both knew who Marion belonged to.

Nicholas sipped his champagne

"God, you're boring." Trevelyan lamented, when Nicholas remained silent. "I've probably met someone *more* boring, but..." He blew out his cheeks, thinking it over. "No. I haven't. Never mind."

Nicholas continued to watch Marion.

"I can still smell the innocence on her. If you were less boring, maybe your virginal little mate would let you fully bed her." Trevelyan opined, ignoring the fact he was being ignored.

Nicholas relished Marion being called *his*, even if it was by a dickhead like Trevelyan. Everything else in that complaint was just white noise.

"But then again, she does say she's marrying you tomorrow." Trevelyan went on thoughtfully. "And she offered to pay me to put a tracking spell on your stony ass." He drank some of his own champagne. "I said I'd do it for free."

Nicholas finally glanced his way.

"I wouldn't wander more than a mile or so away from the woman." Trevelyan advised in a mockingly serious tone, pleased to have finally produced a reaction. "She'll hunt you down, like you're wearing a collar. I had initially thought *you* were the creepily fixated one in the relationship, but Marion might have you beat. It's a very unhealthy dynamic, you know."

Nicholas smiled slightly, not at all worried about being geo-tracked by Marion. He appreciated her fixation on him. It made him feel wanted. And slightly less weird about spying on her, in return.

"You can track her, as well." Trevelyan said, like he'd read Nicholas' mind. "The spell is reciprocal. That's why I agreed to cast it for free. It'll be entertaining to see you two stalking each other around cow pastures and dirt fields. Not that I plan to be in this wasteland for long. Nottingham is already boring me." He made a face. "Everything bores me."

Nicholas disregarded that melodramatic lament, content that Marion cared enough to magically shadow his every move. He went back to watching the grand passion of his life. The dance with Gravol ended and she headed over to referee an argument between Oore and Boulder. As she moved across the room, Nicholas turned, so his eyes could follow her. Like a plant seeking sunlight, he automatically oriented his body to face Marion. It was instinctive. She was his quiet spot in the chaos.

"'Boring' seems to be Marion's type, though." Trevelyan mused, also changing position so he could continue his one-sided conversation. "I mean, she came to this mediocre party with you."

"I abducted her." Nicholas admitted before he could stop himself. "She *had* to come to the party with me."

"Oh, even better!" Trevelyan brightened. "Getting a mate is so much easier, if you use kidnapping." He looked Nicholas up and down. "...Especially for someone like *you*."

"She has a True Love." Nicholas continued, not sure why he bothered. "Robin Hood. That idiot from the foyer, who went out the skylight. He robs from the rich and gives to the poor."

Trevelyan rolled his eyes with exaggerated distain for that idea and emptied his champagne glass.

"The whole kingdom worships him." Nicholas went on. "He's a shiny, blond asshole, who barely even sees Marion, except to steal her money. He just wants a Maid."

"Why is this 'Maid' thing such a *thing* around here?" Trevelyan sounded genuinely confused by someone valuing chastity. "I don't see the point. But then..." He surveyed Nottingham's fanciest gala, with a dismal shake of his head. "This place *is* the boondocks of Hell, so I'm sure you people do a lot of pointless shit. Wrestle in Jell-O. Marry your sheep. Live in mud huts, dressed in smelly bugs and splattered dirt."

"Robin Hood lives in a tree."

"I take it back: *He's* the most boring." Trevelyan

decided with great feeling. "Still, his living arrangements are quite the boon for you. No woman wants to sleep in the rain and snow, with birds shitting on her. You at least offer a roof. Try to work that into the conversation, when you proposition Marion."

"I don't want to proposition Marion." Nicholas snapped. "I want her to love me back."

"Oh." Trevelyan shrugged. "Well, you'll have to kill Robin Hood, then."

"I want to. Obviously. But what will Marion feel afterwards? She might eventually come to hate me for it."

"Don't be such a child. It's just one murder. She'll get over it."

"People don't 'get over' an obsessed gargoyle stalker hanging their True Love."

"Who would even want a True Love that so easily hanged?" Trevelyan seemed baffled as to why this was an issue. "I'd be flattered to have an obsessed stalker clear out the competition for my fair hand. I think it shows initiative."

"That's because you're evil. Marion's not."

Presently, she was off to corral Cragg, who was standing alone in the corner of the ballroom. Nicholas had asked his lieutenants to keep an eye on her, in case any disgruntled partygoers wanted a confrontation, but the request had been wholly unnecessary. Marion hovered around the gargoyles, all on her own. She'd taken the men under her wing.

"But she has so many other attributes that compensate for the lamentable Goodness." Trevelyan was enjoying his new role as a relationship counselor. Mostly because he just liked to talk and talk and *talk*. "Remind her you can provide running water and cooked food. That will smooth the waters, after Hood's untimely demise." He paused and then started speaking slower, like Nicholas might be struggling to keep up. "You people *do* cook food here, yes? You've evolved that far, at least?"

Nicholas pinched the bridge of his nose. "You never found your True Love, I take it."

"No. And I don't plan to. Dragons are far above that

nonsense." He lightly tossed his champagne flute away and the empty glass vanished in midair. "We choose mates for conquest and empire building."

"No wonder your kind are almost extinct."

"*I'm* still here. That's all that really matters."

Nicholas didn't care about the future of the dragons, but if Trevelyan was one of their last hopes, then things were getting dire for them. "Marion wants a marriage like her parents had. She wants True Love. I can't give that to her."

"People say they want a lot of things. Start with fucking her. See how far that gets you." He got a distant look, as if he was tapping into some fantasy. "I suspect the Good girls with the sparks in their eyes all like to be fucked hard by villains. You can just scent it on them."

Nicholas wasn't sure where to even begin responding to that shit. His first instinct was to punch Trevelyan in the throat, but he found he couldn't move.

Trevelyan was introspective, now. "I really want to try one of those girls for myself. Just to see what life and purity and ideas feel like wrapped tight around me. They have magic. I can feel it, but I don't know what kind it is. Most of them aren't magical beings. So why do they have a type of magic that I don't? I'm a dragon!" He looked legitimately irritated by the unfairness of anyone else possessing something he didn't. "I need to investigate it. For science, if nothing else. But those women are so rare, their True Loves always seem to find them first and then lock them away."

"That must be hard for you." Nicholas said sarcastically.

Trevelyan nodded, like he felt terrible about his own suffering. "It's difficult to seduce a Good girl away from her True Love. Believe me. You can get one that *doesn't* sparkle, of course. That's... fine." He shrugged, half-heartedly. "I enjoy knowing I've corrupted their happily-ever-after, even if they never taste quite as sweet as they smell. Goodness is usually a lie, you know. Bland and boring. Often fetid, beneath the gloss."

"Jesus..." Nicholas looked up at the ceiling, at a total

loss as to why he was participating in this conversation.

"The girls I actually want…? The ones who look at you and you can see that extra *something* glistening…? They only give their glow to a chosen few. And then they are dismally loyal to their True Loves. I swear, most of their magic shines right at the bastards." He patted Nicholas' shoulder. "So, I know what you're going through with this Robin what's-his-name. Imagining that primate deep inside Marion… stealing all her light for himself… Well, it isn't a pleasant picture for either of us."

Nicholas jerked away from him and gave his head a clearing shake, because --for some reason-- he hadn't killed the dragon yet. "Why the fuck am I standing here and listening to you talk about Marion? Why am I not ripping your goddamn head from your shoulders and…?" He hesitated.

Hang on.

Why *was* he sharing his deepest thoughts? Why was he talking, *at all?* To Trevelyan, Last of the Green Dragons, of all people? Something wasn't right here. His head felt foggy and…

"Trev?" Marion came marching over and Nicholas lost his moment of clarity. "I need you."

Trevelyan made a hungry sort of sound. "Music to my ears." He murmured.

Nicholas barely heard him, consumed with how utterly amazing his fiancée looked. How utterly amazing she *was*. She stopped beside him and he knew he was the luckiest man ever born.

"Hey, sexy." Marion gave Nicholas a quick kiss, not caring who saw them. She leaned against him, nestling her body close and it was like being touched by starlight. "You still doing okay?"

She knew the noise of the ball bothered him. "I'm fine."

Marion snorted at that assessment. "You've been hanging out with the birthday boy, for half the night. How can you be 'fine?'" The May Day Queen tiara glinted on her head, as she spared Trevelyan a brief glance. "Why are you harassing my groom?"

"I'm bonding with him."

She wasn't convinced. "You have time for a job or what?"

"Anything for you, Marion dear." The dragon couldn't have looked more helpful. His eyes skimmed over her lush body. "Your wish is my command."

Nicholas' grip on Marion's waist tightened, pulling his attention away from her perfection. His eyes narrowed at Trevelyan, back to thinking about killing him.

Wait, *why* wasn't he killing him, again?

"See that big motherfucker over there, flirting with the bartender?" Marion pointed over her shoulder towards Lampwick, the town's blacksmith. The handsome redheaded human was laughing at something the muscular bartender was saying, their hands touching and their eyes devouring each other.

"Which motherfucker, now?" Trevelyan didn't take his attention off her low neckline. "Give me a second to sort through them all."

"Dragon?" Nicholas said quietly.

"Hmmm?"

"I will kill you right here, if you don't stop. *Now.*"

Trevelyan made a face and reluctantly focused on Marion's request. "The man with the shockingly subpar spray-tan?" He guessed with a sigh. "*That* motherfucker?"

"Yes. *Him*. That is Lampwick, winner of the May Day King Pageant. He was my friend Cragg's secret boyfriend, but he broke up with Cragg tonight, crushing his heart. I think he's been playing him all along. He says Cragg has to *pay*, from now on." There was fury in her voice, as she related the tale. "And Lampwick is offering that surfer-guy bartender a blowjob, just to hurt Cragg and drive up the price for his 'companionship.'"

Trevelyan arched a brow. "How entrepreneurial of him."

Nicholas frowned, his gaze seeking out Cragg. The gargoyle was still standing by the wall, looking despondent.

"Lampwick said all this shit about how he was always

too handsome for Cragg. And how no one will ever really love Cragg, because he's a gargoyle. And how he should be thankful for what he's getting." Marion was flushed with the heat of her anger. "I'm *not* having that. The gargoyles are *mine* and I'm going to protect them."

Nicholas felt his heart melt at her words.

"Which is where I come into this soap opera?" Trevelyan guessed. He seemed interested in the love triangle, his green eyes flicking between Lampwick's gloating expression and Cragg's dejected form. "I don't remember which man is which, so I'll hurt either one for a price."

"I want to *destroy* Lampwick's dreams." Marion looked at Trevelyan expectantly. "He's the dude-bro, spray-tanned, human one. Can you do that?"

"What will you pay me for this annihilation?"

Marion glowered at him. "You know there *is* a concept called '*kodamara vadu*.' I learned about it in prison."

"Never heard of it."

"It translates to something like 'a favor between friends.' We do things for each other, because we value our relationship, not because we expect some kind of payment."

"Dear God... Where's the profit in *that?*"

"You really are the worst possible person, Trev."

"But, I'm the very best at magic and isn't that what you're after?"

"Fine. I'll *trade* you for the spell. I have six gold pieces or a stick of gum. Choose."

"How about a kiss?"

"How about you eat shit and die?"

"I'll take the gum."

She slapped it into his hand, like she'd expected that decision all along.

Trevelyan's mouth curved. For once, his smile wasn't tinged with cold disdain.

Nicholas believed Marion about being imprisoned in the WUB Club. How could he not accept most everything she'd told him, at this point? It was hard for his predictable brain to fully conceptualize the idea, but he knew it was true. And he suddenly understood how this bright, mischievous, little creature had miraculously survived being locked up with the vilest evildoers in the world.

Marion identified with outcasts.

Gargoyles, Hatters, Pinocchio, even snarky dragons... she accepted them all as equals. She remembered their birthdays. She treated them with kindness and, if that didn't work, she was willing to fight them face-to-face. There was always respect. Empathy for their feelings. Comradery. A belief that she belonged right there among them, standing on the outside of Good society, plotting to bring it all down in ruin.

Bad folks liked that. They liked *her*. Marion had lasted ten years in prison, because she was *Marion*. And everyone saw her spark.

Marion scowled over at Lampwick, missing Trevelyan's genuine amusement at their exchange. "Make that vain jackass regret he ever set foot out of the stable." She ordered and went hurrying off to comfort Cragg.

Trevelyan kept his eyes on Lampwick. "Does she want me to kill him, do you think?"

Knowing Marion? Probably.

Nicholas cleared his throat. "More in the 'maim' range, would be best." A dead blacksmith on the floor was sure to put a damper on the celebration. "Or we could drag him outside and hang him." Hangings were always neat and tidy.

"No... Maiming's more fun that a quick death."

Magic arced out, green and powerful enough to dim the lights in the chandeliers. Everyone looked up as the lamps flickered. And when they looked down again, Lampwick was sporting a pair of donkey ears.

Literal, brown donkey ears.

They grew out of the top of his skull, like two crescent moons. Jutting about a foot in the air, they began to twitch as they picked up on all the gasps that suddenly filled the room. Lampwick's bartender hookup scrambled backwards in horror. Fingers pointed. Cameras flashed.

Nicholas arched a brow. Marion had said to "Make that vain jackass regret he ever set foot out of the stable" and

Trevelyan had followed her request to the letter. "NIce." He grumbled reluctantly, in an effusive barrage of unsolicited praise.

"I know." Trevelyan smirked without a drop of humility, pleased with the chaos he'd wrought.

Lampwick reached up to feel his head, his grasping hands finding the ears. He gave a shout of alarm that came out as a braying mule sound. The partygoers laughed uproariously. Horrified and humiliated, Lampwick rushed for the door, tripping over his own hooved feet and sobbing out more hee-haws of panic.

As he fled the party, and possibly Nottingham, he stumbled past Cragg and Marion. Cragg looked perplexed as to what was happening. He glanced at Marion, who shrugged like it was all a huge mystery. Then, she sent Trevelyan a thumb's up and a cheerful smile of thanks.

He lifted one shoulder in an arrogant shrug.

Nicholas didn't like Marion smiling at the guy. He didn't like her smiling at anyone but him. "I really hate you, dragon." He muttered.

"Everyone does."

"I hate you the most, though."

"That's because you're an obsessed gargoyle stalker."

Nicholas grunted, because that was probably true.

Trevelyan opened the stick of gum Marion had given him and casually folded it into his mouth. "I can make you human." He offered out of the blue. "My magic is strong enough, and dark enough, and I don't give a shit about rules. I could do it, right now."

Nicholas blinked. For once, he didn't choose to stay silent. He was simply too stunned to think of anything to say.

"We can make a deal, where no one is hurt." Trevelyan's voice was nothing but smooth promises. "Dragons love to make deals, you know. And I'll trade you for something *fair*. Not like the bargain that blockhead Pinocchio made." He leaned closer, his eyes watchful and swirling. "I'll make you a real boy. ...And you give me the woman."

Gargoyles looked up at the night sky and wished for a

moment like this. To become human. To be *alive* in ways that no one could ever question. To have opportunities and choices of your own. To walk the streets and have nobody staring or whispering as you past. Being human would change Nicholas' life and future, forever. Men had killed for the opportunity. They had died for it.

And it was worth literally *nothing* compared to Marion.

"No." Nicholas scoffed. "Not in a million fucking years."

He'd always known Marion would be the cost, if he ever tried to become human. You had to give up what you loved most, if you wanted a wish that big granted. And Marion was the only thing he loved, at all. It was why he'd stopped looking into humanity spells. Because he knew he couldn't pay that price.

At least, he hoped he wouldn't.

If the deal had included harming her, it would have been simple to refuse. He'd never feared that he'd make that trade. Ever. But, magic was insidious. It looked for some weak spot and ego. He'd always been afraid --deep in his heart and soul-- that he'd fall for some trick. In an effort to become human and win Marion, he might lose her forever. She'd forget he existed, or he'd become invisible to her, or some other terrible loophole would steal her away. Even when he had so little of her, he hadn't been willing to chance that outcome.

So, he'd never risked the test.

But, now that moment of reckoning had found him and Nicholas realized he'd worried over nothing. There was no doubt, at all. No temptation to bargain. If he lost Marion, he was dead, anyway.

She was all that kept him alive.

Trevelyan considered the emphatic refusal with a slow smile. "I'll make you human, if you let me have a single, measly night with her, then." He tried. "Just a few hours. You can convince her to do that, surely. What would be the fuss? I won't harm the girl. You know that's not what I want." His voice was hypnotically persuasive. "Marion will be delivered back to your arms, tousled and happy. *You'll* be happy. God knows, *I'll* be happy. Don't you want to make everyone happy?"

"*No.*" Now, it was a warning. And just as emphatic.

"This really is me playing nice. It's a once-in-a-lifetime offer and you know it. Very few of the trapdoors that I usually work into these kinds of deals. A simple, harmless trade." Trevelyan's head tilted. "There's nothing I can offer you to make this happen?"

Nicholas suddenly recalled Marion's words to him, outside the casino:

Being human doesn't give you anything you don't already have. A heart and soul. Thoughts and emotions. Also, you're very attractive. You should stay exactly as you are. You're perfect, Nick.

"No." He said simply. "I'll stay just as I am."

"Don't you want to be really *real?*"

Nicholas wanted to tackle him to the ground and beat the shit out of him. ...But he didn't. For some damn reason. "If Marion was yours, would you make this deal? Would you make *any* deal for your mate?"

Silence.

"Absolutely not." Trevelyan sighed, finally giving up. "Dragons don't share. But few people are as smart as a dragon."

"I'm smart enough to know I already *have* something really real." He met Trevelyan's eyes, so there could be no mistaking the threat in his own. "And I'm keeping her."

Trevelyan chewed his gum, slouching back to being jaded and unconcerned. "Well, it was worth a try. I'm not surprised, though. The girls with the sparks always seem to have True Loves. And the True Loves always turn down my generous offers to buy them. It's very strange, really."

"Robin Hood is Marion's True Love. Not me." Nicholas reminded them both. It hurt to even say the words.

Trevelyan perked up. "So, you're saying I should ask *him*, then?"

There was simply no reason in the world for Nicholas not to hit him. *None.* And yet he didn't hit him. Why? He *wanted* to. He'd hit men with far, *far* less provocation. So why did the dragon still have all his limbs attached? And why did he keep talking to the snarky bastard?

Nicholas' went back to his earlier certainty that something was wrong here, pushing through the fog in his head. There was no way he should be calmly chatting about Trevelyan touching Marion, for any goddamn reason. No way he should be standing there, listening to the dragon's random villainy and insults and ruminations on magic...

Wait.

Trevelyan could do magic.

Goddammit.

He glanced down at his drink suspiciously. "You son of a bitch, did you drug me?"

"You're being paranoid." Trevelyan flicked a dismissive hand. "It's one little truth spell. With a dash of 'non-violence' tossed in, for good measure. Your kind are always so physical and this is a black-tie event."

The spell began to dissipate, now that Nicholas had seen through the enchantment. Once you understood magic was confusing your senses, you could fight through it.

"It speaks well of your commitment to my one-and-only friend, that you refused my offer so readily. Especially, under a truth spell." Trevelyan added, as if Nicholas should give a shit about his opinion. "I've decided to let you keep her." It was hard to tell how much of that entire exchange had been some bizarre dragon-y test.

Nicholas' jaw tightened.

"I expected you to say 'no,' of course, but not *that* quickly." Trevelyan pondered for a beat. "And I was really selling it well, I thought. Perhaps, I'm losing my touch?" He gave a light laugh, as if that was crazy talk. "...No. That can't be it. I'm amazing at everything."

Nicholas' crunched the champagne flute in his stony hand, shattering it to dust.

Trevelyan's gaze flicked to the waterfall of pulverized glass hitting the floor and then to Nicholas' undamaged fist. It finally seemed to occur to him that it would take a lot of dragon-fire to melt rock. His brows tugged together.

Nicholas took a step towards him.

"Well, I'm *bored*." Trevelyan insisted, like that was a legitimate excuse and Nicholas was being totally unreasonable. "It's my birthday and none of the rest of these farmhands are even worth speaking to." Another blasé wave at Nottingham's nobility. "How else can I pass the time, but to play with you? You should be flattered!"

Nicholas' reached out to grab Trevelyan by the front of his tuxedo. It probably cost seven thousand gold pieces and Nicholas's massive fingers ripped a hole straight through it.

"Really?!" Trevelyan snapped, shoving backwards. More fabric shredded. "Fuck! You see? *Physical*. I should turn *you* into a donkey."

"Unmelt the scepter and leave... or I won't let you leave at all." Nicholas stalked closer to the dragon again, closing the distance and looming over him. "I will bury you next to all the other magical shitheads I've killed."

"No, I don't think you will." Trevelyan's smile was back to being a taunt. "Your mate won't appreciate you attacking me. Marion is the one person in the universe who doesn't hate me. She gave me a cupcake for my birthday."

"Was it poisoned?"

"Oh, I hope so. That makes any gift more interesting. Or perhaps she baked a file into it. Marion and I are old prison pals, after all."

"She still likes me more than you, remember?"

"She likes you more than anyone." Trevelyan agreed. It must have been painful for him, because he never agreed with anyone. He thrived on conflict. Green eyes met Nicholas' and for just a second he looked sincere. "Robin Hood can't change her mind about you. Only *you* can."

"He's going to try and steal her back." It drove him crazy to even think about it. "You think I'm going to allow that?"

"The spark I see? It's brightest when she looks at you."

Nicholas' brows slammed down. "Then it's *mine*. Why the fuck are you looking at it, in the first place?"

Trevelyan scowled at that possessive logic. "You didn't know it existed, until I told you. It's some kind of magic. You can't even see it."

"I feel it. I feel Marion's magic every time I look at her." He shook his head. "I have no doubt you see a spark in her. I'm not surprised she glows. But that magic belongs to *me* and you can get your eyes off it. *Now.*"

"You're not even curious to know what that spark *is?*"

"If I investigated every special thing about Marion, I wouldn't have time to eat or sleep. No, I'm fine without discovering the name of her spark. I'm content knowing it's there and aimed at *me.* Instead, I'll dedicate myself to making my bride happy and keeping her far away from dragons and outlaws."

Trevelyan rubbed his forehead, like he couldn't believe how shortsighted Nicholas was being. "Just don't fuck this up." He finally warned. "You won't get another woman like that one. Believe me. I've met you. This is the best you will ever, *ever* do."

Nicholas jabbed a finger at him. "Leave."

"Fine. I'm bored, anyway. I'm not sure why you threw me such a dull party."

"It's *not* your birthday party."

Trevelyan ignored that. "Next year, I want some kind of evil sex show. Possibly with acrobats. I'll send Marion a list of ideas."

"Don't bother."

"Here. A peace offering, before I go." Trevelyan snapped his fingers and the lion-headed scepter appeared in his hand. Had it been that easy for him this whole damn time? "I'm disappointed with how simple it was to find, by the way. It wasn't melted. Just hidden."

Nicholas grabbed the scepter from him, quickly looking it over. "What do you mean it wasn't melted?"

"I mean... it wasn't... melted." Trevelyan repeated in the most condescending tone anyone had ever used. "A locator spell was all I needed."

That didn't make any sense. "Are you sure it's the

right scepter?"

"No, it's *another* ancient, golden, lion-headed scepter buried in Sherwood Forest." Trevelyan drawled out. "Dear God... I'm always surrounded by morons." He turned away, ready to leave. "You can tell Marion I'll be expecting detailed information on my death, very soon."

"Do you see anything special about this thing?" Nicholas called after him, still trying to figure out what the hell was going on with the scepter.

"I don't see anything special about most of the world. That's the whole problem." Trevelyan stopped walking, as if something new had just occurred to him. "Oh, about this Robin Hood person...? The one who pesters Marion, and robbed her, and helped a murderous housekeeper nearly shoot her with an arrow...?"

Nicholas grunted, turning the scepter around in his hands. Nothing about it struck him as particularly important. Why did so many people want this damn thing? And why hadn't it been melted?

"He truly steals gold from the rich and then distributes it to the poor?"

Nicholas snorted. "Supposedly."

Trevelyan made a thoughtful sound and glanced off towards Sherwood. "And Robin Hood keeps all that wealth out in the forest? Behind wooden doors and thatched roofs and whatnot?"

"I assume so." Nicholas glanced up from the scepter, suspicious about the questions. "Why?"

But the dragon was already gone

Chapter Thirty

Carving your own gargoyle: How big is *too* big?

Alan A. Dale- "Nottingham's Naughtiest News"

The party was going well.

The humans mostly looked uncomfortable and haughty, but who cared? The only people who mattered to Marion were the gargoyles and they seemed to be enjoying themselves.

She'd insisted that Nicholas' lieutenants attend the Maypole Ball as guests rather than staff, which was apparently something of a scandal among the bluebloods. Too bad, so sad. The gargoyles lived in the castle. The party was being held at the castle. Why should they be excluded?

There had been some initial wariness about the idea from the men, as well, but they'd given in when she'd pressed. People had a hard time saying no to Marion, especially big, gargoyle-y people. It didn't take long to convince them her idea was right. Now, all six of them seemed happy as clams.

Cragg was in a much better mood, ever since his ex was transformed into a donkey and vanished into ignominy. (That would make *anyone* feel better, really.) He was over by the open bar laughing and drinking with Oore. Rockwell was raiding the buffet table outside. Gravol was listening to the orchestra play, his huge head bouncing along to the music. Even Boulder was smiling, for once. He was scaring all the humans who got within ten feet of him. He loved that.

Sure, the uptight elite of Nottingham weren't thrilled to have armed, inhuman men invading the sanctity of their elaborate ball, but fuck 'em all. Marion was pleased Nicholas' lieutenants were having fun. With her stony in-laws entertained, she was taking a break to plot her break in and reflect.

The rank-and-file palace guards had been dispatched around town, looking for the Wraith. Nicholas had armed the soldiers with hammers and sent them on a house-by-house search of Nottingham.

Nicholas didn't believe a word of Pinocchio's story, but Marion was willing to give the man a chance and her fiancé had gone along with the plan. The gargoyles were questioning the humans and then *softly* rapping them on the hand with a hammer. She'd stressed the "softly" part, although "softly" to a gargoyle would still probably break a few bones. It was all for the greater Good, though. If the suspect was secretly the Wraith, the small blow would kill it. If it wasn't the Wraith, it would just piss the person off.

Marion never minded pissing people off, so it was well worth the risk.

The Wraith hunt had so far proved unsuccessful, but she wasn't giving up. Marion fully intended to hammer-check every single citizen of this God-forsaken kingdom, until she'd located the monster. And if this plan didn't work, at least she'd had the fun of ordering that all the Nottinghamers get hit with hammers.

Huh. Hammering the Nottinghamers. Was there a pun in there someplace?

Beside her, Quarry leaned against the wall eating a plate of fancy desserts. No matter how engrossed they were with the ball, one of the gargoyles was always by her side. It was nice and all, but she had shit to do and they were getting in the way.

"I'm really okay." She assured Quarry. "You can go have fun. I won't mind."

His babysitting was going to make it harder to sneak off and search Nicholas' room, which was her other plan for the evening. Ever since she'd escaped prison, she was coming up with so many great plans it was tough to schedule them all into her day.

"First time I ever saw you was at a party." Quarry said randomly, disregarding her words.

"Really?" Marion blinked. "I don't remember that." She didn't recall ever meeting Quarry before she returned from the WUB Club.

"You wouldn't. Nicholas and some of the higher-ranked boys were assigned to the doors, but I wasn't allowed to come down. The gargoyles carved like me were kept upstairs, for entertainment afterwards."

She cringed a bit.

"But I snuck down to watch the dancing. I was young and interested in the idea of a party. Interested in life beyond a bedroom. I spent all my time locked in there." He sounded matter-of-fact about his miserable existence.

"I'm sorry." Marion told him softly.

Quarry lifted a shoulder in a shrug, like none of it mattered, but he didn't meet her eyes. "Anyway, I saw you come in, dressed in a white gown. Nicholas held the door." He gestured towards the entrance. "You smiled at him, like he was a normal guest at the party and not just a gargoyle. That was remarkable to me." Quarry paused. "He ignored you, of course."

Marion rolled her eyes. "Of course."

"But he watched you for the whole night, like you were made of magic. He never looked away. That gave me hope."

"Why?" She was pretty sure she'd attended that party with Robin.

"Because I knew Nicholas was in love with you."

Marion's insides fluttered.

"Before that, I hadn't realized gargoyles could fall in love. I assumed we were hollowed out of emotions. That's how I always felt, anyway." Quarry glanced at her again. "And I never, *ever* thought that a human might love a gargoyle. But you kept looking over at him, too. All night. I don't think you even knew you were doing it. Your eyes would just scan the room, until you saw Nicholas. Then, you'd smile."

"Sometimes I knew I was looking at Nick. Sometimes it just happened."

"When I watched you and Nicholas, I knew my life could be better. I knew it was *possible*. It's not easy for someone like me to become a palace guardsman. That's not what I was made for."

"It doesn't matter what any of us were made for. It only matters what we *want* to do with our lives."

"Until I saw you smiling at the commander, I didn't know I *could* want anything for my life. Then, I understood that maybe there was some smiling person for me, too. That possibility changed everything. Even if I never find them, the idea saved me." He met her eyes. "Thank you, Marion."

She laid her head sideways, so it rested companionably against his shoulder. "You're welcome."

Quarry glanced down at her and his mouth curved. Not many people had ever touched him in a friendly way. She could tell. "The commander isn't going to like you doing that." He warned, but he didn't dart away.

"He'll have to come over here and complain about it, then."

That remark earned her a chuckle. "I've had my concerns over how it would all pan out, in the end. I knew Nottingham would explode over your relationship. I wasn't sure you'd have the balls to stick with Nicholas, through the fallout. I shouldn't have doubted you, though." He settled back to watch the trouble she was making. "I've never met a ballsier woman."

"You've met a ballsier man?"

"Nope."

"Didn't think so."

Nicholas was already winding his way towards them, a sexy and possessive look on his face.

"Yeah... he's pissed." Quarry surmised.

"Well, he should be over here flirting with me and not bickering with Trevelyan."

"Obviously. You just don't get enough of his attention."

Marion grinned at that dry comment.

Nicholas stopped right in front of them and crossed his arms over his chest.

"Hello, sweet captain of my dreams." Marion said

cheerily. He looked *extremely* handsome in his suit. It was hard to keep her eyes off of him, so she didn't even try.

Their encounter that afternoon had been incredible. Marion had never felt so connected and aroused. When she came apart in his arms, she knew she was home. There had been that brief moment, where she'd accidently asked Nicholas to take care of her and he'd very sincerely agreed, of course. She'd freaked out about that for a second. But, his wicked hand had felt *so good* that she'd soon fallen back under his spell.

Better to just forget about the small lapse and enjoy. That made sense, right?

Right.

Nicholas had claimed his betrothal rights again and again, not stopping until she was limp and drowsy. Then, he'd dressed her in his stolen shirt and tucked her into bed. She'd tried to convince him to join her, as he pressed a gentle kiss to her forehead. After a nap, she would have been more than ready for the main event. But he'd been firmly committed to following his precious betrothal rights rules and had strolled out without succumbing to her feminine whiles.

Marion pouted for a beat.

Her failure to fully seduce him was discouraging, considering their wedding was scheduled for the next day. Who wanted to be a virgin bride, for the second damn time in a row?

Nicholas looked at Quarry.

Quarry held up his hands in a gesture of innocence. "She started it."

Gray eyes swung back to Marion, not doubting that she was the instigator.

She tried and failed to look repentant. "I missed you. I had to lure you over here somehow, didn't I?"

Nicholas grunted, accepting that explanation. He shoved Quarry aside, so he could stand next to Marion.

She cuddled against him. "See? Isn't this better than talking to boring old Trevelyan?"

He arched a brow and looped his arm around her waist, hugging her closer.

Quarry seemed amused by the entire exchange. "I'm going to go someplace else, before I'm demoted."

"Or murdered." Nicholas agreed darkly.

Quarry laughed and popped the last bite-sized dessert into his mouth. "You really think you'd win that fight?" He went wandering off towards the bar to gossip with the others.

Nicholas glanced down at Marion. "None of the men were so playful, before you got here. You're a Bad influence."

"Yeah, but you're all enjoying yourselves a lot more."

Appeased by the truth of that statement, Nicholas kissed the side of her head. "I wasn't hanging out with that asshole dragon for my health, you know. Your fiend of a friend finally did something useful." He held up the scepter.

"Oh my God!" Marion straightened away from him, legitimately shocked. "Trev actually unmelted it? That's amazing! I figured it was --like-- three-to-one he'd just sleep with chambermaids, steal the silverware, and leave when he was bored." She took the scepter, turning it over in her hands. "What's so special about this thing, anyway?"

"I have no idea. But, Trevelyan claims it wasn't actually melted."

She frowned. "L.J. says he put it in the forge himself."

"Either Trevelyan is lying... or the kid is." Nicholas summed up with sheriff-y dispassion. "It hurts me to say it, but I trust the dragon on this one. It's not like you can mistake tossing a scepter into a forge and watching it melt."

Crap.

Under normal circumstances, she'd trust a live cockroach to nest in her hair, before she trusted Trevelyan about anything. But magic was one of the few things he took seriously. He wouldn't lie to her about it.

Marion's mind raced. If Trevelyan was being honest, then there was only one other possibility. "Little John is the Wraith." She said simply.

"Yep." Nicholas agreed like he'd already come to the same conclusion. "Or more accurately, the Wraith is impersonating Little John."

"Shit! Trev said the boy smelled like a bug, but that

was before I knew Wraiths *were* bugs." She winced a bit, thinking it over. "Do you think...?"

Nicholas cut her off, answering her question before she had to ask it. "I think L.J. is dead and there is a monster wearing his skin."

Fuck. Marion closed her eyes. "I *liked* that kid."

"I doubt you even met the actual Little John. He's probably been the Wraith, for a long time."

Her lips parted at that idea. "Well, Robin must know that it's not really Little John, then."

"Hood is involved in the Wraith's whole plot, Marion. Of course, he knows." Nicholas had already passed judgement on her ex, it seemed. "The Wraith can teleport, allegedly. Sometimes L.J. was an illusion, when the Wraith was off being King Richard. Sometimes Richard was an illusion, when it was here being L.J. But, they're *both* the Wraith. They're both its puppets. Hood helped it assume the identities of dead men, so he could profit."

"That's horrible! Not even Trevelyan would do something that despicable and he's the worst person I know." She hesitated. "Well, besides Clorinda."

Nicholas ignored that. "Reasoning it all out, I think we've been used."

She didn't like the sound of that.

"Commander, is it okay if I dance with your girl, again?" Gravol called from his position by the orchestra. "I promise to bring her back."

"She's not my girl." Nicholas answered distractedly.

Marion frowned. Perversely, *not* being called his girl annoyed her, now. Nicholas associated the phrase with safety and home. Of *course*, that meant her! Who else was he even considering for the role?

Gravol wasn't giving up. "Marion, come dance with me, again!" His big, innocent face was alight with happiness.

"Not right now, buddy." Gravol was always following her around, with childlike enthusiasm. It was very cute, but at the moment she needed to concentrate on the dead kid trying to kill them. "How is the Wraith using us?" She asked Nicholas.

"Well, I actually don't have the evidence to back it up…"

Marion cut him off. "Take an educated guess."

"The Wraith would have to impersonate you, to get your memories, right? If we believe Pinocchio, anyway, which is usually a bad idea. But, for argument's sake, once the Wraith *had* your memories, it would know its former plan wasn't going to work, again. What if it decided to try something new?"

"I hate even thinking about that monster wearing my face." Marion muttered.

Gravol came bounding over, undeterred by her refusal. His huge body was outfitted in a gigantic suit, which had taken three seamstresses to finish on time. "Let's go dance!" He suggested eagerly.

"In a second, pal." She patted his massive arm.

Nicholas kept going, ignoring the very large interruption. "Trevelyan says the scepter was buried. So, how in the hell could Hood steal it, when he took the rest of the gold?"

"You think that was an illusion, too?"

"Yes."

"Can we go dance, *now?*" Gravol persisted.

Marion held up a "wait a second" finger.

"The Wraith was trying to *find* the scepter and it used us to help. Nicholas continued, gesturing to it. "It disguised itself as L.J. and planted the idea it was important, knowing that you'd take it from there."

"Why does it even need this thing?" She looked down at the scepter, just as Gravol got bored with waiting and grabbed hold of her.

"Let's go!" He urged excitedly and tugged her towards the dance floor.

The guy was about five times her size, so the move caught her off guard. Marion gave a squeak of alarm. Gravol lifted her right off the ground, without even noticing. The scepter fell from her hand, as she was carted along like a doll.

"Damn it, Gravol." Nicholas sighed in exasperation. "*No!* Put Marion down."

Gravol blinked his big eyes, realizing he'd picked her up. "Whoops." He carefully set Marion back onto her feet. "I'm sorry, Marion. It's just that you're so *small*, I couldn't even tell I was carrying you."

"Saying things like that is why you're my favorite, Gravol." Marion gave him a rueful smile and checked to make sure her May Day Queen crown was still in place. "Don't worry. I'm fine. Let me finish talking to Nick and *then* we'll dance, okay?"

"Okay." He relaxed, seeing she wasn't upset, and went dashing off towards the maypole. Marion gave it about five minutes before he knocked it down.

"You're sure that you're alright?" Nicholas asked, looking her over for injuries.

"Of course. He wouldn't hurt me."

"Not on purpose, but his wrist is thicker than your waist, so..." Nicholas trailed off with a low curse, his eyes on the floor.

Marion followed his gaze and immediately spotted the problem. "Uh-oh."

The scepter was broken. When she'd dropped it, the top had snapped off, so it now lay in two irregular pieces. The lion's head was one section and the golden shaft was the other. The *hollow* golden shaft.

And inside of it was a rolled up piece of paper.

She swooped down to pick it up, quickly unfurling it and scanning the document. Seeing it was some kind of birth certificate.

Seeing it was *Robin's* birth certificate.

"Holy shit!" She blurted out.

Nicholas read it over her shoulder, his forehead creasing. "Aw hell..." He muttered in disgust. "Hood is King Jonathan's secret son? Christ, that's all I need."

Marion looked up at him, her mind whirling.

Nicholas kept scanning the page, his face grim. "It says he was given a name, before his adopted parents rechristened him: David Doncaster." He pointed to it, like maybe she was about to start arguing. "His mother was Guyla *Doncaster*

Gisborn."

"Do you understand what this *means?*" Marion whispered in horror.

"That King Jonathan had an affair with a married housekeeper? That this birth certificate is the reason Hood and the Wraith wanted to find the scepter? That your ex-boyfriend is the heir to a kingdom and you can prove it?"

"No! It means I've kissed my fucking *cousin!*"

Nicholas gave a startled bark of laughter. People turned to gape at him, shocked that the Sheriff of Nottingham found anything amusing outside of hanging people in the courtyard. He quickly sobered, as if the sound had even surprised him. "Sorry." He cleared his throat. "I just… wasn't expecting you to say that."

She had never heard Nicholas actually laugh before. He should do it loudly and often. She wished he hadn't stifled it so quickly, because his uproarious laughter would at least be nice to listen to as her world rearranged itself.

Marion swallowed. "No wonder Robin has been so angry at you." She gestured to the paper. "He hates that you're in charge of Nottingham, instead of him."

"It's probably *part* of why he hates me. You're still the heart of it, though."

Nicholas was wrong. Robin cared *far* more about himself, than he did about Marion. It wasn't even a question. Marion wasn't going to argue about it, though. She was too busy thinking. Did this revelation change anything about her plans to burn Nottingham to ash?

Nope.

In fact, it just made the impending devastation more delightful. As her initial shock faded, triumph took its place. She'd just been dealt a winning hand!

"Richard must've learned about Hood and wanted to stay heir apparent, so he got rid of his brother to hide the truth." Nicholas was busily putting pieces together. "Maybe Jonathan wanted to openly acknowledge his son. Robin was almost of age, by that point, and Jonathan didn't have any other children."

"You think the Wraith saw all this in Richard's memories, when it stole his face?"

"Makes sense." Nicholas grunted. "I guess Hood is the royal lovechild that Alan A. Dale has been investigating for the tabloid." He paused. "I was starting to suspect it was *you*, actually. That maybe your mother and King Jonathan really did..."

"No!" Marion interrupted, shocked he would even consider such a thing. She dragged her attention from the birth certificate. "My mother and father were very happy together. They were True Loves."

"I know." He agreed expressionlessly. "That's why it's the kind of relationship you've always wanted."

"All I want is a relationship with *you*." She corrected. "Now, focus on the downfall of our enemies." She shifted the paper, so he could see its calligraphy-ed glory. "This actually makes sense. Robin was ranting about having 'pure blood,' like some kind of fucking Gyre scumbag, so he must have decided his DNA is..."

Nicholas cut her off. "What's a gyre scumbag?"

"A humans-are-superior-to-everyone, anti-magic cult. Are those losers not around, yet? Well, they will be and they suck." She lifted a shoulder in a resigned shrug. "Anyway, it's typical that Robin would align more with his dead, royal father, rather than his living, housekeeper mother. ...His *formerly* living housekeeper mother. I can't believe he let Guyla sacrifice herself, while he escaped us." She wrinkled her nose. "No, that part I actually *do* believe. What a putz."

"Guyla and Jonathan together seems like the unbelievable part to me." Nicholas sounded perplexed with the image of the dour housekeeper and the golden king secretly dating. "She was always so... unhappy."

"Maybe losing him *made* her unhappy. I think Guyla really loved Jonathan." Marion's eyes narrowed. "And she *hated* my mother. I'll bet, Mom told her best friend, Jonathan, to stop sleeping with that crazy hag."

"Probably sound advice."

"Except Jonathan didn't listen quick enough and Robin

was the result. I knew he was adopted, but..." She slowly shook her head. "He's the real king of Nottingham."

Nicholas sighed in aggravation. "Hood will be even worse at the job than Richard was." He muttered. "Do you *have* to hand him the key to the kingdom?" He nodded towards the notarized page that gave her idiot ex the throne.

Marion scoffed. "Of course not!" Grasping the document between her hands, she casually ripped it in two. "We're not helping Robin become king. Are you kidding me?"

Nicholas' mouth curved.

"The Wraith might have some of my memories, but it doesn't understand a damn thing about me. Not if it thought I'd find this scepter and stop hating that bastard." Marion smirked. "I'm not the weepy damsel in distress, I was before. Now, I'm the wicked bitch of the WUB Club. And *nobody* fucks me over."

"I love it when you're Bad, Marion." He watched her shred the birth certificate into pieces, tension easing from his shoulders.

She tossed the tiny bits of paper to the ground, so they mingled with the party's colorful confetti and were lost forever. "Robin Hood didn't mind stealing our future, last time around. Let's see how he likes it when we hijack his."

"Team Creative Villainy."

A gleeful smile crossed her face. "'Good luck, Robin. ...But, I think we should see other people.'" She mocked, paraphrasing the words he'd used, when she was carted off to jail.

Smoke-colored eyes gleamed. "I'm fine with that idea, just so I'm all the other people you're dating."

"Who else could I have this much fun with?" She agreed. "You know, when she sent me back here, Tansy wanted me to live in peace or some shit. She said she'd hoped I'd rise above my petty need for revenge. But," Marion shrugged, "*nah.*"

"Well, her wish might still come true. You're running out of enemies to destroy, so sooner or later your vengeance will have to stop. Everyone will be dead or crying."

"That's the plan. Still, none of the other paybacks have been *this* satisfying. I'm dedicating it to my father, who watched his life being sold out from under him by that thieving fuck-wad. I *told* you I'd destroy Robin's dreams."

Nicholas looked amused and kind of turned on by her unrepentant evilness. "I'm happy you were right, but we still have some problems here.'

"I know! Should we celebrate with more champagne or a bottle of Richard's best merlot?" She leaned closer. "Drink the merlot *now*, if you want any, because I'm emptying the palace wine cellar at the reception's open bar."

"No, I mean the birth certificate explains why the Wraith and Hood wanted the scepter, but it doesn't explain why they've been targeting you through two timelines."

"Maybe they're jealous I actually *do* have a crown." She pointed to the plastic tiara on her head.

"Or maybe we're still missing a piece of the puzzle. Why try to kill you with puppets, if you're the one they thought would find the scepter? Why did Hood lure you to the tent? It doesn't make any sense."

"Oh, I don't think Robin was in on the marionette attack." She said blithely. "He swore he wasn't and I trust him."

Nicholas was suddenly still. "You trust Hood?" He repeated in a voice lacking all emotion.

"I really can't imagine Robin wanting me dead. He hasn't threatened me, at all, and I know I've been pissing him off." Nicholas would agree with the logic in her words if he considered the facts. He loved facts. "I mean, he actually *has* bitched about my crown, but nothing more dire. Not like the puppet attack. I think the Wraith did it without him."

Silence. Very, very silent silence.

Marion was lost in thought. "Weirdly, I think Robin *likes* that I'm pissing him off, this time around. Have you noticed that?" Her deluded ex was just a glutton for punishment. "I think it turns him on and makes this whole thing a contest. He's seeing me as the grand prize!"

Robin left her at the altar, when she wanted to marry

him. He declared them destined loves, when she dumped him. She would simply never understand it.

Nicholas was thinking, too. Deeply.

Good. He'd see she was right.

"Marion!" Gravol called again. "Come dance!"

"I'm coming, pal." She gave Nicholas a quick kiss on the cheek. "Duty calls." She hurried off to dance with Gravol, missing the way her fiancé stared after her with dark concern.

Chapter Thirty-One

Thirty-one foolproof recipes for avoiding Maid Marion's Bad influence. Don't fall for her tricks, as she brainwashes the rest of Nottingham. We've got the lowdown on all the potions you'll need to stay vigilant.
(You won't *believe* number twenty-two is low-carb!)

Alan A. Dale- "Nottingham's Naughtiest News"

Marion adjusted her rhinestone tiara in the ladies' room mirror, admiring the way it caught the light. Her life in prison had been so sparkle deprived. Fortunately, she was making up for it, now. Her wedding tomorrow would be visible from space. Crates full of sparkles were being brought in by caravan. She'd bought up the supply of everything that glittered in a four-thousand mile radius, so remote sparkle mines had to be accessed, in the deepest mountain ranges of the...

The door slammed open hard enough to rattle the large and tasteful flower arrangements on the vanity counter. Clorinda stood there, a vision in false lashes and righteous fury.

Marion arched a brow. "Did you get an invitation?"

The Maypole Ball was the domain of Nottingham's elites and Clorinda didn't even qualify as a lady-in-waiting, anymore. Not since Marion had fired her (annoyingly toned) ass. And, by the way, it was *super* annoying that Clorinda was still the prettiest girl in all the land, even with a broken nose and a scowl on her face. Marion simply didn't understand how it was possible for such a hateful shrew to look so beautiful, all the time. You'd think Clorinda's withered soul would peek through around the edges.

Maybe it was an evil glamour.

Two random noblewomen were fixing their makeup at the long mirror over the sinks. Marion didn't recall their names. They hesitated, their eyes going from Marion to Clorinda and then back again. They seemed to want to run, but they also feared it might draw attention.

Clorinda strode into the room, like a gunslinger ready for a duel. ...If gunslingers wore pink chiffon ball gowns. "Get out." She snapped at the other women, barely looking their way.

The women couldn't have fled faster if their tampon strings were on fire.

Technically, they outranked Clorinda in the social pecking order, but it didn't matter. They still followed commands, because Clorinda inspired terror wherever she went. It was one reason she'd been a wonderful lady-in-waiting, if you discounted the "ratting Marion out to the tabloids" thing. People had given Marion extra leeway, just to avoid angering Clorinda. No one else in Nottingham was so relentless in their angelic, size-two, treachery.

Marion turned to face her nemesis. "If you want to fight again, this time I'm going to take out some of your teeth."

Clorinda slammed the bathroom door shut and said nothing for a long moment. All that was missing was tumbleweed rolling past, and ominous harmonica music building tension, and someone shouting "draw!" before the big shootout.

Marion waited.

"I did not steal your diary and sell it to Alan A. Dale." Clorinda finally bit off.

Marion's eyebrows shot up. She hadn't been expecting that.

"I take my job seriously." Clorinda went on. "I was *good* at being your lady-in-waiting. Maybe I targeted a few other useless bluebloods, but I left you alone."

"Except you *did* steal my diary. Maybe not in this reality, but in the last..."

Clorinda cut her off. "I don't give a shit about some other reality!"

"That's because you don't remember it! I *do*, though. And while I'm in jail, you take my diary and cash in." Marion snapped. "I thought you were my friend and you betrayed me!"

"We weren't friends! You *paid* me. You can't be friends with someone you pay."

"Of course you can! I paid you, because you *were* my friend. I could've hired a *way* less irritating lady-in-waiting, if I wanted. But I thought you and I... I don't know... *got* each other." In some ways, Clorinda's betrayal had hurt more than Robin's, because Marion had felt closer to her. The pain of it had lasted way longer.

Clorinda crossed her arms over her chest and said nothing.

"I kept paying you, even when I couldn't afford a lady-in-waiting, because I didn't want to see you out of work. And you *know* that, Clory. You saw how I had to fire the rest of the staff, one by one, just to keep above water. But, I kept you with me, right until the end... And you *still* fucked me over."

Clorinda pursed her lips. "Did I come see you in prison?"

"Nope."

Clorinda tilted her head, like she didn't believe that.

"Fine." Marion admitted. "You *tried* to come, but I wouldn't see you. I wasn't in the mood to watch you gloat."

"You always think the worst of me."

"Because you're a being of absolute darkness."

"Granted." Clorinda allowed, because there was simply no arguing the point. "So, maybe in some possible future, I sold your diary to the newspaper."

"Not 'maybe.' It *happens*."

"Alright. But maybe ask yourself *why*."

"For money, of course."

"Yes.! Because I had to eat, you moron!" Clorinda shouted back. "My cousin isn't the king, financing the world's costliest wedding. No one is going to buy me a chocolate moat for *my* reception, filled with little golden gondolas carrying cute hors d'oeuvres and sapphires."

"There won't be any golden gondolas floating around my reception. ...They're platinum."

Clorinda kept talking. "I'm broke, Marion. This dress?" She gestured to the pink chiffon. "That *you* got mustard all over, the other day? It's the only decent one I own!"

Marion glanced at the gown. Clorinda's face was so lovely that it was easy to overlook the clothes she wore, but that garment did seem very familiar. She was pretty sure Clorinda wore it a lot. "I thought that was just your *favorite* dress."

"It's three years out of style!"

"I'm from the future. Everything around here is years out of style."

That distracted Clorinda for a beat. "What happens with dress sleeves next season? I'm hoping they'll be more fitted. I have amazing arms." She held up one supple limb to admire its shape.

"Ya know, I missed all the fall fashion shows, while I was doing time in super-max, so..." Marion trailed off with a taunting shrug.

Clorinda shook her head, like Marion was hopeless. "If you were arrested, I was suddenly out on the street." She continued, back on track. "Who else in Nottingham is dumb enough to hire me? I was probably looking for a way to generate some much needed cash, when I took your diary. I'm positive it wasn't personal."

"It sure felt personal."

"Well, it *wasn't*. Whatever I did, it was just about survival. In fact, I'll bet you that I went to that jail to give you some of the money I'd made. God knows, I'm the only one of us who's resourceful enough to earn gold." Clorinda arched an arrogant brow. "Under those circumstances, I'd do whatever it takes to survive and to keep *you* surviving.

Marion frowned.

"Although, I'm not sure why I'd bother to help you, at all." Clorinda continued dramatically. "You're a lunatic and ungrateful and violent." She gestured to her nose. "*Really* violent. You punched me! And I don't even want to know why you have the gargoyles wandering around town, beating people with hammers."

Marion was still focused on the beginning of that rant. Wait... The funds in her WUB Club commissary account had come from Clorinda?

Crap, that actually made sense.

When she'd first arrived in prison, Marion had used that money to stay alive, bribing guards for extra protection. It had saved her, until she found her footing. She'd assumed the cash came from Robin, which was a stupid guess in retrospect. The man had been stealing her gold, not giving her more. Clorinda was selfish, conniving, and callous... But there was no one else in all of Nottingham who would've tried to make Marion's incarceration a little more comfortable.

Maybe Clorinda hadn't completely abandoned Marion, after all. Maybe there had been some mitigating circumstances to her betrayal. Maybe --in some bizarre, ruthless, self-serving way-- Clorinda had tried to help her.

Maybe.

"How would you know what the other-Clorinda did?" She asked suspiciously.

"Because there is only *one* Clorinda." She gave her blonde curls a haughty toss.

Marion pinched the bridge of her nose at that egocentric response. "Oh for God's sake..."

"It's true! I know everything there is to know about me. And I know that I hate every useless, stuck-up Maid in this kingdom, so I would *happily* wreck their lives for fun and profit. ...Except you, Marion." She shifted uncomfortably. "I never hated you."

Marion dropped her hand from her face and blinked.

Clorinda made an expansive gesture with one graceful hand, like sharing her lack of malice was embarrassing. "You were always kind. To everyone. Even the people who couldn't help you, which was... baffling." She cleared her throat. "But, while you can be a naïve, puritanical, know-it-all, and I'm constantly appalled by your lipstick choices, I still find you somewhat tolerable."

"What's wrong with my lipstick?!"

Clorinda shot her a pitying look. "What *isn't* wrong

with it?"

Marion scowled and turned back towards the mirror to examine the color for herself. "You think I should go darker?"

"Look at your nipples."

Marion automatically glanced down, but everything seemed covered. "What?"

"To find the right shade of lipstick, you look at your nipples and try to match the color." Clorinda made it sound like the most obvious thing in the world. "How do you not know that?"

"I *wish* I had the kind of life where all I had to focus on is the color of my goddamn nipples."

Clorinda sighed. Loudly. "Being a duchess is wasted on you. If *I* was a duchess, I'd focus on catching some rich nobleman and not making out with rugged gargoyles."

It was gratifying someone else noticed how sexy Nicholas was, but still... "Don't look at Nick. He's mine."

Clorinda ignored that. "Actually, I would never be a duchess for long." She decided, as if she'd thought it all through. "I'd already be a *princess*, because I have ambition."

"I have ambition!"

"No. You have *plans*. There's a difference. Plans are focused on a specific goal. Ambition is about bettering your position, through any means necessary." She jabbed a perfectly painted finger at Marion, emphasizing each word. "Any. Means. Necessary. I started out in a hut, but I worked my way up to a lady-in-waiting. You think that was easy?"

"I never really thought about it, at all."

But it was so weirdly like Quarry's story that Marion suddenly saw that it wasn't just Maids and gargoyles that the kingdom oppressed. It was everyone! Shepherdesses, millers' sons, those noble girls only allowed to perform one talent at the talent show... They were *all* locked in boxes. In prisons. Most of them just didn't want to acknowledge it. Instead, they kept the cycle going and going, refusing to see reality and clinging to the broken past.

You needed plans and ambition and maybe a little creative villainy to escape Nottingham's rigidly defined roles.

You needed to be fixated on something that was really *real*.

"Of course you didn't think about where I came from!" Clorinda continued. "If you thought about it, you never would have hired me, in the first place. What kind of noblewoman asks a shepherdess to be her lady-in-waiting?"

Marion nodded in mock agreement, shaking aside her revelation about Nottingham's toxic culture. "Especially such a psychotic one."

"Look who's talking. Ever since your birthday, you've been just as diabolically vindictive as me." She watched Marion closely. "Perhaps we *can* be friends."

"Gosh, I sure hope so." Marion snarked.

Clorinda's mouth curved.

For no reason at all, Marion found herself wanting to grin back. "Kinda-sorta friends." She stipulated. "We're not going to hug and cry and say supportive shit."

"Of course not. We'll just badmouth our enemies and each other, while drinking a lot. And obviously we can do manicures."

"Sounds about right."

"While we're clearing the air, I never used a spell to play the piano better than you." Clorinda tacked on. "I just practice a lot, because princesses need to know how to play the piano. I've concentrated all my energy on getting out of the sheep pasture and into a palace. One day I'll make it all the way to the top. How? Ambition and being a bitch." She smiled righteously. "It's an unbeatable combination for success."

Marion fully agreed with that analysis. "I had enough bitchy ambition to win the May Day Queen pageant, right out from under you."

"Keep the plastic tiara, if it means so much to you. I'm going to figure out how to get a real one, one day." Clorinda sniffed. "But, it was clearly cheating to have your fiancé as judge."

"Says the loser."

"Well, if you can live with yourself for not winning fairly, I'm not…"

Bagheera Kong burst through the door and attacked.

Christ, Marion had picked a hell of a week to quit smoking.

She hit the floor with Bagheera on top of her. Ten minutes before, Marion had been dancing with her handsome groom. Then, she went to the ladies room and all her enemies decided to pounce. It was Nottingham's fault. The place bred miserable people. Sure, Marion had aggravated Bagheera, when she'd told the newspaper the woman had murdered Judge Kong. But, if it wasn't her dead husband ruining her reputation, Bagheera would be angry over something else. Nottinghamers were always unhappy.

Bagheera was wearing a purple evening dress, but that wasn't slowing her down. Her short black hair was slicked back from her face to reveal the hatred in her yellow eyes. "You ruined my life! I've been expelled from the garden club forever! None of my friends will even talk to me!"

"You shouldn't have accused me of seducing your scumbag husband, if you didn't want me to retaliate!" Marion retorted and delivered a four-knuckle punch to Bagheera's throat.

Bagheera was stronger than Marion, and capable of turning into a killer cat, but she didn't have any barbarian combat training. That gave Marion a fighting chance. In hand-to-hand combat with a stronger opponent, you had to strike hard and fight dirty. Actually, you should *always* strike hard and fight dirty. Any worthwhile barbarian warrior would agree.

Bagheera stumbled back, gripping her bruised neck and giving Marion an opportunity to get out from under her. ...And an opportunity to crush the woman's kneecap with her foot. There was a satisfying crunch and Bagheera collapsed backwards. She didn't break any bones, but she dislocated the damn thing. Not too shabby.

With a cry of agony, Bagheera fell into the trashcan, knocking it sideways. Marion rolled out of the way, as Bagheera grabbed the metal receptacle and heaved it at her. A hurricane of crumpled paper towels rained all over the room.

Clorinda shifted to the side, avoiding the melee and throwing up her hands in annoyance. "I'm trying to have a meaningful conversation with you here, Marion. Stop messing around with that tacky cat-person and focus on *me*."

"Can you just give me a second, please?" Marion looked around for a weapon.

Bagheera didn't have to search, because her weapons were attached to her. Rallying through her pain, she went at Marion again, swinging out with her panther-y claws. They grew right out of her hands, her fury aiding in her partial transformation into her feline-form.

Marion used her legs to heave the woman back, scrambling away before she was slashed. Bagheera grabbed for her again, but Marion was already on her feet.

"If you break my crown, I'm going to be pissed." Marion warned angrily. She couldn't take her eyes off the rampaging lunatic to check it for herself, though. Her fighting coach would have her ass if she took her attention away from her opponent. "Clorinda, did she break my crown?"

"No, but your hair's a mess." She gave a nonchalant shrug. "I mean, it's *always* a mess, but now it's even *more* of a mess."

Marion flicked her off, her gaze staying on Bagheera.

"I was going to shape the garden club into the preeminent social organization in Nottingham!" Bagheera shrieked, fully committed to her role as victim. She was trying to stand, but her wounded leg wouldn't totally support her. The injury kept her attack at least partially in check. "I was going to be the best chairperson it ever saw! But then you went and screwed it all up!"

"You attacked me first, in that damn newspaper!"

"You all but *forced* me to kill my husband!"

"You pushed him through that wall, all by yourself!"

"I was temporarily insane! You incited me to violence, when I'm very peaceful and refined..."

Clorinda cut her off with an irritated groan. "Oh my God... Can you stop whining and just go *away*, Bagheera?" Her tone was a perfect distillation of every high school cheerleader who'd ever wrecked the self-esteem of all the chubby kids in class. "Nobody wants you in here. We don't care about your boring problems and your perfume that reeks like death." She arched a mocking brow. "Or is that just Judge Kong?"

Bagheera's head whipped around to glare at her.

Clorinda smirked with all the malice in her blackened heart.

The distraction was just what Marion needed. She snatched the huge vase of flowers from the vanity and crashed it into Bagheera's skull. The woman gave a choked sound of shock, before slumping to the ground in an unconscious pile of cat-fur and taffeta.

Marion and Clorinda stared down at her.

"I can't believe she wore those shoes." Clorinda finally said.

"They're hideous." Marion agreed, breathing hard.

"And totally wrong for the occasion. If you're going to kill someone, you don't go for a three inch heel." Clorinda made a disdainful *tsk* sound. "You choose flats for the practicalities of violence or stilettos for the badass spectacle. The woman has terrible taste. No wonder she's been ostracized."

Marion tore her eyes away from her comatose victim and studied Clorinda for a long beat. It occurred to her that maybe she'd first hired Clorinda because the two of them were more alike than either of them would like to admit.

What the hell... She was doing her best to give all the other villains she knew a second chance, so why not the meanest mean girl in Nottingham?

"You should leave this kingdom." She decided.

Clorinda sent her a frown, misunderstanding that remark. "You want to make this some kind of feud? Because, I'm going to stop being so nice about things, if you keep being so..."

"No, I don't want to be enemies. I told you, I'll be your kinda-sorta friend, so long as you're mine. And *that's* why you should leave." Marion gave a meaningful pause. "Soon."

Clorinda's eyes widened. "You know what's going to happen next and it's Bad?" She surmised, not sounding at all concerned.

"I know things around here are going to take a turn for the fucked, any day now."

Clorinda slowly smiled. "Well, I deserve a vacation, anyway." She bent down to deftly unfasten Bagheera's diamond bracelet and pocketed it for herself. "Hey, do you think she's dead?"

"Not yet. But my fiancé is always happy to hang the assholes who attack me. We can add her to the backlog."

Clorinda chuckled and took Bagheera's earrings, too. "I admire crazed obsession in a man. Now that we're kinda-sorta friends, you should tell me what it's like to sleep with a gargoyle. Is *all* of him stone?"

"Sleeping with Nick is going to be great, and magical, and none of your damn business."

"Going to be?" Clorinda repeated. "Jesus, don't tell me you're *still* a virgin."

"None of your business." Marion repeated firmly.

Clorinda didn't accept such a concept was possible. *Everything* was her business. "Don't be such a dreary little prude. I understood not sleeping with Robin Hood. What would be the point? Just looking at him, I guarantee he's as boring naked, as he is clothed." She fastened her stolen jewels onto her ears. "The way the sheriff stares at you is positively *devouring*. I'm sure he'll be fun in bed."

"Stop imagining my fiancé in bed or I'll bury you in a shallow grave."

Clorinda blithely disregarded that threat, craning her neck to admire her new fortune in diamonds in the mirror. "It's fun that we can chat like this. I've never had a kinda-sorta friend before."

"Shocking." Marion deadpanned.

Clorinda missed the sarcasm. "Other girls always hate me, since I'm so much prettier than them." She made it sound obvious. "Usually, I'm smarter, too. And more motivated to succeed. They just can't stand the competition." She pouted a bit. "There's so much pettiness in the world."

Marion rolled her eyes.

"You don't seem *too* jealous, though." Clorinda

praised, perking up again. "Probably because you're going to marry a man who positively dotes on your plainness. So, we need to make sure that the sheriff doesn't wise up and escape, because that would for *sure* impact our new kinda-sorta friendship."

"So my romance is all about *you?*"

Clorinda blinked. "What else would it be about?"

"Nick and I, maybe?"

"Don't be so self-centered. We're talking about *me*, right now."

Marion sighed and folded a piece of gum into her mouth. "You know, maybe other women hate you because you're a viperous megalomaniac."

"And a natural blonde." Clorinda agreed without a drop of humility. "But, fine. If you're determined to only focus on yourself, consider this: You could have died, just now. Slashed to pieces by this weak, crybaby, social-climber." She absently gestured towards Bagheera. "Do you *really* want to leave this mortal coil without bedding the large, pretty man who's obsessed with you?"

Marion's brows drew together, as she considered that sage advice.

"You need to seduce the Sheriff of Nottingham, Marion. As your kinda-sorta friend, I absolutely *insist* upon it."

"I'm working on that, but..."

Clorinda cut her off. "Working on it?" She echoed in derision. "No. Get it *done*. More than anyone, you should know that wasting time is a lousy idea. Get his pants off and get him into bed. *Tonight*." Clorinda turned back to her and gave a decisive nod. "You'll thank me later."

Chapter Thirty-Two

**Secrets, secrets, secrets!
Celebrity psychics spill the beans on everything Nottingham's biggest names have been hiding!**

Alan A. Dale- "Nottingham's Naughtiest News"

Only Marion would get into a fistfight with a panther.

Nicholas shook his head in exasperation. Oore and Boulder had lugged Bagheera's unconscious body off to the dungeon, while he went upstairs to talk to Marion. A brawl in the ladies' room was a minor occurrence for a woman who lived and breathed creative villainy, of course. She'd been blasé about the entire event, insisting that she was unhurt and just needed to go fix her hair.

Nicholas believed *that* much, at least. Since their conversation about Hood, he was suddenly doubting a lot of other shit, though.

Marion had lied to him.

The thought filled him with dread and pain and fear and loss and rage, because *why* had she lied? For Hood? What else was she lying about? Did she still love the man?

Nicholas' jaw clenched, pushing down the festering jealousy that had been his constant companion for fourteen years and banged a hand on her bedroom door. "Marion, it's Nick." He was surprised at how normal his voice sounded.

"Who else would it be?" She called back. "Come in, pudding-fish. I'm almost done."

"You used 'pudding-fish' before." He entered the room and scanned around the interior, even though he'd been there with her less than six hours before. Now, he was scrutinizing it with new eyes.

Marion was sitting in front of the vanity, re-pinning her

dark hair around her May Day Queen tiara. "I used 'pudding-fish' before?" Her nose wrinkled. "You sure?"

"You were topless on my lap, when you said it. Believe me, I remember the moment vividly."

That earned Nicholas a laugh. Her laugh had always been the most beautiful sound he'd ever heard. "Well, do you like that name any better this time around?"

"No." His gaze searched over the walls and furniture, not seeing anything suspicious.

Nothing seemed out of place. No evidence she was secretly plotting with the most heroic bastard in Nottingham. Of course, Marion was smart. She'd never leave anything incriminating out in the open.

"Guess what?" She said without a care in the world. "Clorinda and I have become kinda-sorta friends. She thinks I should seduce you. I told her I'm working on it."

Nicholas gave a skeptical grunt. Seducing him would literally take one crook of her finger, even now. He went to look out her window for signs of Hood climbing up the trellis. There was nothing. Was he hiding out there in the darkness? Hoping to see a glimpse of her, like Nicholas had done, so many times in the past?

Marion watched Nicholas in the mirror, confused by his restless prowling and lack of reaction to her news. "Anything wrong?"

Just let this go. Don't do anything to jeopardize what you have. Who cares if she still loves Hood? So what if she's lying? At least, she's with you. That's enough.

No. It wasn't enough. Nicholas wanted *everything* from her.

"Nick? She prompted, when he didn't answer her.

He turned to look at her.

"Why are you acting weird?"

He leaned one shoulder against the wall and began asking questions that might destroy him. But, he didn't have a choice. With Marion, he'd never settle for anything that wasn't really *real*. "You got that crown yesterday evening."

"And I've flaunted it ever since. I'm going to wear it to

our wedding. I've already decided." Talking about her extravagant wedding plans always delighted Marion. "We can attach the crown to my veil. It's ninety-two yards of lace made by an extinct kind of singing worm. *Super* expensive. And it hums "Here Comes the Bride!" Wait until you hear."

"Hood escaped custody and went out the skylight yesterday afternoon."

She made a face, like that was a bizarre thing for him to mention. "What does he have to do with my humming lace? Oh! Before I forget, have you ever heard of Pecos Bill, the country singer? Because I feel like…"

Nicholas cut her off. "You said Hood was bitching about you wearing that tiara."

Marion froze, finally putting together what he was getting at.

"How did Hood mention your tiara to you, if you got the tiara *after* you last saw him?" Nicholas finished anyway.

Marion squeezed her face up in the expression of someone who knows they've just made a dumb mistake. "Shit." She muttered and turned from the vanity to frown at him. "Have I mentioned how annoying it is when you go all sheriff-y on me?"

Nicholas waited.

"This is not a big deal." Marion assured him earnestly, seeing he was upset.

He arched a cynical brow.

She studied his face for a moment, her mouth thinning. "You're standing *exactly* the way you were on the night I first arrived."

Was he? He hadn't noticed. It didn't matter. "Have you spoken to Hood today?"

"*No.*"

Nicholas said nothing.

"Really?" She bounded to her feet, like he'd just escalated things into a full-blown argument with his silence. "You *really* want to do this, Nick?"

No, he absolutely *didn't* want to do this. He wanted to toss her on the bed, and make love to her, and hear her talk about the damn extinct worms, and marry her tomorrow. Instead, he was desperately hoping for a semi-logical explanation for her lies. He'd even accept a *vaguely* logical explanation. Logic adjacent. *Anything.*

"Think *very hard* about what you're about to say next." Marion warned, jabbing a finger his way. "Because, I see you thinking things that are guaranteed to get your ass kicked, if you say them to me."

He shook his head at the way she was turning this all around. "This isn't my doing. This is *you*, Marion. I've done nothing wrong." If you discounted the kidnapping that had set this all in motion, obviously.

"I've done nothing wrong, either!"

"So, explain how Hood knew about the tiara."

"Why bother?" Marion scoffed. "You've clearly got it all figured out. I'm secretly pining for Robin..."

Nicholas felt himself flinch.

Marion was busy ranting and didn't notice. "....so I destroyed the document that proved he was king and let you give me four orgasms in a row. It's a fucking master-class in planning, alright."

His body sagged with relief at the sarcasm. "You said yourself Robin likes you better since you've been pissing him off." He got out, not ready to quit. "Whatever you're doing, it seems to be working well."

"This is all a big sadomasochism game? *That's* your great theory?"

"*I don't know what's happening!*" Nicholas bellowed, his calm façade crumbling. The loud sound of his own voice added to the chaos in side of him. "I just know you lied to me!"

"I did *not* lie to you! I haven't seen Robin today. The last time I saw him was with *you*, in the foyer."

Nicholas tried to think. "Explain how Hood knew about the tiara." He ordered, because he was willing to listen to any halfway plausible excuse she offered.

"I don't have to explain anything." She crossed her arms over her chest, defiant and on the offensive. "There's *plenty* that you don't tell me, Nicholas."

His teeth ground together at the name. "*Not* about some other woman. *Not* about my True Love." He emphatically shook his head. "Whatever I keep private, it's *not* the same as when you lie about Hood."

"I am so sick of talking about Robin!" She threw up her hands. "Is he really *that* interesting?"

"You tell me. You're the one who bought a wedding dress and planned to marry the son of a bitch."

Brown eyes narrowed like lasers of icy death. "Do you have something to say about my perfect tulle gown?"

Nicholas wasn't stupid. Insulting that dress was a nonsurvivable event. "No." He said quickly. "Of course not."

Marion watched him, like she was trying to decide how mad she should be about this situation. He wasn't sure why *she* was mad, at all. *He* was the one on the brink of life-ending heartbreak and eternal solitude.

Marion's brain didn't work like everybody else's, though. It was sharper. Less predictable. She was fully capable of leading him down some tangential pathway, so he was distracted and she got to keep all her secrets.

He took a deep breath and tried again. "I believe you didn't see him today." He'd believe anything she told him. "Would you just explain how Hood knew about the damn tiara, please?"

"Oh my God, you're *asking me?*" She mocked. "Instead of just barging in here and accusing me of being some undercover floozy for Sherwood?"

"I never said that. You're making this..."

"You didn't say *anything!*" She interrupted. "You stood there and looked at me like I was guilty of a crime. Do you not trust me?"

Oh, that was rich... "Shall we talk about trust, Marion? Shall we talk about how you can only count on yourself and never me?"

Her lips parted in growing outrage. "*You're* the one who told me that, asshole!"

"No, I didn't."

"The *other*-you did."

"Well, it's not fucking true."

"Isn't it? The first chance you get, you're accusing me of lying to you!"

"You *did* lie to me."

Marion didn't see it that way. "Why are you doing this?" Brown eyes met his and he saw she was on the brink of tears. "Do you *really* believe I'll go back to Robin? Seriously?"

Nicholas hesitated, every doubt in his head slamming to the forefront.

Did he believe that? Hood was her True Love and now the rightful king. Anyone with a positive-digit IQ would see that he was a better groom than a socially-phobic, wickedly-inclined gargoyle. The last few days had given Nicholas just what he always wanted, but they were an aberration. Marion's journey through time had altered her perspective, but it could all change back again, just as fast.

Did he honestly --deep in his heart and soul-- believe that Marion would choose him over Robin Hood forever-after?

Marion's mouth tightened when he didn't come up with an answer fast enough. "Fine." She bit off. "I'll show you the solution to your big mystery." She headed over to the trash can and began rooting around in the discarded papers. "Ridiculous man."

Nicholas watched her, his brows compressing. "What are you...?"

"Robin left *this* one for me, this morning." She came marching back to him, holding two carelessly crumbled pieces of paper. "There was another one on Monday, too, filled with rants about how I'm mistreating him. I already got rid of it." She shoved the larger of the pages into his hand. "Here."

Nicholas blinked, his eyes automatically scanning the note. It was nothing but bullshit excuses for not rescuing Marion, and promises to marry her soon, and bitching about the tiara. He didn't even need the signature to know it was from Hood. This was... it? This was the whole answer to his question?

Oh, thank God.

The relief that went through him drained the strength

from his body. He had to sit down on the edge of the bed, overwhelmed with gratitude that Marion wasn't plotting to leave him.

"This note," she passed him the smaller piece of paper, "was attached to the arrow shot at my head. Different handwriting. You see? Robin didn't try to kill me with the puppets. Just like I said. He's a moron, but he doesn't want me dead."

Nicholas' gaze flicked from one page to the other. She was right. The Wraith must have targeted her without Hood. He wasn't sure what that meant exactly.

"I didn't mention Robin left me notes, because I knew you'd make them a big damn deal and they're *not*." Marion continued. "I just tossed them away and got on with my life."

She'd ignored Hood's pleads to return to him. Nicholas had the evidence of that right in front of him. In the letter, Hood was begging to make her his literal queen. Instead, Marion still proudly wore the plastic tiara Nicholas had placed on her head. It was crystal clear and fully rational.

He felt like he'd just been saved from the darkest pit in Nottingham and dragged back into the sunlight.

Marion wasn't done. "I had no idea you were going to make it *this* big a deal, though." She took a step back from him. "I had no idea you were still so unsure about me."

That made him frown. "I'm sure about you." His love for her was the bedrock of his life.

"Apparently not! You think I might run off with another man, meanwhile our wedding is *tomorrow morning*."

Marion was hurt and furious, with him and he couldn't stand it. The words of that damn dragon came back to him: *"Robin Hood can't change her mind about you. Only you can."* Trevelyan was right. Nicholas needed to fix this.

He tried to think of something to say, but nothing brilliant came to mind. "I'm not unsure about *our* relationship." He tried, hunting for words. "I'm unsure of your relationship with Hood."

"Because you don't trust me." She began pacing around in agitation.

"It's not distrust. I worry you'll change your mind and things will go back to normal. It's... I can't go back to you with *him*..." Nicholas waved a hand towards Sherwood, trying to articulate his jealousy. "For so long, I've watched you with him smiling up at him and loving him and being his girl."

"That was years ago, Nick."

"It was *days* ago, for me. Time has passed for you that hasn't passed for me, yet. It's hard for me to go from kidnapping you on Saturday to marrying you on Wednesday, without some questions about *why*."

Her forehead wrinkled. "You want to postpone the wedding?"

"*No*." The answer was emphatic. "So long as you show up at the church, we're getting married. I just have trouble keeping up, sometimes. ...And I don't like you lying to me about Hood."

"I didn't lie." She sniffed, choosing a hill to die on. "I just didn't tell you everything."

Nicholas wasn't going to let that go unchallenged. "So, you'd accept that, if I tried it as an excuse?" He stood up, again. "You'd be okay with me not 'telling you everything,' if my ex was lurking around and I was lying about her?"

"What ex?" She demanded hotly. "You have an ex? Who is she?"

"No, you're missing the point."

Marion was too enraged to listen. "If I find out some other woman is after you, there will be blood in the streets..."

"There is no other woman!" He interrupted. "But, if there *was*, you'd be just as troubled about her, as I am about Hood." At least, he hoped so. The frantic rush of emotions made it hard to think logically. "Hell, you had that dragon put a tracker on me!"

"That's to *protect* you. So, I can find you, if you're in trouble." She defended righteously. "Saying 'strategic wildflower supplies' isn't always going to be enough of a failsafe. You'll thank me when you survive to see the weekend."

The woman was unbelievable sometimes. "So, you

can protect *me*, but you panic when I say I'll take care of *you?*"

"I don't panic!"

"Bullshit." And since they were having this discussion… "And what the hell do you mean you trust Hood?"

"What? What are you even talking about *now?*"

"Downstairs, you said you trusted Hood not to kill you with puppets."

"Because he didn't try to kill me with puppets! I just *proved* that to you! Jesus! I obviously wouldn't trust Robin with anything important."

"Only your literal life, it seems."

She shot him a glower. "It's like you invent problems."

"You should trust *me* and never him." Nicholas thought that was extremely reasonable.

Marion didn't. Her temper went incandescent. "Until you're standing at the altar, realizing that no one is coming to rescue you, you don't get to judge me for my lack of blind faith in anyone!"

"*I* would come to rescue you. You should have faith in *that.*"

"You're the one who kidnapped me in the first place! *Then you died and left me all alone!*" Marion grabbed a lamp from the nightstand and threw it at him. Well, in his general direction. If Marion had wanted to hit him, he'd be picking lamp pieces out of his hair. Instead, it shattered against the wall about four feet from him.

The breaking porcelain seemed to startle her. Marion's whole body jolt, as she blinked at the destruction in shock. For a brief moment, she was seeing something else. Some other time. Her defenses slipped, her anger fading.

Nicholas saw his opportunity and seized it.

"I would never leave you willingly. The other-me didn't either." He said quietly, trying to articulate what he was certain the former-him felt. "I promise you, I wanted to stay. Leaving you was the hardest part of death."

Wet eyes met his.

"I fuck-up a lot, yes. Like I did just now and I'm *sorry*. I am. I'm not great with words or emotions." Nicholas ran a hand through his hair. "But, I'm trying. I want you badly enough to risk *everything*, Marion. I've bet my heart and soul on you. So, I'm all in."

Her lips parted.

"Good, Bad, or gray-area, I'll hold *nothing* back from you." Nicholas took a step closer to her. "Give me the same."

Marion fled. Turning on her heel, she dashed right out of the room and into the hall.

"Marion!" He called after her, but she'd started running and she didn't look back.

Shit.

Nicholas tipped his head back in frustration. He was left alone with the smell of her perfume, and shards of a broken lamp, and a very real feeling that he'd just fucked-up his whole future

It felt familiar.

Chapter Thirty-Three

The Wedding is Off!
Close sources say the rift is irreparable and Nottingham's most infamous couple is through forever.
Maid Marion rumored to be rebounding with Sir Galahad, after the famous knight is spotted in Nottingham.

Alan A. Dale- "Nottingham's Naughtiest News"

Six years in the future, Marion had a cellmate named Tempest, who was a clockmaker. Tempest, being a clockmaker, liked to fiddle with clocks. Not having any clocks in their cramped cell to fiddle with, she'd made do with fiddling with *locks*. And while she endlessly opened and closed, opened and closed the mechanism of their cell door, she'd talked. A lot.

And Marion had listened.

There hadn't been much else to do, except "unhealthily fixate" on Nicholas. So, when she was taking a break from that all-consuming drive, she'd learned how to identify, repair, and pick locks from Tempest. Inmates were typically happy to pass on their nefarious knowledge to anyone willing to learn. After all, they were bored, too.

Maids might have been blocked from getting a quality education in Nottingham, but Marion really had made up for it in the WUB Club. She'd been an excellent student. Even insanely complicated locks, snapped open thanks to Tempest's teachings and Marion's desire to learn. She'd always known knowledge was its own reward.

The heavy wooden door to Nicholas' bedroom opened and Marion stepped inside. It looked just as it had the night

Nicholas died. The night she'd thrown the lamp at him, and screamed at him, and charged out in a fury.

...The *other* night she'd thrown the lamp at him, and screamed at him, and charged out in a fury.

The man drove her crazy and made her crazy in love, no matter what the timeline.

Her gaze cut over to the nightstand, where she knew he kept the letters she sent, beside his mother's ring. Her lawyer had wanted to use the letters as evidence at trial. She'd told Marion that the safest bet was to say Nicholas had tried to rape her that night, and she'd had to shoot him to save herself. The letters would corroborate the fact he had a "desperate obsession," according to the attorney. Nicholas was a gargoyle. Marion was a Maid. The jury would probably believe her.

Marion had refused to go along with that plan. The letters belonged to Nicholas. She hadn't intended them for him, but they'd ended up right where they were supposed to go. The words in them were his. Just his. And she wouldn't share them with every tabloid reporter and hypocritical jackass in Nottingham.

That decision had probably convicted her.

She didn't regret it.

If she'd sent Nicholas the letters, in the first place, her life would have been very different. For one thing, she probably wouldn't know how to pick locks, because she wouldn't have gone to jail. But, maybe Nicholas would have died anyway. And without meeting Tansy, Marion wouldn't have been able to save him. She would have spent the rest of her linear days without him.

Life and time travel weren't certain, but her love for Nicholas *was*. She wouldn't change a goddamn thing, if it meant risking him. She would go back to prison, right now, to ensure his safety. Then, she'd write him letters.

And Marion knew he'd write her back.

She'd only gotten one letter from Robin, during the war. That had arrived after she threatened to never write him again, unless she received some kind of answer to her hundreds of heartfelt notes. Marion had been upset, when she'd sent that letter. It had been months since he'd left and Robin had never replied to anything. She probably would've continued to write him anyway, because she'd been so committed to their relationship. So blind. But then a response had finally come in the mail and it had washed away all her anger.

It had been a *perfect* letter. Exactly what she'd longed to hear. She'd saved it, treasuring its short, poignant words. The poetry of them.

Reaching into the pocket of her dress, Marion pulled out the tattered paper and sat down on the edge of Nicholas' bed. She smoothed the note against her leg. The words were the same as they'd always been. And, as always, they brought tears to her eyes.

> *Please keep writing.*
> *You're all that keeps me alive.*

Marion stared down at the unsigned letter. At the simple and profound need it conveyed. The bare and desperate emotion expressed in just nine words. ...And she knew that Robin Hood hadn't written it.

She knew Nicholas had.

She'd known back in the WUB Club. Replaying the fight she and Nicholas had had, over and over in her mind. Remembering what he'd said about Robin only reading her first three letters. So how could Robin have known she threatened to stop sending more? Why would he even care? And Nicholas' words had sounded so close to the note Robin supposedly sent. "*I* needed *the letters. I* needed *them to survive. The war was killing me. That's the truth, Marion. I couldn't go on without... I* needed..."

Her.

Nicholas had needed her and he'd sent the note to ensure that she continued to write Robin. Because she was really writing *him*.

In prison, Marion hadn't been able to prove her theory. Now, it would be easy. The unadorned masculine handwriting on her letter was so different than Robin's florid script. If she went over to Nicholas' desk, she could pick up any page with his writing. The plain, block letters on her note would match it. The mystery would be solved.

Except it wasn't a mystery.

Robin didn't show love so openly. Marion wasn't even sure he could *feel* it. She'd been a fool to ever believe that the note came from him. Nicholas, on the other hand, had made it clear how much he longed for Marion. The lengths he'd go to and the lines he'd cross.

Some girls might be a little worried about his endless, possessive need, as a matter of fact. Marion wasn't. Nicholas' "desperate obsession" with her and her "unhealthy fixation" on him were kind of the same thing. It was messy, and all-consuming, and maybe kinda crazy. Shit got stolen, and exes got punched, and locks got picked, and time got traveled, and maybe there was a small amount of protective spying going on, here and there. But that was how they loved each other.

To the brink of absolute madness.

Tonight, she'd intended to "borrow" some of Nicholas' papers to prove herself right. To have hard evidence that he really did love her and it wasn't just her mind playing tricks, like Dr. Ramona had said. Then she could fully trust him. Her plan had seemed cautious and sensible.

Besides, she'd been *pissed* after she stormed out of her bedroom. The man had a hell of a nerve accusing her of lying, when she could prove he was an even bigger one. Her B&E was totally justified and she'd be happy to tell him so, when she waved the letter in his stupid, handsome face. The man was a terrible communicator, ninety-nine percent of the time.

...But the other one percent of the time, he was pretty frigging perfect at it.

Tonight he'd told Marion he was all in on her. Just like she was full speed ahead, all in, no stop with him. That had maybe panicked her a little. And thinking about the former-Nick's death had been upsetting, because she couldn't go through that kind of loss again. It would be a million times worse with this Nick, because she loved him. And now he wanted her to trust him with *everything*. When he'd asked her to try, she'd bolted out of the room.

Marion shut her eyes.

Now that her initial wave of panic faded, she could see things more clearly. It was difficult for Marion to trust people, but she'd been trying with Nicholas. It was difficult for Nicholas, too, but he was trying with her. And they were so close to getting there. They loved each other. She was sure of that. They were partners in life and crime. No one else would ever fit either of them.

So, what the hell was she even doing in his bedroom? This plan to check his handwriting was stupid. What was she going to prove that she didn't already know?

She *already* trusted Nicholas.

The bedroom door slammed open and Nicholas stood framed in the opening.

He'd followed her.

Of course he had. She would have done the same thing, if their positions were reversed. It was part of the "protective spying" thing.

Marion arched a brow at her favorite person in the world. The last of her anger drained away. "This room is less drafty than the rest of the castle. Is that why you chose it?"

Nicholas didn't answer. His eyes darted around, looking for some reason she was in his bedroom. He hated anyone else in his private space, but he didn't seem upset to find her there. It probably helped that she was sitting on his bed.

He slowly eased forward, suspicious that she was doing something sketchy, but clueless as to what it might be. "Are you planting cameras?" He guessed.

"No, not right *now*." She scoffed, because that was silly. "The good ones need to be special ordered. Believe me. I checked."

"I do believe you. But I also *know* you."

"I believe and know you, too."

"Do you?" He didn't seem convinced.

"Yes. I believe you about all of it. Once I calmed down

and thought it over… I heard what you were saying downstairs."

Some of his tension eased. "You did?"

"Yeah. …But, I'm still ordering the cameras, because you could be snatched up, or shot again, or stalked by someone even crazier than me." She needed to keep an eye on him.

Nicholas seemed to give himself a shake. "Marion, I *know* you." He repeated, still suspecting a trap. "So, whatever you're up…"

Marion held up the letter, interrupting him with a gentle rattle of the paper.

Nicholas paled, instantly recognizing it. "Shit." He blurted out.

She wanted to laugh, but she managed to keep her face grave. This plan was even better than her former one. Nicholas deserved to suffer a bit, the jerk. He'd been way out of line with all that Robin shit earlier. Let's see how he liked it when she flipped the script on him.

"Okay. Wait." He held up his palms, like he was approaching a madman with a gun. "You found out about that. But, I can explain it."

"Great! Go ahead. Explain it to me."

Nicholas winced at that daunting task. "Um…" His mouth opened. Closed. Opened again. "I…"

Marion waited.

Nicholas tried again, feeling out the words as he went along. "I wanted those letters." He said at length. Then, he stopped and thought about that justification. "Yes." He gave a satisfied nod, like his richly detailed account made total sense.

"*Why* did you want them?"

Her new question stymied him. "Uh…" He searched for the answer on the ceiling. "Because, I'm obsessed with you?" It came out sounding like a guess.

Marion tilted her head, still waiting for more.

"And… I mean… I should've gotten the letters in the first place." Nicholas decided, warming to his explanation, as he verbalized his reasoning. "It was always supposed to be *me*."

Marion couldn't argue with that.

Nicholas waved a disparaging hand towards Sherwood Forest. "Fuck Hood. If he was too stupid to know the value of the letters...?" He shrugged expansively. "Good! It clears the path, for me. I'll take them all for myself. I'll take everything you'll give me. More even."

"*Why* did you want them?" She asked again. "Why were they so important to you?"

Nicholas hesitated, as if he was delving deep into his own head for the core answer.

Marion waited.

"I missed you." He finally murmured, like he'd only just discovered that simple reason himself.

Now they were getting somewhere.

Nicholas let out a half-scoff, half-chuckle of revelation. "I missed you so much that I couldn't breathe sometimes, Marion. You are my *home*." He met her eyes and she saw all his unbreakable, infinite, maybe-kinda-crazy feelings for her. "The letters made me feel connected to you and I needed that to survive."

Bingo.

That hadn't taken nearly as much effort as she'd anticipated. Nicholas was learning how to communicate, no doubt about it. ...At least with her. Maybe *only* with her. But, that was good enough for Marion.

She got to her feet. "You did a much better job of explaining it this time through, angel kitten."

Nicholas stared at her, suddenly noticing she wasn't screaming or throwing lamps. "You already knew about the letters." He deduced, tension easing from his shoulders.

"I did."

His brows compressed. "'Secrets and stealing.'" He quoted from memory. "You said the last night I was alive, we argued about secrets and stealing." He nodded, putting pieces together. "You found them and we fought. Because I was really, really bad at talking to you, probably."

"Yep. It took me longer to realize you'd written back to me, though." She held up the note he'd sent. "You didn't mention that part.

"I *had* to write you." He pressed the heels of his palms into his eyes. "Jesus, for most of my life, I'd seen you every day. Heard your voice. I made sure I did, even if I had to walk miles to catch a glimpse of you. Now, I was stuck in some goddamn desert. And I had no… you. I *truly* couldn't have survived that for long. I'm not exaggerating. You know I'm not."

Marion understood completely. She'd kept him alive for ten years in her head, because she'd been unable to let him go. And he'd been obsessed way longer than she'd been fixated.

"I was *so far* from you, Marion. All I had was the letters. And then you threatened to stop writing me. You wanted to take them away from me." It almost sounded like an accusation. He frowned, hearing his own words. "…Or you threatened to stop writing *Hood*, I guess. But, I was…"

"They're your letters, Nick." Marion interjected calmly. "Robin never even read them. Everything in them is only between you and me."

That brought him up short. Gray eyes blinked at her. "My letters?" He echoed like the words made no sense.

She nodded.

His gaze went over to the nightstand and then back to her. "I can have them?"

"They've always been yours."

Nicholas processed that idea for a beat. His expression was more vulnerable than she'd ever seen it. "Really?"

She kept her eyes steady. "Really."

Nicholas swallowed. "I wanted you to write me." He whispered. "I wanted it so badly, Marion."

"I did write to you. I just didn't know it." Every single one was addressed to him. "I gave *you* those letters, the moment they were mailed."

His jaw firmed, liking that thought. Triumph glinted on his face. "My letters." This time it was said with possession. "Yes. They're *mine*. And I needed them." He gestured to the note in her hand. "So, I wrote *that* to stop you from…" He trailed off, as a new thought occurred to him. "Wait. You still *have* that damn thing? Why? I didn't even know what to say in

448

it. It took me three days to write two sentences."

"They were two really good sentences."

"Yeah?" He didn't seem convinced.

"As many times as you read your letters…? I'm sure I read mine more."

"Well, it's shorter."

"It's *better*."

"No." He sounded very certain. "It's not. Your letters kept me alive."

"Yours kept *me* alive, Nick. In prison, I became more and more fixated on you. On this." She waved the note again. "It gave me something to focus on. I *knew* you wrote it. It took ages for me to put it all together, but I eventually figured out the truth." It broke her heart, how blind she'd been. "I'm sorry. I knew too much, too late."

He shook his head, pacing around. "No. You have nothing to apologize for. It was *me*. All of it. My fault. My fucking inability to talk to you. My obsession with you." He ran a hand through his thick hair. "I *kidnapped* you, for Christ's sake."

"You're apologizing for kidnapping me?" That would be a first.

"No."

Marion rolled her eyes.

"Kidnapping you has worked out better than I'd ever dreamed! How could I possibly regret it? I'm going to *marry* you tomorrow. Do you know how many stars I wished on for you and now…?" He trailed off with an amazed head shake. "Now, I'm so close to having it all come true. It seems *impossible*. It *is* impossible." His eyebrows compressed, suddenly thinking dark thoughts. "This is impossible."

"Oh no. Things were finally going well. *Now,* what are you…?"

He cut her off. "Something's going to go wrong with this wedding."

"It better *not* go wrong. I have it all planned. Things will be *perfect* or heads will roll. Literally. Cragg has an axe."

Nicholas barely heard her. "I need advice. And my

reverse conscience has been quiet lately. Or saying weird shit. Or I don't agree with it, at all. I need to think of a plan."

"What's a reverse conscience?"

"The voice in my head that gives me all my Bad ideas."

"Well, that's my job."

Nicholas looked at her.

Marion shrugged, because it was true.

He slowly nodded. "*That's* what's going on. You're right. I don't need a reverse conscience anymore, because I have *you,* now. You're the only one I want to talk to and you're the sharpest person I know." He focused on her, like she was about to solve whatever problem he'd just invented. "So... how can I ensure my bride gets to the church? Help me think of a creatively villainous plan. You're great at those."

It was sweet of him to say so. "I'm *going* to be at the wedding, Nick. I'll wear my tulle dress. You'll wear your traditional bycocket hat. And all of Nottingham will be appalled and fuming over the cost of the reception." She sighed in satisfaction. "You don't have to do anything that you haven't already done."

He scowled, only focusing on the final part of that assurance. "Nothing I haven't already done? You mean kidnap you?" He paused, as if some brilliant idea had just entered his head. The man was so unpredictable. "I should kidnap you, again."

"I think technically I'm *still* kidnapped." Marion mused, thoughtfully.

"I'm serious. The wedding is in," he checked the time, "fourteen hours. I could just keep you right here for fourteen hours and I could be *sure*. I'd be sure you'd show up at the church. I'd be sure no one stole you away. I'd be sure nothing went wrong."

"No."

He scowled at her refusal. "This was your idea!"

"It absolutely was *not* my idea. And I'm not staying in this room with you one second after twelve. Not the night before we're married. Are you insane?"

"I can sleep on the floor, if you..."

"It's bad luck!" She interrupted. How did he not know this? "I can't see you on our wedding day, until I walk down the aisle. It's tradition."

He let out a frustrated breath. "I don't care about luck or tradition, Marion."

"So help me God, if you wreck my dream wedding over your stupid paranoia…"

"I'm *saving* your dream wedding, by making sure you show up." He jabbed a big finger at her. "You're kidnapped. Deal with it."

Marion groaned, tilting her head back in exasperation. "Is this about Robin? Are you still worried about him crashing through a church window to rescue me or something?"

"No!" The way he shouted it meant "yes."

"Nicholas…"

"Don't call me that." He muttered and headed back towards the door. "This plan will work. Just give it a chance. I'll get you some food and then you can rest right here. I like seeing you in my bed, anyway."

"Robin's not going to come for me tomorrow." Marion called after him, pushed to the brink of madness by his idiocy. "He didn't in the original timeline, either. That's how you and I ended up married, the last time."

Nicholas stopped short, his hand on the doorknob. His head whipped around to gape at her. "What?"

Marion tried to look casual and probably failed miserably. "We're already married, snookum." She shrugged, her heart pounding as she finally told him the whole truth. "It just hasn't happened, yet."

Chapter Thirty-Four

How It Happened the First Time...

Robin Hood wasn't coming to save her.
Nicholas' heart pounded as Friar Tuck droned through the wedding vows, his eyes cutting around the interior of the church. Gargoyles were stationed everywhere and there was no sign of Robin Hood rushing to Marion's aid. Was that moron seriously going to let this happen?
Shit.
If Hood didn't show up, Marion would be heartbroken.
Nicholas' eyes slipped down to her and saw she was *already* heartbroken. Marion knew Robin wasn't coming. She'd figured it out too and she was sinking into shock. Hood's betrayal had knocked her on her heels. She had no idea what to do now that her perfect hero had been thwarted by...
Nicholas' thoughts skidded to a halt and rewound.
Hood wasn't coming to save Marion.
No one was coming to save her.
A new idea suddenly whirled in his head. An idea so spectacular that he'd never even let himself consciously consider it before. It was already fully-formed in his mind, though, as if he'd been willing it to happen this whole time. Simple and straightforward and stunningly obvious. Gargoyles weren't creative thinkers by nature, but this idea was so dazzling it instantly captured his imagination.
I could just... marry her.
For really *real.*
Nicholas could keep Marion for himself and Robin could die alone in Sherwood. He'd rather catch a wife than an

outlaw. The rest of the church was murmuring, but no one else had given up on Hood's daring rescue. They weren't going to rally quickly enough to stop him. *No one* could stop him. This was the opportunity he'd never dreamed of having.

And Nicholas wasn't a man who missed opportunities.

Marion looked up at him. "Robin's not coming." She whispered and a tear rolled down her perfect cheek. "You can stop all this now. There's no point."

"Isn't there?" He sure as hell saw one.

Friar Tuck paused his speech, like he wasn't sure what to do next. He'd gotten to the part where the couple had to say their vows. His beady eyes darted around, still expecting Robin to magically appear.

Only Robin Hood wasn't coming.

Nicholas realized he was breathing too fast, excitement filling him. If this was going to happen, it had to happen *now*. Before anyone had the presence of mind to protest. Before Marion ran away. Before lightning struck the church, or hyenas attacked, or any other random happenings happened. Before anything, anything, *anything* took her away from him.

"Get on with it." He ordered, glaring at the rotund man.

Friar Tuck scowled, looking for a way out of this.

"Do it or I'll hang you and then find someone who will." Nicholas snarled in the most serious voice he'd ever used in his life.

Friar Tuck heaved an aggravated sigh. "Do you, Nicholas Greystone, Sheriff of Nottingham, take this woman to be your lawfully wedded wife...?"

"I do."

"I wasn't finished." Tuck protested and started over. "Do you, Nicholas Greystone, Sheriff of Nottingham, take this woman to be your lawfully wedded wife, to have and to hold...?"

"Yes. Yes, to *all* of it."

Friar Tuck went back to the beginning again, buying Robin Hood time. "Do you, Nicholas Greystone, Sheriff of

Nottingham, take this woman to be your lawfully wedded wife, to have and to hold, in sickness and in health, 'til death do you part?"

"I do, dammit!"

"Wait, I forgot the 'richer or poorer' part. Let's try, again." Tuck cleared his throat importantly. "Do you, Nicholas Greystone, Sheriff of Nottingham..."

Nicholas had had enough. He leaned closer, talking right over the friar's latest stall-tactics. "We're done." He intoned and no one could have missed the threat. "I. *Do*." He carefully spaced out each word. "Move on."

Tuck's mouth thinned, but he didn't push it any farther. He sensed how little patience Nicholas had remaining. "Fine." He reluctantly turned to Marion. "Do you, Marion Huntingdon..."

Nicholas cut him off. "She does."

"*She* has to say it. ...And there really should be a ring."

Fuck. There *should* be a ring. In fact, there *was* one. His mother's ring had always belonged on Marion's finger. Nicholas had known that since boyhood. It just hadn't occurred to him that this fake wedding would become real, so the ring was still safely stored in his bedroom. He could get it on her finger later. Somehow. Nicholas certainly wasn't taking the time to go and get it now. Not when everything he'd always wanted was on the edge of falling into his granite clutches. He needed to hurry.

"We don't need a ring, for it to be legal." He told Tuck.

"No. Not technically. But tradition says..."

"I don't give a shit about tradition. I care about the vows. Finish them, before I finish *you*."

Tuck grudgingly ran through the whole damn spiel again, speaking as slowly as possible. Nicholas wanted to rip his hair out by the roots.

When the friar was finally done talking there was silence.

Marion hadn't even heard him. She was still staring at Nicholas' chest, a faraway expression on her face.

Nicholas leaned closer to her, drawing her attention.

Marion sniffed, gazing up at him, and Nicholas' heart stuttered in his chest. She was the most beautiful creature he'd ever seen. "Is it over, yet?" She whispered.

"I've given up on Hood coming to your rescue."

"Me too." Luminous brown eyes were filled with humiliated tears.

"When the chips are down, you can't count on True Love to save you, Marion."

Hopefully, she'd listen to that advice and let Hood go. Hopefully, she'd finally understand he was unworthy of her affection and always had been. Hopefully, she'd realized there was another path for her, another man who would do *anything* for her, even if he wasn't her destined mate.

Hopefully, she'd see Nicholas.

Marion swiped a hand across her eyes, still silently crying.

It killed him to see her so sad.

What was he doing? Nicholas hesitated. Her heartbreak was because of him and this new plan would only add to it. Marion was helpless, at the moment. He was preying on her vulnerability, when she'd never done anything but show him kindness. It wasn't her fault that he was so in love with her that it had become an obsession. He should stop this, now. It was the right thing to do and he knew it.

Do not fucking stop, you moron!

Nicholas blinked as the screaming voice of his worst impulses, jarred him back to reality. He was seconds away from having Marion as his wife. For the rest of his life, she would be tied to him. No one else in the universe could be her husband, as long as he breathed. Just Nicholas. She would *have* to give him a chance then, wouldn't she?

His reverse conscience was right this time. He wasn't going to stop. He *couldn't*. Not with that kind of dazzling possibility dangling right in front of him. He wasn't Good or Bad, but he also wasn't stupid.

Nicholas kept his voice low, so only she could hear. His heart was hammering so loudly, he was shocked she couldn't hear that, too. "You want to get out of here, duchess?"

He knew his expression revealed too much of his eagerness, but he couldn't help it and she was in no condition to notice. He wanted her to say "yes" more then he'd ever wanted anything in his life.

She nodded. "Please, Nick."

Hearing her say his name had his insides clenching in need. The name she'd given him and that only she used. His real name. He was so *close* to having her. To having everything he'd never thought he could have.

"Say 'yes' and we're done." He promised. "I'll take care of everything, Marion. We can get an annulment later, if you want. But, right now, let's just finish this and go home." He kept his voice gentle, but his hand tapped on his leg in agitation.

Marion blinked in a bemused fog. "Say 'yes?'" She repeated like his words were some gibberish from the forgotten language of witches.

"Exactly." He was praying that she didn't understand exactly what she was agreeing to. "Trust me and say 'yes.'" She shouldn't trust him, but it was something he'd always longed for and the words were out before he could stop them. "Please, Marion. Trust me. Just this once."

"Yes." She whispered.

Yes!

Nicholas looked back at the friar, his face like a conquering general. "She's mine." He said with ruthless finality.

Tuck paled.

Half the assembled guests cringed.

Racing to the end, without waiting for the friar, Nicholas bent to brush Marion's lips in the quickest kiss imaginable. He had to for the damn wedding scroll to be officially enspelled or he wouldn't have risked it. He doubted anyone but Robin Hood had ever kissed her before. The brush of his lips lasted half a second and it still made his heart lurch.

Marion startled at the contact, as if the kiss had jolted her, too. She blinked up at him, coming out of her shocked trance. "What...?"

"I now pronounce you man and wife." The friar intoned miserably, like he'd just pronounced them dead.

On the lectern in front of him, Marion and Nicholas' names appeared on the formal marriage scroll. Nicholas swallowed hard when he saw his name was spelled out as "Nick Greystone." Right then, he knew that he'd actually done it. That it was all real. The magic binding them was fathomless and older than time. It knew the name he called himself. The one that Marion had given him. It knew who he really was inside.

A marriage scroll was practically unbreakable. Both parties would have to go before a wizard and agree to the dissolution of the marriage, or the document would seal them together forever. And Nicholas would *never* agree to release his stolen bride. With any luck, Marion wouldn't remember what he'd said about an annulment, because it would *never* happen. Atlantis had a better chance of rising from the sea. Gold cursive letters proclaimed Nicholas' claim for everyone to see and he let out a ragged breath.

He'd just grabbed hold of the biggest opportunity of his life. He had Marion.

She gave her head a small shake, more aware since he'd kissed her. "Wait..." She stared at the scroll, like maybe it was a mirage. "What just happened?"

"We just got married."

Marion's head whirled around to gape up at him. Then, she burst out crying.

Shit.

Nicholas instinctively scooped her up and headed up the aisle. Marion's arms wrapped around his neck, clinging to him. It was the first time she had ever reached out to him for comfort. The first time *anyone* had. She wanted Nicholas to soothe her tears. Wanted him to care for her and keep her safe. And that was what *he* wanted, too. It always had been. He *hated* to see her crying. It ate at him. But he had no idea how to fix things, now.

Luckily, they had decades together for him to figure it out. Nicholas would spend all of them trying to win Marion over. He would do whatever it took to make this better for her. To make her smile. Just so she stayed with him, he'd give her every star in the sky. Marion was the entire reason he'd been created. Why he lived and breathed. There was nothing else that mattered to him. Nothing at all.

This woman was his heart and soul.

"I hate you." Marion sobbed out on a hiccupped breath.

He wasn't surprised. "Maybe it will pass."

"I doubt it. I plan on hating you forever-after." She wiped her nose on his uniform. "I still hate Robin more, though."

"Me too. See? We have a lot in common, already."

Marion buried her cheek against his hard shoulder and started crying in earnest again, barely hearing his feeble attempts to cheer her up. "I thought he loved me. But, he didn't. He lied about everything. My whole life was a lie."

Nicholas held her close. "Hood is an idiot." He murmured into her soft hair. He ignored the stunned and horrified faces in the crowd, as he strode by them and out of the church. Every primitive instinct in his body wanted his new wife safely ensconced in his room, where no Nottingham do-Gooder could interfere with his claim. "If it was me, I would have overthrown this whole fucking kingdom to get you back, Marion."

"My True Love abandoned me." She whispered in a shattered voice.

"I know." He kissed the top of her head, intense satisfaction eclipsing the guilt he felt at taking advantage of her misery. "But, I've got you, now. And I'm not going anywhere."

Chapter Thirty-Five

**Interspecies romance: The hot new trend that's redefining modern relationships.
Our foolproof guide on how to attract all the swooniest monsters!**

Alan A. Dale- "Nottingham's Naughtiest News"

Nicholas gazed at her, breathing hard. "We're not married." He shook his head, his eyes swirling with unnamed emotions. "We can't be... Why would you...? No, Robin Hood would..."

Marion cut him off, her voice raised to a yell. "*Robin didn't come to the church!*" She felt her heart pounding, as she tried to make him understand. "Think about it: What would you do, if he didn't show up? Would you just call the wedding off and send me home? Or would you," she shrugged, "grab the opportunity?"

Silence.

...But he carefully closed the bedroom door, shutting them in together. Listening.

"It happened before I even *knew* what was happening." She explained, seeing she had his full attention. "Looking back, you were just thinking so much faster than me." She snapped her fingers in rapid succession to indicate his synapses firing at top speed. "I told you before, you tricked me. I didn't see it coming. At least, I don't *think* I did. Maybe on some level..." She trailed off, because maybe she *had* known? Down in the very Baddest parts of her? "Anyway, I told you at the time that I'd hate you forever-after. But luckily for you, I got over it."

Nicholas stared at her so intently that he didn't even blink.

"You set your mind to your goal and nobody else could

keep up, Nick. You hammered down all the obstacles. I've always admired how determined you are, but that day *no one* could have stopped you."

He gave his head a quick shake, like he wasn't sure he'd heard her right.

"When Robin abandoned me, I was crushed. I was so out of it, I wasn't sure I'd even survive the heartache. You told me to just say 'yes' and you'd take care of everything." She chewed her lower lip. "And so I did."

"You... said 'yes?'"

"I said 'yes.' So did you."

He scoffed at that, the sound a little wild. "Of course *I* would say it. Is that even in question?" He began pacing around, looking at everything but her. Trying to gather evidence, because that was his sheriff-y way. "Did I kiss you?"

"Yep. And our names appeared on the scroll."

"What did my name say? Was it my full name?"

"No. It said 'Nick Greystone.'" She'd noticed that, even in the midst of her breakdown. Only Marion had ever called him "Nick," as far as she knew. It caught her attention that the marriage scroll didn't use his given name and title.

Apparently, the nickname was a pretty big clue for him, because he swallowed convulsively. "You're *sure* it said 'Nick?'"

"I'm positive. I asked you about it later, because it seemed informal. But, you said it was the name that mattered."

Nicholas' breath left him in a wheezing rush.

"But it was all legal and binding." Marion wanted to make sure he knew that and wasn't looking for loopholes. "You're stuck with me, pumpkin."

"And you said 'yes'?" He repeated, like he wanted to be completely, *completely* sure.

"I did. I always say 'yes' to you."

"So... we were married? You and the other me?"

"We *are* married. I'm the same person who stood in that church and *you're* my husband. The other you is still *you*." The magic that sealed marriage contracts was some of the strongest in any land and it was uncomplicated in its certainty.

Not even a Hatter's powers could alter what had happened. "You said the vows to me and you can't take them back."

His head gave an almost imperceptible nod. "I would've said the vows, if I'd had the chance." He agreed dazedly. "I know I would've. Jesus, I would do... *anything.*"

"You did do 'anything.' And you weren't even the least bit sorry about doing it. You just made everything happen and then you walked out of the church, with me in your arms." She paused. "In retrospect, it was kind of awesome. I'm sure you looked like a gladiator. At that moment, though, I was crying too hard to notice.

"I'm sorry."

"No, you're not. Just like I'm not sorry to spring this on you now. Neither of us play fair, when we're trying to capture the other."

He didn't deny that.

Marion kept going, emboldened. "You carried me out of the church and brought me back to the castle, afterwards. No one tried to stop you. Certainly not me. I was in shock, I think. And you were nothing but sweet. You brought me to this room and you tucked me into bed."

He winced slightly at the description, like it hurt him to hear.

"It's true!"

"Nothing I've ever felt for you was 'sweet.'" He scraped a hand through his hair. "Why in the hell would you trust anything I said, at that point? I wouldn't and I'm the one who apparently said it."

"I trust everything you tell me, Nick. ...Even when I'm scared to."

His smoke-colored gaze impaled hers, his heart in his eyes.

Marion arched a brow. "You *didn't* offer to send me home and you *didn't* carry me back to my bedroom here at the castle, though. Instead, you put me in *your* bed." She pointed to it. "And you stood there, watching over me for hours. I didn't process that until much later." She tilted her head. "In prison, I thought up a lot of not-quite-right theories as to your motivations."

His mouth curved the tiniest bit, like he knew *exactly* why his former self had made that choice.

"And then one night, it suddenly occurred to me that you put me in your bed, simply because you were... claiming me." Marion surmised with a shrug. "Robin didn't come to save me and you didn't care. You were *happy*, when he didn't show up at the church. You were *happy* your plan failed. I saw it."

The small smiled grew a bit bigger. "Yes." He agreed. "I must have been the most triumphant son of a bitch in Nottingham. It would have been fucking *glorious*."

"For you, I'm sure it was. I was pissed."

"Obviously."

"For a long time, I was concerned you were only interested in me because of Robin and how much you hate him."

Nicholas rolled his eyes, as if that was the last thing in the world she needed to be concerned about. "Why do you keep worrying about this? I'm not obsessed with you, because I hate Hood. I hate *Hood,* because I'm obsessed with *you*."

"Your obsession *worked*, though. You stole me, fair and square. And the only logical reason to do that was... it simply didn't matter to you that I was Robin's." Marion beamed at him. "You just want me to be *yours.*"

Nicholas watched her like a freezing animal edging nearer to a fire, wanting to get closer, but hesitant to take the risk. "It was always supposed to be me."

"I kinda figured that, when I totally forgot the color of Robin's eyes, but I dreamed about *you* for ten years straight."

Nicholas was quiet for a long moment. "Hood doesn't come to our wedding?" He finally asked, like this was the first time he'd heard that news. Or maybe just the first time he'd really processed it.

Marion sighed in exasperation, prepared to go through it all again.

Nicholas didn't wait for her to answer, before he was nodding to himself in something like satisfaction. "My God...

That moron doesn't come to the wedding." It was a statement, now. He tipped his head back and squeezed his eyes shut. Marion read pure exaltation in his usually stoic expression. "*Fuck,* yes."

Relief filled her, at that very strange, heartfelt prayer of thanks. "I would have let you keep me. If we'd had time together and I had gotten to know you, I would've wanted to keep you, too." She gave a breathless laugh. "I *did* keep you. I haven't gone by 'Marion Huntingdon' since the trial. I was booked into the WUB Club as 'Marion Greystone' and I decided to keep your name. It sounded… right."

Nicholas' chest expanded like he was trying to get enough oxygen.

"When I got back here and saw you again, I knew I had a second chance. I was telling myself to take things slowly with you and not to be rash. …But, how could I?" She lifted her hands helplessly. "How could I waste any time?"

Nicholas opened his eyes and faced her again in confusion. "I don't want to go slow. Why the hell would I want to go slow?"

That was another promising response. "I could have left Nottingham, once I returned." Marion took a step closer to him. "I could have warned you about this murder and just walked away. You couldn't stop me, if I really wanted to escape. But, I stayed here, because I wanted to see if our marriage could be really… real."

His head tilted. "And what did you decide?"

"That *everything* about you is really real, Nick."

His whole body jerked, as if she'd shocked him with an electrical current.

Marion winked at him.

His eyes sharpened, like they always did when she was inviting him to play some Bad game, and he seemed to reach a decision. Clearing his throat, he cut straight to the bottom line. "So, what you're saying is: You owe me a wedding night."

He believed her. He really believed her!

"You talked about an annulment, actually." She whispered, her insides fluttering with happiness.

Nicholas snorted. "See, I was *definitely* lying. I promise you, you *were* never getting away from me. Not in any timeline."

"Ditto. I really do have the security cameras all picked out."

He continued to watch her, his gaze growing more and more intense. That determined, rock-hard core of him had switched on. "Get on the bed." He commanded.

"What?"

"Get on the bed. Unless you want me to take you on the floor. I'm not waiting anymore for what's already mine."

Well, that was unexpected. Marion's eyebrows soared, wondering what interesting game he was playing. "Nick, what...?"

"We're doing this *now*, before you change your mind." He interrupted.

So, not a game, then. He was legitimately worried. Marion enjoyed it when he was sexy and possessive, but this seemed like the beginnings of panic. If she was working through all her baggage, he needed to work through his, too. It was only fair. "Nicholas..."

"I hate it when you call me that. It's not my name. It hasn't been since I was thirteen. You smiled at me and called me 'Nick' and I was reborn."

Oh... *Now*, she understood the signature on the marriage contract.

"Nick." She corrected, refusing to be sidetracked. "You need to let go of your paranoia about Robin."

"I might be your husband, but *he's* still your True Love." Nicholas pointed off towards Sherwood Forest and his strawberry-blonde enemy. "Have you thought about that?"

Marion crossed her arms over her chest. "You still think I'd leave you because some yahoo claimed to be my True Love? I traveled through time for you, jerkoff."

Nicholas was busily unbuttoning his shirt. "Gargoyles don't have True Loves, but I still understand the power of the connection. I can't... And you're..."

Marion waited.

He gave his head another shake, organizing his words. "Your kind thinks True Love trumps wedding vows. You said yourself that True Love was what you always wanted. Like your parents had."

"Yes, but I will never find that with *Robin*." Was he just inventing problems again or was he really this blind? "He isn't a rival for my affections. It isn't even a contest. And if there *was* a contest, you'd have already won." Why was he not seeing this? "Nick, he gets nothing and you get *everything*. I told you that."

He kept talking, too fast and almost frenetic. Still not understanding. "I'm not risking losing you. Jesus, I never even *thought* I'd be this close. You're *married* to me...? And you want to go *slow?*" He made it sound like she'd suggested they go skydiving without parachutes. "No. We're consummating this, *now*."

"Sex won't make us more married." Clearly, it was the only thing that would get through to him, though. She was going to have to show him, because he was beyond listening to logic.

"It *will* make us more married. I can't give you everything you want in a relationship, but I can work with passion. Get on the bed."

She wasn't against the broad strokes of his scheme. Finally sleeping with her husband sounded pretty great. She'd been trying to seduce him for days. But, not this way. Nope. He was only seeing this as some masterplan to keep her from leaving. She needed to take control or this situation would deteriorate into chaos.

And he needed to honest-to-God propose, before the honeymoon started.

Marion pursed her lips. "I'm a Maid. I don't put out, until there's a ring on my finger, gummy-worm."

Nicholas' determined expression faded, replaced by bafflement.

She waggled the back of her bare hand at him.

Comprehension dawned. Nicholas' tension eased at her teasing, like it grounded him again. He stopped undressing and stared at her. "Really?" He asked, with desperate hope in his voice.

"Really." Her eyes pointedly moved towards the nightstand.

Nicholas immediately crossed to it. Digging around in the drawer, he came up with a familiar blue velvet box. "This is yours." He moved to stand in front of her and placed his mother's ring into her palm, folding her hand closed around it. Giving it to her straight from his heart and soul.

And Marion accepted it the same way.

Nicholas seemed dazed as the ring passed easily into her possession. She owned it, now. They both felt it happen, as the rules of the spell were followed. "It's always been yours." He whispered. "I've known it since you smiled at me in Sherwood Forest."

She wrinkled her nose in delight. "First time we met, you fell for me, huh?"

"I'm *still* falling for you. Every single time we meet, I just fall harder."

Butterflies attacked her stomach and he hadn't even touched her. Nicholas could romance a Maid right out of her virtue, with just his pretty words. ...Too bad for all those other girls, he only used his sweet-talking talents on Marion.

Her attention shifted to the magnificent ruby, set in a thick gold band. It was perfect. Just as she remembered. A reminder of both their mothers and a promise for a better future.

"You once told me that stones can absorb feelings from the people around them."

"They can."

"I think people can absorb feelings, too." She tore her eyes away from her shiny new ring and smiled at her shiny new groom. "I felt all these huge, beautiful emotions, once I started hanging around with you. I had no idea *how much* there was to feel, until you, Nick."

Nicholas touched her hair. His eyes had lost that frantic edge and now he was seeing *her*, again. "Be with me and no one else. Forever."

That counted as a genuine proposal! After a decade of being married, she was finally *really* engaged. She quickly extended the ring towards him, excited and happy. "Here."

"No." He shook his head emphatically, refusing to take it. Thinking she was rejecting him. "It's *yours*, Marion. Please. I know that I'm not... But I swear I can..."

Marion cut him off, seizing his wrist. "You have to put it on me." She pushed the ring into his palm. "You're my husband and it's a *wedding band*, dummy."

Nicholas blinked. "Oh." He frowned in deep concentration. "Right." He took the ring from her and carefully slid it onto her finger, like it was a volatile science experiment ready to explode.

Instantly, Marion felt magic lock it in place. Their wedding ceremony hadn't happened yet, but it *had* happened. The vows never went away, because Marion had never let Nicholas go. If she had moved on like a healthily non-fixated person, the "'til death do us part" clause would've clicked in. But, she'd kept him alive in her mind and heart, puzzling and fantasizing about the man's every tiny facial expression, for a decade. Now, the ring was attached to her, until she willingly took it off, proof of their bond. Nothing else could remove it. That was the way wedding spells worked.

"See?" She sniffed back tears. She'd known it. She'd *known* it! "We're still married. It's sealed on my finger." She held out her hand to him.

Nicholas' expression went taut. Wanting to feel it for himself, he gave the ring an experimental tug and groaned when it stayed in place. "You're really mine, Marion."

"You're really *mine*." She corrected. "It's why I came back for you, even though you were a colossal jackass for most of our interactions. We *fit*, you and me."

Nicholas made a choked sound of emotion and then Marion was in his arms. His mouth slanted over hers hungrily. Suddenly, he wasn't rushing through the preliminaries, because of his delusions. He was rushing through them, because he was going absolutely wild for her.

That was *much* better.

Marion wrapped her legs around his waist, as he lifted her straight off the ground and carried her towards the bed. "Do not break my May Day Queen crown. Better yet, I'll just take it off, before you ravish me." She pulled the rhinestone tiara free of her hair and dropped it on the nightstand, as they went by.

"How attached are you to the dress?"

"Rip the damn thing to pieces." She urged. "I love how strong you are." The man could probably carry her for miles with one hand. It was very appealing.

"I love how strong *you* are." He shook his head. "I can't believe all you've done --All you've survived-- to come back to me."

"I would do anything to be here with you." Since her arms were free, she took up where he left off and began yanking his buttons free.

"I would do anything to be with *you*." He easily shifted her weight in his grasp, allowing her to tug off his shirt. "I have done some really shitty 'anythings,' as a matter of fact."

"I'll forgive you, if you take your clothes off." She gave a contented sigh at the sight of his heavily muscled torso. The stony texture of his right side was such a turn on for her. Like a warrior's armor. "I really love your chest."

"I really love *your* chest." He deadpanned and dropped her on the mattress.

Marion laughed, feeling free. She scooted backwards on the bed to give him room to climb on. She didn't get very far.

He grabbed hold of her ankle and dragged her back to the edge. "Where do you think you're going?"

"Nowhere?"

"Nowhere." He affirmed and the rest of his clothes hit the floor in rapid succession. "You're staying right there in my bed. Where you belong."

Her eyes slipped down to his straining erection. She'd never actually seen a naked man in person before. Unless you counted that one evil wizard from Blue Block, whose clothes kept vanishing. She hadn't expected Nicholas to look quite so...

imposing. He hadn't been carved for palace "entertainment," like Quarry, but he was still bigger than average. She was pretty sure, about that. A lot bigger. And there was some rockiness on the right side. And she wasn't so certain...

He seemed to follow her thoughts. "Hey." He climbed onto the mattress, tugging her closer to him, so she couldn't freak herself out by staring. "Don't worry. Everything about us is a perfect fit. I'll make sure of it."

Marion managed a nod and then her clothes were being ripped right off her body. Nicholas didn't seem to care about tearing fabric, just so he could get down to her bare skin. He did take a moment to appreciate her black underwear and then it was gone too. Naked and aching, Marion pressed against him. She felt all fizzy and tight, as he began caressing her. Every time Nicholas touched her, she was gasping with pleasure. He was *amazing* at this.

Wait. What if she was terrible at this?

That sudden worry flickered and she frowned, jolted out of her pleasurable haze. "Tell me if I'm terrible at this." She blurted out.

Nicholas scoffed, as if that was ludicrous. He didn't even bother to lift his head from her breasts. Not that she *wanted* him to stop what he was doing. It was fucking incredible. Marion tried to think through her panting desire. The problem with waiting so long to have sex was expectations and insecurities built simultaneously. She always assumed she'd be a badass at sex. What if she let him down?

Nicholas kissed the inside of her leg and then focused his attention at the very junction of her thighs.

Marion squeaked in sudden alarm, jerking back. "Wait! You can't do that. Husbands don't like to do that."

Nicholas hesitated, his eyes finding hers. "We don't?" He asked dryly. "Says who?"

She struggled to remember who'd told her that rule. "My marriage deportment tutor. When a Maid is eighteen, a marriage expert begins lessons on what her husband will expect and... *Fuck*." She stopped her nervous jabber and pinched the bridge of her nose, hearing how absolutely stupid that sounded.

His mouth curved.

"It's not funny!" She was making a total fool of herself. Ten years in prison had taught her a lot of unMaidenly shit, but it was all theoretical. The hands-on aspects of sex were unknown to her and she was already screwing it up. She could tell. "Damn it, I *hate* being a virgin."

The small curve of Nicholas' lips became a full-blown grin. "Don't worry. You won't be one for much longer."

"I'm serious! I *really* want to do this. And I want to be a cool and awesome badass, but I'm *not*. Dr. Ramona said I have a slight sexual dysfunction. I feel like I'm just going to disappoint you. I should have practiced with someone I didn't care about, but I can't stand the idea of anybody else touching me."

"No, you should absolutely *not* have practiced with anyone else."

"Maybe books, then. I should have read more smut. Rockwell has plenty of smutty books I could..."

Nicholas cut her off. "Marion." He moved to cradle her face in his palms. "You have the most interesting mind in the kingdom. I've always admired that."

She sniffed, feeling a bit mollified. "Thank you."

"...But right now you're being an idiot."

She made an exasperated face at him. "*Really?*"

"Really." He nodded gravely. "Your very fascinating brain is overthinking this. You do *not* have a slight sexual dysfunction. Whatever you need, it's normal and *fine*. There is literally no possibility that you can disappoint me, so long as you're here. I am so obsessed with you I almost have a heart attack every time you touch my hand."

"You're not going to die tomorrow. You die on Thursday and I'm going to make sure that it never happens."

"See? You *are* a badass." He was trying to make her smile.

It worked, much to her irritation.

"Do you want to wait?" He asked in a soft tone.

"No! I've waited long enough for you. I waited *so long* and now I'm... nervous." It killed her to admit that. "I'm too old to be nervous, but I am."

"I'm nervous, too."

"No, you're not."

"No, I'm not." He agreed with a very un-Nicholas-y laugh. She'd never seen the man so ecstatic. "I'm too fucking pleased with myself to be nervous. You are the only thing that matters to me and I somehow got you for my wife! One of the Nick Greystones, in one of these timelines, is a goddamn genius."

Marion gave a snort of amusement. His visible triumph made her feel more self-assured. "I just don't want all Nottingham's bullshit about 'being a perfect bride' to stand between us."

His expression went soft. "There is *nothing* standing between us. If there was, I would knock it down to reach you. I already *did*."

"You did." She smiled a bit. "You captured me."

"I'm obsessed with you. Everyone knows it." He kissed her. "Do what feels right to *you* and forget the rest of Nottingham."

"Fuck 'em all?" She suggested in a lighter tone.

"Family motto." He agreed. "It's just us here."

She took a deep breath. "Just us." It was dumb to be nervous about sleeping with him. He wasn't going to be upset, if she messed up a little. He was having a good time, with her. Just like she was having a good time with him. Together, they were unstoppable.

His thumb caressed the curve of her cheek, seeing her calm. "You don't have to try and be a perfect bride for me, because you're perfect for me *without* trying. Exactly as you are. Be with me and I'm happy."

"I'm happy with you, too." She nodded, feeling relaxed again. "You're right." Of course, she could do this! She'd been anxious over nothing. "Okay. Try it, again." She pushed on his shoulder, guiding him back down her body.

Nicholas was delighted to comply. His lips grazed her stomach, chuckling at the shocked breath she inhaled. "If you don't like what I'm doing, *at any point*, just say so and I'll stop.

Otherwise, I'm doing what I want and we can figure out what works for you."

Marion bit her lower lip, her legs instinctively parting to let him in. "What if there's something that *you* don't like?"

"I'm extremely confident that's not going to happen." His breath rushed over the tight nest of curls at the junction of her thighs. "My God, you smell good."

"I do?" That was nice to hear. And his touch made her heart race. And his hair was so beautifully shiny when she looked down at him. Yeah, this was all going great, again. "Hey, do you think I should...? Holy *shit!*"

He licked her. Deep inside. And Marion forgot everything. Literally *everything*. Time and space reduced down to nothing but her husband's mouth doing very wicked things to her.

"My God!" It was so much! "Oh my *God*." Marion cried out in joy and frustration. His mouth consumed her. Sucking and nipping and devouring. Instead of trying to run, like any proper Maid would have, she eased her thighs farther apart.

"So pretty." He murmured against her saturated flesh, feeling her surrender to his erotic demands. His hands pressed the inside of her legs wider, seizing more ground. "God, I have always wanted to do this to you."

She jolted, feeling exposed, but not really minding it. In fact, this was... incredible. A whimper escaped her.

Nicholas liked the needy sound. "I know, duchess. Just relax. You're going to be tight, so we need you prepared first. Just give me a second to figure out what you need."

She nodded, barely hearing him.

"You're so wet for me already." He groaned, nestling deeper between her thighs.

Her hands tangled in his otherworldly hair. "I can't wait anymore... Please." Her hips began to move against the thrusts of his tongue. "Oh please, Nick."

He liked hearing his name. A lot. His lips shifted a tiny bit to the left and Marion nearly shot off the mattress.

"Right there. Right *there!*" Her thighs tightened

around his head, instinctively holding him to her. Nicholas lavished the spot with attention and a massive orgasm rushed through Marion, blinding and clean. That was all it took. She gasped, clinging to Nicholas for support as her entire world imploded. *"Nick!"*

Nicholas moved his body up to cover hers, before the tremors stopped, trapping her beneath him. He was so *heavy*. The weight of him pressed her deeper into the bed and she loved it.

Nicholas snarled at the submissive sound she made, but he was still trying to soothe her. "I've got you, Marion. Let me in, now. I can't wait anymore for you."

Her legs wound around his hips and he pushed inside of her drenched channel, nearly out of control with desire.

Two things happened simultaneously: Marion felt her virginity give way and she felt the True Love bond snap into place.

She gasped at both sensations, but she wasn't surprised by the knowledge of who Nicholas really was to her. She'd been coming to the realization for a long, long time.

Nicholas seemed positively astonished, though.

He stopped dead. He had been shocked about the wedding, but the news that she was his True Love seemed to freeze him solid. For an endless moment, he just stayed there, deep inside of her, like he was afraid to move. Afraid the bond would somehow go away.

Gray eyes slammed into hers.

Marion smiled and reached up to lay a palm against his face. "Now you get it, right?"

Nicholas swallowed. "Gargoyles can't have a True Love." He got out, like there must have been a mistake and he wasn't sure what to do next. "Everyone says so."

"Well, my unpredictable, passionate, purposeful husband likes to prove everyone wrong."

He blinked, still not processing it.

"Nick?" She prompted, a little worried about his silence.

"Robin Hood isn't your True Love?"

"No."

"You're sure that it's not supposed to be him?"

She shook her head. "It was always supposed to be *you*."

His gaze misted with tears. "Marion." He whispered. Then, his arms were around her and he was holding her tight. Too tight, but that was okay. He buried his face in the curve of her neck and breathed in the scent of her. "Marion."

He began to make love to her in earnest, his rock-hard erection carefully tunneling into her eager body. She'd expected to be uncomfortable, but being impaled and stretched excited her. She was captured and consumed by him. And the texture on his right side was making her crazy, in all the best ways.

His hands caressed her everywhere, holding her tenderly as he entered her, again and again. His mouth tasting her skin, kissing her lips, whispering words of praise and thanks and adoration. It was perfect. Just how she'd always imagined, and she was already so happy, and so aroused, and she'd waited a fucking decade for him.

Her body began heating up for another orgasm, but she wasn't sure she could achieve it. Her flesh still felt so sensitized. Nicholas' determined thrusts jangled every nerve-ending and threatened to drown her in sensation. She instinctively tried to shift away from the heightened pleasure, but he caught hold of her. Grabbing her wrists together, he held her down with one big hand. That only heightened things *more*.

Marion cried out, her nipples jutting up into painful points. The damn things were so responsive to him. They knew he made them happy.

Nicholas made a sound of contented villainy, at her body's eager reception. "That's it. I told you, you're not going anywhere. You're right where you belong." He dipped his head to lick one of the hard berries, as if it was an offering on a menu.

Marion struggled just a tiny bit against his hold, to see what would happen. He didn't let her go and ohGodohGodohGod... Her back arched, pressing more of her breast to his lips. He sucked at it, drawing it into his mouth, grazing it with his teeth. Taking possession.

"Fourteen years, Marion. You've been teasing me for fourteen years. But I've got you, now." His gaze was hot and possessive. "All those times you flounced past me and then looked back over your shoulder to smile...? What did you think? That I'd just let you go?"

"I wasn't... teasing. I was being... friendly..."

"Bullshit. You were teasing. From that day you winked at me in Sherwood, I knew you were trouble." He kissed her, long and deep. "First time I ever jacked-off, I was picturing your Bad little smile. Every time I've ever come in my life, I've thought of you, Marion."

"Oh *God*." She squeezed her eyes shut. She really, really loved it when he was wicked.

His gigantic chest was heaving. "Can you take a little more?" It was a rhetorical question. "Of course you can. You're perfect at this. Perfect for me." He pressed the last length of him tight inside her and let out a low groan. "*Perfect*."

He was so big. So hard. Her hips began to move, trying to accommodate the sheer scale of him. Finding a rhythm that matched his. Lost in the powerful feel of his body. It was all so good. So tight. Rushing at her from all sides. "Please let me come." She begged. She needed it. Needed him. "Please, Nick."

"Fuck yes." His voice was dark with lust. "I want you to come all around me. I want to feel it. I've dreamed about it."

Marion's head thrashed on the pillow, needing relief. "I can't... I can't unless you do something. I don't..."

"I'll take care of you, duchess. Always." He hit some astonishing spot and Marion totally believed his promise. She was swept up in agonizing relief. She screamed his name, her whole body shaking. She was dimly aware of Nicholas finishing with a roar, deep inside of her. Shouting her name.

Then, she was floating between wakefulness and a

blissful haze. She sank into the mattress, secure under his massive weight. She'd known there was *more* and now she had it.

Yeah... she really was a badass.

When she finally opened her eyes, she saw Nicholas propped up on one shoulder, staring down at her. He looked enraptured. She was fairly sure she could've asked for the stars, at that moment, and Nicholas would've started tying together ladders to go get them.

"Thank you, Marion."

If he was trying to build her sexual-confidence, it was one-million percent working. "You're welcome, lamb-chop." Marion yawned and snuggled into the curve of his body. "I told you the letters were yours, didn't I? I put your name right on the top of every one of them."

"'My own True Love.'" Nicholas quoted softly. He touched her hair with a reverent hand. "You started them all that way. Every single one."

Marion smiled, at total peace for the first time in ten years. "Whether I knew it or not, they *did* go to my own True Love. To help him return to me, safe and sound. Just like you were always meant to."

Chapter Thirty-Six

Experts agree: Nottingham's obsession with sex is lowering public discourse.
We must say no to smut!
Which positions and sensual games you should absolutely *never* discuss are discussed on page 4.
Plus, color-coded diagrams of all the most shocking acts to avoid knowing about!

Alan A. Dale- "Nottingham's Naughtiest News"

Later that night, Marion lay on top of her husband, playing with the ends of his spectacular hair. She hadn't stopped touching him.

Nicholas stacked his hands between his head and pillow, watching her with a reverent expression. "You are my favorite person in the world." He said seriously.

"I know." She sent him a saucy grin. "You told me before."

"Did I?"

"Um-hmm. Right after you coerced me into marriage and confessed to secretly reading my most private thoughts."

"It's a wonder you *didn't* kill me dead. I can't imagine any romantic speech from me going very well, at that point. ...Or at any point, really."

"Well, you must've done something right, because I sure fell for your charms."

His mouth curved and Marion's heart skipped a beat.

She leaned up to kiss him smartly. "I did throw that lamp at you, though." She gestured towards the bedside table.

He chuckled, nearly knocking her off his chest in the process.

"You deserved it!" She insisted, hanging on for dear life. "No matter how charming I find you, your kidnapping plan was still a screwed up thing to do to a girl."

"I was desperate."

"And stupid."

"And stupid." He agreed. "But I'm still not sorry. I would do it all again --dying included-- to have you as my wife."

"You *are* a sweet talker, Nick Greystone. It's no wonder I fell so hard for you."

He shifted, so his hands could roam around her naked body. "When I was young, I thought the most heroic bastard in Nottingham was going to win you. I concocted a list of trials that he'd probably have to go through, just to be considered worthy. And I would do them *all*, Marion. I would slay fearsome monsters and overthrow kingdoms." He paused. "Hell, I would even write poetry, which is a lot more terrifying."

"You *did* write me poetry." Her eyes flicked over to the dresser, where his letter sat. "It was beautiful."

He snorted skeptically. "If you're willing to count that, I'm not going to argue."

"And you're supporting me in burning Nottingham to ashes. That counts as overthrowing a kingdom. I'll share the credit with the other half of Team Creative Villainy."

"Generous of you, considering I don't even know what your creatively villainous plan is, yet."

"The details are in flux. I'm waiting to hear back from someone I did time with."

"Oh God. It's not another dragon is it?"

"No, of course not." She waved that aside, focused on flirting with her husband. "So anyway, all you really have left to do is rescue me from some fearsome monster and you're a hero worthy of winning a fair Maid." She batted her lashes.

"Deal." He said simply."

From out of nowhere, his words from the wedding came back to her:

When the chips are down, you can't count on True Love to save you, Marion.

She mentally winced, insecurities jangling a bit.

Nicholas felt her stiffen and read her mind. "Whatever the other-me said to you at the wedding, the words came out wrong." He assured her quietly. "I guarantee it. I would *never* have said anything to hurt you."

She frowned and shook her head. "Of course not. It's nothing. I just..."

He kept talking, ignoring her denial. "And I sure as hell wouldn't have said you couldn't count on your True Love, if I'd known *I* was your True Love. You *can* count on me."

"In my head, I know that."

"Yeah?" He smiled a bit.

"Yes! I know you'll take care of me, the way I'll always take care of you." She chewed on her lower lip. "It's just... instinctive for me to worry, I guess. But, I'm all in with you. I swear."

"I know." His voice was soothing. "Try one of those visualization exercises Rockwell was talking about. Think to yourself: 'If a fearsome monster shows up, all I have to do is run like hell. Because, Nick –who carries a literal *broadsword* to work every day-- will slay a thousand of those fuckers, to keep me safe. I can *always* count on my True Love.'"

Marion snorted in amusement and shook off her anxieties, not wanting to ruin the mood. "That's a very helpful visual to have. Thanks."

"At the end of the visual, I heroically sweep you right off your feet. Did I mention that?"

"Obviously. When I rescue you, here in reality, it's much less dramatic. I just use time travel."

"You protected me with your tiny little body, when Hood was throwing rocks, that day in Sherwood."

Her lips parted in outrage. "*Robin* was the one throwing rocks at you, when we were kids?" Marion hadn't known that. "You should have told me it was him. That evil little fuck..."

Nicholas cut her off, before she got sidetracked. "And during the war, you kept me safe with those letters. Every day, you gave me a reason to survive until the *next* day, because, I didn't want to miss one. You have kept me safe, one way or another, since I was thirteen years old."

Her heart melted. "Lucky for me I did... Because, you

are *my* favorite person in the world, Nick."

Gray eyes glowed. "About time you noticed that." He murmured.

"In the WUB Club, I was thinking about you non-stop. Wishing I'd done things differently. I knew you were my True Love. I mean, I couldn't be completely sure, of course. But I could *feel* it, especially as I embraced my Bad side. I just felt it too late."

"Whatever you needed to do to survive prison is nothing but *Good*." His fingers traced up and down her back. "But, I do appreciate your Bad side. I always have."

She rubbed against one of the stony sections of his chest, liking how the texture felt against her skin. "I would have stayed with you, either way." She wanted him to know that. "True Love or not, I only want to be with you." She chewed on her bottom lip. "Do you forgive me for ever thinking it was Robin?"

"Yes." He scoffed, like the idea of not forgiving her anything was totally foreign to him. "If you chopped my arms off with a chainsaw, I'd forgive you."

Marion wasn't willing to let it drop. "I am *so* sorry, Nick."

He shrugged uncomfortably, like almost marrying someone else was no big deal and she should just forget about the heartache it must've caused him.

Marion tried again. "Last time through, you said you were angry at me, for being with him."

"No." The denial was instant.

"It's okay, if you are. I'd be angry, if you were ever walking around, professing your love for another girl. Like I would *still* be flipping the hell out. It would be a never-ending rampage of that bitch's blood and tears." Being a True Love always meant being a little clingy. And Marion and Nicholas both careened towards *fanatically* clingy. She could only imagine what he'd endured, watching her with another man.

Nicholas kept frowning. "I've never been angry *at* you. I must have been fumbling with words. I'm... I *was* angry that you never really saw me. I needed you and there was nothing I could do about it."

Marion pointedly looked down at her naked body and then up at his face. "Nothing?" She repeated skeptically. "Seems like there *was* something you could do, once you decided to try. When you *let* me see you, it was inevitable that I would choose you."

"You wouldn't have chosen me..."

She cut him off. "Nick... I *did* choose you."

He blinked, listening now.

It was instinctive for him to worry about Robin, the way it was instinctive for Marion to worry about counting on anyone but herself. She thought for a beat, debating what she should reveal about her most private insecurities and how much sharing them might help him.

"Robin tried to talk me into bed a lot of times, over the years. I think it was mostly purity tests, to prove how Good I was." She said slowly. "It wasn't just before he left for war, when he wanted to come on my breasts. He'd ask for something sexual every few months."

Nicholas' eyes sharpened.

"I always said no." She rushed to say, because True Loves were also territorial and Nicholas was more territorial than most. It was because he'd been denied his place for so long. He needed a lot of reassurance. "I knew if I said yes, I'd lose value in Robin's eyes. Being a Maid is all about virginity. So, it's kind of a no-win situation. You have a man trying to seduce you and telling you pretty things. And if you reject him, he blames you for bruising his ego. But if you give in and get seduced, he then blames you for being... less."

"You could never be less, duchess."

Nicholas always knew what to say, even when he didn't *know* that he knew it. She gave him a quick, grateful smile. "He asked me to do all kinds of things. And," she swallowed, "I had no real trouble refusing Robin's advances, even after ten years of being his."

"You're *not* his."

Marion ignored that vehement denial, wanting to get this out. "But after a few days of hanging around with you, here I am. Naked in your bed." Saying all this was idiotic. She *knew* that and still she was saying it, because Nottingham's sexist bullshit had always played havoc on her thoughts. Even when she recognized what was happening, she felt vulnerable to it.

Nicholas studied her, like he was trying to read her mind. "I'm married to you. I'm you're True Love. You've done nothing wrong by sleeping with me. You're right where you're supposed to be."

"I *know*. But," she took a deep breath, "I would've slept with you, anyway."

His head tilted.

"I know me." Marion admitted. "I know how hard I fell, once you let me in. And I know I would be here, with you, even if we *weren't* married and you *weren't* my True Love. Which is *not* what a virtuous Maid should be saying, but..." She trailed off. "I just want you *so much* that nothing else matters."

Silence.

Marion waited, unaccountably nervous.

Nicholas' face broke into a wide grin. "You're honestly worried about this?" He deduced incredulously. "You're worried that I'd be...what?... *unhappy* to hear that you're helpless in the face of my magnetic virility."

"Well, yes!" Marion blinked at his playful tone. "It doesn't speak well of my chastity." That was the primmest thing she'd said in a decade.

"I don't give a shit about your chastity." He said bluntly. "I care that you choose *me*, above everyone else." He shook his head, like he was amazed that she couldn't see this. "It wouldn't have changed anything, if you'd slept with Hood. If you'd slept with the entire Nottingham army, I'd still be pining for you. I'd still respect you and be obsessed with you. I never wanted a Maid. I just want *Marion*."

No other man in the kingdom would have said such a thing.

She exhaled heavily, beaming up at him.

Nicholas paused. "But..." He opened his mouth and then closed it again, hunting for words.

Marion's brows slammed together. "But?" She prompted.

He winced slightly. "Um... since we're sharing... I don't *hate* the fact that you were a virgin...?" It came out as a question. "I don't hate that you gave me something Hood wanted and can never have."

She pursed her lips at his hesitant confession, trying not to laugh.

"I really don't like the man." Nicholas admitted, as if maybe she hadn't noticed before. "I didn't like that you were dating him. I didn't like that everyone thought he had a claim on you. I've been a little jealous."

Marion somehow managed to keep a straight face. "I did notice you were *troubled*, a few times." She agreed in a serious tone.

Nicholas seemed relieved by her unruffled response. "Right. I didn't like watching him touch you or dance with you or talk to you. I didn't like it when you'd smile up at him, like he was a goddamn hero. I once saw you kissing him and I punched a hole in the garden wall, imagining it was his skull."

"The stone wall? Around my house?"

He nodded.

"I *wondered* how that happened! You owe me fifteen gold pieces for repairs, you vandal." She nipped his side in punishment.

Nicholas caught onto her amusement and relaxed. "So, I might possibly feel a bit of vindication, now that he's the one on the outside. You're finally touching *me*, and smiling at *me*, and kissing *me*. Like you always should've been." He cleared his throat. "That's all."

"That's all?" Marion doubted it. She could see there were still darker thoughts in his head. Watching his True Love pledge her devotion to another man had wounded Nicholas. Deeply. Getting it all out was the only way to heal him. "Tell me everything, Nick. I won't be mad, if you want to talk about Robin." She tried a cheeky smile. "I like it when you're sexy and possessive."

Nicholas hesitated.

Marion waited patiently, her chin on his chest. If you gave him time to figure out his own thoughts and settle on the words he needed, he could communicate just fine.

"Well…" Nicholas began in a slow voice, "there is a slight chance I'm pleased that Hood will never be able to call you his True Love, again."

Marion nodded encouragingly.

His jaw tightened at the memories. "I fucking *hated* it when he'd say that. I sometimes think he sensed I hated it, so he'd just do it more. I wanted…" He let out an aggravated breath and trailed off.

"Go on." Marion murmured, he needed to express all his feelings, so they could move past them.

"I wanted *you*. And he had you. And it *killed* me. For years. Every time you'd walk by me and I saw you…" He shook his head. "I knew you were supposed to be mine. I felt it. But, you'd be holding *his* fucking arm. So, I somewhat enjoy the idea that the tables have turned. Hood's alone in those tick-filled woods, while you're crying out my name and begging me to let you come."

"That didn't happen." She denied piously, although it probably had.

"Hood will never know how soft and wet you are… And he'll know that I *do* know. Every time he sees me, he's going to think about what I have and he doesn't." Nicholas smirked a bit. "I may have briefly thought of how *nice* that will be."

For some perverse reason, Marion's insides flipped at his smug expression. She should ask Nicholas to share his thoughts, more often. They were delightfully wicked.

"And there is the remote possibility that I relish him finding out you're my wife. Just mine. That I'll be the one with all your ideas and your heart and your future. And there is nothing he can do to get you back."

"*Nothing.*" Marion agreed firmly.

His eyes were clearer, now. "I really only care about you and me, Marion. That's all that truly matters. I swear it."

"But…" She prompted.

"But... on a petty and very inappropriate level? The news that you're mine, for really *real?* When he hears that?" Nicholas sighed with arrogant anticipation, the cat who ate the canary. "It's going to eat the bastard alive. And I fucking *love* that."

Robin wouldn't really care, but Marion didn't want to spoil Nicholas' fun by pointing that out. "Are you sure you weren't born Bad?" She teased.

He lifted a self-deprecating shoulder. "I know I'm an asshole for thinking about any of this pissing-contest bullshit. It's not even about Hood. It's about *you*. And my terrifying lifelong obsession with you."

"I don't think you have an obsession. At least, not a terrifying one. It's a harmless..."

He outright scoffed, cutting her off. "I need you *so much*, sometimes I can't breathe, Marion. I want my handprints all over your body, so people will see who you belong to." It came out in a rush. "I have memorized those letters you sent. I can *recite* them to you. I know how many kinds of perfume you own and which one you'll pick, depending on your mood. I know the color of your favorite pair of socks. I'm insanely, incurably, *passionately* obsessed with you."

"I'm your True Love. You knew that, on some level, at a very young age." She touched his beautiful face. "So, you sought me out in any way you could. I think all your instincts went into overdrive and you grew a little bit *troubled*, when another man got close. But over all, it was perfectly normal."

"I kidnapped you."

"Okay, *that* part was a bit obsessive."

"I would do worse. I would burn down the world to have you."

"I *am* going to burn down Nottingham, because of what this town did to us." She paused, wrinkling her nose. "But I actually am unhealthily fixated, according to the WUB Club's psych evaluation. I warned you about that, right?"

"Yes. And I'm terrified you'll one day be cured."

"If ten years in prison and your death didn't cure me, nothing will. Just resign yourself to being stalked by a felon forever."

"Deal." He kissed her forehead. "There's a part of me that knows I should give you space to adjust to everything that's happened. ...But I *can't*. It all feels too fragile. I'm paranoid you'll run."

"I'm not going to run."

"You should."

"Nottingham screwed up our perceptions of ourselves. They told you gargoyles weren't worthy of True Love and they told me Maid's shouldn't enjoy sex. It's all bullshit. We just have to sort through the last remnants of the lies and move on with our happily-ever-after, because we *know* better."

He still looked a little pensive. "I can't give you kids." He said randomly. "I'm a gargoyle. We can't reproduce."

Marion rolled her eyes. The man was inventing issues, again. "Do you even *want* kids? Personally, all I want to do was drink on a beach, for the next decade or so."

"I'm happy, just so I have you. You in a bathing suit is a bonus."

"I'm happy with focusing on you in a bathing suit, too. So, problem solved." She cuddled closer to his big body. "But if we change our mind later, carve ourselves a little gargoyle, just as perfect as you."

He was satisfied with that plan. "Deal." He said again. He lifted her hand to rub at the ruby ring gleaming on her finger and was silent for a long moment. She realized he was digging through his emotions, trying to find words. "What I really want is everyone to know you're my True Love and that our marriage is irrevocable." He eventually decided. "Because it *is*, Marion. We'd both have to agree to dissolve it and I'll hang *myself* before I agree to that."

"I don't think it *can* be dissolved." She nuzzled his neck, thrilled that he was sharing all his apprehensions with her. He really did trust her! "The marriage scroll isn't in this timeline. It would have to be destroyed to get divorced and there's no way *to* destroy it. I'm not even sure 'when' it is."

Oh, he liked that quandary. She could feel him swelling beneath her. Marion sent him an arch look through her lashes and licked at his flat nipple enticingly.

He sucked in a breath. "*No.*" He warned. "You'll be too sore." His eyes fluttered closed, as she lapped at his sensitive flesh. "God, you were so *tight*."

"I'm the perfect size." Marion reached down to caress his growing erection. "You're just very, *very* big."

He swallowed. "Was it too much for you?"

"No, I loved it. I want to be a badass at sex. Teach me everything. Don't worry. I'm a really great student."

"Holy God..." He sighed in defeat as she stroked him, helpless against her touch. "You're a Bad influence on me, Marion Greystone."

She smiled at the name. "You like to be wicked. That's why we fit so well, His Grace, Duke of Huntingdon."

Nicholas stilled at the fancy-ass title that would now pass to him. "Shit." He muttered, like it was just occurring to him he'd been elevated to the peerage and he wasn't thrilled with his social climb. "Nobody's gonna approve of a gargoyle being a duke."

"Fuck 'em all." Marion kissed his stomach, her tongue running over the deep muscles, on to far more interesting plans. "You have such a beautiful body."

He seemed startled by that idea. "You think so?"

"Yep. I want to do all kinds of naughty things with it." Her mouth glided south. "Speaking of which... Are you going to miss your betrothal rights, now that we're married?"

"I still *have* my betrothal rights."

She glanced up at him, intrigued. "You want to keep your betrothal rights, even though we're married?"

"Of course. They're mine and I take them seriously."

He *did* take them seriously. She hadn't realized how much until right that minute.

Nicholas didn't look away from her searching gaze. "You handed your body into my hands and I will always keep you safe. Married or not, that will *never* change."

Instead of feeling panicked by that vow, Marion felt oddly reassured. "Okay. She whispered.

He liked that she finally believed his promise. His

pleasure was *very* obvious.

Marion smiled and continued heading south.

Nicholas' hips instinctively bucked, when she found a particularly sensitive spot. "*Shit!* Are you sure you want to be down that far?"

Oh, she was *very* sure.

"Since I've promised to take care of you, too, I want some betrothal rights, as well." She decided. "I think I should get to touch *your* body, for a change." She settled between his legs, her eyes bright with mischief. "And I'm thinking I want to try all the very Bad things Robin wanted from me. Only instead of doing them to *him*... I'm going to give them all to *you*."

He stared at her, his gaze burning hot. "He gets nothing. I get everything."

"Everything." She was pretty sure it would help him get over his final worries about her ex, once and for all. "And don't even think about stopping me. I have certain rights, under the law."

His smile gleamed. "Claim *all* of them, duchess."

She loved it when he was playful with her. "I'm probably not going to be great at this, at first." She warned. The best way to deal with her internal conflicts and insecurities was to face them head-on. "You'll have to teach me what you like."

"I like *you*." No doubt about that. If Nicholas got any more aroused, his erection would explode. "You don't need to worry about being an expert. I promise you. I'm not going to last long, anyway. I'm already too far gone." His fingers tightened on her tousled curls and his arousal nudged her lips. "I've dreamed of you doing this every single time you've smiled at me, for the past ten years."

She rewarded his patience by leaning forward to suckle the very tip of his manhood.

"*Marion!*" His hand fisted in her hair, like he was afraid she'd disappear if he let her go.

Marion's confidence skyrocketed. She adjusted her position to take him deeper, learning as she went. His reactions told her how to move to make him the happiest. Nicholas was usually the quietest man in Nottingham, but sex sure seemed to turn up his volume. He talked a lot in bed and he was *loud*, when he got happy.

"Christ, that's good." He was trying to hold himself motionless, so he didn't frighten her. She could feel the strain in his muscles. "You're so pretty. You're so goddamn pretty, sometimes it hurts to look at you." His body jerked involuntarily and he moaned. "Harder. That's it. Let me in, nice and deep."

There wasn't a single person in the castle who'd missed his ringing praise and vivid instructions. Nicholas had just singlehandedly turned her reputation from innocent maiden to sexual dynamo. Enjoying this immensely, Marion licked her way down his throbbing shaft. The taste and feel of him was intoxicating. Her nipples beaded in response to his arousal, her own body warming. She could do this all day.

Nicholas couldn't.

"Don't stop." He hadn't been kidding about how close to the edge he was. "Please, don't stop."

So, of course, Marion pulled back, just to torment him. He liked to be teased. "Ten years, huh? In this timeline, I was awful young to be fantasizing about."

His eyes were glazed. "I was young, too, so it was legal." He panted. "Believe me. I'm the sheriff."

"That was right around the time I started dating Robin, wasn't it?"

"Yes." The word was stark, all his insecurities closer to the surface. Excellent. This was working. She was about to exorcise them, once and for all.

"That's also when he first asked me to do this. Robin wanted to come in my mouth. He wanted me to swallow all of him. To mark me, I think."

Nicholas didn't like that information. At all.

"I refused, of course." She went on casually. "I was a *very* Good girl, back then."

He saw where this was headed. "I get all the things you wouldn't give him." He reminded her, his voice dark with primitive desire. "I get *everything*."

She blinked with mock innocence. "You want to mark more of me?" Her hand came up to sensually brush the small bite he'd left on her neck and went in for the kill. "Well, I supposed that's only fair, since I'm your girl."

Nicholas paused, his eyes locked on hers. That was the first time she'd accepted the nickname. And when someone gave you a name and you accepted it, it meant something.

"Again." He whispered, need in his voice.

"I'm your girl, Nick." She repeated, giving him the words he wanted. "*Just* yours. And I will keep telling you that, again and again, until you see it's true." Marion pressed a kiss to his stomach. He didn't have a bellybutton. That was so cute. "And I'll keep showing you that you're the only man I want." Her tongue trailed along his skin. "The only man I'd ever choose."

He shuddered in frenzied passion and pushed her head back towards his weeping erection. "Show me, now."

Marion grinned at his desperation and lowered her head. Then, she set about driving him absolutely crazy. Just because she was feeling particularly adventurous, she tried using her teeth on his rigid staff.

"*Fuck!*" His body came right off the bed. "My God... You own every fucking piece of me." He wrapped her hair around his stony hand, guiding her. Watching her.

Claiming her.

"That's so good. Everything about you is Good, Marion. And perfectly Bad. And you're all fucking *mine*." He let out a shout of triumph and then she was swallowing the thick essence of him. Nicholas kept her still, groaning loudly, as he ensured she suckled him dry. "Take it all. That's it. It's all yours."

No Maid would ever tolerate such a primeval display. Marion had told Robin that once and it had been true.

...So, Marion must not be a Maid anymore, because she was incredibly aroused by the wildness of it. The last of her inhibitions fell away. Nottingham's brainwashing didn't really stand a chance against the raw pleasure of Nicholas. She felt like the world's greatest seductress. No one could resist her.

Not even the forbidding Sheriff of Nottingham.

"Thank you, Marion." He whispered.

"Anytime." She moved up his body again, so they could lay face-to-face. Marion was drowsy, but she didn't want to fall asleep. Nicholas seemed to feel the same. She'd never seen the man so calm.

"No more worries about Robin, I take it?" She finally murmured.

"Who?"

Marion grinned at his bored question. "I caused amnesia? Wow, I *am* incredible at sex. You can tell me again how incredible I am at sex. I don't mind."

"You're *incredible* at sex." He assured her, kissing her smiling face.

"You're pretty incredible at it, too." She kissed him back. "Best I ever had."

He chuckled against her mouth.

"But then, *you're* pretty incredible, my own True Love. So, I'm not surprised by your talent."

He blinked at the endearment, lifting his head. "I like that name best." He decided, in a surprisingly intent tone.

Marion met his eyes, seeing he was serious. "A little long for everyday use, isn't it?"

"You can shorten it, if you want. But *that's* the name. It means something." He pressed his lips to the mark he'd left on her neck earlier, years of pent-up desire in the gesture. "It means *everything* to me that I'm your own True Love."

"My love?" She suggested, readily offering more usable versions of what he wanted. "My own? My...?"

"Own." He interrupted, surety in his voice. "I am yours, Marion."

Marion pretended to pout. "You really like 'my own' better than 'beef cake' and 'smookie-wookie.'"

"Much better. Call me that, from now on."

"I'll put it in the rotation." She teased.

Time went by. Marion kept her eye on the clock, even though she didn't really want to. She felt drifty and bonelessly content.

"Do you still want to have the wedding tomorrow?" Nicholas asked at 11:55. He held his stony palm against hers, measuring their different sizes. Instead of being ashamed of his hand, he seemed to like seeing it wrapped around Marion's. "Since we're already married, we could just skip it."

"What about your grand plan to catch Robin at the church?"

"What about it?" All of Nicholas' demons about her ex had been cleansed. He just wanted to focus on their future. His big fingers toyed with hers, replete and confident in his claim. "Hood doesn't even show up. I don't care if he *does* show up. I want to spend the day here in bed with my girl."

"Nice try, but we're having the ceremony. No way am I missing the opportunity to wear my gown. A bride only gets one perfect wedding day, you know."

"Seems like you're getting two."

"The first one *wasn't* perfect, Mr. Kidnapper."

"*Duke* Kidnapper. And it was perfect for me." He gave a lazy shrug. "Because you said 'yes.'"

"I'll say 'yes' tomorrow, too. Only I'll be doing it in ten feet of imported tulle and a rhinestone tiara."

"Fine." Nicholas gave up on his half-hearted arguments, like he was happy either way. He folded their connected hands against his chest, right over his heart. "At least everyone in Nottingham will see you become legally mine. The shock and horror will be fun."

"I'm already yours. In every way possible. Your wife and your girl and your True Love and your home." She squeezed his big fingers. "You're my home, too, Nick."

His smiles came so much easier, now. It was incredible to see. "I could've told you that fourteen years ago."

Marion refused to be distracted by his handsomeness. "It's 11:56." She reluctantly squiggled free of his hold. "I gotta go, before it's too late."

He blinked at her with total incomprehension.

"I have to go back to my room before midnight." She reminded him. "I told you, I can't see you the day of our wedding."

"What? We're already married!"

"That wedding doesn't count! I didn't have my perfect dress on." Speaking of which... How was she going to get back downstairs, since her clothes were shredded and strewn all over the floor?

Nicholas shook his head, refusing to let her escape. It was like trying to evade a mountain with big hands and abandonment issues. "No." The word was absolute. "You're staying in my bed. Right where you belong."

"Nick..."

"*No*." He dragged her back to him, as if she weighed nothing at all. "You're not sleeping apart from me. Not ever again, Marion."

"It's bad luck!"

"I don't give a shit. You're kidnapped. Deal with it." He hugged her even closer than before and sighed with satisfaction, as his huge body wrapped securely around hers. "See? A perfect fit." Hellhounds couldn't have pried her from his hold.

"You're being a little obsessive about this, my own."

He didn't seem worried about his mental health. "I think you had a point, the other day. I think gargoyles can be Good *or* Bad. ...And I think I'm mostly Bad." He kissed her with wicked intent. "Now, don't make me tie you up or neither of us will get any sleep."

Marion surrendered to her latest abduction, with an exasperated shake of her head. "If you jinx our wedding, I am going to be *so* pissed off." She was quiet for a beat, thinking. "Hey, not to be *too* villainous... but I'd be willing to forget about sleep all together, if I can tie *you* up."

For the first time in his life, Nick Greystone laughed uproariously. "Deal."

Chapter Thirty-Seven

Naughtiest News Exclusive:
Behind the Scenes at Maid Marion's Mega-Wedding!
See how all the Mega $$$ were spent!
Hear from the gardeners, chefs, and unicorns who are making it all happen.
Plus, who is the Mega Mystery Guest everyone's talking about?!

Alan A. Dale- "Nottingham's Naughtiest News"

It was quite possibly every tulip in the world.

Nicholas' eyes slowly traveled around the elaborately decorated throne room of the castle. It was the palace's largest space and there wasn't a square inch that wasn't now sparkly, frosted, or bedecked with greenery.

Forests of tulip-covered arches, a glacier ice statue the length of a city block, eighteen photo booths, a cowboy-looking guy in white fringe, a lagoon of chocolate manned by some kind of Oompa-creatures, twinkling lights made from actual diamonds, fifty enchanted instruments scheduled to perform songs specially written for the occasion, a literal waterfall of Carbonated Magic Bean Juice…

Everywhere Nicholas looked he saw more, piled atop more, piled atop *more*.

He couldn't even begin to guess how much it had all cost. There was no way Richard's coffers could pay for it. When the bills came in, they couldn't possibly be paid. Marion had bankrupted the kingdom with this celebration. No doubt that had been her intention. Well, that and throwing a "fuck 'em all" party, just to out-do every other Nottingham bride and scandalize the tasteful elite.

His mouth curved. He so enjoyed her Bad side.

A waiter came by and offered him food off a sterling silver tray. "Canape?"

Nicholas blinked. It was eight in the morning. The reception wasn't for hours. Why were they already serving food?

"It's icen jellyfish eggs from the Moaning Sea." The waiter waggled the tray at him temptingly. "Maid Marion said the staff might get hungry, while we set up the wedding, so we've all been enjoying it." He was dressed in a brand new uniform covered in thick gold braiding. Literally. The threads were gold. "Icen Jelly fish caviar is rare, you know."

No, he didn't know that. Why would he know that? "*How* rare?"

"It takes four magic spells just to process it. One tablespoon could buy you a horse."

Nicholas eyed the overloaded tray. "How much did Marion order?"

"The entire year's harvest, of course."

Of course.

Amused, Nicholas took a dozen horses-worth of rare caviar for his breakfast. It tasted horrible. He doubted Marion would care, just so it drained Nottingham's treasury.

The waiter went off to offer the canapes to Alan A. Dale, who was pestering the cowboy-looking guy. Marion insisted Pecos Bill would be a huge star one day, but presently he seemed like a washed-up nobody from some cactus-y place. Nottinghamers had never heard of him. But, Nottingham was isolated and culturally backwards, so maybe he was famous in other lands. Or maybe not. Either way, Marion was pleased to have him there and that was all that mattered.

Sadly, Pecos Bill wasn't so thrilled to be in attendance.

His squinty gaze cut around the spectacle of lights and flowers in annoyance, as Alan attempted to interview him. Given the ostentatious stage being erected for the cowboy's debut of "My Own True Love," Alan was positive he was someone important in disguise and was demanding to know his secret identity. The more Pecos Bill argued he didn't have a secret identity, the more Alan became convinced that he must secretly be a *huge* celebrity and peppered him with questions.

Pecos Bill was pissed.

Nicholas didn't blame him. He also didn't care.

The cowboy had been shipped in early that morning, slightly against his will. A microphone had been shoved into his hand and he'd been told he was going to sing. He refused, which obviously wouldn't do, at all. Marion had been upset, when Quarry came to tell her Pecos Bill was throwing a fit about his surprise headlining performance.

As the experience abductor in the family, Nicholas had offered to go downstairs and rationally discuss the situation with the obviously temperamental man. A great conversation followed, to Nicholas' way of thinking:

Pecos Bill said he didn't sing.

Nicholas said he could either sing or he could hang.

Pecos Bill said he *wouldn't* sing.

Nicholas said he could either sing or he could hang.

Pecos Bill said he'd alert the local authorities about this kidnapping.

Nicholas said he *was* the Sheriff of Nottingham. ...And the cowboy could either sing or he could hang. Then, he'd pointed out the window to one of the gallows Marion had festively draped with orange blossoms.

Pecos Bill said he'd sing.

Nicholas grunted and walked away. *Nobody* said "no" to his adorable bridezilla.

Just in case Marion's country-western hostage tried to escape, Nicholas made sure the gargoyles were keeping an eye on him. The guards were happy to oblige. They were milling around the vast room, fascinated by Marion's decorating choices.

Gravol was talking to the parrot sommelier, seemingly enchanted by its tiny tuxedo. The dignified bird wore a top hat and was recommending some delightful wine pairings for the frozen jellyfish eggs. Oore was trying to avoid the eighty-nine photographers and videographers recording every second of the preparations. Rockwell was admiring the fountain of champagne at the open bar. It had mermaids swimming in it. *All* the gargoyles seemed to enjoy the open bar and mermaids, actually.

Quarry came over, wryly observing the budgetless extravaganza. "We could've just handed out sacks of money to all the guests. It would've been cheaper."

"Don't give Marion any ideas. She'll make them our party favors."

"The wedding cake is so big it won't fit through the door."

"That's why Marion built it its own special building, out by those gigantic talking flowers." The new cake-house was shaped like a gigantic gazebo and painted in some enchanted color that grew gossamer feathers.

Quarry snickered. "Richard will be glad he's dead, when he gets the bill for all this."

Nicholas glanced at his best man. "I just hope all her enemies show up to be deeply offended. Marion will be disappointed if she went through all this trouble and no one was forever scarred by it."

"Oh, all of Nottingham will be here, just to behold the spectacle." Quarry sounded confident in the townsfolk's bitter jealousy. He was crunching on some kind of intricate hors d'oeuvre dusted with edible glitter and genuine pixie dust. "Ready to go to the church?"

"Yes." As promised, he had a ridiculous bycocket on his head and he felt the long red feather waving around ridiculously. "Boulder and Cragg are getting Marion and then we'll leave. In separate carriages."

She was still convinced he'd jinxed her big day, by insisting she sleep in his bed, the night before. Actually, they hadn't done much sleeping, but Nicholas couldn't even pretend to feel repentant for keeping his little villainess awake and beside him.

To try and rectify the "jinxed" situation, and also make him suffer, Marion had insisted that he couldn't see her all morning.

After she'd seduced him, again.

Marion had been giggling madly as he lifted her against the wall. They'd reenacted her sex dream from the original timeline... minus the wedding dress part. Marion was passionate about keeping her perfect gown unwrinkled, so she'd refused to play any Bad games in it. Yet. He had many wicked plans for the honeymoon, though. Marion would love them. He already knew it.

Until the wedding was over, however, no one was allowed to see or touch the precious tulle confection. She'd keep it hermetically sealed in plastic, if she could.

At the moment, Marion was up in her room getting ready. Personally, Nicholas would have preferred to skip all the preparations, the ceremony, the party, and the guests. Marion already wore his ring. That was all he cared about. And this whole thing was sure to be loud. Although, Marion had given him a wedding gift of earplugs, which was very thoughtful and would probably help. Still, why couldn't they...?

"Commander!" Boulder and Cragg came rushing into the ballroom, interrupting his thoughts. "Marion is gone."

Nicholas couldn't process what the words meant. He turned to look at them blankly. "Gone?"

Boulder's brows were slammed low over his eyes. "Cragg and I went to get her, but she wasn't in her bedroom."

"No." Nicholas shook his head. "She has to be there. She was just getting the dress..."

"She's *gone*, Commander." Boulder interrupted.

Nicholas stared at him, trying to think.

At the May Day Festival, Marion had said the wedding would prove he could trust her feelings for him. That if she didn't show up in her perfect dress, he'd know she'd been lying about wanting to marry him and he could feel vindicated that his worst suspicions had been right, all along.

Only Nicholas didn't feel vindicated. He felt shocked. Gutted. Panicked.

No. This wasn't right.

The other gargoyles began to gather around, wearing various looks of concern.

"This was on the pillow, addressed to you." Cragg handed him a sealed envelope, an uncharacteristically grave expression on his face. "Look, I don't know where she went, but I know she wanted to be *here*. She spent a lot of time planning this wedding and all she talks about is you, Commander. That's not fake."

Nicholas snatched the paper from his hand and tore it open, the way he'd torn open countless other letters from Marion. He instantly knew she was the one who wrote this one, too. No one could have copied the swirling, feminine penmanship so exactly. Not even the Wraith.

Dear Nick,

By the time you read this, I'll be married to Robin. I can come clean now that I'm finally staging my Strategic escape. Our entire engagement has been a sham. I can't believe you were dumb enough to fall for it! You even let me decorate the castle in red and white Wildflowers, like you really thought we'd have a wedding. How stupid are you? No one would ever choose a rock-monster like you, over a hero like Robin. Don't try to follow me. Robin has plenty of Supplies to outlast you. He's brilliant and prepared for anything. He's a king out here in the forest. And soon he'll be king, over all of Nottingham!

Best Wishes,
Marion

Nicholas' read the letter twice, trying to make sense of it through his swirling emotions.

It was a lie.

She wouldn't run off with Robin Hood. No goddamn way. She loved Nicholas. She hadn't said the words, but he *felt* it. He believed in her and in their bond. His analytical sheriff's brain clicked on, even as his emotions were in chaos.

Marion had spent the night curled up in his arms, after giving him her virginity. Why would she do that, if she planned to leave him twelve hours later?

She'd started the good-bye letter with the name he liked. If her feelings for him had all been an incredibly convincing act, surely she would have used "Nicholas," just to drive home the point. Plus, she'd closed the damn thing with "best wishes?" *Best fucking wishes?!*

And how could she possibly marry Hood, anyway? Even if he was wrong about everything else, that part was flat-out impossible. Marion was *already* married to Nicholas. Her letter didn't even mention that small detail.

None of the evidence added up. Something else was happening here.

Rockwell scanned the note over his shoulder, a frown tugging at his face and sending dust particles flying from the crumbling stone. "Wildflowers? Is this my fault? Maybe she's upset because I ordered red and white tulips." He looked around the festooned ballroom. "Like... all of them."

"You idiot!" Oore shouted, ready to blame him for everything.

Strategic. Wildflower. Supplies.

The random capitalization of the three words suddenly jumped out at Nicholas. It wouldn't have been especially noteworthy, unless you'd spent the entirety of your deployment memorizing every loop of her handwriting. Unless you'd had Marion sitting on your lap, while she laughed over "strategic wildflowers supplies" being a secret code, in case something terrible happened. Unless you trusted your wife with your whole heart and soul.

His jaw tightened, dread filling him. This wasn't a good-bye note. This was Marion sending him a distress message.

"Commander?"

He glanced up at Quarry, his mind racing with rage and all-consuming worry.

The other man stared back, his face grim. "When Marion enters a room, she looks for you. She always has. Her eyes skim over everyone else. And when her gaze finally finds you, she smiles." Quarry slowly shook his head. "All she sees is *you*."

"That's what I'm saying!" Cragg cried triumphantly. "Marion loves the commander. She didn't leave of her own freewill. Not after she spent four hours deciding on the perfect place settings for their fifty-two course dinner. They're made of porcelain from that dude in Oz!"

"Even if she *did* leave on her own, we need to get her back." Oore declared righteously. "She belongs to the commander. To all of us. Girls like it when you stalk them. At least, Marion does. I vote we track her down. It's probably what she wants."

Gravol nodded, his eyes wide. "We're going to move to the beach. I'm going to have my own room. Marion said so."

Nicholas rubbed at his temple, barely even hearing the other men. He *knew* Hood would come for her. No one would give Marion up so easily. Fuck! Why had he let her out of his sight? What if something happened to her?

"Maybe it's that dragon playing a trick." Rockwell chimed in. "I've never liked the looks of him."

"His looks look pretty good to me." Cragg muttered. "But I get your point. It could be a spell. Except Trevelyan already left Nottingham, didn't he? Maybe someone else cast it."

Boulder cleared his throat. "I don't think it's a spell. Yesterday, Marion told me she was worried about secret passages, here in the castle." He shifted, uncomfortable that he agreed with the others. Boulder typically liked to take contrary positions as a matter of principle. "Seems like if she was gonna run away, she wouldn't have mentioned an escape route."

Nicholas belatedly realized he should've asked Marion *how* Hood left her those whiny letters. They hadn't come in the mail, which meant they'd probably been left in the castle.

...Which meant Hood had a way *into* the castle.

Marion must have suspected as much, so she'd sent Boulder looking for it. Was it too much to ask for the other half of Team Creative Villainy to tell *him* what the hell was going on in his own house?

Shit!

It was too late to do anything about the tunnels, so he

focused on retrieving his aggravatingly independent wife. His brain slid pieces into place, as he worked out a plan. Kidnapped... Stalking... Tracking... Dragon... Spell... "here" not "there"...

The other gargoyles all began talking over each other, wanting to express their opinion of where Marion went, how to retrieve her, where the secret passage might be, what Trevelyan was plotting, and why Rockwell should have ordered wildflowers instead of tulips.

"Marion is my True Love." Nicholas said, cutting through the chatter, so they would shut up and he could focus on what actually mattered.

The gargoyles all turned to gape at him, falling silent. Having a True Love was completely beyond their expectations. Beings carved from stone never contemplated finding something so extraordinary.

Even Quarry was shocked by the scope of what Nicholas just revealed. "You're sure?" He finally whispered.

"I'm sure."

Nicholas was suddenly sure about everything. His mother had been right. If you committed yourself to something with your whole heart and soul, you inevitably found your purpose. Even if you were a gargoyle. And Marion had been right, too. A purpose wasn't just the things you did. It was *why* you did them. Nicholas' heart and soul belonged to his perfect, troublemaking wife. They were totally committed to her. She was his truth. She was his *why*.

Marion was his purpose.

It had always been her. The dead-him must have realized it, too, when he'd carried her out of the church. Of course he had! How could he possibly miss it? That unpredictable woman was the purpose of his very existence. Without Marion, there *was* no Nick.

"We can have True Loves?" Rockwell seemed awed by the possibility. "You're *completely* sure, Commander?"

"I'm completely sure."

"Holy shit!" Oore blurted out. There was only one way someone who wasn't born Bad could be *completely* sure.

"You slept with Maid Marion? Like all the way?"

Quarry gave him a disgusted whack on the back of his head.

Boulder crossed his arms over his chest. "Told you she was kidnapped." He smugly informed the world at large. "She loves the commander. I knew it the whole time."

Nicholas crumpled the letter in his fist. "Hood took her." He intoned. "The letter says Hood is a king '*here*' in the forest. Not '*there*' in the forest. He's already got her in Sherwood."

Every single gargoyle bought into that explanation without argument. Robin Hood was hated, so they all would have eagerly blamed him even without the evidence. Grunts of agreement and dark scowls filled the room.

"Hood probably came through the secret passage to snatch Marion." Boulder muttered.

"You should've found it when she told you to!" Oore snapped back.

"You didn't find it either!"

"I didn't know it existed. Nobody ever tells me anything. I didn't even know we could have True Loves!"

Nicholas ignored them. "Trevelyan put a tracking spell on Marion and me. It connects us when were more than a mile apart." Determination filled him, blocking out his desperate fear and giving him something to hold onto. "I can find her. I *will* find her."

"Anything wrong, Sheriff?" Alan A. Dale pulled his attention from interrogating Pecos Bill, sensing an even bigger story brewing.

"Not for long." Nicholas started for the door. He'd always been goal oriented and now he had a goal like no other. "I'm just going to get my girl."

Nothing in the world could keep him from Marion's side.

...Unfortunately, that's when the dead king arrived.

Chapter Thirty-Eight

**Countdown of the biggest scandals I've ever covered, as a seasoned and impartial reporter of truth:
Number 2: That time King Jonathan came back.**

Alan A. Dale- "Nottingham's Naughtiest News"

King Jonathan was back!

The beloved ruler of Nottingham was alive and well, after all these years. It was the miracle every citizen had prayed for. Jonathan rode through the cobblestone streets, with an army of knights on white horses. Blue and gold banners flapped in the misty air and, for just a moment, the majesty of the kingdom had been restored. People stopped and gaped as the procession went by, wonder in their eyes.

It was glorious.

It was magical.

It was complete and total bullshit.

There was no way in the world King Jonathan had been resurrected. *None.* Robin Hood's father was dead somewhere in the forest. Nicholas had no doubt about that. He'd been pushed into a shallow grave by Richard, with that damn scepter still on his belt. That's why Trevelyan had claimed it was buried. Jonathan had been carrying the proof of his secret child when he died, not knowing the scepter would be lost along with him. It only made sense, if you examined the evidence.

This was the Wraith.

Nicholas took a beat to review his options, his straightforward mind running scenarios. He couldn't stop this madness without killing a lot of people and killing people would take time. He couldn't waste time. The longer he spent defending the kingdom from the Wraith, the longer Marion was at Hood's mercy. He didn't need a betrothal rights pledge to know guarding his bride took precedence over guarding Nottingham. She took precedence over *everything.*

So really there was only *one* option.

He stalked down the front steps of the castle, already dismissing the spectacle from his mind. He needed to find Marion. Nothing else mattered. Certainly, not this spangled, shiny, patriotic sideshow.

The sight of a living, breathing Jonathan was overwhelming to the not-very-bright citizens, though. The fact that the Nottinghamers were being fooled by the Wraith's elaborate use of power pissed Nicholas off. Magic crackled the air, raising the hairs on Nicholas' arms. There was *so much* dark energy being used to create the procession. Surely, some of the townsfolk could feel it, too. But the illusion was what they wanted to see, so they believed it without question.

"Shit." Quarry muttered from beside him. "Now, what do we do?"

"Rescue my wife." Nicholas kept walking.

Every bit of his rock-hard determination was focused on Marion. The Wraith and Robin Hood might be working together, but *Hood* was the one who had his girl. Therefore, he was the one who died first. Nicholas needed to save his True Love from her backwoodsman of an ex-boyfriend, as quickly as possible. Dealing with the Wraith and Nottingham and everything else would have to wait. Marion was his only focus.

The rest of the guards followed Nicholas, their wary eyes on fake-Jonathan and the small army of knights filling the castle courtyard. The mounted soldiers were illusions, but that didn't make the sight less imposing.

"Stand down, men!" King Jonathan called to the gargoyles with fake joviality.

None of the gargoyles stood down.

The palace guards weren't the passionless, predictable, purposeless robots Nottinghamers believed. They had minds of their own. As a unit, the gargoyles backed Nicholas. They trusted him. They *liked* him. They'd follow his orders, even though disobedience to the crown might mean their own deaths. They were already pulling their swords and backing him up.

In the midst of everything, Nicholas appreciated his family's loyalty.

Fake-Jonathan looked a little perturbed that he couldn't easily seize control of the palace guards. He switched his attention to Nicholas. "Halt, Sheriff!" He proclaimed in a ringing voice. "I have come to reclaim my throne!"

Nicholas kept walking.

The phony-king's pronouncement was met with cheers from the growing crowd. Wide-eyed townsfolk gazed up at fake-Jonathan like he was a messiah. Several hundred young men, who'd grown-up hero-worshipping the dead king, gathered around him. They were ready to blindly follow his commands.

"For too long, Nottingham has suffered under my warmongering brother and his gargoyle henchmen." Fake-Jonathan shouted to the adoring masses. "But now I have returned!"

More cheers. Tears rolled down cheeks. People hugged each other. Much-the-Miller pushed to the front of the crowd, stars in his eyes and righteousness on his face. Nottingham wasn't willing to rally to Robin Hood's aid at the May Day Festival, but they were all-in on their long-lost martyr. Jonathan was the easiest answer to all their problems. They were already blocking the road, preventing the gargoyles from leaving.

"My beloved son, Robin Hood, and I will put this kingdom back in order!" Fake-Jonathan continued. "Richard is dead. The war has ended. Nottingham is back to normal, Good people. All the villains will be expelled from our kingdom, starting with Maid Marion and the gargoyles."

A chant of Jonathan's name began, illustrating Nottingham's approval of the plan. Now, the smallminded populous had a group of dissidents to blame for all their troubles and a flawless hero to smite them down. It was backwards, and mean-spirited, and absurd. ...Just like Nottingham itself.

Nicholas' eyes flashed over to fake-Jonathan, not caring about the crowd's growing enmity. "Move or I will kill you now, instead of later." He warned.

"You dare to speak that way to a king!"

"You're not Jonathan. You're a bug."

Shocked gasps echoed from the townsfolk. They weren't used to hearing him talk at all, let alone insult a "king." Nicholas' popularity was already at an all-time low, because of Marion's "let's hit everyone with a hammer" plan. He'd forgotten to cancel that idea after they'd discovered L.J. was the Wraith, so a lot of people had bruised hands this morning. None of the humans were in the mood to listen to a gargoyle about *anything*.

Fake-Jonathan knew he'd already won the crowd. He looked right at Nicholas and smiled. His eyes were Huntingdon brown. The same as Marion's. ...Only they *weren't* the same. Even from a distance, Nicholas could see they were different. The Wraith couldn't copy people exactly. The eyes were always a little bit wrong.

"What do you mean he's not Jonathan?" Much-the-Miller cried indignantly. "Look at him!"

"Yes, *look* at him." Nicholas agreed impatiently. "It's been a dozen years and he hasn't aged a day!" His handsome face was exactly the same as it had been on the afternoon he disappeared. "You don't think there's some kind of dark magic involved in that?"

"He has excellent genes! He's *royalty*." Much-the-Miller yelled back.

"You said *peasants* were the ones with the hardy genes." The President of the Peasants' Guild had been loudly proclaiming that fact at the May Day festival.

The other man frowned. For half a second, Nicholas thought logic might win out over Nottingham's usual mire of toxic tradition. That Much-the-Miller might break free of the past, the way Marion and the gargoyles had. That he'd choose a new future.

Then, Much-the-Miller shook his head, preferring the simplicity of mindless compliance over following his own judgement. "We all have to play our roles, in this kingdom. I'll never be a pianist. You'll never be anything but a gargoyle. Jonathan will *always* be a king. We need to accept who we really are!"

"I *know* who I really am. I'm Nick Greystone."

Fake-Jonathan shook his head, like he pitied Nicholas. "Bring Maid Marion out and the two of you will receive fair trials, before you hang."

The demand made Nicholas frown. "Marion's not here." Didn't the Wraith know that?

"Of course, she's here. Where else would that fixated bitch be? She's *always* with you."

Nicholas recalled the notes Marion had shown him, indicating the Wraith alone had been behind that puppet show attack. And now Robin Hood wasn't keeping his cricket sidekick apprised of his plans today. Interesting.

Nicholas' wicked-impulses had him exploiting the rift. "Hood took Marion. Didn't he tell you?"

The fake-Jonathan's eyes widened, anger and concern flashing on his face. "You're lying!"

Just for the hell of it, Nicholas gave his best impression of a Trevelyan smirk. "I'm not."

Fake-Jonathan's jaw clenched, proving the dragon's favorite expression was rage-inducing across species. He refocused on swaying the crowd. "Nottingham is too clever to fall for your tricks, rock-monster. Your days of terrorizing these Good people are over. I'm here to restore law and order... for the brilliant, worthy *humans*." There was a gleeful taunt to that final word, because humans were nothing but toys to the Wraith. Puppets it could dance around and masks it could wear.

"Nottingham is for humans!" Someone cried from the back of the crowd.

"Gargoyles aren't even really *real!*" Another voice declared.

"King Jonathan's come back to save us from the Sheriff

of Nottingham!" Much-the-Miller assured them loudly. "We need to listen to our royal champion!"

"King Jonathan is dead. This is an imposter." Nicholas scanned the scores of angry faces before him. He wasn't good with words, but he tried one last time to make them see. "If you were in the war, you know a monster just like this one attacked us, a few nights before Kirklees. It takes the faces of people we trust and uses that trust to its advantage. This is *not* Jonathan."

"It *is* Jonathan, you traitor!" Much-the-Miller bellowed back and the rest of the citizens hooted in agreement.

"Then where has he been for so long? Why is he suddenly coming back now? And where are the knights he rode in with?" Nicholas gestured around, because the illusion of the armed men had already faded. Did they not see that? Did they not *want* to see it?

The crowd descended into muttering and denials. Hostile glares were shot at Nicholas. It had nothing to do with Marion's plan to hit them with hammers or Nicholas' lack of communication skills. In that moment, nothing could have convinced them of the truth. They weren't going to listen to what they didn't want to hear. It was the natural state of Nottinghamers. Throughout the courtyard, there was a refusal to believe what was blatantly obvious to anyone willing to think for themselves.

Nottingham would never, ever change. It was no wonder Marion was so eager to leave it behind.

Fake-Jonathan laughed, confident that the scores of townsfolk were about to assassinate its foes. This was how the monster liked to operate; turning its unsuspecting victims against some target of its choosing. Maybe it thought the gargoyles would hesitate in killing humans, even if the humans were trying to kill them.

Nicholas wasn't hesitating.

Marion was in danger and seconds were ticking by. The Nottinghamers were on their own. He'd given them a chance, but he couldn't save people too stupid to save themselves. He glanced at the other gargoyles. The rest of the men stood behind the lieutenants, awaiting orders. They looked at him, stoically expecting to die fighting for an empty castle.

"We're leaving." Nicholas decided ruthlessly. "Kill anyone who gets in our way."

Dozens of stony eyebrows shot up.

"Kill the Sheriff of Nottingham!" Fake-Jonathan raised a hand over his head in victorious command. "We're taking back my kingdom!"

The crowd roared in agreement, ready to do his bidding. The judgmental townsfolk had no issue at all with their false king's order. They began grabbing up weapons and marching forward, towards the hated gargoyles.

Much-the-Miller led the way. "Kill the sheriff!"

"Kill Maid Marion, too!" Tilda, the witch-practitioner, shrieked from somewhere in the mob. "If she stands with the gargoyles, she doesn't deserve Prince Robin Hood!"

"Get me some arrows and I'll kill them all!" Gilbert Whitehand, Nottingham's second best archer, boasted with bloodthirsty assurance.

Nicholas and the other gargoyles took up defensive positions. They didn't have much of a choice, but none of them were eager to harm civilians. Most of them were only armed with pitchforks and clubs.

"How do we kill *that* thing?" Quarry demanded, his eyes still on the Wraith. "That's the only way we're getting out of here."

"Pinocchio says we need a hammer."

"What?" Quarry flashed him an incredulous look. "Is *that* why the men are going around town, crushing people's fingers? Because I don't remember stopping the last Wraith that way. The human soldiers just shot that fucker with flaming-arrows."

"Pinocchio says it regenerated, because we didn't finish it off with a hammer." Nicholas paused, thinking that idea over. "But anything that little wooden prick tells me, I believe the opposite."

Ordering the palace guards to whack random citizens

with hammers was easy enough and made Marion happy. Nicholas had been willing to give it a try. But wagering his True Love's life on Pinocchio's truthfulness...? Hell, no.

Nicholas glanced Quarry's way. "Do we still have that Oak Major 1000, locked in the armory?"

Quarry warily nodded. "Yeah, but *we* can't use it." Gargoyles sucked at archery. Their large hands snapped bowstrings. "We'd need a human to fire that thing."

"Hood *took* my human." And Nicholas was getting her back, if he had to slay every monster in the world. "The crossbow has a trigger. I'll figure out the rest as I go. Get it. Now."

Quarry took off running towards the castle.

Nicholas started for the Wraith.

Fake-Jonathan bared his teeth in an animalistic snarl and moved towards Nicholas, reacting to the challenge.

Before they could reach each other, an explosion rocked Nottingham. A huge fireball was catapulted against the city walls, detonating in a reverberating crash of flames and destruction. Almost simultaneously, another projectile impacted the roof of the castle, igniting it and propelling stone through the air.

Nicholas hadn't seen anything like it since Kirklees.

More importantly, he hadn't *heard* anything like it.

The sounds were overwhelming. Screams and booms and smashing and horses and crying and breaking and running... It was like being dropped back into the war. Rioting townspeople fled in terror, as rocks and sparks fell onto the courtyard. The wedding staff joined them, evacuating the burning castle and adding to the disorder in the streets.

The gigantic gazebo-shaped building housing the multistory wedding cake collapsed, flooding the cobblestones with exotic strawberries and buttercream. It was a quagmire of panicked pedestrians and white frosting.

Alan A. Dale tripped on the mile-long red carpet lining the castle steps and fell into a decorative arrangement of gigantic talking flowers. The gigantic talking flowers screamed in outrage.

The parrot sommelier flew away as fast as its wings would carry it, its tiny top hat falling off in its haste to escape.

Pecos Bill stood in the middle of the pandemonium, his cowboy hat tipped back on his head and a pissed-off expression on his face. "Damnation, this is one fucked-up day."

More fireballs fell.

Fake-Jonathan wheeled around on his horse, his wrong-eyes wide with surprise and fear. Whatever was happening, it wasn't part of the creature's plan.

Nicholas continued forward, still intending to grab the Wraith. He was more than willing to see what kind of damage he could do, even as the city burned. He blocked out the cacophony of sound ricocheting around in his head, because all that mattered was Marion. Fake-Jonathan was standing between him and his wife, so Nicholas was going to move the bastard. It was that simple.

Spotting Nicholas approaching and the crowd scattering, the Wraith panicked. Spurring his horse, he slammed through the crowd and vanished into the bedlam. People were trampled in the escape, adding to the noise and confusion. There was no way Nicholas could catch up.

But at least the road was clear.

"Commander?" Rockwell's voice was strange. "I think you'd better look at this."

Nicholas' head turned, his gaze fixing on the open portcullis at the city gate.

An army was marching into Nottingham.

Crossing the drawbridge, the men headed up the main street, straight for the castle. Not an illusion or a rabble of angry farmers. An *actual* army. How was that possible? There were safeguards in place at the kingdom's borders. How could hundreds of warriors get past them? More importantly, how long would it take to kill them all, now that they were here?

Too long.

Nicholas scowled.

"Are we supposed to fight?" Oore wanted to know, his attention on the invasion. "Because there's a shit-ton of guys headed this way."

"No." The Wraith and this new army could argue for supremacy, if they chose. Nicholas was *leaving*. "Fuck 'em all." He looked back at the gargoyles. "The kings are dead, the city is dying, and Nottingham doesn't want us here." His voice rang out over the chaos. "I'm going to the beach with my True Love. Are you coming?"

The other men nodded, like that was the most inspiring speech he'd ever given.

Hell, maybe it *was*.

"Good. Let's go." Nicholas headed for the gate, ready to go right through the army, if that's what it took to reach Sherwood. The smoldering palace was his resignation letter. As the army drew closer, Nicholas spotted a new problem with his very straightforward plan to rescue his bride and live happily ever after under a palm tree.

Centaurs.

The invaders were goddamn *centaurs*.

With the heads of men and the bodies of horses and every kind of savage weapon imaginable. And not just *any* centaurs. No. Nicholas recognized the gory signets on their strange armor. A hydra, finger-painted with the blood of their last kill. You couldn't miss it. That was the point. Only the barbarian leader and his chosen men wore that distinctive mark, so their enemies would know to be pissing-their-pants terrified before they died.

Nessus Theomaddox had just arrived in Nottingham.

What the *hell* was happening?

Quarry rejoined him at the front, handing Nicholas the Oak Major 1000. The weight of it in his palm distracted Nicholas for an instant. The heavy weapon was oversized for human soldiers, but it fit his rocky hand surprisingly well.

"Centaurs." Quarry muttered, surveying the opposing forces. "Your wedding day is really not going so well, Commander."

Nicholas had to agree. Maybe he *had* jinxed the damn thing.

Rockwell's crumbling face was pale. "The centaurs will slaughter us."

"I'm not dying today." Nicholas refused to even consider it. Nothing was stopping him from reaching Marion. He had no clue how to quickly kill a centaur, but he was about to find out. Hell, maybe a hammer would work. Quarry had brought one of those, too.

The largest of the centaurs led the army, as they rode towards the burning castle. He halted in the middle of the road, seeing Nicholas' approach, and his gargantuan arms crossed over his bare chest. He wore a horned helmet on his head, and bandolier straps across his torso, and nothing else at all. In his horse-man form, the back half of him was a massive ebony stallion.

Nicholas stopped directly in front of him. "Move." He said flatly.

"You are Nick Greystone?" The centaur demanded in a heavily-accented voice.

There was literally nothing else the man could have said that would have gotten his attention so fast. ...Because there was only one person who ever used that name.

"I'm Nick." He agreed, momentarily startled out of his relentless determination. "You know Marion?"

"Not yet." The centaur reached into one of the bandolier pouches and came up with a folded sheet of paper. "I will, though, if one believes this letter. Your mate is a crafty and treacherous woman. She and I will be friends, I think."

Nicholas blinked, trying to catch up with his wife's newest creatively villainous plan.

"I am Nessus Theomaddox, Lord of the Desert and Mountains."

"Yeah, I figured that. You almost massacred me at Kirklees."

"Ah..." Nessus Theomaddox nodded in fond recollection. "The gargoyle who led his superiors into my trap."

The other gargoyles smiled proudly at that synopsis, their tension easing when they saw the centaurs weren't there to restart the war with them.

Nicholas frowned. "That's not exactly what..."

Nessus Theomaddox kept right on talking. "Yes, I've

fought Nottingham, for many years. It is a corrupt and spiteful land. But, now I rule it all." He shrugged, black eyes scanning the cowering city. "Your mate has given it to me. She believes I should burn this kingdom to the ground."

"Yeah, I figured that, too." Nicholas came forward to take the letter, already knowing what he'd read. It was inevitable. Marion wanted Nottingham destroyed and she was best buddies with every deranged psycho in the world.

Dear Nessus,

You don't know me yet, but I'm from the future. We'll meet in the Wicked, Ugly, and Bad Prison. You teach me how to fight, which I greatly appreciate. I help you with art projects, so the nurses don't hassle you at craft time. We are kinda-sorta friends.

On page two of this letter, I've included a list of all the stuff I remember you telling me, which I think should back up my claim. I mean, how else would I know that your childhood dog was named "Dog"? Sadly, you'll die trying to escape the WUB Club, so I suggest you don't go. You'll soon lose some big battle near the Brocéliande Oasis, which is how you get sent there. I'm pretty sure they torture you first and keep you enslaved for years.

Bottom line: You should move. <u>Immediately.</u>

I recommend taking over Nottingham! On pages three through eleven, I have included some helpful hints on how to avoid the kingdom's barriers and sneak in undetected. My father's library was full of maps. It was no trouble to draw you a route full of shortcuts. (Captain Hook taught me some cartography. You don't know him yet, either, but he was at our craft table.) Anyhow, I hate Nottingham and think it would do much better under your rule. Just spare the innocent and the rare plants.

My husband's name is Nick Greystone. He and the other gargoyles will be leaving Nottingham with me, so you don't need to worry about any resistance. That's all I want in return for the kingdom: A new beginning with my family. Kodamara vadu. You once told me that means a favor between

friends. This favor gives both of us a better future, my friend. Burn Nottingham to ashes and start fresh.
> *Best wishes,*
> *Maid Marion*

Despite the frantic pounding of his pulse and everything around him falling into anarchy, Nicholas felt his mouth curve. Reading her cheerfully bloodthirsty words filled him with hope and connection. His thumb brushed over her familiar handwriting and he drew in a deep breath.

Marion Greystone could write one hell of a letter.

His gaze went up to the centaur. "Your dog was named 'Dog?'" He wasn't great at conversations, but it seemed like a reasonable thing to say, under the circumstances.

"In the centaur language, yes." Nessus Theomaddox shrugged, as if it made perfect sense. "He was a dog."

Nicholas nodded. It made sense to him, too.

"As you can see, I have taken your woman's advice and evaded capture." Nessus went on. "Many enemies are dead and I remain free." Villainous satisfaction radiated in his voice. "Everything she wrote me has proven true. Was she also correct about your desire to leave this land, gargoyle?

"My wife is the sharpest person you'll ever meet." Nicholas said honestly. "She's always right." He handed the paper back to him. "Welcome to Nottingham. It's all yours."

Overthrowing a kingdom for Marion was easier to accomplish than he'd ever expected.

Nessus Theomaddox smirked.

Nicholas was done with talking about this invasion. There didn't seem to be any problems between the gargoyles and the centaur, so he could skip the part where he killed them all. "My wife has been kidnapped. I'm going to go murder the son of a bitch who took her, now."

Nessus Theomaddox grunted, as if that also made perfect sense.

"The castle's that way." Nicholas pointed over his shoulder. "You just set it on fire, so it's hard to miss."

Nessus grunted, again.

"Try not to incinerate all the citizens. They're useless bigots, but they're too stupid to know much better." Nicholas thought for half-a-second. "Okay, that's all you need to understand about running the place. The finances are a mess. But don't worry, the asshole who robs most of your tax revenue is about to die." He started walking, easily looping the bulky Oak Major 1000 around his shoulder. "Good luck with the crown. Move out of my way."

The centaurs shifted aside.

Nicholas and every palace guard headed past them and towards Sherwood Forest. The lieutenants all followed their commander and the soldiers all followed their lieutenants. After years of bitterness and disapproval, the Nottinghamers were finally free from gargoyles.

Just in time for Nessus Theomaddox, barbarian warlord and craft time dropout, to become the undisputed King of Nottingham.

Chapter Thirty-Nine

**Countdown of the biggest scandals I've ever covered, as a seasoned and impartial reporter of truth:
Number 1: Maid Marion breaking up with Robin Hood.
For really *real*.**

Alan A. Dale- "Nottingham's Naughtiest News"

    The Sheriff of Nottingham wouldn't come to save her.

    Nicholas would leave Marion to fend for herself. He'd believe the letter she left. He wouldn't see the secret "strategic wildflower supplies" message alerting him to trouble. He'd go on with his life, barely noticing she was gone. Even if he *did* realize she'd been kidnapped, Robin's forest hideout was too well-guarded and Nicholas was too smart. He wouldn't risk coming here. Not for Marion. She was all alone, just like always.

    When the chips were down, you couldn't count on True Love to save you.

    Marion shut her eyes, blocking out the doubts that plagued her. She *knew* they were lies. She knew that Nicholas loved her, even if the big dummy hadn't actually said the words. She trusted him with her life and heart and body. …But this situation dragged-up all her worst insecurities.

    She was standing in a wedding dress, waiting to be rescued.

    "My gold is *gone!*" Robin ranted, pacing around the Merry Men's open-air hideout. "The entire storeroom is empty!" He swung a hand towards the wooden structure behind him. "How could that have happened? There's no one left to steal it! You had all my followers arrested!"

"Maybe the Wraith took it." Marion suggested, because keeping him screaming about the missing treasure was her best option.

She was tied up with magical ropes, so stalling was the only plan she had, right now. Writing Nicholas that good-bye note had been Robin's idea, but Marion had seized on it as a way to tell him she needed help. Hopefully, her instinctive fears were all bullshit and Nicholas would arrive, if she just bought some time.

They *were* bullshit and he *would* arrive.

Weirdly, the betrothal rights helped to keep Marion reassured about that. Whenever panic threatened, she'd recall his promise to always keep her safe. Noblemen saw betrothal rights as strictly ceremonial, but Nicholas considered them sacred. Marion had given herself into his care and he'd pledged to guard her with his life. He *meant* those words with everything inside of him. Every promise, every smile, every touch was Nicholas swearing his devotion to her. She saw that, now. He took the betrothal vows as seriously as a wedding. Her husband would come for her.

And in the meantime, she'd work on getting herself untied.

"The Wraith did *not* take the gold!" Robin yelled, like she'd insulted him. "Mangiafuoco adores me!"

Was that the Wraith's actual name? Huh. It was quite a mouthful. No wonder it preferred "L.J."

Robin continued freaking out about his missing money. "I was going to use that gold to finance my new utopian kingdom and now it's *gone!*"

"*That's* why you've been stealing the tax revenue? To build that stupid forest realm you're always jabbering about?

"It's not stupid! And I'm not 'stealing.' I'm the *king*. It all belongs to me, by right."

"What about *my* money? That sure as hell didn't belong to you."

"It will when we're married." He shrugged without remorse. "And I put your name next to mine on half the companies I bought, didn't I?" A pause. "I mean, part of that was a liability insurance thing, yeah, but..."

"We're not *getting* married, you thief."

"I'm not the thief here!" Robin pointed to his store room again, his face alight with outrage. "Whoever *robbed* me is the thief. They burned a hole right into the side of the building and carted my gold away! *Tons* of it. How could they even carry so much?" He shook his head. "It had to be magic. It *had* to be."

Marion frowned a bit. Magic? She looked closer at the large wooden structure. Sure enough, one wall had a doorway blazed right through it. Robin had attempted to close it up, by nailing some half-ass boards over the opening, but there was no mistaking the gaping hole.

Or the smoldering handprint left at the scene of the crime, scorched into the wood, like a signature. Even Nicholas would agree that was all the evidence needed to settle on a perpetrator. Dragons loved to mark stuff. And steal stuff. And burn stuff.

And they understood the concept of *kodamara vadu*, even if they didn't want to admit it.

"Trev." Marion nearly smiled, despite the circumstances.

Sometimes she recalled why she'd missed that dickhead so much, when he died in prison. Trevelyan robbing Robin Hood just made all his selfish, dragon-y drama worthwhile. Too bad he hadn't roasted the dipshit alive, while he was at it.

She was pissed at her former boyfriend. Beyond pissed. Her ex was in for a rude awakening when she got out of her bindings and beat the living crap out of him.

Only one man was allowed to abduct Marion and it sure wasn't Robin.

Robin scraped both hands through his hair, coming up with a new theory of the crime. "Maybe the sheriff took the gold. He's always been jealous of me. Did the sheriff take the gold?"

"Nope."

"He must have!" Robin shouted. "Who else could've done it? Everyone in this kingdom loves me, except *him*. He hates that you're my girl and not his."

"If I was yours, you wouldn't have had to knock me out to get me here, you foliage-wearing moron."

Marion had discovered why the castle was always so drafty. There was a network of tunnels connecting the massive fireplaces. Robin had gotten into her bedroom through the hidden access, while she'd been getting dressed. He'd bashed her over the head, before she even realized what was happening.

Which meant he could've saved her from Nicholas, the first time around.

She assumed Robin hadn't shown up, back then, because it would've meant marrying her himself. Robin couldn't have returned her to the Huntingdon estate, because Nicholas would've just stolen her again. And he certainly couldn't have spirited a Maid off into the woods unchaperoned, without a ring on her finger. It was easier for him to just pout and do nothing, at all.

Instead of pissing her off, that realization brought nothing but relief. Thank God her ex-boyfriend was such an immature ass-clown. Spending her life married to him would've been a nightmare. Robin's selfish stupidity had led Marion to her True Love and she'd be forever grateful.

But she was still going to beat the crap out of the kidnapping asshole.

While she was at it, she might beat the crap out of Nicholas, too. Or at least say "I told you so" fifty million times. She'd *told* him sleeping in his bed all night would jinx the wedding, but he hadn't listened. Now, her perfect wedding dress was getting dirty, and her glacier ice sculptures were probably melting, and she was missing Pecos Bill's lighting check, with the heart-shaped, neon spotlight made of moonbeams.

Also, Robin seemed to have some deluded idea that *he* was going to marry her.

So... yeah. That was an issue.

Marion worked on prying the ropes off her wrists. She'd learned a lot about magical knots from Captain Hook, but it was hard to get them untangled with her wrists bound.

"The theft doesn't matter." Robin decided, like he was trying to convince himself. "I won't *let* it matter. I'll just have Greystone arrested, for stealing it. Now that the birth certificate's been found, I'll finally be declared king." He sent her an inquiring glance. "You brought it with you, right?"

The Wraith must know that they'd unburied the scepter, but not what happened next. Marion was glad she got to be the one who broke the sad news.

"The birth certificate hidden in that lion-headed golden staff?"

"Right!"

"The one that proves your King Jonathan's son and the heir to the throne?"

"Of course!"

"The one you tricked me into looking for?"

"Yes! Do you have it?"

"I *did*..." Marion smirked, completely unrepentant. "But, that's the exact birth certificate I destroyed. Whoops."

Robin stopped pacing and turned to blink at her.

"I tore it to pieces, last night." She arched a brow. "Now what, *your majesty?*"

"Wha...?" He said stupidly.

"It's *gone*. So are Richard and Jonathan, so good luck with a DNA test." She adopted a look of mock helpfulness. "It won't prove you're king, but I guess *we* could get one." She gestured between them with her bound hands. "Being that we're *goddamn cousins* and you failed to mention it."

"Second cousins, once removed. Maybe even third cousins. Don't be so dramatic." Robin clearly didn't care much about the dangers of inbreeding. All his focus was on his royal pedigree. "What do you mean you destroyed the birth certificate? You're lying, right? You wouldn't really have done that."

"Except I did." His ruination wasn't nearly as satisfying to witness as she'd imagined. Turned out, she didn't even care enough about Robin to care that she'd successfully wrecked his dreams. He simply didn't matter, at all.

"You've *got* to be lying. Destroying it would take away your chance to be my queen."

One of the knots in her bindings came loose, but Marion still didn't have enough slack to wiggle her hands free. "I don't want to be your queen. Why would I want to be your queen? I'm in love with Nick."

"You're still upset with me, so you're lying." He shook his head, unshakably convinced that he was right. "About all of it."

"I'm *not* lying about any of it."

He didn't want to believe that, so he wouldn't. "I'm about to make everything up to you, Marion. After all your years of patience, I'm finally going to make you my bride. You've earned that."

It amazed Marion that she'd dated this shithead for so long and never killed him out of sheer frustration.

Robin kept talking. "Since Friar Tuck is in prison, thanks to that rock-monster sheriff, I'll marry us myself. Kings are allowed to do that."

"No, they're not. And I'm sick of the bigoted, bullshit names you call gargoyles, so I…"

Robin cut her off, refusing to listen. "You're too pure to understand how the world really works, but I'll help to guide you. This will be a kingdom for humans and Good folk, not those hideous creatures. I'll get rid of all the gargoyles, after we marry."

"How are you going to 'get rid' of Nick? Last time you fought, he broke your jaw."

He moved closer to her, seething. "Just do as you're told, for once! And get that damn crown off your head." He grabbed her May Day Queen tiara and threw it into the bushes. "I don't want you wearing anything *he* gave you to our wedding!"

Marion reached the end of her patience. "*I will never marry you, Robin!*" Her voice echoed endlessly through the dense forest.

His fist clenched and he drew in a deep breath, trying to calm down. "You're emotional and illogical, like all Maids. So much excitement has made you overwrought. Soon, this will all be behind us and everything will go back to normal. We'll be just as we were before."

Marion wasn't sure if he was talking to her or to himself. It didn't matter, because her answer was the same either way. "You wouldn't survive the honeymoon. I'd make sure of it."

"You'll come around, once we're ruling together, side by side." Robin paused, as if evaluating his own words. "...Well, obviously *I'll* be in charge. But, you can raise my heirs." He smiled condescendingly, like he felt in control again. "That's *such* an important job."

"I don't even want children."

He ignored that. "Let's just get this ugly ring off you and..." He tried to pry the massive ruby from her finger, but it didn't budge. The wedding band was sealed tight, courtesy of the strongest magic in the land. Only Marion could remove it and Marion would *never* remove it.

Triumph filled her.

"What the fuck...?" Robin gave the ruby another desperate pull, realization dawning. "What have you done, Marion?" His voice became shrill with shock. "What the fuck have you *done?!*"

"I found my True Love and I married him." She yanked her palm back from Robin. "Not in that order."

Furious blue eyes flew to hers. "You stupid little slut, you *married* him?" He seized her upper arm, not letting her retreat. His grip bit into her flesh, leaving marks. "You let that *creature* --that *thing*-- put his ugly hands on you?! When you were supposed to be pure?" He shook her furiously. "When you were supposed to be *mine?*"

Marion kneed him in the balls. Hard. The green tights offered no protection, at all.

Robin made a high-pitched shrieking sound and hit the forest floor.

"*That's* for my tiara." Marion kicked him, again. Once

you had someone down, you kept hitting them, until he stopped moving. Nessus Theomaddox had drilled that rule into her head, back when he taught her to fight. "And *that's* for my father." The second blow broke bones. His sixth and seventh rib, if she wasn't mistaken. Robin curled into a ball of agony. "And that's for *me*." The third seemed to leave him dazed, possibly because she'd aimed it at his dumb, lying, thieving face.

Marion fully intended to kick Robin right into unconsciousness, but long, bug-like arms suddenly grabbed her from behind and pulled her away. She let out a shout of alarm, as she was lifted off her feet and tossed to the ground. She landed against the side of the burned storage room.

The Wraith stood over her.

It *was* a big cricket. At least that's what it looked like, with a greenish-brown oval-shaped body and long antenna. Only parts of it seemed oddly humanoid, too. Like something out of a science-fiction story, where desperate creatures were morphed together. Jutting limbs and a razor-sharp mandible, and strange silver eyes. It was at least seven feet tall and its insectoid face radiated a crafty intelligence. And hatred. The big cricket *hated* her, in a weirdly personal way.

Marion was used to living with villains of all shapes and sizes, but this being was something else. This was pure malevolence.

Robin made a groaning noise.

The Wraith quickly transformed into L.J., like the monster had never been there, at all. In a matter of seconds, it was an innocent looking teenager, turning towards Robin.

"What is she doing here?" The Wraith demanded in L.J.'s voice. "Why didn't you tell me you were going to bring her to the camp?"

"I'm the king. I don't need to run my decisions past you." Robin ground out, talking through his teeth.

The Wraith looked angry. "Marion has served her purpose. I told you she was the only one in Nottingham capable of finding the scepter and she *did*. Her brain doesn't work exactly like everybody else's. She thinks of shit we can't.

Not even I understand what she's up to half the time and I've seen inside her head! But that's why she's dangerous, too. We *have* to get rid of her."

"I'm not going to kill Marion. I've told *you* that."

"No, you'll just kidnap me and force me to marry you." Marion retorted.

"You *never* want to kill her!" The Wraith raged at Robin, ignoring her snide comment. "In the last timeline, you at least agreed to send her to jail, though. I pieced that together from her memories. This *time* around, you're competing with the sheriff to win her hand!"

"That rock-monster is *not* going to beat me." Robin gritted. "He's not going to steal my girl."

"I'm not your girl."

"She's not your girl!" The Wraith bellowed at the same time. "And this is *not* the plan I put together for us!"

"That plan was stupid from the outset." Marion focused on her dimwitted former boyfriend, because he seemed like the weakest link. "If you have a goddamn shapeshifter on your team, I can think of a thousand better ways to get control of Nottingham and turn it into some bucolic commune."

The Wraith flashed her a killing glare.

"That's what I thought, at first." Robin was still on his back. He clutched at his cracked ribs and crushed privates, one hand on each injury. "But, Mangiafuoco said…"

"Marion's trying to trick you." The Wraith interrupted. "Ignore her."

Marion shook her head. You didn't need a Ph.D. in creative villainy to see all the better schemes the Wraith had skipped over in favor of this one. "Robin, *think*. The Wraith is dragging this thing out to waste your time. That's the only explanation. It could've pretended to be Richard and just *appointed* you to the throne. It could have made up some old woman to swear she was the midwife who delivered little-baby-royal you. It even could have fired Nicholas, if he was in your way."

"Shut up!" The Wraith bellowed.

Robin lay there for a beat, considering Marion's words.

"She's trying to trick you." The Wraith repeated, sounding desperate. "I've worn the faces of half the kingdom and she's the most dangerous one, by far. It's why we've had to change things up, from our original plan. She's seen the future and I've seen inside her head!" It tapped L.J.'s temple. "I know what works this time, because I saw what went wrong before. I knew the scepter wasn't with the sheriff. I knew she could find it for us. And I was right, wasn't I?"

"Marion says she destroyed the birth certificate." Robin complained petulantly. "Can you see if *that's* true?"

A weird flash of triumph passed over the Wraith's face. "She ripped it to pieces." There was a certain smugness in the words, like it had *expected* Marion to destroy the birth certificate. Like it had *wanted* her to. Why? To make Robin angry?

No.

To make Robin angry at *Marion*.

To make him hate her.

"You should have seen this coming!" Robin bellowed at the Wraith. "You should have stopped her! Maids are emotional and illogical. I *told* you that. We never should have relied on her to help us find it, in the first place!"

"I wanted to kill her months ago!" The Wraith snapped back, psychotically intent on convincing Robin to murder her. "*You* were the one who insisted she survive. Now you see that she isn't worth your attention, though! Now, you get that she's never been worthy of..."

"Robin wasn't king in the previous timeline, either." Marion interjected. "I didn't rip up the birth certificate last time. So, why didn't he have his crown?"

Having a villainous education meant exploiting weaknesses. Sowing seeds of discontent between her two enemies seemed like a wise strategy. Marrok Wolf had taught her that, back in the WUB Club. Beneath his charming veneer, the Big Bad Wolf was clever and he took pissing people off to an art form.

Robin managed to sit up, his own self-interest

overcoming his pain. "What?"

"Richard was still king, when I traveled back. ...Which means *the Wraith* was still king." Marion had done her very best to learn nothing about Nottingham when she was locked up, but she felt like she'd have heard about her fuck-knob ex-boyfriend being declared royalty.

"We probably didn't find the scepter before!" The Wraith argued hotly. "Richard's memories got mixed up in my head and I thought it was in the castle."

Marion had no clue if that was true and didn't much care. "Or you wanted to keep power for yourself and steal Robin's throne." She speculated, just to cause trouble. "How could someone as powerful as you not find one little scepter?"

Robin glared over at the Wraith, like he was starting to believe Marion's theory.

"She's lying." The Wraith shouted. "She'll say anything to drive us apart, Robin. *This* is why we need to kill her. Can't you see that? We can't risk her being loose."

Robin scoffed like that was preposterous. "She's just a Maid. She can't really stop me. Not for long. Besides, Marion has the purest blood in Nottingham. *Royal* blood. Stupid slut or not, she's the only one worthy of being my queen."

The Wraith's jaw dropped. "What about me?"

"What *about* you?" Robin retorted in annoyance.

Since they were focused on each other, Marion switched her attention to making her own plans. Ash was all over her wedding dress, so someone needed to die. That much was clear. And the Wraith was a much bigger threat to her than Robin. She had to figure out a way to stop the monster and then she'd deal with her doofus of a...

Her gaze fell on a hammer, sitting on the ground beside her. Robin had been using it to nail boards over the scorched opening in the storeroom wall. Now, it was four inches from her hand.

Pinocchio said hammers killed Wraiths.

"I didn't do all this, so you could marry *her!*" The Wraith shrieked at Robin. "I did it so you could marry *me!*"

Marion's eyebrows shot up, forgetting about the

hammer for a second. *That* was what this was about? Apparently, the Wraith really did adore Robin. Like, *a lot.* Nicholas had been right, when he said that even monsters wanted something.

The Wraith wanted Marion out of the picture, so it could have Robin all to itself.

Of all the possible reasons for it to shoot Nicholas and send her to prison, that was one that had never even occurred to Marion. In retrospect, she wasn't sure why. Wraiths no doubt longed for a partner, just like everyone else. This convoluted plot to grow closer to Robin was less crazy than half the stuff Marion did to win Nicholas. When you were over-the-brink-of-madness fixated on someone, you weren't making the most rational choices.

Robin had never loved anything, so he didn't get that truth. "Marry *you?*" He echoed. "Are you insane?"

"I'm in love with you!" The Wraith shouted, confirming Marion's theory. "I've done *all* of this so we could spend time together. I thought, if I gave you enough time, you'd come to see we were made for each other."

Robin goggled, like the creature was speaking another language.

"I stalled a bit, when it came to making you king. I admit it. I *had* to, though!" The Wraith sounded so impassioned, Marion almost felt sorry for it.

...But it had shot Nicholas in some reality or other, so fuck that cricket.

"You mean, Marion's right!?" Robin gasped, shocked and scandalized that an evil monster would lie. "I could be king *already* and you screwed it up?"

"I didn't know where the scepter was! I swear. When I take on people's faces and memories, things can get muddled. But..." The Wraith lifted its hands and dropped them again. "We *could've* come up with a plan that didn't use the scepter, at all. Fine. I guess that's true."

"I knew it!" Robin glanced at Marion. "I *told* you."

What the hell...? "I told *you*, you colossal moron."

Robin sent her an aggrieved look, as if she was being

ridiculous and he deserved all the credit for everything that had ever happened *ever*. He was incapable of admitting he was wrong, even to himself. The man was the blue-eyed embodiment of Nottingham's stagnant hypocrisy.

The Wraith kept talking. "I needed you to get to know me, before you were swept up in courtly balls and fawning subjects, Robin. I wanted us to have a connection. And I thought we did! I thought you loved me back."

Robin seemed repulsed. "Why would you think *that?*"

"You slept with me, for one thing!"

"Only when you looked like a hot girl, or an elf with three breasts." He paused. "Or that time when you were Sir Galahad, but that's *completely* understandable." His gaze cut over to Marion, again. "You get that's completely understandable, right?"

She nodded, because it was the one thing Robin had said in ages that made sense. Sir Galahad was *Sir Galahad*. Pretty much everybody wanted to sleep with him. Camelot's favorite knight was dazzlingly gorgeous, uniquely talented, and was one day going to revolutionize snack foods.

The Wraith didn't appreciate Robin's reasoning. "So, you lied to me? All this time? That's what you're saying?"

"I never lied about anything. It's obvious we could never be together for really *real*. I'm a human and you're nothing but a giant bug!"

The Wraith's fury went ice cold. Its head tilted in an unsettling way that had Marion reaching for the hammer. "You're prejudice against giant bugs?" It asked Robin quietly.

"I mean, you're not so terrible when you're pretending to be someone normal looking." Robin began to rise to his feet, still gripping his injured side. "But, a king needs heirs and I can't have children with tentacles. The dignity of my new forest kingdom..."

The Wraith bit his head off.

There must've been some praying mantis genes mixed in with the cricket-ness, because the Wraith transformed back into its buggy form and snapped its razor-sharp jaws right around Robin's neck.

Marion let out a choked gasp of horror as her ex-boyfriend was eaten by a monster. Robin's body hit the forest floor, as the Wraith chomped up his skull and swallowed it down.

Holy *shit!*

The Wraith turned its too-intelligent compound eyes her way and now there was a gun in its hand. The same gun that had killed Nicholas in the original timeline. The one from Pinocchio's shop.

Marion's hand tightened on the hammer.

"How should 'King Johnathan' explain this to the humans?" The Wraith's real voice was a garbled vibration of sound, but she understood the words. "I think it should playout as a murder/suicide. You killed Robin and then couldn't live with your crime. So, you shot yourself in the head."

"After I ate his?" Marion got out hoarsely.

"Hmmm... That might be a problem to explain. You're right." It cocked its own head to one side. "We'll just blame the sheriff, then. He slaughtered you both, in a jealous rage, when you left him for Robin Hood."

"No one will believe that."

"People believe what they want to. What *I* want them to." The Wraith taunted. "You're all just puppets. Haven't you learned that by now?" It gave a noise that must have been its version of a laugh. "Besides, I never much liked the sheriff. He was the one who alerted those soldiers to my sibling's ruse at that army camp and got poor Jiminy killed. I've never forgotten that."

"Wait, the Wraith that died in Lyonesse was your...?"

"You think we can't have siblings?" It interrupted harshly. "You think only humans have families and wishes and passions?" It gestured towards Robin's corpse. "You think you're the only group who can feel pain?"

"Of course not. But no matter your species, you don't get to *eat people's fucking heads!*"

"If you hadn't interfered, Robin would still be alive!"

"You're the one who attacked *me!* You tried to kill me with puppets!"

534

"Because, I don't *like* you. Robin wouldn't shut up about the archery contest and winning you back from the sheriff. I lost it, alright?" Now, it sounded defensive. "L.J.'s body is good at shooting arrows, so I sent you that note and got you to the tent. With you gone, I thought Robin would finally see *me*." It jabbed the gun at her. "Why couldn't you just give me my happily-ever-after, you insufferable bitch?"

The Wraith wanted to kill her right then, but it forgot what body it was in. Maybe that was a common problem, because it switched forms so much. Or maybe it was so furious, it wasn't thinking straight. Or maybe it was just human-made weapons tended to be scaled to human hands. Nicholas had complained about the same issue with bows.

Whatever the reason, the Wraith tried to shoot her... and couldn't. Its oddly-shaped fingers didn't fit through the trigger guard. It blinked its bulbous eyes and looked down at the gun in annoyance.

That was all the opening she needed.

Before the creature could eat her alive or transform into L.J. and try shooting again, Marion moved. She couldn't credit any of her WUB Club teachings for the idea. It came from that visualization exercise Nicholas had been encouraging her to try the night before: *"Think to yourself: 'If a fearsome monster shows up, all I have to do is run like hell. Because, Nick —who carries a literal broadsword to work every day-- will slay a thousand of those fuckers, to keep me safe. I can always count on my True Love."*

Grabbing the hammer, Marion ran like hell.

She stumbled to her feet and took off into the woods. Branches reached for her, as she barreled through the underbrush, tangling in her wedding gown. Ten feet of imported tulle was not meant for sprinting through the woods. It weighed her down and she had to awkwardly gather it in her arms.

This dress was not *perfect*.

Marion held onto the voluminous skirts and kept going. What choice did she have? This was victory or death. She might be pudgy and unathletic, but pure adrenaline was coursing through her. Wheezing just meant she was still breathing. That was good enough, for now.

Behind her, she heard gunshots blasting. The Wraith chased after her, trying to shoot her through the trees. Bullets ricocheted off trunks. Marion zigzagged through the woods to avoid them, never slowing down.

Nicholas had told her to run and she listened.

The Wraith was pulling the trigger in rapid succession. Whatever body it was using now, the monster still wasn't used to human weapons. It was used to killing its foes with deceit, not firearms. It was trying to run and aim at the same time. It kept missing Marion, then getting frustrated and shooting more wildly than before. A screaming curse echoed, when the gun finally clicked empty.

Marion smiled at the sound of cricket-y rage and kept moving, deeper into the woods. She would keep going full speed ahead, all in, no stop, until she was back in her wicked husband's arms.

She could already visualize it.

***

The woods were full of Marions.

Everywhere Nicholas looked he saw his wife. She was running, crying, laughing, screaming, walking down paths, lying in the leaves, hurt, dead, climbing up the trees, beckoning him this way and that, and dancing through the shadows of Sherwood's maze-like forest.

The Wraith's magic had never been more distracting. The illusions of Marion were everywhere, constantly drawing his eyes. Dozens of them. Hundreds of them. All moving at once. All beautiful and needing his help. All dressed in wedding gowns.

Magic was hanging in the air so thick it felt like fog. It would've been impossible to find the real Marion through the colossal display, except Trevelyan's powers were even stronger. The dragon had put trackers on Marion and Nicholas, so they could always find each other. When Nicholas focused, he could feel a thread connecting him to his True Love. A thread stretching straight from his heart to hers. All he had to do was follow it.

Nicholas' men were spread out all around him, tense and watchful, as they moved through the woods. Freaked the hell out, but pushing forward. It helped that so many of them had seen these same kinds of tricks played back in Lyonesse and again with King Jonathan's disappearing army in the courtyard.

The Wraith's magic was like that truth spell the dragon had cast on Nicholas at the ball. The fog cleared from your mind, when you realized you were being manipulated. Once you knew all the crazy shit around you was fake, you could fight through the bombardment of chaos and tune it out. The Wraith was doing everything it could to lead the gargoyles off the right path, but they weren't falling for it.

Suddenly, the magic went silent.

The bevy of ghostly-Marion's blinked out of existence as quickly as they'd shown up. Nicholas jolted as the endless mirror-images of his bride flickered off. The lack of Marions was nearly as unsettling as the endless duplicates had been.

He looked around and realized he was standing in the middle of the Merry Men's hideout. All the times he'd looked for this spot, so he could arrest those moronic outlaws, and now that he'd finally found it, he couldn't care less. He just wanted Marion.

Ramshackle building stood around him, with thatched roofs and ill-fitting doors. One of the huts was half-burned. The small village seemed deserted, now. Nothing moved down the walkways between the structures or on the nearby archery practice area.

Where the hell was his wife?

Nicholas turned Rockwell's way. "Rip this fucking place apart."

Rockwell nodded, quickly shouting orders at the men.

Nicholas began peering into the huts, one-by-one, quickly scanning for his wife. She was too close now for the mystical tracker to connect them. Trevelyan said the spell worked when they were a mile apart. Since the pull in his chest was nearly gone, Marion must be within that distance.

Men had been sent to the Wicked, Ugly and Bad prison for thinking less vile things than he was now plotting. He would slaughter Hood in ways that humans had never even *heard* about. There were no limits to how far he'd go to rescue his bride. *None.*

Nicholas had promised Marion that he'd keep her safe. That she could count on him. There was no possible way he'd let her down. He would do anything. Say anything. Fight anything. Kill *anything.* He would save his True Love or die trying. That note Nicholas had sent her during the war was completely honest. The woman was all that kept him alive.

Loving Marion Greystone made him really *real.*

"Uh... Commander?"

There was a "somebody's dead" note to Cragg's tone and it filled Nicholas with a rush of dread. "Where?" He demanded, stalking over to see for himself.

Cragg pointed to the ground and Nicholas immediately spotted the blood. It was impossible to miss. There was a huge pool of it all over the forest floor, spreading out from the body in the center. A body dressed in a familiar, tree-lizard green tunic.

Holy *shit.*

Robin Hood had been murdered.

Emotions swamped him. Instant, dizzying relief, because it wasn't Marion lying there. Then, angry frustration that Nicholas hadn't been the one to kill the smug son of a bitch. And finally, confusion. Why was Hood missing his head?

Nicholas instinctively glanced around, but it wasn't there. It couldn't have rolled far and there wasn't a compelling reason for someone to steal it. Where did it go?

Boulder came up beside him and surveyed the carnage with an approving grunt. "Did Marion do this?" He asked hopefully.

"No." Nicholas had boundless faith in his wife's creative villainy, but she didn't have the upper body strength necessary to cleanly decapitate a full-grown man. Stab Hood? Sure. Castrate him? Likely. But lopping off his head...? How could she even heft a sword that high, when Hood was six inches taller than her?

At least, he *had* been six inches taller than her, back when he still had a skull.

So who had murdered this bastard? Odds said it was the Wraith. They'd fought and the monster had won. Simple and violent. Nicholas' eyes cut over to Quarry, for a second opinion.

Quarry shrugged, like he was thinking the same thing. "Guess Fake-King-Jon didn't like Hood freestyling on his own, when he took Marion." He nudged Hood's body with the toe of his boot. "Too fucking bad."

Nicholas grunted. For most of his life, he'd hated Hood, but seeing his bleeding corpse didn't bring any satisfaction. As much as he'd despised the man, he'd understood his motivations: Robin Hood wanted Marion. There was a strange sort of comfort in that knowledge, because the jackass might be a kidnapper, but at least he needed Marion alive for the wedding. Hood hadn't planned to kill her.

The Wraith didn't need Marion breathing. In fact, it *wanted* her dead. Under the circumstances, Nicholas would have much preferred Marion's ex keep his damn head attached. But, of course, Hood even had to screw *that* part up.

Imbecile.

Mentally seething at the dead man, Nicholas bent down to get a closer look at the body. Still warm. His jaw tightened. They were behind, but not by much. His gaze cut around the thick forest surrounding them. Something glinted in the underbrush. He got to his feet and went over to investigate.

Marion's plastic rhinestone tiara was lying on the ground.

Nicholas scooped it up, his fingers tightening on the plastic. His eyes closed, trying to feel which way she had gone. Wanting some kind of reassurance that she was alright.

Then, he heard a gunshot. Nicholas' eyes snapped open, listening. More gunshots. Echoing in all directions. Not illusions. They were real and most likely aimed at his wife.

Goddamn it.

It was hard to tell where the shots originated, given the way noise carried in the woods. Nicholas was sensitive to sounds, though. He always had been. Most of his life, it had been a liability, but now it helped him get a bearing.

Marion was *that* way.

He got to his feet and started towards the gunshots. "Fan out in this direction." He called to the men. "Chop down every goddamn tree in the forest, if that's what it takes to find Marion."

Chapter Forty

Fashion tips for staying cool for summer: Don't you dare be caught in white this year!

Alan A. Dale- "Neverland's Naughtiest News"

Marion had no idea which direction to go, so she just picked one. Darting between trees, she tried to put as much distance as she could between herself and Robin's camp. The hammer was still gripped tightly in her hand, weighing her down and also making her feel slightly more secure. At least she had a way to kill the Wraith, if it caught up with her.

Hopefully, it *wouldn't* catch up with her, though.

She needed to get back to the castle. For now, that was the clearest plan in her head. She fully intended to squash that monstrous bug, of course. It needed to die at least six times over for all the crap it had done. But, Marion would prefer to slaughter it when she wasn't struggling for oxygen, dressed in thirty-pounds of tulle, and lost in Sherwood. The woods were oppressive and creepy. She wanted to go home to Nicholas.

She thought she could use that tracking spell Trevelyan had put on him to guide her back to the castle, but it didn't seem to be working. Fucking dragon. She was going to kick his ass, when she finally got out of here. But, if she ran in a straight line, sooner or later she'd reach the edge of the forest, right? And if that didn't work, she'd wait until night and try to navigate her way by stars. She knew a little bit about constellations, because back at the WUB Club she'd met a Titan named Astraea who was amazing at…

"Marion, where in the frozen-hells are you?" A very annoyed dragon bellowed.

Her head whipped around. "Trev?" She stopped

running, shocked that he was still in the forest. She'd expected him to be off spending Robin's gold. She instantly forgave him for screwing up the tracking spell. "I'm over here."

"Stay where you are." The dragon shouted from somewhere in the thick grove of trees to her left. "I'll come to you."

"You will?"

"As long as it doesn't take too long. I'm not spending all day in this jungle, hunting around in the bushes for you. I don't like you *that* much."

That sounded just like something Trevelyan would say.

Except the longer she carried the amulet around in her pocket, the more she understood the different powers it was sensing. The dragon's magic was constant and strong. *Very* strong. The pendant went crazy whenever he was near. The Wraith's magic, on the other hand, was more like a buzz. That was why she hadn't realized L.J. and the Wraith were the same person. Trevelyan's colossal magic just overpowered everything else, like a roar drowning out a whisper.

And the necklace wasn't roaring.

She froze, but her mind kept racing. "I thought you left Nottingham, Trev."

"And miss your wedding? You know I'd never do that. There's a dance floor made of magic mirrors."

Bullshit. The *real* Trevelyan wouldn't care about his own wedding, let alone someone else's. Dragons didn't respect outside authority. No one else got to declare them legally wed. *They* decided they were married. The end. They might roll their eyes and tolerate a formal ceremony, but they considered it superfluous. No way would Trevelyan stay in Nottingham just to watch Marion marry Nicholas, regardless of the grand spectacle she'd created. No goddamn way.

That wasn't Trevelyan talking to her.

"We have to hurry and get you out of here." The fake-Trevelyan told her, drawing closer. "Keep talking so I can find you."

Marion's hand tightened on the handle of the hammer. Never mind. She'd just kill the bastard now and get it over with. The Wraith thought it was tricking her, pretending to be her kinda-sorta friend, but she was about to turn the tables on that miserable face-stealing fuck.

"I'm right over here." She called grimly, bracing herself to fight.

"Marion!"

Nicholas's voice sounded from the other direction. Marion's heart jumped. The Wraith couldn't impersonate gargoyles, so that was really him!

"Nick!" Relief and worry swamped her, as she raced for him. The huge skirt of her wedding dress slowed her down again, but it didn't stop her. Nothing would stop her from reaching her husband, before the Wraith somehow murdered him all over again. She shot a quick glance over her shoulder, making sure the monster wasn't following her...

And ran into a big stone wall.

The air rushed out of her lungs, as she collided with an immovable object that suddenly appeared in her path. Losing her balance, she started to fall. One huge hand caught her, pulling her close. And she knew who'd captured her.

Who *always* captured her.

"Nick." His name came out like a prayer. She'd found him and now everything would be okay. Together they could face anything. She smiled up at his handsome, comforting, familiar features...

...And instantly knew it wasn't her True Love.

She would know the really *real* Nicholas anywhere and this wasn't him. The eyes were flat. Cold. *Wrong.* Pinocchio had been lying. Wraiths *could* impersonate gargoyles. She was looking right at one.

Marion felt the blood drain from her cheeks.

The monster wearing her husband's face slowly smiled at her. "You have no idea how long I've waited to kill you. Who the hell do you think you are, trying to interfere with my plans?"

"I'm Marion, the one-and-fucking-only."

What happened next was born from countless hours of barbarian fight training. You struck hard and you fought dirty.

No hesitation. That centaur rule for survival had been drilled into her brain so many times that her body just reacted.

Marion slammed the hammer into the fake-Nicholas' temple with all her strength. The Wraith reared back with an astonished curse, releasing its hold on her and gripping its wound. She had hit it so hard that pus-like blood gushed from the injury, pouring down its chest in a thick, sticky cascade.

For just a moment, Marion thought she had won and the creature would topple over dead. Instead, the Wraith gave its head a clearing shake and righted itself. Its not-quite-right gaze focused on her, glowing with pure hatred.

Marion took a step backwards, her heart pounding. The hammer had *not* killed it. It hadn't even stunned it. It had just pissed it off.

Pinocchio, you damn little liar.

"What did Robin see in you, human?" The Wraith hissed at her in Nicholas' voice.

Marion swallowed hard. "Robin didn't actually care about me and I *certainly* don't care about him. You impersonated me, so you know my thoughts. You see that I'm crazy about Nick."

"Crazy? You should experience the inside of the gargoyle's head, if you want to see crazy." The Wraith spat out. "His obsession for you is absolutely *insane*. Everything you've ever done is taking up space in here. I now know what kind of jam you like on your toast and what your sneeze sounds like. I even know that he fantasizes about kidnapping you at your wedding, ripping the dress off you, and fucking you every way a two-legged body bends."

Hopefully, she'd lived to experience that.

The Wraith was spiraling. "How could you want this depraved creature over *Robin?* I don't understand. Robin was so perfect. A hero!"

"Oh, Robin treated us both like crap." Marion shot back. "That's why you killed him, remember?"

"I loved him and he used me!" The fake-Nicholas' face crumpled in distress and loss. "He was going to leave me to rot, while he went on with his happy life. You could never understand what that kind of betrayal feels like."

"I get wanting revenge on the people who hurt you. Believe me." Marion tried reaching out to the heartbroken creature in front of her, because she suddenly understood it, all too well. "Forget Robin. You can still find your True Love. Once you have them, you'll find a purpose beyond just…"

"I'll never forget Robin!" The Wraith shrieked, cutting her off. "Just like how I'll never forget that you turned him against me, you man-stealing whore!" It lunged for her.

Marion scrambled away, trying to think of some new plan. What the hell was she going to…?

"Marion." Nicholas suddenly said from behind her. "Move."

Marion moved. She didn't even think about it. Nicholas' really *real* voice sounded and she instinctively shifted to the side, trusting him to protect her.

She was still facing the Wraith, looking straight into its wrong eyes, as Nicholas calmly lifted the Oak Major 1000. The repeating crossbow might have been too big for human soldiers to carry around, but it fit gargoyles' larger size just fine.

Nicholas had finally found a bow he could fire.

For a man untrained in archery, he was a quick study. The red laser scope of the weapon helped him aim and his large fingers seemed to have no issue with the trigger. He smashed it down, as arrows flew straight through the fake-Nicholas' heart.

At least, Marion *assumed* that its heart was in its chest and Nicholas had hit it. Who knew the exact anatomy of a cricket? Nicholas seemed to have the same thought, because he kept shooting and shooting and shooting until the massive automatic bow finally clicked empty. In a matter of seconds, steel-tipped arrows covered the fake-Nicholas' entire body. At least a dozen of them went right through to the other side of its torso, turning it into a grotesque pincushion.

Marion cringed. Even knowing it wasn't really her True Love, it was hard to see anything that looked like Nicholas suffering.

Nicholas himself seemed fine with it. Maybe he wasn't thrilled with the phony-him professing his love for Robin Hood.

Nicholas really had detested the man. He tossed the Oak Major 1000 aside and calmly pulled a sword, in case he had to kill his doppelganger some more.

There was no need.

The Wraith was dying. Its body morphed back into its bug-like state, as if by reflex. Spindly limbs curled up against its torso, its long antenna twitching like crazy. Bulbous eyes rolled this way and that. A final spasm shook it and the Wraith toppled backwards on the forest floor. White blood poured out of its countless wounds. A wheezing breath escaped its mandibles and then there was nothing but eerie calm.

It was over.

Marion slowly turned to look at her husband.

Nicholas grunted. "That was the first time I ever shot an arrow."

"You did great for a virgin." Even to Marion's ears, her voice sounded very far away.

Nicholas gave a slow smile, closing the distance between them. "Are you alright?" He ran his wonderfully rough hands over her looking for injuries. "Are you hurt?"

"No... I... Robin took me from my room and said he wanted me to marry him." She was breathless from running and fighting and from her wild emotions. "I told him no. I'm married to *you*. And then the Wraith ate his head."

Nicholas paused in his desperate sweep of her body. "His head got *eaten?* That's what happened to it?"

"Yes! The Wraith was going to eat me, too. But you saved me." Marion could hardly believe he was there. He looked incredible. Invincible. "You came for me." There was wonder in her voice and he heard it.

"Did you think I wouldn't?" He seemed mildly exasperated.

"No, I knew you'd save me. I did." She swallowed. "But, then some small part of me thought maybe you'd believe the note. Maybe, you'd just forget about me." Belated tears filled her eyes, even though her worries had been illogical and she *knew* that. "Or maybe you'd see it was too dangerous to come."

"Marion." He cupped her face with his palms, his expression grave. "I would come for you, if it meant my own death." It was the surest vow he'd ever given her. "I would fight for you until I died... and I would die thinking only of *you*."

A tear traced down her cheek and he brushed it away with his thumb.

Deep inside, Marion knew she could've come up with a plan and beaten the Wraith all by herself. Maybe. ...But she didn't *have* to. She didn't have to do anything alone, ever again. She could *always* count on her True Love.

"I love you." Marion whispered.

Nicholas' mouth curved. "I loved you first."

She gave a watery laugh. "Well, I knew we were True Loves first."

"No. I knew you were my True Love, even when I thought it was impossible for a gargoyle to have one." Nicholas kissed her and the world was right again. "Because, you are the only one I will *ever* truly love." He must have found her plastic tiara somewhere in the woods, because he gently placed it on her head.

Marion was thrilled to have it back. "You have *completely* won yourself a fair Maid." She assured him, feeling better by the minute. "All of a sudden, I'm even swooning over archery. That was amazing! How did you know that would work? Pinocchio said arrows didn't work on Wraiths."

"Anything Pinocchio says, I believe the opposite." Nicholas scoffed. "Kill it with a fucking *hammer?* No, I told you that was bullshit, didn't I?"

She thought for a beat. "Except, I once called *you* a big, blunt hammer, remember? And *you* killed the Wraith." She shrugged. "So, maybe Pinocchio saw something..."

"Or maybe Pinocchio's just a duplicitous scumbag." Nicholas interrupted. "I should have hanged him, long ago." Releasing Marion, he stalked over to ensure the Wraith wasn't regenerating by casually hacking off its head.

Marion winced a bit. Witnessing two decapitations in one day seemed excessive.

Satisfied that the Wraith wouldn't spring back to life,

Nicholas stepped away from the corpse. "Now, we'll have the men burn it to a crisp, just to be sure it's dead. That seemed to finish off the last one in Lyonesse."

Marion wrinkled her nose. "You're ruining the romance of the moment, Nick."

He sent her a baffled look. "Romance?"

"You've heroically slayed the fearsome monster." It was literally the deadest thing she'd ever seen and she'd done time with a necromancer. "Now, we're moving on to the part of the visualization exercise where the most heroic bastard in Nottingham sweeps me off my feet. Not to be all Maidenly, but I'm very much looking forward to it."

His expression softened and he returned to her side. "Me too." Before she knew what was happening, he'd lifted her into his arms.

Marion grabbed hold of his shoulders, as he cradled her against his chest. "Very heroic." She told him, feeling safer than she had in her whole life. "This is exactly what you did after our last wedding."

"All the Nicks know a great plan when we think of it."

Marion rested her head on his shoulder. "You *are* wonderful at plans. Just like me."

"Team Creative Villainy." He kissed her forehead. "Speaking of your nefarious schemes, Nessus showed up this morning, with his barbarian horde and flaming catapults."

"Wow, he got here fast." She made an impressed face. "I forgot how efficient centaurs can be, when it comes to carnage. Great! My revenge on Nottingham can be officially crossed off the list." She made a little check mark in the air. "Now, we'll get married again and everything will be..."

Nicholas cut her off. "Nessus set the castle on fire, so I think the reception is cancelled. At least half the guest list is dead or imprisoned, by now. And I'm sure Pecos Bill's escaped."

"Oh, for God's sake..." Marion sighed in annoyance. "You have no idea how hard that damn cowboy was to track down. This is all *your* fault for jinxing things. I hope you know that."

"You're the one who invited the barbarians to our wedding venue, duchess."

"Well, I didn't know they were invading today!" She made an aggravated sound. "Centaurs have the worst timing. And you look so dashing in a bycocket. I knew you would. I was already envisioning the photos and now it's all ruined."

"Shit, do I still have that dumb hat on?" He looked upward like he might be able to see the long feather. "Wonderful."

Marion disregarded his negativity, thinking things over for a beat. "You know, a beach ceremony would be even *more* amazing in pictures. I never really considered that before!"

"Would I have to wear a bycocket?"

"Of course. We're a family who looks great in hats, so we need to lean into that." Marion snuggled deeper into his arms. Relaxing in his embrace, she turned her attention towards a third wedding day. Sooner or later, they'd get it right. "Seriously, we'll have our next ceremony in Neverland. At sunset... by the ocean... tropical vibes." She hesitated. "Bonus: I could wear a lighter-weight gown." She gestured to the ruined tulle, draped over his arm. "This one isn't so perfect, after all."

"You look beautiful."

He deserved a reward for that lie. "Since the gown is ruined anyway, I guess it would be okay if you kidnapped me later and then demanded that I do very evil things to you, while wearing it." She offered casually. "If you just happened to have any sex fantasies like that."

Nicholas met her eyes.

She arched a brow.

"That dress is fucking *perfect*." Nicholas told her with great feeling.

"Somehow, I knew you'd say that."

He gave her another kiss, like he just couldn't help himself. "I will marry you again and again, wearing whatever you want, in any kingdom you wish." He hesitated. "But..."

"But?"

"But, with Hood dead, you're the last of Nottingham's

royal bloodline."

"So?"

"So, you have a pretty clear claim on the crown, Marion. You can be queen." He explained it all slowly, as if he wasn't sure she understood. "If you want to stay here and rule, I'll make sure it happens. I swear it."

"Nick, have you *seen* this kingdom?"

"Yes."

"Would *you* want to rule over it?"

"Hell no."

"Me neither. I'll stick with my May Day tiara over Nottingham's tacky crown."

"You sure?"

"Yep. I'll admit, it would be fun to be a cruel and tyrannical empress to these yokels, but I'm getting bored with vengeance."

"That's a first."

"I'm not going to become like the Wraith, consumed with hatred and hurt. I'm done with Nottingham forever. I want to focus on *us* and not them. It's time to move on: just me and you and the gargoyles. … And the big golden scepter I'll be melting down to finance our first-class trip to paradise."

He snorted in amusement.

Marion grinned back. "Let's get out of here, my own." She leaned up to kiss him. "We've got a future to plan."

Chapter Forty-One

Starting over in Neverland has been quite an adventure for this reporter.
But, as I fled the barbarian invasion of my homeland to begin this even more truthful newspaper here on the beach, at least one thing has remained consistent:
Wherever she goes, Maid Marion is a Bad influence on *everybody*.

Alan A. Dale- "Neverland's Naughtiest News"

Five Years Later

"I'm in love with Sir Galahad." Tansy said with great feeling. The Hatter wore a bikini top, cutoff shorts, and braids, looking even younger than her nineteen years. "I'm not even kidding."

"Most of the population of the world is in love with Sir Galahad." Marion reminded her.

"But, I'm *passionately* in love with him. I've never met him, and I'm not into knights, but I'd marry that pretty, blond genius right now."

"Wait until the Gala-Chip money starts rolling in, before you propose. Then, you'll *really* be passionately in love. This is just from the Gala-Shoes."

"Ten million pairs of sneakers sold worldwide." Tansy whispered, still awed by the number.

"And we own twenty percent." Marion smiled and watched the mansion being constructed in front of her. She'd done her best to learn everything she could about finances, since she left Nottingham. As she always suspected, she was great at it. "Gala-Chips are where the *real* money is. They get invented any day now. Once they hit shelves, we'll never have to worry about gold again. We're going to be the richest people in Neverland, thanks to Galahad."

"I *so* love him." Tansy reiterated. The magic talisman she had once given Marion was looped around her neck. Marion had given it back to her, when she'd first reunited with her friend and now Tansy never took it off. "Momma can't believe we're going to live *here!*" She gestured towards the massive house taking shape, right on the beach. "It's like a miracle, what you did!"

"What *we* did, kiddo."

In this timeline, Tansy was back to being a teenager, but she was still the same as she'd been in the WUB Club. Only so much happier. Her eyes were bright with emotion, as she looked over at Marion. "Thank you."

Marion rubbed the girl's arm. "Thank *you*." She said simply. "You allowed me to redo my life and now I have *everything*. The least I can do is offer some investment tips."

Marion's initial money-making idea had been simple: Bet big on anything Sir Galahad invented. The man was successful at whatever he tried. She'd put the gold she'd gotten from the sale of her parents' house and all of Nicholas' trust fund into Gala-Gum. That had netted them a not-so-small fortune. Then, she'd dumped most of *that* into Gala-Shoes, which did even better. Also, there was sports gambling. Marrok Wolf made them wealthier with every Wolfball championship.

The Duke and Duchess of Huntingdon were now fuck 'em all rich.

These days, Marion liked to diversify, so she wasn't *just* invested in Galahad-invented products and Marrok's winning streak. She was pretty good at making money, for a Maid who wasn't supposed to learn math. Even Nicholas was shocked by the ever-growing numbers in their bank account.

Speaking of which... "I've gotta get home. Nick says he's got a birthday surprise for me."

"Oooohhhh, sounds *intriguing*." Tansy teased with exaggerated innuendo.

"What would you know about anything 'intriguing'? You're technically still a virgin." She ruffled Tansy's hair.

Tansy made a face at her. "Are you *ever* going to get

tired of that joke?"

Marion laughed in delight. "Maybe on your wedding day." She started down the beach, towards the *new* Huntingdon estate. "Hey, be at my party by seven. Don't forget!"

"When do Hatters ever forget a birthday?" Tansy called after her.

What didn't get invested in stocks got spent on property. The gargoyles needed the space. Nicholas' family had found far greater acceptance outside of Nottingham's rigid social structure. Neverland Beach was a much more diverse community. Some of the men had even started dating locals and none of them ever mentioned paying for the company.

The gargoyles had started their own security force that hired out to help people in need of protection. They were thriving, but they still called the Huntingdon estate home. They seemed most comfortable around each other and with Nicholas in command. Maybe they'd relax, in time. But for now, Marion just bought up more and more land to accommodate their needs. It was no hardship. She loved the gargoyles. Besides, no one ever regretted owning a gigantic private compound on a tropical island.

She waved at Gravol, who was working on a gargantuan sandcastle. "Hey, pal. Where are the others?"

"Jet skis." He pointed out towards the ocean, his attention on creating a perfectly shaped turret. "But I want to finish my castle." He loved building elaborate structures on the shoreline. "It's my biggest one yet."

"And it looks great!" She put a hand on her head, keeping her stylish sunhat in place, as the breeze picked up. "Don't forget the party's at seven."

"Okay, Marion." He continued to happily create his architectural marvel. She had no idea how half of it was staying upright. Gravol was thriving in Neverland, with plenty of attention and lots of time to sculpt his masterpieces on the beach.

Marion headed up the pathway to the gigantic house she'd designed for her family. Wings jutted off in various directions, so each of the lieutenants had privacy. She and Nicholas lived in the center. Their bedroom was a tower that overlooked the endless turquoise sea, because why the hell not?

"Nick?" Marion strolled by the huge pool, across the wide porch, and into the house. She stopped in the entrance to grab the mail off the table.

She'd started up correspondence with half the inmates she'd known in the WUB Club. Bad folks had helped her a lot when she needed it. It was only fair she repay the favor. *Kodamara vadu.* Having found her True Love, made her fortune, and destroyed the dreams of her enemies, Marion was now focused on helping other felons achieve their own happily ever afters. Most of her kinda-sorta friends were unrepentantly horrible, but she was pretty sure she could get a few Baddies on the right track.

It helped that she was willing to invest all their ill-gotten gains. The Creative Villainy Hedge Fund had started out with Marion and gargoyles, but it had grown rapidly once Nessus and the barbarians' loot got involved. Then, Trevelyan realized his stolen Robin Hood cache could be tripled within months and insisted on joining, too. And from there, it had *really* taken off. Now, she had hundreds of investors.

Some Good folk didn't appreciate her making evil-doers piles of gold to carry out their nefarious schemes, but very few were stupid enough to complain above a scandalized whisper. Her clientel were a maniacal bunch.

Marion frowned.

Speaking of maniacal violence, she hadn't heard from Trevelyan lately.

Huh. That wasn't like him. The dragon was always hanging around Neverland. He'd commandeered his own room upstairs. If he didn't at least call for her birthday, then something was wrong and Marion would have to go looking for the dickhead.

Her phone rang and Marion answered it without checking the caller ID. She loved that Neverland wasn't a technological wilderness. Her phone was always on hand, although it would never replace her love of letter-writing. "Hello?"

"I need money."

"Oh for God's sake..." Marion rolled her eyes.

"I don't want to hear your bitching, alright? Just send it. I'm desperate."

"You're *always* desperate. ...In so many, *many* ways."

Clorinda snorted. "Just shut up and send me the money. It's mine, isn't it?"

"I'm the one who makes it. You're just the one who spends it." But, Marion was already initiating the transfer on her phone's screen. When she'd started Tansy's brokerage account, she'd set one up for Clorinda, as well. It was a mistake she lived with every day, because a Clorinda with cash was even more annoying than a broke Clorinda. "I have no idea why I bothered to make you rich."

"Me neither. I think it was some kind of weird power trip."

"I think I'm just too damn nice."

"Like, *literally* no one has ever said that about you. Ever."

"Whatever your problem is this time, I hope it eats you."

"Eat *me*." Clorinda retorted. "Gotta go. Happy birthday, you ancient hag."

"Fuck off, sheep-whore." Marion hung up.

Of all her bizarre kinda-sorta friends, Clorinda was somehow the biggest surprise to her. The two of them were incredibly close, death threats and insults notwithstanding. They fought a lot, but they *liked* fighting each other. Every self-respecting bitch needed a faithful nemesis to sharpen her claws on, after all. No one else seemed to understand their relationship. Hell, even Marion didn't fully understand it. She just accepted that she and Clorinda were going to be sniping at each other and having brunches every Wednesday for the rest of their lives.

"*There*'s my girl." Nicholas came down the stairs. "I thought I was going to have to use that mystical tracker connection to find you." There was a smile on his face and a badly-wrapped package in his hand. "Your surprise arrived."

Marion forgot everything else. "Nick!" She bounded over to her very best friend, jumping up into his arms and twining her legs around his waist. "Gimme, gimme, gimme!"

Nicholas easily supported her with one arm, holding the package out of her reach with his other. The red bow on it was all adorably lopsided. He was awesome at many things, but arts and crafts was not one of them. "Kiss me again, Marion. *Then,* you get your gift."

She grinned at the challenge. Nicholas had gotten so much more secure and playful, over the years. "How nice is the gift?" She asked, pretending to think it over.

"You'll like it. Trust me. Just this once."

Marion trusted him every second of every day. They'd had six weddings, now. Usually some new disaster befell the ceremony and/or reception, screwing up her perfect vision for the event, but it didn't much matter. It was always a dream wedding, because she was marrying the man of her dreams.

Marion leaned forward to press her lips to his.

"Thank you." Nicholas whispered against her mouth. Not breaking the kiss, he carried her across the living room and sat down on the sofa with Marion on top of him. Grasping the rim of her sunhat, he tossed it aside.

Marion glanced over her shoulder to watch it hit the floor. "That's a very expensive hat, you know."

"I'll buy you another one. It'll be my pleasure.' His lips grazed the gold stud she had pierced through her eyebrow. "You look adorable in hats." His hands caressed her, tugging aside her clothes to feel her skin. His big, rocky palm slipped under her flowy dress, past the edge of her swimsuit bottom. Two large fingers squeezed inside of her, thrusting gently.

Marion moaned, her body growing wet for him. It had been almost a day since she'd seduced her husband and her fixation told her that was *far* too long a time apart. Her hips moved to accommodate the size of him, finding a rhythm that would soon bring her to completion. Not being a virgin was yet another perk to her new life.

"Not yet, duchess." He reluctantly removed his hand. "I want you to come against my mouth, after you open your present."

"Oh, this must be a *really* nice gift, if you want *that* kind of kiss for it."

Nicholas smiled, enjoying her teasing. "Open it and see." He nodded to the package, which was now sitting on the couch cushion beside them.

Marion grabbed it up and saw a note was taped to one side.

*For my own True Love,
Then and now and always.*

She blinked against the rush of emotion behind her eyes. "Whoever said you struggled with words?"

"Everyone." He casually held her on his lap, his hands on her waist. "But, you inspire me."

Marion tore the paper off her gift. She'd come to love birthday presents. You just never knew what surprises lay inside. She lifted the lid on the large jewelry box she uncovered. ...And saw her mom's necklace inside.

Marion's lips parted in awe.

"It took me awhile, but I finally found the person who'd bought it." Nicholas said quietly. "I knew I could. I recognized it, from the minute I saw it in that portrait." He watched Marion's face. "My mother made it, you know. It was one of her first pieces. She still had drawings of it, when I was a boy. I always thought it was so beautiful that the woman who owned it must be the most special person in the world." He touched her hair. "...And she is."

Marion stared down at the glowing ruby, for a long moment and then she slowly lifted her eyes to Nicholas'. "In every timeline there is, I am over the brink of madness for you, Nick Greystone."

His mouth curved. "I like this timeline. Let's stay right here, forever after."

"Oh, I plan to. And you're not going *anyplace*. You

might have been the one who abducted me first, but *I'm* the one who's never going to let you go." She arched her pierced-brow. "You're kidnapped. Deal with it."

Thrilled with the dire threat, he lowered his head to kiss her lavishly.

A long time later, Marion was wearing nothing but her giant ruby and a smug smile. She was stretched out on the floor with Nicholas beside her. "I'm such a badass at sex."

Nicholas chuckled, looking blissfully drained. "You really are." He tugged her closer and pressed a kiss to her hair. "'Obsession' isn't a big enough word for how I feel about you."

"Good." Marion snuggled into his embrace, utterly content. "Thank you for my necklace. Did I say that, yet?"

"Just don't wear it near the water, because it'll weigh you down like an anchor."

"*Such* a sweet talker."

His fingers grazed her bare skin, his eyes dancing. "You know, if you *really* want to thank me, I've thought up something new to demand with my betrothal rights."

"That's physically impossible. There isn't anything new you can claim. You have done things to my body that I didn't even know existed, until you were inside of me and doing them."

"There's *always* more I can do to you. I'm extremely creatively villainous. And your necklace got me thinking about Nottingham and Robin Hood. And I suddenly remembered that you once told me that Hood asked to come all over these pretty things." His hand drifted down to brush her breast.

Marion's heartrate sped up. Butterflies attacked her stomach from out of nowhere. The plan was a little bit Bad. Unfamiliar and slightly dirty. It made her feel nervous in all the best ways. She couldn't wait!

"I was a Good girl and refused him." She whispered batting her eyes innocently.

"You've never been a Good girl, duchess."

"Yes, I was! I told Robin no. He got nothing." She sniffed loftily. "...I should probably tell you no, too. It's a *very* wicked thing to ask a Maid."

"I'm a very wicked man." Nicholas's thumb brushed her preening nipple. A rumble of possession sounded in his throat at the sight of her growing arousal. "And I get *everything*." It wasn't a question. It was a command.

She gave a slow smile, loving this. "Yes, Nick."

He massaged her breast with possessive intent. "How much longer until the others come back?"

Marion shook her head. "Sorry, my own. You can't claim your betrothal rights until tonight. I have a lot of stuff that I need to do before the party..." Her phone chimed with a text message alert and she made an aggravated noise. "Hang on." Marion went blindly digging around in her discarded clothes, doing her best not to move too far from his body. "It might be Trev."

"God, I hope not."

"I'm a little worried. He hasn't wished me 'happy birthday,' yet." Trevelyan was usually in Neverland for her celebration. Plus, his own birthday was only a few days away. He *never* missed one of the annual parties she threw for him. "And it's weird that we haven't seen him in so long, right?"

"What you call 'weird,' I call 'a blessing.'" His fingers did something very naughty.

"Stop that. I told you, you have to wait." She batted Nicholas' chest, in flirty amusement. Finally finding her phone, she swiped it open to read the message. "Huh."

"Is it the dragon?"

"No. The message isn't even to me. It's to *you*, because you don't have a phone."

Nicholas made a face. "I don't want a phone. People would call me." He gave a mock shudder at the very idea.

"Well, you might *have* to get one now, I'm afraid." She held up the screen so he could read it. "The Neverland Beach Board of Commissioners just voted you sheriff."

"Shit. I didn't ask for that." He shifted to take the phone from her. "Since when do we even have a sheriff around here?"

"Since now, I guess. You're always at town hall, complaining about the way things are run. Seems like they've thought of a brilliant idea to shut you up."

"I *told* you talking was a terrible idea."

He'd been doing more of it, though. Neverland was a healthier environment for all of them, but the tranquility of the estate, and the noise-blocking effect of the rhythmic waves, especially suited Nicholas. With the house as a quiet spot where he could decompress, he was able to face the rest of the world with less hostility and more comfort.

He frowned in thought, still looking at the phone. "The laws here are ridiculous and no one ever seems to be in charge of enforcing them, though. *Everybody* should be complaining."

"It's an enchanted paradise, Nick. Only you want people ticketed for violating the exact size limits of a beach bonfire."

"Two feet high, three feet around." He quoted absently. "Quarry *knew* that. He deserved that citation."

She bit back a smile.

"This is mostly because your villainous buddies blow into town and the crime rates spikes. I'm sure of it. The Board of Commissioners thinks I'll be able to keep them in line."

"And you will. You were an *excellent* sheriff, back in Nottingham. There was very little recidivism, thanks to the countless hangings."

"They all deserved it." He sent her a dry look. "Can I hang your prison pals? Because I guarantee, they all deserve it, too."

"How about we compromise on building a dank dungeon, with spiked wheels and maces?"

"Deal."

"Does that mean you're taking the job?"

"Why the hell not? 'Nick Greystone, Sheriff of Neverland' has a nice ring to it, don't you think?"

"I think you just want to lock up my kinda-sorta friends and paying clients."

"Well, I'm not a man to miss an opportunity." He tossed the phone aside. "Which is why I'm going to claim my betrothal rights, right now." His eyes were back on her breasts. "At least twice."

"But, there are people coming over..."

"I don't recall any rule saying that I had to wait for my betrothal rights." Nicholas interrupted with a very grave shake of his head. "The law's on my side here."

Marion gave up with a laugh. "You really are the grand passion of my life, you know that?"

"Of course." Nicholas leaned forward to find her lips. "That's my purpose."

Epilogue

How It Happened the Second Time...

No one was coming to save him.

So, Trevelyan would save himself... No matter what it took.

He should have been more careful. Then, things would never have gotten to this point. He could admit that he'd been too complacent. It had just been so long since Trevelyan even thought of Marion's damn note, outlining what she knew about his death. He'd been so sure he'd beaten fate and evaded the other-Trevelyan's mistakes. So positive that he was untouchable.

But he'd been wrong. He hated being wrong. He was a dragon! He was used to being right about everything.

Now, he was stuck in The Wicked, Ugly and Bad Mental Health Treatment Center and Maximum Security Prison. Marion had told him enough to know that this was supposed to be his last day alive. The former-him had been a damn idiot for not confiding more in the girl. It would've been extremely useful to have additional details leading up to this moment. Really, it was the dead-Trevelyan's fault and not his. Not that it would make a difference.

As it was, Marion had related everything she knew. Trevelyan prided himself on never believing anything he personally couldn't see, smell, hear, touch or taste, but Marion had proven herself to be loyal. Trevelyan valued loyalty above *everything.* He trusted that Marion gave him all the information she had to help him avoid this mess.

And he'd followed her instructions!

He hadn't done half the shit she recalled from his rap-sheet. He'd been minding his own business, selling dark magic and only occasionally murdering anyone, but somehow he'd *still* been arrested. That told Trevelyan that this was far bigger than Marion knew. His crimes, past and present, weren't the real reason he was behind bars.

They wanted the spell. *That's* what this was about.

Marion's letter had told him as much, although she hadn't realized it. Neither had he, until it was too late. Now, he recalled everything she'd written, with much greater understanding.

The last day you're alive is May 4th.

His birthday. Birthdays carried a lot of individualized magic. And today was May 4th.

You ate lunch with me in the cafeteria, but something was up with you. You weren't you're usual snarky self. You barely even looked at the Gala-chips I'd stolen for you, as a present.

In this timeline, he hadn't eaten lunch with Marion. She'd changed that part of history. She'd never come to the WUB Club, at all. She was in fucking Neverland with her obsessive gargoyle husband and lots of palm trees. She would try to rescue Trevelyan from prison, of course. He had little doubt Marion would do her best (or her worse) to free him, but it wouldn't work. Not in time.

No one could save Trevelyan, except Trevelyan.

I asked you what was up and you muttered something about a spell you were working on. Then, you sorta looked at me weird and said, "Stay in your cell tonight, Marion." No "Marion dear" shit. You called me "Marion," being all serious. So, I got worried and warned you not to do anything stupid. But you just shook your head and told me, "I don't have another choice. It's this or death. And it will probably be death. No matter what happens, you stay locked in tight." I knew you didn't want me hurt by whatever you were planning, but you got up and left without telling me more.

Trevelyan fully believed he'd attempted to shield the girl. He could count the people he cared about on one finger and Marion was it. But, buried in his warning was a more important message: The other-him had been working on a spell.

And there was only one spell that could be.

So, around 10 pm, I started hearing noises. Explosions.

Screaming. Begging. I did what you said and I stayed in my cell. Other people didn't. They probably wished they had, because they didn't survive long. You had let Nessus Theomaddox free and done something to get the drugs out of his system. He was awake and FURIOUS. I have no idea what moron first decided locking up a centaur warlord was a great idea, but I guarantee they regretted it, once Nessus sobered up.

Recruiting that merciless savage onto his team wasn't such a terrible plan, if Trevelyan did say so himself. The torrents of blood must have been an interesting sight to behold.

I didn't see you, that night. Nessus came by my cell and looked in at me, with those black eyes of his, though. I was scared by the blood all over him, but he just tested the door to make sure it was locked. He grunted when he saw I was safe inside and snapped, "Stay!" at me. Then, he killed some troll who was lurking around my cell, and walked away. I'm not sure if you put him up to checking on me or if he did it on his own.

Either was a possibility. The woman made the damnedest kinda-sorta friends.

Anyway, the whole place was in chaos for hours. Inmates were rioting and killing each other. And there was so much fire! You and Nessus burned most of the prison down. Dwarf guards were dead all over the place. I don't think you even had your magic back, but anyone who got in your way still got slaughtered. One hundred and eight people died.

Not a shabby score. Sadly, Nessus Theomaddox wasn't in the WUB Club, this time around. Marion had changed that part of history, too. The centaur would be no help, even if Trevelyan wanted to risk a repeat of Plan A. ...And honestly Plan A didn't seem like the way to go, regardless of how promising it sounded on paper.

I thought I was going to die that night. I really did. Instead you died, Trevelyan. So did Nessus. I saw his body, out by the Lake of Forgetting, the next day. I never saw what happened to you. Dr. White said later you'd been shot trying to escape, but I never believed that. I think she caught you and killed you slowly, because you wouldn't do something she wanted.

Because he hadn't given her the spell.

Snow White was a vengeful bitch, who ran the prison like her own fiefdom. She would never tolerate any insubordination from a prisoner. Not even a dragon.

No matter what happens you <u>cannot</u> stay in the WUB Club. If they ever arrest you, get out any way you can. I don't care what it takes. ESCAPE. Dr. White will not play fair. I know it. Whatever she was after, she killed you for it last time and this time she might do even worse. I don't want anything to happen to you, Trev. ...Even though you're a dickhead.

He didn't want anything to happen to him, either.

Marion was right. He needed to get out any way he could. Unfortunately, he couldn't cast a spell to escape, thanks to the prison's magic inhibitors. (Who had even invented such vile things? If Trevelyan ever found out, he'd disembowel the bastard on principle.) With his powers woefully blocked and time ticking by, Trevelyan had come up with a simple Plan B. But now *that* was in ruins, too, thanks to his stupid, mangy cell-mate.

Marrok Wolf refused to help Trevelyan blow up the WUB Club, because the moron had some pathetic, moralistic worries about the number of deaths that would result. Trevelyan couldn't have cared less how many people died, just so he wasn't one of them. Sometimes he thought he was the only *real* villain left in the world. Everyone else was a fucking child.

No matter. He'd get revenge on the wolf later for his inexplicable disloyalty. For the moment, he needed to focus on survival. Since magic spells and bombs were off the table, Trevelyan was forced to go with a less elegant solution to his problem.

Plan C was absolutely disgusting, but he'd done it, in order to survive.

He took a deep breath, trying not to breathe in the scent of the naked woman lying beside him. Everyone and everything in the WUB Club hurt his nose, but Snow White smelled absolutely godawful.

Dragons were hyper-aware of fragrances. The stench of Dr. White's cloying, reeking Goodness made him sick. It smelled like rotten syrup mixed with lies. Goodness always had a taint of overly-sweet sweetness, but this woman's sugary scent was infused with something rancid at the base. Decaying. False. It was absolutely repulsive.

Trevelyan had fucked her anyway.

She'd been thrilled when he'd sent word that he'd like some time alone with her. She was use to exploiting male prisoners for her own sexual pleasure, but she'd never had a dragon before. Trevelyan hadn't needed to do much more than show up in her office. Then, she was hustling him into some secret backroom and ordering him to strip. As she had with half the male population of the prison.

It was pitiful. And degrading. And infuriating.

He was halfway-shocked he was able to perform at all, under the circumstances. But, what other option did he have? Even if he gave her the spell she wanted, Snow White would just kill him anyway. So, he'd fucked her in every possible position, until she was exhausted from her multiple orgasms and power-fantasies.

(Trevelyan excelled at *so many* things, but sex and magic really were his best events. He was the first to say so.)

Now, the insidious, smelly bitch was half-asleep beside him, drained and complacent. And Trevelyan had his eyes on the unbarred window across from the bed. *That* was his way out. He already knew it.

"Ramona says you and Marrok were fighting tonight." Snow White murmured, with her eyes closed. "Is that where you got the bruises."

"He looks worse." Probably. Trevelyan had been too enraged to tally all the cuts and contusions they'd inflicted on each other.

"I thought you two were friends."

"I thought so, too."

He should have known better. Trevelyan was all too aware of his own antisocial capabilities. But, when it came to pissing people off, *no one* could rival Marrok. He could drawl out the absolutely perfect remark, at the perfect moment, to incite blackout rage. He'd sent Trevelyan into a screaming fury, earlier that night, and that was a hard thing to accomplish. The wolf had a real gift.

Too bad it was going to get him killed.

"Such a shame that the two prettiest monsters in this cage can't get along." Snow White continued sleepily.

"I'll deal with Marrok." Trevelyan had a long memory and a Bad temper. Sooner or later, the wolf would pay for his betrayal.

"I hope you're not too hard on him. I never saw a handsomer man, in my whole life. His eyes and his body and his hair..." Snow White yawned, her tone dreamy. "The wolf is just *so* beautiful... even if his species isn't as important as a dragon."

No one was as important as Trevelyan. (He was the first to say that, as well.)

She ran a hand over his chest and it was all he could do not to cringe. "Before I send you back to your cell, we need to discuss a spell of yours." Snow White's voice was drifting off. "You're the only one who can cast it and my stepmother is very... Sealing wax isn't..." Her breathing evened out and she was fast asleep.

Trevelyan slowly smiled.

Five minutes later, he was free. The first prisoner to ever escape the WUB Club.

Author's Note

This is not the book I intended to write. Mostly that is Marion's fault.

I wanted to add Robin Hood to the *Kinda Fairytale* series, because... he's Robin Hood. Obviously, he should be here. But these books are generally designed to flip traditional villain and hero roles. I therefore always assumed that Robin would be a real jerk, when he finally showed up.

In fact, if you look back at *Wicked Ugly Bad* (book one of the series) Robin Hood is briefly mentioned in chapter six:

Avenant looked around the group with new enthusiasm. "Who was that pussy who robbed from the rich and gave to the poor and everyone praised *him for his thievery?"*

Please note the past tense (*Seducing the Sheriff of Nottingham* takes place ten years before *Wicked Ugly Bad*) and Avenant's disparaging tone. Granted, Avenant talks about most people in a disparaging tone, but I'm still pretty pleased that my original concept for Robin stayed right on target.

Since Robin was always going to be the villain in my version of the story, it stood to reason that the Sheriff of Nottingham would become the hero. I didn't have a totally clear vision for him in my original concept, but I was a big fan of Richard Armitage's Guy of Gisbourn character in the 2006 BBC *Robin Hood* TV show (to be fair, I am a big fan of everything Richard Armitage does), so generally something like that. Only he'd be less murderous, and more capable, and he doesn't have that horrible hair from season three. Seems simple enough as a starting point, right?

Marion was more difficult to get a handle on, at first. It is important to me that female characters drive a lot of the action in my books. Maid Marion (or "Marian" depending on how you want to spell it) is actually an older character than

Robin Hood. She is traditionally associated with May Day celebrations and, in some of the oldest tales, is a sword-wielding member of the Merry Men. Likewise, I felt like my version of Marion also needed to be able to fight her own battles and be her own person.

On a parallel track, for several years I had wanted to write a contemporary romance where a woman in prison has the chance to redo her life. She was once a polite, refined, beauty queen, but now she's a felon with a chip on her shoulder and she's sent back to change the past. I got two chapters of it written and then I got stuck. This happens to me a lot. I have pieces of dozens of books on my computer, most of which I will never finish. But, they do allow me to try concepts and play with characters. This incomplete bit of story really stayed with me, because I liked the theme of being able to fix your previous mistakes.

One day it occurred to me that *Redoing Your Life* (my tentative title for that unfinished book) and my unstarted Robin Hood project were actually the same story. Marion was the girl in jail and the jail was the WUB Club. This was a real light bulb moment for me. The idea probably came to me in the shower. I get all my best ideas in the shower.

Side note: I've sent out a link to those rough-draft chapters with our Star Turtle Publishing newsletter. If you aren't subscribed and want to read them, please let me know at starturtlepublishing@gmail.com and I'll sign you up. I think you'll see how close those proof-of-concept trial pages for *Redoing Your Life* were to the eventual beginning of *Seducing the Sheriff of Nottingham*.

Anyway, I was pleased with my new, clear vision and I set about writing it with a real sense of purpose. Everything was going to be great! This would not be one of those times were a character derailed me with their unpredictable behavior, because *it's a Robin Hood book!* All I had to do was write Maid Marion returning to Nottingham to clear her name. In the process, she slowly falls in love with the Sheriff of Nottingham. Again, it couldn't be simpler.

This is the part where Marion Huntingdon shows up

and destroys all my dreams.

Marion was *way* more Bad than I anticipated, totally unrepentant about her reign of terror around Nottingham, and she was freaking *crazy* about Nicholas. None of that was planned. Marion didn't "slowly" fall for the Sheriff. She met Nicholas and she was ready to sleep with him on page twenty. I was like "What the hell, Marion? You're not supposed to be doing that!" But she didn't listen. I had to stop and start it all over. She literally didn't care about Robin. At all. It was all Nicholas, all the time. Instead of being reluctantly attracted to the man, she was actively trying to seduce him.

And she didn't have to work real hard.

Marion's reaction to Nicholas shifted Nicholas' reaction to her. Instead of playing the more menacing role I had initially envisioned, he was now staring at her with longing. Marion's creative villainy captivated him. He didn't want to use her as bait for Robin. He wanted her hanging out with him, and talking to him, and smiling at him. He stopped caring about Robin, too, except as a rival for Marion's affections. I have honestly never written two characters more obsessed with each other, right from the outset of their story.

So... I just went with it.

I had to rewrite a bunch of stuff to make them happy, but I usually let characters do what they want. Otherwise none of their actions and dialogue are genuine. If Marion wanted Nick from the beginning, there had to be a reason, right? So, I started thinking about what it might be and that's when it occurred to me that if Robin didn't save her at the wedding, then Marion and Nicholas must have actually gotten married. After I realized that Marion considered him to be her husband from the very first chapter, the rest of the plot solidified for me.

As for developing Nicholas' character, I obviously needed a Sheriff of Nottingham for this book, but the legends don't give him a first name. That was kind of surprising to me. I think that led to the idea of Nicholas valuing names more than most people. It took him awhile to get one. I chose "Nicholas" because... I liked it? It sounded like a good romance novel name, but also passably medieval? The original hero in the original book concept for *Redoing Your Life* was also named Nicholas? All of the above? I don't know. It was just his name.

In the original tales, the Sheriff of Nottingham doesn't have a lot of "OMG, that is *such* a Sheriff of Nottingham thing to do!" details, with regards to his personality. Some elements I felt were essential to the traditional character were: A hatred for Robin Hood, annoyance over stolen taxes, and an affinity for hanging people in the castle courtyard. Nicholas was happy to oblige in assuming those characteristics.

I then decided to make him a gargoyle, because a fairytale book can't *just* have human characters, to my mind. (Although, I do find the Robin Hood legend to be a more "grounded-in-*this*-reality" story, which is reflected in my version of Nottingham having less magical people than other kingdoms.) In any case, Robin Hood has a medieval aesthetic and stone gargoyles decorate medieval buildings, so that made sense for Nicholas' character. It also gave me a starting point for his personality, as someone partially made of stone isn't going to be the warmest, chattiest guy. More importantly, a man partially made of stone is just an interesting "visual" in my head.

As I worked, Nicholas' backstory began to take on some traits similar to Pinocchio. It just seemed like the story tied in with the concept of the gargoyles being created beings. I think my *Kinda Fairytale* series is best when lots of different myths are blended together. *The Adventures of Pinocchio*, in particular, gave me plenty of weird details to toss into the mix and also helped me to clarify some existing ideas I'd had. (Nicholas' "reverse conscience" and the gorilla judge, for example.) I credit Pinocchio's author, Carlo Collodi for his extremely inventive storytelling.

Personally, I found the Disney cartoon *Pinocchio* quite scary as a child. And the 1883 book was downright terrifying in its random cruelty. It's one of the bestselling books of all time. I'm certainly not criticizing it as a work of art. But as an eight year old, I didn't even want my mom to finish reading it to me. I was too upset after (Spoiler Alert!) a certain cricket got smooshed with a hammer. It would no doubt be a different experience, if I revisited it as an adult, but the *Pinocchio* references used here reflect the creepy vibe the story gave me, as a little girl. I think that off-kilter feeling of impending doom works well with Nottingham's decaying atmosphere.

The Looking Glass Campaigns were a big part of *Best Knight Ever* (the fourth book in this series) and the idea of faraway battles dovetailed nicely with King Richard's crusades in the original Robin Hood tales. So, it made sense to me that Nicholas had been fighting in Lyonesse, for a time. The Looking Glass Campaigns had been over for five years in *Best Knight Ever*, which places them in this book's timeline.

I also see letter-writing as kind of olde-timey and romantic, which fits with the Robin Hood stories, in my head. So, I made notes passing around kind of a theme throughout the book. This led to the idea that Nicholas had been receiving Robin's wartime mail from Marion and fell in love with her. And THAT explained why he was so head-over-heels for her, right from the start of the book. Once I started writing Nicholas and Marion's journey out, it all sort of came together for me. These two not-quite Good-not-quite-Bad characters were soon happily wreaking havoc together.

Another side note: *When a Scot Ties the Knot* by Tessa Dare and *Love in the Afternoon* by Lisa Kleypas are historical romances that also heavily feature love letters in their plots. I highly recommend both, if you enjoy the trope.

In all *Kinda Fairytale* books, I always want to incorporate plenty of elements of the primary "original" story into my own writing. Otherwise, what would be the point of using famous myths as a starting point? However, the Robin Hood tales are a bit more stripped-down in their world-building details, when compared to some legends. (For instance, the Camelot myths are *full* of weird stuff.) But still, some pieces of the traditional tales need to be in a Robin Hood book for it to even *be* a Robin Hood book. Merry Men. Sherwood Forest. Bows and arrows. All that stuff's been added over the past eight-hundred years of storytelling. And there are a lot of strange and interesting hats in all the visual media surrounding it. So, I tossed them in, as well. I also borrowed every *Robin*

Hood character name I could find. Including "Clorinda the Shepherdess," who strangely became one of my favorite characters to write. Her self-centered, mean-girl pragmatism made me laugh. And no one annoyed Marion more. Not even Robin.

Adding appropriate "Robin Hood" stuff was made even more complex, because the tales are inextricably linked with *actual* places in England. In my own head, there was simply no way I could set the story anywhere but Nottingham and have it be "Robin Hood" enough. However, my *Kinda Fairytale* stories are not set in the real world. (Obviously.) I therefore decided to take creative license and create my own fictional kingdom of Nottingham, unrelated to the actual city. They just happen to share a name and have a forest. I feel like this compromise was the best way to go about it. In other news, I would very much like to visit the real Nottingham and see the setting for the traditional tales. I think it would be amazing!

Trevelyan, Last of the Green Dragons appears in this book, because I get a surprising number of requests for him, considering he was such a jackass in *Wicked Ugly Bad*. When readers like a character, I try to feature them more. As I said, that story is set a decade after *Seducing the Sheriff of Nottingham*, so I thought it was an interesting chance to go back and see why Trevelyan made some of the choices he did. Most of my "Bad" characters are not such terrible people, once you get to know them. But, Trevelyan works hard to be horrible all the way through. I enjoy his self-centered dialogue and gleeful villainy, so he'll get his own book soon. (I hope.)

A story only comes alive in the readers' heads, so I don't like to impose my exact ideas of what things look like or sound like in a book. I describe events, people, places, etc… the way I "see" them, but everyone's imagination is different. I want to leave some room for personal interpretation from the audience. That said, in *my* head, Marion's May Day Queen talent show performance sounds like a HUGE karaoke version of Celine Dion's *It's All Coming Back to Me Now*. Only kinda mixed with a belted-out performance of "Don't Rain on My Parade" from the musical *Funny Girl*. But also there's a country element and maybe some of Gloria Gaynor's *I Will Survive* and Meatloaf's *Anything for Love* tossed in someplace there, too. Hopefully, that clears everything right up.

As a final note, I want to send a shout-out to my sister and mom, for their help with this book. Early in the writing process, I was trying to find the right resolution to Marion's vengeance against Nottingham. I randomly asked my sister, Elizabeth, "Hey, how would you destroy a city and burn it to ash?" Without looking up from her computer, Liz casually answered, "Hire barbarians." Thus, Nessus and the centaur army were created, which I think tied everything together nicely.

Then, at the end of the writing process, I gave my mom a draft of this book to read. Somewhere around the Maypole Ball chapter, she told me, "I'm surprised Marion's not just hitting everyone with a hammer to find the Wraith." And hell if that wasn't the most Marion idea I'd ever heard! Of *course* she would do that. It immediately got added to the book and made me laugh out loud. I appreciate the help with crafting this story… and knowing that I am not the only crazy one in my family.

If you want to discuss those scary donkeys in Disney's *Pinocchio*, why medieval hats have such strange names, which upcoming books I'm working on, or anything else, you can contact us at **starturtlepublishing@gmail.com**. The same email address can be used to sign up for our mailing list for news about our upcoming books. We also have a Facebook page, which we update fairly regularly, and a new and improved website at www.starturtlepublishing.com. I hope to see you there!

Printed in Great Britain
by Amazon

element and maybe some of Gloria Gaynor's *I Will Survive* and Meatloaf's *Anything for Love* tossed in someplace there, too. Hopefully, that clears everything right up.

As a final note, I want to send a shout-out to my sister and mom, for their help with this book. Early in the writing process, I was trying to find the right resolution to Marion's vengeance against Nottingham. I randomly asked my sister, Elizabeth, "Hey, how would you destroy a city and burn it to ash?" Without looking up from her computer, Liz casually answered, "Hire barbarians." Thus, Nessus and the centaur army were created, which I think tied everything together nicely.

Then, at the end of the writing process, I gave my mom a draft of this book to read. Somewhere around the Maypole Ball chapter, she told me, "I'm surprised Marion's not just hitting everyone with a hammer to find the Wraith." And hell if that wasn't the most Marion idea I'd ever heard! Of *course* she would do that. It immediately got added to the book and made me laugh out loud. I appreciate the help with crafting this story... and knowing that I am not the only crazy one in my family.

If you want to discuss those scary donkeys in Disney's *Pinocchio*, why medieval hats have such strange names, which upcoming books I'm working on, or anything else, you can contact us at **starturtlepublishing@gmail.com**. The same email address can be used to sign up for our mailing list for news about our upcoming books. We also have a Facebook page, which we update fairly regularly, and a new and improved website at www.starturtlepublishing.com. I hope to see you there!

Printed in Great Britain
by Amazon